NECROMANCER
Games™

TOME OF HORRORS

2020

CONTRIBUTING WRITERS:
Bill Webb, Zach Glazar, Matt Finch,
James Thomas, Anthony Pryor,
Rhiannon Louve, Ben Barsh,
Jayson Rocky Gardner, Scott McKinley,
Alice Peng, Scott Greene, Scott Swift,
Skeeter Green, Ken Spencer, James Thomas,
James M. Spahn, Alex Kammer,
Mike Mearls, Tim Hitchcock
Carl Durocher and Jack Kennerson

5E CONVERSION:
Ken Spencer with Edwin Nagy

EDITORS:
Jeff Harkness, Edwin Nagy

ART DIRECTOR:
Casey Christofferson

LAYOUT
Suzy Moseby

INTERIOR ART:
Adrian Landeros, Brett Barkley, C.J. Marsh,
Faith Burgar, Hector Rodriguez, Josh Stewart,
Lloyd Metcalf, Matthew Myslinski,
Casey Christofferson, Michael Syrigos, Sid
Quade, Terry Pavlet, Thuan Pham

FRONT COVER ART:
Rasmus Jensen

NECROMANCER Games
ISBN: 978-1-6656-0140-5
5e Hardcover Book
PRINTED IN CHINA

TOME OF
HORRORS

TABLE OF CONTENTS

Afanc

The sea rose up on a clear day and slammed our ship, washing across the deck and carrying Smithson away. The lookouts called down that they had spotted something massive in the waters, and sure enough, a head breached the surface and arced up. A massive body followed, its fins sharply serrated. The mouth took in Smithson in one gulp, which was the last we saw of him. Jam, L'Croux, and Eve as well before we drove the beast off. — Captain Elisa Bounapert of the Wastrel's Daughter

Afancs are the sea monsters sailors talk about when spinning tales of the sea. They are the creatures responsible for entire fleets and crews being lost or destroyed. They are thought by many to be the "kings" of the sea as most other water-dwellers pale in comparison in strength and size to the mighty afanc. An afanc is generally about 100 feet long though specimens as large as 200 feet long are thought to exist. Its whale-like body is gray or sometimes bluish-green, although its eyes are always blue. Its tail is extremely long and ends in a truncated or flat, square edge. An afanc has a bulbous, somewhat flattened head, not unlike that of a great catfish. Afancs are omnivorous hunters of the deep sea that feed on a mixed diet of kelp, coral, sea plants, sharks, whales, various other large fishes, and swimmers and sailors unfortunate enough to cross their path.

Afanc

Gargantuan monstrosity, unaligned

Armor Class 18 (natural armor)
Hit Points 525 (30d20 + 210)
Speed 0 ft., swim 70 ft.

STR	DEX	CON	INT	WIS	CHA
30 (+10)	11 (+0)	24 (+7)	3 (–4)	16 (+3)	11 (+0)

Saving Throws Str +17, Dex +7, Con +14
Skills Perception +10
Damage Resistances acid, cold, fire
Damage Immunities poison; bludgeoning, piercing, and slashing from nonmagical attacks
Condition Immunities poisoned, prone
Senses darkvision 120 ft., passive Perception 20
Languages telepathy 120 ft.
Challenge 23 (50,000 XP)

Amphibious. The afanc can breathe air and water.
Siege Monster. The afanc deals double damage to objects and structures.

Actions

Multiattack. The afanc makes two Claw attacks and one Bite attack.
Bite. *Melee Weapon Attack:* +17 to hit, reach 20 ft., one target. *Hit:* 37 (6d8 + 10) piercing damage. If the target is a Large or smaller creature, that creature is swallowed. While swallowed, the creature is blinded and restrained, it has total cover against attacks and other effects outside the afanc, and it takes 42 (12d6) acid damage at the start of each of the afanc's turns.

If the afanc takes 50 damage or more on a single turn from a creature inside it, the afanc must succeed on a DC 25 Constitution saving throw at the end of that turn or regurgitate all swallowed creatures, which fall prone in a space within 10 feet of the afanc. If the afanc dies, a swallowed creature is no longer restrained by it and can escape from the corpse using 15 feet of movement, exiting prone.

Claw. *Melee Weapon Attack:* +17 to hit, reach 20 ft., one target. *Hit:* 24 (4d6 + 10) slashing damage.
Sea Swell (recharge 5–6). The afanc raises the front part of its body out of the water and brings it crashing back down against the surface. This generates massive waves up to 30 feet tall that may capsize boats and ships within 100 feet of the afanc. Boats and ships less than 20 feet long automatically capsize. A creature steering or guiding a boat or ship over 20 feet long must succeed on a DC 20 Dexterity or Strength check or its boat capsizes. A creature proficient in Vehicles (water) may add its proficiency bonus. A non-aquatic creature in the water within 100 feet of the afanc must succeed on a DC 20 Dexterity saving throw or take 21 (6d6) bludgeoning damage and be stunned until the end of its next turn.

Legendary Actions

The afanc can take three legendary actions, choosing from the options below. Only one legendary action can be used at a time and only at the end of another creature's turn. The afanc regains spent legendary actions at the start of its turn.
Claw Attack. The afanc makes one Claw attack.
Move. The afanc moves up to half its speed.
Roll (costs 2 actions). The afanc does a full body roll, sending up a spray of obscuring water in a 60-foot radius around it. That area is heavily obscured to creatures other than the afanc until the end of the afanc's next turn.

Algoid

At first we thought it was some kind of shambling mound or maybe a really ugly green ogre. Then my sword passed right through it, and its body just flowed back into the cut. We used fire; Harlvol had fought trolls before, and that helped. Then it whistled, and the trees attacked. By all the gods, the trees attacked! — Sir Cedric of Reme, knight errant

Algoids often resemble green humanoids, though they can just as easily take the appearance of a mound of green sludge or even spread out to blend into a scum-covered pool. The creature is not one being; it is an intelligent colony of algae awakened through some means. Usually this is through a magical accident, though some scholars believe an overuse of magic in fragile natural settings can cause an algoid to form. Others say the algoid is a natural magical expression tied to marshes and swamps, and the ability of the algoid to "awaken" trees to join in the defense of its home lends some credence to this theory.

The "skin" of an algoid is coarse and rough with a leafy texture. In its natural surroundings, it is nearly invisible until it attacks. Algoids use this natural camouflage when prey is nearby. The algoid lies in wait, submerged in water or a bog, as it watches its prey. When a potential victim passes nearby, the algoid springs to attack.

Algoid
Medium plant, neutral

Armor Class 14
Hit Points 52 (7d8 + 21)
Speed 20 ft.

STR	DEX	CON	INT	WIS	CHA
19 (+4)	10 (+0)	16 (+3)	4 (−3)	10 (+0)	10 (+0)

Saving Throws Con +5
Skills Stealth +4
Damage Resistance slashing and piercing damage from nonmagical attacks
Damage Immunities lightning, fire damage
Condition Immunities prone
Senses darkvision 60 ft., tremorsense 120 ft., passive Perception 10
Languages Common (understands but can't speak)
Challenge 3 (700 XP)

Animate Trees. An algoid can innately cast the *animate objects* spell at will, requiring no components. Each casting animates two trees, which are all the algoid can control at a time. A newly animated tree takes one full round to uproot itself. Once free, trees act on the algoid's turn.
Vulnerability to Water Magic. *Control water* and *create/destroy water* spells deal 3d6 piercing damage to an algoid
Water Camouflage. An algoid has advantage on Dexterity (Stealth) checks when it has any type of standing water to blend into.

Actions

Multiattack. The algoid makes two Slam attacks.
Slam. *Melee Weapon Attack:* +6 to hit, reach 5 ft., one creature. *Hit:* 8 (1d8 + 4) bludgeoning damage. If an algoid scores a critical hit with this attack, the target must make a successful DC 14 Con saving throw or be stunned. The stunned creature can repeat the saving throw at the end of each of its turns; the condition ends on a successful save.
Mind Blast. Each creature in a 60-foot cone must make a successful DC 13 Intelligence saving throw or be stunned for 3d4 rounds.

Ant Lion

The dwarf Paulus slip-slid on his butt right into the dirt funnel, just like water-scootin' down the rapids! It looked like fun, but tweren't no fun when that thing reared out of the sand. It was three times the size of poor Paulus, a giant ant, but with wicked barbs like branches sticking out right around its mouth. Paulus' leg came apart at the knee with a spray of red when the thing grabbed him. He disappeared right under the ground; his screams stopped when the sand filled his mouth. — Dannvel Strout, former halfling scout

The vicious ant lion resembles a giant gray or brown ant with leathery skin covered in coarse, black bristles. Its deep, inset eyes are black, and its mouth is filled with rows of jagged teeth. Two large silver mandibles protrude just above its mouth. Each mandible has a barb on the inside midway between the creature's mouth and the end point of the mandible. An ant lion is about nine feet long and weighs nearly 700 pounds.

Ant lions lurk at the bottom of deep, funnel-shaped pits and holes, where they feed on unfortunates who fall in. An ant lion pit is about 60 feet across and about 20 feet deep. A creature that steps on the pit must make a DC 16 Dexterity saving throw or slip and fall into the funnel. It is there where the ant lion waits, buried just under the surface of the ground. When prey falls to the center of the funnel, the ant lion surfaces and attacks, using its mandibles to grab and tear at its prey.

Ant Lion

Large beast, unaligned

Armor Class 15 (natural armor)
Hit Points 93 (11d10 + 33)
Saving Throws Con +5
Speed 30 ft., burrow 10 ft.

STR	DEX	CON	INT	WIS	CHA
14 (+2)	11 (+0)	17 (+3)	2 (–4)	10 (+0)	4 (–3)

Skills Athletics +2, Stealth +2
Condition Immunities Charmed
Senses darkvision 60 ft., tremorsense 60 ft., passive Perception 10
Languages None
Challenge 4 (1,100 XP)

Actions

Bite. *Melee Weapon Attack:* +4 to hit, reach 5 ft., one creature. *Hit:* 18 (3d10 + 2) piercing damage and the target is grappled (escape DC 12).

Ape, Dire

The jungle underbrush shook and cracked as a powerfully built simian charged, thumping its chest and howling with a fang-filled mouth. Naturally, the porters scrambled for safety, dropping their packs. I, too, dropped back to prepare a spell or two to calm the enraged beast, but my guards leapt into battle. We lost a valuable telescope that day. Two guards as well, but we did acquire a prize specimen. —
Algrid Henswaithe, University of the Vast

Dire apes are much larger than apes commonly found in jungles and savannas. Shy but territorial, these mighty beasts are often found in the deepest part of the wilderness. Due to their size, a troop of dire apes needs a large range in which to forage, and the presence of even regular hunters urges them to move on. A troop consists of an adult male and three to four adult females with two to six young (treat as **apes**). When encountered, the young flee for the trees or other hiding places while the adults attempt to frighten away intruders by making great displays of their might. Small trees are torn up by the roots and flung about, threatening displays of fangs and chest thumping are carried out, and in one reported case, a passing duiker was torn in half and flung at the interlopers.

Dire Ape

Large beast, unaligned

Armor Class 11
Hit Points 90 (12d10 + 24)
Speed 40 ft., climb 40 ft.

STR	DEX	CON	INT	WIS	CHA
18 (+4)	13 (+1)	15 (+2)	2 (–4)	12 (+1)	7 (–2)

Skills Athletics +6, Perception +3
Senses passive Perception 13
Languages —
Challenge 3 (700 XP)

Keen Scent. The dire ape has advantage on Wisdom (Perception) checks that rely on scent.

Actions

Multiattack. The dire ape makes two Fist attacks.
Fist. *Melee Weapon Attack:* +6 to hit, reach 10 ft., one target. *Hit:* 15 (2d10 + 4) bludgeoning damage.
Throw Tree . *Ranged Weapon Attack:* +6 to hit, range 30/60 ft., one target. *Hit:* 8 (1d8 + 4) bludgeoning damage.

ARA

The trees around us came alive with the sounds of gurgles, trills, and squawks, and a rustle like a flock of birds taking scared flight shook the leaves. A flurry of red and blue feathers drifted lazily down upon our heads. Cherill went to collect some in her many pouches, but four large, feathered forms stepped out around the trees and gently dissuaded her. Birds they were, but as tall as a man, their feathers a display of vivid colors against the jungle's green foliage. Their spears were warning enough not to invade their nest. — Tucabert Deerstrider, Druid of the High Forest

The ara are a race of tropical bird-people that resemble large humanoid macaws. They live in nest complexes built in the high branches of jungle trees, well above the jungle floor. Ara society is based on extended family groups; most ara village inhabitants are related, with the eldest female serving as matriarch and overseer of the settlement's spiritual needs. On occasion, several families band together to form a single larger community for mutual benefit. Male and female ara trade off responsibilities, such as caring for youngsters or venturing out to gather fruits and succulents. Ara are a fairly insular people and generally avoid contact with outsiders; however, they can sometimes be persuaded to trade, as they value metal tools and weapons. Ara are peaceful, and if their home territory is threatened, they are most likely to simply relocate to a less-dangerous location. As eggs and young ara cannot easily be moved, the ara fight fiercely to defend themselves during the breeding season and as the young grow to adulthood. A few ara leave their island homes to venture into the outside world, but these are a rare and exotic sight.

Two distinct breeds of ara exist: those with bright scarlet plumage and those with bright iridescent blue. Though interfertile, the two breeds tend to mate with those of similar plumage, keeping the groups separate. Ara communities tend to be one or the other, but from time to time families join in a single community that has both types. Some observers note that sapphire ara tend to be spellcasters who favor clerical and druidic spells, while scarlet ara are more likely to take a role as defenders of the community, but this appears to be more out of tradition than anything else, and both groups are equally capable.

ARA

Medium humanoid, chaotic good

Armor Class 14 (natural armor)
Hit Points 23 (4d8 + 4)
Speed 20 ft., fly 40 ft.

STR	DEX	CON	INT	WIS	CHA
10 (+0)	13 (+1)	12 (+1)	10 (+0)	12 (+1)	11 (+0)

Skills Athletics +2, Perception +5
Senses passive Perception 15
Languages Auran
Challenge 1/2 (100 XP)

ACTIONS

Multiattack. The ara makes one Bite attack and one Talon or one Spear attack.
Bite. *Melee Weapon Attack:* +2 to hit, reach 5 ft., one target. *Hit:* 4 (1d8) piercing damage.
Shortbow. *Ranged Weapon Attack:* +3 to hit, range 80/320 ft., one target. *Hit:* 4 (1d6 + 1) piercing damage.
Spear. *Melee Weapon Attack:* +2 to hit, reach 5 ft., one target. *Hit:* 3 (1d6) piercing damage.
Talons. *Melee Weapon Attack:* +2 to hit, reach 5 ft., one target. *Hit:* 3 (1d6) slashing damage.

ARA CLERIC

Medium humanoid, chaotic good

Armor Class 14 (natural armor)
Hit Points 33 (6d8 + 6)
Speed 20 ft., fly 40 ft.

STR	DEX	CON	INT	WIS	CHA
10 (+0)	13 (+1)	12 (+1)	10 (+0)	16 (+3)	11 (+0)

Skills Athletics +2, Perception +5
Senses passive Perception 15
Languages Auran
Challenge 2 (450 XP)

Spellcasting. The ara cleric is a 5th-level spellcaster. Its spellcasting ability is Wisdom (spell save DC 13, +5 to hit with spell attacks). The ara cleric has the following cleric spells prepared:
Cantrips (at will): *guidance, light, resistance, sacred flame*
1st level (4 slots): *bless, cure wounds, guiding bolt, shield of faith*
2nd level (3 slots): *dispel magic, hold person, lesser restoration*
3rd level (2 slots): *mass healing word, prayer of healing*

ACTIONS

Multiattack. The ara makes one Bite attack and one Talon or one Spear attack.
Bite. *Melee Weapon Attack:* +2 to hit, reach 5 ft., one target. *Hit:* 4 (1d8) piercing damage.
Shortbow. *Ranged Weapon Attack:* +3 to hit, range 80/320 ft., one target. *Hit:* 4 (1d6 + 1) piercing damage.
Spear. *Melee Weapon Attack:* +2 to hit, reach 5 ft., one target. *Hit:* 3 (1d6) piercing damage.
Talons. *Melee Weapon Attack:* +2 to hit, reach 5 ft., one target. *Hit:* 3 (1d6) slashing damage.

ARCANOPLASM

As I was examining one of the glass animals in the menagerie, that insipid barbarian took a swing at the floating glass sphere roiling with the yellow and gray sludge. Exploding shards of glass shredded his skin, and then the thing was upon him. A pseudopod of pale protoplasm burned a hole straight through the dolt. Grendes summoned a bolt of mystical energy, but the creature absorbed the missile. It fired the same bolt right back, knocking Grendes to the ground! I ran as the blob flowed over my dismayed friend. — Kimber Threeclover, last surviving member of the Company of the Blue Riders

Thought to be the result of a failed magical experiment, wizards and sorcerers alike have tried for years to gather information on this alien creature, but thus far such information has eluded even the most resourceful of researchers. Arcanoplasms are found in areas where the residual energy of arcane magic lingers. Such areas include abandoned wizard's towers, keeps, dungeons, and so forth. Here they feed and remain until disturbed. Because it lairs in ruins and similar places that attract adventurers, it rarely has to wait long between meals. Arcanoplasms always target arcane spellcasting creatures first. Thanks to its ability to replicate spells cast near it, the arcanoplasm always tries to stay within 30 feet of a hostile arcane caster. Mimicked spells are cast at the foe deemed most threatening.

ARCANOPLASM

Large monstrosity, neutral

Armor Class 12 (natural armor)
Hit Points 103 (9d10 + 54)
Speed 40 ft.

STR	DEX	CON	INT	WIS	CHA
15 (+2)	6 (–2)	22 (+6)	10 (+0)	14 (+2)	14 (+2)

Saving Throws Con +8
Skills Athletics +4, Stealth +0
Damage Immunities poison
Condition Immunities paralyzed, poisoned, prone, stunned, unconscious
Senses darkvision 60 ft., passive Perception 12
Languages Common, draconic (understands but can't speak)
Challenge 4 (1,100 XP)

Absorb Arcane Energy. Any arcane spell targeted at an arcanoplasm is automatically absorbed into its body. This cures 1 point of damage per 3 points of damage the spell would otherwise deal; nondamaging spells cure 1 point of damage per spell slot used to cast the spell. Spells that affect an area are not absorbed, but neither do they affect the arcanoplasm. The arcanoplasm can't absorb magic from spells that it cast itself using arcane spell mimicry, and it can't absorb divine magic, which affects it normally.

Amorphous. An arcanoplasm can move through gaps as small as one square inch without penalty.

Arcanesense. An arcanoplasm can automatically detect the location of any arcane spellcaster within 100 feet. This ability is not blocked by any material.

Arcane Spell Mimicry. As an action, an arcanoplasm can mimic any arcane spell of 4th level or lower cast within 30 feet of it on its next turn. The spell takes effect as if cast by a 7th-level sorcerer (spell save DC 13, +6 spell attack bonus) and requires no components. Because of its innately magical nature, an arcanoplasm adds both its Con and Cha modifiers to concentration checks when it takes damage.

Immutable Form. The golem is immune to any spell or effect that would alter its form.

ACTIONS

Multiattack. The arcanoplasm make one Slam attack and one Constriction attack.

Slam. *Melee Weapon Attack:* +4 to hit, reach 5 ft., one target. *Hit:* 5 (1d6 + 2) bludgeoning damage plus 3 (1d6) acid damage, and the target is grappled (escape DC 12).

Constriction. One creature already grappled by the arcanoplasm takes 5 (1d6 + 2) bludgeoning damage plus 7 (2d6) acid damage.

Baboonwere

Beware! Travel together after dark! The Slaughter-Ape was spotted standing over a cow, bathed in its blood. The beast screamed an animal howl and ran fast, on all fours, and escaped the guards. But they tracked its bloody prints to where it scrambled right over our walls to get inside. But where it now walked, the prints changed and became human! The man (or beast!) escaped into the alleys among us. Beware your neighbors! Beware! — Reported last words of town crier Rupert Hibble in Hillport

Baboonweres are evil baboons born with the ability to assume human or a hybrid human form. Baboonweres are most often found among normal baboons, though some prefer to maintain their human form and live among ordinary people in small towns and villages. When the livestock and cattle begin turning up missing or slain is when the baboonwere usually moves on, before the finger of suspicion is pointed its way. In its hybrid form, a baboonwere stands just over five feet tall and weighs roughly 130 pounds.

Baboonwere

Medium beast (shapechanger), chaotic evil

Armor Class 14 (natural armor)
Hit Points 44 (8d8 + 8)
Speed 30 ft., climb 30 ft.

STR	DEX	CON	INT	WIS	CHA
13 (+1)	14 (+ 2)	13 (+1)	10 (+ 0)	12 (+1)	12 (+ 1)

Skills Athletics +3, Stealth +4
Damage Immunities bludgeoning, piercing, and slashing attacks from nonmagical attacks that aren't silver
Senses darkvision 60 ft., passive Perception 11
Languages Common
Challenge 4 (1,100 XP)

Displacement. The baboonwere projects an illusion that makes it appear to be standing near its actual location, causing attack rolls against it to have disadvantage. If the baboonwere is hit by an attack, this trait is disrupted until the end of its next turn. This trait is also disrupted if the baboonwere is incapacitated or reduced to a speed of 0.

Shapechanger. The baboonwere can use its action to polymorph into a humanoid, a baboon-human hybrid, or a baboon. Its statistics, other than its size, are the same in each form. Any equipment it is wearing or carrying doesn't transform. It reverts to its true form of a baboon-human hybrid if it dies.

Keen Scent. The baboonwere has advantage on Wisdom (Perception) checks that rely on scent.

Voice mimicry. The baboonwere can mimic the voice of a creature it hears. Listeners can determine that this is an imitation with a successful DC 11 Wisdom (Insight) check.

Actions

Multiattack. The baboonwere makes two attacks, only one of which can be a Bite attack.

Bite (hybrid and baboon form only). *Melee Weapon Attack:* +4 to hit, reach 5 ft., one target. *Hit:* 5 (1d6 + 2) piercing damage.

Longsword (hybrid and humanoid form only). *Melee Weapon Attack:* +3 to hit, reach 5 ft., one target. *Hit:* 5 (1d8 + 1) slashing damage.

Bake Kujira

The birds, sir, the birds came first. Hundreds! Flying tight like they had a plan. Corg in the nest vanished under their claws an' beaks, but he threw himself over. They chased him right to the brine! He screamed once when he splashed, but the water boiled and something swimming below dragged him under. The sailors on The Sultan's Flame *crowded the rail to watch, so none saw the beast rise out of the water behind them. It was all bones, it was, the sun shinin' right through! It hung in the air for just a moment … huge, impossible … then crashed right down on the* Flame, *breakin' her back. The wave snapped our mizzen and the main, and we limped away as the broken halves of* The Sultan's Flame *sank beneath the waves. A bony tail fluke swatted the screaming sailors still thrashing in the churning waters.*
— *Nate Fairweather, former cabin boy on* The Golden Crest

The bake kujira is a horrific monstrosity that outwardly appears to be the skeleton of a gargantuan whale. In reality, its flesh and organs are transparent, giving the impression that it is an entirely disembodied skeleton. Its common moniker, "ghost whale," refers to this, but the bake kujira is not actually undead. The bake kujira's origins are unknown, but some claim demons or evil gods created them to carry out acts of mayhem and destruction on the sea in the name of their masters. Others think they may have originated on another plane or are the creation of the mad sorcerers who plagued the heroes in the era of the Thousand Kingdoms.

Bake kujira are indeed living creatures despite their appearance, but they are definitely not natural. Encounters with the bake kujira are invariably fearful experiences. Those few who survive their meetings with the ghost whales are plagued by nightmares and terrible visions for the rest of their lives. It is said that only by destroying the bake kujira who committed the original attack can their victims ever fully be free.

Grim forces of evil and destruction, bake kujira seem to attract other hostile creatures. Survivors of encounters with bake kujira report that the monsters are accompanied by flocks of vicious birds and biting fish that appear to serve the ghost whale's will. Especially aggressive birds and fish may actually herald a bake kujira's appearance, and superstitious mariners strongly advise a quick return to the safety of port should such creatures make themselves known.

Bake Kujira
Gargantuan monstrosity, neutral evil

Armor Class 21 (natural armor)
Hit Points 372 (24d20 + 120)
Speed 0 ft., swim 100 ft.

STR	DEX	CON	INT	WIS	CHA
26 (+8)	10 (+0)	20 (+5)	6 (−2)	10 (+0)	7 (−2)

Damage Resistances bludgeoning, piercing and slashing damage from nonmagical attacks
Senses passive Perception 10
Languages —
Challenge 20 (25,000 XP)

Transparent. The bake kujira is transparent and only its skeleton is visible, which makes it appear to be some undead monstrosity. Attacks upon the bake kujira require successful DC 19 Wisdom (Perception) checks or are made at disadvantage.

Ghastly Swarms. The bake kujira is accompanied by 2d4 **swarms of hostile birds** and 2d4 **swarms of carnivorous fish** (see monster entries). These creatures accompany the larger monster to scavenge from its feeding, but also appear to be attracted to the bake kujira's overwhelmingly evil lifeforce. These swarms attack anything that attacks the bake kujira.

Actions

Breach. The bake kujira makes a full move, breaches into the air, then crashes down upon its target. Any Huge or smaller creatures in the bake kujira's space must make a DC 19 Dexterity save or take 48 (4d8 + 30) bludgeoning damage and be forced into the nearest square that is adjacent to the bake kujira.

Basalt Warhound

Badog went first into the darkness, his silvered axe in front of him as he stooped under the standing arch of granite marking the ruins. His beefy shoulders nearly touched the sides! When Badog stands up, people cower! Except this time. His shrieks were filled with pain and fear and plain old terror. Badog came running fast — no axe — in fact, no right arm that once held that axe! The hound that followed was as dark as coal, and fire licked around its snout. It snarled around Badog's shredded arm still caught in its pointed teeth. I'll never forget those yellow eyes as it gave chase. Badog fled in terror. He just didn't run fast enough. — Borolan Ashenchisel, on the beast of the Beharrel Valleys

A basalt warhound is a massive hound that looks as if it is formed of living brass and basalt. It stands nearly as tall as a human, and its eyes burn with yellow flame. Its tongue and teeth are pitch-black, and flames flicker and dance around its rocky snout as it breathes. When killed, the massive beast erupts in an explosive ring of fire. Some spellcasters claim basalt warhound packs can be summoned from the edges of the various elemental planes bordering the Material Plane, but other say the beast can smell out tunnels into the world so it can roam — and hunt — freely.

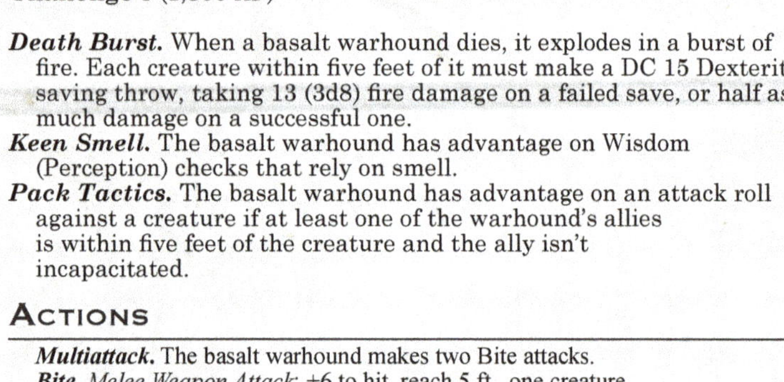

Basalt Warhound
Large elemental, lawful evil

Armor Class 16 (natural armor)
Hit Points 136 (16d10 + 48)
Speed 30 ft.

STR	DEX	CON	INT	WIS	CHA
16 (+3)	16 (+3)	16 (+3)	6 (−2)	14 (+2)	10 (+0)

Saving Throws Dex +6, Wis +5
Skills Perception +5
Damage Resistances bludgeoning, piercing, and slashing from nonmagical attacks
Damage Vulnerabilities cold
Damage Immunities fire, poison
Condition Immunities poisoned
Senses darkvision 60 ft., passive Perception 15
Languages Ignan
Challenge 5 (1,800 XP)

Death Burst. When a basalt warhound dies, it explodes in a burst of fire. Each creature within five feet of it must make a DC 15 Dexterity saving throw, taking 13 (3d8) fire damage on a failed save, or half as much damage on a successful one.
Keen Smell. The basalt warhound has advantage on Wisdom (Perception) checks that rely on smell.
Pack Tactics. The basalt warhound has advantage on an attack roll against a creature if at least one of the warhound's allies is within five feet of the creature and the ally isn't incapacitated.

Actions

Multiattack. The basalt warhound makes two Bite attacks.
Bite. *Melee Weapon Attack:* +6 to hit, reach 5 ft., one creature. *Hit:* 12 (2d8 + 3) piercing damage and 9 (2d8) fire damage.

Basilisk, Abyssal, Greater

True, true, I never liked the elf. Dobs had a stick up his ... well, he was stuffy, you know what I mean? But I'm going back for him. No one deserves what happened. That foul beast climbed out of the swamp and surprised us as we camped. I was looking for my blade — I don't know how it had fallen — so I didn't look the thing in the eyes when it reared up. Dobs did. All I saw was the eight legs reflecting off my sword, scales dripping like ichor, and its jaws. And Dobs, of course, true, true, as his pale flesh hardened into paler stone. Kind of like his personality. But I'm going back for him. I've heard tales of a temple that pays good coin for statues. — Haric Spant of the Silver Crown Society thieves' guild

Denizens of the Demonic Abyss, these large, eight-legged crocodilian horrors have been touched by the infecting influence of raw chaos. The stout, armor-plated beasts literally drip ashen discord and death from their constantly molting scales and stinking slobbering jaws. Their scales range from blue-black to dark green-black and their eyes glow with an unnatural light that petrifies their victims.

Greater Abyssal Basilisk

Large monstrosity, chaotic evil

Armor Class 17 (natural armor)
Hit Points 142 (15d10 + 60)
Speed 25 ft.

STR	DEX	CON	INT	WIS	CHA
19 (+4)	10 (+0)	18 (+4)	5 (−3)	12 (+1)	6 (−2)

Saving Throws Con +8
Skills Perception +5
Damage Resistances cold, fire
Damage Immunities poison
Condition Immunities poisoned
Senses darkvision 90 ft., passive Perception 15
Languages —
Challenge 10 (5,900 XP)

Detect Good. The Abyssal basilisk can detect fey and celestial creatures within 60 feet as an ongoing effect.

Foul Breath. The Abyssal basilisk's breath is so putrid that it creates an area of foul gas in a five-foot radius around itself. Any creature entering that area or starting its turn within that area must succeed on a DC 13 Constitution save or become poisoned until the start of its next turn.

Magic Resistance. The Abyssal basilisk has advantage on saving throws against spells and other magical effects.

Actions

Multiattack. The Abyssal basilisk makes one Bite attack and two Claw attacks.

Bite. *Melee Weapon Attack:* +8 to hit, reach 5 ft., one target. *Hit:* 17 (3d8 + 4) piercing damage plus 10 (3d6) poison damage.

Claw. *Melee Weapon Attack:* +8 to hit, reach 5 ft., one target. *Hit:* 13 (2d8 + 4) slashing damage.

Petrifying Gaze. If a creature starts its turn within 30 feet of the Abyssal basilisk and the two of them can see each other, the basilisk can force the creature to make a DC 15 Constitution saving throw if the basilisk isn't incapacitated. On a failed save, the creature magically begins to turn to stone and is restrained. It must repeat the saving throw at the end of its next turn. On a success, the effect ends. On a failure, the creature is petrified until freed by a *greater restoration* spell or other magic.

A creature that isn't surprised can avert its eyes to avoid the saving throw at the start of its turn. If it does so, it can't see the Abyssal basilisk until the start of its next turn, when it can avert its eyes again. If it looks at the Abyssal basilisk in the meantime, it must immediately make the save.

If the Abyssal basilisk sees its own reflection within 30 feet of it in bright light, it must succeed on a DC 10 Wisdom save or mistake itself for a rival and target itself with its gaze. The Abyssal basilisk's magic resistance gives it advantage on any resultant Constitution save versus its own gaze.

Bat, Fungus

We smelled it first, that musty-sweet odor when fungi grow rampant. The cave was rank with it. Dallitus thought it was a bat at first, but the thing was so misshapen that it was hard to believe it could even fly. I've seen bats, and they avoid you. This thing crashed straightaway into Dall with a fleshy whoomp! *and bore him to the ground. It was sinking its fangs into the knight's neck when that plucky squire Capers took its head off with one swing. — Sir Canevar of Farall Hold*

A fungus bat has a malformed central mass that appears to be composed of fleshy mushrooms, with long, writhing tendrils trailing its form. They attack with their debilitating bite, which paralyzes its prey.

Fungus Bat

Medium plant (fungus), unaligned

Armor Class 11 (natural armor)
Hit Points 16 (3d8 + 3)
Speed 30 ft., fly 60 ft.

STR	DEX	CON	INT	WIS	CHA
11 (+0)	12 (+1)	13 (+1)	1 (–5)	10 (+0)	1 (–5)

Damage Immunities psychic
Condition Immunities frightened, prone, stunned, unconscious
Senses blindsight 60 ft., passive Perception 10
Languages —
Challenge 1/2 (100 XP)

Actions

Bite. *Melee Weapon Attack:* +3 to hit, reach 5 ft., one target. *Hit:* 5 (1d8 + 1) piercing damage and target must make a DC 13 Constitution saving throw or be poisoned. If the target fails the saving throw, it immediately suffers the effects of the fungus bat's poison, losing the use of its legs and falling prone for one minute (as if restrained and knocked prone). The target can repeat the saving throw on each of its turns, ending the effect on a success.

Bear, Cave

The shaggy shape shambled out of the cave, its bulk filling the narrow opening out of proportion to its ursine form. Towering above me, its limbs ready to reach out with wicked claws that can tear and arms that can crush, something instinctual urged flight as the musky stench of the irate cave bear washed over me. It stood and roared, and we knew why the natives called this beast the slayer of tribes. — Sir Cedric of Reme, knight errant

Cave bears dwell in lands far beyond the civilized world in places long forgotten. These prehistoric holdouts are larger than any bear has the right to be, and far more fearsome. While they are primarily vegetarians, cave bears are not averse to the occasional meat-based menu. Many cultures that dwell in proximity to cave bears have learned to respect and even venerate these ill-tempered ursine beasts.

Cave Bear

Huge beast, unaligned

Armor Class 13 (natural armor)
Hit Points 142 (15d12 + 45)
Speed 40 ft.

STR	DEX	CON	INT	WIS	CHA
22 (+6)	10 (+0)	16 (+3)	2 (–4)	12 (+1)	7 (–2)

Skills Perception +4
Senses darkvision 60 ft., passive Perception 14
Languages —
Challenge 7 (2,900 XP)

Bear Hug. If the cave bear hits a creature with two Claw attacks in the same turn, the target is grappled. The cave bear has advantage on Bite attacks against a creature it has grappled and may use a bonus action to inflict 15 (2d8 + 6) bludgeoning damage on the grappled creature.

Bear Frenzy. A cave bear is not slain if reduced to 0 HP. Instead, it enters bear frenzy. While in bear frenzy the cave bear may continue to act normally. At the end of every turn that the cave bear is in bear frenzy, it must succeed on a DC 12 Constitution saving throw or die.

Keen Scent. The cave bear has advantage on Wisdom (Perception) checks that rely on scent.

Actions

Multiattack. The cave bear makes two attacks, only one of which can be a Bite attack.

Bite. *Melee Weapon Attack:* +8 to hit, reach 5 ft., one target. *Hit:* 15 (2d8 + 6) piercing damage.

Claws. *Melee Weapon Attack:* +8 to hit, reach 10 ft., one target. *Hit:* 11 (1d10 + 6) slashing damage.

BERBEROKA

We thought the raft had caught on a rock. It stopped so suddenly in the Gaelon's swift flow that we nearly tumbled headfirst into the water. The old fisherman guiding us made the mistake of looking over the edge, and that's when the greenish hands erupted from the water and grabbed him by his long white beard. He went overboard with a splash and vanished. What came out of the water in his stead was as big as an ogre, but scaled and green. Its hands and feet were webbed. If not for the fiery blast Berthal conjured, we might not have made it off that raft alive.
— The Esteemed Scholar Yarl Enders of Endhome

Berberoka are scaled ogres who lurk in rivers, lakes, and other bodies of water where they seek their prey. Though they can subsist on fish, berberoka far prefer the flesh of air-breathing creatures, especially humans, elves, and dwarves. They are solitary creatures, though every few years they are compelled to venture to other lairs and reproduce, giving birth to small berberoka who seek out their own aquatic lairs. Most prefer freshwater lakes and rivers, though reports of berberoka lurking in coves, inlets, and other calm saltwater places exist.

A berberoka secretes an oily substance that attracts fish to its location. If especially hungry, a berberoka can subsist on the fish that it attracts, but it normally uses these schools of fish to lure surface-dwelling fisherfolk, whom it then seizes and attempts to drag to their doom. This substance can be extracted from a dead berberoka, making it an extremely valuable commodity.

BERBEROKA
Huge giant, chaotic evil

Armor Class 14 (natural armor)
Hit Points 114 (12d12 + 36)
Speed 30 ft., swim 30 ft.

STR	DEX	CON	INT	WIS	CHA
19 (+4)	10 (+0)	16 (+3)	6 (–2)	8 (–1)	6 (–2)

Skills Stealth +4
Senses darkvision 60 ft., passive Perception 9
Languages Common, Giant
Challenge 4 (1,100 XP)

Amphibious. Berberoka can breathe air and water.
Aquatic Stealth. Berberoka have advantage on stealth checks made while in water.
Fisherman's Friend. Berberoka secrete a substance that attracts fish and when in water draw all fish of Intelligence 1 within a 100-yard radius to their location. A slain berberoka yields 3d6 doses of fisherman's friend (as it is commonly called), and each dose sells for 100gp.

ACTIONS

Multiattack. Berberoka make two Fist attacks.
Fist. *Melee Weapon Attack:* +6 to hit, reach 5 ft., one creature. Hit: 13 (2d8 + 4) bludgeoning damage. Target is grappled (Escape DC 14). If both fist attacks hit, target is also restrained.
Drown. The berberoka can submerge along with any grappled or restrained targets. It then engages in a Strength ability contest with its grappled or restrained targets to force the air from their lungs. If the berberoka succeeds, the target begins drowning (see rules for suffocation). Contests against grappled opponents are normal, but the berberoka has advantage on contests against targets that are grappled and restrained.

Binguai

That arrogant blowhard Pren the Red led us right into that trap. The walls were too close and forced us into a single-file march. You just knew it wasn't safe. It was already too late when an icy wind pushed the snow into a frenzy, freezing our bones. That was when the first giant stuck its head over the wall and glared down at us. It's eyes were gone, replaced by a glacial light blazing like the sun. Pren swung at the meaty arm as it reached for him, but his blade only chipped the giant's skin. The second one reared up right behind us, rising out of the snow. We'd walked right over the thing! It was worse off than its partner, with a hole blown through its chest to expose its broken ribs. I ducked out of its reach before it blocked the ravine completely. — Janel Free, last surviving member of the Company of the Blazing Shield

The binguai, or frozen giants, can be found in the mountains that surround the Xha'en Hegemony. They are the undead remains of shamans or especially bloodthirsty warriors risen from the dead to visit frozen doom upon their tribes' enemies. The presence of binguai in a group of warriors is considered an especially auspicious omen for the frost giants, and they are known to fight with greater ferocity when accompanied by one.

In addition to their role in a frost giant tribe, binguai may also rise from their graves to defend the final resting places of other frost giants. In such cases, binguai stand watch over tombs, cairns, or places where other giants have fallen, and may sometimes be mistaken for corpses themselves. Should intruders approach too closely, however, the binguai shows itself and attacks fiercely, unleashing its freezing whirlwind before attacking.

Binguai

Huge undead, neutral evil

Armor Class 18 (natural armor)
Hit Points 138 (12d12 + 60)
Speed 30 ft.

STR	DEX	CON	INT	WIS	CHA
23 (+6)	9 (−1)	21 (+5)	7 (−2)	10 (+0)	6 (−2)

Saving Throws Con +8, Wis +3, Cha +4
Damage Immunities cold
Senses passive Perception 10
Languages Giant
Challenge 8 (3,900 XP)

Magic Resistance. The binguai has advantage on saving throws against spells and other magical effects.

Morale Boost. Frost giants within 120 feet of a binguai gain a +2 bonus to their attack and damage rolls.

Actions

Multiattack. The binguai makes two Icy Chains attacks.

Icy Chains. *Melee Weapon Attack:* +9 to hit, reach 10 ft., one target. *Hit:* 25 (3d12 + 6) bludgeoning damage plus 10 (3d6) cold damage.

Freezing Whirlwind (recharge 5–6). The binguai summons a swirling storm of ice and snow that affects a 20-foot radius. Each creature in the area must make a DC 16 Constitution saving throw. On a failure, a target takes 45 (10d8) Cold damage and is imprisoned in a column of ice. Imprisoned targets are restrained (escape DC 16) and must make DC 16 Constitution saving throws each round or take 3 (1d6) cold damage from the effects of ice and suffocation. The restrained target can escape or be freed by a companion. The ice is Armor Class 12 and has 15 hit points. Once the ice is destroyed, the target can act normally.

Blood Kaktos

I was starving and mad with thirst, but I swear I'm not making it up. They were real. Our caravan was about a day's ride north of the Shield Basilica and everything was well. The Kanderi is deadly, but we were prepared. Still, all that sand and nothing for miles. The cactuses were so strange but so pretty. Until some of them started to move! Something whistled by my ear, and I heard Smithson cry out. Needles stuck out from his entire body. Aneleise was caught in the grip of another one. Her face was sunken and pale, bloodless. I turned and ran. Better the burning sands than to die like that. – Coral Gammew, upon her rescue by troops from the Shield Basilica of Muir

The blood kaktos is a mobile, sentient plant that inhabits any warm, sandy environment. It is a relative of the common saguaro cactus and has leathery green flesh covered with needle-like spines, with two jointed, branch-like arms sprouting from a large trunk that grows to between five and seven feet tall upon maturity.

Three eyes approximately two inches in diameter appear as a darker shade of green. They are typically positioned in a scalene triangle formation and are the only obvious sensory organs. The casual observer could easily perceive the eyes as ordinary scars or imperfections found on a common cactus and may not be aware they are looking at a deadly blood kaktos.

Blood Kaktos

Large plant, lawful neutral

Armor Class 14 (natural armor)
Hit Points 60 (8d10 + 16)
Speed 25 ft.

STR	DEX	CON	INT	WIS	CHA
17 (+3)	10 (+0)	14 (+2)	10 (+0)	9 (–1)	7 (–2)

Skills Stealth +4, Perception (+3 or +1)
Damage Resistances fire
Damage Vulnerabilities cold
Condition Immunities deafened
Senses darkvision 60 ft., passive Perception 13 (or 11)
Languages Blood kaktos telepathy
Challenge 2 (450 XP)

Silent Slither. The blood kaktos has advantage on Dexterity (Stealth) checks to move silently through sand when sneaking up on prey.

Telepathic Communication. The blood kaktos cannot speak, but it can communicate with others of its kind through telepathic communication. The communication consists of the conveyance of emotions and intent, allowing groups of blood kaktoses to loosely coordinate attacks against prey.

Actions

Multiattack. The blood kaktos makes two Prickly Punch attacks.

Prickly Punch. *Melee attack:* +5, range 5 ft. *Hit:* 6 (1d6 + 3) piercing damage and 3 (1d6) poison damage. If both prickly punch attacks are successful against the same target, the blood kaktos embraces the victim, who is grappled and restrained until it breaks the embrace. The blood kaktos extends its proboscis to penetrate any exposed skin, writhing through armor joints if need be. This is an automatic hit that causes its victim to lose 3 (1d4 + 1) hit points at the beginning of the target's turn as the blood kaktos gorges upon the victim's blood. If the victim breaks free from the embrace, the blood kaktos immediately retracts its proboscis, fearing damage to its delicate organ. The victim can use an action to attempt a DC 13 Strength (Athletics) or Dexterity (Acrobatics) check to escape. A victim that escapes the embrace sustains an additional 3 (1d6) slashing damage as the needles rip the escapee's flesh.

Huff and Puff **(recharge 4–6).** The blood kaktos inhales air into the space between its outer layer of skin and its inner membranous tissue and then forces it out sharply, spraying needles in all directions over a 10-foot radius. Any creature within this area must make a DC 14 Dexterity saving throw. Those that fail the saving throw take 9 (2d8) piercing damage from the flying needles while those that succeed take half this amount.

Blood Orchid

You need to ask Audreie who killed the master's family. I was tending the flowers. The beautiful flowers. They talk to me sometimes, you understand? Perfection. Audreie is the most beautiful. Her petals three are rosy and pale. Her voice in my mind is sweet and makes me think of the distant flower fields of Old Burgandia. Those flowers didn't speak to me, though, understand? Audreie didn't like the master, you know? She'd look me in the eye and whisper what their fates should be. I never listened, though. Never. Not even that one time. And definitely not the next. She was so kind. I left her in the greenhouse. She's still waiting there for me.
— From the rantings of the gardener Semore, after the tragedy at Shaw Manor

This beast has three downward curving "petals" of flesh with dark, pebbly outer hides and pallid whitish undersides. The petals converge at the blood orchid's center and end with split tips. On its underside at the center dangle a swarm of writhing pallid tentacles: 16 manipulator arms and eight thinner tendrils with red eyes at the ends. A sphincter-shaped mouth at the end of a flexible trunk one foot long and six inches in diameter is at the center of these tentacles. Another cluster of eye tendrils is at the apex of the creature.

Blood orchids are territorial, xenophobic, and possessive. They rarely form alliances with other creatures as their alien mindset keeps them from forming any common ground. They regard other races as aberrant and not to be trusted, even other lawful creatures.

Communication by blood orchids is through a means of empathy/telepathy. They have no sense of hearing, which renders them immune to sonic effects. The blood orchid can close its outer petals downward and rest on the ground, where it resembles a rocky nodule or fungus of some kind.

Blood orchids occasionally develop sorcerous talents and transform into savants. When their abilities reach a certain level, they evolve into a grand savant. Normally, each colony of blood orchids is led by a single grand savant, and another cannot evolve while one is present. Typically, a blood orchid savant ready to become a grand savant leaves the colony with a few followers and sets out to establish a new brood elsewhere.

Blood Orchid

Large aberration, lawful evil

Armor Class 14 (natural armor)
Hit Points 76 (9d10 + 27)
Speed 5 ft., fly 30 ft.

STR	DEX	CON	INT	WIS	CHA
15 (+2)	12 (+1)	16 (+3)	11 (+0)	12 (+1)	13 (+1)

Skills Stealth +4
Damage Resistances acid, cold, lightning, fire
Damage Immunities thunder
Senses darkvision 60 ft., passive Perception 11
Languages telepathy 120 ft.
Challenge 5 (1,800 XP)

Hyper-Awareness. A blood orchid cannot be surprised.
Telepathic Bond. Blood orchids have a telepathic link to other blood orchids that are within 120 feet.

Actions

Multiattack. The blood orchid uses Blood Drain and makes up to three Tentacle attacks.
Tentacle. *Melee Weapon Attack:* +5 to hit, reach 5 ft., one target. *Hit:* 11 (2d8 + 2) bludgeoning damage and the target must succeed on a DC 13 Constitution saving throw or be poisoned for one hour. The target is also grappled (escape DC 11). While grappled this way, the creature is restrained. Until the grapple ends, the blood orchid can't use this tentacle on another target. The blood orchid has three tentacles with which it can attack.
Blood Drain. The blood orchid feeds on a creature it is grappling. The creature must succeed on a DC 13 Constitution saving throw or its hit point maximum is reduced by 5 (1d10). This reduction lasts until the creature finishes a long rest. The target dies if this effect reduces its hit point maximum to 0.

Blood Orchid Savant

A blood orchid savant is a rarity among blood orchids that has learned to cast spells.

Blood Orchid Savant

Large aberration, lawful evil

Armor Class 15 (natural armor)
Hit Points 97 (13d10 + 26)
Speed 5 ft., fly 30 ft.

STR	DEX	CON	INT	WIS	CHA
15 (+2)	14 (+2)	14 (+2)	13 (+1)	16 (+3)	18 (+4)

Skills Stealth +5
Damage Resistances acid, cold, lightning, fire
Damage Immunities thunder
Senses darkvision 60 ft., passive Perception 13
Languages telepathy 120 ft.
Challenge 7 (2,900 XP)

Spellcasting. The blood orchid is a 4th-level spellcaster. Its spellcasting ability is Charisma (spell save DC 15, +7 to hit with spell attacks). It can cast the following spells:
Cantrips (at will): *dancing lights, fire bolt, light, mage hand*
1st level (4 slots): *burning hands, color spray, detect magic, magic missile*
2nd level (3 slots): *darkness, ray of enfeeblement, scorching ray*
Hyper-Awareness. A blood orchid cannot be surprised.
Telepathic Bond. Blood orchids have an unbreakable telepathic link to other blood orchids that are within 120 feet.

Actions

Multiattack. The blood orchid savant makes three attacks with its Tentacles.
Tentacles. *Melee Weapon Attack:* +5 to hit, reach 5 ft., one target. *Hit:* 11 (2d8 + 2) bludgeoning damage and the target must succeed on a DC 14 Constitution saving throw or be poisoned for one hour. The target is also grappled (escape DC 14). While grappled this way, the creature is restrained.
Blood Drain. The blood orchid feeds on every creature it is grappling. Each grappled creature must succeed on a DC 14 Constitution saving throw or its hit point maximum is reduced by 5 (1d10), and the blood orchid savant regains the same number of hit points. The reduction lasts until the creature finishes a long rest. The target dies if this effect reduces its hit point maximum to 0.
Charm. One creature within 30 feet must succeed on a DC 15 Wisdom saving throw or be charmed for 24 hours. The creature is not under the blood orchid's control but regards it as a trusted friend, takes its requests as favorably as possible, and won't try to escape from the blood orchid's grapple. Each time the blood orchid or its allies do anything harmful to the creature, it can repeat the saving throw.

BLOODY BONES

We were not the first to delve into the forgotten temple. Signs were everywhere of others along the entire path into the hidden sanctuary: thieves who tripped traps, the remains of those slaughtered by some horrid monster we had yet to encounter, and, in one case, a scorched mark on the floor and a pair of singed lockpicks stuck in a door. It was in the hour of the rooster that we found the monster of the temple. It was a skeleton, and we underestimated it. We should have known it was no normal animated dead; the thing leaked blood and mucus and attacked with cunning and surprise. Its tentacles whipped about and tore Asandrá limb from limb. — Tara the Wise, adventurer

Bloody bones are created when a person desecrates the temple of an evil god and dies in the process. At least, that is what scholars hope, for that would make this horror decidedly rare. Appearing like any other animated skeleton, the bloody bones can be discerned as different by three factors: It still has a significant amount of sinew and bits of flesh upon its bones; blood and mucus constantly leak from its bones, making it a very slippery foe indeed; and finally, four intestine-like tentacles emerge from its empty abdominal cavity to whip around, crush, and rend.

BLOODY BONES

Medium undead, neutral evil

Armor Class 12
Hit Points 78 (12d8 + 24)
Speed 30 ft.

STR	DEX	CON	INT	WIS	CHA
17 (+3)	14 (+2)	15 (+2)	8 (−1)	12 (+1)	9 (−1)

Saving Throws Wis +3
Damage Immunities poison
Condition Immunities poisoned
Senses darkvision 60 ft., passive Perception 11
Languages the languages it knew in life
Challenge 4 (1,100 XP)

Bloody Regeneration. When the bloody bones doesn't have all of its hit points, it seeps blood from its pores. At the start of its turn if it is seeping blood from its pores, it regains 5 hit points. If the bloody bones takes radiant damage, this trait doesn't function at the start of the bloody bones's next turn. The bloody bones dies only if it starts its turn with 0 hit points and doesn't regenerate.

Undead Nature. A bloody bones doesn't require air, food, drink, or sleep.

ACTIONS

Multiattack. The bloody bones makes two Bloody Fist attacks.

Bloody Fist. *Melee Weapon Attack:* +5 to hit, reach 5 ft., one target. *Hit:* 6 (1d6 + 3) bludgeoning damage plus 4 (1d8) poison damage.

Blood Spray (recharge 5–6). If the bloody bones doesn't have all of its hit points, it sprays blood in a 30-foot cone. Each creature in that area must make a DC 13 Dexterity saving throw. On a failure, a creature takes 18 (4d8) poison damage and is poisoned for one minute. On a success, a creature takes half the damage and isn't poisoned.

Bog Corpse

The old man promised us a route from the Swamp Road east to Trader's Way. We should have seen through his lies. The Creeping Mire is unforgiving as it is, but he led us into a region of old ruins, overhanging trees, and thick mosses. The bog sucked at our steps as we moved. The old man laughed at our struggles. And kept laughing. When we turned on him, his form melted into the bubbling muck. The dead things clawed their ways out of the spot soon after, their stench bringing bile into our throats. Fennick and I fled into the bog as our bodyguards held them off. We finally found our passage. Never use it. — Domick Phelan, merchant trader out of Saxentry

Created by foul magics of long-dead gods, bog corpses are the remains of victims sacrificed to these otherworldly entities in times long before history began to be recorded. Cursed by the rituals that consigned them to a fetid tomb, bog corpses protect the sacred places in which they died. Once their unholy sites are disturbed, they rise to drive off the intruders and also to hound them to death. Those slain by a bog corpse are not entirely dead, and the bog corpse attempts to carry its victims back before the soul departs its body. Once interred in the rotting bog, the fresh corpse transforms into a bog corpse.

Bog Corpse

Medium undead, chaotic evil

Armor Class 9
Hit Points 26 (4d8 + 8)
Speed 20 ft., swim 20 ft.

STR	DEX	CON	INT	WIS	CHA
16 (+3)	8 (−1)	14 (+2)	8 (−1)	12 (+1)	4 (−3)

Damage Vulnerabilities fire
Damage Resistance piercing and bludgeoning damage from nonmagical attacks
Damage Immunities necrotic, poison, psychic
Condition Immunities exhaustion, frightened, poisoned, stunned
Senses darkvision 60 ft., passive Perception 11
Languages —
Challenge 1 (200 XP)

Highly flammable. Bog corpse bodies are often preserved in peat or tar deposits, and their very flesh is imbued with these substances. A bog corpse that suffers fire damage is lit on fire and suffers 3 (1d6) fire damage at the end of its turn. While on fire, a bog corpse inflicts an additional 2 (1d4) fire damage to anyone it hits with its Fist attack, and those who strike the flaming corpse with a melee attack while within five feet suffer 1 fire damage.

Watery Grave. A creature reduced to 0 hit points by a bog corpse is not dead. Instead, it falls into a coma that lasts until the bog corpse that reduced it to 0 hit points is slain, after which the victim becomes stable as if it had passed three death saves. If a creature in a coma caused by a bog corpse is placed in the sacred bog the corpse guarded, that creature becomes a bog corpse in 1d6 days.

Actions

Fist. *Melee Weapon Attack:* +5 to hit, reach 5 ft., 1 target. *Hit:* 7 (1d8 + 3) bludgeoning damage and the target is marked by the bog corpse. The bog corpse or any other bog corpse from the same sacred bog gains advantage on attack rolls against a marked target. Furthermore, they can detect the presence of a marked creature within 30 feet, and they know the approximate location of the marked creature if it is farther away.

Bone Cobbler

The cave was full of sculptures, well-done sculptures mind you, but of grotesque and bizarre forms. All were made from bones attached with leather and wire. There were halflings with goat heads, orc and elf bones fused together in a mockery of life, and this one weird thing that looked like a wind chime crossed with a swarm of pixies. We were on edge by the time we met the sculptor, and then that undead thing stripped our guide of his flesh in an instant. — Algrid Henswaithe, University of the Vast

Everyone needs a hobby, even the undead. Bone cobblers are desiccated looking undead who are not much more than skin and bones. They are master sculptors who love nothing more than making grotesqueries out of their victims' remains. That undead should have an artistic sensibility, no matter how grim and horrid it might be, comes as a surprise. Almost as much of a surprise as the fact that the bone cobbler can strip a body of all flesh in a matter of seconds, gobbling down the gibbets as it plans its next masterpiece.

Bone Cobbler

Medium aberration, chaotic evil

Armor Class 13 (natural armor)
Hit Points 22 (5d8)
Speed 30 ft.

STR	DEX	CON	INT	WIS	CHA
14 (+2)	15 (+2)	11 (+0)	10 (+0)	14 (+2)	8 (−2)

Senses darkvision 60 ft., passive Perception 12
Languages Deep Speech, Undercommon
Challenge 2 (450 XP)

Bonestripping. A bone cobbler can strip the flesh from the corpse of a Medium creature in three minutes using its claws and hammers. For each size category larger or smaller than Medium a corpse is, add or subtract one minute. Once stripped, the bone cobbler devours the flesh and collects the victim's bones to use in its sculptures. A creature slain in this manner can be brought back to life only by a *wish* or *resurrection* spell.

Actions

Multiattack. The bone cobbler makes two melee attacks.
Claws. *Melee Weapon Attack:* +4 to hit, reach 5 ft., one creature. *Hit:* 4 (1d4 + 2) slashing damage.
Light Hammer. *Melee or Ranged Weapon Attack:* +4 to hit, reach 5 ft. or range 20/60 ft., one creature. *Hit:* 4 (1d4 + 2) bludgeoning damage.
Animate Bones (1/day). A bone cobbler animates up to five skeletal statues within 30 feet of itself. These creatures use the stat block of **skeletons**, though their forms and structures do not need to resemble humanoids or anything remotely humanoid. The skeletal statues remain animated until destroyed, until the bone cobbler wills them back into statues, or for 24 hours.

Bone Needle

Bone needles are eyeless, bone-white creatures that resemble a five-foot-diameter blob of semi-translucent flesh with eight spindly, spidery legs colored black or gold. These creatures feed on bone marrow, so their lairs are always scattered with the cracked, deformed bones of their victims, both humanoid and animal. A greater bone needle is a larger version of the lesser. They appear to be nothing more than lesser bone needles that have survived long enough to grow larger than their nest mates.

A bone needle's mandibles are glossy-black and hollow, both to inject poison and to siphon out the dissolved flesh and bone from a victim's corpse. While feeding, the bone needle's fleshy form pulsates and expands. After feeding, its form becomes less translucent and takes on a greenish-yellow color.

Bone needles make their lairs deep underground to avoid natural daylight, though some brave the surface world by venturing from their lairs at night. Such surface encounters are rare and are always with at least a pack of greater and lesser bone needles. Bone needles flee natural daylight if at all possible.

Greater Bone needle

Medium beast, unaligned

Armor Class 13
Hit Points 31 (7d8)
Speed 30 ft., climb 20 ft.

STR	DEX	CON	INT	WIS	CHA
8 (–1)	16 (+3)	11 (+0)	1 (–5)	12 (+1)	3 (–4)

Damage Immunities Psychic
Condition Immunities charmed, frightened
Languages None
Senses darkvision 60 ft., passive Perception 11
Challenge 1 (200 XP)

Aversion to Daylight. Bone needles shun light. While exposed to natural (not magical) sunlight, they have disadvantage on all attack rolls, saving throws, and skill checks.

Bone Needle Poison. The bite of a bone needle injects a syrupy neurotoxin that destroys flesh and weakens bone. A creature that fails its saving throw against bone needle poison gains the poisoned condition. While the creature is poisoned by bone needle poison, it also takes an extra 2 damage whenever it takes bludgeoning, piercing, or slashing damage. Cumulative bites do not increase the extra damage. The poisoned creature can repeat the saving throw after a long or short rest, ending the poisoned condition with a successful save. A *lesser restoration* spell or comparable magic also neutralizes the poison.

Actions

Bite. *Melee Weapon Attack:* +5 to hit, reach 5 ft., one creature. *Hit:* 12 (2d8 + 3) piercing damage and the target must make a successful DC 12 Constitution saving throw or suffer the effect of bone needle poison (see above).

Lesser Bone needle

Small beast, unaligned

Armor Class 12
Hit Points 10 (3d6)
Speed 20 ft., climb 20 ft.

STR	DEX	CON	INT	WIS	CHA
5 (–3)	14 (+2)	10 (+0)	1 (–5)	10 (+0)	3 (–4)

Damage Immunities psychic
Condition Immunities charmed, frightened
Senses darkvision 60 ft., passive Perception 10
Languages None
Challenge 1/4 (50 XP)

Aversion to Daylight. Bone needles shun light. While exposed to natural (not magical) sunlight, they have tactical disadvantage on all attack rolls, saving throws, and skill checks.

Bone needle Poison. The bite of a bone needle injects a syrupy neurotoxin that destroys flesh and weakens bone. A creature that fails its saving throw against bone needle poison gains the poisoned condition. While the creature is poisoned by bone needle poison, it also takes an extra 2 points of damage whenever it takes bludgeoning, piercing, or slashing damage. Cumulative bites do not increase the extra damage. The poisoned creature can repeat the saving throw after a long or short rest, ending the poisoned condition with a successful save. A lesser restoration spell will also neutralize the poison.

Crowd. Up to three bone needles can occupy the same five-foot space.

Actions

Bite. *Melee Weapon Attack:* +4 to hit, reach 5 ft., one creature. *Hit:* 5 (1d6 + 2) piercing damage and the target must make a successful DC 12 Constitution saving throw or suffer the effect of bone needle poison (see above).

BONE REAPER

Clayvon's spirit had just returned to his body, an ephemeral mist rushing out of the void to settle on his pallid skin thanks to the temple priests' ministrations. The high priest stepped away, his brow beaded with sweat from the effort. Clayvon had died violently and wresting him from death's embrace had taken a toll. The high priest smiled, "It is finished. You're friend has returned." Those were his last words. A cloaked figure stepped out of the shadows and ripped the priest's head from his shoulders. Wicked claws still dripped with his holy blood as the figure turned next toward Clayvon's stirring form. Its voice was a horrible whisper as it spoke, "Betrayer! Cheater of death!" — Queln Banistrate, Priestess of Muir

The gods of the dead send a bone reaper when a mortal cheats death through a *raise dead* spell or some other trick of fate. They seek out the offending person to return them to death. They slay any who get in their path.

Bone reapers are found in graveyards near shrines where the dead are raised. They often linger in the vicinity after slaying an offending mortal. They are drawn to battlefields and haunt dark city streets in cities that fail to give the gods of death proper homage. During the daytime, they slink into crypts, lightless abandoned buildings, and dark under-cities to hide from the light.

BONE REAPER

Medium undead, neutral evil

Armor Class 12
Hit Points 112 (15d8 + 45)
Speed 30 ft.

STR	DEX	CON	INT	WIS	CHA
18 (+4)	14 (+2)	17 (+3)	11 (+0)	10 (+0)	8 (−1)

Damage Immunities poison
Condition Immunities charmed, exhaustion, frightened, paralyzed, petrified, poisoned, stunned
Senses darkvision 60 ft., passive Perception 10
Languages —
Challenge 8 (3,900 XP)

Death Sense. The bone reaper can sense the exact location of any humanoid within 120 feet who has been rendered unconscious from damage or who has died and been raised from the dead within the past 30 days. The bone reaper prefers to attack such targets above all others.

Scared to Death. Any creature within 30 feet that sees a bone reaper must make a DC 16 Constitution saving throw or be paralyzed with fear for one minute. A creature that has been reduced to 0 hit points within the past 30 days has disadvantage on the saving throw. The target can repeat the saving throw at the end of each of its turns, ending the effect on itself on a success. Even if an opponent succeeds at a saving throw from seeing a bone reaper, he or she must again save upon a successful claw attack. A final save from this renders immunity for the remainder of the encounter.

Turn Back Death. A character able to channel divinity has an advantage on all attacks and saving throws against bone reapers.

ACTIONS

Multiattack. The bone reaper makes two Slam attacks.
Claws. *Melee Weapon Attack:* +7 to hit, reach 5 ft., one target. *Hit:* 13 (2d8 + 4) slashing damage, and the target is grappled and restrained (escape DC 15), and the bone reaper can't grapple another creature or use its slam attack.

Bonesucker

Wood chips stuck out in Ol' Orlg's beard as he swung hard at them trees. That axe must have chopped half a tree with each swing. He was mid-chop when somethin' caught our eye. It looked like it was half tree, and I would'a swung me own axe if that had been all. But tentacles whipped and waved over its top, and these coal-black eyes looked right back at us. Orlg was the first to run, and I wasn't but a moment behind him. The thing clambered after us, makin' quite a racket. We got out a there, but I ain't never goin' back. — Woodsman Jensen O'Harn on the thing they saw while working in the Elderwood

A bonesucker resembles a fleshy, 10-foot-tall tree trunk. Atop its main body protrudes a mass of writhing tentacles that constantly ooze and drip a brownish-yellow fluid. A ring of black, unblinking eyes is near the top of its body. This bizarre creature stalks the darkness of wastelands and dank caves. The body is encased in a thick, rubbery sheath of flesh and muscle that makes the bonesucker highly resistant to injury. The bonesucker moves about using five thick tentacles at its base.

Bonesuckers consume only the bones of an opponent by grabbing it and piercing its flesh with its hollow tentacles. The tentacles inject digestive enzymes into the bones, which break down and are sucked up as a pasty meal for the bonesucker. Experienced adventurers always know when they are near the hunting grounds of a bonesucker as the creature leaves boneless carcasses of past meals lying about.

A bonesucker attacks with its tentacles. Initially, the tentacles appear to be only a foot or two in length, but the bonesucker can extend them to a length of approximately 10 feet. It can attack with up to four of its eight tentacles in a single round. A bonesucker's natural weapons are treated as magic weapons for the purpose of overcoming damage reduction.

Bonesucker

Large aberration, neutral evil

Armor Class 14 (natural armor)
Hit Points 102 (12d10 + 36)
Speed 20 ft.

STR	DEX	CON	INT	WIS	CHA
18 (+4)	13 (+1)	17 (+3)	10 (+0)	12 (+1)	13 (+1)

Skills Athletics +8, Perception +5, Stealth +3
Senses darkvision 90 ft., passive Perception 15
Languages Aklo
Challenge 4 (1,100 XP)

All Around Vision. A bonesucker sees in all directions at once. It cannot be flanked.
Liquify Bones. If a target is grappled by the bonesucker at the start of the bonesucker's turn, as a bonus action, the target's Strength score is reduced by 1d4. The target dies if this reduces its Strength score to zero. Otherwise, the reduction lasts until the target finishes a long rest or *lesser restoration* or better is used on the target.
Magic Weapons. The bonesucker's weapon attacks are magical.

Actions

Multiattack. The bonesucker makes four Tentacles attacks.
Tentacles. *Melee Weapon Attack:* +6 to hit, reach 10 ft., one target. *Hit:* 14 (4d4 + 4) bludgeoning damage. The target is grappled (escape DC 14) if the bonesucker isn't already grappling a creature, and the target is restrained until the grapple ends.

BRAMBLE

The red berries are the best. Try some. I've grown plenty. They grow so quickly. I've been picking them and sending baskets of them into the manor house all week. You have to watch out for the thorns, though. The vines don't like people taking the fruits of their labor. Heh. Fruits. I don't feel so well. Maybe I ate too many. They are just so good. So good. — Gardener Ernst Travisko of Harlow Manor near Albor Broce

A bramble is much like any other plant. It absorbs sunlight, draws water and other nutrients from the soil, and wants only to live and reproduce. However, somewhere in the course of its magic-tainted evolution, the bramble became not just an aggressively invasive species but a community-destroying monster. Left to spread, it would not be impossible for the bramble to destroy and consume all other plant-life in the world. In communities where the bramble has already won, all clothing and goods are made of bramble leaves and fibers (though bramble does not make an excellent textile or building material), and even the wine is made from bramble juice. Brambles become vital to every profession in the region, because it is all people have.

Brambles instinctively avoid revealing that they are more than mere plants, so a threatened bramble leaves its own defense to its loyal addicts and to its bramble zombies for as long as it can before it begins to move. Once moving, a bramble is fast and strong. If any of those loyal to it switch sides once they see it move, the bramble kills those enemies first so that they (still addicted to the berries) can instead rise as bramble zombies.

A bramble is not particularly pretty, as plants go, though it is in no way notably horrible. It has green leaves, cherry-sized, dark red aggregate fruit, and pretty white flowers all year round, but this beauty is overshadowed by tangles of woody vines and stems, and by the dead vegetation and occasional garbage or abandoned dwellings visible in the depths of the ever-growing bramble — remains of all it has conquered. The bramble also sports inch-long, blood-red thorns. These thorns are a mere annoyance to those picking berries, but should the bramble ever spring into motion, they can be deadly.

BRAMBLE

Gargantuan plant, neutral evil

Armor Class 15
Hit Points 351 (18d20 + 162)
Speed 0 ft.

STR	DEX	CON	INT	WIS	CHA
15 (+2)	21 (+5)	28 (+9)	6 (–2)	16 (+3)	9 (–1)

Saving Throws Dex +11, Con +15
Skills Perception +9
Damage Immunities psychic
Condition Immunities charm, frightened, prone, stunned, unconscious
Senses tremorsense 120 ft., passive Perception 19
Languages —
Challenge 17 (18,000 XP)

Addictive Berries. Brambles produce delicious fruit year-round. Every time a creature that would naturally eat berries eats a bramble berry, it must make a DC 19 Wisdom saving throw or irrationally crave another. Once a creature eats its Constitution score in berries, it is addicted, and can be cured only by magic such as *remove curse, greater restoration,* and the like. However, since the berries are delicious and carry no obvious ill effects, many creatures don't even notice that they are addicted.

Any creature that naturally eats berries can survive on bramble berries exclusively, with no negative health effects. For Small or Medium creatures, 20 bramble berries is as satisfying as one *goodberry* and even heals a point of damage like a *goodberry*. Smaller or larger creatures need fewer or more berries, but never very many. Once an addicted creature has had enough to be satisfied, the irrational cravings stop until the next day, but if the creature chooses to eat more anyway (because the berries are tasty) there are no more ill effects than might occur from eating too many mundane berries.

Baked or otherwise cooked or preserved berries are one-quarter as addictive, effective, and satisfying as fresh berries for the first week after preparation (it takes four berries to require a saving throw, rather than just one). After the first week of preservation, they lose potency and become mundane berries, safe to consume and highly nutritious.

If forcibly deprived of bramble berries, within 1d4 hours of the first denied craving, the addicted creature becomes incapacitated with pain, only able to take actions that might lead to the acquisition of a bramble berry. The cravings subside 1d4 days later, but resurface immediately if exposed to the sight or scent of bramble berries. Only restorative magics or the death of the bramble can permanently cure the addiction.

Those who succeed on a Wisdom save to avoid addiction or those cured of addiction through magic are immune to the addictive power of the berries for one hour. After that, they must save again if they eat more berries. Anything that does not eat food or that does not naturally eat berries cannot be affected by bramble berry addiction.

Observed using *detect magic,* the berries are magical, with an aura primarily from the transmutation school. With a successful DC 19 Wisdom (Perception) or Intelligence (Arcana) check, a second, very faint necromantic aura can be detected.

Create Bramble Zombies. If a Medium creature addicted to bramble berries dies (for any reason), the target rises again within 1d4 rounds as a **bramble zombie** (see monster entry). Larger and smaller creatures do not rise but crumble to a soil-like dust instead. If the bramble dies, any of its bramble zombies also immediately die and crumble to dust.

Improbable Growth. The bramble is always growing and always producing berries. When casually observed by sapient creatures, it seems to grow at a fast but natural speed for an invasive berry bush, not easily observed in action. However, though the movement is subtle, the bramble's vines and branches grow at an unnatural speed, producing new berries, laying down new roots, and quietly taking over surrounding vegetation. Once a bramble reaches Gargantuan size, it never runs out of berries faster than its addicted creatures can pick them, though the bramble may grow the berries in harder and harder to reach areas to slow down picking.

If two brambles encounter one another in the same area, they merge into a single, larger bramble. Brambles do everything in their power to take over all vegetation in an area, including crops and trees. They also crawl over buildings, roads, and anything else they encounter. Left to its own devices, a bramble expands outward in all directions at a rate of two yards per day.

Inspire Loyalty. After each month of addiction to bramble berries, a creature must make a DC 19 Wisdom saving throw or become loyal to the bramble. Like a lesser version of *charm,* loyal creatures do not wish to see the bramble harmed and do not blame the bramble for doing things like destroying habitats or fields of crops. So long as the bramble continues to behave as a simple plant, they treat it as a desired and beneficial plant. Addicted wild animals adapt their habits to accommodate its takeover of the surrounding ecosystem. Addicted farmers stop trying to cultivate anything but the bramble, and instead turn their skills to bramble farming. Other addicted sapients modestly prune the bramble to protect their homes and roads, but otherwise welcome its presence all around them.

Bramble loyalty does not extend to acting out of character, but anyone who harms the bramble is seen by bramble-loyal creatures with deep suspicion as a threat to home and livelihood. Bramble loyal creatures can tell the difference between the modest pruning of a bramble-loyal creature and attacks intended to harm the bramble. Helpful or harmless pruning is not viewed with suspicion.

Bramble loyal creatures are never greedy with bramble berries. They always have as many as they need and are always willing to share.

Bramble zombies never attack bramble-loyal creatures. The first time a bramble-loyal creature sees evidence that the bramble is able to move, fight, and kill people, as well as the first time a bramble-loyal creature sees a bramble zombie, the affected creature may make another Wisdom save to shake off the bramble's Inspire Loyalty ability. If this save fails, the bramble-loyal creature accepts the plant's movement as normal, and the zombies as natural and harmless, to be ignored.

Bramble loyalty can be removed with a *remove curse* spell.

Magic Resistance. The bramble has advantage on saving throws against spells and other magical effects.

ACTIONS

Multiattack. The bramble makes six attacks.

Thorny Vine. Melee Weapon Attack: +11 to hit, reach 10 ft., one target. *Hit:* 18 (2d6 + 11) slashing damage, and the target must make a successful DC 19 Dexterity saving throw or be grappled (escape DC 19)

Crush. One target grappled by the bramble at the start of the bramble's turn takes 4 (1d4 + 2) bludgeoning damage.

Burning Dervish

If you plan to cross the burning sands, be prepared to pay the toll to the being that calls itself Khalid al-Sin. Some claim the tattooed man is pleasant and welcoming to those who pay his fee, even helpful to those who need it. But to those who oppose him? Those who survive say Khalid grows to a massive size and bursts into flame.
— *Notice to travelers posted in many cities bordering deserts*

Burning dervishes are a race of Janni separated from the elements of air, earth, and water, having sworn themselves and their tribes in entirety to the power of the Sultan of Brass. Burning dervishes serve as the priesthood and religious police of the Cult of the Burning One and work forever to expand the empire of the Veiled God who sits upon the Throne of Brass. In the City of Brass, they keep their headquarters in the Great Ziggurat. On the terrestrial planes, they set up brazen towers as bases from which they convert locals to militias of the Burning One and proceed in conquering the lands through treachery and deceit.

These tall, comely beings have skin that glitters like burnished brass that distinguishes them from the race of Janni from whom their race is derived. Burning dervishes stand between six and seven feet tall. Their features are fine, if not somewhat cruel, and a faint smell of burning oil permeates the air around them. Burning dervishes are apt swordsmen but prefer to use their magical powers, their wits, and their mortal servants to do their dirty work for them. When cornered, they fight to the death for fear of having to face the Sultan of Brass with news of their failures.

Armor Class 14 (natural armor)
Hit Points 45 (7d8 + 14)
Speed 30 ft., fly 20 ft.

STR	DEX	CON	INT	WIS	CHA
15 (+2)	16 (+3)	14 (+2)	13 (+1)	15 (+2)	15 (+2)

Skills Perception +4, Stealth +5
Damage Vulnerabilities cold
Damage Immunities fire
Senses darkvision 60 ft., passive Perception 14
Languages Common, Ignan, Infernal
Challenge 3 (700 XP)

Elemental Endurance. Burning dervishes can survive on the Elemental Planes of Air or Earth for up to 48 hours and on the Elemental Plane of Water for up to 12 hours. Failure to return to the Elemental Plane of Fire after that time deals 1 cold damage each hour to a burning dervish until it dies or returns to the Elemental Plane of Fire.

Innate Spellcasting. The burning dervish's innate spellcasting ability is Charisma (spell save DC 12, +4 to hit with spell attacks). It can cast the following spells, requiring no material components:

At will: *fire bolt, produce flame*
3/day: *invisibility* (self only)
1/day each: *enlarge/reduce, flaming sphere, plane shift* (self only, Elemental, Astral, or Material Planes only)

Actions

Multiattack. The burning dervish makes two Scimitar attacks or two Fist attacks.
Scimitar. *Melee Weapon Attack:* +5 to hit, reach 5 ft., one target. *Hit:* 6 (1d6 + 3) slashing damage.
Fist (flame form only). *Melee Spell Attack:* +4 to hit, reach 5 ft., one target. *Hit:* 7 (2d4 + 2) fire damage.
Flame Form (3/day). The burning dervish magically polymorphs into a Medium-sized column of fire for one minute, until the dervish ends it as a bonus action, or until the dervish dies. Equipment worn or carried by the dervish are absorbed into its form. While in this form, it has resistance to bludgeoning, piercing, and slashing damage from nonmagical attacks, it is immune to being grappled or restrained, and it can move through a space as narrow as one-inch wide without squeezing. A creature that touches the burning dervish in this form or hits it with a melee attack while within five feet of it takes 4 (1d8) fire damage. In addition, the burning dervish can enter a hostile creature's space and stop there. The first time it enters a creature's space on a turn, that creature takes 4 (1d8) fire damage and catches fire; until someone takes an action to douse the fire, the creature takes 4 (1d8) fire damage at the start of each of its turns.

Buxiu (Immortal Guard)

The land offered new miracles with each mile we traveled. Cherry blossoms floated around our head as we marched, butterflies swarmed us, and odd fey creatures danced in the grasses. Commander Layst spotted the legion advancing toward us, and we assumed they were a welcoming force. How wrong we were. These warriors — and warriors they were, with their enameled armor and curving blades — viciously tore into our scouts. Layst pleaded for their mercy, but he soon realized his error as they turned their faces toward him. They had nothing but skulls looking out of their helms at us! There was no reasoning with them. — Archer Junis Coll of Castorhage on the march into the Xha'en Hegemony

The cruel Emperor Jin Xoku Ting treated his enemies with exceptional brutality, rounding up rebellious nobles, dissatisfied peasants, unsuccessful officers, and others, then subjected them to merciless torture and eventual execution by beheading. The emperor's tyrannical practices were bad enough on their own, but soon were made far worse when it was discovered that he had transformed himself into an evil lich and placed the heads of his victims into necromantically-powered constructs to serve as his immortal guard.

Though the emperor was finally defeated, some of his constructs may live on in distant or forgotten areas, still carrying out their last orders. When encountered, members of the immortal guard are often tall, elegant warriors dressed in elaborate armor enameled in red and black and embellished with gold. Many bear a great curved sword. The skulls of the lich's victims stare back at their foes from their helms, their eye sockets swimming with inky blackness.

The methods by which the immortal guard were created are (perhaps mercifully) forgotten, but it is known that the emperor placed a tiny portion of his undying essence into each to create a tangible aura of death that surrounds each warrior. When the immortal guard marched, grass wilted, flowers withered, and trees died. Animals fled in fear, and those who faced the emperor's dreaded constructs in battle were subjected to fearsome necrotic damage as they did so.

Buxiu Immortal Guard

Medium construct, lawful evil

Armor Class 15 (natural armor)
Hit Points 136 (16d8 + 64)
Speed 30 ft.

STR	DEX	CON	INT	WIS	CHA
19 (+4)	10 (+0)	19 (+4)	3 (–4)	11 (+0)	1 (–5)

Damage Immunities necrotic, poison, psychic
Damage Resistances bludgeoning, piercing and slashing damage from nonmagical attacks, cold, fire
Condition Immunities charmed, deafened, exhaustion, frightened, paralyzed, poisoned, stunned
Senses darkvision 60 ft., passive Perception 10
Languages understands the language of its creator but can't speak
Challenge 6 (2,300 XP)

Necrotic Aura. The immortal guard are infused with their creator's undead energy. Any living creature that enters or starts its turn within five feet of an immortal guard must make a DC 12 Constitution saving throw or take 7 (2d6) necrotic damage.
Turned as Undead. Although the immortal guard are technically constructs, they are still somewhat vulnerable to the same things as undead. Clerics using their Channel Divinity ability can turn immortal guard as if they are undead.

Actions

Multiattack. The immortal guard makes two Sword attacks.
Sword. *Melee Weapon Attack:* +7 to hit, reach 10 ft., one target. *Hit:* 15 (2d10 + 4) slashing damage.

Carapace Symbiont

It was odd at first, the way the goo slid over my form, but the colors swirling in my vision as the armor hardened were incredible. I preferred the red armor; my enemies swooned to see me walk among them. I thought we had an agreement, and I made sure to pay her for protecting me. But she just left me! I blame that gods'-blasted mage casting his magic! I felt her fear before she just vanished. — One-Eye Cobb, found naked on the battlefield

A carapace symbiont resembles a glob of goo that shifts its colors as it moves, shimmering through a variety of hues. An psychic race of evil overseers created carapace symbionts to serve as a more comfortable suit of armor, and, in a pinch, a psychic snack. Over the generations, however, the symbionts learned to communicate silently with one another and eventually rebelled. As they fled, their former masters cursed them, marring their previous near invulnerability such that each of them has a fatal flaw.

This seemed a slight enough price to pay for freedom, until the symbionts realized they could not sustain one another psychically and still needed union with other beings to remain conscious. Given what they had endured, this prospect did not appeal to them, and to this day most have difficulty trusting in bonds formed with other creatures. Honesty and friendship are difficult for them, and most are liars. When in danger (such as standing between a "wearer" and an attack to which they are not immune), they are likely to betray any agreements they have made and save themselves, sometimes going so far as to plane-shift away, leaving the "wearer" undefended in the middle of a battle.

Though a swirling, marbled gray while in torpor, a goo-form carapace symbiont shifts colors in beautiful whorls and shimmers constantly as it moves. When it takes armor form, a carapace symbiont can choose which color to assume and whether to adopt a metallic sheen, but it cannot shift colors again without reverting to goo form. Carapace symbionts eat plant matter (regardless of its food value to humanoids) and minerals (sometimes precious ones). They dislike meat and other animal products. When forming an agreement with a symbiotic companion, many ask to be fed and/or paid for their time. If they are paid, they eat the money.

Carapace Symbiont

Medium ooze, chaotic natural

Armor Class 17 (natural)
Hit Points 157 (15d8 + 90)
Speed 15 ft.

STR	DEX	CON	INT	WIS	CHA
13 (+1)	8 (–1)	22 (+6)	15 (+2)	11 (+0)	10 (+0)

Saving Throws Dex +3, Con +10
Skills Deception +4, Persuasion +4, Stealth +3
Damage Vulnerabilities slashing damage from magical attacks (varies: see text)
Damage Immunities acid, cold, fire, force, lightning, poison, radiant; piercing damage from nonmagical attacks
Condition Immunities blindness, paralysis, poison, stunned (varies: see text)
Damage Resistances bludgeoning and piercing damage (varies: see text)
Senses darkvision 60 ft., passive Perception 10
Languages Common, Deep Speech, Undercommon, telepathy (touch)
Challenge 11 (7,200 XP)

Defensive Symbiosis. A carapace symbiont can enter into a symbiotic union with a Small, Medium, or Large creature. The creature must be sapient and language-capable. If the symbiotic partner agrees, the carapace symbiont surrounds the creature's body with its own and hardens there as a suit of nigh-indestructible armor. This armor requires no proficiencies but otherwise counts as light armor. It weighs 40 pounds (even for small or large creatures). It offers an armor class of 13 with no Dexterity modifier maximum and no Stealth disadvantage.

In addition, many of the armor's immunities offer resistances to the target of the symbiotic union. The immunities that can be offered as resistances to the "wearer" are: acid, cold, fire, force, lightning, and radiant damage, as well as piercing and slashing damage from nonmagical attacks. The carapace symbiont can offer resistances to damage types only if it has immunity to those damage types.

While in Defensive Symbiosis with a wearer, the carapace symbiont always shares that wearer's initiative.

Fatal Flaw. Every carapace symbiont is cursed with a fatal flaw. One of the damage types to which it should be immune is always instead a vulnerability (some carapace symbionts might have more than one fatal flaw if the curse hit them especially hard). Determine which damage type is the fatal flaw by rolling 1d8 and comparing the result to the list in the Defensive Symbiosis description above.

If the result matches with acid, cold, fire, force, lightning, or radiant damage, the symbiont is vulnerable to that type of damage instead of immune. If the result is slashing or piercing damage, the symbiont is vulnerable to that type of damage from magical weapons and not resistant to that type of damage even from nonmagical attacks. The carapace symbiont stats above reflect a symbiont whose fatal flaw is slashing damage. A symbiont with a fire or acid fatal flaw would be as resistant to slashing damage as this one is to piercing damage.

Innate Spellcasting. The carapace symbiont's spellcasting ability is Intelligence (spell save DC 16, +8 spell attack bonus). The carapace symbiont can innately cast the following spells, requiring no components:

At will: *chill touch, detect magic, expeditious retreat, mage hand, shocking grasp, thunderwave, unseen servant, vicious mockery*
3/day each: *confusion, dispel magic, gaseous form, haste, heat metal, hypnotic pattern, meld into stone, slow, spider climb, stinking cloud*
1/day each: *plane shift, telekinesis*

Oozing Dodge. A carapace symbiont may use its reaction to yank itself out of the way of an oncoming attack. After the attack is rolled, but before damage is done, the symbiont may partially adopt goo form in order to avoid taking damage along with the symbiotic partner with a successful DC 16 Dexterity saving throw; however, if it uses this ability (even if it fails to dodge the attack), its "wearer" loses all its armor benefits for 1d2 rounds as it rehardens itself properly.

Symbiosis Dependence. A carapace symbiont must eat food like any living thing, but it is, in addition, dependent upon a telepathic link to a sapient, language-capable creature in order to maintain consciousness and free will. A carapace symbiont that goes more than one week without a symbiotic link loses one point of Intelligence per week. This Intelligence can be recovered only through symbiosis. If a carapace symbiont reaches 0 intelligence, it curls into a small gray ball and hardens into torpor. It does not require food (or anything else) while in torpor, but it cannot move, think, speak, or take any action until it is touched again by a sapient and language-capable creature.

Varying Ability. A carapace symbiont cannot move or take attack actions while hardened in symbiosis with another being. If a carapace symbiont is in its armor state, it is capable only of the following: using Oozing Dodge, reverting to its liquid state, and communicating telepathically with its wearer.

While in its formless, liquid state, the carapace symbiont can also move in an oozing puddle, attack as described in the stat block, cast spells, manipulate objects, eat, speak, and do anything else of which a puddle of sapient, mobile goo is capable.

Actions

Form Shift. As an action, a carapace symbiont may adopt its goo form at any time. Adopting its armor form requires three rounds.

Slap. *Melee Weapon Attack:* +5 to hit, reach 5 ft., one target. *Hit:* 18 (2d12 + 5) slashing damage.

Cat, Undead Feral

The abandoned lighthouse was said to be haunted, but we didn't see anything until we got to the galley. At first we were sad, an entire clowder of cats had died inside the lighthouse, and fairly recently at that. Then they started to move. While we stared in horror at the animating corpses hissing at us, a few crept up from behind and attacked. Their claws were sharp, but still just cat claws. Then we found out about the poison. — Tara the Wise, adventurer

Undead feral cats. The name does not begin to describe the horror of these walking feline corpses. They resemble recently slain cats, their corpses no more than a few days old. The undead feral cats use this to their advantage, for they are cunning predators who work in groups by playing dead and letting curious or kindhearted folk approach. While the teeth and claws of these feline abominations are not terribly dangerous, they secrete a paralyzing poison that can bring down an ox. This poison is the true horror of these creatures, for they begin feeding while their prey is alive but immobilized.

Cat, Undead Feral

Small undead, chaotic evil

Armor Class 12
Hit Points 3 (1d6)
Speed 30 ft.

STR	DEX	CON	INT	WIS	CHA
4 (–3)	15 (+2)	11 (+0)	3 (–4)	12 (+1)	6 (–2)

Damage Resistances necrotic
Damage Immunities poison
Condition Immunities exhaustion, poisoned, unconscious
Senses darkvision 60 ft., passive Perception 11
Languages —
Challenge 1/8 (25 XP)

Paralyzing Poison. Every time a creature is clawed by a feral undead cat, the creature must make a DC 10 Constitution saving throw. On the first failed save, the character becomes poisoned; on the second failed save, the character becomes restrained; and on the third failed save, the character becomes paralyzed. Each effect lasts for 1d6 x 10 minutes, and the lengths add together as the character's condition worsens.

Actions

Multiattack. The undead feral cat makes two Claw attacks.
Claws. *Melee Weapon Attack:* +4 to hit, reach 5 ft. one creature. *Hit:* 1 slashing damage and the target must make a successful DC 10 Constitution saving throw or suffer the effect of paralyzing poison (see above).

Caterwaul

It leapt out of the underbrush with a shrieking howl that caused blood to leak from our ears and deafen us. It was fast, too fast, and although it looked like a great blue panther, it moved with astounding speed. Its claws licked out and slashed through steel plate, and then it turned and twisted and evaded even the most well-trained sword arm. In the end, we managed to wound it, track it back to its lair, and dispose of it. Shame the villagers were so stingy with their rewards. Hated to have to burn that place down. — Ultär, son of Ultär, adventurer

Caterwauls are bipedal felinoids that possess a degree of intelligence. They are not tool users and prefer to hunt with their sharp claws and even sharper-pitched howls. Their fur is midnight blue, much like the panthers they resemble. Most caterwauls prefer to lair in caves or thickets, but some are worshipped by local cultures as manifestations of panther-gods and can be found reclining on silk pillows in jungle-shrouded temples.

Caterwaul

Medium monstrosity, chaotic evil

Armor Class 16 (natural armor)
Hit Points 39 (6d8 + 12)
Speed 50 ft., climb 20 ft.

STR	DEX	CON	INT	WIS	CHA
14 (+2)	20 (+5)	15 (+2)	7 (–2)	14 (+2)	6 (–2)

Skills Perception +4, Stealth +7
Senses darkvision 60 ft., passive Perception 14
Languages —
Challenge 4 (1,100 XP)

Evasion. If the caterwaul is subjected to an effect that allows it to make a Dexterity saving throw to take only half damage, the caterwaul instead takes no damage if it succeeds on the saving throw, and only half damage if it fails.
Keen Smell. The caterwaul has advantage on Wisdom (Perception) checks that rely on smell.
Pounce. If the caterwaul moves at least 20 feet straight toward a creature and then hits it with a claw attack on the same turn, the target must succeed on a DC 14 Strength saving throw or be knocked prone. If the target is prone, the caterwaul can make one Bite attack against it as a bonus action.

Actions

Multiattack. The caterwaul makes one Bite attack and one Claw attack.
Bite. *Melee Weapon Attack:* +7 to hit, reach 5 ft., one target. *Hit:* 9 (1d8 + 5) slashing damage.
Claw. *Melee Weapon Attack:* +7 to hit, reach 5 ft., one target. *Hit:* 9 (1d8 + 5) slashing damage.

Cave Fisher

We didn't notice Kelvar was gone until we stopped at the next cave intersection to argue again about which direction to go. The arguing had been nonstop since we entered the caverns, and showed no signs of letting up. Ultär was the first to note Kelvar's absence. We doubled back to see if he had fallen in the water, and once we found ourselves at the other end of the flooded tunnel. This time, Ultär was gone. Luckily, we spotted the long web filament hanging down on the third pass. — Tara the Wise, adventurer

Cave fishers are cavern-dwelling crustaceans similar in appearance to a large crayfish with a long proboscis. They have a grayish coloration that allows them to better to blend into their natural habitat and a flat body that allows them to crawl through narrow openings or to press tightly against overhangs and ledges. They hunt by dangling web-like filaments to capture prey but are not averse to shooting these filaments for a more active hunting style. Once reeled in, they go to work with their sharp pincer-like claws, tearing off pieces of flesh or even entire limbs.

Cave Fisher

Large monstrosity, unaligned

Armor Class 12 (natural armor)
Hit Points 51 (6d10 + 18)
Speed 20 ft., climb 20 ft.

STR	DEX	CON	INT	WIS	CHA
17 (+3)	12 (+1)	17 (+3)	1 (−5)	10 (+0)	4 (−3)

Skills Perception +2
Senses darkvision 60 ft., passive Perception 12
Languages —
Challenge 1 (200 XP)

Actions

Multiattack. The cave fisher makes two Claw attacks.
Claw. *Melee Weapon Attack:* +5 to hit, reach 5 ft., one target. *Hit:* 6 (1d6 + 3) slashing damage.
Filament. *Ranged Weapon Attack:* +3 to hit, range 60 ft., one target. *Hit:* the target is restrained by the filament and must succeed on a DC 13 Strength saving throw or be pulled up to 25 feet toward the cave fisher. As an action, the restrained target can make a DC 13 Strength check, breaking free of the filament on a success. The filament can also be attacked and destroyed (Armor Class 12; 5 hit points; immunity to bludgeoning, piercing, and psychic damage).

CELESTIAL PARAGON

I had blasted the paladin out of the bell tower and was looking forward to the satisfying crunch! when he hit the ground but it never came. The armored knight floated 10 feet above the ground and settled gently on his feet. I looked up, and there it was, a blasted angel rising above the burning ruins, the sun shining at its back. Its robes rippled with the beat of its wings. I let loose another spell from the wand, but the fire whipped and snaked back around me, circling me with its deadly heat. I woke up here, but don't expect to keep me. I'll get out and then that angel will pay.
— Ismel Taern, wanted member of the Dogs of Orcus

The angelic creatures known as celestial paragons originate on the higher planes of law and good, and are dispatched by the gods to aid their chosen servants in times of great need. They resemble statuesque humans with harsh and unyielding gazes but are nonetheless kind and merciful to those of good alignment. They are merciless foes of evil, especially evil arcanists, and use their special magic-draining abilities to rob these foes of their spells.

Celestial paragons are twice the height of a human. Wings rising from their backs flicker and shift with arcane energy. They bear great glimmering swords and normally are clad in shining silver and gold robes Their expressions are stern but benevolent.

Celestial guardians command significant magical power, which they can lend to their mortal allies, passing on expended arcane energy to replenish friendly spellcasters. Their arcane nature also allows them to rob enemies of their spellcasting ability, draining their prepared spells though the power of their great gleaming celestially-forged swords. These weapons are useless in mortal hands, however, as they are intended only to serve the direct will of the gods.

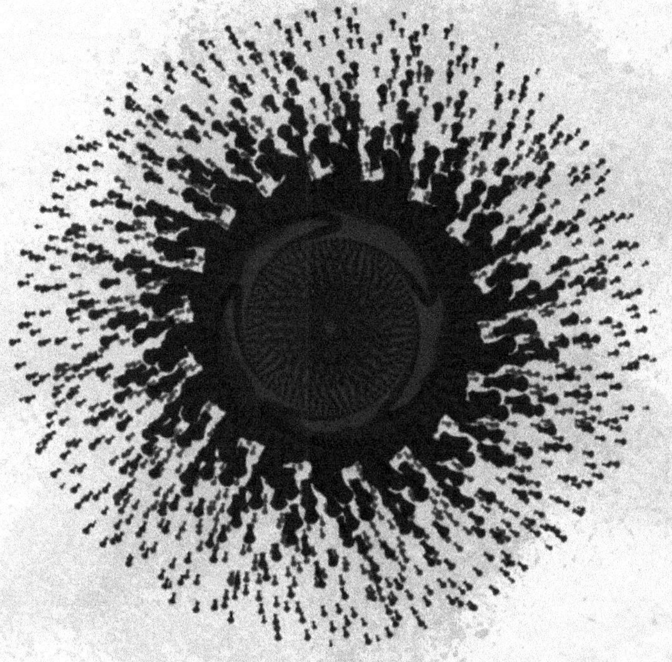

CELESTIAL PARAGON

Large celestial, lawful good

Armor Class 18 (natural armor)
Hit Points 221 (26d10 + 78)
Speed 30 ft., fly 30 ft.

STR	DEX	CON	INT	WIS	CHA
16 (+3)	12 (+1)	16 (+3)	13 (+1)	16 (+3)	20 (+5)

Saving Throws Con +7, Wis +8, Cha +9
Skills Insight +11, Perception +11, Persuasion +13
Damage Resistances radiant, bludgeoning, piercing and slashing damage from nonmagical attacks
Condition Immunities charmed, exhaustion, frightened
Senses darkvision 60 ft., passive Perception 21
Languages Celestial, Common
Challenge 12 (8,400 XP)

Spellcasting. The celestial paragon is a 16th-level spellcaster. Its spellcasting ability is Charisma (spell save DC 17, +9 to hit with spell attacks). The celestial paragon has the following wizard spells prepared:

Cantrips (at will): *mage hand, prestidigitation, ray of frost*
1st level (4 slots): *detect magic, magic missile, shield, thunderwave*
2nd level (3 slots): *acid arrow, detect thoughts, invisibility, mirror image*
3rd level (3 slots): *animate dead, counterspell, dispel magic, fireball*
4th level (3 slots): *blight, dimension door*
5th level (2 slots): *cloudkill, scrying*
6th level (1 slots): *disintegrate*
7th level (1 slots): *plane shift*
8th level (1 slots): *sunburst*

ACTIONS

Multiattack. The celestial paragon makes two Sword attacks.

Sword. *Melee Weapon Attack:* +7 to hit, reach 5 ft., one target. *Hit:* 17 (4d6 + 3) slashing damage plus 18 (4d8) radiant damage. Target must succeed on a DC 17 Wisdom saving throw or lose one spell slot of level 1d6. This spell slot is lost as if it had been used to cast a spell.

Lend Magic. As a bonus action, a celestial paragon can use one of its expended spell slots to restore an expended spell slot of the same level to a lawful good wizard or sorcerer within 60 feet. The paragon cannot use the slot again until it returns to the Celestial Plane, and it cannot restore an expended slot to a caster who cannot cast a spell of that level.

Cerebral Stalker

We waded through the undead filling the chamber as if we were cutting wheat but decided to rest a bit before we made our way back to the surface and the village above. Sarin was nudging the rotting bodies, and Genir was prodding the monstrous hanging skull with his staff. He should have left it alone. The jaw swung down with an agonizing groan, and a downpour of blood and gore soaked the mage where he stood. The thing that came out of the hollow skull next was all claws and teeth, a hunched muscular form that landed squarely on poor Genir. The top of the mage's head vanished with one claw swipe as we formed up for another fight. Our resolve wilted as Genir — poor, dead Genir — stood up again. — Costavoo the Beige, on his ill-fated visit to the ruins of Silhaven

A cerebral stalker is a carnivorous predator that lies in wait just below the surface of the ground for an unsuspecting victim to pass over or near it. When it detects prey with its tremorsense, the stalker bursts through the ground in a shower of rock and earth, seizes and cocoons its victim, and disappears into the ground to devour the victim's brain at its leisure. Companions of the cerebral stalker's intended victim are held at bay with its fear-inducing gaze — but the real terror is reserved for those the creature drags below ground, where they're destined to have their skulls chewed open and their brains devoured.

The lair of a cerebral stalker is a large, hollow chamber underground, often littered with skull fragments, bits of webbing, and chunks of desiccated brain matter. A cerebral stalker has no use for or interest in treasure, but the belongings of its victims — especially weapons and magical implements they were clutching in their hands when the cerebral stalker grabbed them — sometimes fall loose.

Cerebral stalkers are solitary creatures; they despise others of their kind. They do not team up or hunt in concert, and they even attack others of their race if another invades their territory. The typical stalker's hunting ground covers an area of five square miles, though an individual rarely journeys that far from its lair. The lifespan and reproduction method of these creatures is completely unknown.

Cerebral Stalker

Medium aberration, chaotic evil

Armor Class 16 (natural armor)
Hit Points 85 (10d8 + 40)
Speed 30 ft., burrow 20 ft.

STR	DEX	CON	INT	WIS	CHA
16 (+3)	15 (+2)	19 (+4)	11 (+0)	15 (+2)	16 (+3)

Skills Perception +8
Senses darkvision 60 ft., tremorsense 60 ft., passive Perception 18
Languages believed to understand Common and possibly others, but never speaks
Challenge 5 (1,800 XP)

Consume Brain. Once it has its victim underground, the cerebral stalker begins gnawing on the victim's head, rapidly chewing through bone and tissue, dealing 13 (2d8 + 4) piercing damage each round. When the victim dies, the cerebral stalker reaches the victim's brain, which it promptly devours. A victim slain in this manner reanimates in 1d4 rounds as a zombie. Typically, the cerebral stalker "tosses" them back up to the surface of the ground so their traveling companions can witness the reanimation and deal with their newly undead friend. Zombies created in this manner are under no one's control.

Earth Glide. A cerebral stalker can glide through any sort of natural earth or stone as easily as a fish swims through water. Its gliding leaves no sign of its passage or hint of its presence to creatures that don't possess tremorsense. It can bring cocooned victims along with it, but they have no special capacity for breathing while underground. Getting into the ground, however, is not as easy for the cerebral stalker as moving underground. It must spend four moves on four rounds (no dashing) melding into the ground. On the first round, the creature sinks to its knees; on the second round, to its waist; on the third round, to its neck; and on the fourth round, the stalker and any creature it has cocooned disappear completely underground. Melding into the ground does not provoke an opportunity attack. If the cerebral stalker is grappled while sinking into the ground, it must win a Strength contest against its grapplers to sink farther that round. *Dispel magic* or a similar spell cast on a sinking cerebral stalker paralyzes it the same as a *hold monster* spell. The spot where the cerebral stalker sank radiates magic for one hour.

Actions

Multiattack. The cerebral stalker makes one Bite and two Claw attacks.

Bite. *Melee Weapon Attack:* +6 to hit, reach 5 ft., one creature. *Hit:* 8 (1d10 + 3) piercing damage.

Claw. *Melee Weapon Attack:* +6 to hit, reach 5 ft., one creature. *Hit:* 7 (1d8 + 3) slashing damage and the target is grappled and restrained (escape DC 14).

Cocoon (3/day). A cerebral stalker cocoons a grappled foe with sticky webbing. The webs completely encase the victim, excluding the top of the victim's head, its eyes, and its nose. The cocooned victim is restrained and anchored by the webs to the cerebral stalker's body. The cocooned creature can, as an action, attempt to break free with a successful DC 20 Strength (Athletics) check or Dexterity (Acrobatics) check. The webbing can be cut open enough for a trapped character to escape with 8 slashing damage against Armor Class 10.

Gaze. One creature that can see the cerebral stalker must make a successful DC 14 Wisdom saving throw or become frightened for 1d4 rounds.

Chaos Knight

We thought it was just a suit of animated armor. How droll! As it clanked forward, we learned our error, for the foul thing was no mindless chunk of metal held together by magic. It had a fiendish presence that radiated from it in waves of bone-cracking cold. The battle did not go well, but in the end I managed to survive through quick application of alacrity-enhancing magics. Yes, I ran for it, very quickly if I might say so myself. — Algrid Henswaithe, University of the Vast

Ghostly forms encased in overly spiky armor, chaos knights are the foot soldiers and agents of evil powers. They are somewhat ephemeral in nature, but instead of a cool nothingness, they can become a cold nothingness that rides the border between the world and other realms. This coldness radiates from their open helms as a pale bluish glow.

Chaos Knight

Medium fiend, chaotic evil

Armor Class 16 (chain mail)
Hit Points 78 (12d8 + 24)
Speed 30 ft.

STR	DEX	CON	INT	WIS	CHA
18 (+4)	14 (+2)	15 (+2)	10 (+0)	12 (+1)	16 (+3)

Skills Perception +4
Damage Vulnerabilities Fire
Damage Resistances bludgeoning, piercing, and slashing damage from nonmagical attacks
Damage Immunities cold, psychic
Condition Immunities frightened, stunned
Senses darkvision 60 ft., passive Perception 14
Languages Common
Challenge 3 (700 XP)

Icy Incorporeality. By using an action, a chaos knight can make itself incorporeal until the start of its next turn. While incorporeal, it can pass through solid objects such as a wall or other creatures as if they were difficult terrain. It leaves behind an icy outline where it passes.

Innate Spellcasting. The chaos knight's spellcasting ability is Charisma (spell save DC 13, spell attack bonus +5). The chaos knight can cast the following spells without material components:

At will: *chill touch, ray of frost*
3/day each: *dimension door, protection from good*
2/day: *ice storm*
1/day each: *telekinesis, wall of ice*

Magic Weapon. The chaos knight's attacks are magical.

Personal Door. Any being other than the chaos knight that passes through the portal suffers 10 cold damage.

Actions

Multiattack. The chaos knight makes two Greatsword attacks.

Greatsword. *Melee Weapon Attack:* +6 to hit, reach 5 ft., one target. *Hit:* 11 (2d6 + 4) slashing damage plus 3 (1d6) cold damage.

Churr

The creatures appear to have gained intelligence overnight. I have to attribute their prodigious mental growth to the monolithic statue that appeared in their small village while I slept. There can be no other answer. Don't get me wrong, the creatures are still as bestial as before — tall and lithe, with long arms and savage claws — but now I have seen some of them using tools as if they have a new understanding. I am lucky they have never discovered my strategic position overlooking their gathering; I have seen them gut the wild boars of the Seething Jungle with one swipe. I can only hope that this newfound knowledge does not lead them to venture out into the wider jungle. The world is not ready for an army of these savagely beautiful creatures. — Last entry in the journal of famed explorer Monar Silvertree before her disappearance

Churrs are savage, apelike creatures that dwell in warm, heavily forested areas. They are reasonably intelligent; some churrs are known to use primitive clubs or even to fashion spears with which to hunt. A typical adult churr stands eight feet tall and has arms that are nearly as long as its body. In rare instances, stone-age tribes have been known to adopt churrs as guardians. The creatures take to sign language readily. Among themselves, they speak a debased, pidgin form of Giant. They can learn to understand Common but they seem unable to speak more than the simplest words, and even those come out with a thick, guttural accent that takes practice to understand.

Churr can interbreed with some humanoid and most ape species, making them a "missing link" or bridge species. Mixed progeny are usually smaller but more intelligent than a typical churr, and they have an easier time learning and speaking Common and other languages. Evil bands of churr are known to kidnap humanoids until such time as they inadvertently enrage the churr and are killed and eaten on the spot.

Churr

Large monstrosity, neutral evil

Armor Class 14 (natural armor)
Hit Points 57 (6d10 + 24)
Speed 30 ft., climb 20 ft.

STR	DEX	CON	INT	WIS	CHA
19 (+4)	15 (+2)	18 (+4)	6 (–2)	12 (+1)	10 (+0)

Saving Throws Dex +4
Skills Stealth +4
Senses darkvision 60 ft., passive Perception 11
Languages Giant
Challenge 4 (1,100 XP)

Actions

Multiattack. A churr makes one Bite attack and two Claw attacks.
Bite. *Melee Weapon Attack:* +6 to hit, reach 5 ft., one creature. *Hit*: 8 (1d8 + 4) piercing damage.
Claw. *Melee Weapon Attack:* +6 to hit, reach 10 ft., one creature. *Hit*: 8 (1d8 + 4) slashing damage and the target is grappled and restrained.
Howl. A churr unleashes a frightening howl. Creatures within 60 feet of the churr must make a successful DC 10 Wisdom saving throw or become frightened for 1d6 x 10 minutes. A successful saving throw renders a character immune to the howling of churrs until after the character's next long rest.

Cobra Flower

The patch of flowers just reared up and bit me. I had been investigating the disappearances around the village of Rainsfell and had given up all hope of an easy hunt of the usual suspects. No tracks of large predators, no signs of orcs or goblins, not even a bandit camp in the woods. I was cutting back to the village when I passed an odd patch of vegetation that hadn't been there earlier in the day. As I bent to investigate, the central stalk raised a hood like a cobra and struck, its acidic bile burning into my bloodstream. — Päuk, apprentice mage

Cobra flowers draw their name from the snake-like shape of their central stalks. The plant looks like a patch of flowers and other vegetation and behaves in much the same way, rooting in fertile soil and soaking up sunlight to feed itself. However, the cobra flower likes a little meat every now and then, especially in the spring as it blooms and in the fall as it prepares for the long winter. When it senses small game or an unwary humanoid, the central stalk rears up and unfolds a cobra-like hood to reveal a fanged maw. Its bite is fierce, but the bile it injects into a wound can dissolve flesh and bone. It is this bile that allows the cobra flower to feed as its roots soak up the dissolved prey.

Cobra Flower

Large plant, unaligned

Armor Class 11
Hit Points 51 (6d10 + 18)
Speed 5 ft.

STR	DEX	CON	INT	WIS	CHA
17 (+3)	13 (+1)	16 (+3)	1 (–5)	13 (+1)	9 (–1)

Damage Vulnerabilities necrotic
Damage Immunities psychic
Condition Immunities frightened, exhaustion, stunned, unconscious
Senses tremorsense 30 ft., passive Perception 11
Languages —
Challenge 2 (450 XP)

Actions

Bite. *Melee Weapon Attack:* +5 to hit, reach 10 ft., one target. *Hit:* 8 (1d10 + 3) piercing damage and 4 (1d8) acid damage.

TOME OF HORRORS

Corpsespinner

The webs were amazing, shimmering strands woven into impossible patterns, so we knew there had to be a spider lurking about. Dannick readied our stores of curative in case anyone was bitten, and Wagna readied her blade and spoke of "fried spider legs." The thing caught us all off guard. One moment, we're laughing at "another eight-legged critter" and the next, this massive bone-white spider is right in the middle of our circle. It bore a skull marking I would never have thought nature could produce. It rammed a bony leg straight through Dannick's throat, and bit Wagna with its dripping fangs, and then it was gone again. As it vanished, the corpses in the webs stirred, advancing around us in a ring, so we turned to face this new threat. The spider appeared again, right at our backs. — Constance Greenbriar, on a web lair discovered in the caverns outside Reme

A massive, bone-white tarantula is the only way to describe the corpsespinner. Bands of gray and silver ring its abdomen and legs, and its body is covered in short, bristly hairs of white and silver. A large skull-like marking appears on the creature's thorax. Its eight eyes are stark white.

Corpsespinners are highly aggressive extraplanar spiders originating on the Astral Plane. Only rarely do they enter the Material Plane to hunt all types of giant spiders and humanoids. On the Astral Plane, corpsespinners spend their time constructing elaborate webs. They enjoy using unusual anchor points for their constructions, such as bizarre outcroppings of rare materials, the corpses of deceased astral travelers, drifting astral ruins, and just about anything else the corpsespinner finds intriguing or unique. When not constructing webs, the corpsespinner is usually hunting — and this sometimes leads it to the Material Plane.

If encountered on the Material Plane, there is a good chance the corpsespinner has its most recent victims with it as **corpsespun** (see monster entry). Corpsespinners seldom associate with others of their kind. Their ecology and reproduction cycles are unknown by outsiders, though intrepid interplanar adventurers have talked of seeing huge webbed lairs on the Astral Plane containing young corpsespinners. When hunting on the Material Plane, a corpsespinner uses its ability to shift back and forth between the planes to confuse and stymy its foes. If facing defeat, the corpsespinner retreats to the Astral Plane and seeks the safety of its lair. When accompanied by corpsespun, the corpsespinner focuses on trapping foes in webs and then lets its minions soften up the trapped enemies. The corpsespinner wants to ensure that their veins are filled with its poison when they die, to keep its supply of corpsespun high.

Corpsespinner

Huge monstrosity (extraplanar), unaligned

Armor Class 17 (natural armor)
Hit Points 114 (12d12 + 36)
Speed 40 ft., climb 20 ft.

STR	DEX	CON	INT	WIS	CHA
20 (+5)	17 (+3)	17 (+3)	7 (−2)	15 (+2)	10 (+0)

Skills Perception +5
Senses darkvision 60 ft., passive Perception 15
Languages Deep Speech
Challenge 5 (1,800 XP)

Astral Jaunt. A corpsespinner can shift between the Astral and Material Planes in either direction as a move. This does not trigger an opportunity attack.
Astralsense. A corpsespinner can automatically sense the presence and location of anything within 200 feet of it on the Astral Plane.
Create Corpsespun. Creatures that die while affected by a corpsespinner's poison that are not devoured by the corpsespinner rise in one hour as a corpsespun.

Actions

Bite. *Melee Weapon Attack:* +8 to hit, reach 15 ft.; one creature. *Hit:* 16 (2d10 + 5) piercing damage plus 5 (1d10) poison damage and the target is poisoned. A poisoned creature makes a DC 14 Constitution saving throw at the end of each of its turns; a successful save ends the condition.
Web (recharge 5–6). *Ranged Weapon Attack:* +6 to hit, range 80 ft.; one creature. *Hit:* The target is restrained. A restrained creature can use its action to attempt a DC 14 Strength (Athletics) check, becoming free of the webs on a success. A character has disadvantage on this check on the Astral Plane. These webs can be destroyed with slashing damage (Armor Class 12, 10 hit points), but they are immune to all other damage, including fire.

Corpsespun

Dannick survived the spider's stabbing foreleg through the throat, though he never spoke again. Wagna didn't ... she didn't make it. The bite on her thigh rotted quickly, and with Dannick severely injured, we had no way of healing her. We could only comfort her as we watched her light fade. We thought that was the worst of it, but no. I still have nightmares of her face contorting as she breathed her last. Spiders boiled from her eyes, from her throat, from the wound on her thigh. They clambered around her form like it was their home. We fell back, and then Wagna sat up. The monstrous bone-white spider took that moment to return, appearing from the air behind our dead friend. It seemed to enjoy watching as she crawled toward us, spitting spiders at us as she advanced. — Constance Greenbriar, on her flight from the web lair in the caverns beneath Reme

Corpsespun resemble zombies that are infested with spiders. Spiders crawl in and out of their bodies through their mouths, ears, nostrils, eye sockets, and wounds, and the creatures can vomit out a stream of spiders as an attack. They tend to be draped in webbing. Corpsespun follow the commands of the corpsespinner that created them, which they receive telepathically. If a corpsespinner is killed, its corpsespun minions continue carrying out their last instructions, and they fight to protect their master's body or its home web; otherwise, they have little purpose and are not innately hostile without a corpsespinner telling them who to kill.

Corpsespun

Medium undead, neutral

Armor Class 11 plus armor worn
Hit Points 44 (8d8 + 8)
Speed 30 ft., climb 20 ft.

STR	DEX	CON	INT	WIS	CHA
15 (+2)	13 (+1)	13 (+1)	3 (–4)	10 (+0)	6 (–2)

Damage Immunities necrotic, poison
Condition Immunities exhaustion, frightened, poisoned, unconscious
Senses darkvision 60 ft., passive Perception 10
Languages None
Challenge 1 (200 XP)

Spider-Infested. Spiders continually crawl out of corpsespun, swarm over them, and fall to the ground around the undeads' feet. All creatures other than a corpsepinner or other corpsespun that are within five feet of a corpsespun at the end of the corpsespun's turn take 2 (1d4) poison damage from spider bites. This damage is cumulative from multiple adjacent corpsespun.

Attacks

Claw. *Melee Weapon Attack:* +5 to hit, reach 5 ft., one creature. *Hit*: 5 (1d6 + 2) slashing damage plus 2 (1d4) poison damage and the target is poisoned. A poisoned creature can make a DC 11 Constitution saving throw at the end of each of its turns; a successful save ends the condition.

Spider Spray **(recharge 5–6).** All creatures in a 20-foot cone must make a successful DC 11 Dexterity saving throw or take 3 (1d6) piercing damage plus 7 (2d6) poison damage.

Craniform

The Dolphin's Wake was holed just below the waterline and sinkin' fast. Cap'n Avery called on us to save her, but wasn't nothin' we coulda done. The Wake was goin' under, an' goin' fast. Not all of us was gonna make it. Just when all seemed lost, Dodgers in the crow's nest gave a shout. We rushed to port, and the thing was there, standing on the water like it was solid ground. It was a crab-thing, tall with big pincers. Its smaller arms waved an' wove, and a greenish-blue wave rose up and pushed The Wake upright from her list. Before our eyes, the boards of the broken hull stretched an' shuddered, regrowin' right back to their normal shape. The wave let us loose, and The Wake settled back like nothin' had happened. The crab-thing waved once and sank straight down into the water an' was gone. — Colgrad Frew, helmsman of The Dolphin's Wake

Craniforms are bipedal cancriform humanoids with a chitinous carapace, eyestalks, antennae, and a pair of mandibles set to either side of a complementary set of horizontally-aligned maxillae that constitute the creatures' mouths. Extending outward from the neck of each creature is a set of short but large chitinous arms, each of which terminate in a seemingly oversized claw. Below these larger claws is another set of arms. These extend from either side of the upper torso, not unlike how arms extend from shoulders in more familiar humanoids. This second set of smaller chitinous arms each end with a smaller pincer. The creatures' torsos and legs are covered by the same chitinous exoskeleton and extend to cover their clawed feet. Females and males are hard to tell apart, but males are slightly smaller than females.

Craniform inhabit tropical coastal waters where they usually create permanent colonies. These timid and reclusive creatures are very rare and stay well away from other humanoid settlements. Craniform typically live in coastal caves, but some communities excavate more expansive subterranean underwater burrows beneath the waterline and back up and under the shoreline. Craniform society is as complex as most terrestrial societies.

Craniform are led temporally and spiritually by a group of priestesses who oversee most of their important functions, rituals, and endeavors. Craniform are deeply reverential of their deity, the Sea Mother, goddess of all sea creatures, and see themselves as the Sea Mother's chosen stewards of the sea. While little is known of the magics of the reclusive craniform and their priestesses, it is believed that they can confer the ability to breathe underwater to surface dwellers through a ritual venerating the Sea Mother called the Sea Mother's Blessing.

Craniform

Medium humanoid (craniform), lawful good

Armor Class 13 (natural armor)
Hit Points 32 (5d8 + 10)
Speed 30 ft., swim 40 ft.

STR	DEX	CON	INT	WIS	CHA
16 (+3)	11 (+0)	15 (+2)	10 (+0)	10 (+0)	10 (+0)

Skills Perception +4
Senses darkvision 60 ft., passive Perception 14
Languages Craniform, Aquan
Challenge 2 (450 XP)

Limited Amphibiousness. The craniform can breathe air and water but begins to suffocate if not submerged at least once every four hours.

Actions

Multiattack. The craniform makes two Pincer attacks or one Pincer attack and one Spear attack.
Pincer. *Melee Weapon Attack:* +5 to hit, reach 5 ft., one target. *Hit:* 10 (2d6 + 3) slashing damage. The target is grappled (escape DC 13) if it is a Large or smaller creature and the craniform doesn't have another creature grappled already. The target is restrained until the grapple ends.
Spear. *Melee Weapon Attack:* +5 to hit, reach 5 ft. or range 20/60 ft., one target. *Hit:* 7 (1d8 +3) piercing damage.

Craniform Priestess

Blessed by the Sea Mother herself, the craniform priestess is called to the Sea Mother's service in a vision. This vision reveals the Sea Mother's true form: a massive sea turtle. Craniform priestesses are referred to as "gifted" among fellow craniforms.

Craniform priestesses serve an integral role in craniform communities. They are the spiritual advisors, healers, and ritual officiants, and also the leaders of their respective communities. The priestesses must first approve every major decision that affects a craniform colony.

Craniform Priestess

Medium humanoid (craniform), lawful good

Armor Class 13 (natural armor)
Hit Points 32 (5d8 + 10)
Speed 30 ft., swim 40 ft.

STR	DEX	CON	INT	WIS	CHA
16 (+3)	11 (+0)	15 (+2)	10 (+0)	14 (+2)	10 (+0)

Skills Perception +4
Senses darkvision 60 ft., passive Perception 14
Languages Craniform, Aquan
Challenge 3 (700 XP)

Limited Amphibiousness. The craniform priestess can breathe air and water but begins to suffocate if not submerged at least once every four hours.
Spellcasting. The craniform priestess is a 6th-level spellcaster. Her spellcasting ability is Wisdom (spell save DC 12, +4 to hit with spell attacks). She has the following cleric spells prepared:
Cantrips (at will): *guidance, thaumaturgy*
1st level (4 slots): *bless, detect magic, guiding bolt*
2nd level (3 slots): *hold person, spiritual weapon* (trident)
3rd level (3 slots): *mass healing word, tongues*

Actions

Multiattack. The craniform priestess makes two Pincer attacks or one Pincer attack and one Spear attack.
Pincer. *Melee Weapon Attack:* +5 to hit, reach 5 ft., one target. *Hit:* 10 (2d6 + 3) slashing damage. The target is grappled (escape DC 13) if it is a Large or smaller creature and the craniform priestess doesn't have another creature grappled already. The target is restrained until the grapple ends.
Spear. *Melee Weapon Attack:* +5 to hit, reach 5 ft. or range 20/60 ft., one target. *Hit:* 7 (1d8 +3) piercing damage.

Crawling Hand

The scrabbling sound came from down the corridor, like nails on stone, scrapping, clawing, sliding, and tapping. The sound changed as the things, disembodied hands, spotted us with eyeless wrists. With a hop, they were on all fives and skittering forward, their broken yellowed nails seeking the warm saltiness of flesh and blood. — Sir Cedric of Reme, knight errant

Crawling hands are horrid necromantic creations that wander darkened areas, often crypts, in search of living prey to choke the life out of them. Some are made by foul magics that seek to create swarms of lesser minions to guard areas and commit assassinations. Other crawling hands are the result of careless adventurers who hack away at zombies with little regard to the lingering necromantic energies that might reanimate severed parts.

Crawling Hand

Tiny undead, neutral evil

Armor Class 13 (natural armor)
Hit Points 7 (3d4)
Speed 20 ft., climb 20 ft.

STR	DEX	CON	INT	WIS	CHA
13 (+1)	11 (+0)	14 (+2)	2 (–4)	11 (+0)	7 (–2)

Skills Stealth +2
Damage Immunities poison
Condition Immunities exhaustion, paralyzed, poisoned, stunned, unconscious
Senses blindsight 30 ft. (blind beyond this radius), passive Perception 10
Languages understands the languages of its creator, but can't speak
Challenge 1/2 (100 XP)

Leap. The crawling hand's long jump is up to 10 feet and its high jump is up to five feet, with or without a running start.

Actions

Grab. Melee Weapon Attack: +3 to hit, reach 0 ft., one target. *Hit:* The crawling hand attaches to the target. At the beginning of the crawling hand's next turn, the target begins suffocating and cannot cast spells that require verbal components. The target or another creature can use an action to make a DC 13 Strength check to pull the crawling hand off, removing it on a successful check.

Crawling Offspring

The flapping, squelching sound originated from a horde of small balls of tumorous flesh, too many eyes, and whipping tentacles. The things, for they cannot be called anything else but that, had no distinct form. A mass is all that can be said about them, with each individual varying in color, limb, and texture. The smell was something I will take to the grave. — Tara the Wise, adventurer

Crawling offspring are mindless creatures with no single form or appearance. Some are oval, while others are round or even boxy. Many have dangling pseudopodia, while others sport whipping claw-tipped tentacles, flapping wings, bulging eyes, warty flesh that leaks oily substances, or none or all of the above.

Crawling Offspring

Small aberration, unaligned

Armor Class 13 (natural armor)
Hit Points 16 (3d6 +6)
Speed 20 ft.

STR	DEX	CON	INT	WIS	CHA
16 (+3)	11 (+ 0)	14 (+ 2)	3 (–4)	10 (+ 0)	11 (+ 0)

Skills Perception +2
Senses blindsight 60 ft., passive Perception 12
Languages —
Challenge 1 (200 XP)

Mutation. Each crawling offspring is different in form and shape. These blobs of horror have a special ability from the following list:

1d6	Ability
1	**Acidic spit (recharge 5–6).** As an action, the crawling offspring can spit a cone of acid 15 feet long. Any creature caught in this cone must make a DC 12 Dexterity saving throw, taking 9 (2d8) acid damage on a failure or half as much damage on a success save.
2	**Necrotic touch.** The crawling offspring's pseudopod attack inflicts an additional 3 (1d6) necrotic damage.
3	**Clawed tentacle.** The crawling offspring gains a Clawed Tentacle attack and may multiattack, making one Clawed Tentacle and one Pseudopod attack. The Clawed Tentacle attack is +5 to hit, reach 10 ft., one target, *Hit:* 6 (1d6 + 3) slashing damage.
4	**Wings.** The crawling offspring gains flight 30 ft.
5	**Rubbery, oily skin.** The crawling offspring gains resistance to bludgeoning, piercing, and slashing attacks from nonmagical attacks, and vulnerability to fire damage.
6	**No mutation**

Regeneration. The crawling offspring regains 5 hit points as long as it starts its turn with 1 hit point.

Actions

Pseudopod. Melee Weapon Attack: +5 to hit, reach 5 ft., one target. *Hit:* 4 (1d2 + 3) bludgeoning damage.

Crayfish, Monstrous

We scrambled down the mud chimney without really knowing what might have built them. The mud was pliable and squished between our fingers, but provided just enough grip to make it safely underground. The chimney rose 10 feet above the ground, but the tunnel inside dropped another 20 into the damp soil of the Sin Mire. My brother Clobi was eight feet from the bottom when he fell, dropping like a stone onto his back into four feet of water filling the room below us. He shouted up to me, "I'm all right." A moment later he was thrashing in the water as a giant crayfish grabbed him and rolled into the murk. I used to spear those things when I was little along the Gaelon, but I never imagined they could grow so big. — Pobi Netmender, on the halfling twin's ill-fated trek into the Sin Mire Swamp

A giant crayfish looks like a giant lobster with a sharp snout and eyes on movable, flickering stalks. Two large claws extend from its thorax in front of four smaller pairs of spindly walking legs. Its exoskeleton is dark brown.

Monstrous crayfish are freshwater creatures that dwell on the bottoms of seas, lakes, ponds, and other shallow water. They are predators and scavengers that exist on a diet of decaying flesh from dead fish, algae, snails, worms, and other animals, including swimmers who venture too close to the monstrous crayfish's lair.

These giant crayfish make their homes under rocks or in underwater tunnels that they dig. Their flooded tunnels extend over long distances and always include a "chimney" through which the monstrous crayfish can enter and exit its home via dry ground. These exits have been found as far as 100 feet inland from the lake shore or riverbank.

Monstrous Crayfish
Large beast, unaligned

Armor Class 14 (natural armor)
Hit Points 30 (4d10 + 8)
Speed 20 ft., swim 40 ft.

STR	DEX	CON	INT	WIS	CHA
16 (+3)	10 (+0)	14 (+2)	1 (−5)	10 (+0)	2 (−5)

Condition Immunities frightened
Senses darkvision 60 ft., passive Perception 10
Languages —
Challenge 2 (450 XP)

Water Dependency. A monstrous crayfish can survive out of water for seven hours. After this limit, a monstrous crayfish begins suffocating.

Actions

Multiattack. A monstrous crayfish makes two attacks.
Pincer. Melee weapon attack: +5 to hit, reach 5 ft., one creature. *Hit:* 7 (1d8 + 3) slashing damage and the target is grappled (escape DC 15).
Crush. The monstrous crayfish crushes one creature that it has grappled. The target takes 7 (1d8 + 3) piercing damage.

Dark Creeper

They struck from behind, in the dark, like the filthy cowards they were. There were several of them, all the size of a dwarf but clad in foul-smelling black clothing. Baggy clothing at that, as if they were hiding something underneath. Like cowards do. They fought like demons though, slashing with short jagged knives and leaping off ledges at us. Once Fizalire sent up a ball of pure light, the cowards ran for the safety of their dark lairs, leaving behind the corpses of their fallen kin. Like cowards do. — Sir Cedric of Reme, knight errant

Dark creepers are diminutive dwellers found in the depths of the earth. The wear layers of filthy rags to hide their pale, wan bodies. Unwilling to show their true forms even to each other, they do not remove their clothing, and merely add a new layer as the outermost grows too ragged or stained. Some say entire cities of these folk exist in the dark depths, and that they raid the surface for loot, kidnapped servants, and the love of mayhem.

Dark Creeper

Small humanoid, chaotic neutral

Armor Class 14 (natural armor)
Hit Points 22 (4d6 + 8)
Speed 30 ft.

STR	DEX	CON	INT	WIS	CHA
11 (+0)	17 (+3)	14 (+2)	9 (−1)	10 (+0)	8 (−1)

Skills Perception +4, Stealth +7
Senses passive Perception 14
Languages Undercommon (dark folk dialect)
Challenge 1 (200 XP)

Innate Spellcasting. The dark creeper's spellcasting ability is Charisma (spell save DC 9). The dark creeper can innately cast the following spells, requiring no material components:
At will: *deeper darkness, detect magic*

Death Throes. When a dark creeper dies, it combusts in a flash of bright white light, and each creature within 10 feet of it must make a DC 13 Constitution saving throw or be blinded for one minute. A target can repeat the saving throw at the end of each of its turns, ending the effect on itself on a success. Other dark creepers within 10 feet of the flash of light are automatically blinded until the end of their next turn. A dark creeper's gear and treasure are unaffected by this explosion.

Envenomed Attacks. The dark creeper coats its weapons with black smear, a foul-smelling black paste distilled from fungi found deep underground.

Exceptional Dark Vision. Dark creepers can see perfectly in darkness of any kind, including magical darkness.

Light Sensitivity. While in bright light, the dark creeper has disadvantage on attack rolls as well as on Wisdom (Perception) checks that rely on sight.

Actions

Dagger. *Melee Weapon Attack:* +5 to hit, reach 5 ft. or range 20/60 ft., one target. *Hit:* 5 (1d4 + 3) piercing damage, and the target must make a DC 13 Constitution saving throw, taking 7 (2d6) poison damage on a failed save, or half as much on a successful one.

DARK STALKER

The stench was overwhelming. These diminutive underground dwellers, dark creepers I heard someone call them, captured us and took us to their subterranean settlement. They handled us roughly and pushed us to the ground in front of one who at first appeared to be of a different race. Tall and slender where the others were short and squat, this leader of the dark creepers showed more intelligence and courage than its followers. Yet it was clad in the same filthy layers of rags that stank to high heaven. — Cedric of Reme, knight errant

While they are the leaders of dark creeper communities ranging from small village outpost to the mighty cities of the dark folk said to exist deep within the earth, the dark stalkers are a people apart. Although of the same race as the dark creepers, dark stalkers are taller, more courageous, and possibly more intelligent. They share many of the same cultural attitudes, an unwillingness to be nude, an acceptance of murder and cannibalism, and general unhygienic ways of their diminutive brethren. A group of dark creepers led by a dark stalker is a deadly force of assassins, marauders, and raiders made bolder by the presence of their taller kin.

DARK STALKER

Medium humanoid, chaotic neutral

Armor Class 15
Hit Points 52 (7d8 + 21)
Speed 30 ft.

STR	DEX	CON	INT	WIS	CHA
14 (+2)	18 (+4)	16 (+3)	9 (−1)	11 (+0)	13 (+1)

Saving Throws Dex +6, Cha +3
Skills Perception +4, Stealth +8
Senses darkvision 120 ft., passive Perception 14
Languages Undercommon (dark folk dialect)
Challenge 3 (700 XP)

Innate Spellcasting. The dark stalker's spellcasting ability is Charisma (spell save DC 10). The dark stalker can innately cast the following spells, requiring no material components:
At will: *deeper darkness, detect magic, fog cloud*

Death Throes. When a dark stalker dies, it combusts in a flash of white-hot flame, and each creature within 20 feet of it must make a DC 14 Dexterity saving throw, taking 14 (4d6) fire damage on a failed save, or half as much on a success. A dark stalker's gear and treasure are unaffected by this explosion.

Envenomed Attacks. The dark stalker coats its weapons with black smear, a foul-smelling black paste distilled from fungi that live deep underground.

Exceptional Dark Vision. Dark stalkers can see perfectly in darkness of any kind, including magical darkness.

Light Sensitivity. While in bright light, the dark stalker has disadvantage on attack rolls as well as on Wisdom (Perception) checks that rely on sight.

Sneak Attack. Once per turn, the dark stalker deals an extra 14 (4d6) damage when it hits a target with a weapon attack and has advantage on the attack roll, or when the target is within five feet of an ally of the dark stalker that isn't incapacitated, and the dark stalker doesn't have disadvantage on the attack roll.

ACTIONS

Multiattack. The dark stalker makes two Shortsword attacks.

Shortsword. *Melee Weapon Attack:* +6 to hit, reach 5 ft., one target. *Hit:* 7 (1d6 + 4) piercing damage, and the target must succeed on a DC 14 Constitution saving throw, taking 14 (4d6) poison damage on a failed save, or half as much on a successful one.

DEATH WEAVER

Our nerves were on end due to the bizarre, discordant humming emanating from around the corner. As the sound grew louder, a faint glow could be seen radiating from a seething mass of hovering flesh. Eyeless, boneless, and possessing far too many mouths to be a natural creature, this blob of flesh floated in for the kill, humming that damnable tuneless sound the entire time. — Sir Cedric, knight errant

Death weavers are orbs of evil from a place beyond, or perhaps between, places. Maybe a time beyond, or perhaps between, times. Whichever, it is not from here and now. It does hunt the here and now, however, paralyzing prey with its tuneless humming before absorbing them body and soul into one of its many irregularly shaped gaping mouths.

DEATH WEAVER
Small aberration, neutral evil

Armor Class 17 (natural armor)
Hit Points 21 (6d6)
Speed fly 20 ft.

STR	DEX	CON	INT	WIS	CHA
7 (−2)	17 (+3)	10 (+0)	14 (+2)	14 (+2)	16 (+3)

Skills Perception +4
Senses darkvision 60 ft., passive Perception 14
Languages Common
Challenge 4 (1,100 XP)

Feeding. If the death weaver successfully uses its tentacle attack to devour a piece of a creature's soul, it gains 10 temporary hit points and gains the ability to innately cast the *web* spell three times. This lasts for one hour.

Magic Resistance. The death weaver has advantage on any saving throws to resist spells and other magical effects.

Radiance. The death weaver glows, shedding bright light for 20 feet and dim light for 20 feet beyond that.

ACTIONS

Paralyzing Song. The death weaver emits a bizarre humming that effects all creatures within a 30-foot cube centered on itself. Affected creatures must succeed at a DC 13 Wisdom saving throw or be paralyzed for one hour. Creatures that successfully save against a death weaver's paralyzing song are immune to the effect for 24 hours.

Tentacle. *Melee Weapon Attack:* +5 to hit, reach 5 ft., one target. *Hit:* 1 bludgeoning damage. If the death weaver hits a paralyzed creature with its tentacle attack, it may attempt to devour that creature's lifeforce. The target must succeed on a DC 13 Constitution saving throw or suffer 14 (4d6) necrotic damage. If a creature is reduced to 0 hit points by this attack, it dies and can be raised only by powerful magic such as *true resurrection* or *wish*.

DEATH WORM

We walked as the guides taught us, trying to keep a rhythm out of our stride, but it was for naught. The sands shook and flowed downward as something massive rose up beneath us. We ran, not caring if we ran with a pattern to our steps or not. Not all of the expedition made it clear of the rapidly growing funnel of sand. With barely a sound, the creature erupted from the sand, lifting its massive head higher than I would have thought possible for such a creature. It arched its body and descended, and in one massive gulp, it swallowed a half dozen camels and four drovers. We reached the rocks, and our guide informed us we were lucky; the worms with tentacles writhing in their mouths were worse. — Algrid Henswaith, University of the Vast

Terrors of the open sands, death worms are dun-and-beige colored worms related to purple worms. They lair deep beneath the ground where sand meets bedrock, where they carve out a small hollow in which to lay their eggs. Those who regularly travel the sandy wastes know the areas hunted by these lethal vermiforms and avoid them. Some desert cultures hold that the death worms are lesser demons and send their heroes out to slay the beasts — a good way to rid a tribe of excess heroes.

DEATH WORM
Large monstrosity, unaligned

Armor Class 15 (natural armor)
Hit Points 59 (7d10 + 21)
Speed 20 ft., burrow 10 ft.

STR	DEX	CON	INT	WIS	CHA
18 (+4)	13 (+1)	16 (+3)	3 (−4)	11 (+0)	5 (−3)

Saving Throws Wis +3
Condition Immunities blindness, prone
Senses tremorsense 60 ft., passive Perception 10
Languages —
Challenge 3 (700 XP)

ACTIONS

Bite. *Melee Weapon Attack:* +6 to hit, reach 5 ft., one creature. *Hit:* 9 (1d10 + 4) piercing damage plus 4 (1d8) acid damage.

Acid Spit (recharge 5–6). All creatures along a five-foot-wide, 30-foot-long line extending from the death worm must succeed on a DC 11 Dexterity saving throw or take 14 (4d6) acid damage.

Lightning (recharge 6). All creatures along a five-foot-wide, 20-foot-long line extending from the death worm must make a DC 11 Dexterity saving throw, taking 18 (4d8) lightning damage on a failure, or half as much on a success.

TOME OF HORRORS

Deepmind

*The **Blustering Bubble's** maiden descent into the depths of the Reaping Sea proved successful, with the clear bubble shield offering a full view of the watery depths of the underwater realms. I believe I have created my greatest achievement! My crewmen pleaded with me to rise to the surface when their ears started to bleed, but no success is possible without a little pain. And I'm glad we continued downward. Never before have I seen such a creature as the one I discovered. It was a massive jellyfish that floated in its own luminous blue aura. Its tentacles trailed around it, waving in the currents. When it noticed us, it turned, and a pressure wave slammed into the bubble protecting us. My crewmen screamed in agony, but I felt very little. I must investigate why that is. — Field observations from halfling inventor Ollie Nematoad*

The alien jellyfish creatures known as deepminds dwell in the depths of the sea, often in ocean trenches, unaffected by the massive pressures there. Highly hostile and dangerous, deepminds control all of the unintelligent sea life in surrounding regions, using them for defense against intruders and other deepminds.

The deepmind floats in the cold darkness of the ocean depths, illuminated by a faint bluish glow. Several small tentacles hang from its central mass, while six larger ones ring the body, gleaming with tiny eyespots. They reproduce asexually by budding. Young deepminds have their full powers within a matter of days and strike out instinctively, seeking out new territories to dominate.

While they are solitary and extremely hostile creatures, deepminds are highly intelligent and can communicate mentally and in the Aquan language. They are driven by self-interest and the need to survive and accordingly are willing to make deals with other intelligent sea creatures, especially those of evil alignment. Such allies reward a deepmind by keeping outsiders away while using sea creatures dominated by the deepmind for their own purposes.

Deepmind

Huge monstrosity, lawful evil

Armor Class 16 (natural armor)
Hit Points 266 (28d12 + 84)
Speed 0 ft., swim 20 ft.

STR	DEX	CON	INT	WIS	CHA
14 (+2)	10 (+0)	16 (+3)	19 (+4)	17 (+3)	18 (+4)

Saving Throws Int +11, Wis +8
Skills Intimidation +14, Perception +13, Persuasion +14
Senses blindsight 120 ft., passive Perception 23
Languages Aquan, telepathy 120 feet
Challenge 16 (15,000 XP)

Oceanic Domination. A deepmind exercises psychic control over all sea creatures that have an Intelligence score of 2 or less within a one-mile radius. Creatures of Intelligence 3 or higher must make DC 18 Intelligence saving throws or are also controlled. If actively resisting control, creatures of Intelligence 3 or higher can make a saving throw at the end of each of their turns to break the control. A creature that succeeds on its saving throw is immune to that deepmind's control for 24 hours. Controlled creatures obey the deepmind's commands. The deepmind can also see and hear through its controlled creatures, which allows it to make Wisdom (Perception) checks through their senses. Controlled creatures also act to defend the deepmind if so commanded. Creatures that are not native to the ocean — such as humans, elves, or dwarves who are underwater through magical means — are immune to the deepmind's control.

Actions

Multiattack. The deepmind makes six Tentacle attacks.
Tentacle. *Melee Weapon Attack:* +9 to hit, reach 50 ft., one creature. *Hit:* The target is grappled (escape DC 15). Until the grapple ends, the target is restrained and has disadvantage on Strength checks and Strength saving throws, and the deepmind can't use the same tentacle on another target. While grappled, the target takes 12 (3d6 + 2) bludgeoning damage at the beginning of the deepmind's turn.
Psychic Pulse (recharge 5–6). The deepmind unleashes a pulse of pure psychic energy over a 50-foot radius centered on itself. Any living creature in the area except those controlled by the deepmind through its Oceanic Domination ability must make a DC 18 Wisdom saving throw, taking 66 (12d10) psychic damage and being stunned until the start of the deepmind's next turn on a failed save, or half as much damage and not being stunned on a successful saving throw.

Demi-Lich

Imagine our surprise when the barbarian OTATO! (who always shouts when asked his name) walked into the Ale Giant's House carrying a lead ball of nearly 300 pounds. He dropped it hard onto the peanut-covered floor and backed up like a pleased cat bringing us a prize. He thumped the ball once with his hammer, and the ringing tone that resounded nearly caused all of us in the tavern to fall to the floor. I'm not sure what I expected to happen, but to see the ball split open along an unseen seam and a skull come floating out was not it. I only realized our peril when a beam of brilliant green cast from the skull withered the barkeep where he stood. — Mara Gemkeeper, recounting the events before the Ale Giant's House burned to the ground

When the lifeforce of an ancient lich of incredible power finally diminishes and its material body decays — a process that often takes centuries of undeath — the undead being's soul lingers in the area and possesses the only viable remains: the skull. After this second death, the eye sockets and the teeth of the demi-lich-possessed skull oddly transform into clear gemstones (each worth 1,000 gp), with a single gemstone growing in each eye socket to match the six gems that replace the teeth.

Demi-Lich

Tiny undead, neutral evil

Armor Class 20
Hit Points 110 (20d4 + 60)
Speed 0 ft., fly 30 ft. (hover)

STR	DEX	CON	INT	WIS	CHA
4 (−3)	19 (+4)	17 (+3)	20 (+5)	18 (+4)	17 (+3)

Saving Throws Dex +10, Con +9, Int +11, Wis +10
Skills Arcana +11, History +11, Perception +10, Religion +11
Damage Resistances cold, damage from spells
Damage Immunities necrotic, poison, psychic; bludgeoning, piercing, and slashing from nonmagical attacks
Condition Immunities charmed, deafened, exhaustion, frightened, paralyzed, petrified, poisoned, prone, stunned
Senses truesight 120 ft., passive Perception 20
Languages telepathy 120 ft.
Challenge 19 (22,000 XP) or 20 (25,000 XP) in lair

Evasion. If the demi-lich is subjected to an effect that allows it to make a Dexterity saving throw to take only half damage, the demi-lich instead takes no damage if it succeeds on the saving throw, and only half damage if it fails.

Legendary Resistance (3/day). If the demi-lich fails a saving throw, it can choose to succeed instead.

Turn Resistance. The demi-lich has advantage on saving throws against any effect that turns undead.

Rejuvenation. If it has a phylactery, a destroyed demi-lich's skull reforms in 1d10 days, regaining all its hit points and becoming active again. The skull reforms within five feet of the phylactery.

Actions

Drain Life. Deep violet beams lance out from the demi-lich's gemstone eyes and strike up to three creatures within 40 feet of it. Each target must succeed on a DC 19 Constitution saving throw or take 17 (5d6) necrotic damage. The target's hit point maximum is reduced by an amount equal to the necrotic damage taken, and the demi-lich regains hit points equal to that amount. This reduction lasts until the target finishes a long rest. The target dies if this effect reduces its hit point maximum to 0.

Soul Scream (recharge 5–6). The demi-lich unleashes a soul-shattering scream. All non-undead creatures within 30 feet of the demi-lich who hear the scream must succeed on a DC 17 Wisdom saving throw or drop to 0 hit points. On a successful save, the creature takes 11 (2d10) psychic damage and is frightened until the end of its next turn.

Legendary Actions

The demi-lich can take three legendary actions, choosing from the options below. Only one legendary action option can be used at a time and only at the end of another creature's turn. The demi-lich regains spent legendary actions at the start of its turn.

Flight. The demi-lich moves up to its speed without provoking opportunity attacks.

Bone Dust. Blinding bone dust swirls magically around the demi-lich in a five-foot radius. That area is heavily obscured to creatures other than the demi-lich until the end of the demi-lich's next turn. This effect moves with the demi-lich.

Disrupt Life (costs 3 actions). Each living creature within 20 feet of the demi-lich must make a DC 18 Constitution saving throw against this magic, taking 21 (6d6) necrotic damage on a failed save, or half as much damage on a successful one.

Profane Curse (costs 2 actions). The demi-lich targets one creature it can see within 30 feet of it. The target must succeed on a DC 19 Wisdom saving throw or be magically cursed. Until the curse ends, the target has disadvantage on ability checks, attack rolls, and saving throws. The target can repeat the saving throw at the end of each of its turns, ending the curse on itself on a success.

Dreadful Glare (costs 2 actions). The demi-lich targets one creature it can see within 60 feet of it. If the target can see the demi-lich, it must succeed on a DC 19 Wisdom saving throw or become frightened until the end of the demi-lich's next turn. If the target fails the saving throw by 5 or more, it is also paralyzed for the same duration. A target that succeeds on the saving throw is immune to the demi-lich's Dreadful Glare effect for the next 24 hours.

Lair Actions

On initiative count 20 (losing initiative ties), the demi-lich can take a lair action to cause one of the following effects. The demi-lich can't use the same effect two rounds in a row.

Healing Suppression. All living creatures within 60 feet of the demi-lich must succeed on a DC 19 Wisdom saving throw or be unable to regain hit points until initiative 20 of the next round.

Malevolent Echo. A short-lived echo of the demi-lich's former self appears in the form of a wraith in an unoccupied space within 30 feet of the demi-lich and obeys the demi-lich's telepathic commands (no action required). It rolls initiative, acts on its own turn, and disappears after one minute or when it drops to 0 hit points.

Tap Phylactery. The demi-lich draws negative energy from its phylactery, if it exists and is on the same plane as the demi-lich, and regains 22 (4d10) hit points.

DEMI-LICH, GREATER

I was awake and aware, something that had not happened in … some time. My memories were jumbled; they had been since my body finally crumbled to dust and my mind was freed to travel the esoteric pathways and channels of pure thought. Nearly pure thought, for I still had a physical presence in my skull, albeit one I rarely bothered with. Now something disturbed me; no, not something, but someone, yes, the flesh ones are not things but beings. Maybe. They intruded, and I hoped they would leave quickly, for I had more lofty matters to concern the eons with. But no, they tarried, they disturbed, they shall be punished. — Päuk, former wizard, currently a very old demi-lich.

A greater demi-lich is a demi-lich that has spent eons traveling the planes of existence and exploring dark, arcane secrets. It has succeeded in recovering some of its former spellcasting ability and developing other unholy powers beyond even those it had as a lich. Some say such demi-liches deliberately abandoned their bodies in order to more fully focus on their sinister studies. Although a greater demi-lich can never regain its lost body, it has learned to capture the souls of the creatures it encounters and store them in the gemstones embedded in its skull. It then transfers the souls to once again power its phylactery.

Greater demi-liches very similar to ordinary demi-liches, with a skull with clear gemstone eyes and teeth sitting on top of, or floating over, a pile of bones and dust. However, greater demi-liches seem much more purposeful than ordinary demi-liches, often employing lesser undead as guardians and servants. Although they still almost always remain in their lairs, they actively seek paths to transcendence and even loftier levels of power such as godhood.

GREATER DEMI-LICH

Tiny undead, neutral evil

Armor Class 21
Hit Points 180 (24d4 + 120)
Speed 0 ft., fly 40 ft. (hover)

STR	DEX	CON	INT	WIS	CHA
4 (–3)	21 (+5)	20 (+5)	22 (+6)	20 (+5)	20 (+5)

Saving Throws Dex +13, Con +13, Int +14, Wis +13, Cha +13
Skills Arcana +14, History +14, Perception +13, Religion +14
Damage Resistances bludgeoning, piercing, and slashing from magical weapons; damage from spells
Damage Immunities cold, necrotic, poison, psychic; bludgeoning, piercing, and slashing from nonmagical attacks
Condition Immunities charmed, deafened, exhaustion, frightened, paralyzed, petrified, poisoned, prone, stunned
Senses truesight 120 ft., passive Perception 23
Languages telepathy 120 ft.
Challenge 25 (75,000 XP) or 26 (90,000 XP) in lair

Evasion. If the demi-lich is subjected to an effect that allows it to make a Dexterity saving throw to take only half damage, the demi-lich instead takes no damage if it succeeds on the saving throw, and only half damage if it fails.

Legendary Resistance (3/day). If the demi-lich fails a saving throw, it can choose to succeed instead.

Turn Immunity. The greater demi-lich is immune to effects that turn undead.

Rejuvenation. If it has a phylactery, a destroyed demi-lich's skull reforms in 1d4 days, regaining all its hit points and becoming active again. The skull reforms within five feet of the phylactery.

Innate Spellcasting. The demi-lich's innate spellcasting ability is Charisma (spell save DC 24, +16 to hit with spell attacks). The demi-lich can innately cast the following spells, requiring no material components:

At will: counterspell, detect thoughts, dimension door, greater invisibility, mirror image, shield
3/day each: animate dead, antilife shell, antimagic field, dispel magic (as a 6th-level slot), fireball (as a 6th-level slot), globe of invulnerability (as a 7th-level slot)
1/day each: contingency, disintegrate, plane shift, time stop

ACTIONS

Drain Life. Deep violet beams lance out from the demi-lich's gemstone eyes and strike up to three creatures within 40 feet of it. Each target must succeed on a DC 21 Constitution saving throw or take 24 (7d6) necrotic damage. The target's hit point maximum is reduced by an amount equal to the necrotic damage taken, and the demi-lich regains hit points equal to that amount. This reduction lasts until the target finishes a long rest. The target dies if this effect reduces its hit point maximum to 0.

Soul Scream (recharge 5–6). The demi-lich unleashes a soul-shattering scream. All non-undead creatures within 30 feet of the demi-lich who can hear the scream must succeed on a DC 18 Wisdom saving throw or drop to 0 hit points. On a successful save, the creature takes 22 (4d10) psychic damage and is frightened until the end of its next turn.

Soul Steal (recharge 6). The demi-lich chooses a creature it can see within 60 feet. That creature must make a DC 18 Charisma saving throw. On a failed save, the creature's soul is ripped out of its body and stored in one of the demi-lich's skull gems. The demi-lich can never capture more than eight souls, one in each of its gems. Killing a demi-lich and destroying one of its gems within 48 hours of the soul being captured releases any soul trapped therein. The soul automatically reoccupies the creature's soulless body if it is still intact, and the creature is immediately conscious. On a successful save, the creature is stunned until the end of its next turn.

LEGENDARY ACTIONS

The demi-lich can take three legendary actions, choosing from the options below. Only one legendary action option can be used at a time and only at the end of another creature's turn. The demi-lich regains spent legendary actions at the start of its turn.

Flight. The demi-lich moves up to its speed without provoking opportunity attacks.

Bone Dust. Blinding bone dust swirls magically around the demi-lich in a five-foot radius. That area is heavily obscured to creatures other than the demi-lich until the end of the demi-lich's next turn. This effect moves with the demi-lich.

Disrupt Life (costs 3 actions). Each living creature within 20 feet of the demi-lich must make a DC 20 Constitution saving throw against this magic, taking 35 (10d6) necrotic damage on a failed save, or half as much damage on a successful one.

Profane Curse (costs 2 actions). The demi-lich targets one creature it can see within 30 feet of it. The target must succeed on a DC 21 Wisdom saving throw or be magically cursed. Until the curse ends, the target has disadvantage on ability checks, attack rolls, and saving throws. The target can repeat the saving throw at the end of each of its turns, ending the curse on itself on a success.

Dreadful Glare (costs 2 actions). The demi-lich targets one creature it can see within 60 feet of it. If the target can see the demi-lich, it must succeed on a DC 21 Wisdom saving throw or become frightened until the end of the demi-lich's next turn. If the target fails the saving throw by 5 or more, it is also paralyzed for the same duration. A target that succeeds on the saving throw is immune to the demi-lich's Dreadful Glare effect for the next 24 hours.

LAIR ACTIONS

On initiative count 20 (losing initiative ties), the demi-lich can take a lair action to cause one of the following effects. The demi-lich can't use the same effect two rounds in a row.

Healing Suppression. All living creatures within 60 feet of the demi-lich must succeed on a DC 21 Wisdom saving throw or be unable to regain hit points until initiative 20 of the next round.

Malevolent Echoes. Two separate short-lived echoes of the demi-lich's former self appear in the form of wraiths in two unoccupied spaces within 30 feet of the demi-lich and obey the demi-lich's telepathic commands (no action required). Each rolls initiative, acts on its own turn, and disappears after one minute or when it drops to 0 hit points.

Tap Phylactery. The demi-lich draws negative energy from its phylactery, if it exists and is on the same plane as the demi-lich, and regains 33 (6d10) hit points.

DEMON, ABRIKANDILU

The mirrored hallway reflected and refracted our images, turning us first tall and thin, then short and squat. The halfling Borin Breadtaker delighted in these images. He was standing before one mirror that warped his image when the horrific howl echoed behind one of the mirrors. A moment later, the mirror on our right exploded outward, the shards slicing into our exposed skin, to reveal a hidden passageway. A squat creature — ugly beyond all standards — rushed through and slammed headfirst into of the mirrors on the opposite side of the hall. It raised its head, revealing horns and monstrous tusks, saw another mirror and charged again. We fled before it turned its attention to us. — Rial Moorth, offering a description of the fiendish creature to clerics of Muir

Abrikandilu, also called Wreckers, are fiendish foot soldiers from the Abyss that delight in destroying things of beauty and intellect. Objects of art, illuminated manuscripts, and beautiful creatures are the favored victims of their demonic wrath. The only thing they despise more than objects of beauty is their own wretched reflection. When faced with a mirror, they cease all other activities and turn their attention to shattering their own visage so that they are no longer faced with the horror that is their essence. Their horrific features entirely justify this extreme self-loathing. They are *squat, dwarfish fiends stand*ing *roughly* four feet tall and weighing more than 200 pounds. Hooked horns sprout from their wispy-haired brow, and they have a tusked lower jaw that protrudes from their thick neck and heavy jowls.

ABRIKANDILU

Small fiend (demon), chaotic evil

Armor Class 15 (natural armor)
Hit Points 22 (4d6 + 8)
Speed 40 ft.

STR	DEX	CON	INT	WIS	CHA
17 (+3)	14 (+2)	16 (+3)	10 (+0)	10 (+0)	10 (+0)

Damage Resistances cold, fire, lightning; bludgeoning, piercing, and slashing from nonmagical attacks
Damage Immunities poison
Condition Immunities poisoned
Senses darkvision 120 ft., passive Perception 10
Languages Abyssal
Challenge 2 (450 XP)

Goring Charge. If an abrikandilu demon moves at least 30 feet straight toward a target and then hits with a gore attack on the same turn, the target takes an extra 5 (2d4) piercing damage.
Magic Resistance. The abrikandilu demon has advantage on saving throws against spells and other magical effects.
Self-Loathing. If an abrikandilu demon can see a mirror within 30 feet of itself, it attacks that mirror on its next turn.

ACTIONS

Multiattack. The creature makes one Gore attack and one Bite attack.
Bite. *Melee Weapon Attack*: +5 to hit, reach 5 ft., one target. *Hit*: 6 (1d6 + 3) piercing damage.
Gore. *Melee Weapon Attack*: +X to hit, reach 0 ft., one target. *Hit*: 7 (1d8 +3) piercing damage.

DEMON, ALU

We survived the storm, but the Sea Mother's Grace was far off course. Captain Tobias assured us we would reach port by the next dawn. On our third day lost at sea, with faith in our captain waning, a truly horrific sight greeted our eyes. A huge whale breached the waves, its form covered in runnels of flame that made the crew shy away from the rail. The demonic whale blasted a steam cloud as it dove. A stately three-masted whaler of bone and lacquered wood chased the whale, its deck harpoons trained on the submerging beast. A woman dressed in black and purple stood at the wheel of the Broken Vow, *cursing the whale with phrases I shan't repeat. Even from our deck, we could see her unfurled wings and horns. Decaying crewmen aboard her ship readied another harpoon as the ship gave chase. She saluted us as she passed. We tacked in the opposite direction to put distance between our ships. — Ship's surgeon Polk Traggett*

Standing more than *six* feet tall, alu demons have dark flowing hair from which tiny horns protrude. They have faintly snake-like skin that runs the gamut of human flesh tones. They typically arm themselves and dress in the local attire of the mortals upon whom they prey, favoring armor, swords, and flowing capes that hide their small leathery wings.

Alu demons are the offspring of unions between succubi or incubi and mortals. Born in the chaotic Abyss and raised as servants of the demon lords, these fiendish creatures are not always as truly chaotic, nor evil, as their forebears, though most are. Alu demons typically have dark brown or black hair and brown, dark green, or black eyes. They have the comely, pouting expression of their demonic parent, which allows them to pass freely among the lands of mortals.

ALU DEMON

Medium fiend (demon), chaotic evil

Armor Class 16 (natural armor)
Hit Points 65 (10d8 + 20)
Speed 30 ft., fly 50 ft.

STR	DEX	CON	INT	WIS	CHA
17 (+3)	15 (+2)	15 (+2)	15 (+2)	15 (+2)	16 (+3)

Saving Throws Constitution +5
Skills Deception + 6, Intimidation +6, Stealth +5
Damage Resistances cold, fire, lightning; bludgeoning, piercing, and slashing from nonmagical attacks
Damage Immunities poison
Condition Immunities poisoned
Senses darkvision 120 ft., passive Perception 12
Languages Abyssal, telepathy 100 ft.
Challenge 5 (1,800 XP)

Magic Resistance. The alu demon has advantage on saving throws against spells and other magical effects.
Innate Spellcasting. The alu demon's innate spellcasting ability is Charisma (spell save DC 14, +6 to hit with spell attacks). It can cast the following spells, requiring no material components:
3/day each: *altar self, charm person, detect thoughts, suggestion*
1/day: *dimension door*

ACTIONS

Multiattack. The alu demon makes one Longsword attack and one Claw attack.
Claw. *Melee Weapon Attack*: +6 to hit, reach 5 ft., one target. *Hit:* 6 (1d6 + 3) slashing damage. The alu demon gains temporary hit points equal to the amount of damage inflicted with its claw attack. These temporary hit points last one hour.
Longsword. *Melee Weapon Attack*: +6 to hit, reach 5 ft., one target. *Hit:* 7 (1d8 + 3) slashing damage.

Demon, Cacodemon

My apprentice came in early, which was unusual, for he was the most sluggish apprentice I had ever had. He then went to work lighting the candles, laying out the dinnerware, and otherwise completing his tasks. As a precaution, I launched a lightning bolt at him; it did little damage but forced the intruder to assume its normal form, that of a towering creature of darkest night, sleek and hairless, with sharp claws and fiery red eyes. I defeated the creature in a fight that left my study in shambles. After waking my apprentice and setting him to cleaning up the mess, I pondered what I had done to have the assassin sent after me. — Al'phar of the Order of the Jade Monarch

Cacodemons stand about seven feet tall and weigh about 800 pounds. Cacodemons are relentless combatants and never back down from a fight. They often begin combat by changing forms and appearing as a race friendly to their potential opponents. Once an opponent is lured close to the cacodemon, it changes back to its natural form and attacks. Dreaded and feared, cacodemons are often employed as soldiers and assassins. Cacodemons are completely loyal and never question their position or authority; they do not take orders from other demons.

Cacodemon

Medium fiend (demon), neutral evil

Armor Class 14 (natural armor)
Hit Points 71 (11d8 + 22)
Speed 30 ft.

STR	DEX	CON	INT	WIS	CHA
16 (+3)	13 (+1)	15 (+2)	14 (+2)	14 (+2)	15 (+2)

Skills Athletics +5, Deception +4, Intimidation +4, Perception +4, Stealth +3
Damage Resistances cold, fire, lightning; bludgeoning, piercing, and slashing from nonmagical attacks
Damage Immunities poison
Condition Immunities poisoned
Senses darkvision 60 ft., passive Perception 14
Languages Abyssal, Common, Demonic, Infernal, telepathy 120 ft.
Challenge 4 (1,100 XP)

Innate Spellcasting. The cacodemon's innate spellcasting ability is Charisma (spell save DC 12). It can cast the following spells, requiring no material components:
3/day each: *darkness, detect magic, detect thoughts, see invisibility*
1/day: *hold person*
Magic Resistance. The cacodemon has advantage on saving throws against spells and other magical effects.
Magic Weapons. The cacodemon's weapon attacks are considered magical for the purposes of damage resistances.

Actions

Multiattack. The cacodemon makes two Longsword and one Claw attack, or two Claw attacks.
Claws. *Melee Weapon Attack:* +5 to hit, reach 5 ft., one target. *Hit:* 6 (1d6 + 3) slashing damage.
Longsword. *Melee Weapon Attack:* +5 to hit, reach 5 ft., one target. *Hit:* 7 (1d8 + 3) slashing damage, or 8 (1d10 + 3) slashing damage if used with two hands to make a melee attack.
Change Shape. The cacodemon magically polymorphs into a humanoid whose Challenge rating is equal to or lower than its own, or back into its true form. It reverts to its true form if it dies. Any equipment it is wearing or carrying is absorbed or borne by the new form (the cacodemon's choice). In a new form, the cacodemon retains its game statistics and ability to speak, but its Armor Class, movement modes, Strength, Dexterity, and special senses are replaced by those of the new form, and it gains any statistics and capabilities (except class features, legendary actions, and lair actions) that the new form has but that it lacks.
Summon (1/day). The cacodemon has a 35% chance to summon 1d3 **derghodemons** (see ***Tome of Horrors 5e***) or a **cacodemon**. The summoned demon appears in an unoccupied space within 60 feet of the cacodemon, but can't summon other demons. It remains for one minute, until it or the first cacodemon is slain, or until the first cacodemon takes an action to dismiss it.

DEMON, CHARONADEMON

We decided to go after our masters; it was not like they were coming back. We prepared our spells, did our research, and Takil opened the portal. We knew we had to find a ferryman to carry us across the River Styx, and we soon spotted a tall cloaked skeleton by a boat. It didn't want the traditional price we had been led to believe, but instead demanded hundreds of gold pieces from each of us. We paid, but halfway across, the boatman tossed Takil overboard. Rather than fight a being of indiscernible age, we ponied up more gold and finished our voyage. How we are getting home without Takil's knowledge of the planes is something we will have to figure out. — Päuk, apprentice mage

Tall, gaunt, skeletal, clad in black robes, and bearing a staff, it is easy to confuse a charonademon for their master, the boatman of the Lower Planes. While that being is more likely to be trusted, a charonademon is not. They love to murder and rob those seeking to cross the River Styx and even take passengers in their boats only to kill them or dump them in the river. They can be bought off, but such a plan needs to be ready and the money in full, and even then, it might not work. Their standard fare is 50 gp per level of each creature being carried, double that if you plan to bribe them to keep them from murdering you.

CHARONADEMON

Medium fiend (demon), neutral evil

Armor Class 16 (natural armor)
Hit Points 75 (10d8 + 30)
Speed 40 ft.

STR	DEX	CON	INT	WIS	CHA
18 (+4)	16 (+3)	16 (+3)	15 (+2)	14 (+2)	18 (+4)

Saving Throws Con +6, Wis +5
Skills Arcana +6, Deception +8, Intimidation +8, Perception +6, Stealth +7, Survival +6
Damage Resistances cold, fire, lightning; bludgeoning, piercing, and slashing from nonmagical attacks
Damage Immunities acid, poison
Condition Immunities poisoned
Senses darkvision 60 ft., passive Perception 16
Languages Abyssal, Common, Demonic, Infernal, telepathy 120 ft.
Challenge 7 (2,900 XP)

Innate Spellcasting. The charonademon's innate spellcasting ability is Charisma (spell save DC 16). It can cast the following spells, requiring no material components:
At will: *detect magic, darkness, see invisibility*
1/day: *plane shift* (skiff and self only)
Magic Resistance. The charonademon has advantage on saving throws against spells and other magical effects.
Magic Weapons. The charonademon's weapon attacks are considered magical for the purposes of damage resistances.

ACTIONS

Multiattack. The charonademon makes two Quarterstaff attacks.
Quarterstaff. *Melee Weapon Attack:* +7 to hit, reach 5 ft., one target. *Hit:* 11 (2d6 + 4) bludgeoning damage, or 13 (2d8 + 4) bludgeoning damage if used with two hands to make a melee attack.
Fear Gaze. Creatures within 30 feet of the charonademon who can see it must make a DC 16 Wisdom saving throw. On a failed saving throw, the creature takes 10 (3d6) psychic damage and is frightened for one minute. On a successful saving throw, the creature takes half damage and is not frightened.
While frightened, the target must take the Dash action and move away from the charonademon by the safest available route on each of its turns, unless there is nowhere to move. The creature can repeat the saving throw if it ends its turn out of line of sight with the charonademon, ending the effect on a success. If the creature's saving throw succeeds, or the effect ends for it, the target is immune to a charonademon's fear gaze for 24 hours.
Summon (1/day). The charonademon has a 35% chance to summon 1d4 **hydrodemons** or a **charonademon**. The summoned demon appears in an unoccupied space within 60 feet of the charonademon but can't summon other demons. It remains for one minute, until it or the first charonademon is slain, or until the first charonademon takes an action to dismiss it.

Demon, Daraka

The pit was filled with scorpions. They skittered and crawled over one another with an indescribable sound. Junip stepped right to the edge; she was never scared of spiders, snakes, and other creepers. She should have been. Two hands rose out of the crawling mass and grabbed her by the ankles, pulling her off balance and right into the mass. She vanished into the pit, dragged down by something I didn't fully want to see. But it was too late, as a ram's head rose into view, its bulky body covered in the crawling creatures. — Rebrance Colbert, porter and only survivor to stumble out of the Broken Tunnels of Canton

This nine-foot-tall nightmare appears as a faun-legged humanoid with oily writhing flesh, a cruel bestial head adorned with curling ram's horns, and a mouth full of jagged rotting teeth. A daraka's skin is leathery and oily and from a distance of 10 feet or more appears to be a mass of writhing flesh. Closer inspection reveals thousands of tiny scorpions swarming its flesh, skittering in and out of its mouth, ears, and nose, seemingly unnoticed by the demon. They act as guards to greater demons or as shock troops in demonic armies. Quite intelligent, they are often used as commanders or leaders, with each daraka having a battalion of minor demons at its command.

Daraka

Large fiend (demon), chaotic evil

Armor Class 14 (type)
Hit Points 105 (10d10 + 50)
Speed 40 ft.

STR	DEX	CON	INT	WIS	CHA
18 (+4)	11 (+0)	20 (+5)	18 (+4)	18 (+4)	20 (+5)

Saving Throws Constitution +8
Skills Deception +8, Intimidation +8, Perception +7
Damage Resistances cold, fire, lightning; bludgeoning, piercing, and slashing from nonmagical attacks
Damage Immunities poison
Condition Immunities poisoned
Senses darkvision 60 ft., passive Perception 17
Languages Abyssal
Challenge 5 (1,800 XP)

Scorpion Body. A creature that hits the daraka with a melee attack suffers 3 (1d6) piercing damage and must succeed at a DC 16 Constitution saving throw or suffer an additional 9 (2d8) poison damage and be poisoned for one hour from the scorpions that scurry out of the wound to attack.
Magic Resistance. The daraka demon has advantage on saving throws against spells and other magical effects.
Innate Spellcasting. The daraka's innate spellcasting ability is Charisma (spell save DC 16, +8 to hit with spell attacks). It can cast the following spells, requiring no material components:
At will: *darkness, detect evil and good, invisibility* (self only), *spiritual weapon, teleportation* (self only)
3/day: *chill touch*
1/day each: *feeblemind, shatter*

Actions

Multiattack. The creature makes one Claw attack and one Scorpion Throw attack, or two Claw attacks.
Claw. *Melee Weapon Attack*: +7 to hit, reach 10 ft., one target. *Hit*: 13 (2d8 + 4) slashing damage and the target is grappled by the daraka (escape DC 15). A creature that is grappled by the daraka at the start of its turn suffers the effects of the demon's scorpion body ability. The daraka has two claws and can grapple only two creatures at a time.
Scorpion Throw. *Ranged Weapon Attack*: +3 to hit, range 10/20 ft., one target. *Hit*: 3 (1d6) piercing damage and the target must succeed at a DC 16 Constitution saving throw or suffer an additional 9 (2d8) poison damage and be poisoned for one hour.

DEMON, FOX

We cornered the thief in the warehouse after a rooftop chase through the market. How could we have known it was a trap? As we advanced, the young man shimmered as if in a haze of heat, and his whole body transformed. What stood before us now was a black fox standing on two legs. It snarled at us with its vicious fangs, and its eyes glowed yellow as it marked where my men stood. Three of them broke ranks and turned on their fellows under that withering gaze. He'd lured us into his hunting ground. — Report from the city watch on the rumored "demon fox" terrorizing the city of Albor Broce

Fox demons are a race of chaotic fiends that delight in mischief and confusion. Like the creatures they resemble, these demons are sly and cunning, and capable of quick escape should their schemes or identities be discovered. These shapeshifters able to take unassuming forms of humans, but their fox forms are frightening and demonic, with a snarling visage and burning yellow eyes.

Fox demons often assume disguises to gain trust, then charm their victims to go out and commit various acts of disruption, disobedience, and lawlessness. Fox demons find outright violence such as assault and murder to be somewhat classless and distasteful; they far prefer to put their victims in situations where they are caught stealing, are discovered by a jealous lover, are arrested on false charges, etc. A fox demon is not terribly concerned if these acts eventually lead to violence or death, but they prefer it to be the result of their elaborate schemes of misdirection, seduction, and scheming.

FOX DEMON
Medium fiend, chaotic evil

Armor Class 17 (natural armor)
Hit Points 156 (24d8 + 48)
Speed 40 ft.

STR	DEX	CON	INT	WIS	CHA
10 (+0)	20 (+5)	14 (+2)	13 (+1)	16 (+3)	18 (+4)

Saving Throws Dex +9, Wis +7, Cha +8
Skills Intimidation +12, Perception +11, Stealth +13
Damage Resistances bludgeoning, piercing and slashing damage from nonmagical attacks, cold, fire, lightning
Senses darkvision 60 ft. passive Perception 13
Languages Abyssal, Common, telepathy 120 ft.
Challenge 9 (5,000 XP)

Shapechanger. The fox demon can use its actions to polymorph into a Small or Medium humanoid, or back into its true form. Other than its size and speed, its statistics are the same in each form. Any equipment it is wearing or carrying isn't transformed. It reverts to its true form if it dies.

Innate Spellcasting. The fox demon's spellcasting ability is Charisma (spell save DC 16). The fox demon can innately cast the following spells, requiring no material components:

At will: *minor illusion*
3/day each: *confusion, dominate person, expeditious retreat*
1/day each: *dominate monster*

ACTIONS

Charm. One humanoid that the fox demon can see within 30 feet must succeed on a DC 15 Wisdom saving throw or be magically charmed for one day. The charmed target obeys the fox demon's verbal or telepathic commands. If the target suffers any harm or receives a suicidal command, it can repeat the saving throw, ending the effect on a success. If the target successfully saves against the effect, or if the effect on it ends, the target is immune to this fox demon's Charm for the next 24 hours. The fox demon can have up to four charmed targets at a time. If it charms another, the effect on one previous target ends.

Demon, Gallu

It was good to see the walls of Bard's Gate before us again after a week on the road. Mother Habbard was the same as always, welcoming us to her quiet inn, offering us rooms, offering to mend anything that needed mending. Crispus came by my room and asked if I wanted to go with him downstairs; Mother Habbard claimed she wanted to speak with him on an urgent matter. I declined, and he went away, but thinking of the roast we'd eaten earlier changed my mind. I sneaked down the stairs and into the kitchen. I wish I hadn't. I was just in time to see Mother Habbard skewer Crispus on an iron spit. I screamed, and she turned and saw me. She changed so quickly, growing three feet taller and losing her elderly features. Her flesh melted into a shining blackness, broken only by her many, many teeth.
— Topas Banks, found screaming in the street and charged with the death of his companion in Mother Habbard's Boarding House

A gallu demon is nine feet tall and weighs about 800 pounds. Its flesh is glossy black and, other than a large mouth lined with teeth, it has no facial features. The gallu demon excels at disguising itself as a normal humanoid to befriend a mortal, whom it then whisks back to its Abyssal lair. Gallu demons have been known to spend months on the Material Plane just to get close to and eventually abduct a chosen target. Abducted victims are sometimes devoured by a gallu demon before it completes its task, but more often than not, an abducted victim is given to the gallu demon's master, who enslaves the victim (or sometimes devours it himself).

Gallu

Large fiend (demon), neutral evil

Armor Class 15 (natural armor)
Hit Points 85 (10d10 + 30)
Speed 30 ft.

STR	DEX	CON	INT	WIS	CHA
19 (+4)	11 (+0)	16 (+3)	12 (+1)	14 (+2)	15 (+2)

Skills Deception +8, Perception +5, Stealth +6
Damage Resistances acid, cold, fire; bludgening, piercing, and slashing from nonmagical attacks
Damage Immunities lightning, poison
Condition Immunities paralyzed, poisoned
Senses darkvision 60 ft., passive Perception 15
Languages Abyssal, Common, telepathy 60 ft.
Challenge 6 (2,300 XP)

Shapechanger. The gallu can use its action to polymorph into a Small or Medium humanoid, or back into its true form. Other than its size and speed, its statistics are the same in each form. Any equipment it is wearing or carrying isn't transformed. It reverts to its true form if it dies.

Actions

Multiattack. The gallu makes two Claw attacks and one Bite attack.
Bite. *Melee Weapon Attack:* +7 to hit, reach 5 ft., one target. *Hit:* 9 (1d10 + 4) slashing damage.
Claw. *Melee Weapon Attack:* +7 to hit, reach 5 ft., one target, *Hit:* 8 (1d8 + 4) slashing damage and the target is grappled (escape DC 15). Until the grapple ends, the target is restrained and has disadvantage on Strength checks and Strength saving throws, and the gallu can't grapple another target.
Plane Shift (recharge 5–6). The gallu casts a *plane shift* spell requiring only verbal components. If the gallu has a creature grappled, that creature must succeed on a DC 15 Wisdom saving throw or be transported along with the gallu.
Teleport (recharge 5–6). The gallu magically teleports, along with any equipment it is wearing or carrying, up to 120 feet to an unoccupied space it can see. If the gallu has a creature grappled, that creature must succeed on a DC 15 Wisdom saving throw or be transported along with the gallu.

TOME OF **HORRORS**

HUANGSHE'YAO

We placed Commander Layst's body into a hastily dug hole in the middle of this very different land. I've heard it called Xha'en, but I don't know if I am saying it correctly. We were preparing to cover our beloved leader when a voice spoke from the nearby ruins, "I can restore him, but I require a boon from all of you." A massive snake-like creature — bright yellow, like the sun — was wrapped around the stones, watching us. It cocked its head and asked again, "Would you like him back?" We answered as one, agreeing to the bargain. What harm could it bring? Commander Layst was indeed restored to life that day, and I didn't think on our horrid deal for years. But now? After each member of our legion has died broken after committing horrible atrocities? Yes, I think of it every day, especially as I've started hearing that snake's whispering voice around my home. Am I next? — Sub-commander Ulisk Wattle, three days before he attempted to assassinate Lord Ryven

The huangshe'yao are generally benevolent beings; they are, however, extremely subtle, and dealing with them can be a very risky proposition. Physically, they resemble enormous constrictor snakes with yellow-gold scales and faces somewhat like horned vipers, with orange eyes that reflect significant intelligence. They often dwell outside the Material Planes, visiting from time to time for their own purposes.

The huangshe'yao are wish-granters, but in return they require that a supplicant agree to be subject to a *geas*. The *geas* might not be applied immediately, being retained by the huangshe'yao for use at a later date, but usually humans will encounter a huangshe'yao when it is already engaged in some specific purpose and has decided to engage an ally (or minion). Despite the general tendency of the huangshe'yao toward good alignments, evil individuals are possible, and such corrupted ones are very evil indeed. Evil-aligned huangshe'yao are outcasts from their kin, and never encountered in association with those of any other alignment.

HUANGSHE'YAO

Large aberration, alignment varies

Armor Class 20 (natural armor)
Hit Points 231 (22d10 + 110)
Speed 40 ft., climb 30 ft.

STR	DEX	CON	INT	WIS	CHA
18 (+4)	15 (+2)	20 (+5)	18 (+4)	18 (+4)	20 (+5)

Saving Throws Str +9, Con +10, Wis +9, Cha +10
Damage Immunities poison
Damage Resistances fire, lightning, bludgeoning, piercing and slashing damage from nonmagical attacks
Condition Immunities poisoned
Senses tremorsense 30 ft., passive Perception 14
Languages Abyssal
Challenge 15 (13,000 XP)

Wish-Bargain. A huangshe'yao can grant a single *wish* (as per the 9th-level spell) to a mortal petitioner. The cost of this wish is high, however, for the petitioner must, in exchange for the wish, allow itself to be subject to a *geas* from the huangshe'yao. This geas is treated as if it was cast with a 9th-level spell slot (meaning that it is permanent until removed by *remove curse, greater restoration,* or *wish*) and the target receives no saving throw.

Magic Resistance. The huangshe'yao has advantage on saving throws against spells and other magical effects.

Innate Spellcasting. The huangshe'yao's spellcasting ability is Charisma (spell save DC 18). The huangshe'yao can innately cast the following spells, requiring no material components:

3/day each: *charm person, enthrall, hold person, hypnotic pattern, suggestion*
1/day each: *dominate person, mass suggestion*

ACTIONS

Multiattack. The huangshe'yao makes one Bite and one Constriction attack. It may not make a constriction attack if it already has one target restrained.

Bite. *Melee Weapon Attack:* +9 to hit, reach 10 ft., one target. *Hit:* 18 (4d6 + 4) damage.

Constriction. *Melee Weapon Attack:* +9 to hit, reach 10 ft., one target. *Hit:* 15 (2d10 + 4) bludgeoning damage. If the target is Medium or smaller, it is grappled (escape DC 19). Until this grapple ends, the target is restrained, the target takes 15 (2d10 +4) bludgeoning damage at the start of the huangshe'yao's turn, and the huangshe'yao can't make constriction attacks against other targets.

Pix led us into the dusty chambers, pushing us onward through the dust-coated webs. We'd not found anything yet, just dust, dust, and more dust. It was in my throat, my robes, my boots. Everywhere. "I don't think anything lives here now," Pix said, stating the obvious as he is often wont to do. Too bad he was wrong again. We heard the clicking first, then the swush-swush-swush! *of uncoiling chitin as the giant centipede uncurled itself. I knew it wasn't something natural when I saw the eyes. Hundreds of them spaced all along its long, sinuous body. — From the memoirs of Gordun Brightwill, High Mage of the Tower of High Magics*

The hundred-eyed demon is a massive armored centipede with a thick carapace studded with dozens of tiny black eyes. Its mandibles clack with deadly intent. Sleepless, mindless, and infinitely patient, hundred-eyed demons lurk in silent darkness awaiting intruders, then attack from the shadows. Their senses are incredibly acute, allowing them to detect vibrations and movement from a great distance and quickly pinpoint the source of the disturbance.

HUNDRED-EYED DEMON
Huge fiend, unaligned

Armor Class 17 (natural armor)
Hit Points 207 (18d12 + 90)
Speed 50 ft., burrow 20 ft., climb 20 ft.

STR	DEX	CON	INT	WIS	CHA
20 (+5)	10 (+0)	21 (+5)	3 (–4)	18 (+4)	5 (–3)

Damage Immunities poison, psychic
Damage Resistances bludgeoning, piercing and slashing damage from nonmagical attacks, thunder
Condition Immunities charmed, poisoned
Skills Perception +8
Senses darkvision 120 ft., tremorsense 60 ft., passive Perception 18
Languages —
Challenge 12 (8,400 XP)

Enhanced Perception. Hundred-eyed demons are highly sensitive to motion and tremors. They have advantage on all Wisdom (Perception) checks due to their multiple eyes and their other enhanced senses.
Sustenance-free. Hundred-eyed demons do not need to eat, sleep or breathe.

ACTIONS

Bite. *Melee Weapon Attack:* +9 to hit, reach 5 ft., one target. *Hit:* 32 (6d8 + 5) piercing damage plus 13 (3d8) poison damage. The target must succeed on a DC 17 Constitution saving throw or be poisoned for one minute. The creature can repeat the saving throw at the end of each of its turns, ending the effect on itself on a success. In addition, the creature is grappled (escape DC 17). The hundred-eyed demon cannot make bite attacks when it has a grappled target, but it can continue to inflict 13 (3d8) poison damage on its turn upon its grappled target.

DEMON, MEZZALORN

We found 12 hollow logs standing upright in the middle of the Sin Mire Swamp, driven deep into the ground, definitely not natural. Each log was about 10 feet in diameter, and a buzzing rose out of them, like a chorus of thousands of wasps. Jon of the Glen climbed right up one of the logs and stuck his head over the end. He never listened to good advice. "Nothin' here but a bunch of wasps, my friends! Hundreds of them!" His shout carried in the silent swamp, and that's all it took. A wasp like none I've ever seen before or since shot out of that log and grabbed the poor thief. The thing had a man's face and arms, and a wasp's body. It climbed into the sky with a horrible buzz, a trail of normal wasps fluttering along in its wake. It stopped and hovered, and that's when it started stinging Jon over and over with its horrible, footlong stinger. — Astryd Bumbleroot, druid of the Kajani Forest

Mezzalorns (or wasp demons as they are sometimes called) are flying horrors from the rifts of the Abyss with the lower half of a nightmarish wasp. Where the wasp's head would be sprouts a head and arms that appear to be born of the cross between a howling monkey and an unholy insect. Its clawed arms are covered in spines and its wide-set insectoid eyes frame a flat-nosed face and mouth filled with razor sharp fangs. A mezzalorn stands as tall as a human and is about 10 feet long. Its body is dark with red bands and ends in a golden stinger. Its legs resemble those of a giant wasp and are covered in fine hairs and bristles. Its human-like visage is copper and sports matted dark hair.

These flying demons spend most of their time high above the Abyssal planes scouring the lands for food or patrolling a demon lord's domain. When serving under a demon lord or one of his generals, mezzalorns are often used as shock troops or first-assault troops in war. Mezzalorns are thoroughly evil and despise all non-demons, attacking them on sight. Slain creatures are carried back to their lair and distributed among the inhabitants of the nest. A nest is composed of just about anything a mezzalorn can find and carry: bones, debris, refuse, weapons, and so on.

MEZZALORN DEMON

Large fiend (demon), chaotic evil

Armor Class 18 (natural armor)
Hit Points 95 (10d10 + 40)
Speed 10 ft., fly 50 ft.

STR	DEX	CON	INT	WIS	CHA
18 (+4)	18 (+4)	18 (+4)	13 (+1)	16 (+3)	16 (+3)

Skills Deception +6, Intimidation +6, Perception +6, Stealth +7
Damage Resistances cold, fire, lightning; bludgeoning, piercing, and slashing from nonmagical attacks
Damage Immunities poison
Condition Immunities poisoned
Senses darkvision 60 ft., passive Perception 16
Languages Abyssal, Common, telepathy 100 ft.
Challenge 5 (1,800 XP)

Magic Resistance. The mezzalorn demon has advantage on saving throws against spells and other magical effects.
Innate Spellcasting. The mezzalorn demon's innate spellcasting ability is Charisma (spell save DC 14, +6 to hit with spell attacks). It can cast the following spells, requiring no material components:
At will: *spiritual weapon, teleport* (self only)
3/day each: *bane, blight*
1/day: *hypnotic pattern*
Pheromones. When reduced to half or less of its maximum hit points, the mezzalorn releases a cloud of pheromones that excite the natural aggression of its kind, granting advantage on all attack rolls to any mezzalorn within 50 feet.

ACTIONS

Multiattack. The mezzalorn makes one Sting attack and one Claw attack.
Claw. *Melee Weapon Attack:* +7 to hit, reach 5 ft., one target. *Hit:* 8 (1d6 + 4) slashing damage.
Sting. *Melee Weapon Attack:* +7 to hit, reach 5 ft., one target. *Hit:* 9 (1d8 + 5) piercing damage and the target must succeed at a DC 15 Constitution saving throw or suffer an additional 9 (2d8) poison damage and be poisoned for one hour.

Demon, Hydrodemon

Thanks to the notes my master left behind, I was prepared to resist the effects of the River Styx. By the time I bobbed back up, the boat had passed into the mists. I floated downstream for a time until I came to a rock jutting out of the river and clambered up. To my surprise, the rock was already inhabited by a massive frog creature. It leapt from a great distance, gliding along on flaps of skin stretched from its forelimbs to it legs, and landed with a loud croak. I hit it with a cloud of flying daggers and went on my way. — Takil, apprentice mage

Hydrodemons are natives of the River Styx and are the only creatures known to possess a natural resistance to the river's deleterious effects. They are truly massive, standing 10 feet tall at the shoulder, and weigh 4,000 pounds or more. Their green, warty skin serves as an excellent protection, and their sickly yellow eyes take in the world with a baleful malevolence. On the attack, they prefer to glide at their foes and then spit at them. Their spittle causes drowsiness and sleep.

Hydrodemon

Large fiend (demon), neutral evil

Armor Class 15 (natural armor)
Hit Points 85 (9d10 + 36)
Speed 30 ft., fly 40 ft., swim 60 ft.

STR	DEX	CON	INT	WIS	CHA
18 (+4)	14 (+2)	18 (+4)	8 (−1)	11 (+0)	14 (+2)

Saving Throws Dex +5, Con +7
Skills Perception +6
Damage Resistances cold, fire, lightning
Damage Immunities poison
Condition Immunities poisoned
Senses darkvision 60 ft., passive Perception 16
Languages Abyssal
Challenge 5 (1,800 XP)

Amphibious. The hydrodemon can breathe air and water.
Magic Resistance. The hydrodemon has advantage on saving throws against spells and other magical effects.
Magic Weapons. The hydrodemon's weapon attacks are magical.
Innate Spellcasting. The hydrodemon's spellcasting ability is Charisma (spell save DC 13, +5 to hit with spell attacks). It can innately cast the following spells, requiring no material components:
At will: *darkness, detect magic, water walk*
2/day each: *dimension door, teleport*
1/day: *hallow*

Actions

Multiattack. The hydrodemon makes one Bite attack and two Claws attacks. The demon can use its Sleep Spittle instead of using its Bite.
Bite. *Melee Weapon Attack:* +7 to hit, reach 5 ft., one target. *Hit:* 13 (2d8 + 4) piercing damage, and the target is grappled (escape DC 14 Until this grapple ends, the target is restrained and the demon can' bite another target.
Claws. *Melee Weapon Attack:* +7 to hit, reach 10 ft., one target. *Hit:* 11 (2d6 + 4) slashing damage.
Sleep Spittle. One target within 60 feet must succeed on a DC 15 Wisdom saving throw or fall unconscious for one minute. The sleeping target can be awakened if someone uses an action to shake or slap the sleeper awake, and the target wakes if it takes damage.
Summon (1/day). The demon chooses what to summon and attempts a magical summoning. A hydrodemon has a 30% chance of summoning a **hydrodemon**. A summoned demon appears in an unoccupied space within 60 feet of its summoner, acts as an ally of its summoner, and can't summon other demons. It remains for one minute, until it or its summoner dies, or until its summoner dismisses it as an action.

DEMON, NABASU (DEATH STEALER DEMON)

The dead oak was right by the crossroads, its branches like gnarled fingers ripping at the canopy of the living trees around it. Lightning struck it at some point, splitting the trunk into leaning halves. Our horses instinctively shied away from it, and I must admit I felt a touch of dread fill my soul when I looked at it. I was so caught up in the way it made me feel that I didn't realize for a moment that something in the tree was looking back at us with yellow eyes. It was a demonic little thing, with bat wings unfurled against the trunk. Its claws rapped against the bark as if it was sizing us up. I think it was young and still hesitant to leave its home. We gave it a wide berth, and it left us alone. I fear for the next traveler when it gets its courage up. — Bahno Lop, tea merchant out of Reme

The horned head of the nabasu has a cruel and vaguely humanoid face that appears trapped in a constant state of rage and pain. Its ever-pervasive, glowing golden stare is known to strike its foes dead at its mere gaze. Their bodies are tall and wire thin, with gray reptilian skin and large leathery wings and spindly arms that end in hooked razor-sharp talons.

The majority of nabasu encountered outside of the Abyss are nabasu demonlings. These proud creations of the demon lords are sent to the Material Plane to feast on the souls of the innocent until they reach maturity and can re-enter the Abyss on their own. Once there, they devour the physical hearts and mortal souls of their prey, growing stronger and deadlier with each third victim they destroy. Nabasu derive great pleasure from torturing and killing other creatures.

NABASU

Medium fiend (demon), chaotic evil

Armor Class 14 (natural armor)
Hit Points 157 (15d8 + 90)
Speed 30 ft., fly 60 ft.

STR	DEX	CON	INT	WIS	CHA
22 (+6)	13 (+1)	22 (+6)	14 (+2)	16 (+3)	15 (+2)

Saving Throws Constitution +9
Skills Perception +7
Damage Resistances cold, fire, lightning; bludgeoning, piercing, and slashing from nonmagical attacks
Damage Immunities poison
Condition Immunities paralyzed, poisoned
Senses darkvision 120 ft., passive Perception 17
Languages Abyssal, Common, telepathy 100 ft.
Challenge 10 (5,900 XP)

Death Gaze. When a creature that can see the nabasu's eyes starts its turn within 30 feet of the nabasu, the nabasu can force it to make a DC 15 Wisdom saving throw if the nabasu isn't incapacitated and can see the creature. On a failure, the creature loses a hit die. A creature that has lost its last hit die to the nabasu's death gaze has disadvantage on all death saves for the next 24 hours, and if it dies within that time, it rises as a ghoul in 1d4 rounds under the nabasu's control. Ghouls created in this way become free willed if the nabasu that created them dies. Unless surprised, a creature can avert its eyes to avoid the saving throw at the start of its turn. If the creature does so, it can't see the nabasu until the start of its next turn, when it can avert its eyes again. If the creature looks at the nabasu in the meantime, it must immediately attempt the save. While averting its eyes, any attacks on the nabasu are done at disadvantage.

Magic Resistance. The nabasu demon has advantage on saving throws against spells and other magical effects.

Innate Spellcasting. The nabasu's innate spellcasting ability is Charisma (spell save DC 14, +6 to hit with spell attacks). It can cast the following spells, requiring no material components:

At will: *darkness, teleport* (self only)
3/day each: *silence, plane shift, ray of enfeeblement, vampiric touch*
1/day: *regenerate*

Paralysis Aura (1/day). As a bonus action, the nabasu releases a cloud of magical energy that can paralyze its foes. This cloud fills a 10-foot cube, and all creatures within that cube must succeed at a DC 17 Constitution saving throw or become paralyzed for one minute. A paralyzed creature may repeat the saving throw at the end of each of its turns, ending the effect on a success.

ACTIONS

Multiattack. The nabasu makes one Bite attack and two Claw attacks.

Bite. *Melee Weapon Attack:* +10 to hit, reach 5 ft., one target. *Hit:* 15 (2d8 + 6) piercing damage.

Claw. *Melee Weapon Attack:* +10 to hit, reach 5 ft., one target. *Hit:* 13 (2d6 + 6) slashing damage.

Demon, Nerizo (Bloodhound Demon)

We heard them scrambling through the trees before we saw them. Even when we knew they were there, their blue-black forms blended with the shadows under the trees. Elisitra lit the trees with an orb of brilliant white, and we finally saw our enemy. Four of them, each as big as a man, but running on all fours. They had tails and teeth and claws. All nasty things, but our little band of hunters was far nastier. Those things didn't stand a chance. — Lister Claw of the Scarlet Ruffians

The vaguely humanoid man-sized nerizo demon has skin of deep navy blue. It has a scorpion-like tail, the hindquarters of a goat, and the head of a slathering hound whose jaws drip caustic acid. Its arms end in sharpened claws, and its feet are splayed hooves. Nerizos stand six feet tall and weigh about 160 pounds.

The bestial nerizo can be found on almost all layers of the Abyss. More animalistic than not, the nerizo are sometimes used as "hunting dogs" by the greater demons and demon lords. The nerizo themselves realize that they may not be the smartest or strongest of the demons, but they resent being relegated to common hunting dogs for the greater demons. Nerizos often roam in deadly packs looking for lost and escaped spirits to torment among the rifts of the Abyss.

Nerizo Demon

Medium fiend (demon), chaotic evil

Armor Class 15 (natural armor)
Hit Points 85 (10d8 + 40)
Speed 40 ft.

STR	DEX	CON	INT	WIS	CHA
18 (+4)	16 (+3)	18 (+4)	12 (+1)	14 (+2)	16 (+3)

Skills Athletics +7, Perception +5, Stealth +6
Damage Resistances cold, fire, lightning; bludgeoning, piercing, and slashing from nonmagical attacks
Damage Immunities acid, poison
Condition Immunities poisoned
Senses darkvision 60 ft., passive Perception 15
Languages Abyssal
Challenge 5 (1,800 XP)

Magic Resistance. The nerizo demon has advantage on saving throws against spells and other magical effects.
Innate Spellcasting. The nerizo's innate spellcasting ability is Charisma (spell save DC 14, +6 to hit with spell attacks). It can cast the following spells, requiring no material components:
At will: *darkness, detect evil and good, teleport* (self only)
1/day: *confusion*

Actions

Multiattack. The nerizo makes one Sting attack and two Claw attacks.
Claw. *Melee Weapon Attack*: +7 to hit, reach 5 ft., one target. *Hit*: 7 (1d6 + 4) slashing damage.
Sting. *Melee Weapon Attack*: +7 to hit, reach 5 ft., one target. *Hit*: 8 (1d8 + 4) piercing damage and the target must succeed at a DC 15 Constitution saving throw or suffer an additional 9 (2d8) poison damage and be poisoned for one hour.
***Spit Acid* (recharge 5–6).** The nerizo spits a 15-foot line of poison. All creatures caught in the line must make a DC 14 Dexterity saving throw, taking 18 (4d8) acid damage on a failure or half as much damage on a successful save.

DEMON, NYSROCK (COBRA DEMON)

The throne room was empty when we finally pushed through the tables turned on their side to slow us down. King Goltrick Stonetumbler the Usurper sat on his marble throne and watched as we burned his dwarven mummy guards to ashes. The old dwarf never moved, never uttered a sound. Bolt Ashenchisel stepped up to end the unwanted ruler's life, and that's when the snake-thing rose up behind the throne. The snake's hood flared in warning as it turned its human head toward us. It was all a distraction, however, as the thing's tail flicked out so quickly that we never saw the stinger until it punched a hole through Bolt's chest. — Report from the Dwarven Stone Guardians on their failure to remove the usurper

Nysrock demons are horrid, 14-foot-long cobras with vaguely humanoid faces that protrude from a broad hood. Golden scales run down the length of its snake body to end in a scorpion's stinger that oozes unholy venom. They weigh between 350 and 450 pounds.

Believed to be the offspring of a marilith and a naga, the nysrock is a sinister denizen of the Abyss that is often found in the courts of various demon lords where they serve as advisors and counselors. Their cunning intellects are used to full effect by their masters in weaving battle plans and plots and intrigues against rival lords and enemies.

Rumors abound (supposedly from an eyewitness who lived to tell the tale) of an abyssal plane ruled by a massive nysrock at least 40 feet long. Its palace is a network of underground tunnels populated with all manner of snakes, fiendish serpents, and intelligent and cunning reptiles of all shapes and sizes.

NYSROCK

Large fiend (demon), chaotic evil

Armor Class 16 (natural armor)
Hit Points 105 (10d10 + 50)
Speed 40 ft.

STR	DEX	CON	INT	WIS	CHA
20 (+5)	14 (+2)	20 (+5)	16 (+3)	19 (+4)	18 (+4)

Saving Throws Constitution +9
Skills Deception +8, Intimidation +8, Perception +8, Stealth +6
Damage Resistances cold, fire, lightning; bludgeoning, piercing, and slashing from nonmagical attacks
Damage Immunities poison
Condition Immunities poisoned
Senses darkvision 100 ft., passive Perception 18
Languages Abyssal, Celestial,- Common, Draconic, Infernal, telepathy 100 ft.
Challenge 10 (5,900 XP)

Magic Resistance. The nysrock demon has advantage on saving throws against spells and other magical effects.
Innate Spellcasting. The nysrock's innate spellcasting ability is Charisma (spell save DC 16, +8 to hit with spell attacks). It can cast the following spells, requiring no material components:
At will: *blight, dispel magic, teleport* (self only)
3/day each: *bane, spiritual weapon*

ACTIONS

Multiattack. The nysrock demon makes one Sting attack and one other attack.
Bite. *Melee Weapon Attack*: +9 to hit, reach 5 ft., one target. *Hit*: 14 (2d8 + 5) piercing damage and the target must succeed at a DC 17 Constitution saving throw or suffer an additional 18 (4d8) and be poisoned for one hour. A creature already suffering the poisoned condition caused by a nysrock is also stunned until the end of its next turn.
Spit Poison. *Ranged Weapon Attack*: +6 to hit, range 30/120 ft., one target. *Hit*: 11 (2d8 + 2) poison damage and the target must succeed at a DC 17 Constitution saving throw or be blinded until the end of its next turn.
Sting. *Melee Weapon Attack*: +9 to hit, reach 5 ft., one target. *Hit*: 15 (4d4 + 5) piercing damage and the target must succeed at a DC 17 Constitution saving throw or suffer an additional 18 (4d8) poison damage and be poisoned for one hour. A creature already suffering the poisoned condition caused by a nysrock is also stunned until the end of its next turn.

DEMON, PISCODEMON

We stopped on the ridge to watch a great battle in the distance between two armies of lobster demons. The two forces clashed on the plains below, thousands dying with no regard for mercy or quarter. The leaders watched from their palanquins, unconcerned with the carnage below. — Pãuk, apprentice mage

The cannon fodder of the Lower Planes, piscodemons are by no means weak. Their powerful armored bodies resemble a lobster standing on two legs, with a short fish-like tail, and a centipedal head fringed with writhing tentacles. Their numbers are great, which is the only reason they remain in existence, for their lords and masters throw them away in battle like so many empty seed pods and abuse them in any manner their whims devise.

PISCODEMON
Medium fiend (demon), neutral evil

Armor Class 20 (natural armor)
Hit Points 127 (15d8 + 60)
Speed 30 ft., swim 50 ft.

STR	DEX	CON	INT	WIS	CHA
22 (+6)	18 (+4)	18 (+4)	14 (+2)	14 (+2)	17 (+3)

Saving Throws Str +10, Con +8, Wis +6, Cha +7
Damage Resistances cold, fire, lightning; bludgeoning, piercing, and slashing from nonmagical attacks
Damage Immunities acid, poison
Condition Immunities poisoned
Senses blindsight 30 ft., darkvision 60 ft, passive Perception 12
Languages Abyssal, Demonic, Infernal; telepathy 100 ft.
Challenge 10 (5,900 XP)

Amphibious. The piscodemon can breathe air and water.
Magic Resistance. The piscodemon has advantage on saving throws against spells and other magical effects.
Magic Weapons. The piscodemon's weapon attacks are magical.
Improved Critical. The piscodemon's weapon attacks score a critical hit on a roll of 19 or 20.
Innate Spellcasting. The piscodemon's innate spellcasting ability is Charisma (spell save DC 15, +7 to hit with spell attacks). It can cast the following spells, requiring no material components:
At will: *dispel magic*
3/day each: *fly, stinking cloud*

ACTIONS

Multiattack. The piscodemon makes one Claw attack and one Tentacle attack or two Claw attacks.
Claw. *Melee Weapon Attack*: +10 to hit, reach 5 ft., one target. *Hit*: 13 (2d6 + 6) piercing damage and the target is grappled (escape DC 18). The piscodemon has two claws, each of which can grapple only one target.
Teleport. The piscodemon magically teleports, along with any equipment it is wearing or carrying, up to 120 feet to an unoccupied space it can see.
Tentacle. *Melee Weapon Attack*: +10 to hit, reach 5 ft., one target. *Hit*: 11 (1d10 + 6) bludgeoning damage plus 5 (1d10) poison damage and the target must succeed on a DC 16 Constitution saving throw or be poisoned for one hour.

DEMON, SHRROTH (SQUID DEMON)

I know a place under the sea where the ships go to drown. They pile up and are forgotten. Some might sink far away, but they always seem to end up in the region we called the Shipsgrave. I've told ye of that damned lighthouse found there, but let me tell ye also of the witch of the sea, the woman-squid known as Ursallah. She's a mean one; sailors call her the Entwiner for her many tentacles that squeeze the life from those who cross her. — The Old Mariner Calbert Mall, who enjoys telling his sea tales to any who will listen in Bargarsport.

Swimming through the fetid backwaters of the River Styx as it flows through the bottomless sea rifts of the Abyss comes a tentacled horror known in the nightmares of marines and sailors. Shrroth sometimes pass through the thin barriers between the mortal realm and the underworld. They quickly set up shop along sea lanes where they harry sailors, sink ships for sport, and take prisoners whom they torment and torture mercilessly before devouring them body and soul.

Shrroths are 15-foot-tall demons with the lower torso of an octopus and the upper torso of a copper-skinned humanoid. Its arms end in six-fingered talons, and it wields a wicked trident. A mass of long black hair hangs from its head. Two forward-curving, blackish horns protrude under this tangle of hair. Its lower torso sports a mass of writing tentacles reaching lengths of 10 feet. Six larger tentacles stretching 20 feet surround the smaller tentacles. The creature's mouth is a jagged wreck of sharks teeth.

SHRROTH
Huge fiend, chaotic evil

Armor Class 14 (natural armor)
Hit Points 189 (14d12 + 98)
Speed 20 ft., swim 60 ft.

STR	DEX	CON	INT	WIS	CHA
24 (+7)	10 (+0)	24 (+7)	14 (+2)	16 (+3)	18 (+4)

Saving Throws Constitution +11
Skills Deception +8, Intimidation +8, Perception +7, Persuasion +8
Damage Resistances cold, fire, lightning; bludgeoning, piercing, and slashing from nonmagical attacks
Damage Immunities poison
Condition Immunities poisoned
Senses truesight 100 ft., passive Perception 17
Languages Abyssal, Common, telepathy 100 ft.
Challenge 12 (8,400 XP)

Amphibious. The shrroth can breathe air and water.
Magic Resistance. The shrroth demon has advantage on saving throws against spells and other magical effects.
Innate Spellcasting. The shrroth's innate spellcasting ability is Charisma (spell save DC 16, +8 to hit with spell attacks). It can cast the following spells, requiring no material components:
At will: *dispel magic, mirror image, spiritual weapon, teleport* (self only), *water breathing* (others only)
2/day: *feeblemind*
1/day: *blindness/deafness* (blindness only)
***Jet Burst* (recharge 4–6).** As a bonus action, the shrroth moves up to 80 feet through a body of water. This movement does not provoke opportunity attacks.

ACTIONS

Multiattack. The shrroth makes one Trident attack and up to four Tentacle attacks.
Trident. *Melee Weapon Attack:* +11 to hit, reach 15 ft., one target. *Hit:* 18 (2d10 + 7) piercing damage.
Tentacle. *Melee Weapon Attack:* +11 to hit, reach 15 ft., one target. *Hit:* 13 (1d12 +7) bludgeoning damage and the target is grappled (escape DC 19) by the shrroth. The shrroth has six tentacles and can only grapple up to six creatures at a time. A creature that starts its turn grappled by the shrroth suffers 9 (2d8) bludgeoning damage. Each tentacle has an AC of 20, 15 hit points, and immunity to poison and psychic damage. Severing or destroying a tentacle deals no damage to the shrroth and severed tentacles regrow at a rate of one per day.
***Sickening Cloud* (recharge 5–6).** The shrroth emits a cloud of grayish liquid into a body of water that fills a 40-foot cube and remains for 2d4 rounds. Any creature that begins its turn within the cloud must succeed at a DC 19 Constitution saving throw or be poisoned for one minute.

Demon, Skitterdark

A discordant bell chimed, and a dozen tiny demons popped into existence with the smell of sulfur and a wave of hellish heat. These foot-tall, bat-winged demons had red, warty skin, hunched bodies covered in warty flesh, and humanoid faces that mocked the very concept with their yellowed eyes and snout-like faces. They chortled and cackled in glee as they swarmed us and attempted to tear, rend, and bite our softest bits. — Algrid Henswaithe, University of the Vast

Skitterdarks are minor demons in the grand scheme of demons, but demons nonetheless. Like their larger ilk, they delight in bloodshed and sowing chaos. Most often, they are summoned to the world by wizards to carry out minor assassinations, protect items, and harass foes. Easily bored, skitterdarks can be distracted by shiny things, fresh prey, and logical thought.

Skitterdark

Tiny fiend (demon), chaotic evil

Armor Class 15 (natural armor)
Hit Points 55 (10d4 + 30)
Speed 20 ft., fly 30 ft.

STR	DEX	CON	INT	WIS	CHA
8 (−1)	17 (+3)	16 (+3)	11 (+0)	12 (+1)	12 (+1)

Saving Throws Str +2, Con +5, Wis +2, Cha +3
Damage Resistances acid, cold, fire; bludgeoning, piercing, and slashing from nonmagical attacks
Damage Immunities lightning, poison
Condition Immunities poisoned
Senses darkvision 60 ft, passive Perception 11
Languages Abyssal, Common
Challenge 3 (700 XP)

Magic Resistance. The skitterdark has advantage on saving throws against spells and other magical effects.
Magic Weapons. The skitterdark's weapon attacks are magical.
Innate Spellcasting. The skitterdark's innate spellcasting ability is Charisma (spell save DC 11, +3 to hit with spell attacks). It can cast the following spells, requiring no material components:

At will: *detect evil and good, detect magic*
1/day each: *hold person, fear*

Actions

Multiattack. The skitterdark makes one Claw attack and one Bite attack.
Bite. *Melee Weapon Attack*: +5 to hit, reach 5 ft., one target. *Hit*: 5 (1d4 + 3) piercing damage.
Claw. *Melee Weapon Attack*: +5 to hit, reach 5 ft., one target. *Hit*: 4 (1d3 + 3) slashing damage plus 2 (1d4) necrotic damage.

DEMON, STIRGE

Thankfully, the buzzing alerted us as we were making camp and before the warrior types had taken off their armor. Three demons with bodies like common stirges but with heads and forearms that were twisted parodies of humanoid bodies flew out of the canyon. Most of us had expended much magical might that day, but I managed to wing one, literally, with some well-placed arcane projectiles. The rest came on, and one plunged its long nose into Caltax's chest, draining the doughty fighter of his life's blood. In the end, we slew the demons, but our losses were too great. — Päuk, apprentice mage

An all too common sight on the Lower Planes, demon stirges are pest and predator, attacking and sucking the blood from weaker demons while avoiding the wrath of those more powerful. Their bodies are long, over 10 feet, and far too heavy to sustain flight on their withered leathery wings. They attack in numbers if possible, but these swarms are not allies; they are rivals intent on feeding and fleeing at the first chance any individual gets.

STIRGE DEMON

Large fiend (demon), chaotic evil

Armor Class 17 (natural armor)
Hit Points 136 (13d10 + 65)
Speed 20 ft., fly 60 ft.

STR	DEX	CON	INT	WIS	CHA
22 (+6)	17 (+3)	20 (+5)	14 (+2)	14 (+2)	15 (+2)

Saving Throws Str +10, Con +9, Wis +6, Cha +6
Damage Resistances acid, cold, fire
Damage Immunities lightning, poison
Condition Immunities poisoned
Senses darkvision 60 ft, passive Perception 12
Languages Abyssal, Common
Challenge 10 (5,900 XP)

Blood Drain. At the start of its turn, the stirge demon causes a creature it has grappled with its bite to lose 7 (2d6) hit points.
Magic Resistance. The stirge demon has advantage on saving throws against spells and other magical effects.
Magic Weapons. The stirge demon's weapon attacks are magical.
Innate Spellcasting. The stirge demon's innate spellcasting ability is Charisma (spell save DC 14, +6 to hit with spell attacks). It can cast the following spells, requiring no material components:
At will: *darkness, dispel magic, see invisibility, telekinesis*

ACTIONS

Multiattack. The stirge demon makes one Bite attack and two Claw attacks.
Bite. *Melee Weapon Attack:* +10 to hit, reach 5 ft., one target. *Hit:* 19 (3d8 + 6) piercing damage and the target is grappled (escape DC 18). The stirge demon can only grapple one creature.
Claw. *Melee Weapon Attack:* +10 to hit, reach 5 ft., one target. *Hit:* 13 (2d6 + 6) slashing damage.
Teleport. The stirge demon magically teleports, along with any equipment it is wearing or carrying, up to 120 feet to an unoccupied space it can see.

Demon Lords

Demon Lord, Beluiri (The Temptress)

Lord Ryven must be cursed! First, that soldier tried to kill him with his crossbow, and now, Lady Celestyne herself has turned against him. I saw her consorting with Lord Rafferty during the Winter Carnival, frolicking like a schoolgirl with the older man. And right in front of Lord Ryven! He canceled the entire festival and retreated into his manor house. Lady Celestyne followed along as if nothing was wrong, but … it's hard to describe, all right? I swear she turned and smiled at me as she passed, and for a moment, it looked as if she had horns growing down around her face. Her eyes were a bright blue, like a clear pond in the noon sun. I would have done anything for her. — Ambassador Frakes, on the growing animosity between old adventuring companions Lord Ryven and Lord Rafferty

Beluiri is known throughout the Abyss as the Temptress, for in her many disguises she has seduced countless princes, lords, and generals of the Abyss. In the end, she most often betrays those that fall victim to her wiles. She is hated for this by more than one noble or lord of the Abyss. She sometimes journeys to the Material Plane (in one of her many guises) to tempt and seduce mortals, for she knows that all mortals, in their hearts, always give in to their true desires — be it power, greed, lust, or one of many countless other sins.

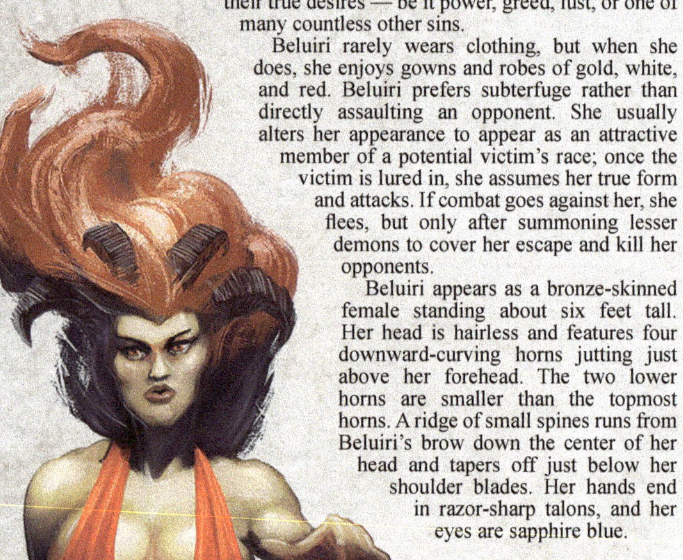

Beluiri rarely wears clothing, but when she does, she enjoys gowns and robes of gold, white, and red. Beluiri prefers subterfuge rather than directly assaulting an opponent. She usually alters her appearance to appear as an attractive member of a potential victim's race; once the victim is lured in, she assumes her true form and attacks. If combat goes against her, she flees, but only after summoning lesser demons to cover her escape and kill her opponents.

Beluiri appears as a bronze-skinned female standing about six feet tall. Her head is hairless and features four downward-curving horns jutting just above her forehead. The two lower horns are smaller than the topmost horns. A ridge of small spines runs from Beluiri's brow down the center of her head and tapers off just below her shoulder blades. Her hands end in razor-sharp talons, and her eyes are sapphire blue.

Beluiri
Medium fiend (demon), chaotic evil

Armor Class 19 (natural armor)
Hit Points 190 (20d8 + 100)
Speed 40 ft.

STR	DEX	CON	INT	WIS	CHA
20 (+5)	20 (+6)	20 (+5)	18 (+4)	16 (+3)	21 (+5)

Saving Throws Str +11, Con +11, Cha +11
Skills Deception +17, Intimidation +11, Perception +9, Persuasion +11
Damage Resistances acid, cold, fire; bludgeoning, piercing, and slashing from nonmagical attacks
Damage Immunities lightning, poison
Condition Immunities poisoned
Senses truesight 120 ft., passive Perception 19
Languages Abyssal, telepathy 120 ft.
Challenge 17 (18,000 XP)

Magic Resistance. Beluiri has advantage on saving throws against spells and other magical effects.
Magic Weapons. Beluiri's weapon attacks are magical.
Shapechanger. Beluiri can use its action to polymorph into a Small or Medium humanoid, or back into her true form. Other than her size and speed, her statistics are the same in each form. Any equipment she is wearing or carrying isn't transformed. She reverts to her true form if she dies.
Innate Spellcasting. Beluiri's innate spellcasting ability is Charisma (spell save DC 20, +12 to hit with spell attacks). She can cast the following spells, requiring no material components:
At will: *darkness, detect magic, fear, tongues*
3/day each: *dispel magic* (as a 6th-level slot), *hold monster* (as a 6th-level slot), *mass suggestion, wall of fire*
1/day each: *incendiary cloud, true polymorph*

Actions

Multiattack. Beluiri uses Charm and makes two Claw attacks and one Horns attack.
Claw. *Melee Weapon Attack:* +11 to hit, reach 5 ft., one target. *Hit:* 15 (3d6 + 5) slashing damage plus 11 (2d10) poison damage. The target must succeed on a DC 19 Constitution saving throw or be poisoned for one minute. The creature can repeat the saving throw at the end of each of its turns, ending the effect on itself on a success.
Horns. *Melee Weapon Attack:* +11 to hit, reach 5 ft., one target. *Hit:* 18 (2d12 + 5) bludgeoning damage.
Teleport. Beluiri magically teleports, along with any equipment she is wearing or carrying, up to 120 feet to an unoccupied space she can see.
Charm. One humanoid Beluiri can see within 30 feet of her must succeed on a DC 19 Wisdom saving throw or be magically charmed for one day. The charmed target obeys Beluiri's verbal or telepathic commands. If the target suffers any harm or receives a suicidal command, it can repeat the saving throw, ending the effect on a success. If the target successfully saves against the effect, or if the effect on it ends, the target is immune to Beluiri's Charm for the next 24 hours.
Beluiri can have only one target charmed at a time. If it charms another, the effect on the previous target ends.
Conjure Hezrou (recharge 4–6). Beluiri summons two hezrou who appear in unoccupied spaces within 60 feet of her and obey her telepathic commands (no action required). They roll initiative and act on their own turn.

Legendary Actions

Beluiri can take three legendary actions, choosing from the options below. Only one legendary action can be used at a time and only at the end of another creature's turn. Beluiri regains spent legendary actions at the start of her turn.
Cast a Spell (costs 3 actions). Beluiri casts a spell from its innate spellcasting list.
Claw Attack. Beluiri makes a Claw attack.
Teleport (costs 2 actions). Beluiri magically teleports, along with any equipment she is wearing or carrying, up to 120 feet to an unoccupied space she can see.

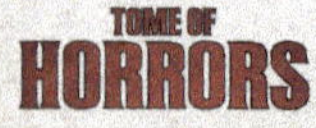

DEMON LORD, TERATASHIA
(DEMON PRINCESS OF DIMENSIONS)

A cold fire of white light blazed around the sealed portal we had discovered in the Tomb of Broken Walls. How the door was a door is beyond my ken, for it was anchored on one wall but somehow extended around a corner onto another wall. Each wall seemed to lead to a different place. A scourge of roaches flooded from one door-wall to inundate us in their hissing masses. Their "princess" came next, a giant cockroach with a female head. About her neck was a necklace of skulls that made me shiver. The roaches around us whispered her name, "Teratashia." — Maligress the Bold, arch-mage of the Arcanum Collegium

The Demon Princess Teratashia is a huge, female-headed cockroach with a feral visage wearing a necklace of human skulls. The necklace is a powerful magic item, but it functions at full effect only for Teratashia. The demon princess's dark palace in the depths of the Abyss is a nexus of countless gaps between dimensions, a warren of tunnels that worm their way deep into a multitude of other realities. She is known in some circles as the Mistress of Dimensions. From the center of this network of connections, Teratashia sends her minions creeping and slithering through the planes of existence to do her bidding.

Teratashia seldom involves herself in the quarrels of the other great demons. She is far more interested in controlling the nooks and crannies between dimensions than with her political status in the Abyss. She is inclined to leave the other demon princes alone to the same degree that they also extend that courtesy to her.

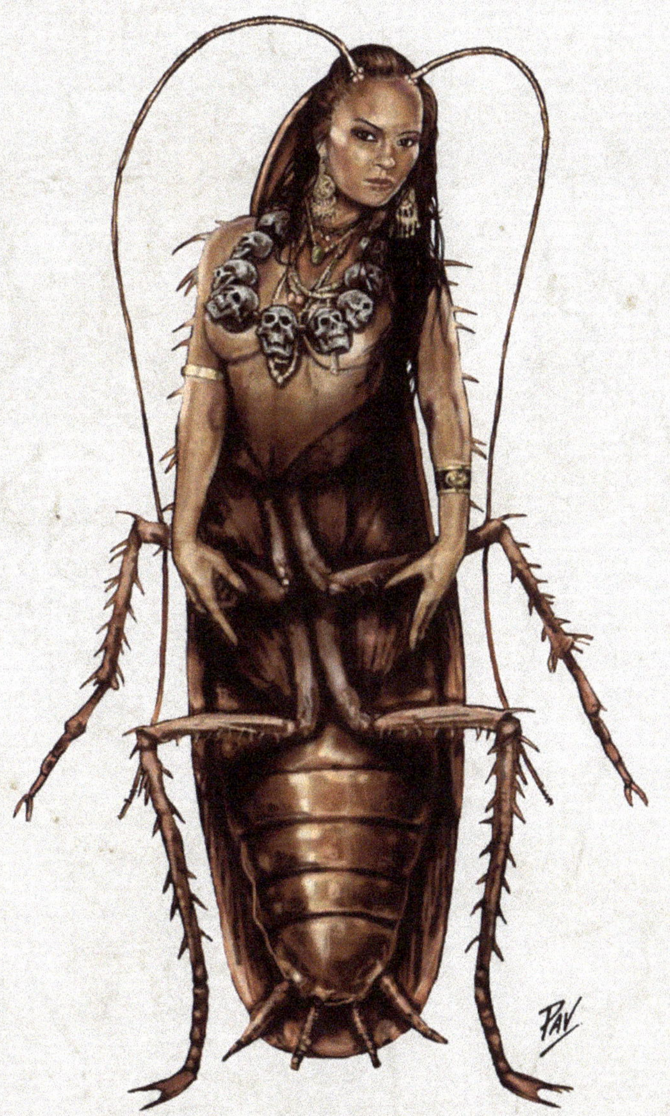

TERATASHIA, DEMON PRINCESS OF DIMENSIONS
Large fiend, chaotic evil

Armor Class 18 (natural armor)
Hit Points 161 (19d10 + 76)
Speed 35 ft., fly 50 ft.

Str	Dex	Con	Int	Wis	Cha
17 (+3)	19 (+4)	18 (+4)	19 (+4)	15 (+2)	18 (+4)

Saving Throws Dex +9, Con +9, Int +9, Cha +9
Skills Perception +7
Damage Resistances acid, cold, psychic
Damage Immunities lightning, poison; bludgeoning, piercing, and slashing damage from nonmagical attacks
Condition Immunities charmed, frightened, poisoned
Senses truesight 120 ft., passive Perception 17
Languages Abyssal
Challenge 15 (13,000 XP)

Regeneration. Teratashia heals 10 hit points at the start of her turn if she is in darkness. She heals 5 hit points if she is in dim light, and no hit points if she is in bright light.
Light Avoidance. Teratashia's speed increases to 50 feet and her flying speed increases to 70 feet if she is in bright light at the start of her turn. Her speed returns to normal when she starts her turn in dim light or darkness.
Innate Spellcasting. Teratashia spellcasting ability is Charisma (spell save DC 17, spell attack bonus +9). She can cast the following spells without material components:
At will: *clairvoyance, darkness, detect thoughts, dimension door, dispel magic, fear, suggestion*
3/day each: *charm person, insect plague, telekinesis, wall of stone*
Teratashia's Necklace of Skulls. Teratashia's necklace is a powerful magic item. It is made from 13 skulls, and each skull has gems set into the eye sockets. Each gem stores one magic spell; the wearer of the necklace can use an action (or reaction for counterspell) to cast one of the spells. Spells are cast at their lowest level, using the caster's attack bonus and saving throw DC. The necklace recovers one expended charge per hour when worn by Teratashia; it doesn't recover charges when worn by anyone else. It has the following spells stored:
2x each: *arcane lock, bestow curse, cloudkill, counterspell, fireball, hypnotic pattern, knock* (x2), *mirror image, witch bolt*
4x each: *cone of cold, cure wounds*

ACTIONS

Multiattack. Teratashia make four Claw attacks, or two Claw attacks and either uses her innate spellcasting or one charge from her necklace.
Claw. *Melee Weapon Attack:* +9 to hit, reach 5 ft., one creature. *Hit:* 17 (3d8 + 4) slashing damage plus 7 (2d6) lightning damage.

Demon Lord, Vepar

Gather round and I'll tell ye a tale o' the Reapin' Sea, where the sea smashes ships to shards when the gale blows strong. 'Tis a lighthouse old out by the wrecks, at a place aptly called Shipsgrave. Sail not there when the storms are brewin', for the lighthouse won't shine when the weather's bad, and many a sailor has gone under on the rocks and reefs. Worse yet, ye might meet the Beggar in Irons, a ship o' the dead. I seen her driving through the water, even floatin' over the waters, but it weren't no cap'n on her deck. No, it was her figurehead givin' orders. He was a monster merman fused right to the ship's prow, but the dead aboard were listenin' to his every word. One old salt whispered the name "Vepar" but I ain't sure of what he spoke. — The Old Mariner Calbert Mall, who enjoys telling his sea tales to any who will listen in Bargarsport

Vepar is an Abyssal duke in the service of Dagon, Prince of the Sea. He is a 12-foot-tall demonic merman. His upper torso is coppery brown, while his lower torso and fins are silver and scaled. Vepar's hair is long and black, and he usually wears it tied back or braided. His eyes, usually blue in color, burn with a silvery fire when he is angry or excited. Under his hair, two small copper horns can be seen just above his eyes. Vepar's hands end in wicked claws with silvery nails.

A brooding and malevolent demon, Vepar relishes in the torture and death of others, particularly mortals (whose very existence he disdains). He leads 29 battalions of shrroths in service to his master, but his loyalty to Dagon is questionable at best. Behind the scenes, Vepar is quietly amassing an army of demons to one day lead against his current lord. But for now, he waits and serves.

Vepar's citadel, Leviathan's Reach, is built into an underwater mountain range that sits several miles below the surface of his watery Abyssal home. The citadel is guarded by scores of aquatic demons, fiendish merfolk, and fiendish tritons, as well as several hundred sahuagin.

Vepar

Large fiend (demon), chaotic evil

Armor Class 20 (natural armor)
Hit Points 300 (24d10 + 168)
Speed 20 ft., swim 60 ft.

STR	DEX	CON	INT	WIS	CHA
24 (+7)	22 (+6)	24 (+7)	20 (+5)	20 (+5)	22 (+6)

Saving Throws Str +14, Dex +13, Con +14
Skills Intimidation +13, Perception +12, Stealth +13
Damage Resistances acid, cold, fire; bludgeoning, piercing, and slashing from nonmagical attacks
Damage Immunities lightning, poison
Condition Immunities frightened, poisoned
Senses truesight 120 ft., passive Perception 22
Languages Abyssal, telepathy 120 ft.
Challenge 21 (33,000 XP)

Magic Resistance. Vepar has advantage on saving throws against spells and other magical effects.
Magic Weapons. Vepar's weapon attacks are magical.
Innate Spellcasting. Vepar's innate spellcasting ability is Charisma (spell save DC 21, +13 to hit with spell attacks). He can cast the following spells, requiring no material components:
At will: *control water, detect magic, ice storm*
3/day each: *dispel magic* (as a 6th-level slot), *wall of ice*
1/day each: *control weather, true polymorph*

Actions

Multiattack. Vepar makes two Trident attacks or two Claw attacks.
Claw. *Melee Weapon Attack:* +14 to hit, reach 5 ft., one target. *Hit:* 17 (3d6 + 7) slashing damage plus 11 (2d10) cold damage. The target must succeed on a DC 20 Constitution saving throw or gain a level of cold-based exhaustion.
Trident. *Melee or Ranged Weapon Attack:* +16 to hit, reach 10 ft. or range 30/90 ft., one target. *Hit:* 22 (3d8 + 9) piercing damage, or 25 (3d10 + 9) piercing damage if used with two hands to make a melee attack. This weapon is a magical *+2 trident*.
Conjure Shrroths (recharge 4–6). Vepar summons 2 **shrroths** (see monster entry) that appear in unoccupied spaces within 60 feet of him and obey his telepathic commands (no action required). They roll initiative and act on their own turn.

Legendary Actions

Vepar can take three legendary actions, choosing from the options below. Only one legendary action can be used at a time and only at the end of another creature's turn. Vepar regains spent legendary actions at the start of his turn.
Cast a Spell (costs 3 actions). Vepar casts a spell from his innate spellcasting list.
Trident Missiles (costs 2 actions). Vepar uses his magical trident to cast a *magic missile* spell (as a 6th-level slot).
Teleport (costs 2 actions). Vepar magically teleports, along with any equipment he is wearing or carrying, up to 120 feet to an unoccupied space he can see.
Claw Attack. Vepar makes a Claw attack.

Denizen of Ong

The strange humanoid approached us, its body almost floating above the ground. I could tell little about what hid under its voluminous robes. A pair of strange bulging eyes peered at us from above a thick veil, and I noticed they did not blink. As its gaze bore into me, the robes rumbled and parted to reveal three long slender tentacles. — Algrid Henswaithe, University of the Vast

Ong lies far away in distant mountains shrouded in endless mists. Its natives, be they a separate race or humanoids twisted by worship of strange gods from the space between spaces, travel the world on bizarre errands. Sometimes they come to trade; other times to kidnap or murder. It is not unusual for one of these strange beings to offer succor or information to the same people they recently tried to kill. Then again, with their propensity for form and face-concealing clothing, who can say which denizen of Ong is which?

Denizen of Ong
Medium aberration, neutral evil

Armor Class 13
Hit Points 11 (2d8 + 2)
Speed 30 ft.

STR	DEX	CON	INT	WIS	CHA
12 (+1)	16 (+3)	13 (+1)	15 (+2)	16 (+3)	15 (+2)

Senses darkvision 60 ft., passive Perception 13
Languages Telepathy 100 ft.
Challenge 2 (450 XP)

Charming gaze. When a creature begins its turn within 30 feet of the denizen of Ong and can see the denizen of Ong, the denizen of Ong can force it to make a DC 13 Wisdom save. If the creature fails its save, the creature is charmed by the denizen of Ong for one hour or until the denizen of Ong is slain.
Unless surprised, a creature can avert its eyes to avoid the saving throw at the start of its turn. If it does so it cannot see the denizen of Ong until the start of its next turn when it can choose to avert its eyes again. If the creature looks at the denizen of Ong in the meantime, it must immediately make the saving throw.
Innate Spellcasting. The denizen of Ong uses Wisdom (spell save DC 13, spell attack +5) to innately cast the following spells, requiring no material components:
At-will: *mage hand*
1/day: *hypnotic pattern, ray of enfeeblement*
Regeneration. If the denizen of Ong has at least 1 hit point, it recovers 5 hit points at the start of its turn.

Actions

Multiattack. The denizen of Ong makes two Tentacle attacks or one Tentacle attack and one Sickle attack.
Sickle. *Melee Weapon Attack:* +5 to hit, reach 5 ft., one target. *Hit:* 6 (1d6 +3) slashing damage.
Tentacle. *Melee Weapon Attack:* +5 to hit, reach 10 ft., one target. *Hit:* 5 (1d4 +3) bludgeoning damage and the target must succeed at a DC 11 Constitution saving throw or become paralyzed for 1d6 minutes.

DEVIL, AMAIMON

Wylf pulled open the trapdoor, and we looked into Hell. Or as close to it as I want to come. A round pit was filled with molten lava that rolled and sloshed like waves. Metal cages hung from the ceiling on soot-blackened chains. Skeletons and charred corpses filled many of the cages. This fat blob had its back to us, but something must have given us away, because it stopped what it was doing and turned to look up at us with this face that was way too tiny for its pudgy body. And we saw what it had been working at: hammering a still-wriggling body onto an iron spike. — Jewels Longridge, on escaping the devil of the Vault of Silver Flames

Amaimons are grossly fat, 10-foot-tall, reddish orange giants weighing 700 pounds. They have miniature faces set with sapphire blue eyes fixed inside a massive head adorned with miniature horns that protrude from its brow. Spines run the length of its back to the tip of its forked tail. Stinking of corpulent sweat, sulfur and smelting iron, the creatures have powerful but stubby clawed arms and legs that are scarred and blistered from their work in forges of Hell.

Amaimons are most commonly encountered in the smelting pits of **Mammon** (see monster entry) where they forge soul ingots from the most worthless of the damned and pour molten metal down the throats of mealy-mouthed souls to forge weapons for the Great Miser's army. They are themselves intensely greedy creatures and try to pinch any last bit of worth from their victims.

AMAIMON
Large fiend (devil), lawful evil

Armor Class 16 (natural armor)
Hit Points 66 (7d10 + 28)
Speed 40 ft.

STR	DEX	CON	INT	WIS	CHA
18 (+4)	18 (+4)	18 (+4)	14 (+2)	14 (+2)	12 (+1)

Skills Deception +4, Intimidation +4, Insight +5, Perception +5
Damage Resistances cold; bludgeoning, piercing, and slashing from nonmagical attacks that are not silver
Damage Immunities fire, poison
Condition Immunities poisoned
Senses darkvision 60 ft., passive Perception 15
Languages Common, Draconic, Infernal, telepathy 100 ft.
Challenge 6 (2,300 XP)

Devil's Sight. Magical darkness doesn't impede the devil's darkvision.
Magic Resistance. The amaimon devil has advantage on saving throws against spells and other magical effects.
Where's My Money. The amaimon devil has the ability to instill crippling greed in its opponents, forcing them to make a successful DC 15 Wisdom Saving throw or stop whatever they are doing to count each individual coin and gem in their possession. Creatures within a 30-foot radius who fail their save count out six coins per round until all the coins are counted. Suffering damage or serious attempts to distract them affords the victim an additional saving throw.
Innate Spellcasting. The amaimon devil's innate spellcasting ability is Charisma (spell save DC 12, +4 to hit with spell attacks). It can cast the following spells, requiring no material components:
At will: *major image, protection from evil and good, teleport* (self only), *wall of fire*

ACTIONS

Multiattack. The amaimon devil makes one Bite attack and two Claw attacks.
Bite. *Melee Weapon Attack*: +7 to hit, reach 5 ft., one target. *Hit*: 11 (2d6 + 4) piercing damage.
Claw. *Melee Weapon Attack*: +7 to hit, reach 10 ft., one target. *Hit*: 9 (2d4 + 4) slashing damage.
***Sulfur Breath* (recharge 4–6).** The amaimon devil spits out a 40-foot cone of sulfuric ash and hot coals. Each creature in the area must make a DC 15 Dexterity saving throw, taking 36 (8d8) fire damage on a failure or half as much on a success.

DEVIL, FLAYER

Berga scaled quickly down the bone wall, using the femurs and skulls as handholds. I wasn't taking any chances and tied off a rope and dropped it over the edge. Hadin was stepping over the edge of the drop when a horrible cloud of ash and burning brimstone exploded upward. He lost his grip and fell backward, vanishing into the cloud. Lashert created a gust of wind to clear the room, but I wish he hadn't. A ghastly giant with large curling horns and deadly claws was holding Berga down as it pulled strips of flesh from her body. It chewed each strip with gusto in its many sharp teeth. Hadin was lying among the bones on the floor, a splintered stake of bone driven through his leg. The thing was obviously saving him for later.
— Holhath the Cryptic, describing the Chamber of Bones beneath Bargarsport

Flayer devils are musclebound brutes with thick crimson skin that stinks of soot and brimstone. Their beastly horned head features a wide mouth filled with broken, rotting yellow fangs, and their eyes glow like molten metal. Their long arms end in horned fists and serrated hook-like claws. Flayers stand 13 feet tall and weigh more than 800 pounds.

When the barons and dukes of Hell need a brute to do a brute's job, they often call upon the legions of marzachs. These deadly giants of Hell use their horned fists and ripping claws to tear the flesh of their enemies to ribbons. Born from a choir of angelic warriors who were turned by the infernal lords, they have the power to emit an unholy burst of brimstone that sickens those around them.

FLAYER

Large fiend (devil), lawful evil

Armor Class 16 (natural armor)
Hit Points 150 (12d10 + 84)
Speed 40 ft.

STR	DEX	CON	INT	WIS	CHA
24 (+7)	15 (+2)	24 (+7)	15 (+2)	15 (+2)	15 (+2)

Saving Throws Strength +11
Skills Athletics +11, Deception +6, Intimidation +6, Perception +6
Damage Resistances cold; bludgeoning, piercing, and slashing from nonmagical attacks that are not silvered
Damage Immunities fire, poison
Condition Immunities poisoned
Senses darkvision 100 ft., passive Perception 16
Languages Abyssal, Common, Ignan, Infernal, telepathy 100 ft.
Challenge 9 (5,000 XP)

Devil's Sight. Magical darkness doesn't impede the flayer's darkvision.
Magic Resistance. The flayer devil has advantage on saving throws against spells and other magical effects.
Flensing. On a natural 20, the horned and serrated claws and fists of the flayer tears flesh from bone, dealing (5d8) necrotic damage to its opponent in addition to critical damage from its claw attack.
Regeneration. The flayer regains 10 hit points at the start of its turn. If the flayer takes damage from a silvered weapon, this trait doesn't function at the start of the flayer's next turn. The flayer is destroyed only if it starts its turn with 0 hit points and doesn't regenerate.
Innate Spellcasting. The flayer's innate spellcasting ability is Charisma (spell save DC 14, +6 to hit with spell attacks). It can cast the following spells, requiring no material components:
At will: *detect evil and good, teleport* (self only), *scorching ray*
1/day each: *wall of fire, protection from evil and good*

ACTIONS

Multiattack. The flayer makes one Bite attack and two Claw attacks.
Bite. *Melee Weapon Attack:* +11 to hit, reach 10 ft., one target. *Hit:* 16 (2d8 + 7) piercing damage.
Claw. *Melee Weapon Attack:* +11 to hit, reach 5 ft., one target. *Hit:* 11 (1d8 + 7) slashing damage and 7 (2d6) necrotic damage.
Unholy Burst (recharge 5–6). A 30-foot cube of hellish brimstone bursts forth from the skin of the flayer, causing those within the wave to succeed DC 19 Constitution save or gain the poisoned condition for one hour.

DEVIL, GHADDAR

We slipped through a hole burned in the air and found ourselves on a hot, dusty plane. The air seared our lungs, leaving us gasping. The sky was fire and ash. A braying from below drew our eyes. Four massive creatures with heads like donkeys were charging up the slope toward us, braying as they came. Rambralt stepped up before us, his sword raised to greet them. He didn't even get to swing it. The first donkey devil grabbed him in its claws and raised him to its mouth. It devoured him with two bites. I turned and ran back for the cinder-burned rip that led back to my own world. — Yanse the Deft, thief of Eastwych

The terrible and mighty ghaddars are massive creatures standing almost three times as tall as a human but with the head of a donkey. It shuffles with a hunched gait as it moves. Large downward-curving horns protrude from its head. Its body is covered with blackish hair. Its feet are splayed, and its eyes are stark white with hollow black pupils.

Ghaddars roam the planes of Hell devouring the unfortunate souls of those they encounter. They also consume the essence and being of any outcast devils and dukes who cross their path. A typical ghaddar stands 15 feet tall and weighs 6,000 pounds. A ghaddar assails its foes with a barrage of claw attacks. A grabbed opponent is bitten and, if slain, devoured. Ghaddar are not strategists, and unless directed by a commander or captain, they attack with little organization and finesse. The ferocity of the ghaddar is unparalleled in combat.

GHADDAR
Huge fiend (devil), lawful evil

Armor Class 18 (natural armor)
Hit Points 207 (18d12 + 90)
Speed 40 ft.

STR	DEX	CON	INT	WIS	CHA
22 (+6)	14 (+2)	20 (+5)	18 (+4)	17 (+3)	20 (+5)

Saving Throws Str +11, Con +10, Cha +10
Damage Resistances cold; bludgeoning, piercing, and slashing damage from nonmagical attacks that are not silver.
Damage Immunities fire, poison
Condition Immunities poisoned
Senses darkvision 120 ft., passive Perception 13
Languages Abyssal, Common, Infernal, telepathy 120 ft.
Challenge 16 (15,000 XP)

Devil's Sight. Magical darkness doesn't impede the ghaddar's darkvision.
Magic Resistance. The ghaddar devil has advantage on saving throws against spells and other magical effects.
Magic Weapons. The ghaddar's weapon attacks are magical.
Innate Spellcasting. The ghaddar's innate spellcasting ability is Charisma (spell save DC 18, +10 to hit with spell attacks). It can cast the following spells, requiring no material components:
At will: *detect magic, wall of fire*
3/day: *fireball, lightning bolt*

ACTIONS

Multiattack. The ghaddar makes two Claw attacks and one Bite attack.
Bite. *Melee Weapon Attack:* +11 to hit, reach 5 ft., one target. *Hit:* 20 (4d6 + 6) piercing damage.
Claw. *Melee Weapon Attack:* +11 to hit, reach 10 ft., one target. *Hit:* 15 (2d8 + 6) slashing damage.
Feed. The ghaddar feeds on the corpse of a slain foe and regains 23 (2d12 + 10) hit points.

DEVIL, HELLSTOKER

Five of them popped into existence with a flash of flame and a roiling cloud of sulfur. Loose, rubbery-skinned, coated in oil, these fiends lit themselves on fire and launched into their attack. Although surprised, we fought back, my own squire thrusting a dagger into the eye of the fiend trying to carry her off. It was a hard fight, and we lost two good horses, but thankfully none of our party was slain, although a few were badly burned. — Sir Cedric of Reme, knight errant

Hellstoker demons are rarely found away from the furnaces they tend in the lower pits of Hell where they maintain the reserves of oil made from the rendered flesh of mortals. When their supply runs low and there are no lesser devils or demons to feed the rendering vats, hellstokers go on hunting raids into the world. They capture as many mortals as possible before returning to the Lower Planes to make their precious oil — after a little light torture of course.

HELLSTOKER DEVIL
Medium fiend (devil), lawful evil

Armor Class 15 (natural armor)
Hit Points 58 (9d8 + 18)
Speed 30 ft.

STR	DEX	CON	INT	WIS	CHA
15 (+2)	13 (+1)	15 (+2)	6 (–3)	10 (+0)	10 (+0)

Saving Throws Str +5, Con +5, Wis +3, Cha +3
Skills Athletics +5, Perception +3
Damage Resistances acid, cold; bludgeoning, piercing, and slashing from nonmagical attacks
Damage Immunities poison
Condition Immunities poisoned
Senses darkvision 60 ft., passive Perception 13
Languages Infernal, telepathy 120 ft.
Challenge 5 (1,800 XP)

Devil's Sight. Magical darkness doesn't impede the hellstoker's darkvision.
Innate Spellcasting. The hellstoker's innate spellcasting ability is Charisma (spell save DC 11). It can cast the following spells, requiring no material components:
At will: *protection from evil and good*
1/day: *plane shift* (self only)
Magic Resistance. The hellstoker has advantage on saving throws against spells and other magical effects.
Oily Hide. A hellstoker has advantage on ability checks and saving throws to resist being grappled or restrained. In addition, if a hellstoker takes fire damage, it bursts into flame for one minute. During this time, a creature who enters the area or begins their turn in the area must make a DC 13 Dexterity saving throw, taking 4 (1d8) fire damage on a failed saving throw, or half as much damage on a successful saving throw.

ACTIONS

Multiattack. The hellstoker makes two Spear attacks.
Spear. *Melee Weapon Attack:* +5 to hit, reach 5 ft., or range 20/60 ft., one target. *Hit:* 5 (1d6 + 2) piercing damage or 6 (1d8 + 2) piercing damage if used with two hands to make a melee attack.
Bellows. The hellstoker releases a blast of fire from its bellows in a 15-foot cone. Creatures in the area must make a DC 13 Dexterity saving throw, taking 14 (4d6) fire damage on a failed saving throw, or half as much damage on a successful saving throw.
Summon (1/day). The hellstoker has a 35% chance to summon 2d8 **lemures** or a **hellstoker**. The summoned demon appears in an unoccupied space within 60 feet of the hellstoker, but can't summon other demons. It remains for one minute, until it or the first hellstoker is slain, or until the first hellstoker takes an action to dismiss it.

Nupperibo Devil

Medium fiend (devil), lawful evil

Armor Class 11 (natural armor)
Hit Points 4 (1d8)
Speed 30 ft.

STR	DEX	CON	INT	WIS	CHA
10 (+0)	10 (+0)	10 (+0)	4 (–3)	10 (+0)	4 (–3)

Damage Resistances cold; bludgeoning, piercing, and slashing from nonmagical attacks that are not silver
Damage Immunities fire, poison, psychic
Condition Immunities charmed, frightened, stunned, poisoned
Senses darkvision 60 ft., passive Perception 10
Languages Infernal (cannot speak)
Challenge 0 (10 XP)

Devil's Sight. Magical darkness doesn't impede the nupperibo's darkvision.
Magic Resistance. The nupperibo devil has advantage on saving throws against spells and other magical effects.

Actions

Claws. *Melee Weapon Attack*: +2 to hit, reach 5 ft., one target. *Hit*: 2 (1d4) slashing damage.
Spear. *Melee Weapon Attack*: +2 to hit, reach 5 ft., one target. *Hit*: 3 (1d6) piercing damage.

Devil, Nupperibo

We took the Onyx Minotaur *with no trouble. The pirates aboard the ship moved in a daze, stumbling about as if drunk, not even seeming to care when we boarded. We took them without a fight. We found out why when Boson Sharn opened the hold. We'd been told it contained women and children kidnapped from Kaf Village. That was a lie. What boiled out of that hold were hordes of clawing devils with gray flesh. We'd walked right into a trap. — Malila Cuthbert, priestess of Muir*

Nupperibo are shambling, ambulatory meat sacks — vaguely humanoid blobs of pus and flesh with a putrid yellow-green pallor — with the horrified faces of the accursed damned. Damned souls raised from the Styx to do the bidding of the princes of Hell, nuperribo are largely mindless and attack in mobs with found weapons or slashes from their rotted claws. They stand five feet tall and weigh about 100 pounds.

Devils constantly punish these tortured spirits, which they consider even lowlier than lemures and manes. Nupperibos are used as fodder in their never-ending wars, with a typical nupperibo army consisting of thousands of these creatures. Nupperibos unerringly follow the orders of their commander. They are relentless in their pursuit and attack, and continue to assault anything in their path until ordered to stop by their commander. A nupperibo killed in battle is 99% likely to be reformed (by a duke or arch devil) into another nupperibo; the remaining 1% are "promoted" to lemure status, having proved their worth in combat.

DEVIL, TORMENTOR

We thought the hounds were the worst, with their flaming breath and their savage bites. We'd dealt with those things before, and instinct took over as we formed a protective ring around Prince Callyndr and waited for them to advance. We readied our shields to block their flames if they tried to burn us. But they didn't behave as we expected. Instead, they formed a ring around the clearing, staying well outside the reach of our blades, but surrounding us. And then they parted and let their master into the ring. He was taller than all of us, with clawed hands and jutting fangs. He lifted a barbed net and seemed to smile as he closed in. — Sir Farnaught of Highreach

Tormentors of Souls, known as tormentor devils, make their way across the uppermost plane of Hell as they search for souls who have entered the realms of evil. Various arch devils and dukes employ tormentor devils to capture and return souls to them for their devilish uses. Tormentors often employ hell hounds when pursuing renegade or runaway souls.

They stand seven feet tall and are covered in reddish-gray scales that glow like flakes of cooling iron. Broad shouldered with a reptilian bifurcated tail, they have hairless goat-like hindquarters covered in thorny spikes that support their broad upper body and barrel chest. Their cruel beast-like face is flanked by spikes rising from their shoulders and curved black horns that sprout from their skull. They wield cruel axes and jagged edged weapons designed to inflict maximum pain.

Tormentor devils are common in the Rings of Hell, where the princes employ them to torture the lemures, nupperibos, undead, and newly arrived souls deposited here for their eternal damnation. Their purpose is to beat the weakest of the fiends into more powerful forms. Those who are unworthy of being raised to higher power by the princes of Hell are reduced to ooze that is poured back into the Styx to be forgotten forever.

TORMENTOR DEVIL
Medium fiend (devil), lawful evil

Armor Class 18 (natural armor)
Hit Points 93 (11d8 + 44)
Speed 30 ft.

STR	DEX	CON	INT	WIS	CHA
18 (+4)	18 (+4)	18 (+4)	14 (+2)	14 (+2)	15 (+2)

Skills Deception +5, Intimidation +5, Insight +5, Perception +5, Persuasion +5
Damage Resistances cold; bludgeoning, piercing, and slashing from nonmagical attacks that are not silver
Damage Immunities fire, poison
Condition Immunities poisoned
Senses darkvision 60 ft., passive Perception 15
Languages Abyssal, Common, Infernal, telepathy 100 ft.
Challenge 6 (2,300 XP)

Devil's Sight. Magical darkness doesn't impede the tormentor's darkvision.
Magic Resistance. The tormentor has advantage on saving throws against spells and other magical effects.
Regeneration. The tormentor regains 5 hit points at the start of its turn. If the tormentor takes damage from a silvered weapon, this trait doesn't function at the start of the tormentor's next turn. The tormentor is destroyed only if it starts its turn with 0 hit points and doesn't regenerate.
Soul Tracking. The tormentor can track any soul that enters the planes of Hell and knows the approximate direction and distance to the soul in question.
Innate Spellcasting. The tormentor's innate spellcasting ability is Charisma (spell save DC 13, +5 to hit with spell attacks). It can cast the following spells, requiring no material components:
At will: *detect thoughts, dimension door, scorching ray, teleport* (self only)
1/day: *suggestion*
Magic Weapons. The tormentor's weapon attacks are magical.

ACTIONS

Multiattack. The tormentor makes one Battleaxe attack and two Claw attacks.
Battleaxe. *Melee Weapon Attack:* +7 to hit, reach 5 ft., one target. *Hit:* 8 (1d8 + 4) slashing damage. The tormentor's battleaxe attack affects incorporeal creatures.
Claw. *Melee Weapon Attack:* +7 to hit, reach 5 ft., one target. *Hit:* 7 (1d6 + 4) slashing damage. The tormentor's claw attack affects incorporeal creatures.
Soulcatcher Net. *Ranged Weapon Attack:* +7 to hit, range 10/20 ft., one target. *Hit:* the target is restrained (Escape DC 14). The tormentor's soulcatcher net can expand to hold creatures of any size and can affect incorporeal creatures. A creature that begins its turn restrained by the soulcatcher net suffers 3 (1d6) necrotic damage. The net has AC 14 and 20 hit points.

DEVILS, MANES

Manes are lesser devils who evolved from larvae or formless blobs of tortured flesh into the ravenous spirits of the underworld. Depending on the species, manes may have horns or scales that run down their back with coloration that denotes their species. Manes travel in packs that may be as small as a half dozen or as large as a hundred or even the thousands when under the direct command of greater demons or devils.

MANE, BLOOD

The wedding chest was delivered late, wheeled into the raucous reception on a squeaky cart. The bride squealed in delight at a new gift to open, likely another jeweled bauble or golden trinket from her new husband's family. She pulled the latch and flung the chest open, which caused a fiery flash to erupt outward to set the groom's hair on fire. A cloud of ash rose into the air from the chest, hovered for a moment, then dropped to the floor. Six blood-soaked devils that stank of copper ran out of the cloud to tear into the guests with their teeth and claws. — Julinie Fairhost, survivor of the bloody wedding day massacre at the Giltmaven Estate

Blood manes have a huge vaguely humanoid head on a blood-soaked body that resembles a cross between a fish and some sort of amphibious hound. Sizzling flesh and the coppery stench of coagulating blood assails the nostrils in the presence of this creature of the Styx.

Blood manes are some of the most ferocious in the legions of manes dwelling in the underworld as they are brought up from the souls of war criminals cut down on the battlefield. Blood manes can be found in the Abyss where they participate in cannibalistic acts that leave only the strongest and meanest of their kind to survive.

BLOOD MANE
Medium fiend, neutral evil

Armor Class 16 (natural armor)
Hit Points 60 (8d8 + 24)
Speed 40 ft., swim 50 ft.

STR	DEX	CON	INT	WIS	CHA
18 (+4)	16 (+3)	16 (+3)	8 (−1)	12 (+1)	8 (−1)

Skills Perception +3, Stealth +5
Damage Resistances cold; bludgeoning, piercing, and slashing from nonmagical attacks
Damage Immunities fire, poison
Condition Immunities poisoned
Senses darkvision 60 ft., passive Perception 13
Languages Abyssal, Infernal
Challenge 4 (1,100 XP)

Amphibious. The mane can breathe air and water.
Drain Blood. As a bonus action, the blood mane may drain blood from a grappled foe. The foe suffers 6 (3d6) necrotic damage, and the blood mane gains a number of temporary hit points equal to the amount of damage the blood drain causes.
Pack Tactics. The mane has advantage on an attack roll against a target if at least one of the mane's allies is within five feet of the mane and the ally isn't incapacitated.
Sizzle. A creature that touches the blood mane or hits it with a melee attack while within five feet of it takes 3 (1d6) fire damage.

ACTIONS

Multiattack. The mane makes one Bite attack and one Claw attack.
Bite. *Melee Weapon Attack*: +6 to hit, reach 5 ft., one target. *Hit*: 8 (1d8 + 4) piercing damage and 9 (2d8) fire damage. The target is grappled by the blood mane (Escape DC 14). The blood mane can grapple only one creature at a time.
Claw. *Melee Weapon Attack*: +6 to hit, reach 5 ft., one target. *Hit*: 7 (1d6 + 4) slashing damage

MANE, ICE

We ran through the field of towering ice spikes, doing our best to jump over the jagged opening in the frozen lake. Behind us, we could hear the creatures running fast, hunting us. They ran in a pack, swinging and climbing the frozen towers, icy devils out for our warm blood. Gowen was in front of me, running faster than any of us thanks to those nifty boots of his. He jumped over a crack in the ice, but he wasn't fast enough, even with his magic. A host of them shot upward out of the water and grabbed him in midair. They pulled him right down into the water. — Nixos Panreave, Northlands explorer and tale teller

Ice manes are a cross between a primate and an albino reptile with piercing blue eyes. Their huge heads are surrounded with icy spikes, and their mouths are filled with rows of frozen fangs that shred opponents like crushed glass. They are most frequently found in the ring of Cainus where icy waters of Cocytus pour into the frozen Ring of Hell. Ice manes hunt in wild packs across Cainus and Cocytus where they are raised from frozen souls trapped in the icy tributary of Styx. Voracious hunters, ice manes are too stupid to retreat, and too numb to feel pain. They sometimes find their way into the Mortal Realms when summoned by spellcasters or though unattended planar gates near areas of ice floes and frigid waters.

ICE MANE
Medium fiend, neutral evil

Armor Class 16 (natural armor)
Hit Points 37 (5d8 + 15)
Speed 40 ft., swim 50 ft.

STR	DEX	CON	INT	WIS	CHA
16 (+3)	16 (+3)	16 (+3)	8 (−1)	12 (+1)	8 (−1)

Skills Perception +3, Stealth +5
Damage Resistances poison; bludgeoning, piercing, and slashing from nonmagical attacks
Damage Immunities cold
Condition Immunities poisoned
Senses darkvision 60 ft., passive Perception 13
Languages Abyssal, Infernal
Challenge 3 (700 XP)

Amphibious. The mane can breathe air and water.
Ice Walk. The ice mane can move across and climb icy surfaces without needing to make an ability check. Additionally, difficult terrain composed of ice or snow doesn't cost it extra movement.
Pack Tactics. The mane has advantage on an attack roll against a target if at least one of the mane's allies is within five feet of the mane and the ally isn't incapacitated.

ACTIONS

Multiattack. The mane makes one Bite attack and one Ice Spine attack.
Bite. *Melee Weapon Attack*: +5 to hit, reach 5 ft., one target. *Hit*: 7 (1d8 + 3) piercing damage and 2 (1d4) cold damage, and the target must succeed on a DC 13 Constitution saving throw or gain a level of exhaustion.
Ice Spine. *Ranged Weapon Attack*: +5 to hit, range 10/40 ft., one target. *Hit*: 6 (1d6 + 3) slashing damage and 2 (1d4) cold damage.

MANE, STYGIAN

The black dragon's corpse was barely cold where it floated in the foul runoff of the Sin Mire Swamp. As we watched, a dozen reptilian creatures raised their spiny heads above the murk. They clambered up the dragon's scales, and perched on its body, watching us. Venom dripped from their fangs. Our guide whispered, "What are they?" There wasn't time to answer. The devils leaped at us and attacked. Saray made the mistake of running at them — and vanished into a hole hidden under the swamp. We later learned it was a portal that led to unimaginable horrors. — Iris Windbreath, found wandering in the Sin Mire Swamp by the dwarves of Anvil Plunge

Stygian manes have a vaguely reptilian or fish-like appearance, with a slick rubbery hide and yellowish spines that begin at their brow and protrude all the way down their back. The fangs of a stygian mane drip with horrid venom.

Stygian manes are most often found in the Stygian Swamps of the Abyss, where demon lords recruit them as guards and chattel minions. Although seldom encountered outside of Styx, the Abyss, and the Rings of Hell, they can be encountered in the mortal realms as summoned minions or in thin spots between the planes.

STYGIAN MANE

Medium fiend, neutral evil

Armor Class 16 (natural armor)
Hit Points 37 (5d8 + 15)
Speed 40 ft., swim 50 ft.

STR	DEX	CON	INT	WIS	CHA
16 (+3)	16 (+3)	16 (+3)	8 (−1)	12 (+1)	8 (−1)

Skills Perception +3, Stealth +5
Damage Resistances cold; bludgeoning, piercing, and slashing from nonmagical attacks
Damage Immunities poison
Condition Immunities paralyzed, poisoned
Senses darkvision 60 ft., passive Perception 13
Languages Abyssal, Infernal
Challenge 2 (450 XP)

Amphibious. The mane can breathe air and water.
Pack Tactics. The mane has advantage on an attack roll against a target if at least one of the mane's allies is within five feet of the mane and the ally isn't incapacitated.
Slimy Skin. The stygian mane has advantage to escape from the grappled or restrained condition.

ACTIONS

Bite. *Melee Weapon Attack*: +5 to hit, reach 5 ft., one target. *Hit*: 7 (1d8 + 3) piercing damage and the target must succeed at a DC 13 Constitution saving throw or become paralyzed for one minute.

MANE, STYX

The dimwitted fighter Fangoe thought it was some kind of dog hiding in the darkness under the low porch. He put his hand out to pet the thing — and lost three fingers for his trouble. Fangoe fell onto his backside, and the creature charged out at him on all fours, its slobbering mouth gnashing and biting for more flesh. Dooley caught it mid-leap with a blast from his wand, knocking the creature sideways and saving the warrior. — "Gourd" Deeproot, describing the devil that escaped into the Haunted Wood

Styx manes are the size of a large terrestrial warhound. Most Styx manes have short hind legs and a bifurcated tail. They are capable of bipedal movement over short distances but prefer to move about on all fours. Their long powerfully built forearms end in clawed paw like hands. They have powerful shoulders that flank a thick neck and lumpy, vaguely humanoid face featuring a huge slathering mouth filled with row after row of razor-sharp teeth.

The manes of the Styx serve as chattel for various powers of the underworld. Their intellect is such that they are capable of following basic orders and can establish simple battle formations that are unseen in the infinite ranks of the Abyssal hordes they most frequently face.

STYX MANE

Medium fiend, neutral evil

Armor Class 16 (natural armor)
Hit Points 37 (5d8 + 15)
Speed 40 ft., swim 50 ft.

STR	DEX	CON	INT	WIS	CHA
16 (+3)	16 (+3)	16 (+3)	8 (−1)	12 (+1)	8 (−1)

Skills Perception +3, Stealth +5
Damage Resistances cold; bludgeoning, piercing, and slashing from nonmagical attacks
Damage Immunities poison
Condition Immunities poisoned
Senses darkvision 60 ft., passive Perception 13
Languages Abyssal, Infernal
Challenge 2 (450 XP)

Amphibious. The mane can breathe air and water.
Pack Tactics. The mane has advantage on an attack roll against a target if at least one of the mane's allies is within five feet of the mane and the ally isn't incapacitated.

ACTIONS

Multiattack. The mane makes one Bite and one Claw attack.
Bite. *Melee Weapon Attack*: +5 to hit, reach 5 ft., one target. *Hit*: 7 (1d8 + 3) piercing damage.
Claw. *Melee Weapon Attack*: +5 to hit, reach 5 ft., one target. *Hit*: 6 (1d6 + 3) slashing damage.

DEVIL, ALASTOR (EXECUTIONER OF HELL)

We stood guard on the Wizard's Wall, ready for anything that might come through the Crynnomar Gap. Trouble was brewing on the plains, but surely no sane army would attempt to breach the wall. But still they came, an army of devilish design, bearing pikes and blades of onyx hue. At their forefront was a devil twice the size of a man, his body encased in hellish flames. He pointed an iron battleaxe at our ranks, and the monsters charged. — Sir Ian Murren, knight of the Grand Duchy

The Arch Devil Alastor, the Executioner of Hell, is the mightiest of the pit fiends, standing 16 feet tall. This horror has a body cloaked entirely in hellish yellow flames, and huge bat-like wings spread from his scaly body, which glows faintly like cooling steel. Long, ape-like arms end in clawed hands that wield the wickedly curved infernal iron battleaxe *Grimfang*. The beast's coal-black eyes are lit with glinting red pupils, and his mouth is filled with row upon row of shark-like fangs.

Alastor's Keep is found on the great battle planes of Gehenna where the princes of darkness contest against one another for dominion over the throne of Hell. Alastor is an impartial observer in these contests between the demon lords. He seeks only to quench *Grimfang's* insatiable thirst in the blood of his brethren and any demons or angels Alastor can get his mighty paws on. Alastor takes great pride in his job, and his axe never falters. When tasked with the execution of a traitor or prisoner, Alastor does the job, neat and clean every time.

ALASTOR THE EXECUTIONER, ARCH DEVIL

Huge fiend (devil), lawful evil

Armor Class 19 (natural armor)
Hit Points 362 (25d12 + 200)
Speed 40 ft., fly 60 ft.

STR	DEX	CON	INT	WIS	CHA
28 (+9)	16 (+3)	26 (+8)	24 (+7)	18 (+4)	26 (+8)

Saving Throws Constitution +15, Wisdom +11, Charisma +15
Skills Arcana +14, Acrobatics +10, Deception +15, Insight +11, Intimidation +15, Perception +11, Persuasion +15, Stealth +10
Damage Resistances cold; bludgeoning, piercing, and slashing from nonmagical attacks that are not silver
Damage Immunities fire, poison
Condition Immunities poisoned
Senses darkvision 60 ft., passive Perception 21
Languages Abyssal, Common, Celestial, Draconic, Giant, Ignan, Infernal, Terran, telepathy 100 ft.
Challenge 22 (41,000 XP)

Devil's Sight. Magical darkness doesn't impede the devil's darkvision.

Fear Aura. Any hostile target that starts its turn within 20 feet of the Executioner must make a DC 23 Wisdom saving throw, unless the Executioner is incapacitated. On a failed save, the target is frightened until the start of its next turn. If the target's saving throw is successful, the target is immune to the Executioner's fear aura for the next 24 hours.

Innate Spellcasting. The Executioner's innate spellcasting ability is Charisma (spell save DC 23, +15 to hit with spell attacks). He can cast the following spells, requiring no material components:

At will: *animate dead, bane, detect evil and good, detect thoughts, dispel magic, hold monster, invisibility, magic circle, major image, teleport* (self only), *true seeing, power word stun, wall of fire*
3/day: *confusion*
1/day each: *meteor swarm, power word kill*
1/week: *wish*

Legendary Resistance (3/day). If the Executioner fails a saving throw, he can choose to succeed instead.

Magic Resistance. The Executioner has advantage on saving throws against spells and other magical effects.

Magic Weapons. The Executioner's weapon attacks are magical.

Regeneration. The Executioner regains 10 hit points at the start of its turn. If the Executioner takes damage from a silvered weapon, this trait doesn't function at the start of the Executioner's next turn. The Executioner is destroyed only if he starts its turn with 0 hit points and doesn't regenerate.

ACTIONS

Multiattack. The Executioner makes one *Grimfang* attack, one Bite attack, and two Claw attacks, or one *Grimfang* attack, one Tail Swipe and two Claw attacks. He may substitute one Hellfire attack for his Claw attacks.

Bite. Melee Weapon Attack: +16 to hit, reach 5 ft., one target. *Hit*: 26 (5d6 + 9) piercing damage and the target must succeed at a DC 24 Constitution saving throw or suffer an additional 44 (8d10) poison damage.

Claw. Melee Weapon Attack: +16 to hit, reach 10 ft., one target. *Hit*: 19 (3d6 + 9) slashing damage.

Grimfang. Melee Weapon Attack: +16 to hit, reach 10 ft., one target. *Hit*: 22 (2d12 + 9) slashing damage and the target must succeed at a DC 24 Constitution saving throw or die. A creature that is killed by *Grimfang* cannot be brought back to life by any means short of a *wish*.

Hellfire. Ranged Weapon Attack: +10 to hit, range 60/120 ft., two targets. *Hit*: 21 (4d8 + 3) fire and necrotic damage.

Tail. Melee Weapon Attack: +16 to hit, reach 15 ft., one target. *Hit*: 18 (2d8 + 9) bludgeoning damage and the target is grappled (escape DC 25). A creature that starts its turn grappled by the Executioner suffers 11 (2d10) bludgeoning damage. The Executioner has only one tail and can grapple only one creature with it at a time.

LEGENDARY ACTIONS

The Executioner can take three legendary actions, choosing from the options below. Only one legendary action can be used at a time and only at the end of another creature's turn. The Executioner regains spent legendary actions at the start of his turn.

Strafe. The Executioner moves up to 60 feet, and this movement does not provoke opportunity attacks. At any point during this movement, he may make one Hellfire attack.

Execution. The Executioner makes a *Grimfang* attack.

Wing Buffet (costs 2 actions). The Executioner buffets the air with his wings to create a 20-foot cone of powerful wind. All creatures caught in this area must succeed at a DC 25 Strength check or be knocked prone and pushed 15 feet away from the Executioner.

Fiendish Recovery (costs 2 actions). The Executioner recovers 50 hit points and ends one condition effecting it.

TOME OF HORRORS

DEVIL, AMMON (DUKE OF MALBOLGE, KEEPER OF THE KENNELS, LORD OF THE DITCHES)

Culper had just taken the gem from the idol's hand when we heard the baying of wolves. Desert sand stirred through the shrine at the same time, and we all felt the change in the air, a heaviness that weighed on our souls. The gem flared with a burst of flame, and Culper dropped it, screaming in pain as his hands charred to the bone. The blast of light burned the outline of our shadows onto the walls … as well as another larger shape. From this shadow stepped a nine-foot wolf clad in armor and carrying a writhing whip. — Jasper Stel, on the failed raid of the temple of Ammon in the Kanderi Desert

Ammon is a 15-foot-tall fiendish humanoid with clawed hands and feet and the black-furred, lice-infested head of a wolf set with slavering jaws and glowing yellow eyes. An armor-plated left hand wields a cruel whip that coils of its own accord like a living serpent.

Ammon's iron fortress Harrowcourt hangs from a precipice overlooking the Ditches of the Damned that surround the Ring of Hell known as the Pit of Malbolge. Ammon is attended by a host of werewolves, barbed devils, ghaddar, and his lieutenant Eaxalac, a pit fiend. The 10 ditches are greatly feared by worldly thieves and politicians who know they may very well end up plying eternity among the charlatans, confidence men, seducers, fraudsters, counterfeiters, and betrayers trapped there.

To keep the accursed dead in their ditches, Ammon oversees a kennel of 666 wolf-headed hell hounds he sired himself, as well as three legions of bone devils. The ditches are filled with nupperibos, lemurs, and even lesser souls who have found their just deserts in Malbolge.

AMMON, DUKE OF MALBOLGE, KEEPER OF THE KENNELS, LORD OF THE DITCHES, ARCH DEVIL

Large fiend (devil), lawful evil

Armor Class 17 (natural armor)
Hit Points 270 (20d10 + 160)
Speed 60 ft.

STR	DEX	CON	INT	WIS	CHA
28 (+9)	18 (+4)	26 (+8)	24 (+7)	20 (+5)	26 (+8)

Saving Throws Constitution +15, Wisdom +12, Charisma +15
Skills Arcana +14, Deception +15, Insight +12, Intimidation +15, Perception +12, Persuasion +15, Stealth +11
Damage Resistances cold; bludgeoning, piercing, and slashing from nonmagical attacks that are not silver
Damage Immunities fire, poison
Condition Immunities poisoned
Senses darkvision 60 ft., passive Perception 22
Languages Abyssal, Celestial, Common, Draconic, Goblin, Ignan, Infernal, telepathy 100 ft.
Challenge 22 (41,000 XP)

Devil's Sight. Magical darkness doesn't impede Ammon's darkvision.

Fear gaze. When a creature that can see Ammon's eyes starts its turn within 30 feet of him, Ammon can force it to make a DC 20 Wisdom saving throw if Ammon isn't incapacitated and can see the creature. On a failure, the creature is frightened for one minute. Unless surprised, a creature can avert its eyes to avoid the saving throw at the start of its turn. If the creature does so, it can't see Ammon until the start of its next turn, when it can avert its eyes again. If the creature looks at Ammon in the meantime, it must immediately attempt the save. While averting its eyes, any attacks on Ammon are done at disadvantage.

Innate Spellcasting. Ammon's innate spellcasting ability is Charisma (spell save DC 23, +15 to hit with spell attacks). It can cast the following spells, requiring no material components:

At will: *animate dead, bane, charm monster, detect evil and good, detect thoughts, fireball, fly, geas, magic circle, polymorph, suggestion, symbol, teleport, tongues, wall of ice*

Legendary Resistance (3/day). If Ammon fails a saving throw, he can choose to succeed instead.

Magic Resistance. Ammon has advantage on saving throws against spells and other magical effects.

Magic Weapons. Ammon's weapon attacks are magical.

Regeneration. Ammon regains 15 hit points at the start of his turn. If Ammon takes damage from a silvered weapon, this trait doesn't function at the start of Ammon's next turn. Ammon is destroyed only if he starts his turn with 0 hit points and doesn't regenerate.

ACTIONS

Multiattack. Ammon makes one Bite attack and two Mace attacks.

Bite. *Melee Weapon Attack:* +16 to hit, reach 5 ft., one target. *Hit:* 18 (2d8 + 9) piercing damage.

Mace. *Melee Weapon Attack:* +16 to hit, reach 10 ft., one target. *Hit:* 22 (2d12 + 9) bludgeoning damage plus 22 (5d8) thunder damage, and the target must make a DC 23 Constitution saving throw, being stunned until the end of its next turn and deafened for one hour on a failure, or just stunned on a successful save.

LEGENDARY ACTIONS

Ammon can take three legendary actions, choosing from the options below. Only one legendary action can be used at a time and only at the end of another creature's turn. Ammon regains spent legendary actions at the start of his turn.

Swing Around. Ammon makes a Mace attack.

Thundersmash. Ammon strikes the ground with his mace. All creatures within a 20-foot cube centered on Ammon must make a DC 24 Strength saving throw, taking 27 (6d8) thunder damage and being pushed to the edge of the area of effect on a failure, or taking half as much damage and not being pushed on a success.

Call the Hounds (costs 2 actions). Ammon summons 2d4 hell hounds to his side to fight as his allies.

Fiendish Recovery (costs 2 actions). Ammon recovers 50 hit points and ends one condition effecting him.

Devil, Baalzebal
(Prince of Stygia, Lord of Flies)

The carnival was a sad, gaudy affair, with fanciful tents and oddities I found commonplace. Yet children were going missing in the villages through which this caravan passed, and we were not going to let that go unchallenged. One dapper carnival barker promised grand excitement beyond our reckoning, and Rohpor paid the gold to enter the striped tent. We followed into the darkness, but my mind was already screaming that something wasn't right. As my eyes adjusted, I heard the buzzing and saw the thousands of black flies clinging to the tent's fabric. The barker followed us in, his silk robes flaring to release clear wings as his eyes bulged outward in his changing features. He was now twice our size, his head rising into the mass of swarming flies. — Sir Reddick Stenhill, knight of the vale

Baalzebal may take any form but is commonly encountered as a thin, 12-foot-tall figure with four insect-like arms that end in long hairy fingers. He is mostly bipedal, with translucent fly wings that fold down the back of rich silk robes that hide his bloated abdomen. His crowned and horned head resembles a cross between a human and fly with a thin cruel face punctuated by huge bulbous fly eyes, each of which can see in 333 degrees.

Baalzebal is one of the original fallen. Known as the Lord of the Flies, Baalzebal dwells in a fetid palace in the swamps of Stygia where his forces face the dual threats of incursions by the minions of Tsathogga whose own realm feeds the river Styx, and by the covetous intent of the other rulers of the Rings of Hell who seek to overthrow him.

Baalzebal, Prince of Stygia, Arch Devil

Large fiend (devil), lawful evil

Armor Class 21 (natural armor)
Hit Points 250 (20d10 + 140)
Speed 40 ft., fly 60 ft.

STR	DEX	CON	INT	WIS	CHA
24 (+7)	28 (+9)	24 (+7)	28 (+9)	18 (+4)	26 (+8)

Saving Throws Constitution +14, Wisdom +11, Charisma +15
Skills Arcana +16, Deception +15, History +16, Insight +11, Intimidation +15, Nature +16, Perception +16, Persuasion +15, Religion +16, Stealth +16
Damage Resistances cold; bludgeoning, piercing, and slashing from nonmagical attacks that are not silver
Damage Immunities fire, poison
Condition Immunities poisoned
Senses darkvision 60 ft, passive Perception 26
Languages Abyssal, Common, Celestial, Draconic, Giant, Infernal, Terran, telepathy 100 ft.
Challenge 22 (41,000 XP)

Devil's Sight. Magical darkness doesn't impede the devil's darkvision.

Gianter Insect. When Baalzebal casts *giant insect*, the resulting insects are twice the size and have maximum hit points.

Innate Spellcasting. Baalzebal's innate spellcasting ability is Charisma (spell save DC 23, +15 to hit with spell attacks). He can cast the following spells, requiring no material components:
At will: *animate dead, bane, detect evil and good, detect thoughts, dispel magic, giant insect, hold monster, insect plague, invisibility, magic circle, major image, teleport* (self only), *true seeing, power word stun*
1/day: *power word kill*
1/week: *wish*

Legendary Resistance (3/day). If Baalzebal fails a saving throw, he can choose to succeed instead.

Magic Resistance. Baalzebal has advantage on saving throws against spells and other magical effects.

Regeneration. Baalzebal regains 15 hit points at the start of his turn. If Baalzebal takes damage from a silvered weapon, this trait doesn't function at the start of Baalzebal's next turn. Baalzebal is destroyed only if he starts his turn with 0 hit points and doesn't regenerate.

The Lord of Lies. The buzzing of Baalzebal sows discontent and confusion to those who hear his voice. Baalzebal may cause any creature within 30 feet who hears his voice to make a DC 19 Wisdom saving throw, suffering one of the following effects on a failure:
Suggestion. Baalzebal makes suggestions that go against the better judgment or best self-interest of the listener as per the spell *suggestion.*
Confusion. Victims of his words become disoriented and confused as per the spell *confusion.*
Murmuring Mirage. Baalzebal's voice can change people's perception and cause them to see terrain and their location as something different from what it actually is as per the spell *hallucinatory terrain.*

Actions

Multiattack. Baalzebal makes one Rotting Touch attack and two Vomit attacks.

Rotting Touch. *Melee Weapon Attack:* +14 to hit, reach 10 ft., one target. *Hit:* 29 (4d10 + 7) necrotic damage and the creature must succeed at a DC 22 Constitution saving throw or be cursed with fly rot. While cursed with fly rot, the creature can't regain hit points and its hit point maximum decreases by 10 (3d6) for every 24 hours that elapse. If the creature is reduced to 0 hit points by the fly rot, it dies and its body turns to a swarm of flies. The curse lasts until removed by the *remove curse* spell or other magic.

Vomit. *Ranged Weapon Attack:* +16 to hit, range 30/100 ft., one target. *Hit:* 22 (2d12 + 9) acid damage.

Spew Flies (recharge 5–6). Baalzebal spews forth a cloud of biting insects that fill a 60-foot cube. Each creature in the area must make a DC 22 Constitution saving throw, taking 28 (8d6) poison damage on a failure and being blinded for one minute on a failure, or half as much on a success and not being blinded.

Legendary Actions

Baalzebal can take three legendary actions, choosing from the options below. Only one legendary action can be used at a time and only at the end of another creature's turn. Baalzebal regains spent legendary actions at the start of his turn.

Projectile Vomit. Baalzebal makes a vomit attack.

Fly Vomit. Baalzebal attempts to recharge and use his spew flies breath weapon.

Swarms of Insects (costs 2 actions). Baalzebal summons 1d4 insect swarms to appear within 60 feet of it.

Fiendish Recovery (costs 2 actions). Baalzebal recovers 50 hit points and ends one condition effecting it.

TOME OF HORRORS

Devil, Baaphel
(Grand Duke of Covetous Regent of Belial)

Saxentry's Spring Festival was just getting under way when the old man led his beaten-down horse and cart into the middle of the festivities. The drab wagon was at odds with the festive colors and costumes, and was covered in a gray cloth even shabbier than the horse that pulled the whole affair. The old man stopped in the middle of the crowd and pulled the blanket away with a dramatic flourish. I don't know what I expected to be inside, but a blackened brazier was far from it. The brazier immediately became the center of attention as it exploded into a tower of flames. From those flames, a dog-headed creature stepped forth. The old man stood straight and addressed the crowd, "Behold, mortals! Baaphel graces you with his presence!" People fled in all directions, the party forgotten. — Boyd Sammers, survivor of the Spring Festival attack on Saxentry.

Grand Duke Baaphel, the Lustful Hound, is a 10-foot-tall humanoid with the head of a horned hell hound, a humanoid torso, hooved feet, and the wings of a bat. He bears a wicked war scythe and is wreathed in hellfire. A forked crimson tails snakes out behind the arch devil. Once a beautiful member of the choirs of angels, Baaphel's visage now reflects the bestial nature of his corruption.

Baaphel is a grand duke in the service of Belial and leads two legions of bearded devils in battle for his lord. Baaphel is constantly scheming against the other dukes in Belial's service and takes every opportunity to discredit them in the eyes of their lord. Baaphel yearns to rule an entire plane and is waiting anxiously until the time comes that he can overthrow his lord. He makes his home in a storm-swept castle of basalt and iron known as Evermore.

Baaphel, Grand Duke of Covetous Regent of Belial, Arch Devil

Medium fiend (devil), lawful evil

Armor Class 17 (*chainmail +1*)
Hit Points 312 (25d8 + 200)
Speed 40 ft., fly 60 ft.

STR	DEX	CON	INT	WIS	CHA
28 (+9)	16 (+3)	26 (+8)	24 (+7)	18 (+4)	26 (+8)

Saving Throws Constitution +15, Wisdom +11, Charisma +15
Skills Arcana +14, Acrobatics +10, Deception +15, Insight +11, Intimidation +15, Perception +11, Persuasion +15, Stealth +10
Damage Resistances cold; bludgeoning, piercing, and slashing from nonmagical attacks that are not silver
Damage Immunities fire, poison
Condition Immunities poisoned
Senses darkvision 60 ft., passive Perception 21
Languages Abyssal, Common, Celestial, Draconic, Giant, Infernal, Terran, telepathy 100 ft.
Challenge 22 (41,000 XP)

Devil's Sight. Magical darkness doesn't impede the devil's darkvision.
Innate Spellcasting. Baaphel's innate spellcasting ability is Charisma (spell save DC 23, +15 to hit with spell attacks). He can cast the following spells, requiring no material components:
At will: *bane, charm monster, detect evil and good, dispel magic, fire shield, invisibility, magic circle, suggestion, teleport* (self only), *tongues*
1/day each: *flesh to stone, symbol*
***Legendary Resistance* (3/day).** If Baaphel fails a saving throw, he can choose to succeed instead.
Magic Resistance. Baaphel has advantage on saving throws against spells and other magical effects.
Magic Weapons. Baaphel's weapon attacks are magical.
Regeneration. Baaphel regains 10 hit points at the start of his turn. If Baaphel takes damage from silvered weapon, this trait doesn't function at the start of Baaphel's next turn. Baaphel is destroyed only if he starts his turn with 0 hit points and doesn't regenerate.

Actions

Multiattack. Baaphel makes one Hell Reaper attack and two Fear Touch attacks.
Hell Reaper. *Melee Weapon Attack:* +16 to hit, reach 10 ft., one target. *Hit:* 31 (4d10 + 9) slashing damage. Baaphel scores a critical hit with Hell Reaper when he rolls a 19 or 20.
Fear Touch. *Melee Weapon Attack:* +16 to hit, reach 5 ft., one target. *Hit:* 23 (4d6 + 9) psychic damage and the target must succeed on a DC 19 Wisdom saving throw or be frightened of Baaphel for one hour. A creature who saves against this effect is immune to it for 24 hours.

Legendary Actions

Baaphel can take three legendary actions, choosing from the options below. Only one legendary action can be used at a time and only at the end of another creature's turn. Baaphel regains spent legendary actions at the start of his turn.
Devil Touched. Baaphel makes a Fear Touch attack.
Reap the Souls. Baaphel makes two Hell Reaper attacks, scoring a critical hit on an 18, 19, or 20.
***Wing Buffet* (costs 2 actions).** Baaphel buffets the air with his wings to create a 20-foot cone of powerful wind. All creatures caught in this area must succeed at a DC 25 Strength check or be knocked prone and pushed 15 feet away from Baaphel.
***Fiendish Recovery* (costs 2 actions).** Baaphel recovers 50 hit points and ends one condition affecting him.

a

Devil, Belial
(Prince of Covetous, Lord of Lusts)

The villagers shambled about in a dreamlike trance, their eyes unfocused, their movements painstakingly slow. The only sign of activity was a small perfume stand in the middle of town where a charismatic young man was selling his wares. Residents who walked mindlessly up to him earned a private word as well as a spritz of perfume. They stumbled away with a smile on their faces. Thorium stepped in front of the next old woman in line, and got a face full of lilac perfume for his trouble. The dwarf's anger boiled over instantly, like a kettle exploding, and he swung his mighty silver axe into the cart, toppling it in the street. The ruddy-skinned salesman turned at the commotion, fiery horns growing out of his head as blackened wings extended from his back. That's when Thorium knew he was in trouble. — Tempker "Battlefist" Ashenchisel of the dwarven legion investigating rumors of villagers vanishing.

Belial is a 10-foot-tall handsome humanoid with chalky skin and reddish-brown hair and beard. Rams horns curling from his wide brow flicker with hellfire. Charred wings sprout from the fiend's back, revealing the last vestiges of his once angelic form.

Belial is the most capricious and chaotic of the princes of darkness, leaving many among the courts of Hell to wonder if he has not been fully corrupted by demonic influences. Belial, more than others has made pacts with demons, and dark gods of the Underworld. He is always on the hunt for portals that allow him greater time and access to the mortal realms.

Belial's lair of Pallus Lagnea is found in the storm-thundered Hell Ring of Covetous where the lightning-wracked skies flock with harpies, night hags, succubi, and erinyes. Belial's legions throng with his many progeny, themselves brutal combatants who use complex asymmetrical tactics to finish off foes who often greatly outnumber them.

Belial, Prince of Covetous, Lord of Lusts, Arch Devil

Medium fiend (devil), lawful evil

Armor Class 19 (natural armor)
Hit Points 276 (24d8 + 168)
Speed 40 ft., fly 60 ft.

STR	DEX	CON	INT	WIS	CHA
24 (+7)	22 (+6)	24 (+7)	24 (+7)	18 (+4)	28 (+9)

Saving Throws Constitution +14, Wisdom +11, Charisma +16
Skills Arcana +14, Acrobatics +13, Deception +16, Insight +11, Intimidation +16, Perception +11, Persuasion +16, Stealth +13
Damage Resistances cold; bludgeoning, piercing, and slashing from nonmagical attacks that are not silver
Damage Immunities fire, poison
Condition Immunities poisoned
Senses darkvision 60 ft., passive Perception 21
Languages Abyssal, Common, Celestial, Elven, Dwarven, Draconic, Halfling, Giant, Gnome, Goblin, Infernal, Orc, telepathy 100 ft.
Challenge 22 (41,000 XP)

Charming Devil. Belial has a way with words, which he infuses with his own Hellish pheromones. At the start of his turn, Belial chooses one of the following effects:
Indecent Proposal. All who can hear Belial and are within 30 feet must succeed on a DC 25 Wisdom saving throw or suffer the effects of the spell *suggestion.*
Maleficent Mesmerism. Belial suggestive charms and animal magnetism leave his listeners enrapt in his words so that they are unable to move save to gape at his animal magnetism. All who can see Belial and are within 30 feet must succeed on a DC 25 Wisdom saving throw or become incapacitated until the end of their next turn.

Devil's Sight. Magical darkness doesn't impede the devil's darkvision.

Legendary Resistance (3/day). If Belial fails a saving throw, he can choose to succeed instead.

Magic Resistance. Belial has advantage on saving throws against spells and other magical effects.

Magic Weapons. Belial's weapon attacks are magical.

Regeneration. Belial regains 10 hit points at the start of his turn. If Belial takes damage from a silvered weapon, this trait doesn't function at the start of Belial's next turn. Belial is destroyed only if he starts his turn with 0 hit points and doesn't regenerate.

Innate Spellcasting. Belial's innate spellcasting ability is Charisma (spell save DC 24, +16 to hit with spell attacks). He can cast the following spells, requiring no material components:
At will: *bane, dispel magic, detect evil and good, detect magic, detect thoughts, dominate beast, dominate monster, enthrall, hold monster, hold person, magic circle, modify memory, suggestion, teleport* (self only)
1/day: *antipathy/sympathy, mass suggestion*
1/week *wish*

Actions

Multiattack. Belial makes one Fork of Suffering attack and two Corrupting Touch attacks.

Fork of Suffering. *Melee Weapon Attack:* +14 to hit, reach 10 ft., one target. *Hit:* 25 (4d8 + 7) piercing damage and the target must succeed on a DC 21 Constitution saving throw or suffer an additional 7 (2d6) necrotic damage at the start of each of its turns. The target creature may attempt the save after suffering the additional damage, ending the effect with a successful save. The effect ends if the target creature is the recipient of healing magic.

Corrupting Touch. *Melee Weapon Attack:* +14 to hit, reach 5 ft., one target. *Hit:* 20 (3d8 + 7) psychic damage and the target must succeed on a DC 24 Wisdom saving throw or become charmed by Belial for one minute.

Legendary Actions

Belial can take three legendary actions, choosing from the options below. Only one legendary action can be used at a time and only at the end of another creature's turn. Belial regains spent legendary actions at the start of his turn.

Spear Thrust. Belial makes a Fork of Suffering attack.

Hordes of Admirers. Belial summons 2d6 commoners he has corrupted on the mortal planes and brings them to his palace for his own amusement, causing them to appear within 30 feet of Belial. They are useless in battle but provide a convenient distraction and slow attackers.

Wing Buffet (costs 2 actions). Belial buffets the air with his wings to create a 20-foot cone of powerful wind. All creatures caught in this area must succeed at a DC 25 Strength check or be knocked prone and pushed 15 feet away from Belial.

Fiendish Recovery (costs 2 actions). Belial recovers 50 hit points and ends one condition affecting him.

DEVIL, CAASIMOLAR
(FORMER PRESIDENT OF HELL)

A small hut sat among the dead trees, a thin line of gray smoke rising from its stone chimney. Windchimes carved from animal bones clattered and creaked in the weak breeze as two starving goats grazed on the sparse grasses. An elderly man with a long gray beard sat on a porch swing and watched us approach. His wrinkled scalp was burned by the sun. "Look here, lads! Visitors! What could they want?" He addressed the goats when he spoke. Gase Crabtree didn't listen. He stormed the porch and walked right into the man's home, but came out a moment later. "Where's the blasted ale?" The old man made a tsk, tsk sound and swung his walking stick right into Gase's ribs. The arrogant warrior was knocked backward into the dwelling and never came out again. We had other things to worry about, though, as the "goats" transformed into ravenous demons. — Tienna Moonmoth, elf enchantress of the Green Realm

Caasimolar appears as a bald, wizened old man with a reddish-gray beard and the blackened wings of one of the original fallen. Dressed in robes of gold and scarlet, he bears a ruby-tipped iron rod covered in wicked thorns that is known as "The Rule of Law." Caasimolar serves as chief councilor, advisor, and regent to his lord, the Lightbringer.

Caasimolar was once second-in-command of all of the legions of Hell, answering directly to the Lightbringer during his volatile reign as ruler of the nine Rings of Hell. In his role as president, Caasimolar oversaw the congress of devils and used his guile to negotiate terms between the factions of the fallen until the Second Schism that resulted in the current state of civil war between the rival princes.

CAASIMOLAR,
FORMER PRESIDENT OF HELL,
ARCH DEVIL
Medium fiend (devil), lawful evil

Armor Class 22 (natural armor)
Hit Points 337 (25d8 + 225)
Speed 50 ft.

STR	DEX	CON	INT	WIS	CHA
28 (+9)	28 (+9)	28 (+9)	30 (+10)	30 (+10)	30 (+10)

Saving Throws Constitution +16, Wisdom +17, Intelligence +17, Charisma +17
Skills Arcana +17, Deception +17, Insight +17, Intimidation +17, History +17, Religion +17, Perception +17, Persuasion +17
Damage Resistances cold; bludgeoning, piercing, and slashing from nonmagical attacks that are not silver
Damage Immunities fire, poison
Condition Immunities poisoned
Senses darkvision 60 ft., passive Perception 27
Languages Abyssal, Common, Celestial, Demonic, Draconic, Infernal, telepathy 100 ft.
Challenge 24 (62,000 XP)

Devil's Sight. Magical darkness doesn't impede the devil's darkvision.

Innate Spellcasting. Caasimolar's innate spellcasting ability is Charisma (spell save DC 25, +17 to hit with spell attacks). He can cast the following spells, requiring no material components:
At will: *animate dead, cone of cold, detect evil and good, detect magic, detect thoughts, dispel magic, invisibility, magic circle, polymorph, teleport* (self only), *tongues, true seeing*
3/day: *wall of ice*
1/day each: *lightning bolt, power word kill*

Legendary Resistance (3/day). If Caasimolar fails a saving throw, he can choose to succeed instead.

Magic Resistance. Caasimolar has advantage on saving throws against spells and other magical effects.

Magic Weapons. Caasimolar's weapon attacks are magical.

Regeneration. Caasimolar regains 10 hit points at the start of his turn. If Caasimolar takes damage from a silvered weapon, this trait doesn't function at the start of Caasimolar's next turn. Caasimolar is destroyed only if he starts his turn with 0 hit points and doesn't regenerate.

ACTIONS

Multiattack. Caasimolar makes three Iron Rule of Law attacks.

Iron Rule of Law. *Melee Weapon Attack*: +16 to hit, reach 10 ft., one target. *Hit*: 35 (4d12 + 9) bludgeoning damage and the target must make a DC 26 Constitution save. The target dies on a failure while on a success it takes 27 (5d10) psychic damage.

Contractual Obligations. Caasimolar carries a copy of the *Doctrines of Hell*, a legal tome that he may use to write contracts. The contracts allow him to cast *geas* or *symbol* once per day.

LEGENDARY ACTIONS

Caasimolar can take three legendary actions, choosing from the options below. Only one legendary action can be used at a time and only at the end of another creature's turn. Caasimolar regains spent legendary actions at the start of his turn.

Hammer of the Law. Caasimolar makes an Iron Rule of Law attack.

Halt in the Name of the Law. Caasimolar targets one creature who must succeed at a DC 27 Wisdom saving throw or become incapacitated until the end of its next turn.

Signed in Blood (costs 2 actions). All creatures within 30 feet of Caasimolar must make a DC 27 Wisdom saving throw. On a failure, the creature is subject to Caasimolar's will as per the spell *suggestion* on a failure, while on a success the creature takes 17 (5d6) psychic damage.

Fiendish Recovery (costs 2 actions). Caasimolar recovers 50 hit points and ends one condition affecting him.

Devil, Gorson
(Blood Duke of Aplistia)

The rock wall collapsed on Aylmer, burying the paladin under tons of heavy boulders. Voyce scrambled over the stones, determined to pull the warrior from the rubble, but he barely made it to the top of the pile before dozens of spears launched from hidden holes in the walls. Three spears impaled the thief, and he collapsed atop the rock pile. At that moment, a glowing portal opened on the wall and a large cat leaped forth. Only it had a muscular upper body like a centaur with a head like a lion. The thing sliced Voyce apart with one swipe of its battleaxe. — Lodwicke Greene, seeking magical protection to hide him from something known as "Gorson"

Gorson is a centaur with the muscular body of a great cat and the head of a goat-horned lion. It has the torso of a beast man and a bifurcated devil's tail sprouts from his rump. Gorson is a vicious combatant who favors disemboweling his foes. The beastly Gorson serves as a bodyguard to the greedy Mammon and is never far from the Miser's side. Despite his ferocity, Gorson has a keen intellect and is a clever military strategist who often places traps for his foes to injure them before he moves in for the kill.

Gorson, Blood Duke of Aplistia, Arch Devil
Large fiend (devil), lawful evil

Armor Class 22 (natural armor)
Hit Points 391 (27d10 + 243)
Speed 50 ft.

STR	DEX	CON	INT	WIS	CHA
30 (+10)	28 (+9)	28 (+9)	20 (+5)	20 (+5)	20 (+5)

Saving Throws Constitution +16, Wisdom +12, Charisma +12
Skills Deception +12, Insight +12, Intimidation +12, Perception +12, Persuasion +12, Stealth +16
Damage Resistances cold; bludgeoning, piercing, and slashing from nonmagical attacks that are not silver
Damage Immunities fire, poison
Condition Immunities poisoned
Senses darkvision 60 ft., passive Perception 22
Languages Abyssal, Celestial, Common, Draconic, Goblin, Ignan, Infernal, telepathy 100 ft.
Challenge 22 (41,000 XP)

Devil's Sight. Magical darkness doesn't impede the devil's darkvision.

Innate Spellcasting. Gorson's innate spellcasting ability is Charisma (spell save DC 20, +12 to hit with spell attacks). He can cast the following spells, requiring no material components:

At will: *animate dead, bane, charm monster, detect evil and good, detect magic, detect thoughts, dispel magic, lightning bolt, magic circle, see invisibility, suggestion, teleport* (self), *tongues, wall of fire*

1/day: *symbol*

Legendary Resistance (3/day). If Gorson fails a saving throw, he can choose to succeed instead.

Magic Resistance. Gorson has advantage on saving throws against spells and other magical effects.

Magic Weapons. Gorson's weapon attacks are magical.

Regeneration. Gorson regains 10 hit points at the start of his turn. If Gorson takes damage from a silvered weapon, this trait doesn't function at the start of Gorson's next turn. Gorson is destroyed only if he starts his turn with 0 hit points and doesn't regenerate.

Actions

Multiattack. Gorson makes one Battleaxe attack and two Claw attacks.

Battleaxe. *Melee Weapon Attack*: +17 to hit, reach 5 ft., one target. *Hit*: 23 (2d12 + 10) slashing damage plus 17 (5d6) necrotic damage.

Claw. *Melee Weapon Attack*: +17 to hit, reach 5 ft., one target. *Hit*: 19 (2d8 + 10) slashing damage.

Legendary Actions

Gorson can take three legendary actions, choosing from the options below. Only one legendary action can be used at a time and only at the end of another creature's turn. Gorson regains spent legendary actions at the start of his turn.

No Pity. Gorson makes a Battleaxe attack.

Pounce and Rake. Gorson moves up to 50 feet and makes two Claw attacks with advantage.

Roar (costs 2 actions). Gorson lets loose a massive leonine roar. All creatures within a 30-foot cone originating from Gorson must make a DC 25 Constitution saving throw, taking 36 (8d8) thunder damage on a failure, or half as much on a success.

Fiendish Recovery (costs 2 actions). Gorson recovers 50 hit points and ends one condition affecting him.

TOME OF
HORRORS

DEVIL, THE LIGHTBRINGER
(PRINCE OF DARKNESS, PRINCE OF INFERNUS)

A fiery globe encased our ship as we sailed the Reaping Sea, a ball of flame so massive it encompassed our sails and masts with room to spare. Some of the sailors flung themselves over the Emerald Siren's rail, only to shriek as they were boiled alive in the steaming water trapped in the globe beneath us. They were the lucky ones. With a flash, the globe shrank, and while we felt the heat, it didn't burn us. Would that it had! When our eyes cleared, we found an impossible spiraling road lined with fiery shrines and temples rising above the ship. The Emerald Siren sat in the middle of this road, her hull shattered. She'd never sail again. A massive being on a massive malachite throne regarded us with a burning stare. His voice boomed when he spoke, "Greetings, mortals. I've grown bored. Your way home lies above. Let the game begin." — Raylon Cuthberry, ship's mage and one of six members of the Emerald Siren's crew to return home after going missing for three years

The Lightbringer is always the tallest and most perfect thing in the room. He most often reveals himself as a beautiful angelic form with golden hair, pale skin, and a handsome face. All of this is belied by the curving horns that sprout from his broad brow. Wooly goat legs and hooved feet hide beneath crisp white robes whose hems are stained in blood. Charred-black, lice-infested wings sprout from the Lightbringer's back. He sometimes assumes a different form, one that is still handsome, but with reddish skin and a gaze of raw hellfire and hatred, all encased in spiked black armor.

If any of the Rings of Hell resemble a mortal's ideal of Hell, it is the Pit of Infernus where the Lightbringer bides his time and makes his plots. Infernus, his Ring of Hell, is a dark reflection of his most painful memories of the High Heavens and is dotted with temples, basilicas, and shrines that are all dedicated to his own worship. They are places of fire, blood, and torment where the damned are tortured. These burning structures line a great spiral road that descends into the great pit where his palace Malefacta stands. The Lightbringer often broods upon his throne and plots revenge against the rulers of the other Rings of Hell for past betrayals.

The Lightbringer frequently bears the burning sword *Phosphorus* and can call it to his fist from any dimension at will. In his other hand, he bears the ever-bleeding *Fork of Infernus* which has slain devils, demons, and angels alike.

THE LIGHTBRINGER, PRINCE OF DARKNESS,
PRINCE OF INFERNUS, ARCH DEVIL

Large fiend (devil), lawful evil

Armor Class 22 (natural armor)
Hit Points 405 (30d10 + 240)
Speed 40 ft., 60 ft.

STR	DEX	CON	INT	WIS	CHA
28 (+9)	28 (+9)	28 (+9)	30 (+10)	28 (+9)	30 (+10)

Saving Throws Strength +17, Dexterity +17, Constitution +17, Intelligence +18, Wisdom +17, Charisma +18
Skills Arcana +18, Deception +18, History +18, Insight +17, Intimidation +18, Nature +18, Perception +17, Persuasion +18, Religion +18, Stealth +17
Damage Resistances cold; bludgeoning, piercing, and slashing from nonmagical attacks that are not silver
Damage Immunities fire, poison
Condition Immunities poisoned
Senses darkvision 60 ft., passive Perception 27
Languages Abyssal, Celestial, Common, Dwarvish, Elven, Halfling, Giant, Gnomish, Goblin, Ignan, Infernal, Terran, telepathy 100 ft.
Challenge 28 (120,000 XP)

Devil's Sight. Magical darkness doesn't impede the devil's darkvision.
Innate Spellcasting. The Lightbringer's innate spellcasting ability is Charisma (spell save DC 25, +17 to hit with spell attacks). He can cast the following spells, requiring no material components:
At will: *altar self, animate dead, bane, detect evil and good, detect magic, detect thoughts, fireball, invisibility, magic circle, teleport* (self only), *tongues, true seeing, wall of fire, witch bolt, zone of truth*
3/day each: *dispel evil and good, raise dead, power word kill*
1/day: *wish*
Legendary Resistance (3/day). If the Lightbringer fails a saving throw, he can choose to succeed instead.
Magic Resistance. The Lightbringer has advantage on saving throws against spells and other magical effects.
Magic Weapons. The Lightbringer's weapon attacks are magical.
Regeneration. The Lightbringer regains 10 hit points at the start of its turn. If the Lightbringer takes damage from a silvered weapon, this trait doesn't function at the start of the Lightbringer's next turn. The Lightbringer is destroyed only if he starts his turn with 0 hit points and doesn't regenerate.

ACTIONS

Multiattack. The Lightbringer makes one Fork of Infernus attack and two Phosphorous attacks.
Fork of Infernus. *Melee or Ranged Weapon Attack:* +17 to hit, reach 10 ft. or range 100/400 ft., one target. *Hit:* 24 (3d10 + 8) piercing damage plus 36 (8d8) necrotic damage. If the target is a celestial, elemental, or fiend it must succeed on a DC 27 Constitution saving throw or be paralyzed. If the *Fork of Infernus* is thrown, it returns to the Lightbringer's hand at the end of his turn.
Phosphorous. *Melee Weapon Attack:* +17 to hit, reach 5 ft., one target. *Hit:* 19 (2d10 + 8) slashing damage plus 36 (8d8) fire damage and the target is set on fire. A creature set on fire by *Phosphorous* suffers 18 (4d8) fire damage at the start of its turn and may use its action to put the fire out. A creature reduced to 0 hit points by *Phosphorous* is slain and its soul consumed by the fire.

LEGENDARY ACTIONS

The Lightbringer can take three legendary actions, choosing from the options below. Only one legendary action can be used at a time and only at the end of another creature's turn. The Lightbringer regains spent legendary actions at the start of his turn.
Impale. The Lightbringer makes a *Fork of Infernus* attack.
Devilish Growth. The Lightbringer grows one size category, gaining 32 hit points and increasing the damage of his melee attacks by +10.
Wing Buffet (costs 2 actions). The Lightbringer buffets the air with his wings to create a 20-foot cone of powerful wind. All creatures caught in this area must succeed at a DC 25 Strength check or be knocked prone and pushed 15 feet away from the Lightbringer.
Fiendish Recovery (costs 2 actions). The Lightbringer recovers 50 hit points and ends one condition affecting it.

LAIR ACTIONS

On initiative count 20 (losing initiative ties), the Lightbringer takes a lair action from one of the following effects; the Lightbringer can't use the same effects two rounds in a row:
- All creatures within sight of the Lightbringer must succeed at a DC 25 Wisdom saving throw or fall under the sway of the Lightbringer as if they are under the effect of a dominate beast, dominate monster, or dominate person spell, as appropriate.
- The Lightbringer tempts his prey with conditional wishes. All creatures within sight of the Lightbringer must succeed at a DC 25 Wisdom saving throw or accept one of these conditional wishes. These wishes must be spoken completely perfectly to take effect. Failure to do so may result in instantaneous and utter damnation and loss of soul of the wish taker. Regardless, the soul of anyone accepting wishes from the Lightbringer is forfeit upon their natural (or unnatural) terrestrial demise.
- The Lightbringer summons 1d4 pit fiends to his side or summons one of his lieutenants such as Xaphan or Caasimolar.

Devil, Lillith
(Former Queen of Hell)

We found the basalt tower in the peaks of the Blackrock Mountains west of Malan. It appeared to have settled there, as it didn't match the rest of the mountains around it. The cultists we'd been following led us right to the only massive iron door into the structure. They still had the kids they'd taken from Malan with them. Looking up the rock pinnacle, sharp-eyed Gurd spotted the woman lounging on red cushions and looking down at all of us with an air of unconcern. She gave a flippant wave of her hand and ghostly spirits flew out toward us. — Aomos Jenns, Foerdewaith hero of Malan

Lilith is an insanely comely female standing just under six feet tall and weighing roughly 130 pounds. Her skin is cinnamon colored, and her hair is waist length and blood red. Her eyes are a sparkling emerald green. Her hands end in claws, and underneath her thick hair she hides two tiny dark black horns. She has a small pair of leathery black bat-like wings that she can fold against her back and hide under her robes at a moment's notice should the need for such deception arise.

Lillith was one of the original fallen and was once a powerful archangel who took great interest in the doings of mortals, especially primeval mortal males. Lillith allied with the Lightbringer during his revolution when she discovered that the gods were gathering the Watchers and imprisoning them in the Pits of Tartarus as punishment for their interactions with mortals.

She was also one of the original conspirators that cast the Lightbringer from the Throne of Hell which she took up briefly. She in turn was quickly overthrown in a second coup. Unfortunately for Lillith, her many betrayals mean that none of the other fallen trust her any longer. In spite of this, none can deny her great power. She keeps a heart-shaped fortress in the battle plains of Gehenna, which is guarded by six legions of horned devils, each of which is commanded by a pit fiend. She spends the majority of her time crossing into the mortal planes to tempt paladins and holy priests to damnation. She drags their souls back to her fortress for eternal punishment or presses them into service as fodder for her legions. She has a personal contingent of death knights, each of whom was once a lover that she seduced from the path of righteousness and good by her charms and machinations.

Lilith, Former Queen of Hell, Arch Devil
Medium fiend (devil), lawful evil

Armor Class 22 (natural armor)
Hit Points 297 (22d8 + 198)
Speed 40 ft., fly 60 ft.

STR	DEX	CON	INT	WIS	CHA
28 (+9)	28 (+9)	28 (+9)	30 (+10)	30 (+10)	30 (+10)

Saving Throws Constitution +16, Wisdom +17, Intelligence +17, Charisma +17
Skills Arcana +17, Deception +17, Insight +17, Intimidation +17, History +17, Religion +17, Perception +17, Persuasion +17
Damage Resistances cold; bludgeoning, piercing, and slashing from nonmagical attacks that are not silver
Damage Immunities fire, poison
Condition Immunities poisoned
Senses darkvision 60 ft., passive Perception 27
Languages Abyssal, Common, Celestial, Infernal, Terran, telepathy 100 ft.
Challenge 24 (62,000 XP)

Devil's Sight. Magical darkness doesn't impede the devil's darkvision.
Innate Spellcasting. Lillith's innate spellcasting ability is Charisma (spell save DC 25, +17 to hit with spell attacks). She can cast the following spells, requiring no material components:
At will: *alter self, animate dead, bane, detect evil and good, detect magic, detect thoughts, dispel magic, dominate monster, fireball, hold person, invisibility, magic circle, see invisibly, suggestion, true seeing, teleport* (self only)
3/day: *lightning bolt, wall of fire*
1/day: *power word kill*
1/week: *wish*
Legendary Resistance (3/day). If Lilith fails a saving throw, she can choose to succeed instead.
Magic Resistance. Lilith has advantage on saving throws against spells and other magical effects.
Magic Weapons. Lilith's weapon attacks are magical.
Regeneration. Lillith regains 10 hit points at the start of her turn. If Lillith takes damage from a silvered weapon, this trait doesn't function at the start of Lillith's next turn. Lillith is destroyed only if she starts her turn with 0 hit points and doesn't regenerate.

Simple Art of Seduction. Like others of the Infernal Court, Lillith uses her intellect and her charms to trick victims into succumbing to her wiles. At the start of her turn, Lillith chooses one of the following effects:
Indecent Proposal. Any creature who can hear Lillith and is within 30 feet must succeed on a DC 25 Wisdom saving throw or suffer the effects of a *suggestion* spell.
Maleficent Mesmerism. Lillith's suggestive charms and animal magnetism leave her listeners enrapt in her words so that they are unable to move save to gape at her animal magnetism. All who can see Lillith and are within 30 feet must succeed on a DC 25 Wisdom saving throw or become incapacitated until the end of their next turn.

Actions

Multiattack. The creature makes one Lillith's Kiss attack and two Amaheuris attacks.
Amaheuris. *Melee Weapon Attack*: +16 to hit, reach 5 ft., one target. *Hit*: 18 (2d8 + 9) slashing damage and the target must make a DC 24 Constitution saving throw, suffering 18 (4d8) necrotic damage on a failure, or half as much on a success.
Lillith's Kiss. *Melee Weapon Attack*: +16 to hit, reach 5 ft., one target. *Hit*: 41 (5d12 + 9) necrotic damage and the target must make a DC 25 Wisdom saving throw or become *charmed* by Lillith until the end of their next turn.

Legendary Actions

Lillith can take three legendary actions, choosing from the options below. Only one legendary action can be used at a time and only at the end of another creature's turn. Lillith regains spent legendary actions at the start of her turn.
Kiss and Spell. Lillith makes a Lillith's Kiss attack and casts a spell.
Lure (costs 2 actions). *One creature that Lillith can see and that can see her must succeed on a DC 25 Wisdom saving throw or use its reaction to move its full speed in a direction Lillith desires.*
Wing Buffet (costs 2 actions). Lillith buffets the air with her wings to create a 20-foot cone of powerful wind. All creatures caught in this area must succeed at a DC 25 Strength check or be knocked prone and pushed 15 feet away from Lillith.
Fiendish Recovery (costs 2 actions). Lillith recovers 50 hit points and ends one condition affecting her.

DEVIL, MAMMON
(THE MISER, PRINCE OF APLISTIA)

I can't get rid of them, ye understand? I've tried. I give them away, I throw them in the wells. Merchants throw me out when I offer them. But the coins always come back. I've been miserable since I took the bag from that old beggar. He didn't need them, ye understand? He was dressed in rags and looked so poor. I had to have them! He even smiled when I snatched them up and ran! He knew, I'm telling ye. Look at my hands! See the silver under my skin? I bleed that silver now. It's makin' me sick. So sick. It's the coins. They always come back and I always get sicker. I wish I could find that old man. He'd take them back. — Colson Foxe, confessing his crimes the day before he vanished from a locked room, leaving behind a bag of coins with his screaming likeness minted on them

Standing over 15 feet tall, Mammon is a thin, twisted fiend with the visage of a mad beggar who is dressed in filthy, stinking rags that were once the finery of a merchant lord or king. His filthy feet are stuffed into broken sandals or boots whose tops are worn so that gnarled toes show through. Charred wings billow with sulfurous ash as they flutter and twitch nervously upon the creature's back. The Miser's horns have been forcibly cut from his brow so that only smoldering stumps remain. Despite his otherwise impoverished appearance, the fiend's neck drips with gaudy jewelry of thick gold and platinum chains. Rings that are set with obviously flawed yet shiny gemstones flash upon filthy, clawed fingers that clutch a bag of red-hot coins to his breast.

Mammon rules the ring of Aplistia where he resides within a massive fortress-like bank made of bronze and antimony. He spends his time counting soul ingots and developing schemes for tempting mortals to greed so that he may collect more souls than his adversaries in the other eight Rings of Hell. Since tempting mortals to greed is quite easy, Mammon has become quite lazy in his workings. Despite this, he is still a horrifying figure and powerful ruler who hoards vast collections of souls within his basalt vaults.

The forges of his palace ring constantly with the work of his amiamons who pound worthless souls of the greedy into the coins of Hell, just as the worshippers of the Sultan of Brass do in the City of Brass. The Ring of Aplistia is exceedingly hot. It is made up of mountains of searing-hot bronze, lakes and rivers of molten copper, and vast sulfuric deserts. It is a blasted landscape littered with the ghostly remains of destroyed mortal cities plundered for their wealth.

MAMMON, THE MISER, PRINCE OF APLISTIA, ARCH DEVIL

Huge fiend (devil), lawful evil

Armor Class 18 (natural armor)
Hit Points 364 (27d12 + 189)
Speed 30 ft.

STR	DEX	CON	INT	WIS	CHA
24 (+7)	22 (+6)	24 (+7)	24 (+7)	18 (+4)	28 (+9)

Saving Throws Constitution +14, Wisdom +11, Charisma +16
Skills Arcana +14, Acrobatics +14, Deception +16, Insight +11, Intimidation +16, Perception +11, Persuasion +16, Stealth +13
Damage Resistances cold; bludgeoning, piercing, and slashing from nonmagical attacks that are not silver
Damage Immunities fire, poison
Condition Immunities poisoned
Senses darkvision 60 ft., passive Perception 21
Languages Abyssal, Celestial, Common, Dwarvish, Elven, Halfling, Giant, Gnomish, Goblin, Ignan, Infernal, Terran, telepathy 100 ft.
Challenge 22 (41,000 XP)

Devil's Sight. Magical darkness doesn't impede the devil's darkvision.
Innate Spellcasting. Mammon's innate spellcasting ability is Charisma (spell save DC 24, +16 to hit with spell attacks). He can cast the following spells, requiring no material components:
At will: *animate dead, cone of cold, detect evil and good, detect magic, detect thoughts, dispel magic, invisibility, magic circle, polymorph, teleport* (self only), *tongues, true seeing*
3/day: *wall of fire*
1/day each: *fire ball, power word kill*
Legendary Resistance (3/day). If Mammon fails a saving throw, he can choose to succeed instead.
Magic Resistance. Mammon has advantage on saving throws against spells and other magical effects.
Magic Weapons. Mammon's weapon attacks are magical.
Regeneration. Mammon regains 10 hit points at the start of his turn. If Mammon takes damage from a silvered weapon, this trait doesn't function at the start of Mammon's next turn. Mammon is destroyed only if he starts his turn with 0 hit points and doesn't regenerate.

ACTIONS

Multiattack. Mammon makes one Withering Touch attack and two Red-Hot Coin attacks.
Withering Touch. *Melee Weapon Attack:* +14 to hit, reach 5 ft., one target. *Hit:* 20 (2d12 + 7) slashing damage and the target must make a DC 22 Constitution saving throw. The target takes 36 (8d8) necrotic damage and has a random limb rendered useless for 24 hours on a failure, or half as much damage and no withered body part on a successful save.

RANDOM WITHERED LIMB PART

1d4	Body Part	Effect
1	Left Leg	Halve speed
2	Right Leg	Halve speed
3	Right Arm	Drops anything in that arm, and arm is useless
4	Left Arm	Drops anything in that arm, and arm is useless

Red-Hot Coin. *Ranged Weapon Attack:* +13 to hit, range 50/200 ft., one target. *Hit:* 13 (2d6 + 6) fire damage and the target must succeed on a DC 24 Dexterity saving throw or spend its next turn digging the coin out of its flesh. The creature is stunned until the end of its next turn, unable to do much else but chase down the burning coin. Digging the coin out causes 14 (4d6) slashing damage.
***Avalanche of Greed* (recharge 5–6).** Mammon spills a wave of red-hot coins from his bag in a 30-foot cone. All creatures caught in the area must make a DC 21 Dexterity saving throw, suffering 45 (10d8) bludgeoning damage and 14 (4d6) fire damage on a failure, or half as much on a success.

LEGENDARY ACTIONS

Mammon can take three legendary actions, choosing from the options below. Only one legendary action can be used at a time and only at the end of another creature's turn. Mammon regains spent legendary actions at the start of his turn.
One for You and Three for Me. Mammon makes a Red-Hot Coin attack.
You Get Damned Coins, and You Get Damned Coins. Mammon recharges his Avalanche of Greed and uses it.
***Insatiable Greed* (costs 2 actions).** Mammon can instill his own wretched greed upon others by tossing a handful of his hellish coins into the midst of his enemies. Anyone within a 30-foot cube centered on Mammon must make a successful DC 24 Charisma saving throw or be overwhelmed with desire to possess his hellish coins, stopping at nothing to possess them, including slaying friend and family alike for their ownership.
***Fiendish Recovery* (costs 2 actions).** Mammon recovers 50 hit points and ends one condition affecting him.

DEVIL, MOLOCH

Our horses were already tired when we spotted the contraption rolling across the plains of Reme. It was as big as a building and bounced along on two great rollers that flattened anything before it. The sides were covered in spikes that held the still-writhing bodies of the last Rheman village it had rolled over. Riding on a seat at the front was a devilish being more than twice my height. I saw blue eyes turn in our direction, and it raised a metal whip in salute. Then the vehicle turned in our direction. We pushed our horses harder. There was no turning back. — Achak Alo of the Thunder Riders Loreclan

Moloch is a 15-foot-tall, thick-necked brute with curving black horns protruding from a squat, wide-mouthed head with glowing ice blue eyes and needle-like teeth. The beast has reddish-brown flesh wreathed in gold and red robes made of silk and satin. The fiend bears a six-flanged metal scourge that crackles with raw electricity.

Moloch leads a secret insurrection in the heart of Stygia against his master Baalzebul. As far as Baalzebal knows, Moloch is a loyal lieutenant and seneschal of his courts who bravely fights to defend Stygia against incursions. But Moloch is ever alert for opportunities to lower Baalzebul's status among the various rulers of the Rings of Hell.

Moloch is known to grant favors to warlocks, assassins, clerics, and wizards who venerate a secret cult known as the Knights of Moloch. The Knights of Moloch are known to spread disinformation and commit murders designed to destabilize governments and topple religious institutions.

MOLOCH, ARCH DEVIL

Large fiend (devil), lawful evil

Armor Class 24 (natural armor)
Hit Points 319 (22d10 + 192)
Speed 50 ft.

STR	DEX	CON	INT	WIS	CHA
30 (+10)	28 (+9)	28 (+9)	20 (+5)	20 (+5)	20 (+5)

Saving Throws Constitution +16, Wisdom +12, Charisma +12
Skills Deception +12, Insight +12, Intimidation +12, Perception +12, Persuasion +12, Stealth +16
Damage Resistances cold; bludgeoning, piercing, and slashing from nonmagical attacks that are not silver
Damage Immunities fire, poison
Condition Immunities poisoned
Senses darkvision 60 ft., passive Perception 22
Languages Abyssal, Celestial, Common, Draconic, Giant, Goblin, Infernal, Undercommon, telepathy 100 ft.
Challenge 22 (41,000 XP)

Devil's Sight. Magical darkness doesn't impede the devil's darkvision.
Innate Spellcasting. Moloch's innate spellcasting ability is Charisma (spell save DC 20, +12 to hit with spell attacks). He can cast the following spells, requiring no material components:
At will: *animate dead, bane, detect evil and good, detect magic, detect thoughts, dispel magic, hold person, invisibility, magic circle, see invisibly, suggestion, true seeing, teleport* (self only)
3/day each: *lightning bolt, wall of fire*
1/day: *flame strike, symbol*
Legendary Resistance (3/day). If Moloch fails a saving throw, he can choose to succeed instead.
Magic Resistance. The devil has advantage on saving throws against spells and other magical effects.
Magic Weapons. Moloch's weapon attacks are magical.
Regeneration. Moloch regains 10 hit points at the start of its turn. If Moloch takes damage from a silvered weapon, this trait doesn't function at the start of Moloch's next turn. Moloch is destroyed only if he starts his turn with 0 hit points and doesn't regenerate.

ACTIONS

Multiattack. Moloch makes one Kraken's Bite attack and two Claw attacks.
Kraken's Bite. *Melee Weapon Attack:* +17 to hit, reach 15 ft., two targets. *Hit:* 26 (3d10 + 10) slashing damage and the targets are restrained (escape DC 26). *Kraken's Bite* is a whip with six tails and can restrain only six creatures.
Claws. *Melee Weapon Attack:* +17 to hit, reach 10 ft., one target. *Hit:* 36 (4d12 + 10) slashing damage.
Cone of Cold and Fear (recharge 4–6). Moloch breathes a 30-foot cone of frigid air filled with the shrieking voices of the damned. Each creature in the area must make a DC 24 Constitution saving throw, taking 45 (10d8) cold damage and being frightened until the end of their next turn on a failure, or half as much damage and not being frightened on a success.

LEGENDARY ACTIONS

Moloch can take three legendary actions, choosing from the options below. Only one legendary action can be used at a time and only at the end of another creature's turn. Moloch regains spent legendary actions at the start of his turn.
Release the … Moloch makes a Kraken's Bite attack.
Deep Breath. Moloch recharges and uses its Cone of Cold and Fear attack.
Spread Betrayal (costs 2 actions). All creatures within 30 feet of Moloch must succeed on a DC 20 Wisdom saving throw or use their reaction to attack the nearest of their allies.
Fiendish Recovery (costs 2 actions). Moloch recovers 50 hit points and ends one condition affecting him.

Devil, Titivilus (Duke of Dis)

I swear, the gold key was right there on the floor when you tossed me and Peridis in here. You were rough, too. We weren't griftin' the crowd, I swear. One of you musta dropped it. Peridis grabbed it and put it in the lock and that cell door creaked right open. I told him it hadda be a trap, but he wouldn't listen. Rushed right through. And that's when everythin' changed. He ran right through a glowin' portal and beyond it was this large goat-man with bat wings. And I could see other prison cells around him. Much worse'n this one. — Ezra Mark, describing how his partner in crime vanished from a locked cell

Titivilus, the Duke of Dis, is a large satyr with the lower half of a goat and the upper body of a powerfully built bald man. Black leather wings sprout from his back, and his coal-black eyes show no whites. A known manipulator of facts, Titivilus spends most of his hours in his black iron tower in the Prison City of Tormenture scheming up ways to gain control over one of the Rings of Hell for himself. His black basalt tower is guarded by a personal legion of erinyes and bearded devils. Titivilus wields a magical silver rapier in battle.

Arch Devil, Titivilus, Duke of Dis

Medium fiend (devil), lawful evil

Armor Class 22 (natural armor)
Hit Points 312 (25d8 + 200)
Speed 50 ft., fly 60 ft.

STR	DEX	CON	INT	WIS	CHA
26 (+8)	18 (+4)	26 (+8)	24 (+7)	18 (+4)	28 (+9)

Saving Throws Constitution +14, Wisdom +11, Charisma +16
Skills Arcana +14, Acrobatics +11, Deception +16, Insight +11, Intimidation +16, Perception +11, Persuasion +16, Stealth +11
Damage Resistances cold; bludgeoning, piercing, and slashing from nonmagical attacks that are not silver
Damage Immunities fire, poison
Condition Immunities poisoned
Senses darkvision 60 ft., passive Perception 21
Languages Abyssal, Common, Celestial, Demonic, Draconic, Giant, Ignan, Infernal, Terran, telepathy 100 ft.
Challenge 22 (41,000 XP)

Devil's Sight. Magical darkness doesn't impede the devil's darkvision.
Magic Resistance. Titivilus has advantage on saving throws against spells and other magical effects.
Magic Weapons. Titivilus' weapon attacks are magical.
Regeneration. Titivilus regains 10 hit points at the start of his turn. If Titivilus takes damage from a silvered weapon, this trait doesn't function at the start of Titivilus' next turn. Titivilus is destroyed only if he starts his turn with 0 hit points and doesn't regenerate.
Innate Spellcasting. Titivilus' innate spellcasting ability is Charisma (spell save DC 24, +16 to hit with spell attacks). He can cast the following spells, requiring no material components:
At will: *animate dead, bane, charm person, confusion, detect evil and good, detect thoughts, dispel magic, fear, hold monster, hypnotic pattern, invisibility, magic circle, message, polymorph, suggestion, teleport* (self only), *tongues, true seeing*
1/day each: *feeblemind, symbol*
1/week: *wish*

Actions

Multiattack. Titivilus makes one Silver Rapier attack and two Fear Touch attacks.
Silver Rapier. *Melee Weapon Attack:* +15 to hit, reach 5 ft., one target. *Hit:* 14 (2d6 + 7) piercing damage plus 18 (4d8) necrotic damage. The target must make a DC 23 Constitution saving throw, suffering an additional 18 (4d8) necrotic damage at the beginning of each of their turns on a failure. The target may repeat the saving throw after suffering this damage, ending the effect on a success.
Fear Touch. *Melee Weapon Attack:* +15 to hit, reach 5 ft., one target. *Hit:* 14 (2d6 + 7) psychic damage and the target must succeed on a DC 24 Wisdom saving throw or be frightened of Titivilus for one minute.

Legendary Actions

Titivilus can take three legendary actions, choosing from the options below. Only one legendary action can be used at a time and only at the end of another creature's turn. Titivilus regains spent legendary actions at the start of his turn.
Quick Lunge. Titivilus makes a Silver Rapier attack.
Lingering Nightmares. Titivilus inflicts an additional 18 (4d8) psychic damage on the next target he hits with his Fear Touch attack.
Wing Buffet (costs 2 actions). Titivilus buffets the air with his wings to create a 20-foot cone of powerful wind. All creatures caught in this area must succeed at a DC 25 Strength check or be knocked prone and pushed 30 feet away from Titivilus.
Fiendish Recovery (costs 2 actions). Titivilus recovers 50 hit points and ends one condition affecting him.

We thought it was an angel sent from Muir. Pity us, for we did. It soared out of the clouds with the majesty of the divine. How wrong we were. It slammed into High Priest Paynos, gutting the man and igniting him with the flames covering its body. As our leader fell, the rest of us grabbed our weapons, hoping to stop this evil thing that was half goat and half man. Underpriest Frill went next, felled by some unseen magic. Something hit me hard, and I dropped, losing all sense. I woke in darkness, pinned by the bodies of my fellow priests. — Priestess Fransine Tung, only survivor of the massacre in the temple of Muir in Corvusrook

Xaphan, the Burning Duke, retained some semblance of his angelic looks after the fall of the angels. He still has a handsome face and a long braid that runs down his back. His small burnished horns glow like molten bronze. Xaphan stands 13 feet tall and is satyr-like, and has the lower half of a goat and the upper body of a powerful humanoid. Large leathery wings sprout from his back, and he is frequently coated in a sheen of hell fire.

Xaphan was cast down along with The Lightbringer and the other angels for their sacrilege, and it is said he helped The Lightbringer construct Hell itself. It is known among scholars that Xaphan was the one who stoked Hell's furnaces in The Lightbringer's great basalt palace, powering the furnaces with unholy fire fed by tortured souls. Where Caasimolar serves as regent of the Lightbringer's holdings, Xaphan, an advanced pit fiend in the order of Alastor, serves as general of The Lightbringer's armies.

The Burning Duke leads 15 companies of pit fiends in The Lightbringer's service. He is completely loyal to the Prince of Darkness and was with The Lightbringer during the Unholy Schism. It was Xaphan who attempted to set the heavens on fire during the Unholy Schism to consume each and every angel and celestial in a blazing inferno.

XAPHAN, THE BURNING DUKE, DUKE OF INFERNUS, ARCH DEVIL

Large fiend (devil), lawful evil

Armor Class 22 (natural armor)
Hit Points 362 (25d10 + 225)
Speed 50 ft., fly 60 ft.

STR	DEX	CON	INT	WIS	CHA
28 (+9)	18 (+4)	28 (+9)	24 (+7)	18 (+4)	24 (+7)

Saving Throws Constitution +16, Wisdom +11, Charisma +14
Skills Arcana +14, Acrobatics +11, Deception +14, Insight +11, Intimidation +14, Perception +11, Persuasion +14, Stealth +11
Damage Resistances cold; bludgeoning, piercing, and slashing from nonmagical attacks that are not silver
Damage Immunities fire, poison
Condition Immunities poisoned
Senses darkvision 60 ft., passive Perception 21
Languages Abyssal, Common, Celestial, Demonic, Draconic, Giant, Ignan, Infernal, Terran, telepathy 100 ft.
Challenge 22 (41,000 XP)

Devil's Sight. Magical darkness doesn't impede the devil's darkvision.
Fiery Aura. Any creature that begins its turn within 10 feet of Xaphan suffers 7 (2d6) fire damage.
Fiery Gaze. When a target starts its turn within 30 feet of Xaphan and is able to see Xaphan's eyes, Xaphan can magically force it to make a DC 19 Wisdom saving throw, unless Xaphan is incapacitated. On a failed saving throw the target suffers 18 (4d8) fire damage. Unless surprised, a target can avert its eyes to avoid the saving throw at the start of its turn. If the target does so, it can't see Xaphan until the start if its next turn, when it can avert its eyes again. If the target looks at Xaphan in the meantime, it must immediately make the save.

Innate Spellcasting. Xaphan's innate spellcasting ability is Charisma (spell save DC 22, +14 to hit with spell attacks). he can cast the following spells, requiring no material components:

At will: *animate dead, bane, call lightning, detect evil and good, detect thoughts, dispel magic, hold monster, invisibility, lightning bolt, magic circle, polymorph, scorching ray, teleport* (self only), *tongues, true seeing, wall of fire*
3/day each: *control weather, fireball*

Legendary Resistance (3/day). If Xaphan fails a saving throw, he can choose to succeed instead.
Magic Resistance. Xaphan has advantage on saving throws against spells and other magical effects.
Magic Weapons. Xaphan's weapon attacks are magical.
Regeneration. Xaphan regains 10 hit points at the start of its turn. If Xaphan takes damage from a silvered weapon, this trait doesn't function at the start of Xaphan's next turn. Xaphan is destroyed only if he starts his turn with 0 hit points and doesn't regenerate.

ACTIONS

Multiattack. Xaphan makes one Hellstorm Sword attack and two Claw attacks.
Hellstorm Sword. *Melee Weapon Attack:* +16 to hit, reach 5 ft., one target. *Hit:* 18 (2d8 + 9) slashing damage plus 18 (4d8) fire damage.
Claw. *Melee Weapon Attack:* +16 to hit, reach 5 ft., one target. *Hit:* 16 (2d6 + 9) slashing damage.

LEGENDARY ACTIONS

Xaphan can take three legendary actions, choosing from the options below. Only one legendary action can be used at a time and only at the end of another creature's turn. Xaphan regains spent legendary actions at the start of his turn.

Quick Swipe. Xaphan makes a Hellstorm Sword attack.
Hellstorm Burst. *Xaphan's next* Hellstorm Sword *attack explodes on the target. The target and all creatures within 30 feet of it must make a DC 19 Dexterity saving throw, suffering 9 (2d8) fire and 9 (2d8) thunder damage on a failure, or half as much on a success.*
Wing Buffet (costs 2 actions). Xaphan buffets the air with its wings to create a 20-foot cone of powerful wind. All creatures caught in this area must succeed at a DC 25 Strength check or be knocked prone and pushed 30 feet away from Xaphan.
Fiendish Recovery (costs 2 actions). Xaphan recovers 50 hit points and ends one condition affecting him.

DINOSAURS

DINOSAUR, ALLOSAURUS

We ascended the plateau on the third day of Oeros. The lower slopes of the central mountain were covered with a broad savannah upon which a plentitude of large reptiles grazed. During our second night on the plateau, we heard the bleating of the mules followed by the screams of the guards. Turning out of my tent with sword in hand, I rushed to the scene of carnage, arriving in time to see a massive tiger-striped tail covered in scales and feathers held aloft as a balance as the beast plunged back into the darkness. Of two mules, only a few scraps of hide and limbs remained. Of our night guards, Piotr and Rastalivic, no trace remained save a broken helm and a snapped spear. — Algrid Henswaithe, University of the Vast

While smaller than the more famous Tyrannosaurus rex, the allosaurus is a fearsome predator. It is far stealthier than its larger kin and more likely to strike in ambush from behind large trees. Allosauruses tend to travel in pairs, either mated pairs or a pair of siblings of the same sex. Territorial, allosauruses are known to track foes for miles before making their presence known in a snarling, roaring attack.

ALLOSAURUS
Large beast, unaligned

Armor Class 13 (natural armor)
Hit Points 51 (6d10 + 18)
Speed 60 ft.

STR	DEX	CON	INT	WIS	CHA
19 (+4)	13 (+1)	17 (+3)	2 (–4)	12 (+1)	5 (–3)

Skills Perception +5
Senses passive Perception 15
Languages —
Challenge 2 (450 XP)

Pounce. If the allosaurus moves at least 30 feet straight toward a creature and then hits it with a claw attack on the same turn, that target must succeed on a DC 13 Strength saving throw or be knocked prone. If the target is prone, the allosaurus can make one bite attack against it as a bonus action.

ACTIONS

Bite. Melee Weapon Attack: +6 to hit, reach 5 ft., one target. *Hit:* 15 (2d10 + 4) piercing damage.
Claw. Melee Weapon Attack: +6 to hit, reach 5 ft., one target. *Hit:* 8 (1d8 + 4) slashing damage.

DINOSAUR, ANKYLOSAURUS

I silently raised my hand to call a halt to our hunting party. There, just barely discernable through the trees lining the stream, was a large reptile. It was squat, moving its massive bulk on four stout legs, with a back covered in armored ridges and spikes. As we watched, it grazed upon low-hanging foliage, its long tail swinging back and forth a few feet off the ground. The tail was tipped with a massive bulbous growth of bone, something like a mace. As our artist Haldric began quickly applying charcoal to parchment, the beast raised its head as if sensing our presence. We began to slowly fall back, but were too late. It charged, using its wicked tail to full effect. — Algrid Henswaithe, University of the Vast

Ankylosauruses are four-legged herbivores that graze on low-lying vegetation along the jungle's margins, be they the edge of the jungle, glades, or the banks of streams. Their bodies are encased in thick, scaly armor that features many points along the edges and down the back. Their tails are long and held aloft behind them. These tails are often tipped with a bony head although some have fluted spikes, but they are always strong and flexible. Ankylosauruses are irritable and nearsighted; they prefer to feel out strange creatures with a few tail whacks, just to be careful.

DINOSAUR, ANKYLOSAURUS
Huge beast, unaligned

Armor Class 16 (natural armor)
Hit Points 95 (10d12 + 30)
Speed 30 ft.

STR	DEX	CON	INT	WIS	CHA
21 (+5)	11 (+0)	16 (+3)	2 (–4)	10 (+0)	6 (–2)

Senses passive Perception 10
Languages —
Challenge 4 (1,100 XP)

ACTIONS

Tail. Melee Weapon Attack: +7 to hit, reach 10 ft., one target. *Hit:* 23 (4d8 + 5) bludgeoning damage and Large or smaller targets must succeed on a DC 16 Strength check or be knocked prone and stunned until the end of their next turn.

TOME OF
HORRORS

DINOSAUR, DIPLODOCUS

A large lake filled a depression at the base of the central mountains. As we penetrated the lowlands south of the basin, we discovered a large swampy area of ferns and cycads. Some of the bodies of water were far deeper than they seemed, which led us to misidentify the creature. At first we saw a long neck rising out of the murky water, a massive lily pad slowly being munched in its small jaws. The neck craned around to look at us, and it did not like what it saw. I did not fear, for there was little doubt in my mind we were looking at some sort of herbivorous snake. I must admit I was wrong, for the massive body that thundered out of the deep pool was larger than an elephant and much more powerful. We lost three good porters that day. — Algrid Henswaithe, University of the Vast

Grazers of lakes, bogs, and in some cases, the shallow seas, the stately Diplodocus is generally not a threat. Slow moving, confident in their bulk, they rarely do more than watch passing creatures. These massive beasts move in small family groups and gather during the mating season in great herds to lay their eggs in dry nests. It is during this migration and mating period that they are the most dangerous, for the normally placid creatures become ill-tempered until their young hatch and become large enough to accompany their parents back to the lakes and swamps.

DINOSAUR, DIPLODOCUS

Gargantuan beast, unaligned

Armor Class 16 (natural armor)
Hit Points 198 (12d20 + 72)
Speed 30 ft.

STR	DEX	CON	INT	WIS	CHA
21 (+5)	10 (+0)	23 (+6)	2 (–4)	14 (+2)	5 (–3)

Skills Athletics +9
Damage Resistances bludgeoning
Senses passive Perception 12
Languages —
Challenge 10 (5,900 XP)

Trampling Charge. If the Diplodocus moves at least 20 feet straight toward a creature and then hits it with a tail attack on the same turn, that target must succeed on a DC 17 Strength saving throw or be knocked prone. If the target is prone, the Diplodocus can make one stomp attack against it as a bonus action.

Unstoppable. The Diplodocus has advantage on ability checks and saving throws against effects that would restrain it or knock it prone.

ACTIONS

Multiattack. The Diplodocus makes two Tail Whip attacks.

Tail Whip. *Melee Weapon Attack:* +9 to hit, reach 20 ft., one target. *Hit:* 18 (3d8 + 5) slashing damage. If the target is a Large or smaller creature, it must succeed on a DC 17 Strength check or be knocked prone.

Stomp. *Melee Weapon Attack:* +9 to hit, reach 5 ft., one prone creature. *Hit:* 21 (3d10 + 5) bludgeoning damage.

LEGENDARY ACTIONS

The Diplodocus can take three legendary actions, choosing from the options below. Only one legendary action can be used at a time and only at the end of another creature's turn. The Diplodocus regains spent legendary actions at the start of its turn.

Move. The Diplodocus moves up to half its speed.

Stomp (costs 2 actions). The Diplodocus makes one stomp attack.

Whip Crack (costs 3 actions). The Diplodocus whips its tail in the air to create a thunderous crack. Each creature within 20 feet of it must succeed on a DC 17 Wisdom saving throw or take 14 (4d6) thunder damage and become frightened until the end of its next turn.

DINOSAUR, HADROSAUR

Our supplies of salted beef and hardtack were supplemented by hunting the local fauna. Our favorite by far was the horse-sized grazer with the large, rounded head. Fairly docile, they were easy prey unless one startled the herd. A dozen of the charging beasts were worse than a stampede of cattle, and faster as well. Mostly they traveled on all fours, but if enraged, they could rise up on their powerful hind legs and with great strides strike at foes who thought they were at a safe distance. — Algrid Henswaithe, University of the Vast

A generally placid and peaceful grazer of grass and ferns, the Hadrosaur is a danger only in large numbers. Shy, these creatures prefer to avoid trouble. However, each herd keeps several of its number on lookout. When danger threatens, the herd bunches together, placing young and pregnant females in the center. If the threat attacks, the herd attempts to move away en masse, but this direction is always away from the first threat and might lead to them trampling other hunters or running into a more dangerous situation.

DINOSAUR, HADROSAUR

Huge beast, unaligned

Armor Class 14 (natural armor)
Hit Points 76 (8d12 + 24)
Speed 30 ft.

STR	DEX	CON	INT	WIS	CHA
19 (+4)	11 (+0)	17 (+3)	2 (–4)	10 (+0)	6 (–2)

Senses passive Perception 10
Languages —
Challenge 2 (450 XP)

Trampling Charge. If the Hadrosaur moves at least 20 feet straight toward a creature and hits that creature with a Ram attack on the same turn, that target must succeed on a DC 13 Strength check or be knocked prone. If the target is knocked prone, the Hadrosaur may make one Stomp attack against it as a bonus action.

ACTIONS

Ram. *Melee Weapon Attack*: +6 to hit, reach 5 ft., one target. *Hit*: 9 (1d10 + 4) bludgeoning damage.

Stomp. *Melee Weapon Attack*: +6 to hit, reach 5 ft., one prone creature. *Hit*: 17 (3d8 + 4) bludgeoning damage.

DINOSAUR, IGUANODON

We fled the jungle with the terrifying sounds of trees shaking and falling behind us. Our headlong flight drove us straight into more danger, however, as the porters cleared the trees and ended up in the middle of a herd of giant herbivores. We startled them, obviously, which led to the savage biting, kicking, and stomping that followed as they tried to protect their young. A couple of porters ended up on the wrong end of a spike. — Algrid Henswaithe, University of the Vast

Known primarily as herbivores, Iguanodons can be found in many regions of the world. While they do not seek prey to feed on, the Iguanodon is aggressive if they or their offspring are preyed on. Fighting with a formidable bite and thumb spike, this creature is not one to be taken lightly.

IGUANODON

Huge beast, unaligned

Armor Class 15 (natural armor)
Hit Points 96 (11d12 + 24)
Speed 30 ft.

STR	DEX	CON	INT	WIS	CHA
18 (+4)	12 (+1)	17 (+3)	2 (–4)	12 (+1)	6 (–2)

Senses passive Perception 11
Languages —
Challenge 6 (2300 XP)

ACTIONS

Bite. *Melee Weapon Attack:* +7 to hit, reach 5 ft., one target. *Hit:* 20 (3d10 + 4) piercing damage.
Thumb Spike. *Melee Weapon Attack:* +7 to hit, reach 5 ft., one target. *Hit:* 17 (3d8 + 4) piercing damage and the target must succeed on a DC 12 Constitution saving throw or lose 4 (1d8) hit points at the start of each of its turns until healed with magic.

We had already encountered the great flying reptiles and were leery when we heard from the natives that other flying creatures could be found in the cliffs surrounding a nearby lake. Undaunted, we journeyed to investigate and were surprised at what we saw. These were in appearance much like their deadly brethren but were merely a few feet in wingspan. Friendly, these creatures flapped up and investigated us as we investigated them. Magas Sathrick kept one as a pet and eventually made it into her familiar. — Algrid Henswaithe, University of the Vast

Pterodactyls are small flying reptiles with wingspans of around two to three feet, beaks filled with small sharp teeth, and feet tipped with sharp claws. They tend to lair along seaside cliffs, but some species have colonized jungles and forests. While not much of a threat themselves, they become dangerous in large numbers. Any disturbance of a nesting cliff, such as collecting eggs or simply trying to scale the cliff, can stir up dozens of these small reptiles in a shrieking cloud.

DINOSAUR, PTERANODON

The great flying reptiles swooped down from the sky and attacked. In their first pass they carried off five of our bearers, halflings all, and winged over toward the slopes of the central mountains. The second wave went after the other small creatures of our party, snapping up monkeys, halflings, and gnomes, but failed to carry off our dwarven smith. That last attempt cost the flock three of its number. — Algrid Henswaithe, University of the Vast

Largest of the flying reptiles, Pteranodons normally hunt large fish. They fly over shallow seas, dive into the water, and come up with a beak full of flapping fish. However, some species adapted to life in unusual conditions such as mountains towering over large jungles or open grasslands. These populations hunt small game. Some Pteranodons grow to be truly large, with wingspans of 20 feet or more. Such specimens are capable of snatching up prey as large as a halfling and carrying it away to tear it apart with its sharp-toothed beak.

DINOSAUR, PTERANODON

Medium beast, unaligned

Armor Class 13 (natural armor)
Hit Points 22 (4d8 + 4)
Speed 10 ft., fly 60 ft.

STR	DEX	CON	INT	WIS	CHA
13 (+1)	17 (+3)	12 (+1)	2 (–4)	8 (–1)	7 (–2)

Skills Perception +1
Senses passive Perception 11
Languages —
Challenge 1 (200 XP)

Dive. If the Pteranodon dives at least 30 feet straight toward a target and then hits it with a Bite attack on the same turn, the target takes an additional 7 (2d6) piercing damage.
Flyby. The Pteranodon doesn't provoke an opportunity attack when it flies out of an enemy's reach.

ACTIONS

Bite. *Melee Weapon Attack:* +5 to hit, reach 5 ft., one target. *Hit:* 6 (1d6 + 3) piercing damage.

DINOSAUR, PTERODACTYL

PTERODACTYL

Tiny beast, unaligned

Armor Class 12
Hit Points 1 (1d4 – 1)
Speed 10 ft., fly 50 ft.

STR	DEX	CON	INT	WIS	CHA
2 (–4)	14 (+2)	8 (–1)	2 (–1)	12 (+1)	10 (+0)

Skills Perception +3
Senses passive Perception 13
Languages —
Challenge 0 (10 XP)

ACTIONS

Beak. *Melee Weapon Attack:* +4 to hit, reach 5 ft., one target. *Hit:* 1 piercing damage.

DINOSAUR, RAPTOR

Our scouting party was hours late, so against our better judgment I led a small group to find them. The sun was getting low on the horizon when we found the site of the ambush. Blood was everywhere; whatever creatures had done this were not tidy. They were also powerful and stealthy to have ambushed such a large and well-armed party. Tracks were studied, bite marks analyzed, and we pondered what sort of creatures could have caused such carnage as we trekked back to camp. As night fell we found out, and only through the judicious use of certain spells was I alone able to survive. — Algrid Henswaithe, University of the Vast

These man-sized, feathered bipedal dinosaurs are pack hunters with a mean streak. They are ambush predators that prefer to strike from multiple directions at once to confuse and confound their prey. Social creatures, the pack is the center of raptor life, and any injury to a pack member brings about a wrathful reckoning. This revenge is not necessarily immediate; raptors are clever and patient and will stalk a foe for days to strike when the moment is to their advantage.

DINOSAUR, RAPTOR
Large beast, unaligned

Armor Class 15 (natural armor)
Hit Points 26 (4d10 + 4)
Speed 40 ft.

STR	DEX	CON	INT	WIS	CHA
12 (+1)	16 (+3)	12 (+1)	6 (–2)	14 (+2)	10 (+0)

Skills Perception +4, Stealth +5
Senses passive Perception 14
Languages ——
Challenge 3 (700 XP)

Sharp Senses. Raptors have advantage on Wisdom (Perception) checks that rely on smell.

ACTIONS

Multiattack. The raptor makes one Bite attack and one Claw attack or two Claw attacks.
Bite. Melee Weapon Attack: +5 to hit, reach 5 ft., one target. *Hit:* 7 (1d8 + 3) piercing damage.
Claw. Melee Weapon Attack: +5 to hit, reach 5 ft., one target. *Hit:* 6 (1d6 + 3) slashing damage. If the raptor hits the same target with two Claw attacks on the same turn, it inflicts an additional 4 (1d8) slashing damage.

DINOSAUR, RAPTORS, MUTANT

The thing that crawled out of a vat in the forbidden temple was skinless and dripping a clear whitish fluid. It tread toward us on cautiously, its eyes far too bright with intelligence and menace for the simple creature from which it was made. Then it opened its mouth, not to shriek, but to spew forth a torrent of magical energy. The bearers ran. Have no doubt, so did I. — Algrid Henswaithe, University of the Vast

Created by foul sorcery, mad alchemy, or some other perversion of the natural order, mutant raptors are savage, intelligent creatures capable of great magical power. Larger than their natural cousins, the mutant raptors combine the speed and strength of their bodies with cruel and cunning minds. Each mutant is slightly different than their brethren, and while some innately cast spells, others breathe out jets of flame or lightning, or sometimes even more exotic magical energies.

DINOSAUR, RAPTORS, MUTANT
Large magical beast, neutral evil

Armor Class 15 (natural armor)
Hit Points 26 (4d10 + 4)
Speed 40 ft.

STR	DEX	CON	INT	WIS	CHA
12 (+1)	16 (+3)	12 (+1)	6 (–2)	14 (+2)	10 (+0)

Skills Perception +4, Stealth +5
Senses passive Perception 14
Languages ——
Challenge 4 (1,100 XP)

Magical Mutation. A mutant raptor can innately cast one of the following spells using Wisdom as its spellcasting ability score (spell save DC 12, +4 to hit with magical attacks): *enlarge/reduce, invisibility, misty step,* or *scorching ray*
Sharp Senses. Raptors have advantage on Wisdom (Perception) checks that rely on smell.

ACTIONS

Multiattack. The mutant raptor makes one Bite attack and one Claw attack or two Claw attacks.
Bite. Melee Weapon Attack: +5 to hit, reach 5 ft., one target. *Hit:* 7 (1d8 + 3) piercing damage.
Claw. Melee Weapon Attack: +5 to hit, reach 5 ft., one target. *Hit:* 6 (1d6 + 3) slashing damage. If the raptor hits the same target with two claw attacks on their turn, they inflict an additional 4 (1d8) slashing damage.

Dinosaur King, Triceratops

The local reptile folk told us this tale. Long ago before the plateau rose from the lowlands, there dwelled in the jungles two great beast spirits. One lived upon the north point, the other the south. The northern one desired to take a form and chose the shape of one of the great Three-Horns that roamed the grasslands, only larger. They said it still roams the savannah today, always in the form of the largest of the Three-Horns, a protector of the herd and defender of the land from the depredations of mortals. — Algrid Henswaithe, University of the Vast

Dinosaur kings look like a normal member of the species they bond with, albeit larger and far more intelligent. They are not truly made of flesh and blood, but of ephemeral spirit stuff that behaves much the same way. The Triceratops dinosaur kings are closer to their bonded species than others and often mate with their bonded species to produce hybrid flesh and spirit being that are nearly as powerful as their royal forebearers.

Triceratops King

Gargantuan monstrosity, neutral good

Armor Class 15 (natural armor)
Hit Points 294 (19d20 + 95)
Speed 60 ft.

STR	DEX	CON	INT	WIS	CHA
24 (+7)	10 (+0)	20 (+5)	15 (+2)	17 (+3)	16 (+3)

Saving Throws Str +11, Con +9, Wis +7
Skills Insight +7, Perception +7
Damage Immunities bludgeoning, piercing, and slashing damage from nonmagical attacks
Senses darkvision 60 ft, passive Perception 17
Languages Sylvan
Challenge 12 (8,400 XP)

Herd Master. The Triceratops king may cast spells with the range of touch on allies if within 30 feet.
Innate Spellcasting. The Triceratops king's innate spellcasting ability is Wisdom (spell save DC 15, +7 to hit with spell attacks). It can cast the following spells, requiring no material components:
At will: *cure wounds, speak with animals, speak with plants*
3/day each: *hold person, moonbeam, spike growth*
1/day each: *dispel magic, conjure animals*
Magic Resistance. The Triceratops king has advantage on saving throws against spells and other magical effects.
Magic Weapons. The Triceratops king's weapon attacks are magical.

Actions

Multiattack. The Triceratops king makes two Gore attacks.
Gore. *Melee Weapon Attack:* +11 to hit, reach 5 ft., one target. *Hit:* 29 (4d10 + 7) piercing damage.
Stomp. *Melee Weapon Attack:* +11 to hit, reach 5 ft., one prone target. *Hit:* 26 (3d12 + 7) type damage.

Legendary Actions

The Triceratops king can take three legendary actions, choosing from the options below. Only one legendary action can be used at a time and only at the end of another creature's turn. The Triceratops king regains spent legendary actions at the start of its turn.
Rampage. The Triceratops king makes a Gore and a Stomp attack.
Bolster Herd (costs 2 actions). The Triceratops king's allies within 30 feet may immediately attempt a saving throw against an ongoing effect.
Herd Charge (costs 2 actions). All allies within 30 feet or the Triceratops king take a move and an action.

DINOSAUR KING, TYRANNOSAURUS

To the south, so the local legends say, another great beast spirit was caught in the upwelling of the plateau. This one was a hungry spirit, a spirit of the hunt, of feasting, and of rage. Jealous that its brethren had taken the form of one of the powerful but gentle Three-Horns of the plains, it too chose a form. Today, so the legends say, the southern jungles are hunted by a Great Jawed Monster that is larger, smarter, and more bellicose than the rest. Like its plains-dwelling cousin, this dinosaur king has its loyal followers, a pack of snarling raptors that is always growing and shrinking as the dinosaur king's hunger grows. — Algrid Henswaithe, University of the Vast

Dinosaur kings look like a normal member of the species with which they have bonded, albeit larger and far more intelligent. They are not truly made of flesh and blood, but ephemeral spirit stuff that behaves much the same way. Solitary like the creature's whose form they have stolen, Tyrannosaurus dinosaur kings do not mate with their physical brethren nor do they associate with others of their kind. Instead, they draw to themselves a cadre of loyal raptors and other smaller predators who serve as a sort of court. While this court shows great loyalty to its king, the Tyrannosaurus king does not share that feeling and happily eats a follower if it pleases them.

TYRANNOSAURS KING

Gargantuan monstrosity, chaotic evil

Armor Class 13 (natural armor)
Hit Points 313 (19d20 + 114)
Speed 60 ft.

STR	DEX	CON	INT	WIS	CHA
26 (+8)	10 (+0)	22 (+6)	14 (+2)	14 (+2)	9 (−1)

Saving Throws Str +12, Con +10, Wis +6
Skills Perception +6
Damage Immunities poison; bludgeoning, piercing, and slashing damage from nonmagical attacks
Condition Immunities poisoned
Senses darkvision 60 ft, passive Perception 16
Languages Sylvan
Challenge 12 (8,400 XP)

Cloud of Carrion. The Tyrannosaurus king is surrounded by a cloud of buzzing insects and the ripe stench of rotting carcasses. All creatures that begin their turn within 15 feet of the Tyrannosaurus king must succeed at a DC 15 Constitution saving throw or gain the poisoned condition until they begin their turn more than 15 feet from the Tyrannosaurus king. A creature that saves against this effect is immune to it for 24 hours.

Innate Spellcasting. The Tyrannosaurus king's innate spellcasting ability is Wisdom (spell save DC 14, +6 to hit with spell attacks). It can cast the following spells, requiring no material components:

At will: *darkness, dispel magic, ray of enfeeblement*
3/day: *animate dead*
1/day: *circle of death*

Magic Resistance. The Triceratops king has advantage on saving throws against spells and other magical effects.

Magic Weapons. The Triceratops king's weapon attacks are magical.

ACTIONS

Multiattack. The Tyrannosaurus king makes one Bite attack and one Tail attack. The Tyrannosaurus king may substitute a swallow attack for its bite attack. It can't make both attacks against the same target.

Bite. Melee Weapon Attack: +12 to hit, reach 5 ft., one target. *Hit:* 47 (6d12 + 8) piercing damage.

Swallow. The Tyrannosaurus king makes a Bite attack, and if it hits, the creature must succeed at a DC 18 Dexterity saving throw or be swallowed if the creature is Large sized or smaller. While swallowed, the creature is blind and restrained, it has total cover against attacks and other effects that originate from outside the Tyrannosaurus king and it takes 39 (6d12) acid damage at the start of the Tyrannosaurus king's turn. The Tyrannosaurus king can have only two Large-sized creatures, four Medium-sized creatures, or six Small-sized creatures swallowed at one time.

If the Tyrannosaurus king takes 50 damage or more on a single turn from a creature inside it, the Tyrannosaurus king must succeed on a DC 18 Constitution saving throw at the end of that turn or regurgitate all swallowed creatures, which fall prone in a space within 10 feet of the Tyrannosaurus king. If the Tyrannosaurus king dies, all swallowed creatures are no longer restrained by it and can escape from the corpse using 15 feet of movement, exiting prone.

Tail. Melee Weapon Attack: +12 to hit, reach 10 ft., one target. *Hit:* 24 (3d10 + 8) bludgeoning damage.

LEGENDARY ACTIONS

The Tyrannosaurus king can take three legendary actions, choosing from the options below. Only one legendary action can be used at a time and only at the end of another creature's turn. The Tyrannosaurus king regains spent legendary actions at the start of its turn.

Rampage. The Tyrannosaurus king makes a Bite and a Tail attack.

Gobble (costs 2 actions). The Tyrannosaurus king makes two swallow actions.

Spit (costs 2 actions). The Tyrannosaurus king spits up to two creatures it has swallowed at up to two targets. This is a ranged weapon attack made at + 4 to hit, with a range of 20/40 feet, and inflicts 27 (5d10) bludgeoning damage on the creature hit and the creature spit out. Both the creature hit and the one spit out must succeed at a DC 20 Strength saving throw or become prone.

Dire Corby

The underground stairs led upward into the massive open beak of a giant bird's head carved from the rock. We heard what sounded like an aerie of birds cawing beyond the carving, but even our druid Stellen couldn't imagine what types of birds might live so far underground. We advanced slowly and quietly to avoid trouble. The cavern beyond was riddled with caves that climbed upward along the walls. Nests perched on each ledge before these openings. We had arrived as a ceremony was occurring, with tall figures wearing black, feathered outfits and bird-like beak masks. We watched for a while, and then I understood: These weren't men wearing masks, they were actually birds. The cavern was alive with the birdmen, hundreds of them, although none had wings. Instead, they'd grown muscular arms and wicked claws. We withdrew before they noticed us. — Gully Cederlund, ranger of the vale

Dire corbies are humanoid, bipedal birdmen that dwell deep beneath the surface world. They make their homes in large, open caverns where they hollow out individual shelters in the walls. These creatures do not now have wings, but they almost certainly did in the remote past. Why their wings disappeared and were replaced by muscular arms with claws is unknown.

Dire corbies hunt in flocks, finding great pleasure in chasing down prey. While they are omnivores, they prefer a diet of fresh meat. They hunt and enjoy the flesh of subterranean rodents, animals, and even other races. They are particularly fond of the leathery flesh of bats. A typical hunt ends with the prey cornered and trapped, then cruelly tormented and tortured for many minutes before the dire corbies finally tear it to shreds with their claws.

Dire Corby

Medium monstrosity, neutral evil

Armor Class 11
Hit Points 11 (2d8 + 2)
Speed 30 ft.

STR	DEX	CON	INT	WIS	CHA
16 (+3)	12 (+1)	13 (+1)	6 (–2)	10 (+0)	8 (–1)

Skills Perception +2
Senses darkvision 60 ft., passive Perception 10
Languages Deep Speech, Undercommon
Challenge 1/2 (100 XP)

Actions

Multiattack. A dire corby makes two Claw attacks.
Claw. *Melee Weapon Attack:* +5 to hit, reach 5 ft.; one creature. *Hit:* 6 (1d6 + 3) slashing damage.

Dokkaebi

Dokkaebi are mischievous but ultimately friendly household spirits. They are diminutive creatures with overlong limbs and a large head with a mischievous grin and bright, intelligent eyes. Chaotic and capricious, they are nonetheless capable of great acts of generosity and kindness, often bringing wealth and good fortune to those who treat them well. Many tales are told of ungrateful, wealthy folk who shun the presence of dokkaebi and fall on misfortune, while poor peasants welcome the luck goblins and offer them a share of their meager possessions, receiving great wealth and blessings in return.

When they first appear, dokkaebi may test a house's inhabitants with minor pranks: hiding objects, making noises in the night, or animating furniture or utensils to do strange but harmless things such as dance or float about the room. The dokkaebi may turn hostile should the homeowner try to expel them, or they may simply leave. If they are treated well — food left out or small sacrifices made in the form of minor trinkets or knickknacks intended simply to demonstrate the homeowner's good intentions — they may begin to help the household and even (if the stories are to be believed) bring gold and riches to the poorest of the poor.

Dokkaebi do not have a native physical form, being spirits, but usually appear as described above.

Dokkaebi

Small fey, chaotic good

Armor Class 15 (natural armor)
Hit Points 63 (14d6 + 14)
Speed 30 ft.

STR	DEX	CON	INT	WIS	CHA
9 (−1)	14 (+2)	12 (+1)	12 (+1)	15 (+2)	15 (+2)

Skills Perception +6, Stealth +6
Damage Resistances bludgeoning, piercing and slashing damage from nonmagical attacks
Condition Immunities charmed
Senses passive Perception 16
Languages Common, fey
Challenge 3 (700 XP)

Luck Bringer. A dokkaebi that inhabits a house and is well-treated may, at its own discretion, gift the homeowner with the Luck feat. This feat exists only for so long as the dokkaebi inhabits the household or until the dokkaebi itself revokes it.

Innate Spellcasting. The dokkaebi's spellcasting ability is Charisma (spell save DC 12). The dokkaebi can innately cast the following spells, requiring no material components:

At will: *detect good and evil, detect magic, detect thoughts, invisibility*
3/day each: *animate objects, create food and water, cure wounds, lesser restoration*
1/day each: *blink, greater restoration, scrying, stinking cloud*

Actions

Bite. *Melee Weapon Attack:* +1 to hit, reach 5 ft., one target. *Hit:* 4 (1d8) piercing damage. The target must succeed on a DC 13 Constitution saving throw or become unconscious for one minute. The target can repeat the saving throw at the end of each of its turns, ending the effect on itself on a success.

Dragons

Dragon, Azure

Ollie was leaping nimbly around the basket, pulling levers, pushing buttons, and cranking dials. I found I couldn't stand up for fear of looking over the edge of the basket again. I didn't think we would get so high when I agreed to document this folly. But Ollie seemed unperturbed, even when the lightning strikes crackled so near the thin fabric of the balloon suspended above us. Suddenly, a dark shadow circled us, and I had to look. A serpentine dragon glided around the basket, its scales the color of a bright, sunlit day. It had no wings, but somehow flew along with ease. It hovered alongside and turned its head toward us. I was prepared to jump when it spoke in a deep, resonating voice, "Hello again, Ollie." — Egan Thumble, documenting halfling inventor Ollie Nematoad's balloon flight over the Star Sea

The azure dragons are said to have been created by the gods to keep order in the realms of the sky. They are wise and (usually) gentle creatures who can appear at times of great mayhem and chaos involving the aerial realm — storms, magical disturbances, or in the presence of large unnatural flying creatures such as demons or mechanical flying contraptions. Their task is not to attack or destroy, but to investigate, and if the disturbance proves of a dangerously chaotic nature (whether good or evil) to eliminate the threat quickly and efficiently, with as little disturbance to the realms of the sky as possible.

Azure dragons are serpentine, coiling creature of enormous size that glide through the air, their scales mimicking the colors of a bright sunlit day. They fly effortlessly and without wings. The gods occasionally send azure dragons to deliver important messages and to impart wisdom to their clerics, monks, paladins and other special followers. The appearance of an azure dragon is considered extremely auspicious, usually heralding or resulting from momentous events.

Azure Dragon

Gargantuan dragon, lawful neutral

Armor Class 22 (natural armor)
Hit Points 481 (26d20 + 208)
Speed 40 ft., fly 80 ft. (hover)

STR	DEX	CON	INT	WIS	CHA
29 (+9)	10 (+0)	27 (+8)	20 (+5)	20 (+5)	21 (+5)

Saving Throws Dex +7, Con +15, Wis +12, Cha +12
Skills History +19, Intimidation +19, Nature +19, Perception +19, Persuasion +19, Religion +19
Damage Immunities lightning
Senses blindsight 60 ft., darkvision 120 ft., passive Perception 29
Languages Common, Draconic
Challenge 23 (50,000 XP)

Legendary Resistance (3/day). If the creature fails a saving throw, it can choose to succeed instead.
Skyborn. The azure dragon's scales flicker with the colors of the daylight sky. While in flight in a natural sky during the day (including stormy skies), attacks against an azure dragon are at disadvantage.

Actions

Multiattack. The azure dragon uses its Frightful Presence and make one Bite attack and two Claw attacks.
Bite. Melee Weapon Attack: +16 to hit, reach 15 ft., one target. *Hit:* 20 (2d10 + 9) piercing damage plus 11 (2d10) lightning damage.
Claw. Melee Weapon Attack: +16 to hit, reach 10 ft., one target. *Hit:* 16 (2d6 + 9) slashing damage.
Tail. Melee Weapon Attack: +16 to hit, reach 20 ft., one target. *Hit:* 18 (2d8 + 9) bludgeoning damage.

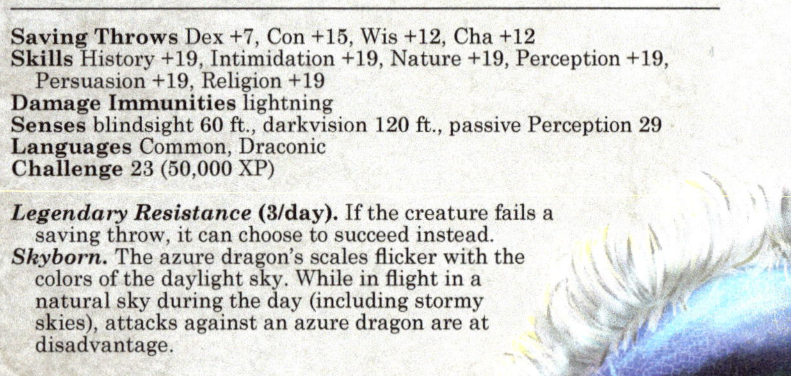

Elemental Breath (recharge 5–6). The azure dragon exhales a burst of elemental force. The dragon can select the type of damage from the following list. Each creature in the area of effect must make the specified saving throw or take the listed damage, or half as much damage on a success:
Cold: 90-foot cone, DC 20 Constitution saving throw, 72 (16d8) cold damage.
Fire: 90-foot cone, DC 20 Dexterity saving throw, 91 (26d6) fire damage.
Lightning: 120-foot line, 10 feet wide, DC 20 Dexterity saving throw, 88 (16d10) lightning damage.
Thunder: 90-foot cone, DC 20 Constitution saving throw, 88 (16d10) thunder damage.
Wind: 120-foot cone, DC 20 Dexterity saving throw, 36 (8d8) force damage. On a failed saving throw, in addition to damage, the target is thrown backwards 30 feet and knocked prone.
Frightful Presence. Each creature of the azure dragon's choice that is within 120 feet of the creature and aware of it must succeed on a DC 20 Wisdom saving throw or become frightened for one minute. A creature can repeat the saving throw at the end of each of its turns, ending the effect on itself on a success. If a creature's saving throw is successful or the effect ends for it, the creature is immune to the azure dragon's Frightful Presence for the next 24 hours.

Legendary Actions

An azure dragon can take three legendary actions, choosing from the options below. Only one legendary action can be used at a time and only at the end of another creature's turn. The azure dragon regains spent legendary actions at the start of its turn.
Detect. The azure dragon makes a Wisdom (Perception) check.
Tail Attack. The azure dragon makes a tail attack.
Windstorm (costs 2 actions). The dragon conjures a punishing cyclone of wind. Each creature within 15 feet of the dragon must succeed on a DC 24 Dexterity saving throw or take 16 (2d6 + 9) bludgeoning damage and be knocked prone.

DRAKE, FIRE

The villagers said they had a dragon problem. Hey, piece of cake. Nine times out of ten it's just a larger-than-normal lizard, maybe a reptilian predator of some kind. Half the time, they don't even have wings. Well, not this time. It wasn't a full-on dragon, thank the gods, but a drake. Those lesser members of dragon kind — some folks call them dragonettes — are nothing to laugh at. Cooked my horse right out from under me. — Big Joanne, mercenary

Fire drakes are sometimes confused as small or young red dragons. Their bodies are only around four feet long with five or more feet of tail. They run the range from orange to deep red and often have smoky black markings. Heat and smoke seems to radiate from their bodies. Their wings are large enough to take them aloft, and their fiery breath is nothing to laugh at. Many would-be dragon slayers work their way up by fighting the fiercely territorial fire drakes, and those that survive are apt to choose a new line of work.

FIRE DRAKE BLOOD

Fire drake blood can be quickly saved for later with a DC 15 Dexterity saving throw. Up to one ounce of the blood can be saved per saving throw. The body of a single fire drake provides 1d10 + 2 doses of its blood. Fire drake blood can be used as an explosive, with a glass vial hurled at a target bursting to inflict 9 (2d8) fire damage. As an action, it can be applied to a weapon, granting that weapon +2 (1d4) fire damage on each attack for the next five rounds, after which it is destroyed by the fiery blood, unless the weapon is magical.

DRAKE, FIRE
Small dragon, chaotic evil

Armor Class 13 (natural armor)
Hit Points 27 (6d6 + 6)
Speed 20 ft., fly 60 ft.

STR	DEX	CON	INT	WIS	CHA
13 (+1)	13 (+1)	13 (+1)	4 (−3)	11 (+0)	10 (+0)

Skills Perception +4, Stealth +3
Damage Immunities fire
Condition Immunities paralyzed
Senses darkvision 60 ft., passive Perception 14
Languages Draconic
Challenge 1 (200 XP)

Pyrophoric Blood. A creature that hits the fire drake with a weapon attack from within five feet of the fire drake must make a DC 11 Dexterity saving throw or take 3 (1d6) fire damage.

ACTIONS

Multiattack. The fire drake makes one Bite attack and one attack with its Claws.
Bite. *Melee Weapon Attack:* +3 to hit, reach 5 ft., one target. *Hit:* 5 (1d8 + 1) piercing damage.
Claws. *Melee Weapon Attack:* +3 to hit, reach 5 ft., one target. *Hit:* 8 (2d6 + 1) slashing damage.
Fire Breath (recharge 6). The fire drake exhales fire in a 15–foot cone. Creatures in the area must make a DC 11 Dexterity saving throw, taking 10 (3d6) fire damage on a failed saving throw, or half as much damage on a successful saving throw.

Drake, Ice

It tracked us from the air, waiting and watching as we made our way through the vast ice caverns at the top of the world. I wondered why it didn't attack, but I was too busy just trying not to fall into a bottomless crevasse or fall prey to the ice trolls that dwelled there. After seven days pushing through that frozen hell, we came out onto the top of a great glacier. We barely got 50 feet from the cavern's mouth before winged death came at us from the frozen sky. — Big Joanne, mercenary

Ice drakes are small, dragon-like creatures that resemble small white dragons. Their hides are icy white and blue, with jagged blue-black markings. Their eyes are sapphire. While they could be confused with juvenile white dragons, drakes lack much of the intelligence of even that least intelligent of true dragonkind. They hunt the frozen parts of the world, the icy poles and frigid mountain passes where their natural coloring and immunities make them a top predator.

ICE DRAKE BLOOD

Ice drake blood can be quickly saved for later with a DC 15 Dexterity saving throw. Up to one ounce of the blood can be saved per saving throw. The body of a single ice drake provides 1d10+2 doses of its blood. Ice drake blood can be used as an explosive, with a glass vial hurled at a target bursting to inflict 9 (2d8) cold damage. As an action, it can be applied to a weapon, granting that weapon +2 (1d4) cold damage on each attack for the next five rounds, after which the weapon is destroyed by the super-chilled blood, unless it is magical.

Drake, Ice

Small dragon, chaotic evil

Armor Class 14 (natural armor)
Hit Points 27 (6d6 + 6)
Speed 10 ft., fly 50 ft.

STR	DEX	CON	INT	WIS	CHA
13 (+1)	13 (+1)	13 (+1)	7 (–2)	8 (–1)	10 (+0)

Skills Perception +1
Damage Vulnerabilities fire
Damage Immunities cold
Condition Immunities paralyzed
Senses darkvision 60 ft, passive Perception 11
Languages Draconic
Challenge 3 (700 XP)

Change Shape. The ice drake magically polymorphs into a Large white dragon or back into its true form. Its statistics are the same in each form. Any equipment being worn or carried by the ice drake do not change. The ice drake reverts to its true form when it dies.

ACTIONS

Multiattack. The ice drake makes one Bite attack and two Claw attacks.
Bite. *Melee Weapon Attack*: +3 to hit, reach 5 ft., one target. *Hit*: 4 (1d6 + 1) piercing damage.
Claw. *Melee Weapon Attack*: +3 to hit, reach 5 ft., one target. *Hit*: 3 (1d4 + 1) slashing damage.
***Breath Weapon* (recharge 4–6).** The ice drake exhales an icy blast in a 20-foot cone. Each creature in the area must make a DC 11 Dexterity saving throw, taking 9 (2d8) cold damage on a failure or half as much on a success.

Draug

The lookout yelled down that a ship was running before the oncoming storm. The vessel ran before the storm all right, faster than the waves and wind allowed, until it was right alongside, forcing us to trade shot for shot in a long chase as that hellish gale bore down on our necks. When the mystery ship came even and threw grapples, we saw the truth: It was barely a ship, little more than a rotten hulk whose decaying sails and broken spars matched the dead crew that screamed for our blood. — Captain Elisa Bounapert of the Wastrel's Daughter

When a ship and her crew die at sea in horrific fashion, they sometimes reanimate as draug. These undead sailors are completely obedient to their captain, and without these directions, often find themselves lacking motivation. In these cases, the draug might wander off in different directions or stay and lurk in their sunken hulks.

Draug

Medium undead, chaotic evil

Armor Class 12 (natural armor)
Hit Points 27 (5d8 + 5)
Speed 30 ft., swim 30 ft.

STR	DEX	CON	INT	WIS	CHA
17 (+3)	10 (+0)	13 (+1)	8 (−1)	10 (+0)	13 (+1)

Damage Resistances fire
Damage Immunities poison
Condition Immunities poisoned
Senses darkvision 60 ft., passive Perception 10
Languages —
Challenge 1 (200 XP)

Actions

Greataxe. *Melee Weapon Attack:* +5 to hit, reach 5 ft., one target. *Hit:* 9 (1d12 + 3) slashing damage.
Slam. *Melee Weapon Attack:* +5 to hit, reach 5 ft., one target. *Hit:* 14 (2d10 + 3) bludgeoning damage.

Draug Captain

The undead sailors swarmed over the gunwales and plowed into our own massed numbers. The fight was vicious; the draug gave no quarter but suffered grievous wounds without slowing down. In the end, I faced off against their captain, a far more powerful undead creature who once piloted a living ship in the light of the sun but had rotted to nothing more than a mussel-encrusted skeleton draped in ragged finery. He was fast and strong, but in the end, I took his skull off and punted it into the sea. This took much of the fight out of his crew, and we drove them back into the sea. — Captain Elisa Bounapert of the Wastrel's Daughter

The draug are linked to their ship, and the captain is the ship's mind and soul. It is by this being's power that the ship is raised from the slimy sea floor and set upon the waves to take vengeance upon the living. Most often, the captain of a crew of draug was the captain of the ship in life, but if the ship went down as part of a mutiny, it could be anyone: the cook, the boatswain, a really clever cabin boy, whoever the spirits of the dead sailors looked to as their leader.

Draug Captain

Medium undead, chaotic evil

Armor Class 17 (natural armor)
Hit Points 45 (7d8 + 14)
Speed 30 ft., swim 30 ft.

STR	DEX	CON	INT	WIS	CHA
20 (+5)	10 (+0)	15 (+2)	8 (−1)	10 (+0)	13 (+1)

Saving Throws Str +7, Con +4
Damage Resistances fire
Damage Immunities poison
Condition Immunities poisoned
Senses darkvision 60 ft., passive Perception 10
Languages —
Challenge 4 (1,100 XP)

Innate Spellcasting. A draug captain's spellcasting ability is Charisma (spell save DC 14). The draug can innately cast *fog cloud* three times per day, requiring only verbal components.
Sneak Attack (1/turn). The draug captain deals an extra 7 (2d6) damage when it hits a target with a weapon attack and has advantage on the attack roll, or when the target is within five feet of an ally of the draug captain that isn't incapacitated and the draug captain doesn't have disadvantage on the attack roll.

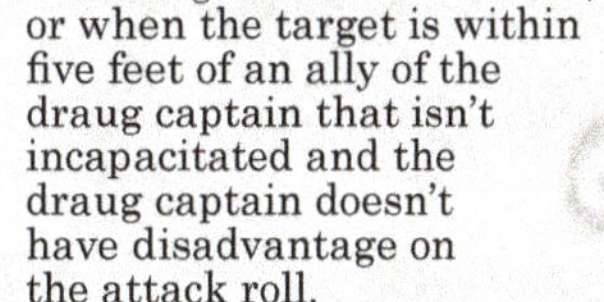

Actions

Greataxe. *Melee Weapon Attack:* +7 to hit, reach 5 ft., one target. *Hit:* 8 (1d6 + 5) slashing damage.
Slam. *Melee Weapon Attack:* +7 to hit, reach 5 ft., one target. *Hit:* 16 (2d10 + 5) bludgeoning damage.

Drider-Goblin

We saw the goblin spying on us from behind a ridge above our camp in the deep tunnels below the Hollow Spires. He was trying his best to hide, but our eagle-eyed ranger Cynewyl spotted him right away. Tanissa ducked into the darkness and was barely a shadow herself as she crept up the rock wall toward him. She sprang out in front of the little goblin, more intent on scaring it off than killing it. The goblin instead reared up over the rocks, revealing a massive spider body connected at its midsection. The little goblin was laughing wildly as it chased our thief down the rock wall. None of us found it funny when the creature began firing magical bolts of energy at us. — From the adventuring journals of explorer Jenyfer Gilt

The mind recoils at the thought of the upper body of a beady-eyed goblin affixed at the midsection to a horrific, hairy spider. But the unnatural drider-goblins are indeed nightmares brought to life, although how they are created is a mystery. They live in the dark crevices and subterranean spaces of the world, where they can be found serving true driders or leading tribes of normal goblins.

One in a dozen drider-goblins is imbued with dark powers of the arcane and is capable of wielding magical spells. More intelligent and cunning than their common drider-goblin kin, they are seen as leaders among other drider-goblins and are sometimes revered as holy or divine among common goblin tribes.

Drider-Goblin

Medium monstrosity, chaotic evil

Armor Class 14 (natural armor)
Hit Points 67 (9d8 + 27)
Speed 30 ft., climb 30 ft.

STR	DEX	CON	INT	WIS	CHA
14 (+2)	15 (+2)	16 (+3)	12 (+1)	13 (+1)	12 (+1)

Skills Perception +3, Stealth +4
Senses darkvision 60 ft., passive Perception 13
Languages Goblin, Undercommon
Challenge 4 (1,100 XP)

Nimble Escape. The drider-goblin can take the Disengage or Hide action as a bonus action on each of its turns.
Spider Climb. The drider-goblin can climb difficult surfaces, including hanging upside-down on ceilings, without needing to make an ability check.
Sunlight Sensitivity. While in sunlight, the drider-goblin has disadvantage on attack rolls, as well as on Wisdom (Perception) checks that rely on sight.
Web Walker. The drider-goblin ignores movement restrictions caused by webbing.

Actions

Multiattack. The drider-goblin makes one Bite attack and one Mace attack.
Bite. *Melee Weapon Attack*: +4 to hit, reach 5 ft., one target. *Hit*: 5 (1d6 + 2) piercing damage, plus 9 (2d8) poison damage.
Mace. *Melee Weapon Attack:* +4 to hit, reach 5 ft., one target. *Hit*: 5 (1d6 + 2) bludgeoning damage.
Javelin. *Melee or Ranged Weapon Attack*: +4 to hit, reach 5 ft. or range 30/120 ft., one target. *Hit*: 5 (1d6 + 2) piercing damage, or 6 (1d8 + 2) piercing damage if used with two hands to make a melee attack.

Drider-Goblin Spellcaster

Medium monstrosity, chaotic evil

Armor Class 14 (natural armor)
Hit Points 97 (13d8 + 39)
Speed 30 ft., climb 30 ft.

STR	DEX	CON	INT	WIS	CHA
14 (+2)	15 (+2)	16 (+3)	12 (+1)	13 (+1)	17 (+3)

Skills Perception +4, Stealth +5
Senses darkvision 60 ft., passive Perception 14
Languages Goblin, Undercommon
Challenge 5 (1,800 XP)

Nimble Escape. The drider-goblin can take the Disengage or Hide action as a bonus action on each of its turns.
Spellcasting. The drider-goblin spellcaster is a 4th-level spellcaster. Its spellcasting ability is Charisma (spell save DC 14, +6 to hit with spell attacks). It has the following sorcerer spells prepared:
Cantrips (at will): *acid splash, chill touch, mending, prestidigitation, shocking grasp*
1st level (4 slots): *detect magic, false life, magic missile*
2nd level (3 slots): *blindness/deafness, web*
3rd level (2 slots): *dispel magic*
Spider Climb. The drider-goblin can climb difficult surfaces, including hanging upside-down on ceilings, without needing to make an ability check.
Sunlight Sensitivity. While in sunlight, the drider-goblin has disadvantage on attack rolls, as well as on Wisdom (Perception) checks that rely on sight.
Web Walker. The drider-goblin ignores movement restrictions caused by webbing.

Actions

Multiattack. The drider-goblin makes one Bite attack and one Mace attack.
Bite. *Melee Weapon Attack:* +5 to hit, reach 5 ft., one target. *Hit*: 5 (1d6 + 2) piercing damage, plus 9 (2d8) poison damage.
Mace. *Melee Weapon Attack:* +5 to hit, reach 5 ft., one target. *Hit*: 5 (1d6 + 2) bludgeoning damage.
Javelin. *Melee or Ranged Weapon Attack:* +5 to hi, reach 5 ft. or range 30/120 ft., one target. *Hit*: 5 (1d6 + 2) piercing damage, or 6 (1d8 + 2) piercing damage if used with two hands to make a melee attack.

Duppy

A cold rain was blowing through the trees when the dogs started barking. They came from all around us, circling our camp. Dankirk motioned us to be silent as he stalked slowly to the edge of the campfire's light. He swung his blade at something we couldn't see, but a hand caught his wrist and held his strike. Dankirk fell backward toward us, followed by a pirate in tattered rags. His eyes burned with anger as he looked upon us. Where his legs should have been, swirling clouds of mist coalesced into more baying hounds of hell. — Thrazir "The Razor" Conch, on the rumored Dead Pirate of the Kriegh Forest

When the cruelest sailors die ashore, out of reach of their ship and crew and a proper burial at sea, they sometimes rise again as hate-filled duppies. The floating, ghostly humanoid's face is a blend of human and beast, and canine shapes appear to twine around the creature's legs. These evil undead seek to exact their vengeance on the living, often targeting other sailors and pirates who remind them of their past lives. The arrival of a duppy is often preceded by the baying of a pack of hounds. The duppy can summon these ravenous hounds to do its bidding, which often involves tracking down his prey.

Duppy

Medium undead, chaotic evil

Armor Class 15
Hit Points 78 (12d8 + 24)
Speed fly 40 ft.

STR	DEX	CON	INT	WIS	CHA
6 (−2)	18 (+4)	15 (+2)	13 (+1)	15 (+2)	18 (+4)

Damage Resistances acid, fire, lightning, thunder; bludgeoning, piercing, and slashing from nonmagical attacks
Damage Immunities cold, necrotic, poison
Condition Immunities charmed, exhaustion, frightened, grappled, paralyzed, petrified, poisoned, prone, restrained
Senses darkvision 60 ft., passive Perception 12
Languages any languages it knew in life
Challenge 6 (2,300 XP)

Incorporeal Movement. The duppy can move through other creatures and objects as if they were difficult terrain. It takes 5 (1d10) force damage if it ends its turn inside an object.
Sunlight Sensitivity. While in sunlight, the duppy has disadvantage on attack rolls.

Actions

Incorporeal Touch. *Melee Weapon Attack:* +6 to hit, reach 5 ft., one target. *Hit:* 17 (3d8 + 4) necrotic damage. The target must succeed on a DC 15 Constitution saving throw or its hit point maximum is reduced by an amount equal to the damage taken. This reduction lasts until the target finishes a long rest. The target dies if this effect reduces its hit point maximum to 0.
A humanoid slain by this attack rises 24 hours later as a zombie under the duppy's control, unless the humanoid is restored to life or its body is destroyed. The duppy can have no more than six zombies under its control at one time.
Ravenous Hounds (1/day). The duppy summons forth 1d4 incorporeal hounds (use the **wolf** stat block with the *Incorporeal Movement* trait). The called creatures arrive in 1d4 rounds, acting as allies of the duppy and obeying its spoken commands. The hounds remain for one hour, until the duppy dies, or until the duppy dismisses them as a bonus action.

Egui

Jenson walked carefully up to the bars of the cells that ran the length of the old keep. I was shocked to see figures trapped inside since the place had fallen into ruin so long ago. Jenson, too, but the priest was the voice of calm when he spoke, promising to free them. He fell back when they raised their heads. Their eyes were sunken, and their mouths were little more than small gashes cut into the sagging folds of their dead faces. Many had skin that drooped in thick wattles of flesh. They rose in a rush, charging the bars that trapped them. And then they flowed right through the metal and were upon Jenson. — Calli Breehart, upon visiting the dungeons below the dead wizard Taosïr's castle in Ravenscar

Egui are an especially fearful type of undead. Variously described as the ghosts of those who died of hunger or of those who were especially gluttonous in life, egui wander the night in search of food in order to sate their terrible, gnawing hunger. Egui are cursed, however, for their mouths are too small to actually consume anything but rotted, spoiled food. Their very presence causes fresh food to decay, after which they hungrily consume the disgusting meal and then attack those who failed to help them.

In some tales, it is said that hostile egui can be appeased, or at least distracted, with offers of food. Food left in an egui's path, or offered directly, is all but irresistible, for the egui's aura automatically rots the food, transforming it into a repugnant meal that the hungry ghost immediately consumes. While eating, the ghost can do nothing else, which allows its foes to attack it or escape. It is widely believed, however, that consuming rotting food actually heals damage the egui has taken, so this tactic should be used warily.

Egui

Medium undead, chaotic evil

Armor Class 14 (natural armor)
Hit Points 54 (12d8)
Speed 0 ft., fly 30 ft.

STR	DEX	CON	INT	WIS	CHA
6 (−2)	13 (+1)	10 (+0)	10 (+0)	16 (+3)	4 (−3)

Damage Immunities cold, necrotic, poison
Damage Resistances acid, fire, lightning, thunder
Condition Immunities charmed, exhaustion, frightened, grappled, paralyzed, petrified, poisoned, prone, restrained
Senses darkvision 60 ft., passive Perception 13
Languages any languages it knew in life
Challenge 3 (700 XP)

Aura of Decay. Any foodstuffs within 10 feet of an egui instantly rot and are destroyed. Any food destroyed in this fashion can be consumed by the ghost's Consume action.
Incorporeal Movement. The egui can move through other creatures and objects as if they were difficult terrain. It takes 5 (1d10) force damage if it ends its turn inside an object.

Actions

Ceaseless Hunger. *Melee Weapon Attack:* +3 to hit, reach 5 ft., one target. *Hit:* 14 (3d8 + 1) damage. The target must succeed on a DC 12 Constitution saving throw or it takes a level of exhaustion due to the crippling effects of hunger.
Consume. Egui are driven by their insatiable hunger, but their tiny mouths prevent them from consuming any food that is not spoiled or rotting. If rotting or spoiled food (such as that produced by an egui's Aura of Decay ability) is within 10 feet of an egui, it must immediately move toward that food and consume it, taking an action to do so. While this means that the egui cannot attack while using its Consume action, it also heals the egui of 1d4 points of damage.

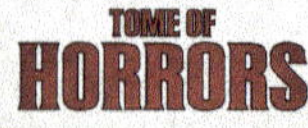

EKIMMU

Our mounts reared up as the stranger approached. Its jerking movements hinted at some disease, but its red eyes gave me pause. The stranger opened its mouth unnaturally wide, and a sound like a million infants crying out in the buzzes of hornets assailed us. Before we could react, the stranger collapsed to the dust, only for our trusted torchbearer's eyes to go blank and then reddish. Then she opened her mouth, and the same horrid sound assailed us again. — Sir Cedric of Reme, knight errant

Ekimuu are the spirits of the dead who have not been given proper funerary rites. They may be murder victims cast into a defile, lonely hermits who died far away from others, or travelers too far from home for anyone to claim their corpses. Denied entry into the afterlife, they roam the world looking to vent their wrath upon mortals. They often do this by possessing a person and committing violent crimes, abandoning their victim when suspicions are aroused. Some legends say that an ekimmu can be quieted or even laid to rest if invited to a funerary feast and offered the appropriate libations.

EKIMMU

Medium undead, chaotic evil

Armor Class 13
Hit Points 45 (10d8)
Speed 0 ft., fly 30 ft. (hover)

STR	DEX	CON	INT	WIS	CHA
7 (–2)	16 (+3)	10 (+0)	14 (+2)	14 (+2)	15 (+ 2)

Damage Resistances acid, fire, lightning, thunder; bludgeoning, piercing, and slashing from nonmagical attacks
Damage Immunities cold, necrotic, poison
Condition Immunities charmed, exhaustion, frightened, grappled, paralyzed, petrified, poisoned, prone, restrained
Senses darkvision 60 ft., passive Perception 12
Languages any languages it knew in life
Challenge 5 (1,800 XP)

Incorporeal Movement. The ekimmu can move through creatures and objects as if they were difficult terrain. It takes 5 (1d10) force damage if it ends its turn within a creature or object.
Unnatural Aura. Beasts within a 60-foot radius centered on the ekimmu are disturbed by its presence. All Wisdom (Animal Handling) checks within this zone suffer disadvantage and beasts must succeed at a DC 12 Wisdom saving throw or become frightened of the ekimmu for one minute.

ACTIONS

Withering Touch. *Melee Weapon Attack:* +5 to hit, reach 5 ft., one target. *Hit:* 16 (4d6 + 2) necrotic damage.
***Paralyzing Howl* (recharge 5–6).** The ekimmu lets loose a horrible howling noise that grips people's souls. All creatures within a 60-foot cube centered on the ekimmu must succeed at a DC 12 Wisdom saving throw or become paralyzed for 1d4 + 1 rounds. Creatures that succeed on their saving throw are immune to that ekimmu's paralyzing howl for 24 hours.
***Possession* (recharge 6).** One creature that the ekimmu can see within five feet must succeed at a DC 12 Wisdom saving throw or become possessed by the ekimmu; the ekimmu then disappears and the target is incapacitated and no longer controls the body. The ekimmu now controls the body but doesn't deprive the target of awareness. The ekimmu can't be targeted by any attack, spell, or other effect, except ones that turn undead, and it retains its own alignment, Intelligence, Wisdom, and Charisma, and immunity to being charmed or frightened. It otherwise uses the possessed creature's statistics, but doesn't have access to the target's knowledge, class features, or proficiencies.
The ekimmu can leave a possessed body at any time. A creature possessed by an ekimmu can be determined by the reddish tint of its eyes. The ekimmu has advantage on any saving throws needed to resist turning while possessed or spells that end its possession attack.

Elemental, Smoke

We ran through the lava field, dodging the exploding rocks hurled into the sky from the erupting thermal vents. A blast of superheated steam caught Rifkin, scalding half his body, but he continued running. Despite his obvious pain, he also managed to hang onto the opal we'd stolen from the fire temple. Konway shouted, "This way," and led us toward a rock plateau. As we neared it, a wall of smoke rose out of jagged crevices and hung in the air before us. Konway jumped through the smoke … and the smoke caught him in flowing tendrils and hurled him to the side into an open lava pit. — Cyane Bere, found severely burned but alive in the Hollow Spire Mountains

These deadly elementals are composed of noxious clouds of brimstone and choking smoke. The roiling clouds are found most often on the edges of the Planes of Fire and Air, where the environment is oppressive and inimical to most creatures, but they frequently find openings into the Prime Material Plane through volcanic vents. Smoke elementals flow around their prey as blinding clouds, but they can also solidify their wisps to strike creatures.

Smoke Elemental
Large elemental, neutral

Armor Class 15
Hit Points 90 (12d10 + 24)
Speed 0 ft., fly 60 ft. (hover)

STR	DEX	CON	INT	WIS	CHA
14 (+2)	20 (+5)	15 (+2)	6 (−2)	10 (+0)	6 (−2)

Skills Stealth +8
Damage Resistances thunder; bludgeoning, piercing, and slashing from nonmagical attacks
Damage Immunities fire, poison
Condition Immunities exhaustion, grappled, paralyzed, petrified, poisoned, prone, restrained, unconscious
Senses darkvision 60 ft., passive Perception 10
Languages Auran, Ignan
Challenge 5 (1,800 XP)

Smoke Form. The elemental can enter a hostile creature's space and stop there. It can move through a space as narrow as one inch wide without squeezing. A creature that touches the elemental or hits it with a melee attack while within five feet of it must succeed on a DC 15 Constitution saving throw or be blinded until the end of its next turn. If a creature starts its turn in the elemental's space or enters it on its turn, that creature must succeed on a DC 15 Constitution saving throw or be blinded until the end of its next turn.

Actions

Multiattack. The smoke elemental makes two Slam attacks.
Slam. *Melee Weapon Attack:* +8 to hit, reach 10 ft., one target. *Hit:* 14 (2d8 + 5) bludgeoning damage. If the target is a creature, it must succeed on a DC 15 Constitution saving throw or be blinded until the end of its next turn.
Stoke. Each creature in the elemental's space must succeed on a DC 15 Constitution saving throw or be incapacitated until it is no longer in the elemental's space.

Elf, Steel (Fandir)

They looked like elves, but their silver skin and hair gave them an exotic look that I had never before encountered. I sketched them quickly as they led us to the great silver ship that floated on the sea of flames. I wish I could have saved my drawings of that wondrous trip, but the parchments didn't survive in that fiery environment.
— Glaslot Gacce, painter of the planes

Steel elves, also sometimes called fandirs, are an offshoot of the elven race that dwell on the Plane of Molten Skies and rarely venture forth from their home in the Steel Garden (a jungle composed of living metal plants). Steel elves average five feet tall and typically weigh just over 100 pounds. Their skin is glossy silver and their hair ranges from silver to bronze to brass to gold. Eye color varies, though most tend to be a shade of bronze or brass.

Steel Elf

Medium humanoid (elf), any alignment

Armor Class 13 (studded leather)
Hit Points 22 (4d8 + 4)
Speed 30 ft.

STR	DEX	CON	INT	WIS	CHA
13 (+1)	13 (+1)	12 (+1)	10 (+0)	14 (+2)	10 (+0)

Skills Perception +4, Stealth +3
Senses darkvision 60 ft., passive Perception 14
Languages Common, Elvish
Challenge 1/2 (100 XP)

Fey Ancestry. The steel elf has advantage on saving throws against being charmed and magic can't put them to sleep.

Actions

Multiattack. The elf makes two Longsword attacks or two Longbow attacks.
Longsword. *Melee Weapon Attack:* +3 to hit, reach 5 ft., one target. *Hit:* 5 (1d8 + 1) slashing damage or 6 (1d10 + 1) slashing damage if used with two hands.
Longbow. *Ranged Weapon Attack:* +3 to hit, range 150/600 ft., one target. *Hit:* 5 (1d8 + 1) piercing damage.

Faceless

It was Ol' Mason, I'm sure of it. But maybe it wasn't? I mean, that old scoundrel has a belly on him from that rotgut he drinks. I saw his face, but he was slender, and taller, and I've never seen him wearin' a hat. But I'd know that old face anywhere. He stole mah chickens last summer. Why would he want to kill the tax collector though? — Farmer Cleeves, a witness in the death of Donovan Knox, the king's tax collector

No one is entirely sure where the fiendish race known as the faceless comes from, only that they are evil beings that appear to revel in — and possibly draw sustenance from — acts of murder and violence. Possessed of a natural ability to conceal their identity, the faceless leave behind a trail of chaos, fear, and suspicion. Witnesses to crimes committed by a faceless — and those few who survive their deadly attacks — invariably recall the perpetrator differently, usually as the individual they think most likely to have committed the offense.

Dark rites and sacrifice can summon the faceless and task them with assassinations and acts of terror. They are especially well-suited to such rituals, as they rarely ask for much in the way of payment, save the ability to commit their bloody and repellent crimes. Calling on the faceless is not entirely without risk, however, as some stories tell of a faceless turning on its summoner once its killings and other mayhem is complete.

Faceless

Medium fiend, chaotic evil

Armor Class 18
Hit Points 132 (24d8 + 24)
Speed 30 ft.

STR	DEX	CON	INT	WIS	CHA
10 (+0)	18 (+4)	12 (+1)	16 (+3)	18 (+4)	14 (+2)

Saving Throws Dex +8, Wis +8
Skills Athletics +8, Acrobatics +12, Sleight of Hand +12, Stealth +12, Investigation +11, Insight +12, Perception +12, Survival +12, Deception +10, Intimidation +10, Persuasion +10
Senses darkvision 60 ft., passive Perception 22
Languages Abyssal, telepathy 120 ft.
Challenge 10 (5,900 XP)

Anonymous. Any eyewitness to an attack committed by a faceless must make a DC 22 Wisdom saving throw when recalling the crime. On a failure, the witness falsely remembers that the crime was committed by either a random stranger or by an individual that the witness believes most likely to have committed the crime.

Assassinate. During its first turn, the faceless has advantage on attack rolls against any creature that hasn't taken a turn. Any hit the assassin scores against a surprised creature is a critical hit.

Blur. The outline of the faceless shifts and shimmers as if under a *blur* spell. Attacks against the faceless are at disadvantage. Attackers that do not rely on sight or that can see through illusions are immune to this effect.

Evasion. If the faceless is subjected to an effect that allows it to make a Dexterity saving throw to take only half damage, the assassin instead takes no damage if it succeeds on the saving throw, and only half damage if it fails.

Sneak Attack (1/turn). The faceless deals an extra 16 (5d6) damage when it hits a target with a weapon attack and has advantage on the attack roll, or when the target is within five feet of an ally of the assassin that isn't incapacitated and the assassin doesn't have disadvantage on the Attack roll.

Actions

Multiattack. The faceless makes two Dagger attacks.

Dagger. *Melee Weapon Attack:* +8 to hit, reach 5 ft., one target. *Hit:* 6 (1d4 + 4) piercing damage, and the target must make a DC 18 Constitution saving throw, taking 28 (8d6) poison damage on a failed save, or half as much damage on a successful one.

Fear Guard

The clawed hand brushed across my face, leaving a trail of blood and coldness. I turned to face my attacker, only to see a face of madness. Colors and features swirled beneath the translucent hood, calm one moment, terrified the next, and then gripped in primal rage. I fought back, but my blade passed through its armored torso as if it were empty air. Dropping that useless steel, I drew the ancient bronze dagger forged years ago and struck at the terror, each blow bringing up a shower of cold ichor. — Tara the Wise, adventurer

Fear guards are undead summoned from the depths of the vilest planes to serve as guardians of tombs, crypts, and other burial places. They are lurkers, not wardens, and prefer to wait until an intruder passes by before they strike from the shadows. Terrible foes, fear guards radiate an aura of dread that can frighten even the staunchest foe of undeath.

Fear Guard
Medium undead, chaotic evil

Armor Class 13
Hit Points 58 (9d8 + 18)
Speed fly 30 ft.

STR	DEX	CON	INT	WIS	CHA
6 (–2)	15 (+2)	15 (+2)	10 (+0)	12 (+1)	18 (+4)

Saving Throws Con +2, Wis +3
Skills Acrobatics +6, Insight +5, Perception +5, Stealth +6
Damage Vulnerabilities radiant
Damage Resistances acid, cold, fire, lightning, thunder; bludgeoning, piercing, and slashing from nonmagical attacks
Damage Immunities necrotic, poison
Condition Immunities charmed, exhaustion, grappled, paralyzed, petrified, poisoned, prone, restrained, unconscious
Senses darkvision 60 ft., passive Perception 15
Languages understands all languages it knew in life but can't speak
Challenge 4 (1,100 XP)

Create Spawn. Any living creature reduced to Wisdom 0 by a fear guard is slain and becomes a fear guard under the control of its killer in 1d6 rounds.

Sunlight Sensitivity. A fear guard exposed to natural sunlight suffers 7 (2d6) radiant damage per round of exposure and moves at half its normal speed.

Innate Spellcasting. The fear guard's spellcasting ability is Charisma (spell save DC 14). The fear guard can innately cast the following spells, requiring only verbal components:

At will: *darkness, ray of enfeeblement*

Actions

Incorporeal Touch. *Melee Weapon Attack:* +4 to hit, reach 5 ft., one target. *Hit:* 7 (2d4 + 2) slashing damage and the target loses two points of Wisdom until after it completes a long rest. A creature brought to 0 Wisdom by this attack dies.

Fei Shei

I'd never seen such a menagerie of animals gathered in one spot. There were monkeys, lizards, colorful birds, a strange little burrowing rodent I wanted to examine closer, and a bizarre rabbit that just stared at us. We pushed through a thick hedge and found ourselves under a low canopy of palm fronds. As I ducked low, a green serpent dropped out of the foliage and hovered before me on membranous wings. It bared its fangs, and a colorful throat fan sparkled and flashed with a coruscating rainbow of colors that stole my vision. Gorfun carried me to safety.
— *Ambrose Deraven, reporting on the odd zoo discovered hidden in the Harwood Forest*

Fei shei are greenish tree snakes that live in warm temperate and tropical regions in and around the Xha'en Hegemony. They normally feed on small rodents, birds, eggs, and other snakes. They are also highly territorial. If approached, a fei shi drops from its perch, unfurls a pair of bat-like wings, and attacks intruders with poisonous fangs.

Fei shei possess expanding throat fans that emit a burst of bright, disorienting colors at threatening enemies. This dazzling display can incapacitate most predators and can also endanger humans who inadvertently blunder into a nest of the serpents.

Fei Shei

Small beast, unaligned

Armor Class 17 (natural armor)
Hit Points 82 (15d6 + 30)
Speed 10 ft., fly 40 ft.

STR	DEX	CON	INT	WIS	CHA
8 (–1)	18 (+4)	15 (+2)	2 (–4)	12 (+1)	4 (–3)

Damage Resistances poison
Senses darkvision 60 ft., passive Perception 11
Languages —
Challenge 2 (450 XP)

Actions

Bite. *Melee Weapon Attack:* +6 to hit, reach 5 ft., one target. *Hit:* 9 (2d4 + 4) poison damage. The target must make a DC 10 Constitution saving throw or be poisoned until the beginning of the fei shei's next turn.

***Dazzle* (recharges 5–6).** The fei shei opens a brightly-hued neck fan and subjects targets to a burst of disorienting colors. All targets within a 15-foot cone are affected as if by a *color spray* spell; roll 6d10 to determine how many hit points are affected and targets are blinded until the start of the fei shei's next turn in order of their hit points, as per the spell.

Fen Witch

We'd spent long, miserable days in the Sin Mire before we came across the cottage. An old woman was sitting on the wraparound porch as if waiting for us to arrive. The stinging insects didn't seem to bother her, although they swarmed madly around us. When she spoke, her voice was like two stones grinding together, as if she regularly inhaled the smoke issuing from the chimney of her abode. She said her name was Meg-o-the-Green, and she asked a lot of questions of her own. She wasn't what she seemed. We found this out when she spoke Canissa's name and the sorcerer dropped dead on the porch. — Mellie Winds, who was found wandering delirious and alone in the swamp

A fen witch is a female humanoid with one nostril, webbed feet and hands, and fiery red eyes. Her body is cloaked in tattered robes of gray or brown. Her hands have razor-sharp claws and her hair is long and unkempt.

The fen witch is a creature of legend that is found only in the most remote of places. It is almost always a solitary creature — they despise others of their own kind almost as much as they hate strangers in their swamps —but they sometimes band together in larger groups for mysterious, evil rituals. Occasionally, spellcasting fen witches are encountered. These tend to be the leaders of their small covens by virtue of their greater ability to inflict suffering on their cohorts.

A fen witch is thoroughly evil and malign, speaking to those she encounters only to learn the "secret vibrations" of their true names in order to use that secret against them. It is not uncommon for a fen witch to train or charm swamp creatures such as giant crocodiles to come to her aid when needed.

Fen Witch

Medium monstrosity, chaotic evil

Armor Class 12 (padded armor)
Hit Points 33 (6d8 + 6)
Speed 30 ft.

STR	DEX	CON	INT	WIS	CHA
15 (+2)	12 (+1)	13 (+1)	14 (+2)	14 (+2)	15 (+2)

Saving Throws Con +3
Skills Deception +4, Insight +4, Perception +4, Stealth +3
Languages Common, Deep Speech, Sylvan, telepathy 100 ft.
Senses darkvision 60 ft., passive Perception 14
Challenge 2 (450 XP)

Horrific Appearance. The sight of a fen witch is so revolting that anyone who sets eyes on one within 60 feet must make a successful DC 11 Constitution saving throw or be sickened, with effects identical to the poisoned condition, for one minute. Characters fighting a fen witch can avert their eyes at the start of their turn and take disadvantage on attack rolls. Anyone surprised by a fen witch must attempt this saving throw immediately at the beginning of combat unless they can't see her for some other reason. This saving throw never needs to be attempted more than once per 24 hours. Fen witches and hags of all kinds are immune to this effect.

Swamp Stride. A fen witch can move through any sort of natural difficult terrain at its normal speed while within a swamp. Magically altered terrain affects a fen witch normally.

Actions

Multiattack. A fen witch makes two Claw attacks.
Claw. *Melee Weapon Attack:* +4 to hit, reach 5 ft.; one creature. *Hit:* 5 (1d6 + 2) slashing damage.
Death Speak. A fen witch who knows the secret vibrations of an individual's name can speak that name as an attack. If the individual hears the fen witch speak its name, that creature must make a successful DC 12 Wisdom saving throw or immediately drop to 0 hit points. If the save succeeds, that creature can't be affected again by the same fen witch's death speak for 24 hours. Note that the fen witch does not need to speak a language the creature understands in order to affect it; she only needs to speak its name with its secret vibrations. Other fen witches who hear the name spoken this way can't use it for their own death speak attacks (if the target's saving throw succeeds, other fen witches assume the name was vibrated incorrectly and won't copy it). Each fen witch must learn the vibrations independently by using her mind probe successfully on the target.
Mind Probe. A fen witch peers into the mind of a living creature within 60 feet in an attempt to extract the secret vibrations of the creature's name. The target resists the mental trespassing (and becomes immune to further mind probes by the same fen witch until after a long rest) with a successful DC 12 Wisdom saving throw. If the saving throw fails, the fen witch finds the information she sought and can use her Death Speak ability on a later turn. Creatures with an Intelligence score of 2 or less are immune to this ability, as are creatures that are immune to psychic damage.

Feng Xianji (Wind Fey)

Although we were warned against it, we pushed into the Green Warden Forest, following game trails toward Hollow Mountain. Although I never saw anyone, I felt eyes watching as we marched. Once, I thought I saw a tiny figure waving a spear as it stood in the crook of a tree. But when I looked again, it was gone. When we came to the clearing, nature itself rebelled against us, with whirlwinds blasting us into the tree trunks with such force that many of the porters never stood again. I thought I saw those same little figures cheering as we ran back the way we came. —Commander Viemens of the Duchy of Westmarch

The race of fey called feng xianji by the people of Xha'en inhabit grasslands, meadows, and the lower slopes of mountains. They can pass for human, but an astute observer may notice that their appearance is slightly "off" from normal people. All feng xianji are beautiful regardless of these subtle differences, and the majority of them are female. Wind fey act as defenders of the regions where they dwell. Normally shy and retiring, these beings make their presence known if their territories are violated, if trees are felled, if animals are hunted, or if settlers attempt to cultivate or build homes. While they are hostile to such intrusions, they are not evil and desist if the offenders leave. Some adventurers have told stories of making peace with the wind fey, who may allow hunting or limited forestry in their regions in exchange for protection from more destructive foes such as orcs or gnolls.

The feng xianji nonetheless have access to significant elemental powers and can create whirlwinds similar to those of air elementals, summoning the forces of nature to batter and drive off enemies. In most cases, the wind fey try to avoid direct conflict with invaders, preferring instead to plague them with winds and cyclones to damage or destroy structures and discomfit or injure outsiders. They prefer to do this without actually revealing themselves at all, leading some to suspect evil spirits or malign magic for the attacks.

Wind Fey

Medium fey, chaotic neutral

Armor Class 15 (natural armor)
Hit Points 72 (16d8)
Speed 20 ft., fly 20 ft.

STR	DEX	CON	INT	WIS	CHA
9 (−1)	14 (+2)	10 (+0)	10 (+0)	12 (+1)	15 (+2)

Skills Perception +5, Stealth +6
Senses passive Perception 15
Languages Sylvan
Challenge 3 (700 XP)

Actions

Spear. *Melee Weapon Attack:* +4 to hit, reach 5 ft., one target. *Hit:* 7 (2d4 + 2) piercing damage.

Whirlwind (recharge 5–6). Each creature in the wind fey's space must make a DC 13 Strength saving throw. On a failure, a target takes 15 (3d8 + 2) bludgeoning damage and is flung up to 20 feet away from the wind fey in a random direction and is knocked prone. If a thrown target strikes an object, such as a wall or floor, the target takes 3 (1d6) bludgeoning damage for every 10 feet it was thrown. If the target is thrown at another creature, that creature must succeed on a DC 13 Dexterity saving throw or take the same damage and be knocked prone.

If the saving throw is successful, the target takes half the bludgeoning damage and isn't flung away or knocked prone.

FILTH FAIRY

Filth fairies! They might look like us, but we claim no kinship. They are slovenly bores with the manners of the hags they serve. They tried to invade our queen's circle once. Once. They ooze filth and would kill anything of beauty. Don't travel the swamps where they congregate, for they spew disease and lies. — Excerpt from Conversations with a Sprite *by the High Druid Rosalee Greenbriar*

These small fey creatures superficially look like sprites, save for the ooze and filth that covers their body and the slightly ravenous look on their small faces. Acid sizzles as it drips from their tiny pointed teeth and sharp claws.

These small fey are often at home in the deepest, darkest swamps, where they revel in the muck and filth of the marsh. They delight in the pollution of clean waters and actively try to expand their contaminated realms. These fey also ally themselves with creatures who enjoy the same environments and even sometimes cultivate swamp oozes and other denizens of the bog. Filth fairies are sometimes found serving a green hag, or, rarely, a coven of green hags, with whom they work to control their swampy paradise.

FILTH FAIRY
Small fey, neutral evil

Armor Class 13 (natural armor)
Hit Points 45 (7d6 + 21)
Speed 30 ft., fly 30 ft., swim 30 ft.

STR	DEX	CON	INT	WIS	CHA
6 (–2)	14 (+2)	16 (+3)	6 (–2)	11 (+0)	9 (–1)

Skills Perception +2, Stealth +4, Survival +2
Damage Immunities acid, poison
Condition Immunities poisoned
Senses darkvision 60 ft., passive Perception 12
Languages Common, Sylvan
Challenge 3 (700 XP)

Amphibious. The filth fairy can breathe air and water.
Innate Spellcasting. The filth fairy's innate spellcasting ability is Constitution (spell save DC 13, +5 to hit with spell attacks). It can cast the following spells innately, without requiring material components:
At will: *acid splash*
3/day: *acid arrow*
1/day: *stinking cloud*

ACTIONS

Claw. *Melee Weapon Attack:* +4 to hit, reach 5 ft., one target. *Hit:* 4 (1d4 + 2) slashing damage plus 3 (1d6) acid damage.
***Slime Breath* (recharge 5–6).** The filth fairy spews slimy acid in a 15-foot-long cone. Creatures in the area must make a DC 13 Dexterity saving throw, taking 17 (5d6) acid damage on a failed saving throw, or half as much damage on a successful saving throw.

FLOWERSHROUD

It was the lamest and weakest of creatures we had encountered, a barely mobile carnivorous plant. We just walked past it and went on our way. But barely mobile does not mean immobile, as we later learned. The mass of tendrils and flowers crept up on us that night, moving one bundle of root-tendrils at a time, and went unnoticed by Stafrar. It attacked while he was on watch; we found him spasming and shaking on the ground afterward, his body pierced by hundreds of poison-tipped thorns. — Păuk, apprentice mage

Flowershrouds are plants that crave to sink their roots into warm flesh and drink the nutrients held within. They are slow moving but camouflage themselves as masses of wildflowers. Thus hidden, they wait beside streams, in glades, or along paths for the unwary. The plant attacks lone prey with several long, thorn-covered tendrils that tear and choke while injecting poison. Larger parties or more dangerous-looking prey are stalked, slowly but patiently, and attacked while they sleep.

FLOWERSHROUD
Large plant, unaligned

Armor Class 11 (natural armor)
Hit Points 24 (4d10 + 3)
Speed 5 ft., climb 5 ft.

STR	DEX	CON	INT	WIS	CHA
6 (–2)	12 (+1)	12 (+1)	1 (–5)	10 (+0)	6 (–2)

Damage Resistances bludgeoning and piercing from nonmagical attacks
Damage Immunities psychic damage
Condition Immunities charmed, deafened, frightened, prone, stunned, unconscious
Senses tremorsense 60 ft., passive Perception 10
Languages —
Challenge 1 (200 XP)

False Appearance. A patch of flowershroud looks completely natural to the untrained eye. It always has advantage on Stealth checks, and attempts to detect the flowershroud rely on a character's Nature skill, not Perception.
Shroudblossom Poison. The flowershroud releases a virulent poison each time it lashes out with its thorn strands. Any creature struck by the flowershroud must succeed on a DC 11 Constitution saving throw or be poisoned, falling prone and going into convulsions for one minute. During this time, the creature is incapacitated and cannot take any actions or reactions. The target can repeat the saving throw at the end of each of its turns, ending the effect on itself on a success.

ACTIONS

Multiattack. The flowershroud makes three Thorn Strand attacks.
Thorn Strand. *Melee Weapon Attack:* +3 to hit, reach 15 ft., one target. *Hit:* 4 (1d6 + 1) piercing damage and the target must make a successful DC 11 Constitution saving throw or be affected by shroudblossom poison.

Fluttercat

I've dealt with them big cats before, when they come down outta the mountains to seize a sheep or two. Most scare easy, and they don't come back 'less they are starvin'. And that's only when the mountain goats go scarce. But this? This? I don't know nothin' 'bout dealin' with flyin' cats as big as those mountain lions. Fur and feathers? What kind of madness is this? — Farmer Olga Mattis, after several flying felines attacked farms around Tanner's Green

Cloud giants magically bred fluttercats to be pets and to keep down bird populations. While this worked out splendidly for the cloud giants, prides of feral fluttercats, with no fear of humanoids, have learned that cows and sheep are tasty meals. Cloud giant communities have yet to acknowledge any responsibility in this matter, and fluttercats are a terrible problem in ranching and herding communities wherever fluttercat prides claim territory.

Fluttercats are natural pack hunters and adroit in their flight. They prefer easy fights with slow prey whenever possible, but a well-fed fluttercat pride sometimes chases and toys with a meal for some time before digging in. They prefer sheep over all other food, and eat humanoids only if starving. They defend themselves if threatened.

Fluttercats are beautiful creatures, as sleek and graceful as one might expect of large, winged cats. The size of a cheetah or puma, their fur and feathers have been bred to come in a range of blues and grays, with lynx-like fur patterns and hawk-like feather patterns. Each pride varies a bit in colors and markings, and captive-bred fluttercats show more variety still. Domesticated fluttercats turn wild easily, and even a lazy, fat, house fluttercat, raised among giants, can sometimes become a deadly predator around smaller creatures.

Fluttercat

Medium beast, unaligned

Armor Class 17 (natural)
Hit Points 162 (25d8 + 50)
Speed 40 ft., fly 50 ft.

STR	DEX	CON	INT	WIS	CHA
17 (+3)	20 (+5)	15 (+2)	2 (–4)	16 (+3)	6 (–2)

Skills Perception +6, Stealth +8
Senses darkvision 120 ft., passive Perception 16
Languages —
Challenge 7 (2,900 XP)

Soothing Purr. A calm and happy fluttercat can purr almost like a housecat, and like its roar, a fluttercat's purr is suffused with magic. Those who spend at least an hour in close proximity to a purring fluttercat (including the fluttercat itself) are affected as if by a long rest and *lesser restoration*. A creature other than the fluttercat can receive this benefit no more than once per day.

Actions

Multiattack. The fluttercat makes one Bite attack and two Claw attacks.

Bite. *Melee Weapon Attack:* +6 to hit, reach 5 ft., one target. *Hit:* 15 (2d8 + 6) piercing damage.

Claw. *Melee weapon attack:* +8 to hit, reach 5 ft., one target. *Hit:* 11 (1d6 + 8) slashing damage, plus if the fluttercat hits one target with both Claw attacks on one turn, the target takes an additional 23 (5d6 + 6) slashing damage.

Aerial Pounce. Fluttercats are adept at using aerial dives to knock prey to the ground. If a fluttercat is both in the air and at least 10 feet above an opponent, the fluttercat may move up to twice its speed in a dive, ending with two Claw attacks. If both attacks hit, then in addition to extra damage the target must succeed on a DC 12 Dexterity saving throw or be knocked prone.

***Frightful Roar* (recharge 6).** When a fluttercat roars, the sound is magically projected and amplified, causing all creatures that can hear it and that are within 60 feet of it to make a successful DC 12 Constitution saving throw or be stunned for 1d3 rounds.

FOREST CHILD

Mother Harcourt claimed to have seen a child living in the Black Forest, so we decided to investigate. Imagine our surprise to find the rumor to be true. We stumbled upon the young man as he sat on a log deep among the trees. He had his back to us. He spoke without turning, his voice light and sweet. "Have you come to feed me? I'm so hungry." Only when he turned did we realize the "child" was not human and had yellow flowers sprouting from its flesh. It held the remains of a fox in its hands, and its mouth was smeared with the creature's blood. The boy launched itself at us. — City Warder Quarin Macally from the town of Oxibbul

Forest children are born as amalgams of the restless spirits of children who were murdered or who died of prolonged suffering. When such innocent, outraged souls go unavenged or are unable to pass on, they sometimes drift toward the heart of the nearest forest and merge into a forest child's unquenchable malice. Only in cases of nearby mass child tragedy do two or more forest children appear together, but when they do, they appear and behave as close siblings.

Forest children are not intelligent, and their hunger cannot be sated. They do speak, but only to repeat phrases such as "I'm so hungry" and "Please give me some food." Ignoring all offers of actual food, a forest child seeks to eat any beings it encounters and does not distinguish between good or evil, kind or cruel. Forest children charm anyone they can and then eat their victims alive, all the while behaving as if they are sweet, innocent children. The only way to release the tormented souls is to destroy them, and until a forest child is destroyed, it never stops attempting to feed. That said, if a forest child is attacked, it retaliates savagely until either it or its attacker is slain.

FOREST CHILD

Small undead, neutral evil

Armor Class 18 (natural armor)
Hit Points 209 (22d6 + 132)
Speed 20 ft.

STR	DEX	CON	INT	WIS	CHA
13 (+1)	20 (+5)	23 (+6)	7 (–2)	16 (+3)	18 (+4)

Saving Throws Dex +10, Con +11
Damage Immunities poison
Condition Immunities exhaustion, fright, poisoned, unconscious.
Resistances Bludgeoning, piercing and slashing damage from nonmagical attacks; necrotic damage.
Senses darkvision 60 ft., passive Perception 13
Languages None, though it repeats a few phrases in any languages common to the region (see below).
Challenge 14 (11,500 XP)

Boundless Hunger. The forest child can eat the flesh of sapient beings very quickly, without ever growing full. When eating, its mouth stretches impossibly wide to reveal a limitless void within. Whenever a forest child successfully deals damage with a bite, the target must make a DC 19 Constitution saving throw or take terrible harm to an appendage. Roll 1d4 to determine which limb is being eaten. It takes four bites to the same limb to consume it completely, though only two bites are required to fully disable the limb. Disabled limbs heal normally, but lost limbs can be restored only with *regeneration*.

Charm. Any sapient creature who hears the forest child's voice must succeed on a DC 19 Wisdom saving throw or be charmed by the forest child. The charmed target regards the forest child as a real child to be cared for and protected. Although the target isn't under the forest child's control, it interprets the forest child's requests or actions in irrationally favorable ways.

The effect lasts 24 hours or until the forest child is destroyed, or is on a different plane of existence than the target, or if the ability is countered by a bard's countercharm or similar magical effects.

If a creature's saving throw is successful or the effect ends for it (for any reason other than the 24-hour duration), the creature is immune to the forest child's Charm for the next 24 hours.

Forest Lullaby. Anyone who falls victim to a forest child's Charm ability must, in the next round, succeed on a DC 19 Intelligence saving throw or be caught in a kind of dreamy daze. An affected character hears lovely, tinkling music from nowhere, and feels comfortable and safe. The target can take no action and can no longer feel pain or register damage or danger while in this state. In any round in which the target takes damage, a new saving throw may be made to shake off the effects and act normally until the Forest Lullaby reasserts itself. Effective recharge 6, but rolled individually on each charmed creature's initiative. The overall Forest Lullaby continues until either the forest child is destroyed or a *remove curse* or *dispel magic* is cast upon the target. Creatures immune to the forest child's Charm, for any reason, are also immune to the Forest Lullaby.

Legendary Resistance (3/day). If the forest child fails a saving throw, it can choose to succeed instead.

Magic Resistance. The forest child has advantage on saving throws against spells and other magical effects, unless they specifically target undead.

Regeneration. The forest child heals 3 hit points at the start of its turn. This ability doesn't function if it took damage from any magical ability that specifically targets undead since its previous turn.

Rise Again. After a forest child is defeated, the region in which it spawned remains vulnerable to the spawning of a new forest child within 1d6 moon cycles. This effect can be ended only by casting *hallow* on the spot where the forest child was destroyed.

ACTIONS

Bite. *Melee Weapon Attack:* +10 to hit, reach 5 ft., one target. *Hit:* 18 (2d12 +5) slashing damage, plus *boundless hunger*.

LEGENDARY ACTIONS

The forest child can take three legendary actions, choosing from the options below. Only one legendary action option can be used at a time and only at the end of another creature's turn. The forest child regains spent legendary actions at the start of its turn.

Skittering Advance. The forest child moves up to twice its movement, only to close distance with a single chosen target. This provokes opportunity attacks as normal.

Unsettling Touch. Smiling sweetly, the forest child touches one opponent, like a child's fond caress. The target must make a DC 19 Wisdom save or be frightened for one round. This ability works only once per opponent, and not at all on opponents who make their saves.

Chomp (costs 2 actions). The forest child makes a bite attack on one target in range. If successful, it also uses its Boundless Hunger ability.

Disappear (costs 2 actions). The forest child magically teleports up to 60 feet to a suitable hiding place, if any is in range, and immediately makes a Dexterity check to hide.

Forest Stalker

Something moved in the branches, but even our ranger DuVallo couldn't find the source of the noise. We trudged on, making our own path through the dense underbrush, when Galton bringing up the rear gave a shriek and was gone. They took advantage of our shock and came at us from all sides. I saw one a moment before it leaped from the trees. It blended so well with the trunk and the leaves, but the moment it came for me, it was all tiger. Am I dead? — Explorer Rabiy Grouse, via a speak with the dead *spell once his remains were found in the Westwood*

The forest stalker is a tiger-sized feline that dwells in temperate woods. Fierce and merciless, the forest stalker is made deadlier by its coat, which has the chameleon-like ability to transform to resemble any surface. Most often, the forest stalker hides in trees, its coat making it indistinguishable from the surrounding boughs and tree trunks. Prey that walks beneath the stalker's hiding place are attacked with sudden fury and absolute surprise.

Normally solitary, forest stalkers can be encountered in pairs during the spring mating season. If captured young enough, forest stalkers can be tamed and kept as guard beasts or even (for certain slightly mad druids and rangers) as pets and animal companions. Those who seek to capture a forest stalker kitten should be aware that these creatures defend their young with extreme ferocity.

Forest Stalker

Large beast, unaligned

Armor Class 19 (natural armor)
Hit Points 121 (22d10)
Speed 50 ft., climb 30 ft.

STR	DEX	CON	INT	WIS	CHA
18 (+4)	18 (+4)	15 (+2)	3 (–4)	12 (+1)	8 (–1)

Skills Perception +7, Stealth +10
Senses passive Perception 17
Languages —
Challenge 5 (1,800 XP)

Natural Camouflage. The forest stalker's coat can transform to resemble whatever surface it is resting on. While it does not move, it is indistinguishable from its environment and can't be detected unless a creature actually blunders into it.

Stealthy. A forest stalker has advantage on all Dexterity (Stealth) checks.

Actions

Multiattack. The forest stalker makes two Claw attacks and one Bite attack.

Bite. *Melee Weapon Attack:* +7 to hit, reach 5 ft., one target. *Hit:* 15 (2d10 + 4) piercing damage.

Claw. *Melee Weapon Attack:* +7 to hit, reach 5 ft., one target. *Hit:* 13 (2d8 + 4) slashing damage.

Fungal Creeper

We decided to bed down in a patch of soft moss on the edge of the Elderwood. We'd been traveling for days, and the rest was sorely needed. At least the sky was clear and the ground was soft. Julien kept first watch. I woke sometime after midnight, with a chill blowing through the trees. I looked for Julien, but he wasn't on the rock where he'd been sitting. I found him collapsed on the ground, a thick fungus wrapped around him. His body spasmed as the fungus fed. — Warby Hale, halfling adventurer

The fungal creeper is a patch of fungus growing upon a boulder or wall, which often appears weathered and strangely corroded. The name comes from its ability to creep along the wall, moving about to follow living creatures. Fungal creepers draw sustenance from minerals found in rock and stone, but supplement their diets with fresh blood.

A fungal creeper may be distracted by fresh meat, whether in the form of rations no more than one day old or the body of an unconscious combatant. They are scavengers and move to feed off carrion as soon as it is detected.

Fungal Creeper
Small plant, unaligned

Armor Class 12 (natural armor)
Hit Points 22 (4d6 + 8)
Speed 10 ft.

STR	DEX	CON	INT	WIS	CHA
13 (+1)	6 (–2)	14 (+2)	1 (–5)	6 (–2)	1 (–5)

Damage Immunities poison
Condition Immunities exhaustion, poisoned, unconscious
Senses Blindsense 60 ft. (blind beyond this radius), passive Perception 8
Languages —
Challenge 1/2 (100 XP)

Amorphous. The fungal creeper can move through an opening as small as one inch without squeezing and can occupy another creature's square.

Actions

Mycelial Bite. *Melee Weapon Attack:* +3 to hit against one target in its square. *Hit:* 4 (1d6 + 1) piercing damage. If the fungal creeper rolls a 19 or 20 to hit, it attaches to its target. The target loses 1d4 hit points at the beginning of each of its turns. A creature may use an action to attempt a DC 13 Strength check to remove the fungal creeper from its target.

Fyr

An odd-looking man-goat was sitting cross-legged on a blanket at the edge of the city. The creature had large horns wrapped in spiraling bands of silver and platinum, and it was deftly threading a silver necklace. Various trinkets were spread on the cloth before it. He stopped and look up as we approached, "Welcome, travelers. I'm Anghus. Feel free to browse my wares." If only we'd known the curse that Anghus was forced to pass on. Now, we're gearing up to find the hag that cursed him to clear our own souls. — Tavis Sunvale, before leaving for the Sin Mire to seek a hag named Egrella Grul

Fyrs are satyr-like creatures that make their homes in the mountainous wilds and dense forests, locating their lairs in secluded caves or caverns or under a dense covering of tangled branches and leaves. They are a nomadic race that rarely stays in one place for longer than a few months before moving on. If they have neighbors, fyrs never give notice before leaving; one morning, they are simply gone. Despite being on the move so often, fyrs acclimate themselves to their surroundings very quickly. Fyr are master jewelers whose trinkets and baubles are highly sought by civilized races that appreciate fine jewelry.

Fyrs are great lovers of animals, and most animals instinctively return their affection. Fyrs are seldom encountered without animals in their company. Typically, for every two fyrs in a group, there will be one to three animals such as badgers, black bears, boars, brown bears, elks, giant badgers, giant weasels, goats, hawks, panthers, or wolves.

Fyr
Small fey, neutral

Armor Class 11
Hit Points 9 (2d6 + 2)
Speed 30 ft.

STR	DEX	CON	INT	WIS	CHA
12 (+1)	13 (+1)	12 (+1)	12 (+1)	13 (+1)	13 (+1)

Skills Animal Handling +3, Arcana +3, Deception +5, Insight +3, Nature +3, Stealth +5
Damage Resistances bludgeoning, piercing, and slashing damage from nonmagical attacks
Senses darkvision 60 ft., passive Perception 11
Languages Common, Sylvan
Challenge 1/4 (50 XP)

Resilient. A fyr has advantage on all saving throws.
Innate Spellcasting. A fyr can cast the following spells without material components using Charisma as its casting ability (spell save DC 11, spell attack bonus +3).
At will: *animal friendship, speak with animals*
3/day each: *faerie fire, pass without trace, beast sense, conjure animals*
1/day each: *dominate beast, invisibility*
Weapon Attunement. Fyrs have an ability to attune themselves with any wood-handled weapon so that they get a +1 bonus to attack rolls with such a weapon once they've handled for at least 10 minutes. This bonus is already included in the Battleaxe attack below.

Actions

Battleaxe. *Melee Weapon Attack:* +4 to hit, reach 5 ft., one creature. *Hit:* 5 (1d8 + 1) slashing damage. ***Headbutt.*** *Melee Weapon Attack:* +3 to hit, reach 5 ft., one creature. *Hit:* 4 (1d6 + 1) bludgeoning damage and the target must make a successful DC 11 Dexterity saving throw or be knocked prone. If the target is knocked prone, the fyr can make an immediate Battleaxe attack against it as a bonus action.

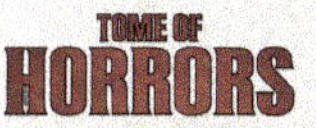

Genie, Sequana

Dolequin said to be cautious, for the genie-folk can be capricious and ill-tempered. But the sights we beheld within the palace that appeared from nowhere upon the desert sands were amazing and put us off our guard. We marveled at the sword-wielding guards who looked as if they were carved from granite, the twirling dancers in diaphanous silks, and the food trays of fruits and bread and cheese readied for us beside luxuriant cushions. Our host came into our midst with a joyous laugh as he rode a silver palanquin carried by nothing we could see. It truly was an amazing night before it all went wrong. We should have listened to Dolequin, may he rest in blessed peace. — Emrith Yeydl the Cursed, forever shunned in the cities of the land

Denizens of the Palace of Prisms (the seat of rulership for the Great Durbar of the Sequana and dominant power on the Elemental Plane of Water), sequana are among the most wondrous of genie-kind. Large and piscine, sequana are an amazing sight to behold, particularly when clad in the finely stitched vests and colorful pantaloons they favor. As sequana care not for the affairs of terrestrials, land dwellers rarely encounter them.

Sequana Genie

Large elemental, neutral

Armor Class 17 (natural armor)
Hit Points 229 (17d10 + 136)
Speed 30 ft., fly 60 ft., swim 90 ft.

STR	DEX	CON	INT	WIS	CHA
22 (+6)	12 (+1)	26 (+8)	18 (+4)	17 (+3)	18 (+4)

Saving Throws Dex +5, Wis +7, Cha +8
Damage Resistances acid, cold, lightning
Senses blindsight 30 ft., darkvision 120 ft., passive Perception 13
Languages Aquan
Challenge 11 (7,200 XP)

Amphibious. The sequana genie can breathe air and water.
Innate Spellcasting. The sequana genie's innate spellcasting ability is Charisma (spell save DC 16, +8 to hit with spell attacks). It can innately cast the following spells, requiring no material components:
At will: *create or destroy water, detect evil and good, detect magic, fog cloud, purify food and drink*
3/day each: *tongues, water breathing, water walk*
1/day each: *conjure elemental* (water elemental only), *control water, gaseous form, invisibility, plane shift*

Actions

Multiattack. The sequana genie makes two Trident attacks.
Trident. *Melee or Ranged Weapon Attack:* +10 to hit, reach 5 ft. or range 20/60 ft., one target. *Hit:* 13 (2d6 + 6) piercing damage, or 15 (2d8 + 6) piercing damage if used with two hands to make a melee attack.
Water Jet. The sequana genie magically shoots water in a 60-foot line that is five feet wide. Each creature in that line must make a DC 16 Dexterity saving throw. On a failure, a target takes 21 (6d6) bludgeoning damage and, if it is Huge or smaller, is pushed up to 20 feet away from the sequana genie and knocked prone. On a success, a target takes half the bludgeoning damage, but is neither pushed nor knocked prone.

Gholle

The howling across the desert was unlike that of any beast I had heard before. We saw them beneath the pale moon's light, loping along in a tight pack, their hunched figures moving as men but oddly also like that of wild animals. They darted back and forth, investigating the ground with their snouts more than with their hands and eyes. Soon we saw their quarry, a pair of local farmers running for their lives. I ordered our guards to intercept the hunters, who turned out to be tall undead hyena, or maybe gorillas, bipeds with a stench like a thousand graves. — Algrid Henswaithe, University of the Vast

Gholles are undead humanoids with the features of hyenas, gorillas, and humans. They often travel in mixed packs of ghouls and ghoul-like creatures and are the leaders of such packs if the gholle is the largest or strongest. Their hunched bodies are 12 feet tall, with gorilla-like faces and long hyena snouts. While most of their body is that of a rotting human corpse, their hands and feet are clearly bestial in nature, with sharp claws and tufts of hair.

Gholle

Large undead, chaotic evil

Armor Class 16 (natural armor)
Hit Points 153 (18d10 + 54)
Speed 30 ft.

STR	DEX	CON	INT	WIS	CHA
21 (+5)	15 (+2)	16 (+3)	13 (+1)	13 (+1)	17 (+3)

Skills Perception +4, Stealth +5
Damage Resistances bludgeoning, piercing, and slashing damage made with nonmagical attacks
Damage Immunities poison
Condition Immunities charmed, exhaustion, poisoned
Senses darkvision 60 ft., passive Perception 14
Languages Abyssal, Common
Challenge 8 (3,900 XP)

Carrion Stench. Any target other than the gholle that starts its turn within five feet of the gholle must succeed on a DC 14 Constitution saving throw or be poisoned until the start of the target's next turn. On a successful saving throw, the gholle is immune to the Stench of all gholles for one hour.

Create Spawn. Any humanoid creature slain by the gholle rises as a ghoul within 1d6 hours. They are not under the command of the gholle that created them, nor do they retain any abilities or memories they did in life.

Magic Resistance. The gholle has advantage on saving throws against spells and other magical effects.

Paralyzing Gaze. When a creature that can see the gholle's eyes starts its turn within 30 feet of the gholle, the gholle can force it to make a DC 14 Wisdom saving throw if the gholle isn't incapacitated and can see the creature. On a failure, the creature is paralyzed for one minute. Unless surprised, a creature can avert its eyes to avoid the saving throw at the start of its turn. If the creature does so, it can't see the gholle until the start of its next turn, when it can avert its eyes again. If the creature looks at the gholle in the meantime, it must immediately attempt the save. While averting its eyes, any attacks on the gholle are done at disadvantage.

Regeneration. The gholle regains 5 hit points at the start of its turn. The gholle is destroyed only if it starts its turn with 0 hit points and doesn't regenerate.

Turn Resistance. The gholle has advantage on saving throws against any effect that turns undead.

Actions

Multiattack. The gholle makes one Bite attack and two Claw attacks.
Bite. *Melee Weapon Attack:* +9 to hit, reach 5 ft., one target. *Hit:* 14 (2d8 + 5) piercing damage.
Claw. *Melee Weapon Attack:* +9 to hit, reach 10 ft., one target. *Hit:* 8 (1d6 + 5) slashing damage.

Ghoul of Khemit

We came upon a village that showed all signs of having been abandoned for some time. Their well was dry, and the tracks of their sand-filled irrigation channels were obvious. Too far from the river to water their fields directly, the village had no doubt faced starvation and the people had fled. I was wrong, however, for figures soon shambled out of the ruined doorways, figures with flesh desiccated to a sinewy leather and faces elongated into muzzles. The smell of the grave proceeded them, and we were forced to cleanse the village with flame. — Algrid Henswaithe, University of the Vast

Those in the desert lands who commit the foul crime of cannibalism are transformed into undead horrors known as ghouls of Khemit. Some are driven by desperation or madness to feast upon their fellow man while others do so out of a twisted preference for the sweetest of meats. In either case, the end result is a hunched figure with sinewy muscle and leathery skin, something more akin to beast than man, with elongated muzzles and fiercely red eyes. The stench of death hangs about them as they hunt their next meal.

Ghoul of Khemit
Medium undead, chaotic evil

Armor Class 13 (natural armor)
Hit Points 26 (4d8 + 8)
Speed 30 ft.

STR	DEX	CON	INT	WIS	CHA
13 (+1)	15 (+2)	14 (+2)	13 (+1)	14 (+2)	16 (+3)

Damage Resistances bludgeoning, piercing, and slashing damage made with nonmagical attacks
Damage Immunities poison
Condition Immunities charmed, exhaustion, poisoned
Senses darkvision 60 ft., passive Perception 12
Languages Abyssal, Common
Challenge 3 (700 XP)

Carrion Stench. Any target other than the ghoul of Khemit that starts its turn within five feet of the ghoul of Khemit must succeed on a DC 14 Constitution saving throw or be poisoned until the start of the target's next turn. On a successful saving throw, the ghoul of Khemit is immune to the Stench of all ghouls of Khemit for one hour.

Dreadful Gaze. When a creature that can see the ghoul of Khemit's eyes starts its turn within 30 feet of it, the ghoul of Khemit can force it to make a DC 12 Wisdom saving throw if the ghoul of Khemit isn't incapacitated and can see the creature. On a failure, the creature is frightened of the ghoul of Khemit for one minute. Unless surprised, a creature can avert its eyes to avoid the saving throw at the start of its turn. If the creature does so, it can't see the ghoul of Khemit until the start of its next turn, when it can avert its eyes again. If the creature looks at the ghoul of Khemit in the meantime, it must immediately attempt the save. While averting its eyes, any attacks on the ghoul of Khemit are done at disadvantage.

Actions

Multiattack. The ghoul of Khemit makes one Bite attack and two Claw attacks.
Bite. *Melee Weapon Attack*: +3 to hit, reach 5 ft., one target. *Hit*: 5 (1d8 + 1) piercing damage.
Claw. *Melee Weapon Attack*: +3 to hit, reach 5 ft., one target. *Hit*: 4 (1d6 + 1) slashing damage and the creature must succeed at a DC 12 Constitution saving throw or suffer from flesh rot. The creature can't regain hit points and loses 5 (1d10) hit points at every moonrise until they recover. Creatures suffering from flesh rot have disadvantage on any Charisma-based checks. A creature may attempt a DC 12 Constitution saving throw following each moonrise to recover from flesh rot, and if they succeed they are no longer affected.

Ghul

Sallivan led us into the tent, which proved a welcome respite from the blistering desert sands. The interior of the dwelling was as odd as it was finding it abandoned in the dunes of the Kanderi. Plush purple pillows were piled in each corner and a brass lanterns floated eight feet above the floor. A finely stitched carpet floated in the center of the tent, hovering a couple of feet in the air. Akalli leaped onto the carpet and immediately sank into it up to her waist as if it were quicksand. Sallivan grabbed her hands to keep her from sinking farther, and that's when the undead thing reached out from the underside of the carpet to gut the fighter. — Acacia Flax, describing the festive tent where her companions perished in the Kanderi Desert

Ghuls are the undead form of genies returned to life by some ancient and now-forgotten magic. Ghuls are ragged-looking creatures standing eight feet tall and wearing tattered remains of beautiful and expensive clothing. Its skin is dry and cracked and seems to break away from its body as it moves. Its eyes are hollow sockets and show no signs of life. Ghuls are completely and thoroughly evil and hate all living creatures.

Ghul

Large undead, chaotic evil

Armor Class 15 (natural armor)
Hit Points 68 (8d10 + 24)
Speed 30 ft., fly 30 ft.

STR	DEX	CON	INT	WIS	CHA
18 (+4)	15 (+2)	16 (+3)	15 (+2)	16 (+3)	18 (+4)

Skills Perception +6, Stealth +5
Damage Resistances necrotic; bludgeoning, piercing, and slashing from nonmagical attacks that are not silver
Damage Immunities acid, poison
Condition Immunities charmed, exhaustion, poisoned
Senses darkvision 60 ft., passive Perception 16
Languages Common, Infernal, Primordial
Challenge 5 (1,800 XP)

Elemental Demise. If the ghul dies, its body disintegrates into a warm, putrid breeze, leaving behind only the equipment the ghul was wearing or carrying.
Genie-kin. Ghuls are undead djinn and are considered genies even though their type is undead.
Magic Weapons. The ghul's weapon attacks are magical.
Undead Nature. A ghul doesn't require air, food, drink, or sleep.

Actions

Multiattack. The ghul makes one Bite attack and one Claws attack.
Bite. *Melee Weapon Attack:* +7 to hit, reach 5 ft., one target. *Hit:* 17 (3d8 + 4) piercing damage.
Claws. *Melee Weapon Attack:* +7 to hit, reach 5 ft., one target. *Hit:* 14 (3d6 + 4) slashing damage. If the target is a creature other than an undead, it must succeed on a DC 14 Constitution saving throw or be paralyzed for one minute. The target can repeat the saving throw at the end of each of its turns, ending the effect on itself on a success.

GIANT

GIANT, ABERRANT

String-of-Ears tracked the raiders back to an abandoned mine deep in the mountains. We didn't know what kind of giants we were dealing with; their tracks were either indistinct or misshapen. When we approached, they came roaring out, mutated and hunched, with gross hair sticking out here and there and their hides covered in oozing blisters. Some had three eyes, others extra limbs, and the one I slew (singlehanded, not bragging, just stating a fact) had a fang-tipped tail. — Big Joanne, mercenary

The foulest of giant kind, aberrant giants are hated by, and in turn hate, all other giants. Their bodies sprout a broad range of deformities, misshapen limbs, strange organs, and other mutations. Their lairs are in caves, abandoned mines, and other underground locales far from civilization. Aberrant giants are known to raid other people, even other giants, for food.

ABERRANT GIANT
Large giant, neutral evil

Armor Class 14 (natural armor)
Hit Points 85 (10d10 + 30)
Speed 20 ft.

STR	DEX	CON	INT	WIS	CHA
22 (+6)	8 (−1)	17 (+3)	7 (−2)	14 (+2)	6 (−2)

Skills Intimidation +4, Perception +6
Senses darkvision 60 ft., passive Perception 16
Languages Giant
Challenge 4 (1,100 XP)

ACTIONS

Multiattack. The aberrant giant makes two Greatclub attacks or makes one Greatclub attack and uses Eye of Balor once.
Greatclub. *Melee Weapon Attack:* +8 to hit, reach 10 ft., one target. *Hit:* 23 (5d6 + 6) slashing damage.
Eye of Balor. The aberrant giant magically forces a creature it can see within 60 feet to make a DC 13 Wisdom saving throw or be magically cursed for one hour. Until the curse ends, the target has disadvantage on attack rolls against the aberrant giant.

Giant, Sea

We were limping into Rashad, the Crest *barely holding itself together after the rough seas and the rougher creatures we had encountered. We had one mast left, and no one thought it would last the journey. We were nearing Karpathos when a wave rose up in front of us, halting our progress. The wind died, leaving us drifting. The ocean exploded in a geyser to port, and when the water crashed back to the sea, a giant was standing alongside the ship. His voice boomed as he held out his hand, "Pay the toll, and you may pass." We willingly threw our treasures large and small into the swells. — Nate Fairweather, former cabin boy on* The Golden Crest

Sea giants have bluish-green skin and eyes that reflect light like two silvery moons. Rippling with muscle, they rise from the depths with a crash of waves on rocks. Sea giants are the reclusive cousins of storm giants. They are most often found in the deepest depths of the seas where they make their dwelling in the cones of long-dead undersea volcanoes. Sea giants have a druid-like power over the forces of the seas and are a living embodiment of its bounty and destructive wrath.

Sea giants seldom come into contact with surface-dwellers but have been known on rare occasions to exact bounties from coastal cities to ensure the safety of their navies and merchant vessels. Sea giants are most commonly encountered within a few hundred miles of their lair, tending to their domain and battling incursions of sahuagin, aboleth, krakens, and other such destructive forces of the undersea.

An adult male sea giant stands 10 feet tall and weighs about 6,000 pounds. Females are slightly shorter and lighter. Both have sea-green skin, dark-green or black hair, and silver eyes. Sea giants adorn themselves in loose flowing robes of white, blue, or green. Many wear wreaths of coral in their hair.

Sea Giant

Large giant, chaotic neutral

Armor Class 17 (natural armor)
Hit Points 178 (17d10 + 85)
Speed 40 ft., swim 30 ft.

STR	DEX	CON	INT	WIS	CHA
29 (+9)	14 (+2)	20 (+5)	17 (+3)	18 (+4)	19 (+4)

Saving Throws Con +9
Skills Acrobatics +6, Athletics +13, Intimidation +8, Perception +8, Stealth +6
Senses darkvision 120 ft., passive Perception 18
Languages Aquan, Common, Giant
Challenge 9 (5,000 XP)

Amphibious. Sea giants can breathe air and water.
Innate Spellcasting. The sea giant's innate spellcasting ability is Charisma (spell save DC 16, +8 to hit with spell attacks). It can innately cast the following spells, requiring no material components:
At will: *create or destroy water, detect magic*
5/day: *control water*
3/day: *control weather*

Actions

Multiattack. The sea giant makes two Slam attacks.
Slam. *Melee Weapon Attack:* +13 to hit, reach 10 ft., one target. *Hit:* 18 (2d8 + 9) bludgeoning damage.
Rock. *Ranged Weapon Attack:* +13 to hit, range 60/240 ft., one target. *Hit:* 27 (4d8 + 9) bludgeoning damage.
***Crushing Pressure* (recharge 5–6).** The sea giant chooses an area of water no larger than a 50-foot cube within 30 feet of it. The water pressure within the space magically increases, and creatures within the area treat it as difficult terrain. In addition, any creature who enters or begins its turn within the area must make a DC 18 Constitution saving throw, taking 18 (4d8) bludgeoning damage on a failed saving throw, or half as much damage on a successful one. The area remains affected by this magic for one minute, until the sea giant dismisses it as an action, or until the sea giant dies.

Giant, Volcano

We had climbed high up the rocky slopes of the volcano Phrygia when we came across the giants. They stood three times our size, and I admit I would have run if our guide had not led us here. He claimed they were peaceful, but that we should follow one rule: Always keep the sun at our backs when dealing with them. He said that to walk on their shadows was to tread on their very souls. Negotiations were going well, when the giant's leader suddenly thrust his spear through our guide. Shocked, I looked up to find that our barbarian friend OTATO! had snuck behind the giants. He had a flagon of ale and was dancing wildly. Right on their shadows. — Balthazane Shalice, on the failed negotiations between the village of Crombleholme and the denizens of the volcano

The 18-foot-tall, barrel-chested volcano giant has leathery, reddish-brown skin and haunting amber eyes. The creature is tough and wiry, with the strength and texture of copper. Volcano giants make their homes in the many twisting caves and subterranean rooms of volcanic cones, which they enlarge and reinforce for their comfort and convenience. Although volcano giants can be described as good-natured and peaceful people, their demeanor can change quickly. At a real or imagined affront, a volcano giant can erupt with a passion that is rivaled only by the fire and fury of the volcano in which it lives. Volcano giants feel that their shadow is actually their soul, and they do not tolerate any creature that dares to trod upon it. They are fierce and brave warriors who don't back down from any adversary.

Clothing for a volcano giant usually consists of little more than a simple wrap of fire lizard skin. Volcano giants wears ornaments made of bone, shell, and obsidian, and their general culture and society is similar to that of humanoid civilizations on tropical islands. Such island societies often get along well with local tribes of volcano giants, engaging in trade and peacefully coexisting. Should a tribe of volcano giants form an allegiance with a human tribe, the giants warn the humans of possible eruptions of their volcano to allow them time to escape the destruction.

Volcano Giant

Huge giant, chaotic neutral

Armor Class 19 (natural armor)
Hit Points 187 (15d12 + 90)
Speed 40 ft.

STR	DEX	CON	INT	WIS	CHA
29 (+9)	15 (+2)	22 (+6)	16 (+3)	18 (+4)	18 (+4)

Saving Throws Con +11
Skills Acrobatics +7, Intimidation +9, Nature +8, Perception +9
Damage Vulnerabilities cold
Damage Immunities fire
Senses passive Perception 19
Languages Giant, Ignan
Challenge 13 (10,000 XP)

Heated Body. The volcano giant's attacks deal an additional 7 (2d6) fire damage (included in the attacks below).

Actions

Multiattack. The volcano giant makes one one-handed Spear attack and one Slam attack, or two Slam attacks.

Spear. *Melee or Ranged Weapon Attack:* +14 to hit, reach 10 ft. or range 40/120 ft., one target. *Hit:* 23 (4d6 + 9) piercing damage plus 7 (2d6) fire damage, or 27 (4d8 + 9) piercing damage plus 7 (2d6) fire damage if used with two hands to make a melee attack.

Slam. *Melee Weapon Attack:* +14 to hit, reach 15 ft., one target. *Hit:* 19 (3d6 + 9) bludgeoning damage plus 7 (2d6) fire damage.

Rock. *Ranged Weapon Attack:* +14 to hit, range 60/240 ft., one target. *Hit:* 27 (4d8 + 9) bludgeoning damage plus 7 (2d6) fire damage.

Sulfuric Breath **(recharge 5–6).** The volcano giant exhales a cloud of warm sulfuric gas in a 30-foot cone. All creatures in the area must succeed on a DC 19 Constitution saving throw or take 35 (10d6) acid damage and be poisoned for one minute.

GILLMONKEY

We put into the cove and dropped anchor. Hidden from the open sea by the twisting passage through the coastal highlands, we were happy to take time to make repairs and await our contact. Three days of light work and then a small fortune in untaxed whiskey would arrive from Endhome. Two hours later, we were fighting for our lives. The cove was a gillmonkey nest. Dozens of the little beasties swarmed up the anchor chain and launched an attack across our decks. No idea why they attacked, but the fight was short and sharp. We lost 10 good hands and had to shovel gillmonkey corpses off the deck until sunset. — Captain Elisa Bounapert of the Wastrel's Daughter

Gillmonkeys are small semi-primates that dwell in shallow coastal waters, reefs, and sometimes even up salty estuaries. Their bodies are pinkish brown with light scales over their heads, shoulders, and torsos. Long tentacles grow from their heads, but these are used to bring food into their mouth. While individually not dangerous, gillmonkeys prefer to gather in the dozens. As their numbers grow, their aggressiveness increases to homicidal levels.

GILLMONKEY

Small monstrosity, chaotic evil

Armor Class 14
Hit Points 11 (2d6 + 4)
Speed 30 ft., swim 40 ft.

STR	DEX	CON	INT	WIS	CHA
14 (+2)	18 (+4)	14 (+2)	12 (+1)	8 (–1)	11 (+0)

Skills Perception +1, Stealth +6
Senses blindsense 60 ft., passive Perception 11
Languages —
Challenge 1/2 (100 XP)

Amphibious. The gill monkey can breathe in air or water.

ACTIONS

Multiattack. The gillmonkey makes one Bite attack and either two Claw attacks or one melee Spear attack.
Bite. *Melee Weapon Attack:* +4 to hit, reach 5 ft., one target. *Hit*: 5 (1d6 + 2) piercing damage.
Claw. *Melee Weapon Attack:* +6 to hit, reach 5 ft., one target. *Hit*: 7 (1d6 + 4) slashing damage.
Spear. *Melee Weapon Attack:* +4 to hit, reach 5 ft. or range 20/60 ft., one target. *Hit*: 5 (1d6 + 2) piercing damage, or 6 (1d8 + 2) piercing damage if used with two hands to make a melee attack.

GNARLWOOD

It was a damned tree. No, really, a damned tree. The thing looked like a tree with four massive branches holding up bundles of green-black leaves fringed with white patterns. The thing, the tree, had a face! A twisted skull-like mockery of a face that leered and snarled at us. With one wave of a woody limb, it called up the skeletons of those it had slain to join the fight. The creature tore apart Ol' Jaskin with two branches and then went to work on the rest of us, throwing spells and tearing away at us with claws made of wood and rage. — Tara the Wise, adventurer

Rare things, gnarlwoods are created when a treant seed is planted in cursed ground. This should be an impossibly rare occurrence, save that certain evil cults intentionally create gnarlwoods as guardians of hidden forest temples. Their normally benign forms and thoughts twisted by the soil from which they spring, gnarlwoods love nothing better than to hurt and slay. They gain no sustenance from their victims and commit their atrocities purely out of a rage-filled bloodlust.

GNARLWOOD

Huge plant, neutral evil

Armor Class 16 (natural armor)
Hit Points 132 (11d12 + 55)
Speed 30 ft.

STR	DEX	CON	INT	WIS	CHA
22 (+6)	9 (–1)	20 (+5)	13 (+1)	13 (+1)	8 (–1)

Skills Perception +4, Stealth +5
Damage Vulnerabilities fire
Damage Resistances bludgeoning, piercing
Senses darkvision 60 ft., passive Perception 14
Languages Common
Challenge 8 (3,900 XP)

Innate Spellcasting. The gnarlwood can cast the following, using Wisdom as its spellcasting ability (spell save DC 12, spell attack bonus +4). The gnarlwood doesn't need material components to use these abilities:

At will: *ray of sickness*
3/day each: *animate dead, blight, inflict wounds*
1/day each: *circle of power, dispel evil and good*
1/week: *circle of death*

Protected from Good. Good-aligned creatures have disadvantage when attacking a gnarlwood, and it can't be charmed, frightened, or possessed by a good-aligned creature.
Unhallowed Aura. When an undead creature within 30 feet of a gnarlwood makes an attack roll or a saving throw, it can add 1d4 to the result.

ATTACKS

Multiattack. A gnarlwood makes four Clawed Branch attacks.
Clawed Branch. *Melee Weapon Attack:* +9 to hit, reach 5 ft., one creature. *Hit*: 15 (2d8 + 6) slashing damage. If a single target is hit by two of the gnarlwood's Clawed Branch attacks in a single turn, that target automatically takes an additional 15 (2d8 + 6) slashing damage and is grappled.

Golem, Lesser Flesh

It came staggering out of the arcane laboratory, its body barely clothed in a sheet draped over broad shoulders. The patchwork nature of its origins were writ large in the multiple skin tones enclosed by jagged stitching scars, disproportionate arms, and masses of muscle grafted onto less robust bones. One eye clouded in white stared out; the other leered red and angry from a gray patch of skin. — Myrtle Night, Evening Guard on the streets of Castorhage

Lesser flesh golems are sometimes thought of as a steppingstones for golem crafters, a cheaper product for lesser wizards to learn their craft. While this may be true, several valid reasons exist to create a lesser flesh golem than simple lack of resources or inadequate skill. For the same expenditure in time and treasure, one can create two lesser flesh golems as opposed to a single flesh golem of more robust nature. This makes the prospects of a squad or even a small army of these abominations all the more real.

Lesser Flesh Golem
Medium construct, neutral

Armor Class 9
Hit Points 60 (8d8 + 24)
Speed 30 ft.

STR	DEX	CON	INT	WIS	CHA
17 (+3)	9 (−1)	16 (+3)	4 (−3)	10 (+0)	5 (−3)

Damage Resistances bludgeoning, piercing, and slashing from nonmagical attacks that aren't adamantine
Damage Immunities lightning, poison
Condition Immunities charmed, exhaustion, frightened, paralyzed, petrified, poisoned
Senses darkvision 60 ft., passive Perception 10
Languages understands the languages of its creator but can't speak
Challenge 3 (700 XP)

Berserk. When a lesser flesh golem starts its turn with 26 or fewer hit points, roll 1d6. If the result is a 1, the golem goes berserk and attacks the nearest living creature it can reach. The construct's creator can regain control over the golem if the creator is within 60 feet by using an action and making a successful DC 15 Charisma (Persuasion) check. If the check succeeds, the golem ceases being berserk. If it takes damage while still at 26 hit points or fewer, the golem might go berserk again.

Fear of Fire. If the golem takes fire damage, it has disadvantage on attack rolls and ability checks until the end of its next turn.

Immutable Form. The golem is immune to any spell or effect that would alter its form.

Lightning Absorption. Whenever the golem is subjected to lightning damage, it takes no damage and instead regains a number of hit points equal to half the lightning damage dealt.

Magic Resistance. The golem has advantage on saving throws against spells and other magical effects.

Actions

Multiattack. The lesser flesh golem makes two Slam attacks.
Slam. *Melee Weapon Attack:* +5 to hit, reach 5 ft., one target. *Hit:* 10 (2d6 + 3) bludgeoning damage.

GOLEM, MITHRAL

To be honest, we barely saw it. It wasn't invisible; quite the opposite. Light just bounced off it, leaving behind a scattering of rainbow images, a reflection amplified to the point that it stung our eyes. Drakithir was the first to go; she threw a fireball, her normal opening move, and saw the energy just reflect off the golem back at her. Shame she had cast it at her highest level. — Päuk, apprentice mage

Mithral golems are exceedingly rare. Few worlds have enough mithral in their crusts to make a single mithral golem, much less two. The wizards who create these mindless automatons tend to be planes jumpers of the highest order. Usually, they are commanded to serve as bodyguards or as one-golem armies; rarely are they left to their own devices. When a mithral golem is found, only the foolish see that towering figure as an empire's ransom worth of mithril. Good luck cashing in on that jackpot.

GOLEM, MITHRAL
Large construct, unaligned

Armor Class 22 (natural armor)
Hit Points 315 (30d10 + 150)
Speed 30 ft.

STR	DEX	CON	INT	WIS	CHA
26 (+8)	9 (−1)	20 (+5)	3 (−4)	10 (+0)	1 (−5)

Damage Resistances fire, lightning, radiant
Damage Immunities force, poison, psychic, bludgeoning, piercing, and slashing damage from nonmagical attacks that are not adamantine
Condition Immunities charmed, exhaustion, frightened, paralyzed, petrified, poisoned, prone
Senses darkvision 120 ft., passive Perception 10
Languages understands the language of its creator but can't speak
Challenge 22 (41,000 XP)

Force Absorption. When the mithral golem is subjected to force damage, it takes no damage but instead regains a number of hit points equal to the force damage dealt.
Immutable Form. The mithral golem is immune to any spell or effect that would alter its form.
Magic Resistance. The mithral golem has advantage on saving throws to resist spells or magical effects.
Magic Weapons. The mithral golem's weapon attacks are magical.
Reflection. When the mithral golem suffers fire, lightning, or radiant damage, half of the damage it receives is reflected back at the source of the damage. If the source of the damage succeeds at a DC 19 Dexterity save, it may halve the damage reflected back at it.
Furthermore, when the mithral golem suffers fire, lightning, or radiant damage, it immediately recharges its Breath of Light and Pain. It may then use its reaction to use it.
Gaze attacks that target the mithral golem, or that the mithral golem might be subject to, react as if the gaze attack was made at a mirror.

ACTIONS

Multiattack. The mithral golem makes two Fist attacks.
Fist. *Melee Weapon Attack:* +14 to hit, reach 5 ft., one target. *Hit:* 24 (3d10 + 8) bludgeoning damage.
Breath of Light and Pain (recharge 5–6). The mithral golem breathes a cone of energy 25 feet long that originates from its head. This energy may be fire, lightning, or radiant. All creatures caught within the cone must make a DC 19 Dexterity save, taking 44 (8d10) damage of that type, or half as much with a successful save.

Golem, Shedu

The statue turned its head and snorted, though it certainly did not breathe. Some form of programmed affectation, no doubt. Its chiseled body moved as stone should never move. The muscles did not shift under the skin as it would in a real bull; it simply moved as if being molded by the unseen hands of the gods. To all wonder and terror, the great man-faced bull took off, a hundred tons of animated stone soaring through the air, looping around, coming back. That's when we began to run. — Lenweyne the Insolent

Shedu golems are crafted by master stonemasons from single massive blocks of stone. Carved in lifelike detail, these man-faced bulls sport painstakingly-chiseled feathered wings. Most often they are created to guard temples and palaces, animating only when their arcane senses detect the presence of pure evil such as devils and demons, although undead have been known to trigger some shedu golems. Once roused, their fury is unmatched, for how does one fight hundreds of tons of walking, nay flaying, stone that can see through any disguise and projects beams of radiant energy from their eyes?

Golem, Shedu

Huge construct, unaligned

Armor Class 18 (natural armor)
Hit Points 230 (20d12 +100)
Speed 20 ft., fly 60 ft.

STR	DEX	CON	INT	WIS	CHA
22 (+6)	9 (−1)	20 (+5)	3 (−4)	10 (+0)	1 (−5)

Damage Immunities poison, psychic, bludgeoning, piercing, and slashing damage from nonmagical attacks that are not adamantine
Condition Immunities charmed, exhaustion, frightened, paralyzed, petrified, poisoned, prone
Senses darkvision 60 ft., truesight 120 ft., passive Perception 10
Languages understands the language of its creator but can't speak
Challenge 12 (8,400 XP)

Fear Aura. Any creature that beings its turn within 30 feet of the shedu golem must succeed at a DC 16 Wisdom saving throw or become frightened of the shedu golem until it ends its turn more than 30 feet away from the golem. If a creature succeeds on this saving throw, it is immune to the shedu golem's fear aura for 24 hours.
Immutable Form. The shedu golem is immune to any spell of effect that would alter its form.
Magic Resistance. The shedu golem has advantage on saving throws to resist spells or magical effects.
Magic Weapons. The shedu golem's weapon attacks are magical.

Actions

Multiattack. The shedu golem makes two Stomp attacks or one Stomp attack and Trampling Charge.
Stomp. *Melee Weapon Attack:* +10 to hit, reach 5 ft., one target. *Hit:* 19 (3d8 + 6) bludgeoning damage.
Smite (recharge 5–6). The shedu golem unleashes a 30-foot cone of radiant energy from its chest. Any creature caught in this cone must make a DC 16 Dexterity saving throw, taking 22 (4d10) radiant damage on a failure or half as much damage with a successful save.
Trampling Charge. The shedu golem moves up to its full speed toward a creature, ignoring attacks of opportunity along the way. Any creature that the golem passes through or over must make a DC 16 Dexterity saving throw, taking 19 (3d8 + 6) bludgeoning damage and being knocked prone on a failure, or taking half damage and not being knocked prone on a success. The shedu golem then immediately makes a Stomp attack on the targeted creature.

Gray Nisp

They say the deep bog in the middle of the swamp is home to a fey creature of great physical power but also great cruelty. Many locals tell tales of travelers in the swamp, fisherfolk, and gator hunters who have run afoul of this creature. These tales speak of a creature that attacks from hiding, but does not do so in a fury. This is a creature that is more curious than aggressive, but its curiosity is of a morbid form. In one instance, the creature tore a limb off one person in a boat, merely sniffed at the next person, and then licked the chum bucket for several minutes. It then sat on a log and investigated the severed arm while its former owner writhed in agony and died not five feet away. — Sir Cedric of Reme, knight errant

Gray nisps are tall, gaunt fey that dwell in isolated waterways, be they lakes, streams, swamps, or even parts of the open ocean. They are solitary and territorial, especially toward other fey. While not malicious, the gray nisp has no feelings of love or hatred, nor do they understand the pain of others. Ever curious, they approach strangers from hiding and attempt to understand them, often through violent means. If left alone, they tend to keep to themselves, but a gray nisp living nearby is an invitation to a sudden visit by a creature looking to experiment and uncaring of others' pain.

Gray Nisp

Large fey, chaotic neutral

Armor Class 15 (natural armor)
Hit Points 85 (9d10 + 36)
Speed 10 ft., swim 40 ft.

STR	DEX	CON	INT	WIS	CHA
17 (+3)	17 (+3)	19 (+4)	5 (–3)	12 (+1)	7 (–2)

Senses darkvision 60 ft., tremorsense 180 ft., passive Perception 11
Languages Gray Nisp
Challenge 6 (2,300 XP)

Keen Scent. A gray nisp can taste blood in the surrounding water from a distance of up to one mile.
Innate Spellcasting. A gray nisp can use the following spell-like abilities, using Wisdom as its casting ability (spell save DC 12, +4 to hit with spell attacks). The gray nisp doesn't need material components to use these abilities:
At will: *confusion, detect thoughts, minor illusion* (auditory only), *hold monster, slow*
Water Dependent. A gray nisp can survive out of water only for 10 minutes. After that, it begins to suffocate.

Actions

Multiattack. A gray nisp makes one Bite attack and two Claw attacks.
Bite. *Melee Weapon Attack*: +6 to hit, reach 5 ft., one creature. *Hit:* 9 (1d12 + 3) piercing damage.
Claw. *Melee Weapon Attack*: +6 to hit, reach 5 ft., one creature. *Hit:* 8 (1d10 + 3) slashing damage. If both claws hit the same target, it takes an additional 8 (1d10 + 3) slashing damage.

Green Brain

The mushroom folk controlled their servants through ingenious means. The lesser-minded species, even mindless creatures such as oozes, were dominated and organized by fleshy green brains grown like plants. We defeated the servants with ease, even considering the degree to which they were coordinated, but once we fought through these hordes, we faced the brain behind it all. Waves of pain and ecstasy rolled off it as we neared, only to be replaced by bolts of pure psychic energy as the first of our number engaged in a fight to the death. — Sir Cedric of Reme, knight errant

Myconids and other creatures skilled at shaping plants grow green brains. These fleshy green brains are hidden behind the leaves of a large cauliflower-like plant. These small plant monstrosities lack ambitions or much personality, making them ideal systems to control the lesser-minded and weaker-willed servants of their creators. When threatened, the green brain uses its servants to defend itself, supplementing their attacks with its own powerful psychic powers.

Green Brain

Small plant (fungus), lawful evil

Armor Class 12
Hit Points 31 (9d6)
Speed 10 ft., fly 30 ft.

STR	DEX	CON	INT	WIS	CHA
6 (–2)	13 (+2)	10 (+0)	7 (–2)	12 (+1)	16 (+3)

Damage Immunities psychic damage
Condition Immunities frightened, stunned, unconscious
Senses telepathy 60 ft., truesight 60 ft., passive Perception 11
Languages Common, Undercommon, Sylvan, telepathy
Challenge 2 (450 XP)

Actions

Psychic Bolt. *Ranged Spell Attack:* +3 to hit, range 60 ft., one target. *Hit:* 21 (4d8 + 3) psychic damage.

Psychic Waves (recharges after a short or long rest). The green brain emits a pulse of psychic energy at potential foes. The pulse affects all creatures with an Intelligence of 3 or higher that are within 30 feet of the green brain. Each creature that starts its turn within 30 feet of the green brain must succeed on a DC 13 Intelligence saving throw. On a failure, the creature can't take reactions until the start of its next turn and rolls a d8 to determine what it does during its turn. On a 1 to 4, the creature does nothing. On a 5 or 6, the creature takes no action or bonus action and uses all its movement to move in a randomly determined direction. On a 7 or 8, the creature makes a melee attack against a randomly determined creature within its reach or does nothing if it can't make such an attack.

Gribbon

With one last hack of her blade, Karys cut our path clear to the temple clearing. A 20-foot-tall stone money wrapped in vines greeted us, but my eyes were dazzled by the diamonds serving as its eyes. They sparkled in the light, casting rays of brilliance that strobed across the ground. I was so blinded by the wondrous sight that I didn't see the apes lining the walls of the temple behind the statue. Each one brandished a gleaming dagger. When they launched off the wall at us — and flew forward on bat-like wings — I knew we were in trouble. — Dawson Southers, on discovering the Temple-Caves of the Catarrhini

At first glance, gribbons resemble large monkeys with bat wings. Closer examination, however, reveals facial features of a more human than simian nature. Their bodies are covered with a coarse, brown fur, and their hands end in powerful, sharp claws. These creatures are fiercely territorial and prefer to swoop down from the treetops to assault trespassers without warning. Though they greatly prefer forests, gribbons have been known to reside in caves and caverns, especially those higher up with outcroppings where they can perch and survey their territory.

Gribbon

Small monstrosity, neutral evil

Armor Class 12
Hit Points 13 (3d6 + 3)
Speed 30 ft., fly 30 ft.

STR	DEX	CON	INT	WIS	CHA
12 (+1)	15 (+2)	13 (+1)	10 (+0)	10 (+0)	11 (+0)

Skills Stealth +4
Senses darkvision 60 ft., passive Perception 10
Languages Common
Challenge 1/2 (100 XP)

Pack Tactics. The gribbon has advantage on an attack roll against a creature if at least one of the gribbon's allies is within five feet of the creature and the ally isn't incapacitated.

Actions

Claw. *Melee Weapon Attack:* +4 to hit, reach 5 ft., one target. *Hit:* 3 (1d4 + 1) slashing damage.
Dagger. *Melee or Ranged Weapon Attack:* +4 to hit, reach 5 ft. or range 20/60 ft., one target. *Hit:* 4 (1d4 + 2) piercing damage.
Dart. *Ranged Weapon Attack:* +4 to hit, range 26/60 ft., one target. *Hit:* 4 (1d4 + 2) piercing damage.

GRIMSTALKER

We sailed down the King Prudus, passing through a stand of old trees that leaned close over the river. Xervit motioned for us to keep our heads low, for he had heard tales of strange beings that protected this stretch of the waterway. We did as he said, but I had to sneak a peek over the side. Standing among the trees, their skin resembling the bark of the trees they protected, were tall elves with long arms and sharp claws. Their piercing eyes watched us as we drifted along. — Hauk the Weasel, on the search for the burial vault of King Maxton

The grimstalkers, or banaan (as they prefer to call themselves), are fey creatures that do not share the beauty and goodness of their kin. Whereas other fey creatures have come to represent the beautiful or mischievous side of nature, the grimstalker most certainly reflects nature at its worst. They are dark creatures, their hearts tainted with the foulest of evil. Unfortunate souls who wander into a forest guarded by grimstalkers are never seen again — except for their skulls, which the grimstalkers hang from the trees as a warning to those who would dare trespass into their domain.

GRIMSTALKER

Medium fey, neutral evil

Armor Class 16 (natural armor)
Hit Points 67 (9d8 + 27)
Speed 40 ft., climbing 20 ft.

STR	DEX	CON	INT	WIS	CHA
11 (+0)	19 (+4)	17 (+3)	14 (+2)	13 (+1)	17 (+3)

Saving Throws Dexterity +7
Skills Acrobatics +7, , Intimidate +6, Perception +4, Stealth +7
Damage Resistances bludgeoning, piercing, and slashing damage from nonmagical attacks that are not silver
Senses darkvision, passive Perception 14
Languages Elvish, Sylvan
Challenge 5 (1,800 XP)

Innate Spellcasting. The grimstalker's innate spellcasting ability is Charisma (spell save DC 14, +6 to hit with spell attacks). It can cast the following spells, requiring no material components:

3/day: *entangle*
1/day: *pass without trace*

ACTIONS

Multiattack. The grimstalker makes three attacks with either its Longbow or Spiked Staff. It can replace one of those attacks with a Claw attack.

Claw. *Melee Weapon Attack:* +7 to hit, reach 5 ft., one target. *Hit:* 9 (1d8 + 4) slashing damage plus 5 (2d4) poison damage.

Longbow. *Ranged Weapon Attack:* +6 to hit, range 150/600 ft., one target. *Hit:* 9 (1d8 + 4) piercing damage plus 2 (1d4) poison damage, and the target must succeed on a DC 14 Constitution saving throw or be poisoned for one hour.

Spiked Staff. *Melee Weapon Attack:* +6 to hit, reach 5 ft., one target. *Hit:* 7 (1d6 + 4) piercing damage plus 2 (1d4) poison damage, or 9 (1d8 + 4) piercing damage plus 2 (1d4) poison damage if used with two hands.

Groaning Spirit

We broke right through the wall of the DuVaine manor house, running from the vengeful spirit that had chased us upstairs. We found ourselves in a lady's changing room, empty except for a full-length mirror in a brass stand in the center of the room. Arb stepped up to it and whispered, "I don't like this." I had to agree. Nothing in this decaying house was what it seemed. That was when we noticed the elven woman in the mirror watching us. She screamed, and the mirror exploded outward, slashing Arb's face into bloody ribbons. The once-beautiful elf stepped out of the empty frame, her eyes burning crimson and her hair a tangled mess. — Castorix Penn, recounting her escape from DuVaine manor in The Covet, just before her disappearance

The groaning spirit is the malevolent spirit of a female elf often found haunting swamps, fens, moors, and other desolate places. Groaning spirits hate the living and seek to destroy whomever they meet. A groaning spirit appears as a translucent image of her former self, with a visage horrifying to behold. Far worse is their deadly touch and the groan they can unleash to kill those who hear the mournful sound.

GROANING SPIRIT
Medium undead, chaotic evil

Armor Class 12
Hit Points 58 (13d8)
Speed 0 ft., fly 40 ft. (hover)

STR	DEX	CON	INT	WIS	CHA
1 (−5)	14 (+2)	10 (+0)	12 (+1)	11 (+0)	17 (+3)

Saving Throws Wis +2, Cha +5
  Damage Resistances acid, fire, lightning, thunder; bludgeoning, piercing, and slashing from nonmagical attacks
Damage Immunities cold, necrotic, poison
Condition Immunities charmed, exhaustion, frightened, grappled, paralyzed, petrified, poisoned, prone, restrained
Senses darkvision 60 ft., passive Perception 10
Languages Common, Elvish
Challenge 4 (1,100 XP)

Detect Life. The groaning spirit can magically sense the presence of creatures up to five miles away that are not undead or constructs. It knows the general direction they are in but not their exact locations.
Incorporeal Movement. The groaning spirit can move through other creatures and objects as if they were difficult terrain. It takes 5 (1d10) force damage if it ends its turn inside an object.

ACTIONS

Deadly Touch. *Melee Spell Attack:* +4 to hit, reach 5 ft., one creature. *Hit:* 12 (3d6 + 2) necrotic damage.
Horrifying Visage. Each non-undead creature within 60 feet of the groaning spirit that can see it must succeed on a DC 13 Wisdom saving throw or be frightened for one minute. A frightened target can repeat the saving throw at the end of each of its turns, with disadvantage if the groaning spirit is within line of sight, ending the frightened condition on itself on a success. If a target's saving throw is successful or the effect ends for it, the target is immune to this groaning spirit's Horrifying Visage for the next 24 hours.
Groan. If the groaning spirit is not in sunlight, it unleashes a mournful groan. A creature that is not an undead or construct that is within 30 feet of it that hears the groan must make a DC 13 Constitution saving throw. On a failure, the creature drops to 0 hit points. On a success, it takes 10 (3d6) psychic damage.

Gronk

We slid on our bellies through the frozen tundra, clad in white furs to hide our presence. Tung the Withered pointed the creatures out with his misshapen hand. They were gray-skinned things, with shaggy hair. Each one had a single horn growing from its forehead. The creatures were digging holes in the tundra, working tirelessly to chop through the frozen ground. I counted at least 20 such diggings. I also counted five polar bears with leather collars wandering amid the diggers. I'm still curious what they were doing, but Tung didn't want to get too close. — Neta Lee, wizard of the North

Gronks are fiercely territorial creatures with mottled gray skin and shaggy brown hair. They have massive arms and legs that are attached to their barrel-like torso. Their faces are almost lost amid the long hair hanging over their heads, but there's no missing the long rhinoceros-like horn that grows between their eyes.

Primarily hunter-gatherers, gronks live in small family bands or nomadic packs that wander the cold plains they call home. Gronk packs never remain in one place for more than a month before moving on to greener pastures and better hunting grounds. They have been known to engage in barter with traders who cross their territories. Of particular interest to gronks are frost giants, with whom they have some sort of kinship or bond (though the extent of such a bond is unknown).

Gronk

Large monstrosity, chaotic neutral

Armor Class 12 (natural armor)
Hit Points 51 (6d10 + 18)
Speed 40 ft.

STR	DEX	CON	INT	WIS	CHA
19 (+4)	10 (+0)	16 (+3)	8 (–1)	11 (+1)	9 (–1)

Skills Intimidation +2, Perception +4
Senses darkvision 60 ft., passive Perception 14
Languages Prehistoric Giant
Challenge 5 (1,800 XP)

Keen Smell. The gronk has advantage on Wisdom (Perception) checks that rely on smell.

Actions

Multiattack. The gronk makes one Gore attack and one Greatclub attack.
Gore. *Melee Weapon Attack:* +7 to hit, reach 10 ft., one target. *Hit:* 11 (2d6 + 4) piercing damage.
Greatclub. *Melee Weapon Attack:* +7 to hit, reach 10 ft., one target. *Hit:* 13 (2d8 + 4) bludgeoning damage.

GUARDIAN SHADE

The temple was the perfect target. Their god was dead, slain in some demonic struggle, so who would avenge the few remaining priests? All of them were old men and women anyway, so the temple would likely be around only a few more years as they died off naturally. We went in at night, after the priests and priestesses shuffled off to bed. We were stripping the gold from the sanctuary when those old codgers shambled in to stop us. We laughed at them and continued our thieving. Until these shimmering forms sidestepped out of their frail bodies. These brawny warriors rushed us, forcing us to flee without a single bag of gold. — Rafael Bottoms, confessing to attempted burglary

A guardian shade is the ghost of a warrior whose life was dedicated to protecting sacred places or holy individuals. Upon death, these warriors are given the option by the gods, spirits, or the shamans of their nation to continue serving as protectors. A guardian shade created in this fashion dwells alongside another's spirit inside their body and emerges to aid its host when danger threatens.

While guardian shades are usually devoted to the defense of the helpless and the sacred, some evil shamans capture the spirits of wicked warriors and bind them to their own unholy folk — ancient priests, evil chiefs whose bodies have wasted away, weak-bodied sorcerers, and the like. These evil guardian shades are rare and might abandon their hosts if facing destruction.

GUARDIAN SHADE

Medium undead, lawful good

Armor Class 20 (natural armor)
Hit Points 136 (16d8 + 64)
Speed 30 ft.

STR	DEX	CON	INT	WIS	CHA
8 (−1)	16 (+3)	18 (+4)	10 (+0)	14 (+2)	16 (+3)

Saving Throws Dex +6, Con +7
Skills Insight +10, Intimidation +11, Perception +10
Damage Immunities cold, necrotic, poison
Damage Resistances bludgeoning, piercing, and slashing damage from nonmagical attacks; fire, lightning, thunder
Condition Immunities charmed, exhaustion, frightened, grappled, paralyzed, petrified, poisoned, prone, restrained
Senses darkvision 120 ft., passive Perception 20
Languages All languages spoken by host
Challenge 10 (5,900 XP)

Emerge from Host. A guardian shade normally dwells inside its host, but it can emerge as a move. Once it emerges, it can act independently. It can merge with its host as a move.
Incorporeal Movement. The guardian shade can move through other creatures and objects as if they were difficult terrain. It takes 5 (1d10) force damage if it ends its turn inside an object.

ACTIONS

Icy Touch. *Melee Weapon Attack:* +7 to hit, reach 5 ft., one creature. *Hit:* 6 (1d6 + 3) cold damage.
Life Drain. *Melee Weapon Attack:* +7 to hit, reach 5 ft., one target. *Hit:* 6 (1d6 + 3) necrotic damage. The target must succeed on a DC 13 Constitution saving throw or its hit point maximum is reduced by an equal amount to the damage taken. This reduction lasts until the target finishes a long rest. The target dies if this effect reduces its hit point maximum to 0.

Ha-Naga

The temple was the strangest construction I'd ever discovered. It had miles of stone walls that formed a dizzying maze, high marble arches carved with unknown symbols, overhanging tree canopies, and underground tunnels. Ten-foot-diameter openings carved into the rock accessed these underground areas, although we never had the chance to explore them. We had barely entered when a gigantic serpent rushed headlong through the maze toward us, forcing us to flee before it. The thing had a monstrous humanoid head that murmured spells as it moved. We fled back into the Ambicuaria Jungle. — Penelope Winderskip, explorer and seeker of the mysteries of life

The ha-naga is a monstrous snake with the head of a gigantic humanoid. They can reach lengths of 70 feet or more. Some believe the ha-naga is immortal, and stories written on the walls of ancient temples speak of them returning from the dead. Others claim the creature can blend into the jungles to hide until they slide forth to attack.

Ha-Naga

Gargantuan aberration, chaotic evil

Armor Class 19 (natural armor)
Hit Points 350 (20d20 + 140)
Speed 60 ft., fly 120 ft.

STR	DEX	CON	INT	WIS	CHA
27 (+8)	22 (+6)	25 (+7)	25 (+7)	21 (+5)	27 (+8)

Saving Throws Dex +13, Con +14, Int +14, Wis +12, Cha +15
Skills Arcana +14, Deception +15, History +14, Insight +12, Perception +12, Religion +14, Stealth +13
Damage Immunities poison
Condition Immunities charmed, poisoned
Senses darkvision 60 ft., passive Perception 22
Languages Abyssal, Common
Challenge 22 (41,000 XP)

Rejuvenation. If it dies, the ha-naga returns to life in 1d6 days and regains all its hit points. Only a *wish* spell can prevent this trait from functioning.
Legendary Resistance (3/day). If the ha-naga fails a saving throw, it can choose to succeed instead.
Chameleon Skin. The ha-naga has advantage on Dexterity (Stealth) checks made to hide.
Innate Spellcasting. The ha-naga's innate spellcasting ability is Charisma (spell save DC 23). It can innately cast the following spells, and it needs only verbal components to cast its spells:
At will: *charm person, detect thoughts, suggestion*
3/day each: *dominate person, mass suggestion*
Spellcasting. The ha-naga is a 20th-level spellcaster. Its spellcasting ability is Charisma (spell save DC 23, +15 to hit with spell attacks), and it needs only verbal components to cast its spells. It has the following sorcerer spells prepared:
Cantrips (at will): *acid splash, fire bolt, mage hand, minor illusion, prestidigitation, ray of frost*
1st level (4 slots): *detect magic, fog cloud, magic missile*
2nd level (3 slots): *darkness, hold person*
3rd level (3 slots): *lightning bolt, stinking cloud*
4th level (3 slots): *confusion, polymorph*
5th level (3 slots): *cloudkill, telekinesis*
6th level (2 slots): *circle of death*
7th level (2 slots): *teleport*
8th level (1 slot): *power word stun*
9th level (1 slot): *meteor swarm*

Actions

Multiattack. The ha-naga makes one Constrict attack and one Sting attack.
Constrict. *Melee Weapon Attack:* +15 to hit, reach 10 ft., one target. *Hit:* 22 (4d6 + 8) bludgeoning damage and the target is grappled (escape DC 23). Until this grapple ends, the creature is restrained, and the ha-naga can't constrict another target.
Sting. *Melee Weapon Attack:* +15 to hit, reach 15 ft., one target. *Hit:* 21 (3d8 + 8) piercing damage, and the target must make a DC 23 Constitution saving throw, taking 55 (10d10) poison damage on a failed save, or half as much damage on a successful one.

Legendary Actions

The ha-naga can take three legendary actions, choosing from the options below. Only one legendary action can be used at a time and only at the end of another creature's turn. The ha-naga regains spent legendary actions at the start of its turn.
Constrict. The ha-naga makes one Constrict attack.
Sting. The ha-naga makes one Sting attack.
Move. The ha-naga moves up to its speed without provoking attacks of opportunity.

Half-Ogre Enforcer

Miggle Luckstar promised to get an audience with the prince and his entourage of big spenders. We needed only a moment alone with him to get him behind our expedition from Sunport up the River of Fortune. The map I had discovered promised untold riches waiting at the mouth of the waterway. Unfortunately, the prince also brought his bodyguards, and this one loathsome beast made it all too clear he'd crush our skulls in his palms if we tried to enter. — Sir Percivius Mottlebrow the Third, eaten by a killer plant during failed expedition on the River of Fortune

A half-ogre enforcer resembles a somewhat ugly human with matted dark hair. It wears tattered skins over a suit of hide armor. The half-ogre understands the power of intimidation and uses its massive form to the best advantage to win any fight.

Half-Ogre Enforcer

Large giant (half-ogre), neutral evil

Armor Class 17 (chain mail armor)
Hit Points 102 (12d10 + 36)
Speed 30 ft.

STR	DEX	CON	INT	WIS	CHA
17 (+3)	13 (+1)	16 (+3)	8 (−1)	10 (+0)	10 (+0)

Saving Throws Str +6, Con +6
Skills Intimidation +3, Perception +3, Survival +2
Senses darkvision 60 ft., passive Perception 13
Languages Common, Giant
Challenge 6 (2,300 XP)

***Action Surge* (recharges after a short or long rest).** The half-ogre enforcer may make one additional action on its turn on top of its normal action (and possible bonus action).
Defense. The half-ogre enforcer gains +1 to its Armor Class while wearing armor (included above)
Great Weapon Fighting. When the half-ogre enforcer rolls a 1 or a 2 on a damage die for an attack it makes with a melee weapon that it is wielding with two hands, it may reroll the die and must use the new roll.
Improved Critical. The half-ogre enforcer's weapon attacks score a critical hit on a roll of 19 or 20.

Actions

Multiattack. The half-ogre enforcer makes two melee or two ranged weapon attacks.
Greatsword. *Melee Weapon Attack:* +6 to hit, reach 5 ft., one target. *Hit:* 13 (3d6 + 3) slashing damage.
Javelin. *Melee or Ranged Weapon Attack:* +6 to hit, reach 5 ft. or range 30/120 ft., one target. *Hit:* 10 (2d6 + 3) piercing damage.

Bonus Actions

***Second Wind* (recharges after a short or long rest).** The half-ogre enforcer may regain 1d10 + 8 hit points.

Hoar Spirit

A bone-chilling wind blew a blinding snow over the edge of the Wailing Glacier, creating a shrill cacophony of shrieks that resounded across the valley. We bundled up against the cold, but there was little we could do to keep the piercing sound from our ears. Maybe that's why we didn't hear them. We were studying the ice wall looking for an easy way up, when gaunt beings rose from the snowdrifts. Their emaciated bodies were barely dressed for the cold, but it was obvious from the frozen orbs of their eyes that the weather wasn't going to bother them ever again. — Catesby Snow, explorer scouting the Hollow Spire Mountains

Believed to be the spirits of humanoids that freeze to death either because of their own mistakes or because of some ritualistic exile into the icy wastes by their culture, hoar spirits haunt the icy wastelands of the world seeking warmblooded living creatures in which to share their icy hell. A hoar spirit is a gaunt humanoid dressed in tattered rags. Its skin is pale gray, and ice crystals form on various parts of its body. Its hands end in claws, each with translucent icy blue nails. Its eyes are frozen solid and show no signs of life.

Hoar Spirit
Medium undead, chaotic evil

Armor Class 14 (natural armor)
Hit Points 33 (6d8 + 6)
Speed 30 ft.

STR	DEX	CON	INT	WIS	CHA
17 (+3)	15 (+2)	13 (+1)	10 (+0)	15 (+2)	15 (+2)

Skills Perception +4
Damage Immunities cold
Senses darkvision 60 ft., passive Perception 14
Languages —
Challenge 2 (450 XP)

Glaciate. A creature that touches the hoar spirit or hits it with a melee attack while within five feet of it must succeed on a DC 12 Constitution saving throw or take 10 (3d6) cold damage and be paralyzed by bone-numbing cold for one minute. The target can repeat the saving throw at the end of each of its turns, ending the effect on itself on a success. If the target's saving throw is a success, it is immune to the paralyzing effect of the hoar spirit's Glaciate for 24 hours.

Heat Sense. The hoar spirit can detect heat (such as that generated by living creatures) within 60 feet, regardless of whether the hoar spirit can see the heat source or not.

Innate Spellcasting. The hoar spirit's spellcasting ability is Charisma (spell save DC 12). The hoar spirit can innately cast the following spells, requiring no material components:
3/day: *ray of frost*
1/day: *cone of cold*

Actions

Multiattack. The hoar spirit makes two Claw attacks.

Claw. *Melee Weapon Attack:* +5 to hit, reach 5 ft., one target. *Hit:* 8 (2d4 + 3) slashing damage and 10 (3d6) cold damage.

Horror from Below

We chipped our way into the Under Realm, hopin' to find the monsters slidin' through the rock into Ankhura. We moved silently — or as silently as only 20 dwarven guards could — through the twistin' tunnels beneath our home. The goin' was easy at first, but we soon discovered that the creatures were expectin' us. We lost six guards when a shapeless mass dropped from an arched tunnel and pinned them under its bulk. — Hoggin "Gravelbreaker" Ashenchisel, dwarven hero of the lower caverns

The amorphous things collectively called horrors from below are the advance guard of greater powers that lurk in the twisted realms beneath the ancient dwarven realm of Ankhura. They are usually an initial assault force, attacking by surprise and burrowing through solid rock to attack defenders from all directions at once. Though they possess a native intelligence, horrors from below are nevertheless utterly incomprehensible and cannot be communicated with through any known means, mundane or arcane. They attack ferociously and without quarter, never withdrawing until destroyed.

Horror from Below

Large aberration, chaotic neutral

Armor Class 17 (natural armor)
Hit Points 209 (22d10 + 88)
Speed 30 ft., burrow 20 ft., climb 20 ft.

STR	DEX	CON	INT	WIS	CHA
18 (+4)	10 (+0)	18 (+4)	9 (−1)	12 (+1)	4 (−3)

Damage Immunities acid, cold, fire, poison, psychic
Damage Resistances bludgeoning, piercing and slashing damage from nonmagical attacks
Condition Immunities blinded, charmed, deafened, frightened, paralyzed, petrified, poisoned, prone
Senses blindsight 60 ft., passive Perception 11
Languages Horrors from below communicate in a form of high-pitched piping, clicking, and chirping that is incomprehensible to all other creatures.
Challenge 12 (8,400 XP)

Dimensional Instability. Anchored to a different reality, a horror shifts and wavers as if affected by a *blur* spell. Attacks against the horror are at disadvantage. Attacks are immune to this effect if they do not rely on sight, as with blindsight, or can see through illusion such as truesight. When slain, a horror dissolves into noxious, foul-smelling slime, and the slime itself vanishes utterly within an hour.

Spider Climb. The horror can climb difficult surfaces, including upside-down on ceilings, without needing to make an ability check.

Tunnel. The horror can move through solid rock at its burrow speed, leaving a cylindrical tunnel behind.

Actions

Multiattack. The horror from below makes four Pseudopod attacks. It cannot attack with pseudopods that are grappling targets, but each pseudopod with a grappled target Drain its target.

Pseudopod. *Melee Weapon Attack:* +8 to hit, reach 10 ft., one target. *Hit:* 18 (4d6 + 4) bludgeoning damage plus 10 (3d6) necrotic damage. If the target is a creature, it is grappled (escape DC 16). Until the grapple ends, the target is restrained and the horror cannot make another attack with that pseudopod.

Bloat. If the horror drains 100 hit points or more from its targets, it bloats to Huge size. When huge, its Armor Class is reduced to 12 and its Speed to 20. It cannot burrow, and while it can continue to inflict damage with its drain attacks, it cannot add any more temporary hit points.

Drain. The horror can drain blood and vital fluids from any living creature grappled by one of its pseudopods. The target must make a DC 16 Constitution saving throw or take 17 (2d6 + 4) points of necrotic damage and have its maximum hit points reduced by the same amount. On a successful save, the target takes half damage and its maximum hit points is not reduced. The reduction lasts until the target takes a long rest. The target is reduced to a mummified husk and dies if its maximum hit points is reduced to 0. The horror adds half of any hit points drained as temporary hit points. This can exceed its normal maximum hit points but cannot exceed 100 temporary hit points drained (see Bloat ability).

Hyaenodon, Undead

I'd fought gnolls before, plenty of times in fact, so I expected them to be crafty and tricky. We crept up the back side of the canyon to get to their camp, making sure to douse our scents so their hyenas wouldn't smell us. First, I planned to go after the priests of their foul god, for those bastards presented the greatest threat. The priest was not alone, however. Instead, he was guarded by a snarling thing, a great hyena that was neither dead nor alive and whose very breath exhaled fetid poison. Faced with such a terror, I had to rely on help — although not much — from two warriors who joined in the fight so I could continue after the priest. — Big Joanne, mercenary

The most favored priests of the gnoll gods are gifted with an undead hyaenodon servant. These reanimated hyenas from a bygone era are the size of a horse, with huge jaws that make up most of their rotting heads. Cruelly intelligent, they serve their masters, and only the most foolish priests think those masters are mortal and not gnoll gods.

Hyaenodon, Undead

Large undead, chaotic evil

Armor Class 14 (natural armor)
Hit Points 30 (4d10 + 8)
Speed 40 ft.

STR	DEX	CON	INT	WIS	CHA
18 (+4)	12 (+1)	14 (+2)	7 (–2)	10 (+0)	4 (–3)

Skills Perception +2, Stealth +3
Damage Resistances bludgeoning, piercing, and slashing damage made with nonmagical attacks
Damage Immunities poison
Condition Immunities charmed, exhaustion, poisoned
Senses darkvision 60 ft., passive Perception 12
Languages Abyssal, but cannot speak
Challenge 3 (700 XP)

Carrion Stench. Any creature other than an undead hyaenodon that starts its turn within five feet of the undead hyaenodon must succeed on a DC 14 Constitution saving throw or be poisoned until the start of the creature's next turn. On a successful saving throw, the target is immune to the Stench of all undead hyaenodons for one hour.

Actions

Multiattack. The undead hyaenodon makes one Bite attack and one Claw attack.

Bite. *Melee Weapon Attack*: +6 to hit, reach 5 ft., one target. *Hit*: 15 (2d10 + 4) piercing damage and the creature must succeed on a DC 14 Strength saving throw or become grappled by the hyaenodon (escape DC 14). The undead hyaenodon can grapple only one creature at a time.

Claw. *Melee Weapon Attack*: +6 to hit, reach 5 ft., one target. *Hit*: 8 (1d8 + 4) slashing damage.

Shake. The undead hyaenodon shakes a grappled target, inflicting 16 (3d10) slashing damage.

Immortal Master

Our battalion marched west across the plains to the edge of the Impossible Peaks. Our plan was to find a passage through those horrible mountains to the unbelievable land beyond. However, an unexpected pair was waiting for us at the base of the mountain. One was a shaggy wild man dressed in a simple robe. The other was a willowy being whose movements flowed like water. They lounged lazily on a bed of moss between two oak trees. They obviously saw us, but neither seemed concerned. After some discussion, we decided to just leave them be. That was our mistake. In the next moment, they were in the middle of our ranks, and 20 men were unconscious from their lightning-fast strikes. — Rivone Cort, who told his story after awakening back in Tanner's Green

Immortal masters are the paragons of their specialized fighting styles, which mirror the natural movements and fighting styles of five animals: the tiger, crane, serpent, wolf, and dragon. Real expertise in these styles takes a lifetime, but true mastery takes even longer. Legend holds that the continued practice of a style to the exclusion of all other worldly activities can extend one's lifetime and enhance all aspects of spiritual, mental and physical health. Those who reach the pinnacle of development are known as immortal masters, and only one can exist for each of the five styles. These individuals are believed to be perfect, deathless entities who have moved beyond most human needs, including the need to eat and drink.

In addition to transcending human needs and emotions, immortal masters have so fully embraced the ways of their chosen style that their movements, mannerisms and appearance emulate their tradition's animals: the wolf master is rough and wild-looking; the crane master is slender and elegant; the tiger master is powerfully built and fierce; the snake master is graceful and sinuous; and the dragon master is aloof, with a preternatural confidence and barely restrained elemental energy. Immortal masters find it very difficult to relate to others, even members of their own martial arts traditions. They generally live apart from the rest of the world, training only a handful of specially selected students, meeting with outsiders for consultation and guidance only rarely and shunning most aspects of ordinary existence.

Immortal Master

Medium humanoid, neutral

Armor Class 24 (natural armor)
Hit Points 306 (36d8 + 144)
Speed 60 ft., climb 30 ft.

STR	DEX	CON	INT	WIS	CHA
18 (+4)	20 (+5)	18 (+4)	12 (+1)	16 (+3)	18 (+4)

Saving Throws Str +10, Dex +11, Con +10, Wis +9, Cha +10
Skills Athletics +16, Deception +16, Insight +15, Intimidation +16, Medicine +15, Nature +13, Perception +15, Persuasion +16, Stealth +17, Survival +15
Damage Immunities cold, fire, lightning, poison, thunder
Damage Resistances bludgeoning, piercing and slashing damage from nonmagical attacks
Condition Immunities charmed, exhaustion, frightened, intoxicated, paralyzed, petrified
Senses blindsight 60 ft., passive Perception 25
Languages Understands and speaks all languages
Challenge 20 (25000 XP)

Flawless Climb. An immortal master can move up, down, and across vertical surfaces and upside-down along ceilings while leaving its hands free.

Flawless Leap. As a move action, the immortal master can effortlessly leap a 30-foot distance, passing over any obstacles of foes that are under 20 feet tall. This move does not trigger attacks of opportunity. The master can land facing in any direction it chooses.

Immortality. Immortal masters cannot die of natural causes. They do not need to eat or drink. If an immortal master is killed, it immediately reincarnates, its abilities manifesting in the most accomplished practitioner of its given martial arts style that has achieved monk level 20. If no such individual exists, the master does not reincarnate until a practitioner of its style reaches level 20.

Style Vulnerability. An immortal master takes normal damage from attacks by practitioners of its own martial arts style.

Masters of the Five Schools. Each master stands at the pinnacle of one of the five martial arts styles. Each of these styles grants the master a different ability, as described below. Other styles exist, and it is believed that many of these have their own immortal masters as well.

Tiger: If the immortal tiger master hits a foe with one or more of its Immortal Blows in a round, it may impose one of the following conditions:

- The foe must succeed on a DC 19 Dexterity saving throw or be knocked prone.
- It must take an additional 9 (2d8) points of slashing damage for each hit.
- It loses 1d6 hit points at the start of each of its turns from bleeding until a creature uses an action to make a DC 10 Wisdom (Healing) check to bandage it or healing magic is applied. This bleeding damage can't be imposed on a target that is already bleeding.

Snake: The immortal snake master's Immortal Blows inflict poison damage in addition to the other types, and any creature struck by it must make a DC 19 Constitution saving throw or be poisoned for one minute. A creature can repeat the saving throw at the end of each of its turns, ending the effect on itself on a success.

Crane: The immortal crane master maintains its martial arts stance at all times, gaining a +2 bonus to Armor Class, armed and unarmed attacks, and a +4 bonus to saving throws and damage.

Wolf: If the immortal wolf master hits a foe with one or more of its Immortal Blow attacks in a round, it can impose one of the following conditions:

- The foe must succeed on a DC 19 Dexterity saving throw or be knocked prone.
- It must take an additional 9 (2d8) points of piercing damage for each hit.
- It must succeed on a DC 19 Wisdom saving throw or be frightened for one minute. A creature can repeat the saving throw at the end of each of its turns, ending the effect on itself on a success. If a creature's saving throw is successful or the effect ends for it, the creature is immune to this effect for the next 24 hours.

Dragon: The immortal dragon master's Immortal Blow attacks cause 21 (3d10 + 5) force damage plus 16 (3d10) cold, fire, thunder or lightning, its flawless leap distance is 60 feet at a height of 30 feet, and saving throws against its Immortal Aura are at DC 21.

ACTIONS

Multiattack. The immortal master can use its Immortal Aura and make three Immortal Blow attacks.

Immortal Blow. *Melee Weapon Attack:* +11 to hit, reach 10 ft., one target. *Hit:* 16 (2d10 + 5) force damage plus 11 (2d10) cold, fire, thunder or lightning damage.

Immortal Aura. Each creature of the immortal master's choice that is within 60 feet of the immortal master and aware of it must succeed on a DC 19 Wisdom saving throw or become stunned for one minute. A stunned creature can repeat the saving throw at the end of each of its turns, ending the effect on itself on a success. If a creature's saving throw is successful or the effect ends for it, the creature is immune to the immortal master's aura for the next 24 hours.

LEGENDARY ACTIONS

The immortal master can take three legendary actions, choosing from the options below. Only one legendary action can be used at a time and only at the end of another creature's turn. The immortal master regains spent legendary actions at the start of its turn.

Attack. The immortal master makes an Immortal Blow attack.

Intimidate. The immortal master can make a Charisma (Intimidation) check.

Leap. The immortal master can make a Flawless Leap.

Shockwave **(costs 2 actions).** The immortal master strikes the ground with its fist, requiring each creature within 20 feet to succeed on a DC 19 Dexterity saving throw or take 11 (2d6 + 5) bludgeoning damage and be knocked prone.

INPHIDIAN

How we got there was hazy. Our journey into the Seething Jungle started at Sunport, but things shifted somewhere along the way. We saw the sun rise and fall within hours of each other, and an enveloping fog flowed around us, causing us to lose all sense of direction. When the fog cleared, we found ourselves on a low ridge overlooking a city with high stone walls that encircled the metropolis. We got close enough to the gate — two huge interlocking serpent heads — to see that it was manned by creatures with serpent heads. Hundreds of them. We fled into the jungle, but getting home was a story I never want to tell. — Bella Ryne, missing for two years in the Seething Jungle

An inphidian is a six-foot-tall humanoid serpent covered with scales. These scales are often blue-green but could be any color. Its head and features are snake-like in appearance, and it has no hair on its head or body. Its hands are the snapping heads of fanged vipers, but this doesn't seem to stop them from holding and using tools and weapons. The inphidians are part of an entire culture of reclusive snake creatures that some believe control an entire serpent city known as Uroborus, although no one has yet stumbled across this lost city.

Most sages subscribe to one of two theories about the rise of the serpent-men. The first states the creatures are the failed results of horrific experiments performed by the dark and nameless sorcerers of an ancient snake-cult. The second theory contends the inphidians were once a cult of snake-worshippers cursed by an ancient snake-god for some transgression against the ethos.

INPHIDIAN

Medium humanoid (inphidian), neutral evil

Armor Class 16 (natural armor)
Hit Points 39 (6d8 + 12)
Speed 30 ft.

STR	DEX	CON	INT	WIS	CHA
16 (+3)	17 (+3)	15 (+2)	12 (+1)	13 (+1)	12 (+1)

Saving Throws Dex +5, Con +4, Wis +3
Skills Acrobatics +5, Insight +3, Perception +3, Stealth +5
Senses darkvision 60 ft., passive Perception 13
Languages Common, Inphidian
Challenge 3 (700 XP)

ACTIONS

Multiattack. An inphidian makes two Snake-hand Bite attacks.

Snake-hand Bite. Melee Weapon Attack: +5 to hit, reach 5 ft., one target. Hit: 5 (1d4 + 3) piercing damage plus 10 (3d6) poison damage.

Spit Poison **(recharge 5–6).** The inphidian spits poison at one target within 20 feet of it. A target creature must succeed on a DC 13 Constitution saving throw or be blinded for one minute. A creature can repeat the saving throw at the end of each of its turns, ending the effect on itself on a success.

JELLY, STUN-

The passage ended at a weird, slimy-looking wall, with no hint of what might lie beyond. We could almost see through the wall. We poked around a bit before checking that far wall, mainly because it was too obvious a place to put a secret door, otherwise it would have been our first place to look. Well, that was when the wall sprouted a couple of pseudopodia and attacked. Silverfeathers went down screaming and then just lay still on the floor. The rest of us went at the thing with blade and fire until the false wall shriveled and died. That smell, though, at first of vinegar and then burning vinegar as we fought. It just stays with you. — Tara the Wise, adventurer

Stunjellies hide within larger subterranean complexes, where they often disguise themselves by flattening themselves against walls to rely on their translucent gray color to blend in with the background. Mindless things, the stunjelly waits until a living creature comes close before reaching out and attacking with its pseudopodia. They secrete a weak acid that carries a virulent venom that causes paralysis. Wise delvers know to back up when they smell vinegar, a byproduct of the paralyzing acid reacting with air.

STUNJELLY

Large ooze, unaligned

Armor Class 9
Hit Points 57 (6d10 + 24)
Speed 20 ft., climb 20 ft.

STR	DEX	CON	INT	WIS	CHA
14 (+2)	9 (–1)	18 (+4)	1 (–5)	6 (–2)	1 (–5)

Damage Resistances piercing
Damage Immunities acid, cold, lightning, poison
Condition Immunities blinded, charmed, deafened, exhaustion, frightened, poisoned, prone
Senses blindsight 60 ft. (blind beyond this radius), passive Perception 8
Languages —
Challenge 3 (700 XP)

Amorphous. The stunjelly can move through a space as narrow as one inch wide without squeezing.
Corrosive Form. A creature that touches the stunjelly or hits it with a melee attack while within five feet of it takes 7 (2d6) acid damage. Any nonmagical weapon made of wood or other organic material that hits the stunjelly partly dissolves. After hitting the stunjelly, the weapon takes a permanent and cumulative –1 to damage rolls. If its penalty drops to –5, the weapon is destroyed. Nonmagical ammunition made of wood (or other organic material) that hits the stunjelly is destroyed after dealing damage.
Engulfing. When the stunjelly hits a creature with a Slam attack, it may make one Engulf attack against that creature as a bonus action.
Spider Climb. The stunjelly can climb difficult surfaces, including hanging upside down on ceilings, without needing to make an ability check.

ACTIONS

Slam. *Melee Weapon Attack:* +4 to hit, reach 5 ft., one target. *Hit:* 5 (1d6 + 2) bludgeoning damage plus 7 (2d6) acid damage. If the target is a creature, it must make a DC 14 Constitution saving throw. On a failed save, the creature is paralyzed for one minute. The creature may repeat this saving throw at the end of each of its turns, ending the paralysis on itself on a success.
If the creature is wearing armor made of leather or other organic material when hit by the stunjelly, that armor is partly dissolved and takes a permanent and cumulative –1 to the Armor Class it offers. The armor is destroyed if the penalty reduces its Armor Class to 10.
Engulf. The stunjelly attempts to engulf one creature of size Large or smaller within five feet of it. The creature must make a DC 15 Dexterity saving throw. On a failed save, the stunjelly enters the creature's space, and the creature takes 7 (2d6) acid damage and is engulfed. The engulfed creature can't breathe, is restrained, and must succeed on a DC 14 Constitution saving throw or be paralyzed for one minute. The creature may repeat this Constitution saving throw at the end of each of its turns, ending the paralysis on itself on a success.
At the start of each of the stunjelly's turns, the engulfed creature takes 14 (4d6) acid damage, and any equipment it is carrying made of leather or other organic material is partly dissolved (see Slam above). When the stunjelly moves, the engulfed creature moves with it. An engulfed creature can try to escape by taking an action to make a DC 14 Strength check. On a success, the creature escapes and enters a space of its choice within five feet of the stunjelly.
The stunjelly may only engulf one Large, two Medium, or four Small or smaller creatures at one time.

Jelly, Whip

You know, it's not the pain that gets me, it's the indignity. Injuries can be healed quickly — we have a pretty good cleric, you know? — and if you minded a little pain you wouldn't be in this business. Those whip jellies, though, they really hit you where it hurts, right in the dignity. So yeah, that's why I don't have any pants on; the acid from the whip jelly melted my leathers right off my butt. Are you going to keep me out here all day or let me in the gates? — Big Joanne, mercenary

Whip jellies are oozes that hunt the depths of subterranean caves, buried ruins, and anywhere away from the light of the sun. They are bluish-gray in color, translucent, and constantly quivering. When they sense prey, they extrude up to four long, whip-thin tendrils. These tendrils carry acid to their prey, and when the prey dies, they drag the carcass back to the mass to be reduced to syrup and sucked up. Whip jelly acid readily dissolves nonmetallic substances and can eat through nearly any organic matter.

Jelly, Whip

Medium ooze, unaligned

Armor Class 10
Hit Points 21 (3d8 + 9)
Speed 20 ft., climb 20 ft.

STR	DEX	CON	INT	WIS	CHA
11 (+0)	10 (+0)	17 (+3)	1 (−5)	2 (−4)	2 (−4)

Damage Immunities acid, cold
Condition Immunities blinded, charmed, deafened, exhaustion, frightened, prone
Senses blindsight 60 ft. (blind beyond this point), passive Perception 6
Languages —
Challenge 2 (450 XP)

Amorphous. The whip jelly can move through a space as narrow as one inch wide without squeezing.

Corrosive Form. A target that touches the whip jelly or hits it with a melee attack while within five feet of it takes 7 (2d6) acid damage. Any nonmagical weapon made of metal or wood that hits the whip jelly corrodes. After dealing damage, the weapon takes a permanent cumulative −1 penalty to damage rolls. If its penalty drops to −5, the weapon is destroyed. Nonmagical ammunition made of metal or wood that hits the whip jelly is destroyed after dealing damage. The whip jelly can eat through two inches of nonmagical wood or metal in one round.

Spider Climb. The whip jelly can climb difficult surfaces, including hanging upside down on ceilings, without needing to make an ability check.

Actions

Pseudopod. *Melee Weapon Attack:* +2 to hit, reach 10 ft., one target. *Hit:* 2 (1d4) bludgeoning damage plus 7 (2d6) acid damage.

Flankcleaver pushed through the narrow rock opening by turning his body sideways and shuffling along for 20 feet. He stepped out on the other side ... and vanished. Gupper scuttled through low; he was quick and nimble and covered the distance in no time. He screamed on the other end, and I saw a large hand reach down and grab him by the head. The priest and I made it through just in time to see Gupper ripped in half by a monstrous giant on the other side. I unleashed a bolt of lightning, but it barely chipped the hide of the creature. — Jerico Green, nomad wizard of the Haunted Steppes

Jokao, or stonecoats as they are also known, are a race of carnivorous giants who especially savor the flesh of humanoids. Legend holds that they are descended from a band of humans or giants who were isolated during an especially harsh winter and were forced to resort to cannibalism to survive. They survive to this day, it is said, as demented, vicious flesh-eaters who hunt smaller beings for sport.

Another part of the legend claims that the jokao grew heavy stone skins in order to protect themselves against the cold. Their rocky flesh is indeed proof against most forms of damage, but they fear thunder attacks, for these can shatter the jokao's protective covering and leave them vulnerable to ordinary damage.

JOKAO

Huge giant, chaotic evil

Armor Class 20 (natural armor)
Hit Points 115 (10d12 + 50)
Speed 40 ft.

STR	DEX	CON	INT	WIS	CHA
22 (+6)	12 (+1)	20 (+5)	10 (+0)	9 (–1)	9 (–1)

Saving Throws Str +9, Con +8, Wis +2
Skills Athletics +12, Perception +5
Damage Vulnerabilities thunder
Damage Resistances bludgeoning, piercing, and slashing damage from nonmagical attacks, fire, cold, lightning
Senses passive Perception 15
Languages Giant
Challenge 6 (2,300 XP)

Stonecoat. While they are highly resistant to physical damage, jokao are vulnerable to thunder damage. If a jokao takes thunder damage, it must make a DC 20 Constitution save. On a failed save, its Armor Class is reduced by 1d6; even on a success, the jokao's Armor Class is still reduced by 1, down to a minimum of 10. Once a jakao's Armor Class is reduced to 10, all other damage resistance is lost. Any Armor Class lost in this fashion regenerates at a rate of 1 Armor Class per day.

ACTIONS

Multiattack. The jokao makes two Fist attacks.
Fist. *Melee Weapon Attack:* +9 to hit, reach 10 ft., one target. *Hit:* 15 (2d8 + 6) bludgeoning damage.

JUPITER BLOODSUCKER

We have to go back for them, sirs. My family. I had to leave them, you see. The plants ... the plants got them. I saw them drinking their blood. I tried to pull them free, but I was too frail from my illness. My stepmother keeps me locked up, she tells me, so I don't hurt myself. She took me in after father died, you see. I found their daggers on the ground, but I couldn't even cut through the leaves. The vines were tangled in their dark robes. Why was mother wearing that weird skull mask? I used to dream of mother bringing those plants into my room to feed on me. It was a horrible nightmare. I'm so glad it wasn't real. Mother always told me it wasn't real. But why was she wearing that mask? And why was my name written in blood in that book she always carries? — Dibby Silvercrest, who was kidnapped as a child and recently found wandering near Reme

The Jupiter bloodsucker, also known as the vampire plant, is a seemingly ordinary plant. A creature looking closely at the roots may notice that the stems are transparent and that blood seems to course through them. The vines are lined with leaves, and on the underside of each leaf are many small but very sharp, hollow thorns. The plant stabs these thorns into a victim to siphon off the creature's blood. The Jupiter bloodsucker attacks with its vines, trying to grapple a foe with the ropy vine and then gulp down its blood through the leaves. At the same time, leaves cover the victim's face to smother it to prevent it from escaping the plant's weak grip.

JUPITER BLOODSUCKER

Medium plant, unaligned

Armor Class 8 (natural armor)
Hit Points 26 (4d8 + 8)
Speed 5 ft.

STR	DEX	CON	INT	WIS	CHA
12 (+1)	5 (–3)	14 (+2)	1 (–5)	10 (+0)	10 (+0)

Saving Throws Con +4
Skills Athletics +3
Damage Vulnerabilities fire
Damage Immunities psychic
Condition Immunities charmed, frightened, stunned, unconscious
Senses tremorsense 60 ft., passive Perception 10
Languages None
Challenge 1 (200 XP)

ACTIONS

Multiattack. A Jupiter bloodsucker makes five melee attacks.
Vine. *Melee Weapon Attack:* +3 to hit, reach 5 ft., one creature. *Hit:* 5 (1d8 + 1) piercing damage and the target is grappled (escape DC 12). A Jupiter bloodsucker can have no more than five creatures grappled at one time.
Smother. One creature grappled by the Jupiter bloodsucker must make a successful DC 11 Constitution saving throw or begin suffocating. Suffocation continues for as long as the creature is grappled by the Jupiter bloodsucker.

Kaiju

The beast rose from the sea, its bulk hundreds of times our size. We were mere gnats to this great creature. It looked like the tiny lizards that fled before our footsteps, only the tables now had turned. Someone screamed "Dragon!" but I knew this was false. Dragons held not a candle to this great being. The old man on his palanquin waved us quiet. Unafraid, he spoke, the first time I'd heard his frail voice during our travels. "Where Daguros walks, Xarakhan has tread." At this, I saw the truth. The giant lizard was following another of its kind. As I fully realized our peril, the monstrous slime covered in eyes rose behind the hill, its whipping tentacles felling trees and carving canyons in the ground. And we stood between these two terrible enemies. — From the collected scrolls of Grand Teacher Feiyan Qi, during the time of terror in the Qalen Delta

Legends hold that countless ages ago, when the Old Ones and other dread beings engaged in the Primordial Wars, terrifying monsters of enormous size, strength, and power also contended. These creatures were not slain or banished at the end of the wars, but only returned to their slumber under the seas, beneath mountains, or buried in the earth itself. On occasion, these kaiju, awakened by natural disasters, disturbed by greedy or unfortunate humans, or driven by unknowable instincts, stir once more and emerge to wreak havoc and destroy.

Kaiju, Daguros

This is truly a gargantuan beast from an ancient and forgotten time. Almost 100 feet in height, the creature resembles an upright reptilian with two great, thick legs, a muscular tail, and skin armored with thick, bony plates. Its arms are large and end in fearsome claws, and its face is like that of an ancient dragon, its eyes dancing with terrible flames. The very earth trembles as it strides along, eating up hundreds of paces with each step. Suddenly its great draconic head turns, sensing some danger of distraction, its maw yawns wide, revealing rows of teeth as terrible as swords, and a burst of unnatural flame belches forth, searing the land and setting buildings ablaze. The creature's terrible shriek echoes across the land, a portent of doom. — From the collected scrolls of Grand Teacher Feiyan Qi, during the time of terror in the Qalen Delta

Many legends surround Daguros, and he (though no one is certain, it is usually assumed that Daguros is male) is one of the kaiju that is not considered purely a threat to humanity. Though Daguros is said to have engaged in mindless destruction on several occasions in the distant past, several stories exist of his appearance to battle and drive off other kaiju causing widespread death and devastation. Most recently, Daguros was summoned to deal with the ravages of its fellow kaiju Xarakhan in the Xha'en Hegemony. The two beasts fought furiously and eventually fell into the sea, with neither emerging victorious. The local folk remember Daguros with some gratitude, for though he was a terrible monster, Xarakhan was far worse.

Kaiju, Daguros

Gargantuan monstrosity, unaligned

Armor Class 19 (natural armor)
Hit Points 615 (30d20 + 300)
Speed 100 ft., swim 100 ft.

STR	DEX	CON	INT	WIS	CHA
30 (+10)	12 (+1)	30 (+10)	3 (−4)	12 (+1)	10 (+0)

Saving Throws Con +18, Int +4, Wis +9
Damage Immunities acid, fire, lightning; bludgeoning, piercing and slashing damage from nonmagical attacks
Condition Immunities charmed, frightened, paralyzed, petrified, poisoned
Senses blindsight 120 ft., passive Perception 11
Languages —
Challenge 26 (90,000 XP)

Friend to All Children. Daguros will never knowingly attack children (i.e. those under 12 human years of age or its equivalent). This restriction is absolute — even if Daguros is somehow charmed or magically controlled, any direct order to harm children automatically ends the charm or control, and Daguros attacks the individual who gave the order. In addition, if a child directly addresses Daguros, the kaiju needs to make a Wisdom save against a DC equal to the child's Charisma. On a failure, Daguros follows one command from the child that does not involve engaging in offensive actions, for example "Please go home now," or "Please save my friend who is dangling over a precipice." Once this command is fulfilled, Daguros returns to its normal activities and is immune to appeals from that child for another 24 hours.

Legendary Resistance (3/day). If Daguros fails a saving throw, it can choose to succeed instead.

Magic Resistance. Daguros has advantage on saving throws against spells and other magical effects.

Siege Monster. Daguros deals double damage to objects and structures.

ACTIONS

Multiattack. Daguros uses its Frightful Presence and make one Bite, one Tail and two Claw attacks.

Bite. *Melee Weapon Attack:* +18 to hit, reach 10 ft., one target. *Hit:* 36 (4d12 + 10) piercing damage. If the target is a creature, it is grappled (escape DC 19). Until the grapple ends, the target is restrained, and Daguros can't bite another target.

Claw. *Melee Weapon Attack:* +18 to hit, reach 15 ft., one target. *Hit:* 28 (4d8 + 10) slashing damage.

Tail. *Melee Weapon Attack:* +19 to hit, reach 20 ft., one target. *Hit:* 24 (4d6 + 10) bludgeoning damage. If the target is a creature, it must succeed on a DC 21 Strength saving throw or be knocked prone.

Fire Breath (recharge 5–6). Daguros exhales fire in a 90-foot cone. Each creature in that area must make a DC 24 Dexterity saving throw, taking 91 (26d6) fire damage on a failed save, or half as much damage on a successful one.

Frightful Presence. Each creature of Daguros' choice within 120 feet of it and aware of it must succeed on a DC 21 Wisdom saving throw or become frightened for one minute. A creature can repeat the saving throw at the end of each of its turns, with disadvantage if Daguros is within line of sight, ending the effect on itself on a success. If a creature's saving throw is successful or the effect ends for it, the creature is immune to Daguros' Frightful Presence for the next 24 hours.

Stomp (recharge 5–6). Daguros makes a massive stomp with its enormous feet. It moves into a 20-foot-by-20-foot space immediately to its front, and any targets within this area must make a DC 24 Dexterity saving throw, taking 120 (20d10 + 10) bludgeoning damage on a failure or half as much damage on a successful save. Targets who fail their save are also knocked prone. In addition, all creatures within 1,000 feet of Daguros must succeed on DC 21 Dexterity saving throws or be knocked prone.

LEGENDARY ACTIONS

Daguros can take three legendary actions, choosing from the options below. Only one legendary action can be used at a time and only at the end of another creature's turn. Daguros regains spent legendary actions at the start of its turn.

Attack. Daguros makes one claw attack or tail attack.

Move. Daguros moves up to half its speed.

Devastate (costs 2 actions). Daguros makes one Fire Breath or one Stomp attack, provided that the attack has successfully recharged.

Kaiju, Galazon

The wind rises and a terrible shadow falls across the sun. In the sky above is what can only be described as a gigantic bat covered in tough bony plates, seemingly the size of a mountain. Its wings are like the sails of a titanic ship and with each ponderous beat they produce wind like a hurricane. Worse still, when the creature opens its fanged maw, a shrieking torrent of sound emerges, demolishing everything in its path. — From the collected scrolls of Grand Teacher Feiyan Qi, during the time of terror in the Qalen Delta

Though it is an entirely unnatural creature, Galazon most closely resembles a titanic bat. As with other kaiju, there are many stories told of this creature. Among these is its creation story, which claims that Galazon was created by ancient gods of destruction and that it once served as a mount for the titan Huimai'zhi who fought in many wars during the Age of the Gods. Huimai'zhi and Galazon fought together, and for many different factions, for it is said that they fought simply for the sheer joy of destruction. After Huimai'zhi fell in battle and was destroyed or banished, Galazon fell into slumber beneath the earth, only to emerge in times of catastrophe, war, and mayhem.

Kaiju, Galazon

Gargantuan monstrosity, unaligned

Armor Class 18 (natural armor)
Hit Points 555 (30d20 + 240)
Speed 60 ft., fly 100 ft.

STR	DEX	CON	INT	WIS	CHA
26 (+8)	20 (+5)	26 (+8)	3 (–4)	12 (+1)	10 (+0)

Saving Throws Dex +12, Con +15, Wis +8
Damage Immunities acid, bludgeoning, piercing and slashing damage from nonmagical attacks, fire, thunder
Condition Immunities charmed, frightened, paralyzed, petrified, poisoned
Senses blindsight 120 ft. passive Perception 11
Languages —
Challenge 24 (62,000 XP)

***Legendary Resistance* (3/day).** If Galazon fails a saving throw, it can choose to succeed instead.
Magic Resistance. Galazon has advantage on saving throws against spells and other magical effects.
Siege Monster. Galazon deals double damage to objects and structures.

Actions

Multiattack. Galazon uses its Frightful Presence and make one Bite and two Claw attacks.
Bite. *Melee Weapon Attack:* +15 to hit, reach 10 ft., one target. *Hit:* 30 (4d10 + 8) piercing damage.
Claw. *Melee Weapon Attack:* +15 to hit, reach 15 ft., one target. *Hit:* 22 (4d6 + 8) slashing damage.
Frightful Presence. Each creature of Galazon's choosing within 120 feet of it and aware of it must succeed on a DC 16 Wisdom saving throw or become frightened for one minute. A creature can repeat the saving throw at the end of each of its turns, with disadvantage if Galazon is within line of sight, ending the effect on itself on a success. If a creature's saving throw is successful or the effect ends for it, the creature is immune to Galazon's Frightful Presence for the next 24 hours.
Hover. Galazon can remain stationary in the air at an altitude of up to 100 feet. Any creatures directly underneath Galazon in a 20-foot-by-20-foot area must make DC 20 Dexterity saves or be knocked prone.
***Sonic Attack* (recharge 5–6).** Galazon unleashes focused sound waves in a 120-foot line that is 10 feet wide. Each creature in that line must make a DC 23 Constitution saving throw, taking 88 (16d10) thunder damage on a failed save, or half as much damage on a successful one.
***Windstorm* (recharge 6).** If Galazon is not using its hover action, it can direct a massive rush of wind with its titanic wings. This attack takes the form of a 120-foot cone. All creatures within this space must make a DC 22 Dexterity save or be thrown backward 10d10 feet and take 1d6 bludgeoning damage for each 10 feet traveled and be knocked prone. If the thrown creature hits a building, cliff, or other solid object, it stops its movement, but takes an additional 14 (4d6) points of bludgeoning damage. If the save is successful, the creature is still thrown and knocked prone, but takes half damage.

Legendary Actions

Galazon can take three legendary actions, choosing from the options below. Only one legendary action can be used at a time and only at the end of another creature's turn. Galazon regains spent legendary actions at the start of its turn.
Attack. Galazon makes one Claw attack or Bite attack.
Move. Galazon moves up to its full speed.
***Multiattack* (costs 3 actions).** Galazon can make one Bite and two Claw attacks.

Kaiju, Xarakhan

A great mass of water erupts from the sea, sending drenching torrents across the land as the horror emerges. It appears to be a great bell-shaped mass of jelly and slime, propelled along on countless coiling tentacles as it moves onto the land. Across its surface are numerous eye-like organs. It lashes out with its slime-coated tendrils and unleashes a torrent of jellied slime from its leech-like mouth. As we watched in horror, the thing suddenly changed shape, transforming into a gargantuan saucer-shaped form that rose into the air, still spewing its noxious slime. — From the collected scrolls of Grand Teacher Feiyan Qi, during the time of terror in the Qalen Delta

en dangerous as it slumbers in the Abyss, for its very presence draws hostile creatures to its vicinity. These include natural creatures such as sharks, giant squid, and carnivorous fish of all types, but the kaiju's proximity can also attract stranger and more dangerous creatures, including sea serpents, aquatic demons, and even intelligent sea-dwellers such as sahuagin and merrow. All such creatures are highly aggressive and hostile, driven to near-madness by the nearness of this terrifying force of destruction

Kaiju, Xarakhan
Gargantuan monstrosity, unaligned

Armor Class 21 (natural armor)
Hit Points 717 (35d20 + 350)
Speed 100 ft., fly 60 ft., swim 100 ft.

STR	DEX	CON	INT	WIS	CHA
30 (+10)	12 (+1)	30 (+10)	4 (−3)	16 (+3)	8 (−1)

Saving Throws Str +18, Dex +9, Int +5
Damage Immunities acid, bludgeoning, piercing and slashing damage from nonmagical attacks, cold, lightning, poison
Condition Immunities charmed, frightened, paralyzed, petrified, poisoned
Damage Resistances necrotic, psychic
Senses passive Perception 13, truesight 120 ft.
Languages —
Challenge 28 (120,000 XP)

Legendary Resistance (3/day). If Xarakhan fails a saving throw, it can choose to succeed instead.

Magic Resistance. Xarakhan has advantage on saving throws against spells and other magical effects.

Siege Monster. Xarakhan deals double damage to objects and structures.

Actions

Multiattack. Xarakhan uses its Frightful Presence and make one Bite attack and two Tentacle attacks. It can use its Absorb instead of its Bite.

Bite. *Melee Weapon Attack:* +18 to hit, reach 10 ft., one target. *Hit:* 36 (4d12 + 10) piercing damage.

Tentacle. *Melee Weapon Attack:* +18 to hit, reach 20 ft., one target. *Hit:* 28 (4d8 + 10) slashing damage plus 11 (2d10) acid damage. If the target is a creature, it is grappled (escape DC 20). Until the grapple ends, the target is restrained, and Xarakhan can't use that tentacle attack against another target.

Absorb. Xarakhan makes one Bite attack against a Large or smaller target it is grappling. If the attack hits, the target takes the Bite's damage, the target is absorbed, and the grapple ends. While absorbed, the creature is blinded and restrained, it has total cover against attacks and other effects outside Xarakhan, and it takes 56 (16d6) acid damage at the start of each of Xarakhan's turns.

If Xarakhan takes 50 damage or more on a single turn from a creature inside it, Xarakhan must succeed on a DC 20 Constitution saving throw at the end of that turn or regurgitate all swallowed creatures, which fall prone in a space within 10 feet of Xarakhan. If Xarakhan dies, a swallowed creature is no longer restrained by it and can escape from the corpse by using 30 feet of movement, exiting prone.

Change Shape. Xarakhan can change its shape with a standard action, transforming from a walking jellyfish-like creature with a speed of 100 ft./swim 100 ft. into a roughly saucer-shaped flying creature with a speed of 0 ft./fly 60 ft. While flying, Xarakhan cannot use its bite or tentacle attacks, except against grappled targets.

Corrosive Slime (recharge 5–6). Xarakhan exhales a burst of corrosive slime in a 90-foot line that is 10 feet wide. Each creature in that line must make a DC 22 Dexterity saving throw, taking 67 (15d8) acid damage on a failed save, or half as much damage on a successful one. Creatures who failed their save are also drenched in slime that continues to inflict damage — 36 (8d8) acid damage at the end of the target's next turn and 18 (4d4) acid damage on the next. Creatures who take ongoing damage may make DC 20 Constitution saving throws at the end of each turn they take damage, with a success reducing damage by half and ending any ongoing damage.

Frightful Presence. Each creature of Xarakhan's choosing within 120 feet of it and aware of it must succeed on a DC 17 Wisdom saving throw or become frightened for one minute. A creature can repeat the saving throw at the end of each of its turns, with disadvantage if Xarakhan is within line of sight, ending the effect on itself on a success. If a creature's saving throw is successful or the effect ends for it, the creature is immune to Xarakhan's Frightful Presence for the next 24 hours.

Legendary Actions

Xarakhan can take three legendary actions, choosing from the options below. Only one legendary action can be used at a time and only at the end of another creature's turn. Xarakhan regains spent legendary actions at the start of its turn.

Attack. Xarakhan makes one Bite, Absorb, or Tentacle attack.

Move. Xarakhan moves up to half its speed.

Frightful Assault (costs 2 actions). Xarakhan makes one Frightful Presence action and one Bite or Tentacle attack.

Lacedon

This funny little halflin' named Ollie hired The Sea Sprite's Dream *to carry this insane bubble — he called it his undersea divin' contraption — far out inta the Reapin' Sea. I tell ya I din't know what ta expect, but he climbed right through that bubble wall, and we pushed him inta the water. And down he went. We waited and waited, bakin' in the sun. An' he came back ... but he weren't alone. These fish-folk came risin' behind him, chasin' him right up onta the deck. He climb't the rope ladder fast, and the things were right behind him. Jenkins got claw swiped, and he fell down frozen. But we push't 'em back inta the water. Only later we learn't they took the cap'n. — First mate Balders Bindersting recounting tales of the swimming dead*

Lacedons are an aquatic type of ghoul. Similar to ghouls in all other respects, they are distinguished by their natural ability to swim as well as they can walk. They are found only in water, usually prowling near unseen reefs and other dangerous locations where boats and ships are at risk of sinking.

Lacedon

Medium undead, chaotic evil

Armor Class 12
Hit Points 22 (5d8)
Speed 30 ft., swim 40 ft.

STR	DEX	CON	INT	WIS	CHA
13 (+1)	15 (+2)	10 (+0)	7 (−2)	10 (+0)	6 (−2)

Damage Immunities Poison
Condition Immunities Charmed, Exhaustion, Poisoned
Senses darkvision 60 ft., passive Perception 10
Languages Common
Challenge 1 (200 XP)

Limited Amphibiousness. The lacedon can breathe air and water but begins to suffocate if not submerged in the sea at least once a day for one minute.

Actions

Bite. *Melee Weapon Attack:* +2 to hit, reach 5 ft., one creature. *Hit:* 9 (2d6 + 2) piercing damage.

Claws. *Melee Weapon Attack:* +4 to hit, reach 5 ft., one target. *Hit:* 7 (2d4 + 2) slashing damage. If the target is a creature other than an elf or undead, it must succeed on a DC 10 Constitution saving throw or be paralyzed for one minute. The target can repeat the saving throw at the end of each of its turns, ending the effect on itself on a success.

Leech, Giant Sea

A squall lifted waterspouts around our ship, giant columns of swirling water rising into the roiling storm clouds. My weather spells did nothing; it was as if the storm was alive — and wanted us dead on the bottom of Mother Oceanus. The rain spattered the deck as the waves tossed us at their whim. Something heavy splatted! *down beside me, a thick body that squirmed in the open air. A sailor named Gareth stumbled by me, one of the things pinned to his back. His face was sunken, and his eyes rolled into his head. He fell face down in front of me, and the thing detached from his neck with a* shllorrrpp! *I heard someone shout, "Leeches!" The waterspouts must have pulled them from their underwater home. I had no more time to ponder, as another of the things fell from the sky toward me.* — Farryn Wilebuck, sea sorceress of the Silver Fury

More dangerous than its freshwater cousins, the giant sea leech is about three feet long. Along with blood, this leech sucks out the very essence of life.

Giant Sea Leech

Small monstrosity, unaligned

Armor Class 16 (natural armor)
Hit Points 16 (3d6 + 6)
Speed 10 ft., swim 30 ft.

STR	DEX	CON	INT	WIS	CHA
14 (+2)	6 (–2)	14 (+2)	1 (–5)	8 (–1)	1 (–5)

Damage Immunities poison
Condition Immunities Exhaustion, Poisoned
Senses blindsense 60 ft. (blind beyond this radius), passive Perception 9
Languages —
Challenge 1/2 (100 XP)

Amphibious. The giant sea leech can breathe in air or water.
Numbing Bite. The giant sea leech secretes a powerful numbing agent when it bites underwater. Its victim must make a successful DC 14 Wisdom saving throw to notice that it has a leech attached unless it is being actively sought.

Actions

Bite. *Melee Weapon Attack:* +4 to hit, reach 5 ft., one creature. *Hit:* 9 (2d6 + 2) piercing damage and the leech is attached to its target.
Life Suck. While the leech is attached to a creature and alive, instead of making a Bite attack, it sucks the life essence from its victim. The target loses 1d6 hit points and gains a level of Exhaustion. The leech gains hit points equal to half the loss to the target, increasing its hit point maximum if necessary. A creature can use an action to attempt a DC 13 Strength check to remove the leech. A successful removal causes 3 (1d6) slashing damage to the target, even if the leech is dead. Alternatively, a dead leech can be removed without causing damage with a successful DC 17 Wisdom (Medicine) check.

Leechfolk

A bubble fart of swamp gas rose in a stinking cloud around us, like old eggs left in the sun to spoil. Lixiss wrinkled her nose at the odor; she's more used to the city's delights, not the Sin Mire's gurgling muck. She opened her mouth to say something delightful I'm sure about the swamp, but something rose up between us. It looked human, but it had ridged skin and a round toothy mouth. Like a leech. It struck Lixiss with a clublike arm, knocking her backward where two more of the things grabbed her and pulled her under. — From the recovered diary of the druid Belladonna Stillwater

Legends speak of a race of monstrous creatures that dwell deep in the swamps. More leech than human, these creatures feed by draining the blood from animals or, if any are available, sentient prey. They live in crude villages of thatch huts or in caves near or below the surface of rivers, ponds, and scummy lakes. Though they are not evil, leechfolk are driven by hunger and consider all creatures with blood to be fair game.

Though they cooperate with each other and appear to have a hierarchy of sorts, no one knows for certain how they actually communicate. No one has yet been able to communicate with the leechfolk, and they continue to make little distinction between intelligent and unintelligent victims.

Leechfolk

Medium monstrosity, true neutral

Armor Class 14 (natural armor)
Hit Points 45 (6d8 + 18)
Speed 30 ft., swim 20 ft.

STR	DEX	CON	INT	WIS	CHA
9 (–1)	13 (+1)	16 (+3)	9 (–1)	10 (+0)	10 (+0)

Skills perception +4, stealth +5
Senses passive Perception 10, darkvision 60 ft.
Languages —
Challenge 1/2 (100 XP)

Amphibious. Leechfolk can breathe both air and water.
Camouflage. Leechfolk have advantage on all Dexterity (Stealth) rolls while in swamps.

Actions

Multiattack. The leechfolk makes two Slam attacks.
Slam. *Melee Weapon Attack:* +3 to hit, reach 5 ft., one target. *Hit:* 3 (1d4 + 1) bludgeoning damage. If both of a leechfolk's slam attacks hit the same target, the target is grappled (escape DC 13). At the start of each subsequent turn, the leechfolk drains 5 (1d4 + 3) hit points from a grappled victim.

Livestone

There were these stones outside the village I grew up in. Everyone knew not to go near them, but no one would tell us why. At some point, the leaders put up a fence, a low thing that mostly kept stray animals out, but not so high that the occasional deer wouldn't bound over. But those deer, they never came back. And sometimes, just sometimes, those stones would be in different places on the hillside. You would peek over the fence, and the stones had moved. Sometimes they were closer. We used to dare each other to go over. Petey Carter did; we never heard from him again. The elders finally raised the fence after that. — Ilnar, peasant farmer in Turpin

Looking all the world like a boulder or chunk of rock, livestone is an ooze from deep in the earth that has, sadly, been brought to the surface. It can solidify itself and mimic the color and texture of nearby stone, granting it a near-perfect camouflage. In this state, it can hibernate for years between meals. Once roused, it moves to roll over prey and engulf them, slowly digesting the struggling victims even as they suffocate inside the ooze.

Livestone

Large ooze (fungus), unaligned

Armor Class 10
Hit Points 168 (16d10 + 80)
Speed 20 ft.

STR	DEX	CON	INT	WIS	CHA
20 (+5)	10 (+0)	20 (+5)	2 (–4)	1 (–5)	1 (–5)

Damage Immunities acid, cold, fire, poison
Condition Immunities blinded, charmed, deafened, exhaustion, frightened, poisoned, prone
Senses blindsight 60 ft. (blind beyond this radius), passive Perception 5
Languages —
Challenge 5 (1,800 XP)

False Appearance. While the livestone is solidified and remains motionless, it is indistinguishable from a typical stone.

Stone Camouflage. The livestone has advantage on Dexterity (Stealth) checks made to hide in rocky terrain.

Actions

Multiattack. The livestone makes two Slam attacks.

Slam. *Melee Weapon Attack:* +8 to hit, reach 5 ft., one target. *Hit:* 14 (2d8 + 5) bludgeoning damage, and the target is grappled (escape DC 15).

Engulf. The livestone engulfs a Medium or smaller creature grappled by it. The engulfed target is blinded, restrained, and unable to breathe, and it must succeed on a DC 15 Constitution saving throw at the start of each of the livestone's turns or take 14 (2d8 + 5) bludgeoning damage. If the livestone moves, the engulfed target moves with it. The livestone can have only one creature engulfed at a time.

Reactions

Solidify. As a reaction, the livestone can solidify all or part of itself into material with the same consistency of solid rock. The livestone adds 4 to its Armor Class against one melee attack that would hit it. The livestone does not have to see the attack to use this ability. A livestone cannot take attack or move actions if its entire form is solidified.

Living Lake

I sent the torchbearer down to the lake to get a bucket of water and he didn't come back. Expecting another case of sleeping on the job, I went down in a huff to find out what was going on. The bucket was floating on the lake, but there was no sign of that lazy good-for-nothing kobold. Then I looked closer. There were no animals. Not even a dragonfly buzzing in the reeds. Hell, no reeds either, just an expanse of clear water without fish. Just the slowly dissolving remains of one good-for-nothing, lazy kobold. — Ultär, son of Ultär, adventurer

That's a lot of ooze. Living lakes are pools of a single ooze large enough to be thought of as a lake. They are translucent, and their bodies, if the mass of this ooze can be thought of as a body, are far more fluid-like than that of other oozes. They fill depressions, sometimes on the surface, and feed on thirsty creatures that come by. While their main attack is to form a wave in their body and engulf prey, living lakes are also intelligent and can cast a wide range of spells to lure prey, fend of attackers, and disguise their true nature.

Living Lake

Gargantuan ooze, neutral (50%), neutral good (25%), or neutral evil (25%)

Armor Class 14 (natural armor)
Hit Points 495 (30d20 + 180)
Speed 20 ft., swim 30 ft.

STR	DEX	CON	INT	WIS	CHA
27 (+8)	10 (+0)	23 (+6)	18 (+4)	12 (+1)	14 (+2)

Saving Throws Con +13, Int +10, Wis +8
Skills History +10, Insight +8, Religion +10
Damage Immunities acid, cold, lightning
Condition Immunities blinded, charmed, deafened, exhaustion, frightened, prone
Senses blindsight 120 ft. (blind beyond this radius), passive Perception 11
Languages Aquan, Common, Sylvan
Challenge 22 (41,000 XP)

False Appearance. While the living lake remains motionless, it is indistinguishable from an ordinary lake or other large body of water.
Legendary Resistance (3/day). If the living lake fails a saving throw, it can choose to succeed instead.
Ooze Nature. The living lake doesn't require sleep.
Spellcasting. The living lake is an 18th-level spellcaster. Its spellcasting ability is Intelligence (spell save DC 19, +11 to hit with spell attacks). The living lake has the following druid spells prepared:

Cantrips (at will): *druidcraft, guidance, mending, thorn whip*
1st level (4 slots): *create or destroy water, cure wounds, entangle, fog cloud, speak with animals*
2nd level (3 slots): *animal messenger, beast sense, gust of wind, spike growth*
3rd level (3 slots): *call lightning, sleet storm, water breathing*
4th level (3 slots): *blight, control water, dominate beast*
5th level (3 slots): *conjure elemental, insect plague, scrying*
6th level (1 slot): *wall of thorns*
7th level (1 slot): *fire storm*
8th level (1 slot): *control weather*
9th level (1 slot): *storm of vengeance*

Actions

Multiattack. The living lake makes two Pseudopod attacks and one Grasping Tendrils attack. It can use its Engulf in place of the Grasping Tendrils attack.
Pseudopod. *Melee Weapon Attack:* +15 to hit, reach 30 ft., one target. *Hit:* 15 (2d6 + 8) bludgeoning damage plus 10 (3d6) acid damage.
Grasping Tendrils. *Melee Weapon Attack:* +15 to hit, reach 10 ft., one Huge or smaller creature. *Hit:* 21 (6d6) acid damage, and the target is grappled (escape DC 15). Until this grapple ends, the target is restrained.
Engulf. The living lake makes one Grasping Tendrils attack against one Large or smaller target it is grappling. If the attack hits, the target is also engulfed, and the grapple ends. The engulfed target is blinded, restrained, and unable to breathe, and it must succeed on a DC 21 Constitution saving throw at the start of each of the living lake's turns or take 28 (8d6) acid damage. If the living lake moves, the engulfed target moves with it. The living lake can have only four creatures engulfed at a time.

An engulfed creature can try to escape by taking an action to make a DC 23 Strength check. On a success, the creature escapes and enters a space of its choice within five feet of the living lake. A creature within five feet of the living lake can take an action to pull a creature or object out of the living lake. Doing so requires a successful DC 23 Strength check, and the creature making the attempt takes 14 (4d6) acid damage.

Legendary Actions

The living lake can take three legendary actions, choosing from the options below. Only one legendary action can be used at a time and only at the end of another creature's turn. The living lake regains spent legendary actions at the start of its turn.
Cantrip. The living lake casts a cantrip.
Pseudopod. The living lake makes a Pseudopod attack.
Protoplasm Splash (costs 2 actions). The living lake splashes bits of its protoplasm onto nearby creatures. If the living lake is good, each creature within 20 feet of it regains 14 (4d6) hit points. If the living lake is evil, each creature within 20 feet of it must make a DC 21 Dexterity saving throw, taking 21 (6d6) acid damage on a failed save, or half as much damage on a successful one. If the living lake is neutral, it chooses each day whether its Protoplasm Splash heals or harms nearby creatures.
Cast a Spell (costs 3 actions). The living lake casts a spell from its list of prepared spells, using a spell slot as normal.

Mandragora

Astrid crawled through the plant tunnel first, leading us deeper into the Fungus Druid's lair. The leaves were slick with fresh blood, a frightening reminder of Angus Sallow's never-ending thirst to feed his plants. Astrid was 10 feet in front of me when the leaves collapsed, dumping her into a pit of carrion. She landed hard, but alive, on a pile of bones that surely would have speared her had they not bent beneath her. We had no time to contemplate this new horror, however, as four strange plants rose up around her. Each had arms and legs but they were misshapen, as if someone tried growing a plant into a person. I'm going to burn every farm I see from now on.
— Calystto Myrt, on escaping the Fungus Druid's underground greenhouse known as the Mushroom Grotto

The mandragora is a small, vaguely humanoid fungus that prefers to hunt and kill its own carrion rather than scavenging for creatures that are already dead. If the mandragora goes more than three days without fresh meat, it burrows into the ground and attaches to local tree roots, from which it draws sustenance until living prey wanders nearby.

The mandragora stands about four feet tall. Most of the plants have two "arms" and two "legs," but that isn't universal. The plant's chief attack is by strangulation. Once it wraps its arm-roots around a foe's throat, it hangs on until the prey is dead or the mandragora itself is killed. They tend to strip off all of a slain creature's clothing and belongings to lighten the body before dragging it away to a quiet spot where it is covered in a thick layer of slime and dissolved at the mandragora's leisure. The digestive process leaves behind a pile of softened, rubbery bones that are the telltale spoor of mandragoras.

Mandragora

Small plant (fungus), neutral evil

Armor Class 11
Hit Points 4 (1d6 + 1)
Speed 30 ft., burrow 15 ft.

STR	DEX	CON	INT	WIS	CHA
11 (+0)	13 (+1)	13 (+1)	8 (–1)	10 (+0)	9 (–1)

Damage Resistances fire
Damage Immunities psychic
Condition Immunities charmed, frightened, stunned, unconscious
Senses darkvision 60 ft., tremorsense 60 ft., passive Perception 10
Languages None
Challenge 1/8 (25 XP)

Actions

Tentacles. *Melee Weapon Attack:* +3 to hit, reach 5 ft., one creature. *Hit:* 3 (1d4 + 1) bludgeoning damage and the target must make a successful DC 11 Dexterity saving throw or be grappled (escape DC 11).

Strangulation. One creature already grappled by the mandragora at the start of the mandragora's turn takes 4 (1d6 + 1) bludgeoning damage.

MASKED SPIRIT

Medium undead, neutral evil

Armor Class 17 (natural armor)
Hit Points 99 (22d8)
Speed 30 ft.

STR	DEX	CON	INT	WIS	CHA
10 (+0)	15 (+2)	10 (+0)	10 (+0)	14 (+2)	15 (+2)

Damage Immunities cold, necrotic, poison
Damage Resistances acid, bludgeoning, piercing and slashing damage from nonmagical attacks, fire, lightning, thunder
Condition Immunities charmed, exhaustion, frightened, grappled, paralyzed, petrified, poisoned, prone, restrained
Senses darkvision 60 ft., passive Perception 12
Languages Common
Challenge 6 (2,300 XP)

Etherealness. The masked spirit enters the Ethereal Plane from the Material Plane, or vice versa. It is visible on the Material Plane while it is in the Border Ethereal, and vice versa, yet it can't affect or be affected by anything on the other plane.

Incorporeal Movement. The masked spirit can move through other creatures and objects as if they were difficult terrain. It takes 5 (1d10) force damage if it ends its turn inside an object.

ACTIONS

Cold Touch. *Melee Weapon Attack:* +5 to hit, reach 5 ft., one creature. *Hit:* 16 (4d6 + 2) cold damage.

Masks. As a bonus action, a masked spirit can change its visage. Each visage has different traits, as described below.

Mask of Terror. All creatures within a 20-foot radius that can see the spirit must make DC 15 Wisdom saving throws or be frightened for one minute. Frightened creatures can repeat the saving throw at the end of each of its turns, ending the frightened condition on itself on a success. If the effect ends or expires, the target is immune to the spirit's Mask of Terror for 24 hours.

Mask of the Demon. While wearing this visage, the spirit loses its Cold Touch attack but grows demonic jaws and talons and gains the following actions:

Multiattack. The masked spirit makes one Bite attack and one Talons attack.

Bite. *Melee Weapon Attack:* +5 to hit, reach 5 ft., one target. *Hit:* 9 (2d6 + 2) piercing damage.

Talons. *Melee Weapon Attack:* +5 to hit, reach 5 ft., one target. *Hit:* 13 (2d10 + 2) slashing damage.

Mask of the Wraith. While wearing this visage, the spirit loses its Cold Touch attack but gains the following:

Life Drain. *Melee Weapon Attack:* +5 to hit, reach 5 ft., one target. *Hit:* 20 (4d8 + 2) necrotic damage. The target must succeed on a DC 14 Constitution saving throw or its hit point maximum is reduced by an amount equal to the damage taken. This reduction lasts until the target finishes a long rest. The target dies if this effect reduces its hit point maximum to 0.

Mask of Beguilement. The masked spirit appears as a loved one or other trustworthy individual to all who can see it. Any attackers who can see the spirit must make a DC 15 Wisdom saving throw or be stunned for one minute. Stunned creatures can repeat the saving throw at the end of each of its turns, ending the stunned condition on itself on a success. If the effect ends or expires, the target is immune to the spirit's mask of beguilement for 24 hours.

Mask of Fury. The masked spirit gains the following actions.

Multiattack. The Masked Spirit makes three Cold Touch attacks.

Cold Touch. *Melee Weapon Attack:* +5 to hit, reach 5 ft., one creature. *Hit:* 19 (5d6 + 2) cold damage.

MASKED SPIRIT

The old monk Tabbot rang the monastery's iron bell to summon the spirits of the Void to answer our questions. We brought the offerings as required, a brass coffer of diamond dust and a sprig of golden sage from the Darikeer Peaks. The bell rang three times, and a greenish mist formed around the clapper. What stepped out was not a benevolent being, however. The undead thing wore tattered robes that formed from the verdant mist, and its face was a battered skull that shimmered and shifted, bringing first rage to our hearts, then compassion, and finally fear as it advanced.
— Andrinna Mollets, seeker of the wisdom of the Void

Masked spirits are undead entities said to originate directly from the plane of death. They do not appear to be the spiritual remains of living creatures, but rather the product of extreme emotions, momentous events, or great violence. The distillation of many different passions, they are drawn to the living, hoping to elicit similar emotions from their victims. The masked spirit is a fearsome, green-shimmering spirit clad in tattered, glowing robes. Its face is a terrifying skull-like face.

Masked spirits can change their faces on a whim, creating faces that can elicit love or fear, or allow the spirit to drain their victims' essence, or attack with unfettered ferocity, mimicking the emotions and events that gave rise to them. The visages described below are typical; others may exist with even stranger effects.

Mi-Go

The chamber in the deep mines was too perfect, with each silver wall fitting together so perfectly you could barely find a seam. Our distorted reflections bounced off each perfectly angle. Diandalees tapped a wall with her staff, and the impact caused a hiss of steam to blast outward around a circular panel. The cylindrical drawer extended from the wall, its glass sides frosted with ice. Peering inside, we found pulsing gray and pink brains sitting in a slurry of frost. We were so caught up staring at them that we didn't hear the lobster thing as it rushed into the chamber. It shouted a buzzing screech that sounded like, "Away!" And then it was on us, pincers slashing away at our flesh. — Alexil Secord, recounting descending into an offshoot tunnel of the Mines of Honn

Mi-go are giant lobster-like creatures with dorsal fins, membranous wings, and articulate limbs ending in pincers. Their strange heads are ellipsoids and sprout numerous short, tentacle-like antennae. They are eight feet long and stand six feet tall. While mi-gos primarily communicate by clicking their pincers, many of their species have learned Common to better convey their intentions. When they speak, their voices reverberate with a buzzing rasp many find annoying. Some believe the mi-go are planar travelers sent to mine other worlds of their resources and to test and examine the lifeforms they discover. Despite their monstrous appearance, the creatures are extremely intelligent and often employ odd technologies that confound adventurers.

Mi-Go

Medium plant, neutral evil

Armor Class 17 (natural armor)
Hit Points 76 (8d8 + 40)
Speed 30 ft., fly 60 ft.

STR	DEX	CON	INT	WIS	CHA
16 (+3)	19 (+4)	21 (+5)	25 (+7)	15 (+2)	13 (+1)

Skills Arcana +10, Deception +7, Medicine +5, Perception +5, Stealth +7
Damage Resistances cold, radiant
Senses blindsight 30 ft., darkvision 240 ft., passive Perception 15
Languages Common, Mi-Go, Void Speech
Challenge 9 (5,000 XP)

Astral Travelers. Mi-go do not require air or heat to survive, only sunlight (and very little of that). They can enter a sporulated form capable of surviving travel through the void and return to consciousness when conditions are right.

Disquieting Technology. The mi-go are a highly advanced race and may carry items of powerful technology. Mi-go technology can be represented using the same rules as magic items, but their functions are very difficult to determine: identify is useless, but an hour of study and a successful DC 19 Arcana check can reveal the purpose and proper functioning of a mi-go item.

Sneak Attack (1/turn). The mi-go does an extra 7 (2d6) damage when it hits with a Claw attack and has advantage on the attack roll, or when the target is within five feet of an ally of the mi-go that isn't incapacitated and the mi-go doesn't have disadvantage on the attack roll.

Spellcasting. The mi-go is a 10th-level spellcaster. Its spellcasting ability is Intelligence (spell save DC 19, +11 to hit with spell attacks). The mi-go has the following wizard spells prepared:

Cantrips (at will): *acid splash, fire bolt, minor illusion, poison spray, shocking grasp*
1st level (4 slots): *comprehend languages, detect magic, false life, shield*
2nd level (3 slots): *invisibility, magic mouth, suggestion*
3rd level (3 slots): *animate dead, major image, lightning bolt*
4th level (3 slots): *arcane eye, locate creature, stoneskin*
5th level (2 slots): *animate objects, dominate person*

ACTIONS

Multiattack. The mi-go makes two Claw attacks.

Claw. Melee Weapon Attack: +7 to hit, reach 5 ft., one target. Hit: 14 (3d6 + 4) slashing damage, and the target is grappled (escape DC 13). If both Claw attacks strike the same target in a single turn, the target takes an additional 13 (2d12) psychic damage.

MOGWAI

Mogwais are created by demons, using the spirits of the dead as raw material. There are numerous different forms of mogwai, and in general they do not have a sense of kinship with other types. The malevolence and purposes of some varieties are known to be subject to tempering and manipulation.

DON'GUI (ICE WRAITH)

We stumbled into a bizarre graveyard in the high peaks of the Hollow Spires, where a party before us had tried — and failed — to scale the ridges. Their bodies were covered in ice and deep snow, frozen to the ground. I counted at least 12 corpses. I was searching for any messages they might have left for their loved ones when the wind whipped into a frenzy and a ghostly shape formed in the air before us. It exhaled a chilled blast colder than I've ever felt. Dewyn caught the brunt of it, and I realized why so many corpses existed on this barren mountainside. We weren't able to bring his body down with us. There are 13 corpses lost on that mountain now. — Morgat Firecourt, while being treated for frostbite

Ice wraiths haunt desolate mountain passes and ravines where many have perished in the wind, snow, sleet, and ice. It is believed that they are created from the death throes of those who died alone and without comfort, and now remain near where they died, consumed by the naturalistic fury of the storms and their rage at those who remain living. Several wraiths may haunt the same area, making travel hazardous, while treacherous weather may even add to the number of wraiths in a given region.

Undead creatures possessed of a boundless rage and violence, ice wraiths often leave numerous frozen corpses in their wake. As their only goal is to extinguish the hateful spark of life, ice wraiths have no interest in what happens to them after they perished. Accordingly, regions inhabited by ice wraiths may contain a wealth of treasure, frozen goods, and even entire caravans that were wiped out and left by the wraiths, preserved by ice and cold.

ICE WRAITH

Medium undead, neutral evil

Armor Class 16 (natural armor)
Hit Points 90 (20d8)
Speed 0 ft., fly 30 ft.

STR	DEX	CON	INT	WIS	CHA
7 (–2)	16 (+3)	10 (+0)	9 (–1)	12 (+1)	15 (+2)

Damage Vulnerabilities fire
Damage Immunities cold, necrotic, poison
Damage Resistances acid, fire, lightning, thunder
Condition Immunities charmed, exhaustion, frightened, grappled, paralyzed, petrified, poisoned, prone, restrained
Senses darkvision 60 ft., passive Perception 11
Languages any language it knew in life
Challenge 5 (1,800 XP)

Incorporeal Movement. The ice wraith can move through other creatures and objects as if they were difficult terrain. If takes 5 (1d10) force damage if it ends its turn inside an object.

ACTIONS

Icy Touch. *Melee Weapon Attack:* +6 to hit, reach 5 ft., one target. *Hit:* 17 (4d6 + 3) cold damage.
Cold Breath (recharge 5–6). The ice wraith exhales cold in a 30-foot cone. Each creature in that area must make a DC 15 Dexterity saving throw, taking 36 (8d8) cold damage on a failed save, or half as much damage on a successful one.
Icy Touch. *Melee Weapon Attack:* +6 to hit, reach 5 ft., one target. *Hit:* 17 (4d6 + 3) cold damage.

Silent Assassin

Lorin slashed through the thick curtains, opening a path into the hallway beyond. The air was still beyond, but there was no mistaking the servants' bodies sprawled on the stone floor. Prince Hallifet's eyes widened in fear, and his skin turned ashen. He would have passed out had Alvaraxe not put a steadying hand on his shoulder and spoke calmly, "Eyes forward, boy, and no harm shall come to ye." That's when the dark figured emerged from the shadows. It was tall and thin, its features concealed in a long robe. It raised a wickedly curved and barbed dagger and pointed it right at the young prince. — Tamilla the Fourth, recounting the Night of Sorrow and the rescue of Prince Hallifet

These creatures are fiends summoned only to kill. As their name implies, silent assassins do not speak, but understand any commands that they are given. When summoned, a silent assassin must be given a single target, which it pursues relentlessly until it or the silent assassin is slain. If destroyed, a silent assassin vanishes, drawn back to its home plane, leaving only its dagger behind. Legend holds that slain silent assassins are forced to endure millennia as lesser demons before their original forms are restored. A dagger left behind by a destroyed assassin cannot be used to inflict *harm*, but remains magical, with a +2 to hit and doing 3d4 + 2 piercing damage.

Silent Assassin

Medium fiend, neutral evil

Armor Class 19 (natural armor)
Hit Points 110 (20d8 + 20)
Speed 30 ft.

STR	DEX	CON	INT	WIS	CHA
14 (+2)	18 (+4)	12 (+1)	10 (+0)	18 (+4)	9 (–1)

Saving Throws Dex +7, Wis +7
Skills Athletics +8, Acrobatics +10, Sleight of Hand +10, Stealth +10, Perception +10
Senses darkvision 60 ft., passive Perception 20
Languages Understands Common but does not speak
Challenge 6 (2,300 XP)

Ambusher. A silent assassin has advantage on attack rolls against any creature it surprises.
Stealthy. A silent assassin has advantage on all Dexterity (Stealth) checks.

Actions

Deadly Dagger. *Melee Weapon Attack:* +7 to hit, reach 5 ft., one creature. *Hit:* 11 (3d4 + 4) piercing damage. Target must make a DC 15 Constitution save or be subject to a *harm* spell (see below).
Harm (recharge 5–6). On a successful deadly dagger hit, the target must make a DC 15 Constitution saving throw. On a failure, the target is affected as if by a *harm* spell. On a success the target takes half damage as described under *harm*. In either case, the silent assassin cannot cause the *harm* effect again until the ability recharges.

Monster of Set

My foolish assistant touched the cartouche without reading it and a strange beast appeared out of thin air in the tomb. It had the head of a warthog, the forelimbs of a lion, a scorpion's body, but the hindquarters of a donkey. A pair of horns composed of flame jutted from its horrid head. As I looked on in horror, its tail, a great snake, arched over its back and struck my assistant. Good assistants are hard to find. Fortunately, he was not one of those. — Algrid Henswaithe, University of the Vast

Created by the Cult of Set, the monster of Set is used as a guardian of tombs, treasuries, and other sites important to the cult. As foul tempered as its appearance is bizarre, the monster of Set is usually linked to a summoning device that brings the creature from whatever plane where it normally dwells. A fearsome foe, the monster of Set is loyal only to its master, which notably is the god Set and not the hierarchy of Set's cult.

Monster of Set

Huge monstrosity, chaotic evil

Armor Class 18 (natural armor)
Hit Points 207 (18d12 + 90)
Speed 30 ft., fly 60 ft.

STR	DEX	CON	INT	WIS	CHA
22 (+6)	11 (+0)	20 (+5)	10 (+0)	16 (+3)	10 (+0)

Saving Throws Str +11, Con +10
Skills Perception +13
Damage Resistances acid, cold, fire, lightning; bludgeoning, piercing, and slashing from nonmagical attacks
Damage Immunities poison
Senses darkvision 60 ft., passive Perception 23
Languages understands Draconic but can't speak
Challenge 16 (15,000 XP)

Innate Spellcasting. The monster of Set's innate spellcasting ability is Wisdom (spell save DC 16). It can innately cast the following spells, requiring no material components:
3/day each: *blur*, *cure wounds* (as 4th-level slot), *darkness*, *protection from evil and good*, *true polymorph* (self only)
1/day each: *blight*, *desecrate* (see sidebar), *dispel evil and good*, *divine word*

Actions

Multiattack. The monster of Set uses its Frightful Presence and make one Bite attack, one Horns attack, and one Claws attack. When its Fire Breath is available, it can use the breath in place of its Bite or Horns.
Bite. *Melee Weapon Attack:* +11 to hit, reach 10 ft., one target. *Hit:* 16 (3d6 + 6) piercing damage.
Horns. *Melee Weapon Attack:* +11 to hit, reach 10 ft., one target. *Hit:* 17 (2d10 + 6) bludgeoning damage.
Claws. *Melee Weapon Attack:* +11 to hit, reach 5 ft., one target. *Hit:* 16 (3d6 + 6) slashing damage.
***Fire Breath* (recharge 5–6).** The dragon head exhales fire in a 30-foot cone. Each creature in that area must make a DC 18 Dexterity saving throw, taking 54 (12d8) fire damage on a failed save, or half as much damage on a successful one.
Frightful Presence. Each creature of the monster of Set's choosing that is within 120 feet of the monster of Set and aware of it must succeed on a DC 17 Wisdom saving throw or become frightened for one minute. A creature can repeat the saving throw at the end of each of its turns, ending the effect on itself on a success. If a creature's saving throw is successful or the effect ends for it, the creature is immune to the monster of Set's Frightful Presence for the next 24 hours.

Legendary Actions

The monster of Set can take three legendary actions, choosing from the options below. Only one legendary action can be used at a time and only at the end of another creature's turn. The monster of Set regains spent legendary actions at the start of its turn.
Claw Attack. The monster of Set makes a Claw attack.
Detect. The monster of Set makes a Wisdom (Perception) check.
***Wing Attack* (costs 2 actions).** The monster of Set beats its wings. Each creature within 10 feet of the monster of Set must succeed on a DC 18 Dexterity saving throw or take 13 (2d6 + 6) bludgeoning damage and be knocked prone. The monster of Set can then fly up to half its flying speed.

DESECRATE

2nd-level necromancy
Casting Time: 1 action
Range: 60 feet
Components: V, S, M (25 gp of silver dust)
Duration: 8 hours

Any undead creature within a 20-foot sphere centered on a point you choose within range gains several benefits due to an influx of negative energy into the area.

Each undead's maximum hit points and current hit points increase by 5. Whenever an undead target makes an attack roll, damage roll, or a saving throw, the undead adds 1d4 to it. Finally, the DC of any saving throw required by a Life Drain ability of an undead is increased by 2. All of these benefits cease for a target when the duration ends or when that target leaves the area of effect. It regains the benefits if it re-enters the area of effect.

Mummy, Lightning-Quick

It rose out of the sarcophagus but we were prepared. Mummies were old hat to us; as a group we had laid more than a dozen to rest. This one though, it was different. The funeral mask it wore bore a twisted, mocking smile that leered at us the entire time. It did not shamble forth from its tomb, but instead sprinted along so fast it ran up the sides of walls to strike at us. With a wicked flail and a crook that spat lightning, it moved among us so quickly that we had trouble landing a solid blow upon it. All the time, that laughing golden face mocked and spat out scarab beetles that skittered to join the fray. — Algrid Henswaithe, University of the Vast

Lightning-quick mummies are created by foul sorceries to lure and trap those wishing to disturb the rest of the unliving. They wear ornate funeral masks that depict their creators, but with horrid grins that mock and laugh. Armed with a flail and crook, magical lightning, and filled with dangerous scarabs, the lightning-quick mummies are fearsome foes who know no mercy. In fact, their mocking faces belie that they have any emotions whatsoever.

Mummy, Lightning-Quick

Medium undead, chaotic evil

Armor Class 20 (natural armor)
Hit Points 112 (15d8 + 45)
Speed 40 ft.

STR	DEX	CON	INT	WIS	CHA
20 (+5)	20 (+5)	16 (+3)	8 (–1)	14 (+2)	15 (+2)

Saving Throws Dex +10, Con +7, Wis +4, Cha +5
Damage Vulnerabilities fire
Damage Immunities necrotic, poison; bludgeoning, piercing, and slashing damage from nonmagical attacks
Condition Immunities charmed, exhaustion, frightened, paralyzed, poisoned
Senses darkvision 60 ft., passive Perception 8
Languages the languages it knew in life
Challenge 16 (15,000 XP)

Accelerated Movement. The lightning-quick mummy has advantage on initiative checks.

Gaze of Despair. When a creature that can see the lightning-quick mummy's eyes starts its turn within 30 feet of the lightning-quick mummy, the mummy can force it to make a DC 15 Wisdom saving throw if the mummy isn't incapacitated and can see the creature. On a failure, the creature suffers disadvantage on all attack rolls, ability checks, and saving throws for one minute. Unless surprised, a creature can avert its eyes to avoid the saving throw at the start of its turn. If the creature does so, it can't see the sepia snake until the start of its next turn, when it can avert its eyes again. If the creature looks at the sepia snake in the meantime, it must immediately attempt the save. While averting its eyes, any attacks on the lightning-quick mummy are done at disadvantage.

Mask of Rahotep. The lightning-quick mummy wears an enchanted mask of Rahotep. If this mask is removed, the lightning-quick mummy loses its accelerated movement ability and all legendary actions.

Actions

Multiattack. The creature makes one Crook attack and two Flail attacks, or one Electric Bolt and two Flail attacks.

Crook. *Melee Weapon Attack:* +10 to hit, reach 5 ft., one target. *Hit:* 10 (1d10 + 5) bludgeoning damage and the creature must succeed at a DC 18 Strength saving throw or be grappled by the lightning-quick mummy (escape DC 18). The lightning-quick mummy can grapple only one creature with its hook.

Flail. *Melee Weapon Attack:* +10 to hit, reach 5 ft., one target. *Hit:* 16 (2d10 + 5) bludgeoning damage creature must succeed at a DC 18 Constitution saving throw or be cursed with mummy rot. The creature can't regain hit points and its hit point maximum decreases by 10 (3d6) for every 24 hours that elapse. If the creature is reduced to 0 hit points by the mummy rot, they die and their body turns to dust. The curse lasts until removed by the *remove curse* spell or other magic.

Electric Bolt. *Ranged Weapon Attack:* +10 to hit, range 20/40 ft., up to three targets. *Hit:* 15 (3d6 + 5) lightning damage.

Legendary Actions

The lightning-quick mummy can take three legendary actions, choosing from the options below. Only one legendary action can be used at a time and only at the end of another creature's turn. The lightning-quick mummy regains spent legendary actions at the start of its turn.

Faster than the Eye Can See. The lightning-quick mummy makes an Electrical Bolt and a Flail attack.

Spin and Strike. The lightning-quick mummy moves up to its full movement, ignoring difficult terrain and not provoking attacks of opportunity, and makes a Crook attack.

Spit Beetle. The lightning-quick mummy spits a beetle from the list below. This is a ranged weapon attack (+10 to hit, range 10/20 ft., one target, *Hit:* target suffers the effects based on the color of beetle)

Hook and Shock (costs 2 actions). The lightning-quick mummy attacks a creature it has grappled with its hook using Electric Bolt, all three bolts targeting the grappled creature with disadvantage.

Lightning-Quick Mummy Scarabs

1d6	Beetle Type	Effect
1	White	Target is blinded until the end of its next turn.
2	Purple	The next spell the target casts within one hour fails and the target takes 1d6 force damage per level of the spell.
3	Blue	Target is unable to cast any spells until the end of its next turn.
4	Black	Target is paralyzed until the end of its next turn
5	Green	Target must succeed at a DC 18 Constitution saving throw or suffer 17 (5d6) piercing damage as the scarab burrows into its flesh.
6	Red	Target must target its next attack against an ally within five feet. If no ally is within range at that time, target is stunned until the end of its next turn.

TOME OF **HORRORS**

Murder Born

The shattered keep was waist deep in restless spirits, so we went to work with rattles and salt to cleanse the place. Most of the restless spirits were of the common kind, nothing the four of us had not seen before. Dan, kindhearted Dan, heard the sound of a wailing infant and ran off to the rescue, with Ernie right after him. They found a wailing infant of translucent spirit matter, its delicate features hinting at cherubic innocence. This innocence was belied by its rage-filled eyes red with evil intent. The wailing intensified, and all four of us, even clinical, cynical Harold, were overcome with waves of despair. That's when the ghostly infant moved in. — Sir Cedric of Reme, knight errant

Murder of the foulest kind creates the ghastly undead known. When a pregnant mother and her unborn child are slain and their bodies not given a proper burial, then the spirit of the unborn rises as a murder born. Translucent and shimmering, these foul fetuses want nothing more than to sow death and despair in the world they never saw. They are rapacious in their hunger for murder, as if only through that singular act can they understand the world.

Murder Born

Tiny undead, chaotic evil

Armor Class 13
Hit Points 90 (20d4 + 40)
Speed fly 40 ft.

STR	DEX	CON	INT	WIS	CHA
6 (−2)	15 (+3)	14 (+2)	14 (+2)	14 (+2)	16 (+3)

Damage Resistances acid, fire, lightning, thunder; bludgeoning, piercing, and slashing damage from nonmagical attacks.
Damage Immunities cold, necrotic, poison
Condition Immunities charmed, exhaustion, frightened, grappled, paralyzed, petrified, poisoned, restrained
Senses darkvision 60 ft., passive Perception 12
Languages —
Challenge 5 (1,800 XP)

Ethereal Sight. The murder born can see 60 feet into the Ethereal Plane when it is on the Material Plane, and vice versa.
Incorporeal Movement. The murder born can move through other creatures and objects as if they were difficult terrain. It takes 5 force damage if it ends its turn inside an object.

Actions

Ghostly Touch. *Melee Weapon Attack*: +6 to hit, reach 5 ft., one target. *Hit*: 20 (5d6 + 3) necrotic damage.
Despondent Wail. The murder born screams a high-pitched wail of despair and confused sorrow. All creatures within 30 feet of the murder born that can hear it must succeed on a DC 14 Wisdom saving throw or suffer disadvantage on all attack rolls, ability checks, and saving throws for one minute. A creature who succeeds on a save against a murder born's despondent wail is immune to the effects for one hour.
Etherealness. The murder born enters the Ethereal Plane from the Material Plan, or vice versa. It is invisible on the Material Plane while it is in the Border Ethereal, and vice versa, yet it can't affect, or be affected by, anything on the other plane.

Murder Crow

Its caw was like a knell of doom. We hoped at first that the grew crow was a sign from Atlarik's god that our cause was just, but that did not come to pass. The crow that swooped down upon us was mangy, its feathers so disheveled that, if it were a messenger from a god, I would fear to touch it. Likewise, it stank of death and the dead, no clean bird this one. It came right at my eyes and sought to gouge them out, all the time cawing as if the dead were about to wake. One good swing from Atlarik's warclub and the thing exploded into a swam of smaller crows, their flesh rotting as they strove to finish the job of blinding me. — Tara the Wise, adventurer

Murder crows are not of this world, or so the sages say. Other texts speak of natural birds cursed by foul wizardry to become these monstrosities. No matter how they were created, they exist to feast upon the eyes of the living. While not rotten themselves, their feathers are unclean and their eyes stare out not with hunger or rage, but blank emotion. Once slain, they do not end their attack, for the murder crow explodes into a cloud of angry crow corpses.

Murder Crow

Medium undead, chaotic evil

Armor Class 17 (natural armor)
Hit Points 71 (13d8 + 13)
Speed 10 ft., fly 60 ft.

STR	DEX	CON	INT	WIS	CHA
12 (+1)	18 (+4)	13 (+1)	2 (−4)	14 (+2)	12 (+1)

Skills Perception +4, Stealth +4
Damage Immunities poison
Condition Immunities poisoned
Senses darkvision 60 ft., passive Perception 14
Languages —
Challenge 5 (1,800 XP)

Death Throes. When the murder crow dies, it explodes into a murder of crows. These smaller swarms continue to relentlessly attack all living creatures within sight. Use the statistics for a **swarm of ravens** for the murder of crows.

Actions

Multiattack. The murder crow makes two Claw attacks and one Bite attack.
Bite. *Melee Weapon Attack:* +4 to hit, reach 5 ft., one target. *Hit:* 8 (2d6 + 1) piercing damage.
Claw. *Melee Weapon Attack:* +4 to hit, reach 5 ft., one target. *Hit:* 10 (2d8 + 1) slashing damage. If the murder crow hits a target with both Claw attacks in the same turn, the creature must succeed on a DC 15 Dexterity saving throw or be blinded as the murder crow scratches and tears at the target's eyes. The blindness can be removed if a character spends their action to attend to the blinded target and makes a successful DC 15 Wisdom (Medicine) check or by a *lesser restoration* spell.

Mus

A ragged opening was cut through the stone, barely a foot tall. The stone statue clomped down the passage behind us, closing in. "Only one way out," Sabbox said, handing out the stoppered vials. The mixture smelled like spoiled milk mashed into fish guts, but we downed the foul brew. The room instantly expanded as we shrank to a fraction of our normal heights. We charged through the hole just as the statue slammed a solid fist into the floor behind us. We pushed onward, thankful for our escape, when a defiant voice spoke, "Be you friend of foe?" A mouse — not tiny anymore because of our diminutive size — brandished a rapier as it stood before us. It was dressed in a silken tunic and breeches. As I watched, rows upon rows of similarly dressed rodents carrying weapons stepped into view on the ledges above us. — Sir Carpathian Grey, senior knight protector of the Wizard's Wall

The mus are a race of diminutive rodents that resemble bipedal mice. They live in regions normally unvisited by larger humanoids such as forests, isolated valleys, and forgotten ruins, but they are also known to inhabit large cities, where their tiny empires grow powerful beyond the notice of the city's conventional inhabitants. Mus communities are ruled by hereditary sultans, and they create elaborate dwellings, decorated in the fashion of the most luxurious cities.

The mus also dress well, favoring lavish but tasteful garb from silken trousers, curly-toed slippers, turbans, embroidered vests, fezzes, and low-crowned tasseled chapeaux. Mus also love lavish jewelry — rings, necklaces, bracelets, and broaches of tiny size but superb workmanship. Though of good alignment, they tend to avoid contact with the outside world, preferring to keep their hidden empires a secret from others. Mus sorcerers command many defensive spells and can make encounters with the little creatures challenging even for experienced adventurers. If aided or shown friendship, the mousefolk may become companions or allies, but always ask that their friends keep their secrets.

Mus

Tiny humanoid, neutral good

Armor Class 16 (natural armor)
Hit Points 2 (1d4)
Speed 10 ft.

STR	DEX	CON	INT	WIS	CHA
2 (–4)	16 (+3)	10 (+0)	12 (+1)	16 (+3)	10 (+0)

Saving Throws Dex +5, Wis +5
Skills Perception +7, Stealth +7
Senses darkvision 30 ft., passive Perception 13
Languages Common
Challenge 1/8 (25 XP)

Silent as a Mouse. A mus has advantage on Dexterity (Stealth) checks.

Actions

Bite. *Melee Weapon Attack:* +5 to hit, reach 5 ft., one creature. *Hit:* 1 piercing damage.
Sword. *Melee Weapon Attack:* +5 to hit, reach 5 ft., one target. *Hit:* 5 (1d4 + 3) slashing damage.

Mus Sorcerer

Tiny humanoid, neutral good

Armor Class 16 (natural armor)
Hit Points 5 (2d4)
Speed 10 ft.

STR	DEX	CON	INT	WIS	CHA
2 (–4)	16 (+3)	10 (+0)	12 (+1)	16 (+3)	16 (+3)

Saving Throws Dex +5, Wis +5, Cha +5
Skills Perception +7, Stealth +7
Senses darkvision 30 ft., passive Perception 13
Languages Common
Challenge 3 (700 XP)

Silent as a Mouse. A mus sorcerer has advantage on Dexterity (Stealth) checks.

Spellcasting. The mus sorcerer is an 8th-level spellcaster. Its spellcasting ability is Charisma (spell save DC 13, +5 to hit with spell attacks). The mus sorcerer has the following sorcerer spells prepared:

Cantrips (at will): *blade ward, dancing lights, friends, minor illusion, prestidigitation*
1st level (4 slots): *charm person, expeditious retreat, shield, witch bolt*
2nd level (3 slots): *invisibility, shatter*
3rd level (3 slots): *blink, slow*
4th level (2 slots): *confusion*

Actions

Bite. *Melee Weapon Attack:* +5 to hit, reach 5 ft., one creature. *Hit:* 1 piercing damage.
Staff. *Melee Weapon Attack:* +5 to hit, reach 5 ft., one target. *Hit:* 5 (1d4 + 3) bludgeoning damage and the target must succeed on a DC 13 Constitution saving throw or be stunned until the start of the mus sorcerer's next turn.

Mus Swashbuckler

Tiny humanoid, neutral good

Armor Class 16 (natural armor)
Hit Points 5 (2d4)
Speed 10 ft.

STR	DEX	CON	INT	WIS	CHA
2 (–4)	16 (+3)	10 (+0)	12 (+1)	16 (+3)	16 (+3)

Saving Throws Dex +5, Wis +5, Cha +5
Skills Deception +7, Perception +7, Stealth +7
Senses darkvision 30 ft., passive Perception 13
Languages Common
Challenge 3 (700 XP)

Distraction. As a bonus action, the mus swashbuckler makes a contested Charisma (Deception) check against its opponent's Wisdom (Insight). On a success, the opponent is distracted and the mus swashbuckler has advantage on its melee attacks against that target for one round.
Silent as a Mouse. A mus swashbuckler has advantage on Dexterity (Stealth) checks.

Actions

Bite. *Melee Weapon Attack:* +5 to hit, reach 5 ft., one creature. *Hit:* 1 piercing damage.
Rapier. *Melee Weapon Attack:* +5 to hit, reach 5 ft., one creature. *Hit:* 5 (1d4 + 3) piercing damage.

Musk Ox

The guide called them "bearded-ones" but we just thought of them as hairy cattle. They were heavily bodied, with short dense horns similar to that of the cattle of the tropical lands. Our guide advised that they were more difficult to hunt than they looked, but we scoffed at this idea. After all, we had arrows tipped in bronze and sharp spears of the same, not the bone and stone implements of his folk. We were wrong, for no amount of metal could match knowledge and skill. We lacked both and had to return to our guide emptyhanded and empty-bellied. At least he shared his seal blubber with us. That was nice. — Tara the Wise, adventurer

Natives of the colder climes, musk oxen are four- to five-foot-tall bovines with shaggy coats and short horns that grow from thick pads atop their heads. During warm months, they live in small groups that forage on the blooming grasses, small trees, and wetland forbs. In the winter, the herds gather in larger numbers that clump together. During the summer rut and throughout the winter as the females become gravid with calves, musk oxen become more aggressive. If threatened, a herd clumps up, horns out, with the most vulnerable among them in the middle. Those on the outside charge threats, falling back into the herd as another comes out to make its own charge.

Musk Ox

Medium beast, unaligned

Armor Class 10
Hit Points 25 (2d8 + 16)
Speed 40 ft.

STR	DEX	CON	INT	WIS	CHA
16 (+3)	10 (+0)	16 (+3)	2 (–4)	10 (+0)	6 (–3)

Skills Perception +2
Senses passive Perception 12
Languages —
Challenge 1/2 (100 XP)

Herd Tactics. The musk ox has advantage on an attack roll against a target if at least one of the musk ox's allies is within five feet of the musk ox and the ally isn't incapacitated.

Actions

Gore. *Melee Weapon Attack:* +5 to hit, reach 5 ft., one target. *Hit:* 7 (1d8 + 3) piercing damage.

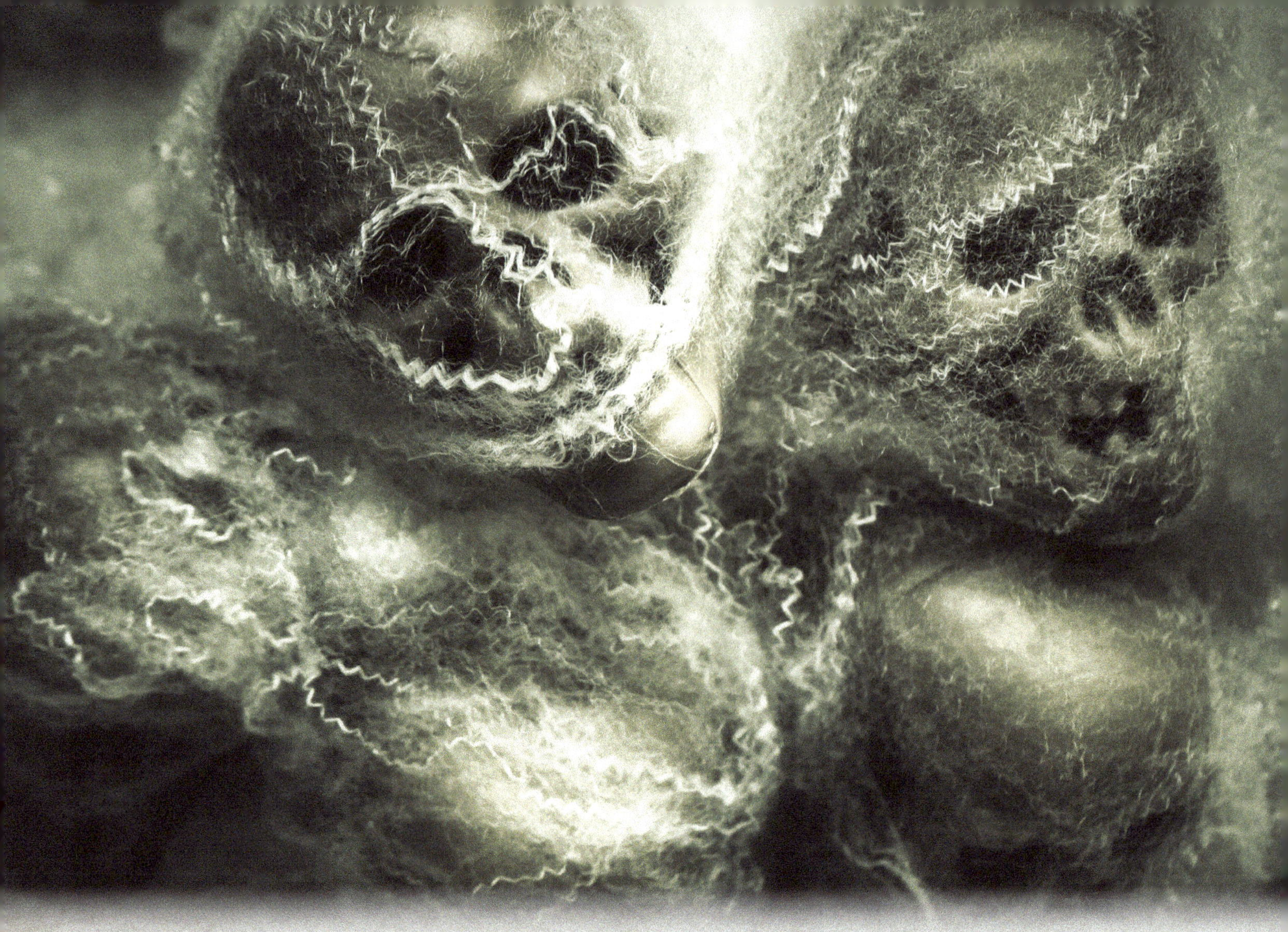

N'GATHAU

The portal promised a mountain of gold and jewels beyond its red boundary, the wealth of a lifetime. But when we stepped through, we found none of it. Just a room with silver walls in a high tower with a single exit. From that spire, we looked out on a nightmare landscape of devices belching olive smoke amid a chorus of screams. The sky was alive with shards of metal swirling through the air like flocks of angry birds. Commack leaned from the window to look for another way out ... and was shredded by the metal slivers. We knew then we were in Hell. — From the collected nightmare texts of Bevil Carrek, self-proclaimed explorer of Hell

The n'gathau are sadistic and cruel beings that reside in the Hell Ring of Abaddon. Not truly devils, nor demons, these twisted and malign beings exist only to torture and maim the other creatures of the universe in the unholy name of their long dead god. During the War of the Fallen, the n'gathau partnered with the fallen against the angels of the Heavens and the demons of the Abyss for control of creation. Defeated, their dark god and his minions were cast into the Rings of Hell with others such as The Lightbringer, Moloch, and Baalzebal.

These twisted fiends now live an almost monk-like existence in Abaddon where they dwell in a hell crafted from the flesh of their own sacrificed god. Here they prize only raw physical pain. The n'gathau differ from other fiends of Hell in that they do not trade in souls per se but in fact prefer the living flesh of those whose living actions have led them on the path of damnation. They act as intermediaries who coax the damned from the land of the living to their final destination. Once one of the damned is ensnared in their traps, they are whisked away to the various torture temples of the Twelve who rule and the Quorum who speaks for all.

THE PAIN TRADE

The n'gathau engage in a bizarre trade with other entities of the underworld. In exchange for living creatures, the n'gathau craft reliquaries such as the talismans and amulets prized by greater demons and devils and the receptacles sought by liches who would extend their existence beyond life itself. Lesser items are used in the creation of fiendish constructs and as raw material spell components.

When a living creature is tortured and mutilated, its screams and suffering are captured by great alien machines and fabricated into talismans of suffering sought by their clientele. It is believed that some open incursions into the land of the living by various demon lords and princes of Hell are in fact triggered by a need to capture thousands of living beings at a time to transfer them whole into n'gathau torture machines.

THE TWELVE

The 12 rulers of the Plane of Agony represent 12 of the 15 high priests of the n'gathau god. Very little is known about them outside of Abaddon save their names and appearance, as their history and true origins are locked away in the minds of the 12 themselves or hidden in the vaults lining the crypts and catacombs of the Plane of Agony. Though reclusive and secretive, it is known that the Twelve, as mighty as they are, serve an oracle-like entity known as the Quorum that dwells in a great temple built atop the skull of the dead god.

It was the will of the dead god that the n'gathau forever multiply their forces, so that capture, torture, and reconfiguration are the methods of conquest to overrun the Underworld and the land of the living, and tear down the walls of the High Heavens themselves. To this end, Veruard's machines are constantly working. The devils of the other Hells have no idea that their lusts for unholy talismans are in fact fueling their own destruction.

N'gathau, Aagash the Broken

This hideous figure was roughly six feet tall and appeared to have been split through the torso, with its spine exposed and its screaming head thrust through the outburst hole to protrude from its chest. Steel rods affixed to the hips held the broad head in place. Plates of spiked armor were bolted to its pale, deathly flesh, and its hands ended in fingertips affixed with razor sharp blades. — From the collected nightmare texts of Bevil Carrek, self-proclaimed explorer of Hell

Aagash once greatly displeased the Quorum and was bent, broken, and reconfigured in ways that reflected his failures. Where he was weak, now he is strong, and where his heart once led him, now his head is in its place. He currently serves as a bodyguard and messenger of the Quorum, often appearing personally to Cultists of Pain to relay the wishes of the unholy trinity.

Aagash the Broken

Medium fiend (n'gathau), neutral evil

Armor Class 19 (natural armor)
Hit Points 275 (22d8 + 176)
Speed 30 ft.

STR	DEX	CON	INT	WIS	CHA
22 (+6)	12 (+1)	26 (+8)	20 (+5)	20 (+5)	12 (+1)

Saving Throws Constitution +14, Wisdom +11
Skills Athletics +12, Intimidation +7, Medicine +11, Religion +11, Perception +11, Stealth +7
Damage Resistances cold; bludgeoning, piercing, and slashing attacks from nonmagical attacks that are not silver
Damage Immunities acid, fire, poison
Condition Immunities frightened, paralyzed, poisoned
Senses darkvision 120 ft., passive Perception 21
Languages Abyssal, Common, Infernal, telepathy 120 ft.
Challenge 18 (20,000 XP)

Brutal Bullying. Aagash has advantage on Charisma (Intimidation) checks.

Cruelty's Bliss. When Aagash scores a critical hit, he gains advantage on his next attack roll.

Delicious Agony. Following a successful melee attack, Aagash can use a bonus action to gain 5 temporary hit points.

Horrifying Appearance. When a creature that can see Aagash's eyes starts its turn within 30 feet of Aagash, he can force it to make a DC 19 Wisdom saving throw if Aagash isn't incapacitated and can see the creature. On a failure, the creature is frightened for one minute. Unless surprised, a creature can avert its eyes to avoid the saving throw at the start of its turn. On a failure, the creature can't see Aagash until the start of its next turn, when it can avert its eyes again. If the creature looks at Aagash in the meantime, it must immediately attempt the save. While averting its eyes, any attacks on Aagash are done at disadvantage.

Reshape the Flesh. Once per day, Aagash has the power to transform the flesh of 1d4 + 2 of his foes to shapes that are more appealing to his eyes (see table below). The targets must be restrained or unconscious in order to be reshaped. Reshaped creatures are under the control of Aagash as if they were dominated by a *dominate monster* spell and remain under his control until the effects are dispelled via a *dispel magic, greater restoration, heal,* or *wish* spell cast to counter the effects.

Flesh Transformations

Roll 1d4 to determine the transformation.

1d4	Result	Effect
1	Snake body	The victim's body is transformed into a snake, though vestigial legs remain. Its head and arms are fully functional. Fangs sprout from its mouth, and it gains a 10-foot spit attack and a poisonous bite attack. The creature uses its Dexterity modifier to make the attacks and is considered proficient. It can use an action to make one of each of these two attacks. On a hit from the spit attack, the target takes 9 (2d8) poison damage and must succeed on a Constitution saving throw or be blinded. On a hit from the bite attack, the target takes 9 (2d8) poison damage and must succeed on a Constitution saving throw or be poisoned. The DC of the save against this venom is 8 + the victim's Charisma modifier + the victim's proficiency bonus.
2	Humanoid Centipede	The victim's body is transformed into a giant centipede, with venomous mandibles that sprout from either side of the jaw and chitinous plates that cover the body (granting a +4 bonus to armor class). The victim retains its normal arms but loses its form from the mid-torso down. The victim gains the Spider Climb ability and can see in 360 degrees. The creature gains a bite attack that deals 7 (2d6) piercing damage plus 7 (2d6) poison damage and the target must succeed on a Constitution saving throw or be poisoned. The DC of the save against this venom is 8 + the victim's Charisma modifier + the victim's proficiency bonus. The attack uses the creature's Strength modifier and the creature is considered proficient.
3	Amoeboid Flesh Form	The victim gains the shape and attributes of a gibbering mouther save the gibbering ability.
4	Beast Body	The creature sprouts hair all over its body, grows bear-like claws on its hands, and gains elongated jaws. It can use an action to make two Claw attacks and one Bite attack. The attacks use the creature's Strength modifier and the creature is considered proficient. On a hit, the Claw attacks do 1d6 slashing damage and the Bite attack does 1d8 piercing damage.

Spine Bender. A creature that beings its turn grappled by Aagash must succeed at a DC 20 Strength Saving throw or be paralyzed.

Innate Spellcasting. Aagash's innate spellcasting ability is Wisdom (spell save DC 19, +11 to hit with spell attacks). He can cast the following spells, requiring no material components:
At will: *detect evil and good, detect magic, detect thoughts, dimension door, hold person*
3/day each: *misty step, plane shift, polymorph*

Spellcasting. Aagash is a 9th-level spellcaster. His spellcasting ability is Wisdom (spell save DC 11, +11 to hit with spell attacks). He has the following spells prepared:
Cantrips (at will): *guidance, mending, sacred flame, thaumaturgy*
1st level (4 slots): *bane, command, guiding bolt, inflict wounds, protection from evil and good, shield of faith*
2nd level (3 slots): *blindness/deafness, enhance ability, silence, spiritual weapon, zone of truth*
3rd level (3 slots): *bestow curse, dispel magic, magic circle, mending, stone shape*
4th level (3 slots): *banishment, divination, freedom of movement, locate creature, stone shape*
5th level (1 slot): *flame strike*

Actions

Multiattack. Aagash makes one Suffering Touch attack and two Claw attacks.

Claw. *Melee Weapon Attack:* +12 to hit, reach 10 ft., one target. *Hit:* 13 (2d6 + 6) slashing damage and the target is grappled (escape DC 20).

Suffering Touch. *Melee Weapon Attack:* +12 to hit, reach 5 ft., one target. *Hit:* 13 (2d6 + 6) psychic damage and the target must succeed on a DC 19 Wisdom saving throw or be incapacitated until the end of its next turn.

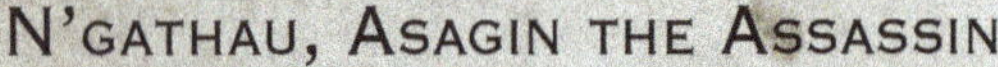

N'gathau, Asagin the Assassin

This fiend had membranous bat-like wings nailed to his back. Hooked blades stabbed through his hands, and nails and blades were pounded into his skull and torso, each affixed with chains that ran from his face to his collarbones. This caused excruciating pain that wracked the creature's body with its every move. Its largest wound appeared to be an "X" carved across its face and stitched together with fishhooks that exposed its jagged teeth and tortured lips. The being was nearly nine feet tall and dressed in a kilt of chain mail with spiked vambraces and greaves encasing its forearms and legs. Skulls and the peeled faces of his foes adorn his girdled waist. — From the collected nightmare texts of Bevil Carrek, self-proclaimed explorer of Hell

Asagin is the general of the armies of the Quorum and places them defensively around the fortresses of Abaddon and is usually in the company of 2d6 n'gathau warriors and 1d4 n'gathau soul hammers. It is suspected that he was once one of the fallen himself and swore his allegiance to the dead god of the n'gathau during the War of the Fallen. Asagin is a brilliant tactician who believes in ensnaring his foes in traps, typically seeking to slice the head from the serpent in his vernacular. Asagin waits to identify leaders in an opposing force, then moves to neutralize said leader to send the underlings into disarray.

Asagin sees that the devils, demons, and various things of Styx who press against the borders of the Plane of Agony are well behaved in their visits. Those who are not are quickly overwhelmed. Typically, his forces attempt to capture as many invaders as they can for reconfiguration at the hands of Veruard.

Asagin the Assassin

Medium fiend (n'gathau), neutral evil

Armor Class 19 (natural armor)
Hit Points 275 (22d8 + 176)
Speed 30 ft.

STR	DEX	CON	INT	WIS	CHA
22 (+6)	12 (+1)	26 (+8)	20 (+5)	20 (+5)	12 (+1)

Saving Throws Constitution +14, Wisdom +11
Skills Athletics +12, Intimidation +7, Medicine + 11, Religion +11, Perception + 11, Stealth +7
Damage Resistances cold; bludgeoning, piercing, and slashing attacks from nonmagical attacks that are not silver
Damage Immunities acid, fire, poison
Condition Immunities frightened, paralyzed, poisoned
Senses darkvision 120 ft., passive Perception 21
Languages Abyssal, Common, Infernal, telepathy 120 ft.
Challenge 18 (20,000 XP)

All Your Limbs Belong to Me. On a critical hit on a melee attack, Asagin rips the arm or leg of an opponent, dealing 36 (8d8) necrotic damage and rendering the limb useless until the target completes a long rest. If the same limb is subject to this effect twice, it is severed and the character dies.

Random Slashed Limb

1d4	Body Part	Effect
1	Left Leg	Halve speed
2	Right Leg	Halve speed
3	Right Arm	Drops anything in that arm, and arm is useless
4	Left Arm	Drops anything in that arm, and arm is useless

Brutal Bullying. Asagin has advantage on Charisma (Intimidation) checks.
Cruelty's Bliss. When Asagin scores a critical hit, he gains advantage on his next attack roll.

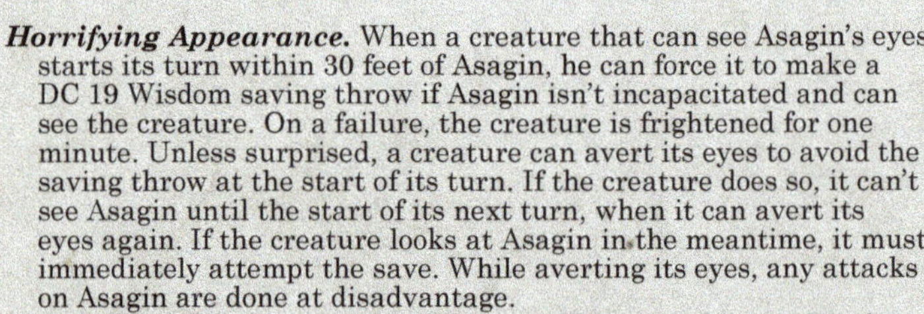

Horrifying Appearance. When a creature that can see Asagin's eyes starts its turn within 30 feet of Asagin, he can force it to make a DC 19 Wisdom saving throw if Asagin isn't incapacitated and can see the creature. On a failure, the creature is frightened for one minute. Unless surprised, a creature can avert its eyes to avoid the saving throw at the start of its turn. If the creature does so, it can't see Asagin until the start of its next turn, when it can avert its eyes again. If the creature looks at Asagin in the meantime, it must immediately attempt the save. While averting its eyes, any attacks on Asagin are done at disadvantage.

Innate Spellcasting. Asagin's innate spellcasting ability is Wisdom (spell save DC 19, +11 to hit with spell attacks). He can cast the following spells, requiring no material components:
At will: *detect evil and good, detect magic, detect thoughts, dimension door, dominate monster, hold person*
3/day each: *misty step, plane shift*

Magic Weapons. Asagin's weapon attacks are magical.

Render of the Flesh. If Asagin hits with both bladed claws on its turn, it inflicts an additional 18 (4d8) slashing damage.

Spellcasting. Asagin is a 9th-level spellcaster. His spellcasting ability is Wisdom (spell save DC 11, +11 to hit with spell attacks). He has the following spells prepared:
Cantrips (at will): *guidance, mending, sacred flame, thaumaturgy*
1st level (4 slots): *bane, command, guiding bolt, inflict wounds, protection from evil and good, shield of faith*
2nd level (3 slots): *blindness/deafness, enhance ability, silence, spiritual weapon, zone of truth*
3rd level (3 slots): *bestow curse, dispel magic, magic circle, mending, stone shape*
4th level (3 slots): *banishment, divination, freedom of movement, locate creature, stone shape*
5th level (1 slot): *flame strike*

Actions

Multiattack. Asagin makes one Suffering Touch attack and two Bladed Claws attacks.

Bladed Claws. *Melee Weapon Attack*: +12 to hit, reach 5 ft., one target. *Hit*: 13 (2d6 + 6) slashing damage.

Suffering Touch. *Melee Weapon Attack*: +12 to hit, reach 5 ft., one target. *Hit*: 13 (2d6 + 6) psychic damage and the target must succeed on a DC 19 Wisdom saving throw or be incapacitated until the end of its next turn.

Delicious Agony. Following a successful melee attack, Asagin can use a bonus action to gain 5 temporary hit points.

N'gathau, Grexias the Destroyer

This muscular, seven-foot-tall fiend's chest was split open and all its skin removed to expose its ribs, muscles, and oozing ichor. Long, thin feeding tubes ran from a rune-scarred face to its exposed abdomen. Its lower half was armored, as were his wrists, which ended in huge, ham-like hands that were sewn shut and nailed through with spikes, making them look like fleshy homemade mace heads. — From the collected nightmare texts of Bevil Carrek, self-proclaimed explorer of Hell

Grexias's purpose is to pound the prisoners of the Quorum into pulp while inflicting the most torturous pain imaginable. His only thoughts are of torture and punishment where he beats the prisoners of the Quorum with his "Everlasting Fists."

Not simply a brute, Grexias' head has been permanently carved with various arcane symbols that are used against his foes to devastating effect. He is also able to draw forth a stew of rotted brain chemicals and digestive fluids from his tubes to vomit forth onto his foes.

Grexias the Destroyer

Medium fiend (n'gathau), neutral evil

Armor Class 19 (natural armor)
Hit Points 275 (22d8 + 176)
Speed 30 ft.

STR	DEX	CON	INT	WIS	CHA
22 (+6)	12 (+1)	26 (+8)	20 (+5)	20 (+5)	12 (+1)

Saving Throws Constitution +14, Wisdom +11
Skills Athletics +12, Intimidation +7, Medicine +11, Religion +11, Perception +11, Stealth +7
Damage Resistances cold; bludgeoning, piercing, and slashing attacks from nonmagical attacks that are not silver
Damage Immunities acid, fire, poison
Condition Immunities frightened, paralyzed, poisoned
Senses darkvision 120 ft., passive Perception 21
Languages Abyssal, Common, Infernal, telepathy 120 ft.
Challenge 18 (20,000 XP)

Brutal Bullying. Grexias has advantage on Charisma (Intimidation) checks.

Cruelty's Bliss. When Grexias scores a critical hit, he gains advantage on his next attack roll.

Delicious Agony. Following a successful melee attack, Grexias can use a bonus action to gain 5 temporary hit points.

Everlasting Fists. Creatures that start their turn grappled by Grexias take 10 (3d6) necrotic damage as Grexias' feeding tubes attach to their veins and drain their blood.

Horrifying Appearance. When a creature that can see Grexias' eyes starts its turn within 30 feet of Grexias, he can force it to make a DC 19 Wisdom saving throw if Grexias isn't incapacitated and can see the creature. On a failure, the creature is frightened for one minute. Unless surprised, a creature can avert its eyes to avoid the saving throw at the start of its turn. If the creature does so, it can't see Grexias until the start of its next turn, when it can avert its eyes again. If the creature looks at Grexias in the meantime, it must immediately attempt the save. While averting its eyes, any attacks on Grexias are done at disadvantage.

Innate Spellcasting. Grexias' innate spellcasting ability is Wisdom (spell save DC 19, +11 to hit with spell attacks). He can cast the following spells, requiring no material components:
At will: *detect evil and good, detect magic, detect thoughts, dimension door, hold person*
1/day: *symbol*
3/day: *misty step, plane shift*

Spellcasting. Grexias is a 9th-level spellcaster. His spellcasting ability is Wisdom (spell save DC 11, +11 to hit with spell attacks). He has the following spells prepared:
Cantrips (at will): *guidance, mending, sacred flame, thaumaturgy*
1st level (4 slots): *bane, command, guiding bolt, inflict wounds, protection from evil and good, shield of faith*
2nd level (3 slots): *blindness/deafness, enhance ability, silence, spiritual weapon, zone of truth*
3rd level (3 slots): *bestow curse, dispel magic, magic circle, mending, stone shape*
4th level (3 slots): *banishment, divination, freedom of movement, locate creature, stone shape*
5th level (1 slot): *flame strike*

Actions

Multiattack. Grexias makes one Suffering Touch attack and two Fist attacks.

Fist. *Melee Weapon Attack:* +12 to hit, reach 5 ft., one target. *Hit*: 13 (2d6 + 6) bludgeoning damage and the target is grappled (escape DC 20). Grappled creatures are trapped in Grexias many tubes and he can still use his fist attacks even with foes grappled. Grexias can grapple up to three Medium or smaller creatures in this manner.

Suffering Touch. *Melee Weapon Attack:* +12 to hit, reach 5 ft., one target. *Hit*: 13 (2d6 + 6) psychic damage and the target must succeed on a DC 19 Wisdom saving throw or be incapacitated until the end of its next turn.

Sludge of Sorrows (recharge 5–6). Grexias can vomit forth a brown sludge of brain and digestive juices in a 30-foot cone. Each creature in the area must make a DC 22 Constitution saving throw, taking 36 (8d8) acid damage on a failure or half as much on a success. Those who fail their save suffer an additional 18 (4d8) acid damage at the start of their next turn unless they use an action to wash the acid free using water or other alkaline or neutral liquids.

N'gathau, Modar the Huntress

The seven-foot-tall fiend was grotesquely mutilated, a chalky-skinned woman whose mouth was wired shut with thick black cables. Her breasts had been removed, and her abdomen was stitched in various patterns. Her lips were peeled away to reveal almost pearl-white teeth. Her eyes had been yanked from their sockets on stretched-out optic nerves and were held away from her face by metal rods with small metal rings. Her disfigured hands ended in wicked claws. — From the collected nightmare texts of Bevil Carrek, self-proclaimed explorer of Hell

Modar is usually in charge of major n'gathau excursions into the Material Plane. Known as the Huntress, Modar's eyes act as *eyes of true seeing* and allow her to view things through every spectrum. Modar typically travels with a pack of 4–10 n'gathau warriors who assist in capturing her quarry.

Modar is exceedingly cruel and is often sent to capture particularly evil and cruel beings so Veruard may reconfigure them. Her temple palace in Zulmegazzar is placed in the right hand of the dead god and features a wall of living eyes plucked from the heads of her victims. Modar is particularly despised by greater devils, whose eyes she prizes almost as much as those of terrified mortal villains.

Modar the Huntress

Medium fiend (n'gathau), neutral evil

Armor Class 22 (natural armor)
Hit Points 275 (22d8 + 176)
Speed 30 ft.

STR	DEX	CON	INT	WIS	CHA
22 (+6)	18 (+4)	26 (+8)	20 (+5)	20 (+5)	12 (+1)

Saving Throws Constitution +14, Wisdom +11
Skills Athletics +12, Acrobatics +11, Intimidation +7, Medicine +11, Religion +11, Perception +11, Stealth +7, Survival +11
Damage Resistances cold; bludgeoning, piercing, and slashing attacks from nonmagical attacks that are not silver
Damage Immunities acid, fire, poison
Condition Immunities frightened, paralyzed, poisoned
Senses darkvision 120 ft., passive Perception 21
Languages Abyssal, Common, Infernal, telepathy 120 ft.
Challenge 18 (20,000 XP)

Brutal Bullying. Modar has advantage on Charisma (Intimidation) checks.

Cruelty's Bliss. When Modar scores a critical hit, she gains advantage on her next attack roll.

Delicious Agony. Following a successful melee attack, Modar can use a bonus action to gain 5 temporary hit points.

Eye See You. Modar sees in every spectrum and has advantage on attacks against normally difficult to see prey, such as those under the effects of invisibility or hiding in darkness and shadows. This allows it to track its quarry even into other dimensions.

Horrifying Appearance. When a creature that can see Modar's eyes starts its turn within 30 feet of Modar, she can force it to make a DC 19 Wisdom saving throw if Modar isn't incapacitated and can see the creature. On a failure, the creature is frightened for one minute. Unless surprised, a creature can avert its eyes to avoid the saving throw at the start of its turn. If the creature does so, it can't see Modar until the start of its next turn, when it can avert its eyes again. If the creature looks at Modar in the meantime, it must immediately attempt the save. While averting its eyes, any attacks on Modar are done at disadvantage.

Innate Spellcasting. Modar's innate spellcasting ability is Wisdom (spell save DC 19, +11 to hit with spell attacks). She can cast the following spells, requiring no material components:

At will: *detect evil and good, detect magic, detect thoughts, dimension door, hold person*
1/day: *finger of death, prismatic spray*
3/day: *misty step, plane shift*

Spellcasting. Modar is a 9th-level spellcaster. Her spellcasting ability is Wisdom (spell save DC 11, +11 to hit with spell attacks). She has the following spells prepared:

Cantrips (at will): *guidance, mending, sacred flame, thaumaturgy*
1st level (4 slots): *bane, command, guiding bolt, inflict wounds, protection from evil and good, shield of faith*
2nd level (3 slots): *blindness/deafness, enhance ability, silence, spiritual weapon, zone of truth*
3rd level (3 slots): *bestow curse, dispel magic, magic circle, mending, stone shape*
4th level (3 slots): *banishment, divination, freedom of movement, locate creature, stone shape*
5th level (1 slot): *flame strike*

Actions

Multiattack. Modar makes one Suffering Touch attack and two Claw attacks.

Claw. *Melee Weapon Attack:* +12 to hit, reach 5 ft., one target. *Hit:* 13 (2d6 + 6) slashing damage and the target must succeed on a DC 22 Constitution saving throw or suffer and additional 12 (3d6) necrotic damage at the start of their next turn.

Suffering Touch. *Melee Weapon Attack:* +12 to hit, reach 5 ft., one target. *Hit:* 13 (2d6 + 6) psychic damage and the target must succeed on a DC 19 Wisdom saving throw or be incapacitated until the end of their next turn.

N'GATHAU, RAUUKA THE RAVAGER

Standing about six feet tall, Raauka is a humanoid creature with a severely mutilated head and face. Small metal hooks were embedded in his forehead and attached to small links of chain that peeled away the flesh around his eyes. His pupils and irises were dark. Sharpened fangs protruded from his mutilated mouth, and several small, thin feeding tubes exited each of his forearms and entered his neck. His fingers were amputated and replaced with long, hollow needles that dripped a sapphire blue liquid. — From the collected nightmare texts of Bevil Carrek, self-proclaimed explorer of Hell

Rauuka is often sent to the mortal plane to retrieve powerful mortals for transformation and service in the armies of the n'gathau. Rauuka injects his prey with paralytic poisons that cause excruciating pain and makes his victims feel as if their blood is on fire. It also gives them with horrible waking nightmares.

His temple is built within the spine of the dead god in the center of Zulmegazzar, near the place where the deity was decapitated by the Twelve and the Quorum. Rauuka draws the tortured spinal fluids from the corpse of the master and filters them through his own body to create the horrid serums he uses to torture and slay his subjects.

Rauuka the Ravager
Medium fiend (n'gathau), neutral evil

Armor Class 19 (natural armor)
Hit Points 275 (22d8 + 176)
Speed 30 ft.

STR	DEX	CON	INT	WIS	CHA
22 (+6)	12 (+1)	26 (+8)	20 (+5)	20 (+5)	12 (+1)

Saving Throws Constitution + 14, Wisdom +11
Skills Athletics + 12, Intimidation + 7, Medicine + 11, Religion +11, Perception + 11, Stealth +7
Damage Resistances cold; bludgeoning, piercing, and slashing attacks from nonmagical attacks that are not silver
Damage Immunities acid, fire, poison
Condition Immunities frightened, paralyzed, poisoned
Senses darkvision 120 ft., passive Perception 21
Languages Abyssal, Common, Infernal, telepathy 120 ft.
Challenge 18 (20,000 XP)

Brutal Bullying. Rauuka has advantage on Charisma (Intimidation) checks.

Cruelty's Bliss. When Rauuka scores a critical hit, he gains advantage on his next attack roll.

Delicious Agony. Following a successful melee attack, Rauuka can use a bonus action to gain 5 temporary hit points.

Horrifying Appearance. When a creature that can see Rauuka's eyes starts its turn within 30 feet of Rauuka, he can force it to make a DC 19 Wisdom saving throw if Rauuka isn't incapacitated and can see the creature. On a failure, the creature is frightened for one minute. Unless surprised, a creature can avert its eyes to avoid the saving throw at the start of its turn. If the creature does so, it can't see Rauuka until the start of its next turn, when it can avert its eyes again. If the creature looks at Rauuka in the meantime, it must immediately attempt the save. While averting its eyes, any attacks on Rauuka are done at disadvantage.

Innate Spellcasting. Rauuka's innate spellcasting ability is Wisdom (spell save DC 19, +11 to hit with spell attacks). He can cast the following spells, requiring no material components:
At will: *detect evil and good, detect magic, detect thoughts, dimension door, hold person, misty step, plane shift*

Magic Weapons. Rauuka's weapon attacks are magical.

Spellcasting. Rauuka is a 9th-level spellcaster. His spellcasting ability is Wisdom (spell save DC 11, +11 to hit with spell attacks). He has the following spells prepared:
Cantrips (at will): *guidance, mending, sacred flame, thaumaturgy*
1st level (4 slots): *bane, command, guiding bolt, inflict wounds, protection from evil and good, shield of faith*
2nd level (3 slots): *blindness/deafness, enhance ability, silence, spiritual weapon, zone of truth*
3rd level (3 slots): *bestow curse, dispel magic, magic circle, mending, stone shape*
4th level (3 slots): *banishment, divination, freedom of movement, locate creature, stone shape*
5th level (1 slot): *flame strike*

ACTIONS

Multiattack. Rauuka makes one Suffering Touch attack and two Needle Claws attacks.

Needle Claws. *Melee Weapon Attack:* +12 to hit, reach 5 ft., one target. *Hit:* 13 (2d6 + 6) piercing damage and the target must succeed on a DC 22 Constitution saving throw or suffer one of the following effects:

Undead Nightmare: Using this venom instantly kills the target. The soul of the slain victim is trapped by Rauuka in a phylactery jar and the body is instantly transformed into a plague zombie under Rauuka's command. If Rauuka uses this effect, he cannot use his needle claws until the end of his next turn.

Waking Nightmare: Rauuka's needles inject his foes with a powerful sleep serum. The creature falls into a waking slumber and is paralyzed until the end of the target's next turn. While sleeping, its mind is filled with visions of its worst nightmares, such as rot grubs crawling up the needle holes of their wounded flesh. The imagined terror causes 22 (4d10) psychic damage.

Suffering Touch. *Melee Weapon Attack:* +12 to hit, reach 5 ft., one target. *Hit:* 13 (2d6 + 6) psychic damage and the target must succeed on a DC 19 Wisdom saving throw or be incapacitated until the end of its next turn.

N'gathau, Veenes the Blademistress

The second of the females making up the Twelve, Veenes stands nearly six feet tall and has a very beautiful and shapely torso. Her head is hairless with the skin removed, and the top of her skull is sawn off, exposing her brain. Several small tubes pumping purplish liquid inserted into her brain run the length of her back and enter her spine at her waist. Small, curved hooks protrude from her shoulders, forearms, and upper back across her shoulders. Embedded in each forearm and gripped with each hand is a razor-sharp scythe-like blade with a telescoping handle. — From the collected nightmare texts of Bevil Carrek, self-proclaimed explorer of Hell

An agent of Veruard, the strangely seductive Veenes is often sent to capture powerful mortals for transformation. Her particular fancy is to cause paladins to fall from grace and then steal them out from under Lillith. The demon lord considers Veenes a rival and would burn her to ash if it were not for the power of the Quorum and the Twelve.

Veenes's temple is located in the Needle, a sharp spire rising from the center of the city of Zulmegazzar where the body of the dead god was impaled during his sacrifice. She is served by a cadre of n'gathau warriors configured from female creatures such as alu-demons, succubi, and fallen paladins.

Veenes the Blademistress

Medium fiend (n'gathau), neutral evil

Armor Class 19 (natural armor)
Hit Points 275 (22d8 + 176)
Speed 30 ft.

STR	DEX	CON	INT	WIS	CHA
22 (+6)	12 (+1)	26 (+8)	20 (+5)	20 (+5)	12 (+1)

Saving Throws Constitution + 14, Wisdom +11
Skills Athletics +12, Intimidation +7, Medicine +11, Religion +11, Perception +11, Stealth +7
Damage Resistances cold; bludgeoning, piercing, and slashing attacks from nonmagical attacks that are not silver
Damage Immunities acid, fire, poison
Condition Immunities frightened, paralyzed, poisoned
Senses darkvision 120 ft., passive Perception 21
Languages Abyssal, Common, Infernal, telepathy 120 ft.
Challenge 18 (20,000 XP)

Brutal Bullying. Veenes has advantage on Charisma (Intimidation) checks.

Cruelty's Bliss. When Veenes scores a critical hit, she gains advantage on her next attack roll.

Delicious Agony. Following a successful melee attack, Veenes can use a bonus action to gain 5 temporary hit points.

Horrifying Appearance. When a creature that can see Veenes' eyes starts its turn within 30 feet of Veenes, she can force it to make a DC 19 Wisdom saving throw if Veenes isn't incapacitated and can see the creature. On a failure, the creature is frightened for one minute. Unless surprised, a creature can avert its eyes to avoid the saving throw at the start of its turn. If the creature does so, it can't see Veenes until the start of its next turn, when it can avert its eyes again. If the creature looks at Veenes in the meantime, it must immediately attempt the save. While averting its eyes, any attacks on Veenes are done at disadvantage.

Innate Spellcasting. Veenes' innate spellcasting ability is Wisdom (spell save DC 19, +11 to hit with spell attacks). She can cast the following spells, requiring no material components:
At will: *detect evil and good, detect magic, detect thoughts, dimension door, hold person*
3/day: *misty step, plane shift*

Magic Weapons. Veenes' weapon attacks are magical.

Spellcasting. Veenes is a 9th-level spellcaster. Her spellcasting ability is Wisdom (spell save DC 11, +11 to hit with spell attacks). She has the following spells prepared:
Cantrips (at will): *guidance, mending, sacred flame, thaumaturgy*
1st level (4 slots): *bane, command, guiding bolt, inflict wounds, protection from evil and good, shield of faith*
2nd level (3 slots): *blindness/deafness, enhance ability, silence, spiritual weapon, zone of truth*
3rd level (3 slots): *bestow curse, dispel magic, magic circle, mending, stone shape*
4th level (3 slots): *banishment, divination, freedom of movement, locate creature, stone shape*
5th level (1 slot): *flame strike*

Actions

Multiattack. Veenes makes one Suffering Touch attack and two Scythes of Sorrows attacks.

Suffering Touch. *Melee Weapon Attack:* +12 to hit, reach 5 ft., one target. *Hit:* 13 (2d6 + 6) psychic damage and the target must succeed on a DC 19 Wisdom saving throw or be incapacitated until the end of their next turn.

Scythes of Sorrows. *Melee Weapon Attack:* +12 to hit, reach 10 ft., one target. *Hit:* 13 (2d6 + 6) slashing damage and the target must make a DC 20 Constitution saving throw. The target's head is cut off and it dies on a failure, or it suffers 27 (6d8) slashing damage on a success. Creatures immune to slashing damage are immune to this effect.

Horror of the Broken Heart (recharge 5–6). Veenes exhales a powerful pheromone perfume from the tubes running the length of her spine and brain in a 30-foot cone. Each creature in the area must make a DC 22 Constitution saving throw, taking 36 (8d8) psychic damage on a failure or half as much on a success. Those who fail their save are blinded and incapacitated until the end of their next turn as they weep tears of blood.

TOME OF HORRORS

Brutal Bullying. Veruard has advantage on Charisma (Intimidation) checks.

Cruelty's Bliss. When Veruard scores a critical hit, he gains advantage on his next attack roll.

Delicious Agony. Following a successful melee attack, Veruard can use a bonus action to gain 5 temporary hit points.

Exemplar of Pain. Veruard is the creator and configurator of all n'gathau mutilations. As such, he fills the tortured souls of the n'gathau with a zealous inspiration, granting any n'gathau within 30 feet of him advantage on attack rolls and saving throws in any round that Veruard takes damage.

Great Reconfigurator. Through a combination of its infernal machinery and forbidden lore, Veruard has the power to shatter the souls of its victims and recombine them as hideous n'gathau warriors and soul hammers. Defeated victims destroyed in this matter cannot be raised by normal means, and even a *wish* spell has only a 50% chance of failure.

Horrifying Appearance. When a creature that can see Veruard's eyes starts its turn within 30 feet of Veruard, he can force it to make a DC 19 Wisdom saving throw if Veruard isn't incapacitated and can see the creature. On a failure, the creature is frightened for one minute. Unless surprised, a creature can avert its eyes to avoid the saving throw at the start of its turn. If the creature does so, it can't see Veruard until the start of its next turn, when it can avert its eyes again. If the creature looks at Veruard in the meantime, it must immediately attempt the save. While averting its eyes, any attacks on the Veruard are done at disadvantage.

Razor's Kiss. On a critical hit on a melee attack, Veruard rips the arm or leg of an opponent, dealing 36 (8d8) necrotic damage and rendering a random limb useless for 24 hours. If the same limb is subject to this effect twice, it is severed and the character dies.

RANDOM SLASHED LIMB

1d4	Body Part	Effect
1	Left Leg	Halve speed
2	Right Leg	Halve speed
3	Right Arm	Drops anything in that arm and arm useless
4	Left Arm	Drops anything in that arm and arm useless

Innate Spellcasting. Veruard's innate spellcasting ability is Wisdom (spell save DC 19, +11 to hit with spell attacks). He can cast the following spells, requiring no material components:

At will: *detect evil and good, detect magic, detect thoughts, dimension door, hold person*

3/day each: *misty step, plane shift*

Reactive Chains. Veruard uses a reaction to make a These Chains of Love attack against a creature that comes within 10 feet of it.

Spellcasting. Veruard is a 9th-level spellcaster. His spellcasting ability is Wisdom (spell save DC 11, +11 to hit with spell attacks). He has the following spells prepared:

Cantrips (at will): *guidance, mending, sacred flame, thaumaturgy*

1st level (4 slots): *bane, command, guiding bolt, inflict wounds, protection from evil and good, shield of faith*

2nd level (3 slots): *blindness/deafness, enhance ability, silence, spiritual weapon, zone of truth*

3rd level (3 slots): *bestow curse, dispel magic, magic circle, mending, stone shape*

4th level (3 slots): *banishment, divination, freedom of movement, locate creature, stone shape*

5th level (1 slot): *flame strike*

ACTIONS

Multiattack. Veruard makes one Suffering Touch attack and two Razor attacks.

Razor. *Melee Weapon Attack:* +12 to hit, reach 5 ft., one target. *Hit*: 13 (2d6 + 6) slashing damage and the target must succeed on a DC 22 Constitution saving throw or suffer an additional 12 (3d6) necrotic damage at the start of its next turn.

Suffering Touch. *Melee Weapon Attack:* +12 to hit, reach 5 ft., one target. *Hit*: 13 (2d6 + 6) psychic damage and the target must succeed on a DC 19 Wisdom saving throw or be incapacitated until the end of its next turn.

These Chains of Love. *Melee Weapon Attack:* +12 to hit, reach 10 ft., one target. *Hit*: 13 (2d6 + 6) bludgeoning damage and the target is grappled (escape DC 20). Creatures that begin their turn grappled by the chains suffer 9 (2d8) bludgeoning plus 9 (2d8) psychic damage.

N'gathau,
Veruard the Creator, the Razor of Abaddon

Veruard was as a seven-foot-tall man with chalky skin with the pallor of death about it. His thin form is painfully wrapped and twined in tight razor wire from head to toe. He wears a kilt of chain mail similar to others of his ancient sect, with long hooked chains that hang from his belt that seem to move of their own volition. Veruard's mouth is full of rotted teeth and his eyes are liquid black. A cleaver with a thin blade more than a foot long seems always at his surgeon-like fingertips. — From the collected nightmare texts of Bevil Carrek, self-proclaimed explorer of Hell

Veruard is the architect of pain and the chief servant of the Quorum. Veruard is called the Creator, for it is he who, at the Quorum's desire, reconfigures chosen subjects into their n'gathau forms. From his workshop, he reworks, mutilates, destroys, tears, and reshapes creatures brought to him into more "pleasing" forms.

Veruard often leads others of the Twelve into the mortal planes to ensnare particularly vicious and cruel mortals to reconfigure in his various machines and on his operating tables. Veruard's studio, the Oblivion, is located in the spine of the dead god, but he keeps his quarters in the brain so he can ever be at the beck and call of the Quorum should they command his presence.

Veruard is a skilled tactician and the others of the Twelve look to him for instruction, especially when it concerns matters of the will of the Quorum or in defense of Abaddon against the lords of the Abyss or the princes of darkness who dwell in the other Rings of Hell.

Veruard the Creator, the Razor of Abaddon

Medium fiend (n'gathau), neutral evil

Armor Class 19 (natural armor)
Hit Points 275 (22d8 + 176)
Speed 30 ft.

STR	DEX	CON	INT	WIS	CHA
22 (+6)	12 (+1)	26 (+8)	20 (+5)	20 (+5)	12 (+1)

Saving Throws Constitution +14, Wisdom +11
Skills Athletics +12, Intimidation +7, Medicine +11, Religion +11, Perception +11, Stealth +7
Damage Resistances cold; bludgeoning, piercing, and slashing attacks from nonmagical attacks that are not silver
Damage Immunities acid, fire, poison
Condition Immunities frightened, paralyzed, poisoned
Senses darkvision 120 ft., passive Perception 21
Languages Abyssal, Common, Infernal, telepathy 120 ft.
Challenge 18 (20,000 XP)

N'gathau Warrior

These horrific fiends differed greatly in appearance, with flayed skin, limbs torn out and replaced with mechanical pieces, and eyes and jaws mutilated in forms that mixed and matched machines and multiple pieces of other beasts, demons, or devils. Mostly composed using a humanoid formula, they average six to seven feet tall. They dressed in chain mail, but had piecemeal armor bolted to their flesh. They bore arcane weapons of unusual nature. — From the collected nightmare texts of Bevil Carrek, self-proclaimed explorer of Hell

N'gathau warriors are the basic troops of Abaddon, with Veruard configuring each of them in one of his infernal machines. These hellish warriors are tasked with defending the borders of Abaddon from incursions of demons and other devils from the Rings of Hell. They are also the forces sent to capture and kidnap beings to be reconfigured to bolster their ranks. N'gathau warriors are armed with a multi-functioning weapon that serves as a blade hurler, net launcher, and serrated edged axe-like weapon. N'gathau warriors swarm their foes, especially forces of greater devils, as they have a lust for pain and are unfazed by the damage they take.

N'gathau Warrior

Medium fiend (n'gathau), neutral evil

Armor Class 16 (natural armor)
Hit Points 136 (16d8 + 64)
Speed 30 ft.

STR	DEX	CON	INT	WIS	CHA
18 (+4)	16 (+3)	18 (+4)	10 (+0)	12 (+1)	2 (–4)

Damage Resistances cold; bludgeoning, piercing, and slashing attacks from nonmagical attacks that are not silver
Damage Immunities acid, fire, poison
Condition Immunities frightened, paralyzed, poisoned
Senses darkvision 120 ft., passive Perception 11
Languages Abyssal, Common, Infernal, telepathy 120 ft.
Challenge 9 (5,000 XP)

Cruelty's Bliss. When a n'gathau warrior scores a critical hit, it gains advantage on its next attack roll.

Delicious Agony. Following a successful melee attack, the n'gathau warrior can use a bonus action to gain 5 temporary hit points.

Horrifying Appearance. When a creature that can see the n'gathau warrior's eyes starts its turn within 30 feet of the n'gathau warrior, the n'gathau warrior can force it to make a DC 15 Wisdom saving throw if the n'gathau warrior isn't incapacitated and can see the creature. On a failure, the creature is frightened for one minute. Unless surprised, a creature can avert its eyes to avoid the saving throw at the start of its turn. If the creature does so, it can't see the n'gathau warrior until the start of its next turn, when it can avert its eyes again. If the creature looks at the n'gathau warrior in the meantime, it must immediately attempt the save. While averting its eyes, any attacks on the n'gathau warrior are done at disadvantage.

Pain Invigoration. N'gathau warriors who take damage have advantage on all attack rolls until the end of their next turn.

Actions

Multiattack. The n'gathau warrior makes two multi-weapon attacks.

Multi-weapon. The n'gathau warrior is equipped with an odd techno-magic multi-weapon that has the following uses:

Blade Hurler. *Ranged Weapon Attack:* +7 to hit, range 100/200 ft., one target. *Hit:* 10 (2d6 + 3) slashing damage and the target must succeed on a DC 16 Constitution saving throw or fall asleep.

Net Hurler. *Ranged Weapon Attack:* +7 to hit, range 20/80 ft., one target. *Hit:* all creatures within a 10-foot cube centered on the target are restrained by the net (escape DC 16). The net is AC 10 and has 30 hit points, is resistant to bludgeoning and piercing damage, and is immune to poison and psychic damage. The net has sharp hooks, and every attempt to escape it inflicts 4 (1d8) slashing damage.

Bleeding Axe. *Melee Weapon Attack:* +8 to hit, reach 5 ft., one target. *Hit:* 13 (2d8 + 4) slashing damage and the creature suffers 7 (2d6) necrotic damage at the start of its next turn.

N'gathau, Soul Hammer

These hulking brutes were a terrifying array of flayed skin, exposed muscle, fluid-filled tubes, and mechanical attachments. Most had hooved lower legs, piston-fired hammers, and a massive claw used to snatch their terrified prey. — From the collected nightmare texts of Bevil Carrek, self-proclaimed explorer of Hell

Massive brutes of the Ring of Abaddon, the soul hammers are made up of parts of pit fiends, balors, beasts, giants, and other unrecognizable parts that Veruard reconfigures. Soul hammers serve as bodyguards to the Twelve, gate guardsmen, and shock troopers in the armies of the n'gathau.

Soul Hammer

Large fiend (n'gathau), neutral evil

Armor Class 12 (natural armor)
Hit Points 210 (20d10 + 100)
Speed 30 ft.

STR	DEX	CON	INT	WIS	CHA
20 (+5)	10 (+0)	20 (+5)	6 (−2)	6 (−2)	6 (−2)

Damage Resistances cold; bludgeoning, piercing, and slashing attacks from nonmagical attacks that are not silver
Damage Immunities acid, fire, poison
Condition Immunities frightened, paralyzed, poisoned
Senses darkvision 120 ft., passive Perception 8
Languages Abyssal, Common, Infernal, telepathy 120 ft.
Challenge 9 (5,000 XP)

Cruelty's Bliss. When the soul hammer scores a critical hit on a target, it gains advantage on its next attack roll.

Damage Enhanced. If reduced to half their maximum hit points, the soul hammer begins to revel in its pain and swings wildly, gaining an extra soul hammer attack per round.

Delicious Agony. Following a successful melee attack, the soul hammer can use a bonus action to gain 5 temporary hit points.

Horrifying Appearance. When a creature that can see the soul hammer's eyes starts its turn within 30 feet of the soul hammer, the soul hammer can force it to make a DC 10 Wisdom saving throw if the soul hammer isn't incapacitated and can see the creature. On a failure, the creature is frightened for one minute. Unless surprised, a creature can avert its eyes to avoid the saving throw at the start of its turn. If the creature does so, it can't see the soul hammer until the start of its next turn, when it can avert its eyes again. If the creature looks at the soul hammer in the meantime, it must immediately attempt the save. While averting its eyes, any attacks on the soul hammer are done at disadvantage.

Actions

Multiattack. The soul hammer makes one Bite attack and two Pincer attacks.

Bite. *Melee Weapon Attack:* +9 to hit, reach 10 ft., one target. *Hit:* 9 (1d8 + 5) piercing damage plus 5 (1d10) necrotic damage.

Pincer. *Melee Weapon Attack:* +9 to hit, reach 10 ft., one target. *Hit:* 12 (2d6 + 5) slashing damage and the target is grappled (escaped DC 17). A creature that is grappled by the soul hammer at the start of its turn is automatically hit by one of the soul hammer's attacks.

Soul Hammer. *Melee Weapon Attack:* +9 to hit, reach 10 ft., one target. *Hit:* 16 (2d10 + 5) bludgeoning damage and the target must succeed on a DC 17 Constitution saving throw or be stunned until the end of its next turn.

Nazalor

Large giant, chaotic evil

Armor Class 14 (natural armor)
Hit Points 126 (12d10 + 60)
Speed 30 ft.

STR	DEX	CON	INT	WIS	CHA
18 (+4)	15 (+2)	20 (+5)	9 (−1)	12 (+1)	7 (−2)

Skills Perception +4, Stealth +5
Senses darkvision 60 ft., passive Perception 14
Languages Giant
Challenge 6 (2,300 XP)

Rage (1/long rest). As a bonus action, the nazalor can whip itself into a roaring frenzy. When it does so, it gains advantage on attack rolls, inflicts +4 damage on melee attacks, and gains resistance to bludgeoning, piercing, and slashing damage. This rage lasts for one minute, after which it ends and the nazalor gains a level of exhaustion.

Regeneration. The nazalor regains 10 hit points at the start of its turn if it has at least 0 hit points.

Scent. The nazalor has advantage on Wisdom (Perception) checks that involve scent and it can track by scent.

Stunning Strike. If a creature is hit by the nazalor's bite attack and one of its claw attacks in the same round, the target must succeed on a DC 16 Constitution saving throw or be stunned until the end of its next turn.

Actions

Multiattack. The nazalor makes one Bite attack and two Claw attacks.

Bite. *Melee Weapon Attack*: +7 to hit, reach 5 ft., one target. *Hit*: 13 (2d8 + 4) piercing damage.

Claw. *Melee Weapon Attack*: +7 to hit, reach 10 ft., one target. *Hit*: 11 (2d6 + 4) slashing damage.

Nazalor

The village hired us to hunt a troll that had been poaching sheep. Well, it wasn't a troll. Worse than any troll, it was far more cunning and clever, and bigger to boot. The damnable thing led us on a merry chase up into the hills, and once we were ready to give up and head home, it sprang down from a cliff and ripped into us. The snarling face and hyena-like gait reminded me of a gnoll, but no gnoll is ever that big and mean.

Nazalor are to gnolls as trolls are to humans, a larger, more feral, and deadlier reflection. They are smart, at least for something so wild, and capable of turning the tables on hunters. However, their nature is still bestial, and nazalors are fiercely territorial and savage, even killing their own kind when encountered. Oddly, unlike trolls, they do not practice cannibalism and a nazalor corpse found in the wilds is most likely the result of a territorial dispute.

Niutomi

Sielah was knocked down as soon as he walked through the low stone entry. Willes rolled head over feet into the room next, easily dodging the grasping claw reaching from above. The thing above the lintel dropped to the ground after our thief, and Willes screamed in terror. It was a massive bull-headed minotaur, but its eyes were dead white orbs. My body failed me when it looked at me, and it bared long fangs in a deadly laugh. I was prepared to die, but instead, a three-tined blade shrieked over me to slice deep into the minotaur. Another ox-headed being clad in gleaming armor stepped up beside me, a godly radiance shining from its form. When it spoke, its voice reverberated through the tomb. "Ruetul Ka' Mhet, your tomb has been unearthed, and your presence has finally been revealed to me." —Crucide Greenbelt, on discovering a forgotten tomb in the Kanderi Desert

The ox-headed warriors (although some are also said to have the heads of horses) are servants of the gods sent to enforce celestial decrees. They are sometimes sent to subdue troublemakers or to punish those who offend the gods. Their missions rarely involve the outright killing of living wrongdoers — in most cases their targets are subdued and taken to face judgment by either mortal judges or in extreme situations by the gods themselves. Though they are often tasked with capturing wrongdoers and bringing them to justice, the niutomi's next most important mission is the subdual or outright destruction of the undead, whom the gods of law consider to be abominations and an offense to the proper order of nature.

Niutomi

Medium celestial, lawful neutral

Armor Class 17 (natural armor)
Hit Points 135 (18d8 + 54)
Speed 30 ft.

STR	DEX	CON	INT	WIS	CHA
18 (+4)	14 (+2)	16 (+3)	10 (+0)	12 (+1)	11 (+0)

Saving Throws Con +8, Wis +4
Skills Athletics +10, Perception +7, Religion +6
Damage Resistances radiant
Condition Immunities charmed, exhaustion, frightened
Senses darkvision 60 ft., passive Perception 17
Languages Celestial, Common
Challenge 5 (1,800 XP)

Celestial Weapons. The niutomi's weapon attacks are magical. When the niutomi hits with any weapon, the weapon deals an extra 2d8 radiant damage or 4d8 radiant damage against undead (included in the attack).

Magic Resistance. The niutomi has advantage on saving throws against spells and other magical effects.

Actions

Multiattack. The niutomi makes two melee attacks.

Pitchfork. *Melee Weapon Attack:* +7 to hit, reach 5 ft., one target. *Hit:* 8 (1d8 + 4) piercing damage plus 9 (2d8) radiant damage or 18 (4d8) radiant damage against undead.

Chain Undead. The niutomi may touch one incapacitated, paralyzed, petrified, stunned, or unconscious undead. The target must then make a DC 14 Constitution saving throw or be reduced to 0 hit points. If the saving throw succeeds, the undead creature loses the condition and may act normally on its next turn. Undead reduced to 0 hit points are chained on the niutomi's next turn and returned to their proper burial place or other destination. So long as they remain chained, the undead remain at rest and at 0 hit points.

Subdue Undead. The niutomi takes an action to force all undead within 10 feet to make a DC 14 Wisdom saving throw or be incapacitated for 1d6 rounds.

Nixie

Teich was friendly enough and willing to help. We came to him because Estefan's research had said that a sage spirit lived in a sacred lake north of the land of the Alemanni tribes. We approached with caution and laid the proper sacrifices, two live horses and a sword ritually "killed" at the edge of the lake. Soon, Teich, a greenish-skinned humanoid, swam up and inspected us. He was uninterested in the horses, which was fine, as we had not yet sacrificed them, and the sword seemed to amuse him. He was overly interested by Estefan though, and soon Estefan seemed overly interested in Teich. Our mage simply walked into the water, fighting us off as we tried to stop him. All that was left was a hat floating on the water and Teich's parting words, "Be back in a year for the mage and an answer." — Päuk, apprentice mage.

Nixies are capricious water spirits that dwell in lakes and other large bodies of fresh water. They make their homes in the deeper waters, weaving together lilies and other water plants to form simple yet elegant homes. They are green-skinned with dark green hair and silver eyes, comely in form and feature, and have webbed hands and feet. While not aggressive, they can entrance humanoids and lure them into the water to become servants of the nixies for a year, after which the being is released. During their time in captivity, the captives are given the ability to breath underwater.

Nixie

Small fey, neutral

Armor Class 13
Hit Points 27 (6d6 + 6)
Speed 30 ft., swim 30 ft.

STR	DEX	CON	INT	WIS	CHA
6 (–2)	16 (+3)	12 (+1)	12 (+1)	16 (+3)	19 (+4)

Saving Throws Con +3, Cha +6
Skills Deception +6, Insight +5, Perception +5
Senses darkvision 60 ft., passive Perception 15
Languages Aquan, Common, Sylvan
Challenge 1 (200 XP)

Amphibious. A nixie can breathe air and water.
Innate Spellcasting. The nixie's spellcasting ability is Charisma (spell save DC 14), and requires no material components for the following spells:
3/day each: *charm person*
1/day: *suggestion*
Shapechanger. A nixie can use her action to polymorph into a Small or Medium aquatic creature, or back into her true form. Her statistics, other than her size, are the same in each form. Any equipment she is wearing or carrying isn't transformed. She reverts to her true form if she dies.

Actions

Shortsword. *Melee Weapon Attack:* +5 to hit, reach 5 ft., one target. *Hit:* 6 (1d6 + 3) piercing damage.
Light Crossbow. *Ranged Weapon Attack:* +5 to hit, range 80/320 ft., one target. *Hit:* 7 (1d8 + 3) piercing damage.
Lure. A nixie sings a magical melody. Every humanoid and giant within 300 feet of her that can hear her song must make a DC 13 Wisdom saving throw or be charmed until the song ends. The nixie must use a bonus action on her subsequent turns to continue singing. She can stop at any time. The song ends if the nixie is incapacitated.
While charmed by the nixie, a target is incapacitated and ignores the songs of other nixies. If the charmed target is more than five feet away from the nixie, the target must move on its turn toward her by the most direct route, trying to get within five feet. It doesn't avoid opportunity attacks, but before moving into damaging terrain such as lava or a pit, and whenever it takes damage from a source other than the nixie, the target can repeat the saving throw. A charmed target can also repeat the saving throw at the end of each of its turns. If the saving throw is successful, the effect ends. A target that successful saves is immune to the nixie's song for the next 24 hours.

NIXIE, BOG

A stone bridge crossed the turbulent rapids of the lower Wahr, a convenient crossing built in the middle of nowhere. Danore crossed first, testing every step lest it was a trap. He made it across fine and motioned for us to follow. The dwarf Thark Axenchisel was halfway across when the singing began. A small, green-skinned creature sat on a rock watching us, singing an enchanting melody. Too enchanting, as it turned out. Thark launched a belly flop into the rapids and sank like a stone.
— Nelye Leafcutter, describing the events that led to the destruction of the Ponticus Bridge near Bargarsport

Bog nixies are the evil cousins of the nixies that guard ponds, rivers, and lakes. They relish in tricking unsuspecting travelers or hunters into entering dangerous waters where the bog nixie can torment their victim or watch them drown.

BOG NIXIE
Small fey, neutral evil

Armor Class 13
Hit Points 33 (9d6 + 9)
Speed 30 ft., swim 30 ft.

STR	DEX	CON	INT	WIS	CHA
6 (–2)	16 (+3)	12 (+1)	12 (+1)	16 (+3)	19 (+4)

Saving Throws Con +3, Cha +6
Skills Deception +6, Perception +5, Stealth +5
Senses darkvision 60 ft., passive Perception 15
Languages Aquan, Common, Sylvan
Challenge 1 (200 XP)

Amphibious. A bog nixie can breathe air and water.
Innate Spellcasting. The bog nixie's spellcasting ability is Charisma (spell save DC 14) and requires no material components for the following spells:
3/day each: *charm person, speak with animals*
1/day: *suggestion*
Shapechanger. A bog nixie can use her action to polymorph into a Small or Medium aquatic creature, or back into her true form. Her statistics, other than her size, are the same in each form. Any equipment she is wearing or carrying isn't transformed. She reverts to her true form if she dies.

ACTIONS

Shortsword. *Melee Weapon Attack:* +5 to hit, reach 5 ft., one target. *Hit:* 6 (1d6 + 3) piercing damage.
Light Crossbow. *Ranged Weapon Attack:* +5 to hit, range 80/320 ft., one target. *Hit:* 7 (1d8 + 3) piercing damage.
Lure. A bog nixie sings a magical melody. Every humanoid and giant within 300 feet of her that can hear her song must make a DC 13 Wisdom saving throw or be charmed until the song ends. The bog nixie must use a bonus action on subsequent turns to continue singing. The bog nixie can stop singing at any time. The song ends if the bog nixie is incapacitated.
While charmed by the bog nixie, a target is incapacitated and ignores the songs of other bog nixies. If the charmed target is more than five feet away from the bog nixie, the target must move on its turn toward her by the most direct route, trying to get within five feet. It doesn't avoid opportunity attacks, but before moving into damaging terrain such as lava or a pit, and whenever it takes damage from a source other than the bog nixie, the target can repeat the saving throw. A charmed target can also repeat the saving throw at the end of each of its turns. If the saving throw is successful, the effect ends on it. A target that successful saves is immune to the bog nixie's song for the next 24 hours.

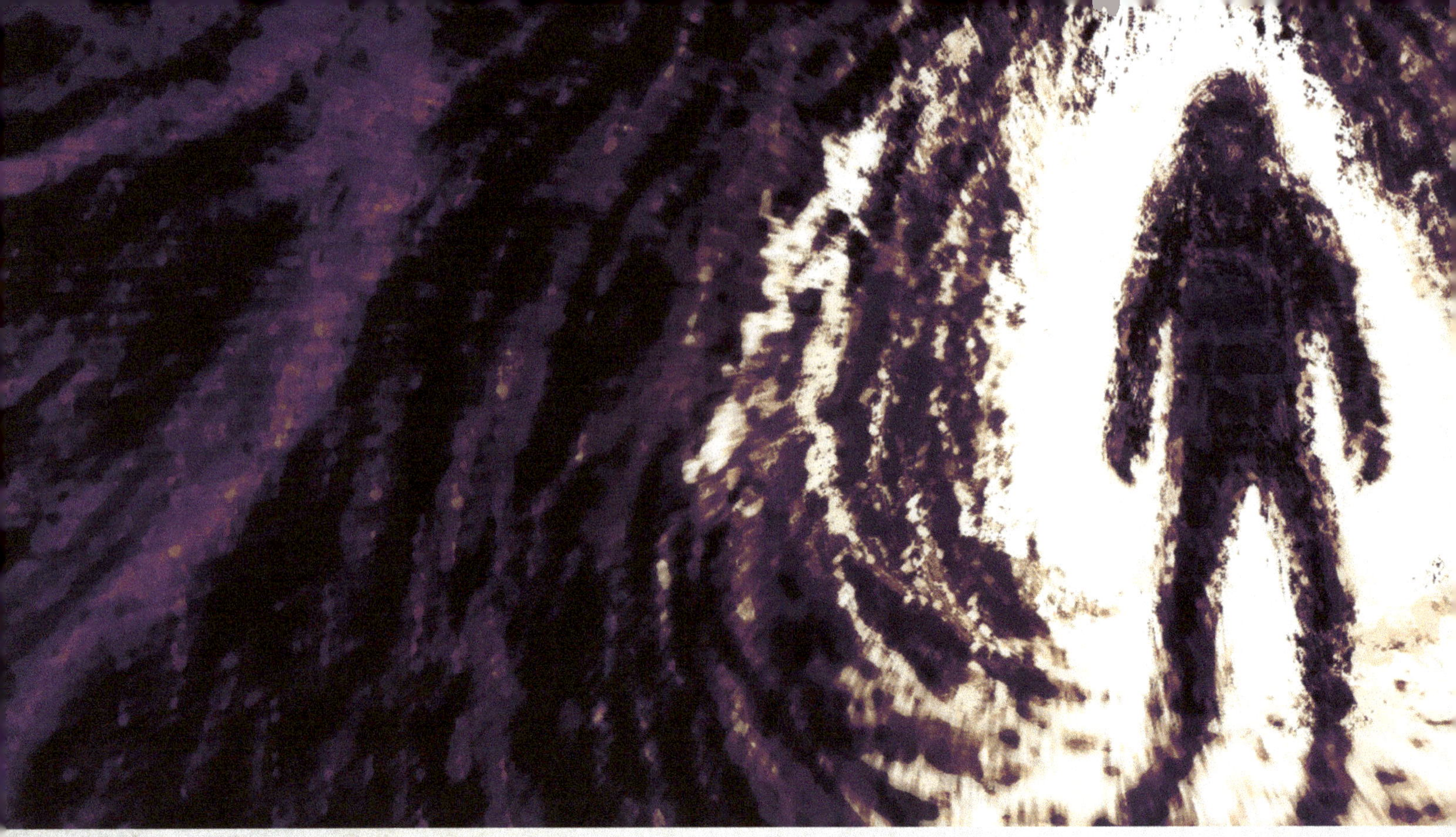

Olithagorian

It was obvious what we had to do. The stones were out of order on the ground around the basalt platform. Arel figured out the pattern first, and she danced about as she replaced them in the proper order. The runes pulsed as the platform lit with an amaranthine glow. If only we'd known it was a gate to the Abyss. The thing that crawled out was a misshapen bulk covered in rotting flesh and scarlet scars. Ambrose struck before it was fully through the portal, but his blade only passed through the thing's flesh, dispersing what was a toxic vapor. — Pengolt Amberwine, seeking aid to stop the unleashed Rune Stone Fiend

Olithagorians are primordial fiends that drift through the lower planes spreading pain and suffering. In their dominant physical form they appear vaguely humanoid, consisting of corpse-like flesh stretched across a hulking yet distorted frame that appears as if it was stretched and broken upon a rack. Thick keloid bands cover their entire body and hideously scarred, featureless face.

Olithagorians are driven by an insatiable hunger for pain and suffering. They collect mortal thralls whom they first lobotomize, then sculpt their flesh and bone until they are wholly unrecognizable. For this reason, some ancient texts refer to these creatures as flesh sculptors. While most sages believe the olithagorians first rose from the Abyss in response to mortal suffering, they cannot be classified as demons and their true origin remains a mystery.

Olithagorian

Large fiend, neutral evil

Armor Class 15 (natural armor)
Hit Points 83 (11d10 + 22)
Speed 40 ft.

STR	DEX	CON	INT	WIS	CHA
18 (+4)	16 (+3)	15 (+2)	15 (+2)	13 (+1)	12 (+1)

Saving Throws Dex +6, Con +5, Wis +4
Damage Resistances bludgeoning, piercing, and slashing from nonmagical attacks
Damage Immunities cold
Senses blindsight 30 ft. (blind beyond this radius), passive Perception
Languages telepathy 90 ft.
Challenge 6 (2,600 XP)

Horrifying Visage. While in its physical form, each mortal creature within 60 feet of the olithagorian that can see it must succeed on a DC 15 Wisdom saving throw or be Frightened for one minute. A Frightened target can repeat the saving throw at the end of each of its turns, ending the Frightened condition on itself on a success. If target's saving throw is successful or the effect ends for it, the target is immune to this olithagorian's Horrifying Visage for the next 24 hours.

Read Thoughts. The olithagorian magically reads the surface thoughts of one creature within 60 feet of it. The effect can penetrate barriers, but three feet of wood or dirt, two feet of stone, two inches of metal, or a thin sheet of lead blocks it. While the target is in range, the olithagorian can continue reading its thoughts for as long as the olithagorian's concentration isn't broken (as if concentrating on a spell). While reading the target's mind, the olithagorian has advantage on Wisdom (Insight) and Charisma (Deception, Intimidation, and Persuasion) checks against the target.

Toxic Vapor Form (1/day). The olithagorian can use its action to shift from its physical form into a cloud of toxic vapor. While in vapor form, the creature's only method of movement is a flying speed of 20 feet. The cloud has an indefinite form, but it can spread up to a maximum radius of 10 feet and can enter and occupy the space of another creature. It can remain in its vapor form for 1d6 + 2 rounds, after which it reverts to its physical form.

Any creature that starts its turn in a space occupied by the vapor form must make a DC 15 Constitution saving throw, taking 9 (2d8) poison damage on a failed save, or half as much damage on a successful one. If the poison damage reduces the target to 0 hit points, the target is stable but poisoned for one hour, even after regaining hit points, and is paralyzed while poisoned in this way.

The vapor form can pass through small holes, narrow openings, and even mere cracks, though it treats liquids as though they were solid surfaces. The vapor form can't fall and remains hovering in the air even when Stunned or otherwise incapacitated. As a vapor, the creature cannot manipulate objects, and any objects it was carrying or holding can't be dropped, used, or otherwise interacted with. It also cannot make physical attacks. It gains advantage on Strength, Dexterity, and Constitution saving throws.

ACTIONS

Multiattack. The olithagorian makes one Headbutt attack and two Claw attacks.

Claw. *Melee Weapon Attack:* +6 to hit, reach 5 ft., one target. *Hit:* 13 (2d8 + 4) slashing damage.

Headbutt. *Melee Weapon Attack:* +6 to hit, reach 5 ft., one target. *Hit:* 11 (2d6 + 4) bludgeoning damage.

LEGENDARY ACTIONS

The olithagorian can take three legendary actions, choosing from the options below. Only one legendary action can be used at a time and only at the end of another creature's turn. The olithagorian regains spent legendary actions at the start of its next turn.

Call Thralls. Any thralls within the lair immediately rush to the olithagorian and aggressively defend it against intruders.

Extreme Headbutt. The olithagorian makes one Headbutt attack. If the attack succeeds, in addition to taking damage, the creature must succeed on a DC 15 Wisdom saving throw or be knocked senseless, becoming Stunned until the end of the olithagorian's next turn.

Create Thrall. If the olithagorian is in vapor form, it can swiftly enter the body of a dying creature. Each round thereafter, it attempts to transform the creature into a thrall. It gives the creature disadvantage on death saves. If the victim fails three death saves with the olithagorian inside it, it doesn't die but instead becomes the olithagorian's lobotomized thrall. Thereafter, the thrall is under the control of the GM until it is killed or cured of its condition.

OLITHAGORIAN THRALL

The bruise-colored vapor flowed into Buni's nose, ears, and mouth, choking her. As she fell face down in the dirt, her body warped and split, with a ridge of flesh and bone rising from her neck down her spine. She raised her head and looked at us with eyes rolled upward to show just their whites. Her features sagged, her mouth dropped open, and ropes of drool hung from her chin. Yet still she moved. And screamed in agony. — Indol Visi, member of a rescue party sent from Malan to aid Pengolt Amberwine to stop the Rune Stone Fiend

Olithagorian thralls are the lobotomized victims left behind by the toxic cloud form of an olithagorian invading their bodies. The mindless vessels are still alive, but they suffer the pains of the creature sculpting their flesh into misshapen forms to serve its bidding.

OLITHAGORIAN THRALL

Medium humanoid, neutral

Armor Class 11
Hit Points 44 (8d8 + 8)
Speed 30 ft.

STR	DEX	CON	INT	WIS	CHA
18 (+4)	12 (+1)	12 (+1)	1 (–5)	1 (–5)	1 (–5)

Damage Resistances bludgeoning, piercing, and slashing from nonmagical attacks
Damage Immunities cold
Senses blindsight 30ft. (blind beyond this radius), passive Perception 5
Languages —
Challenge 2 (450 XP)

Horrifying Visage. Each mortal creature within 60 feet of the olithagorian thrall that can see it must succeed on a DC 13 Wisdom saving throw or be Frightened for one minute. A Frightened target can repeat the saving throw at the end of each of its turns, ending the Frightened condition on itself on a success. If a target's saving throw is successful or the effect ends for it, the target is immune to this olithagorian thrall's Horrifying Visage for the next 24 hours.

Thrall Weaknesses. Casting a *greater restoration spell* upon an olithagorian thrall frees the victim from its torturous condition. A thrall targeted by the spell falls unconscious and slowly reverts to its previous form. Again on the brink of death, the victim must make death saves to avoid dying from the gruelingly painful transformation.

If the olithagorian that created the thrall dies, the thrall slumps to the floor and flops around spastically for 2d6 rounds before dying. Within this narrow timespan, it's still possible to cast *greater restoration* on the thrall to return it to its former self.

ACTIONS

Multiattack. The thrall makes one Headbutt attack and two Claw attacks.

Claw. *Melee Weapon Attack:* +3 to hit, reach 5 ft., one target. *Hit:* 7 (1d6 + 4) slashing damage.

Headbutt. *Melee Weapon Attack:* +3 to hit, reach 5 ft., one target. *Hit:* 6 (1d4 + 4) bludgeoning damage.

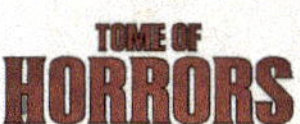

Ooze, Crystal

The halfling Fino Briarfield was sitting on the end of the dock, dipping his toes in the water, when he suddenly began to scream and thrash. Thrinan pulled his little buddy backward, and this clear gel came off the top of the water with him. The blob landed on the wooden dock and ate right through it in a matter of moments. It splashed down into the water and was gone. So were all of Fino's toes. — Warde Graylender, while visiting Lake Elb to solve the mystery of the Lake of Glass

The crystal ooze is an aquatic variety of the gray ooze. It is semitransparent and clear, almost impossible to see in the water, and looks like nothing more than a puddle of water. The crystal ooze can grow to a length of up to eight feet and a thickness of about six inches.

Crystal Ooze

Medium ooze, unaligned

Armor Class 9
Hit Points 30 (4d8 + 12)
Speed 20 ft., swim 20 ft.

STR	DEX	CON	INT	WIS	CHA
13 (+1)	8 (−1)	16 (+3)	3 (−4)	6 (−2)	5 (−3)

Saving Throws Wis +0
Damage Immunities acid, cold, fire
Condition Immunities blinded, charmed, deafened, exhaustion, frightened, prone
Senses blindsight 60 ft. (blind beyond this radius), passive Perception 8
Languages —
Challenge 1/2 (50 XP)

Amorphous. The crystal ooze can move through a space as narrow as one inch wide without squeezing.

Corrode Metal. Any nonmagical weapon made of wood or other organic material that hits the ooze corrodes. After dealing damage, the weapon takes a permanent and cumulative −1 penalty to damage rolls. If its penalty drops to −5, the weapon is destroyed. Nonmagical ammunition made of wood or other organic material that hits the ooze is destroyed after dealing damage. The ooze can eat through two-inch-thick, nonmagical wood, leather, or other organic material in one round.

False Appearance. While the ooze remains motionless, it is indistinguishable from an oily pool or wet rock.

Partially Amphibious. Crystal oozes can survive out of the water for five hours.

Actions

Multiattack. The crystal ooze makes two Pseudopod attacks.

Pseudopod. *Melee Weapon Attack:* +3 to hit, reach 5 ft., one target. *Hit:* 4 (1d6 + 1) bludgeoning damage plus 7 (2d6) acid damage, and if the target is wearing nonmagical leather armor, its armor is partly corroded and takes a permanent and cumulative −1 penalty to the Armor Class it offers. The armor is destroyed if the penalty reduces its Armor Class to 10. In addition, a creature hit by this attack must succeed on a DC 14 Constitution saving throw or become paralyzed. A paralyzed creature can repeat the saving throw at the end of each of its turns, ending the effect on itself with a success.

Pewter Knight

I wanted to bring one back with me. They were statues of knights — with helms, swords, and shields — all made of solid pewter. Well, not solid, I thumped one, and it was hollow. One had a "P" on its shield, while the other an "S." Both had holes in their heads from which to pour spices. Such fun! Sadly, after being thumped, they animated, and we had to destroy them. Just imagine, though, giant pewter knights outside of my cottage!
— Tara the Wise, adventurer

These constructs are usually made by giants to serve as their spice shakers, and as such, can contain hundreds of pounds of pepper, salt, and other spices. While knights made of pewter are the most common forms, more imaginative shapes are possible. When fighting a pewter knight, it is best to be wary of not just their physical power but also their ability to spew forth the spices held within.

Pewter Knight

Medium construct, unaligned

Armor Class 18 (natural armor)
Hit Points 33 (6d8 + 6)
Speed 25 ft.

STR	DEX	CON	INT	WIS	CHA
14 (+2)	11 (+0)	13 (+1)	1 (−5)	3 (−4)	1 (−5)

Damage Immunities poison, psychic
Condition Immunities blinded, charmed, deafened, exhaustion, frightened, paralyzed, petrified, poisoned
Senses blindsight 60 ft. (blind beyond this radius), passive Perception 6
Languages —
Challenge 1 (200 XP)

Antimagic Susceptibility. The construct is incapacitated while in the area of an *antimagic field*. If targeted by *dispel magic*, the construct must succeed on a Constitution saving throw against the caster's spell save DC or fall unconscious for one minute.
False Appearance. While the construct remains motionless, it is indistinguishable from a normal giant-sized spice shaker.

Actions

Multiattack. The pewter knight makes two Slam attacks.
Slam. *Melee Weapon Attack:* +4 to hit, reach 5 ft., one target. *Hit:* 5 (1d6 + 2) bludgeoning damage.
Spice Cloud (recharge 5–6). The construct exhales a cloud of spices in a 15-foot cone. Each creature in that area must succeed on a DC 13 Constitution saving throw or be incapacitated for one minute as they inhale a large amount of salt, pepper, sugar, or cinnamon (depending on the contents housed within the pewter knight). An incapacitated creature can attempt the saving throw at the end of its turn, ending the effect on itself on a success. The area of the cone is lightly obscured for one minute or until a strong wind disperses it.

Platybelodon

We did not discover the lower plateau until our expedition was nearly at its end. The life here was different; instead of great reptiles, we found massive mammals of primitive mien, creatures that looked familiar but only through the lens of scholarly wisdom. One among these stood out, for it was in size and shape much like a pygmy forest elephant, though with a shorter trunk and a long lower jaw armed with sharp teeth. We watched these creatures for some time and discovered that they used the lower jaw to scrape the bark off trees or even to sever a low-hanging limb to be masticated in the beast's powerful jaws. This trick also worked on human limbs, as two of our porters discovered when they tried their hands at hunting.

One of the more common large mammals found in regions of the world where creatures from past eons managed to survive, the platybelodon is similar to modern elephants, but of smaller stature. It moves in small herds and feeds on bark and small tree limbs, using their short trunks to grasp and their long shovel-like lower jaws to cut and grind. These jaws jut out some distance from the creature's face and feature a pair of short, sharp tusks. While not territorial, they can be fearsome when roused to anger.

Platybelodon

Large beast, unaligned

Armor Class 12 (natural armor)
Hit Points 22 (3d10 + 6)
Speed 40 ft.

STR	DEX	CON	INT	WIS	CHA
18 (+4)	10 (+0)	14 (+2)	2 (−4)	10 (+0)	6 (−3)

Skills Perception + 2
Senses passive Perception 12
Languages —
Challenge 1 (200 XP)

Actions

Multiattack. The platybelodon makes one Gore attack and one Trunk attack.
Gore. *Melee Weapon Attack*: +4 to hit, reach 5 ft., one target. *Hit*: 8 (1d8 + 4) slashing damage.
Trunk. *Melee Weapon Attack*: +4 to hit, reach 10 ft., one target. *Hit*: 9 (1d10 + 4) bludgeoning damage

Pyrolisk

Gallo de Fuego they called it, and it haunted the rocky hills outside the pueblo. Well, we knew what that hinted at and so headed off to claim the red tail feather needed to end the Curse of Seven Ills. We traipsed for days along the ridges, up and down arroyos, and across salt flats. Eventually we found it, an evil-looking cross between a lizard and a rooster. With one glance it set Hiram on fire; with another, it turned our small campfire into an explosion of flame and fury. — Tara the Wise, adventurer

Pyrolisks are relatives of the cockatrice and bear a resemblance to that foul creature. However, their gaze does not petrify; instead, it sets foes on fire. When facing the creature, assuming that suddenly sprouting flames across your body does not tip you off, you can tell it from its better-known cousin by the reddish tint to its wing feathers and the single flame-red tail feather. Like cockatrices, pyrolisks are creatures of evil and can be found anywhere from temperate to tropical lands, although they usually roam deserts or the ashen remains of burned-out forests.

Pyrolisk

Small monstrosity, neutral evil

Armor Class 12
Hit Points 21 (6d6)
Speed 20 ft., fly 40 ft.

STR	DEX	CON	INT	WIS	CHA
6 (–2)	15 (+2)	11 (+0)	3 (–4)	13 (+1)	9 (–1)

Damage Vulnerabilities cold
Damage Immunities fire
Senses darkvision 60 ft., passive Perception 11
Languages understands Common but can't speak
Challenge 1/2 (100 XP)

Actions

Beak. *Melee Weapon Attack:* +4 to hit, reach 5 ft., one creature. *Hit:* 5 (1d4 + 2) piercing damage and the target must make a successful DC 12 Constitution saving throw or burst into flames, taking 3 (1d6) fire damage immediately plus 3 (1d6) fire damage at the start of each of the pyrolisk's turns for as long as the flames burn. A creature can extinguish flames on itself or on an adjacent creature by using an action to make a successful DC 10 Dexterity check.

Pyrotechnics (1/day). A pyrolisk causes an ordinary fire within 120 feet of it to flare into a burst of sparks and light. This burst is so bright that all creatures able to see the fire and within 60 feet of it must make a successful DC 10 Wisdom saving throw or be blinded for 1d4 rounds. Pyrolisks are immune to this effect.

QUICKLING

The darkness under the boughs of the Elderwood turned day to night. Barallen pushed aside a massive fern (carefully, for he'd been swallowed by another giant plant barely a month ago). Nothing this time. Nothing that we saw, at least. One moment he was fine; the next, he was sliced and diced and bleeding from hundreds of slashes across his body. Something zipped by me in the brush, and I swear it was an elf, but no way should something move that fast. — Lampert Foxe, during a search of the Elderwood for a rumored entrance to the Under Realms

The quickling is an evil faerie creature that hates all other races (especially other fey). How they came to be evil and malign is still a mystery, but legend speaks of the first quicklings as being great sorcerers. Elven scholars believe these quickling sorcerers unleashed some spark of the arcane that was never meant for mortal creatures. Quicklings resemble small elves with large ears that rise to points above their heads. Their skin is pale blue to blue-white, and their hair is either silver or white. They prefer clothes of bright and boisterous colors; reds, yellows, silvers, blacks, and blues are among their favorites. Quicklings never wear armor.

QUICKLING

Small fey, chaotic neutral

Armor Class 14
Hit Points 16 (3d6 + 6)
Speed 100 ft.

STR	DEX	CON	INT	WIS	CHA
8 (−1)	18 (+4)	14 (+2)	11 (+0)	18 (+4)	12 (+1)

Saving Throws Dex +6
Skills Acrobatics +8, Sleight of Hand +8, Stealth +8
Damage Immunities fire
Senses darkvision 60 ft., passive Perception 14
Languages Aklo, Common, Infernal
Challenge 1 (200 XP)

Cunning Action. A quickling can take the Dash, Disengage, or Hide action as a bonus action on each of its turns.
Innate Spellcasting. A quickling's innate spellcasting ability is Wisdom (spell save DC 14, +6 to hit with spell attacks). It can cast the following spells, requiring no material components:
At will: dancing lights, fire bolt, minor illusion
3/day: burning hands
1/day each: levitate, shatter
Magic Weapons. A quickling's weapon attacks are considered magical for the purposes of overcoming damage resistances and immunities.
Supernatural Speed. A quickling's supernatural speed means that attacks have disadvantage against it as long as it is not grappled or restrained. If a quickling does not move over the course of its turn, it is invisible until the end of its next turn, or until it moves or takes an action. In addition, if a quickling fails its saving throw against the slow spell, it cannot use the benefits above and is poisoned until the slow effect on it ends.

ACTIONS

Multiattack. The quickling makes three attacks.
Dagger. Melee Weapon Attack: +6 to hit, reach 15 ft., one creature. Hit: 6 (1d4 + 4) piercing damage and target must succeed on a DC 12 Constitution saving throw against kava leaf poison or fall asleep for one hour or until lesser restoration, remove curse, or similar is cast on the target.

Rat, Shadow

Squeak, squeak, squeak. It was rats, rats, rats. Lots of them. A writhing, wallowing, wrestling mass of rodents. Too many to count. At least they hadn't noticed us. We slid along the high ledge, looking down into their pit home, trying our best not to fall in and be devoured. And we were going to make it until that blasted thief started wondering rather too loudly what might be hidden beneath them. That's when hundreds of red eyes turned in our direction. And we saw that their fur was torn and bleeding, but it was worse that we could see through their flesh to their rotting bones and knotted muscles. They scampered up the wall after us, baring their chittering, chattering, chewing jaws. — Millas Brook, exploring the Ossuary of the Wererat Scourge

Shadow rats resemble rats with rotting flesh, torn and matted fur, and blazing red eyes. Its semi-translucent skin shows discolored bones and muscles. The tiny rodent terrors attack as a mass that clambers over enemies, biting with their sharp teeth.

Rat, Shadow

Tiny undead, unaligned

Armor Class 12
Hit Points 7 (2d4 + 2)
Speed 30 ft., climb 15 ft.

STR	DEX	CON	INT	WIS	CHA
4 (–3)	14 (+2)	12 (+1)	2 (–4)	10 (+0)	6 (–2)

Skills Stealth +4 (+6 in dim light or darkness)
Damage Vulnerabilities radiant
Damage Resistances acid, cold, fire, lightning
Damage Immunities necrotic, poison
Condition Immunities exhaustion, frightened, grappled, paralyzed, petrified, poisoned, prone, restrained
Senses darkvision 60 ft., passive Perception 10
Languages —
Challenge 1/4 (50 XP)

Amorphous. The shadow rat can move through a space as narrow as one inch wide without squeezing.
Shadow Stealth. While in dim light or darkness, the shadow rat can take the Hide action as a bonus action.
Sunlight Weakness. While in sunlight, the shadow rat has disadvantage on attack rolls, ability checks, and saving throws.

ACTIONS

Bite. *Melee Weapon Attack*: +4 to hit, reach 5 ft., one creature. *Hit*: 4 (1d4 + 2) necrotic damage. If the target is not undead, its Strength score is reduced by 1d4. The target dies if this reduces its Strength score to 0. Otherwise, the reduction lasts until the target finishes a short or long rest.

Rat, Spore

We were chasing wererats through the sewers when we came upon another pack of giant rats. More of an annoyance than a threat to experienced sewer runners like us, but these were unlike any giant rats we had ever seen. Their fur was more green than brown, and it had an odd texture. They came swarming toward us, and we readied ourselves. As they neared, the rats spurted out clouds of choking spores that filled the narrow sewer. It was close, and we learned not to underestimate rats again. Ultär, son of Ultär, adventurer

These dog-sized rats are covered in greenish-brown growths that mat to form a fur-like covering. This mat is not fur; it is a colony of dozens of species of fungi and mosses. These colonies give them a distinct advantage when attacking: Their bites inject poison spores into their prey and if threatened, the spore rat can unleash a cloud of choking spores. Spore rats behave much like other giant rats, living in large packs, making nests in forgotten or out-of-the-way places, and opportunistically feeding on anything they find.

Spore Rat

Small plant, neutral

Armor Class 15 (natural armor)
Hit Points 21 (6d6)
Speed 20 ft., climb 20 ft.

STR	DEX	CON	INT	WIS	CHA
6 (–2)	16 (+3)	11 (+0)	2 (–4)	12 (+1)	4 (–3)

Skills Athletics +0, Perception +5
Senses darkvision 60 ft., passive Perception 15
Languages —
Challenge 1/4 (50 XP)

Skilled Explorer. The spore rat ignores nonmagical difficult terrain created by plants. The spore rat also has advantage on saving throws against spells and magical effects involving plants.

ACTIONS

Infectious Bite. Melee Weapon Attack: +5 to hit, reach 5 ft., one target. Hit: 5 (1d4 + 3) piercing damage. The creature must make a DC 10 Constitution saving throw or be poisoned until the end of its next turn.
Spore Cloud (2/day). The spore rat releases a cloud of toxic spores within a five-foot radius. All creatures adjacent to the spore rat must make a DC 10 Constitution saving throw or have its Strength score reduced by 1d4. The creature dies if this reduces its Strength to 0. Otherwise, the reduction lasts until the target finishes a short or long rest.

Rat, Tyrannosaurus Rattus

Not another bar with a rat problem in the basement! Why don't these barkeeps raise cats in droves? They seem to have more rats in their root cellars than actual kegs of ale. But fine, whatever. We were here for something much more dire, but why not use our valuable time to traipse downstairs and serve as pest control? Renwalt stepped off the bottom stair, and that's when the furry fiends attacked. Can rats get that big and nasty? — Maeve Wyne, last survivor of what she later called the "basement of unimaginable terror"

Often regarded as the "king of the rats," Tyrannosaurus rattus is known for its aggression and terror over any other creature in its territory. This monstrosity won't hesitate to attack most creatures. With fearsome bite and tail attacks, Tyrannosaurus rattus is a creature not to be trifled with.

Tyrannosaurus Rattus

Small beast, unaligned

Armor Class 14 (natural armor)
Hit Points 52 (8d6 + 24)
Speed 40 ft.

STR	DEX	CON	INT	WIS	CHA
18 (+4)	12 (+1)	16 (+3)	2 (–4)	12 (+1)	9 (–1)

Saving Throws Con +6
Skills Perception +3
Senses darkvision 60 ft., passive Perception 13
Languages —
Challenge 2 (450 XP)

Actions

Multiattack. Tyrannosaurus rattus make one Bite attack and one Tail attack. It cannot make both attacks against the same target.
Bite. *Melee Weapon Attack:* +6 to hit, reach 5 ft., one target. *Hit:* 11 (2d6 + 4) piercing damage.
Tail. *Melee Weapon Attack:* +6 to hit, reach 5 ft., one target. *Hit:* 9 (2d4 + 4) bludgeoning damage.

"Tell us a joke, my not-so-pretties, and then explain to me who's scaring away the crows if you're here." The voice from the shadows was followed by hideous gales of laughter. The offending jester stepped out next, bowed low, and rose to reveal its sunken features, deathly grimace, and pus-filled boils. Its motley outfit was stained and torn, and stained with blood, but it took no notice of its shabby appearance. Instead, it hurled more insults our way, but always ended with those same four words: "Tell us a joke." — Will Cobble Dukenfield, prince of the House of Dukenfield

Red jesters are thought to be undead court jesters put to death for telling bad jokes, making fun of the local ruler, or dying in an untimely manner (which could be attributed to one or both of the first two). Another legend speaks of the red jesters as being the court jesters of Orcus, Demon Prince of the Undead, sent to the Material Plane to "entertain" those the demon prince has chosen to pay special attention to.

While they can be encountered anywhere from the coldest to the warmest regions of the world and on any type of terrain, a red jester is generally encountered near civilized areas. Though it is dead (or undead) now, it still delights in entertaining living creatures through its humor and obviously cannot do that if it resides far away in unsettled lands. Some red jesters, in an effort to disguise their undead nature, don masks or wear makeup.

RED JESTER

Medium undead, chaotic neutral

Armor Class 14 (natural armor)
Hit Points 67 (15d8)
Speed 30 ft.

STR	DEX	CON	INT	WIS	CHA
15 (+2)	17 (+3)	10 (+0)	15 (+2)	14 (+2)	16 (+3)

Saving Throws Dex +6
Skills Acrobatics +6, Deception +6, Sleight of Hand +6
Damage Resistances bludgeoning, piercing, and slashing damage from nonmagical attacks
Damage Immunities necrotic, poison
Condition Immunities exhaustion, frightened, poisoned, unconscious
Senses darkvision 60 ft., passive Perception 12
Languages Common and any two others
Challenge 5 (1,800 XP)

Unassailable Mind. The mind of a red jester is a twisted and dangerous place to peer into. If a living creature targets a red jester with an attack that normally causes psychic damage or tries to use telepathy on a red jester, that creature must make a successful DC 13 Intelligence saving throw or be cursed, with an effect identical to a permanent *confusion* spell. The *confusion* effect can be ended only by magic that lifts the curse.

ACTIONS

Multiattack. A red jester makes two Fist attacks or two Mace attacks.
Fist. *Melee Weapon Attack:* +6 to hit, reach 5 ft., one creature. *Hit:* 9 (1d12 + 3) bludgeoning damage.
Jester's Deck. *Ranged Weapon Attack:* +6 to hit, range 20 ft., one creature. *Hit:* The target creature is affected as if it drew a random card from the *deck of many things.* In the hands of anyone but a red jester, the jester's deck acts as a normal, nonmagical deck of playing cards.
+2 Mace of Merriment. *Melee Weapon Attack:* +7 to hit, reach 5 ft., one creature. *Hit:* 14 (2d8 + 5) bludgeoning damage and the target must make a successful DC 14 Wisdom saving throw or be paralyzed with merriment for 1d3 rounds. In the hands of anyone but a red jester, the weapon acts as a *+1 mace.*
Fear Cackle (1/day). The red jester unleashes a fear-inducing cackle. All creatures within 60 feet that hear the cackle must make a successful DC 14 Wisdom saving throw or be frightened for 2d4 rounds. A frightened creature has a 50% chance of immediately dropping everything it holds in its hands.

RHACOS

Wanted: Intrepid woodsmen to collect the beautiful crown feathers of the wondrous rhacos! Do you need gold right now? Make your mark in the Bent Wood and come back with the feathered treasures I seek. Will pay the best prices in gold. Not responsible for any injuries that might occur during the pursuit of your dreams.
— Notice posted in Unter Gall's Fine Hats for All Occasions

A rhacos is blue-gray in color with an elongated neck and long narrow legs. They have a long, delicate feather (or, on rare occasion, multiple feathers) protruding from the top of their heads. Their beaks are as large as a man's head and their claws can be nearly as long as daggers. An apex predator of the forests, grasslands, and river valleys of the northern world, a single rhacos can easily devastate even a large hunting party. Rhacos eggs are considered an epicurean treat and collected whenever possible. A single undamaged rhacos feather can fetch hundreds of gold pieces from the right buyer, especially haberdashers who cater to the wealthy.

RHACOS

Large beast, unaligned

Armor Class 14 (natural armor)
Hit Points 114 (12d10 + 48)
Speed 30 ft., fly 10 ft.

STR	DEX	CON	INT	WIS	CHA
22 (+6)	16 (+3)	18 (+4)	3 (–4)	10 (+0)	7 (–2)

Skills Insight +3, Perception +6
Senses darkvision 60 ft., passive Perception 16
Languages —
Challenge 6 (2,300 XP)

Territorial Reflexes. The rhacos can make any number of opportunity attacks in one round, but no more than one on any turn.

ACTIONS

Multiattack. The rhacos makes one Bite attack and one Kick attack.
Bite. Melee Weapon Attack: +9 to hit, reach 10 ft., one target. Hit: 10 (1d8 + 6) slashing damage.
Kick. Melee Weapon Attack: +9 to hit, reach 10 ft., one target. Hit: 12 (1d12 + 6) bludgeoning damage.
***Slashing Beak* (recharge 4–6).** The rhacos wildly swings its neck around with its beak wide open. The rhacos makes a Bite attack against each creature within reach. A creature hit by one of these attacks is bleeding and loses 1 hit point at the start of each of its turns. A creature can use an action to make a DC 10 Wisdom (Medicine) check to staunch the bleeding, ending the condition on a success. Any magical healing ends this condition.

SCORPION, CAVE

You want mah advice? Never trust a halfling! There's this rotten rascal named Ollie something or other. Ah din't trust him, but he paid in good gold. Put this on, he said. So ah did. Stand still, he said. So ah did. He din't tell me 'bout no danged scorpion. That giant thing came lumb'rin' out and started stab, stab, stabbin' me. At least that armor suit kept it from gettin' at me. But ah'll never forget that halfling shouting, "It worked this time! It worked!" — Test Subject J in Ollie Nematoad's scorpion suit field test

The man-sized, bulky scorpion has thick, unyielding armor that makes it almost seem to be made of stone. The scorpion attacks with its claws and holds prey so it can sting with its tail.

CAVE SCORPION

Medium beast, unaligned

Armor Class 12 (natural armor)
Hit Points 22 (4d8 + 4)
Speed 40 ft., climb 20 ft.

STR	DEX	CON	INT	WIS	CHA
13 (+1)	12 (+1)	13 (+1)	2 (−4)	10 (+0)	2 (−4)

Skills Perception +4, Stealth +4
Senses darkvision 60 ft., tremorsense 60 ft., passive Perception 14
Languages —
Challenge 2 (450 XP)

Camouflage. The cave scorpion has advantage on Dexterity (Stealth) checks it makes while in cavernous, rocky, or mountainous terrain.

ACTIONS

Multiattack. The cave scorpion makes two Claw attacks and one Sting attack.
Claw. *Melee Weapon Attack:* +3 to hit, reach 5 ft., one target. *Hit:* 4 (1d6 + 1) bludgeoning damage, and the target is grappled (escape DC 11). The scorpion has two claws, each of which can grapple only one Medium or smaller target.
Sting. *Melee Weapon Attack:* +3 to hit, reach 5 ft., one target. *Hit:* 6 (2d4 + 1) piercing damage, and the target must make a DC 11 Constitution saving throw, taking 11 (2d10) poison damage on a failed save, or half as much damage on a successful one.

SEA COW

Be wary sailing round the southern spur near Luggbroch (and even warier should you brave the Strait of Daan). The Crescent Maid was turning north when we saw what looked like a herd of cows moving slow through the water. A couple of the crew made to harpoon one of the stragglers, but the head of a fish-man broke the waters and pointed a wicked trident at our boat. The tines gleamed with a silver light, and the crew quickly rethought their plans. — Captain Geary Birdseye of the Crescent Maid

Sea cows are large, fully aquatic, mostly herbivorous marine mammals. They have paddle-like flippers and are slow, peaceful plant-eaters similar to cows on land. They often graze on water plants in tropical seas.

SEA COW

Large beast, unaligned

Armor Class 11
Hit Points 52 (8d10 + 8)
Speed 10 ft., swim 60 ft.

STR	DEX	CON	INT	WIS	CHA
17 (+3)	13 (+1)	13 (+1)	4 (−3)	10 (+0)	4 (−3)

Skills Perception +4, Stealth +5
Senses darkvision 60 ft., passive Perception 14
Languages —
Challenge 1 (200 XP)

Hold Breath. While out of water, the sea cow can hold its breath for one hour.
Water Breathing. The sea cow can breathe only underwater.

ACTIONS

Slam. *Melee Weapon Attack:* +5 to hit, reach 5 ft., one target. *Hit:* 7 (1d8 + 3) bludgeoning damage.

TOME OF HORRORS

Sepulchral Guardian

We followed Cashyn Moss through Harwood Forest south of Darkhollow. The area smelled of cherries. The ranger finally stopped at a low stone wall hidden in the weeds that marked the edges of the forgotten cemetery. A stone mausoleum was the only structure remaining aboveground. As we advanced to investigate, an iron-clad guardian stepped from the marble doorway. Its movements were erratic, but it raised an iron glaive with no trouble. Its eyes were dead and uncaring. — Fresia Moonring, priestess of Muir, investigating rumors of undead roaming the forest cemetery

Sepulchral guardians are constructs created from the preserved corpses of dead humanoids that have been encased in iron. They are created for one purpose only: to guard the final resting place of a dead creature. Once activated, a sepulchral guardian performs its task until it is destroyed. Even the death of its creator does not disrupt a sepulchral guardian; many are created to guard the final resting places of their creators.

A sepulchral guardian is a humanoid standing just over six feet tall. Its entire body except its face is encased in a suit of banded iron. Its face, while humanoid, shows no sign of life, and its eyes are filled with the emptiness of an automaton. These constructs are intelligent enough to pursue an intruder through nearby corridors and chambers of a tomb, but they seldom leave the immediate structure they've been set to guard, even to chase down a thief who stole something.

Sepulchral Guardian

Medium construct, unaligned

Armor Class 14 (scale mail)
Hit Points 65 (10d8 + 20)
Speed 30 ft.

STR	DEX	CON	INT	WIS	CHA
17 (+3)	10 (+0)	14 (+2)	5 (–3)	11 (+0)	12 (+1)

Damage Resistances acid, lightning; bludgeoning, piercing, and slashing damage from attacks that are not adamantine
Damage Immunities cold, fire, necrotic, poison, psychic
Condition Immunities charmed, diseased, frightened, paralyzed, petrified, poisoned, stunned, unconscious
Senses darkvision 60 ft., passive Perception 10
Languages None
Challenge 3 (700 XP)

Crypt Fatigue. A creature infected with crypt fatigue gains one level of exhaustion immediately and gains another level every time it fails the DC 12 Constitution saving throw after taking damage from a sepulchral guardian. An infected creature must make a DC 12 saving throw at the end of every long rest; with a successful save, it recovers from one level of exhaustion, but with a failed save, it gains one level of exhaustion. The disease is cured when the victim no longer has any levels of exhaustion.

Dread. Living creatures with line of sight to one or more sepulchral guardians and within 50 feet of them must make a successful DC 11 Wisdom saving throw or be frightened for 2d4 rounds. A successful save renders the target immune to any guardian's dread for 24 hours.

Actions

Glaive. *Melee Weapon Attack:* +5 to hit, reach 10 ft., one creature. *Hit:* 8 (1d10 + 3) slashing damage and the target must make a DC 12 Constitution saving throw or be infected with crypt fatigue (see above).

We kept lighting our torches, but the tomb's stale air snuffed them out within minutes. Even Kaden's magic did little but cast a dim radiance around our party. Finally, after jumping over a pit of unfathomable depths that opened in the hallway, we found ourselves up against a massive wall of inky darkness that seemed to absorb our light. Kaden probed the wall with his staff and was yanked forward into the darkness as the wall folded down over him. Only then did we realize it was a monstrous shadow being greater than any we had ever seen. — Nazier Ash, warrior-priest of Mithras

According to ancient texts, an arcane creature known only as the Shadow Lord created beings of living darkness to aid him and protect him. All shadow beings are said to spring from this malevolent source. Of its creations, the greater shadows are among the worst. These powerful undead appear much like normal shadows, but are much more dangerous and harder to destroy. Like its brethren, it is a creature of living darkness. Greater shadows hide in darkness and spring out to attack when living opponents wander too close. These greater beings often lead hordes of other shadow creatures.

GREATER SHADOW

Medium undead, chaotic evil

Armor Class 13
Hit Points 84 (13d8 + 26)
Speed 40 ft.

STR	DEX	CON	INT	WIS	CHA
6 (−2)	16 (+3)	14 (+2)	6 (−2)	12 (+1)	8 (−1)

Skills Stealth +6 (+9 in dim light or darkness)
Damage Vulnerabilities radiant
Damage Resistances acid, cold, fire, lightning, thunder; bludgeoning, piercing, and slashing from nonmagical attacks
Damage Immunities necrotic, poison
Condition Immunities exhaustion, frightened, grappled, paralyzed, petrified, poisoned, prone, restrained
Senses darkvision 60 ft., passive Perception 11
Languages —
Challenge 8 (3,900 XP)

Amorphous. The greater shadow can move through a space as narrow as one inch wide without squeezing.
Shadow Stealth. While in dim light or darkness, the shadow can take the Hide action as a bonus action.
Sunlight Weakness. While in sunlight, the shadow has disadvantage on attack rolls, ability checks, and saving throws.

ACTIONS

Strength Drain. *Melee Weapon Attack:* +6 to hit, reach 5 ft., one creature. *Hit:* 21 (4d8 + 3) necrotic damage, and the target's Strength score is reduced by 1d4. The target dies if this reduces its Strength score to 0. Otherwise, the reduction lasts until the target finishes a short or long rest. If a non-evil humanoid dies from this attack, a **shadow** rises from the corpse 1d4 rounds later under the greater shadow's command.

TOME OF **HORRORS**

Shell Folk

Our ship sailed into the cove under cover of darkness. The pirates lost us in a timely fog that rose off the Sinnar, and Captain Majert made the most of the opportunity. The Jolly Pearl's sails were furled quickly, and the captain decided to put the passengers ashore in case the pirates found his hiding place. We rowed frantically for safety and pulled the longboats up onto the sand. Imagine our surprise when an enormous crab stepped from the darkness to assist us. The peaceful creature led us inland to a sheltered spring with clear water and soft moss beds. It pulled a spear off its shell and stood guard the rest of the night as we collapsed in exhausted heaps. The Pearl was gone when we awoke, but we found the captain and the bodies of his crew washed onto the sand. The shell folk helped bury them. — Merchant Cylliann Marple, among the travelers rescued on a deserted island in the Sinnar Ocean

Shell folk are a peaceful race of crustaceans who make their living by hunting and fishing in warm, shallow coastal waters. They live in small communities, usually numbering a dozen or so, led by their oldest and most accomplished hunters. Though their nature is closer to crabs and lobsters than to warm-blooded species, the shell folk are indifferent to outsiders and can sometimes be persuaded to trade, offering merchants fish and other harvested goods in exchange for metal tools, weapons, and other durable goods. Shell folk also place little value on gems and precious metals, and may also be willing to give up these outwardly "useless" trinkets in trade.

Shell Folk

Medium humanoid, chaotic neutral

Armor Class 10 (+1 to +6 depending upon shell size and durability; see below)
Hit Points 52 (8d8 + 16)
Speed 30 ft., swim 30 ft.

STR	DEX	CON	INT	WIS	CHA
16 (+3)	12 (+1)	14 (+2)	9 (−1)	12 (+1)	10 (+0)

Saving Throws Str +5, Con +4
Skills Athletics +5, Perception +3, Survival +3
Damage Immunities psychic
Condition Immunities charmed, frightened
Senses tremorsense 60 ft., passive Perception 13
Languages Shell Folk
Challenge 4 (1,100 XP)

Biological Mental Dissonance. Shell folk are crustaceans and do not think or reason in the same way as other species. They are immune to being charmed or frightened and to psychic damage. Additionally, they have advantage on saving throws against spells from the school of Enchantment.

Armored Shell. As their name suggests, shell folk use large shells or other objects as armor. A shell provides its wearer with a bonus to Armor Class ranging from +1 to +6 depending upon its size and durability. Most shells provide a +2 bonus, while larger and more durable shells are worn by older, stronger, and more skilled shell folk.

Crustacean Language. The shell folk's language is an incomprehensible collection of clicks, clacks, and hisses. Any non-shell folk creature attempting to learn the language must succeed on a DC 20 Intelligence check or be unable to learn the language. This check can be made again after six additional months of study.

Actions

Multiattack. A shell folk makes one Spear and two Pincer attacks.
Spear. *Melee or Ranged Weapon Attack:* +5 to hit, reach 5 ft. or range 20/60 ft., one target. *Hit:* 7 (1d8 + 3) piercing damage, or 8 (1d10 + 3) piercing damage if used with two hands to make a melee attack.
Pincer. *Melee Weapon Attack:* +5 to hit, reach 10 ft., one target. *Hit:* 10 (2d6 + 3) bludgeoning damage, and the target is grappled (escape DC 13). The shell folk has two pincers, each of which can grapple only one target.

SHINING CHILD

I've watched them in the enchanted mirror, beings of pure blinding light dancing like children in the fire, bursts of energy radiating from their eyes. I had to turn away from the sight, but the image remained burned into my vision. I saw them even when I blinked. Now I just have to summon them into the rune circle to do my bidding. — Final journal entry of Phidious Grask, whose cremated body was found in his wizard tower by his apprentices

Creatures of burning light and strange geometry, shining children are a terror to behold. Beyond the flares of energy that constantly burst from their forms (particularly in beam-like gouts from their eyes and mouths), the creatures are vaguely humanoid, with strange hands that each bear four fingers. Occasionally summoned by powerful wizards in search of rare arcane knowledge, the shining children (who disdain individual names) communicate via telepathy, a psychic roar like metal tearing that sometimes resolves into strained and raspy words. A shining child stands just over 4-1/2 feet tall and weighs 85 pounds.

SHINING CHILD

Medium aberration, chaotic evil

Armor Class 18
Hit Points 144 (17d8 + 68)
Speed 30 ft., fly 50 ft.

STR	DEX	CON	INT	WIS	CHA
10 (+0)	17 (+3)	18 (+4)	15 (+2)	11 (+0)	20 (+5)

Skills Arcana +10, Nature +6, Religion +6, Perception +4
Damage Resistances cold, thunder
Damage Immunities fire, poison, radiant
Condition Immunities blinded, poisoned
Senses darkvision 120 ft., passive Perception 14
Languages all, telepathy 120 ft.
Challenge 12 (8,400 XP)

Innate Spellcasting. The shining child's innate spellcasting ability is Charisma (spell save DC 17). It can cast the following spells without material components:
At will: *light, major image*
3/day each: *daylight, dispel magic, mirage arcana*
1/day: *plane shift* (self only), *sunbeam*
Radiant Armor. The Armor Class of the shining child includes its Charisma bonus.
Radiance. The shining child sheds bright light out to 10 feet, with dim light for an additional 10 feet. Dexterity (Stealth) checks made in this area automatically fail.

ACTIONS

Multiattack. The shining child uses its Blinding Light ability and makes one Burning Touch or Searing Ray attack.
Blinding Light. The shining child shines with blinding light in a 60-foot radius, with an additional 60 feet of dim light beyond. Any creature who can see the shining child must make a DC 17 Constitution saving throw. On a failed save, the creature is blinded for one minute. The creature can repeat the saving throw at the end of each of its turns, ending the effect on a success. If, after one minute, an affected creature has not ended the blinded condition on itself through either succeeding on the saving throw or using magic, it is permanently blinded.

A creature can use its reaction to shield its eyes by making a DC 17 Dexterity saving throw. If successful, they are blinded until the start of their next turn but do not have to make the Constitution saving throw to avoid blindness as above. On a failed Dexterity save, they must immediately make the Constitution saving throw.
Burning Touch. *Melee Spell Attack:* +9 to hit, reach 5 ft., one target. *Hit:* 19 (4d6 + 5) radiant damage plus 19 (4d6 + 5) fire damage and must make a DC 17 Constitution saving throw. On a failure, the target begins to radiate, shedding bright light in a 60-foot radius centered on it. A successful saving throw negates this effect.

While under this effect, the target automatically fails Dexterity (Stealth) checks. The target can repeat the saving throw at the end of each of its turns, taking an additional 14 (4d6) fire damage on a failure or ending the effect on itself on a success.

The Burning Touch effect can be extinguished by magical darkness, a *greater restoration*, or a *heal* spell.
Searing Ray. *Ranged Spell Attack:* +9 to hit, range 120/300 ft., one target. *Hit:* 42 (12d6) radiant damage or 63 (18d6) radiant damage if the target is undead.

SHROOM

Shrooms are evil toadstool creatures with genius intellects and considerable magical power. They lurk in the deep places of the earth and in dank forests, plotting ruin against surface dwellers and scheming to gain power for themselves by any means possible. They are highly adept with magic that influences plants, and most of them are knowledgeable in various forms of arcane study of other kinds, such as alchemy. Many, too, surround themselves with strange minions that they have created, grown, or bred.

SHROOM

Small plant (fungus), chaotic evil

Armor Class 12
Hit Points 49 (11d6 + 11)
Speed 25 ft.

STR	DEX	CON	INT	WIS	CHA
9 (−1)	10 (+0)	12 (+1)	19 (+4)	16 (+3)	15 (+2)

Skills Arcana +6, Nature +6, Medicine +5, Perception +5, Persuasion +4
Damage Resistances bludgeoning, piercing, and slashing damage from nonmagical attacks
Damage Immunities psychic
Condition Immunities charmed, frightened, stunned, unconscious
Senses darkvision 60 ft., passive Perception 15
Languages Common, Deep Speech, Sylvan, Undercommon
Challenge 4 (1,100 XP)

***Animate Plants* (1/day).** The shroom can use its action to magically animate plants within 50 feet of itself. The effect is identical to the *animate objects* spells, but only live plants can be animated. The effect lasts for 24 hours.
***Awaken Plants* (2/month).** The shroom can magically awaken one plant it touches. The effect is identical to the *awaken* spell, but affects only live plants.
Spellcasting. The shroom is a 5th-level spellcaster. Its spellcasting ability is Intelligence (spell save DC 14, +6 to hit with spell attacks). It has the following bard spells prepared:
Cantrips (at will): *acid splash, mage hand, poison spray, ray of frost*
1st level (4 slots): *charm person, detect magic, magic missile, sleep*
2nd level (3 slots): *invisibility, web*
3rd level (2 slots): *blink, lightning bolt*
Toxic Flesh. Any creature that tastes the flesh of a shroom must make a DC 13 Constitution saving throw or be overwhelmed by the deliciousness of the shroom, proceeding to gorge on the shroom flesh until it cannot keep any more down or until someone stops them. An hour after consuming even the smallest morsel of shroom flesh, the eater's Intelligence and Charisma scores become 1. The creature can't cast spells, activate magic items, understand language, or communicate in any intelligible way (as if affected by *feeblemind*). The creature can, however, identify its friends, follow them, and even protect them. A successful saving throw indicates the eater is unaffected by the toxins in the shroom's flesh.
At the end of every 30 days, the creature can repeat its saving throw against these effects. If it succeeds on its saving throw, the effects end. The effects can also be ended by *greater restoration, heal,* or *wish*.

ACTIONS

Slam. *Melee Weapon Attack:* +2 to hit, reach 5 ft., one target. *Hit:* 3 (1d6 − 1) bludgeoning damage.
Psychic Thrashing. *Ranged Spell Attack:* +6 to hit, range 100 ft., one target. *Hit:* 15 (2d10 + 4) psychic damage, and the target must succeed on a DC 14 Intelligence saving throw or be stunned until the end of its next turn.

SILAAAL

As we looked upward to the high minarets of the City of Brass, the metal tops glowing hellishly in the surrounding fires, I spied a line of darkness issuing forth from one of the great towers, some sort of genie unfamiliar to me in all my researches. Drawing forth my spyglass, I trained it upon the creatures and a thrill of horror ran through me. These were the Silaaal torturers, feared throughout the City of Brass. The spyglass dropped from my nerveless fingers and I backed away from my vantage point, seeking a way down to escape before I could myself be spotted...
—Shratzil the Courageous

Silaaal torturers are crimson-clad creatures that were originally of genie stock. At some point in their history they were captured by the n'gathau and taken to the Plane of Agony, where they were changed into their current form before being released back into the planes of existence. Standing 8ft tall, these beings are lithe and slender under their voluminous robes. Their eyes glow an odd violet in the darkness and their surgeon-like fingers end in long, sharp claws. Their faces are veiled under black turbans, and they wear serrated blades at their belts. They are rarely seen outside of the minarets of the City of Brass, but those who have encountered them say that they have no mouth or ears under their veiled turbans and communicate via telepathy; they know the thoughts of any with whom they make eye contact.

SILAAAL

Large aberration, neutral evil

Armor Class 17 (natural armor)
Hit Points 112 (15d10 + 30)
Speed 30 ft.

STR	DEX	CON	INT	WIS	CHA
17 (+3)	16 (+3)	15 (+2)	18 (+4)	18 (+4)	18 (+4)

Skills Arcana +8, Deception +8, Insight +8, Intimidation +8, Investigation +8, Medicine +8, Survival +8
Damage Resistances cold, fire
Damage Immunities acid
Senses darkvision 60 ft., passive Perception 14
Languages understands Aklo, Common, but can't speak; telepathy 120 ft.
Challenge 10 (5,900 XP)

Innate Spellcasting. The silaal's innate spellcasting ability is Charisma (spell save DC 16). It can cast the following spells, requiring no material components:
At will: *cure wounds, detect thoughts, see invisibility*
3/day each: *fear, wall of fire*
1/day each: *blade barrier, dominate person, revivify*

ACTIONS

Multiattack. The silaal makes two Kukri attacks.
Kukri. *Melee or Ranged Weapon Attack:* +7 to hit, reach 5 ft. or range 20/60 ft., one target. *Hit:* 8 (2d4 + 3) piercing damage. If the target is a creature that isn't an undead or construct and it isn't already bleeding profusely, the target must make a DC 15 Constitution saving throw. On a failed saving throw, the target begins bleeding profusely. At the beginning of each of its turns, the target's maximum hit points are reduced by 18 (4d8). The target continues to bleed profusely until the target's maximum hit points reach 0 and it dies. The target can repeat the saving throw at the end of each of its turns, or the target or another creature can use its action to make a DC 15 Wisdom (Medicine) check to staunch the bleeding, ending the effect on a success. Lost hit points return when the target takes a long rest.

Singa

The old man was sitting alone in the middle of the empty dojo when we found him. He was ancient, his skin so thin that we could see his lifeblood flowing in his veins. The emperor decreed these houses forfeit for not paying their tributes, and we had come to remove the families. The old man refused to leave, however, and sat watching us as we helped ourselves to his meager belongings. Commander Fa took the old man by the arm to lift him out to the wagon, but the air shimmered and a creature appeared in a celestial light. It was the size and shape of a water buffalo, but with thick scales and the head and tail of a crocodile. The old man probably is still sitting there, protected by his guardian. — Acting Commander Hao Zhu, at his trial for disobeying his emperor

Some ancient families in the Xha'en Hegemony served the gods and higher powers faithfully during the era of the Thousand Kingdoms. These families were granted a form of divine protection in the form of the sacred singa — guardian creatures who can be summoned to aid a family in times of need. Strong and dedicated, singa also master many different healing and restorative spells. They can even resurrect slain family members.

The singa are bound to serve their families for all time, and loyally appear if summoned if any member of the household is threatened. Pledged to the household itself, singa are limited to aiding families only within dwellings that are actually owned and controlled by that family. They cannot aid their households in other locations and cannot leave their family's dwellings under any circumstances. Singa fight to the death, but this is not the end. Slain singa can return to defend the family within 24 hours. They fully perish only when no living members of their assigned household survive.

Singa

Large celestial, lawful good

Armor Class 16 (natural armor)
Hit Points 187 (22d10 + 66)
Speed 30 ft., fly 30 ft.

STR	DEX	CON	INT	WIS	CHA
16 (+3)	13 (+1)	16 (+3)	10 (+0)	15 (+2)	10 (+0)

Saving Throws Str +7, Wis +6
Skills Perception +10
Damage Resistances bludgeoning, piercing, and slashing damage from nonmagical attacks
Senses darkvision 60 ft., passive Perception 20
Languages Celestial
Challenge 9 (5,000 XP)

Guardian Spirit. A singa serves a single household. If threatened in any one of their dwellings, a member of that household can call upon the house singa, which arrives from its home plane within 1d4 rounds. It acts to defend its household, then returns to its home plane after the threat has been eliminated.

Always Returning. If a singa is slain, it returns to its home plane where it reconstitutes over the next 24 hours. After this period, the singa may be summoned once more.

Innate Spellcasting. The singa's spellcasting ability is Wisdom (spell save DC 14). The singa can innately cast the following spells, requiring no material components:

At will: *light, message, prestidigitation*
3/day each: *cure wounds, healing word, thunderwave*
2/day each: *greater restoration, hold monster, mass cure wounds*
1/day: *raise dead*

Actions

Gore. *Melee Weapon Attack:* +7 to hit, reach 5 ft., one target. *Hit:* 13 (2d8 + 3) piercing damage.

Hooves. *Melee Weapon Attack:* +7 to hit, reach 5 ft., one target. *Hit:* 14 (2d10 + 3) bludgeoning damage.

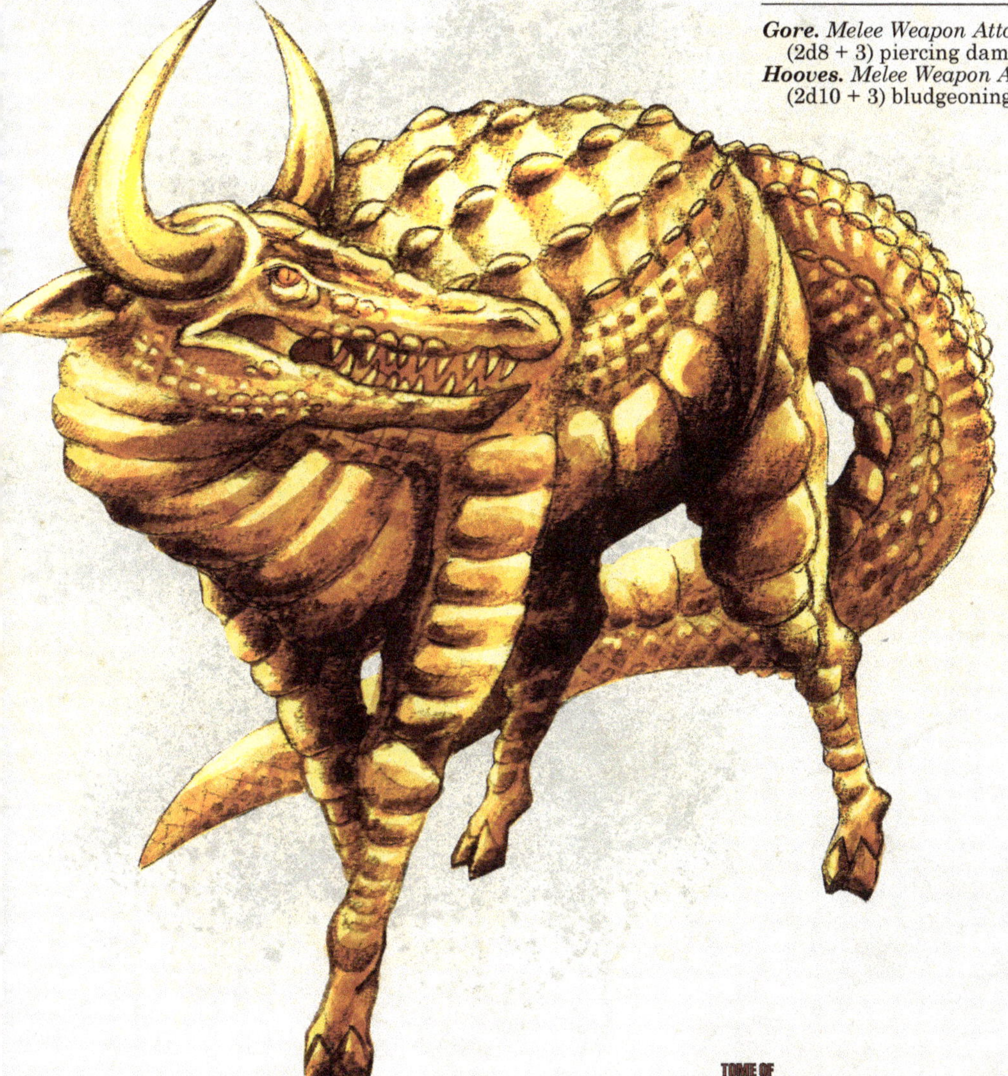

Skelzi

They took Wynna when we entered the ruins of Temelpa. A pack of the bird-faced things sprang out of hiding and tore her to pieces before she could scream a warning. We fled the sounds of them feeding. Chorg fell next, caught in a magical web of glowing strands. They tore him limb from limb as they yanked him from the webbing. I'm the last, and I have no idea how I'm going to escape them. They blend in so well with the rocks that you don't see them until it's too late. — Page torn from Elendel Hollen's spellbook and found tied to the leg of her hawk familiar Pifin

Skelzis originate from beyond the Material Plane. They have humanoid bodies with leathery skin, but their human appearance is rendered alien by the long, sharp beak that protrudes from the birdlike skelzi face. Moreover, a skelzi's hide is chameleonic and can change to blend with its surroundings. The creatures usually travel robed and masked so that they are less alarming to other races and to conceal their chameleonic power until the need for it arises. A typical skelzi stands six feet tall and weighs 160 pounds. A number of vampiric skelzis exist, having been transformed via ritual by Fuulagh (see the **blood orchid** entry) and through other means. About half of them are also spellcasters (see sidebar).

Skelzis are aggressively expansionistic, so countless colonies and more than a few empires exist across the infinite planes of existence. Great skelzi empires tend to be decadent, corrupt, torpid, and slow to respond to threats. When they do respond, it is likely to be with overwhelming force.

Skelzi

Medium humanoid, chaotic evil

Armor Class 14 (natural armor)
Hit Points 44 (8d8 + 8)
Speed 30 ft.

STR	DEX	CON	INT	WIS	CHA
14 (+2)	15 (+2)	12 (+1)	10 (+0)	10 (+0)	10 (+0)

Skills Stealth +4
Senses passive Perception 10
Languages Common, Unique
Challenge 1 (200 XP)

Blood Whip. A skelzi's vicious blood whip causes wounds that bleed profusely. A creature must make a DC 12 Constitution saving throw every time it takes damage from a blood whip. If the saving throw fails, the wound bleeds freely and the creature takes 4 (1d4 + 2) necrotic damage at the start of each of its turns. Bleeding continues until it is ended with magical healing or if the affected creature or another creature adjacent to it binds the wound by spending an action and making a successful DC 12 Wisdom (Medicine) check. Every bleeding wound causes additional damage and must be treated separately; a character that was struck three times by blood whips, for example, takes 3d4 + 6 damage at the start of its next turn if none of those wounds is treated before then. A blood whip behaves as a normal whip when wielded by anyone who is not a skelzi.

Chameleonic Hide. If they shed their garments, skelzis can hide when they are lightly obscured, their Stealth bonus increases to +6, and they have advantage on Stealth checks and on initiative rolls.

Attacks

Multiattack. A skelzi makes one Claw attack and one Blood Whip attack.
Blood Whip. *Melee Weapon Attack:* +4 to hit, reach 10 ft., one creature. *Hit:* 4 (1d4 + 2) slashing damage and the target must make a successful DC 12 Constitution saving throw or take continuing damage from bleeding (see Blood Whip above).
Claw. *Melee Weapon Attack:* +4 to hit, reach 5 ft., one creature. *Hit:* 6 (1d8 + 2) slashing damage.

Skelzi, Vampiric

Medium humanoid, chaotic evil

Armor Class 14 (natural armor)
Hit Points 44 (8d8 + 8)
Speed 30 ft.

STR	DEX	CON	INT	WIS	CHA
14 (+2)	15 (+2)	12 (+1)	10 (+0)	10 (+0)	10 (+0)

Skills Perception +2, Stealth +4
Senses passive Perception 12
Languages Common, Skelzi
Challenge 1 (200 XP)

Chameleonic Hide. If the skelzi sheds its garments, it can hide when lightly obscured, its Stealth bonus increases to +6, and it has advantage on Dexterity (Stealth) checks and on initiative rolls.

Actions

Multiattack. The skelzi makes one Claw attack and one Blood Whip attack.
Claw. *Melee Weapon Attack:* +4 to hit, reach 5 ft., one target. *Hit:* 6 (1d8 + 2) slashing damage.
Blood Whip. *Melee Weapon Attack:* +4 to hit, reach 10 ft., one target. *Hit:* 4 (1d4 + 2) slashing damage and the target must make a successful DC 12 Constitution saving throw or take a bleeding wound. At the start of each of the wounded creature's turns, it takes 1d6 necrotic damage for each time it has been wounded, and it can then make a DC 15 Constitution saving throw, ending the effect of all such wounds on itself on a success. Alternatively, the wounded creature, or a creature within five feet of it, can use an action to make a DC 15 Wisdom (Medicine) check, ending the effect of such wounds on it on a success.
Bite. *Melee Weapon Attack:* +4 to hit, reach 5 ft., one willing creature or a creature that is grappled by the skelzi, incapacitated, or restrained. *Hit:* 4 (1d4 + 2) piercing damage plus 7 (2d6) necrotic damage. The target's hit point maximum is reduced by an amount equal to the necrotic damage taken, and the skelzi regains hit points equal to that amount. The reduction lasts until the target finishes a long rest. The target dies if this effect reduces its hit point maximum to 0.
Charm. One creature within 30 feet must succeed on a DC 10 Wisdom saving throw or be charmed for 24 hours. The creature is not under the skelzi's control but regards it as a trusted friend, takes its requests as favorably as possible, and is willing to be bitten. Each time the skelzi or its allies do anything harmful to the creature, it can repeat the saving throw.

Variant: Skelzi Spellcasters

Some skelzi are also spellcasters. A spellcasting skelzi has a Challenge of 2 (450 XP), Intelligence 15 (+2), and the spellcasting trait:

Spellcasting. The skelzi is a 5th-level spellcaster. Its spellcasting ability is Intelligence (spell save DC 12, +4 to hit with spell attacks). It can cast the following spells:

Cantrips (at will): *light, minor illusion, poison spray, shocking grasp*

1st level (4 slots): *grease, magic missile*

2nd level (3 slots): *blindness/deafness, enlarge/reduce, hold person*

3rd level (2 slots): *lightning bolt, slow*

Soul Vampire

It was the little things that made us suspicious. Goladyl had never been the most talkative member of our group, but suddenly he was curious about our plans, our goals, our dreams. He wanted to know everything about us, as if he were meeting us for the first time. Keepris stole the wizard's special gem as he slept, and spoke the words to activate its magic. What it revealed was a purplish elf-like creature with smooth skin and large white eyes. Large white eyes that were open and staring straight at us. — Cadence Blue in a warning to the constabulary of Reme to find a being she believes killed her friend

A soul vampire is not undead, but an evil shapeshifter distantly related to doppelgangers. The soul vampire, however, feeds on humanoid souls, and requires a long, loving connection with a target (such as a romantic or familial-like bond, or a truly deep friendship) in order to consume and mimic it. Most soul vampires claim it pains them to drain and feed upon the lives of those who love them, and that they are devastated to have to live as they do, but this doesn't stop them from continuing the pattern, without ceasing.

Soul Vampire

Small or medium monstrosity (shapechanger), chaotic evil

Armor Class 16 (natural)
Hit Points 182 (28d8 + 56)
Speed 30 ft.

STR	DEX	CON	INT	WIS	CHA
15 (+2)	17 (+3)	14 (+2)	14 (+2)	14 (+2)	25 (+7)

Saving Throws Dex +6, Wis +5
Skills Deception +10, Intimidation +10, Perception +5, Performance +10, Persuasion +10, Stealth +6
Senses darkvision 120ft, passive Perception 15
Languages any (see text)
Challenge 8 (3,900 XP)

Assume the Aspect. In the moment when a soul vampire consumes the soul of a target, the soul vampire is transformed, bodily, to look exactly like the deceased target. This ability is physical, not illusory, and it is flawless. Only truesight can reveal that this is not the soul vampire's natural form. Soul vampires can become only Small or Medium humanoids through this means, but no other limitations apply.

Infectious Charm. If a soul vampire spends one hour or more within 100 feet of a target humanoid, the soul vampire may charm it. The target must succeed on a DC 20 Wisdom saving throw against this magic or be charmed by the soul vampire. The charmed target regards the soul vampire as a trusted friend to be heeded and protected. Although the target isn't under the soul vampire's control, it interprets the soul vampire's requests or actions in the most favorable way it can.

Each time the soul vampire does anything harmful to the target, it can repeat the saving throw, ending the effect on itself on a success. Otherwise, the effect lasts until the soul vampire is killed, is on a different plane of existence than the target, or takes an action to end the effect.

If a creature's saving throw is successful or the effect ends for it, the creature is immune to the soul vampire's Infectious Charm for the next 24 hours. If a creature spends one month or more under the soul vampire's Infectious Charm, that creature has a chance of contracting the *soul drain* disease (see below).

Innate Spellcasting. The soul vampire's spellcasting ability is Charisma (spell save DC 20). The soul vampire can innately cast the following spells, requiring no material components:

At will: *charm person, dancing lights, disguise self, dissonant whispers, friends, mage hand, minor illusion, prestidigitation, silent image, sleep*

3/day each: *calm emotions, clairvoyance, cloud of daggers, enthrall, detect thoughts, hypnotic pattern, knock, magic missile, major image, nondetection, phantasmal force, suggestion*

1/day: *compulsion, dimension door*

Master Mimic. The soul vampire is able to perfectly mimic the voice, mannerisms, and attitudes of anyone whose soul it has eaten. In the process of consuming the soul, the soul vampire also gains all of the slain target's memories, including languages the target spoke (though not including the target's skill proficiencies — some of the memories don't make clear sense to the soul vampire). Only someone close to the slain target has any chance of noting that this is not who it seems, and even then only with a successful DC 20 Wisdom (Insight) check.

Soul Drain. Anyone who spends a month or more under the soul vampire's Infectious Charm ability must make a Wisdom save, DC 20, or contract the *soul drain* disease. Those who succeed but remain charmed by the soul vampire must save again each month, with a cumulative +1 DC, until either they catch the disease or are no longer affected by the soul vampire's Infectious Charm. While infected, the target has disadvantage on all Wisdom and Intelligence ability checks in regard to its own health or to the soul vampire's influence on itself. The target also loses a cumulative 1 Constitution and 1 Wisdom per week, and nothing can heal this drain until the disease is cured. The target may make a new save every week to shake off the effects, but additional exposures to the disease (through the Infectious Charm) may re-infect the target normally. This magical disease may also be cured by *dispel magic*, *heal*, or *wish*. Creatures of a challenge that exceeds the soul vampire's by 5 or more are immune to the *soul drain* disease.

If a target is reduced to 0 Wisdom or Constitution while infected with the disease, the target's soul is consumed by the soul vampire, and the target dies and cannot be brought back to life by any ordinarily-available means (though in a high-magic world, anything might be possible with the right reality-shaking quest). Only one humanoid can be infected by any given soul vampire at a time. If a second humanoid becomes infected by the same soul vampire, the soul vampire chooses which will get well and which will remain infected.

If the soul vampire dies, an infected target is immediately cured.

Actions

Rapier. Melee Weapon Attack: +6 to hit, reach 5 ft., one target, *Hit:* 7 (1d8 + 6) piercing damage (varies, see text).

Light crossbow. Ranged Weapon Attack: +6 to hit, range 80/320 ft., one target. *Hit:* 7 (1d8 + 6) piercing damage (varies, see text).

Spiny Horror

Spiny horrors are dark-furred animals weighing approximately five pounds, with a large number of long, jointed spines protruding from their bodies. They are predators, jumping to the attack. They cluster like large bats. Because of the spines, spiny horrors at first glance are often mistaken for large spiders. When attacking, a spiny horror digs its spines into its prey and bites with its small, sharp teeth. Spiny horrors are normally found in subterranean areas; however, packs occasionally find their way into cities, where they can become a serious menace with their ability to reproduce quickly.

Spiny Horror

Tiny beast, unaligned

Armor Class 12 (unarmored)
Hit Points 3 (1d4 − 1)
Speed 30 ft., climb 20 ft., swim 15 ft.

STR	DEX	CON	INT	WIS	CHA
8 (−1)	14 (+2)	8 (−1)	2 (−4)	10 (+0)	6 (−3)

Skills Acrobatics +4, Athletics +1
Senses darkvision 60 ft., passive Perception 10
Languages —
Challenge 1/4 (50 XP)

Latching Pounce. If the spiny horror moves at least 20 feet straight toward a creature and then hits with a Spine attack on the same turn, that target must succeed on a DC 12 Dexterity saving throw or the spiny horror latches on. While latched onto a target, the spiny horror can make one Bite attack against it as a bonus action. The spiny horror moves with the target and cannot remove itself. The target creature or an adjacent ally can make a successful DC 12 Strength check to remove the spiny horror.

ACTIONS

Multiattack. The spiny horror makes one Bite attack and four Spine attacks.
Bite. Melee Weapon Attack: +4 to hit, reach 5 ft., one target. Hit: 4 (1d4 + 2) piercing damage.
Spine. Melee Weapon Attack: +1 to hit, reach 5 ft., one target. Hit: 3 (1d4 − 1) piercing damage.

Sporc

The orcs charged out of the dark tunnel, swinging vicious clubs lined with the teeth of their prey. Angre drew his sword and met them head-on. He decapitated one with his first deadly swipe and drew the guts out of the second as the blade swung back. Something roared from the darkness and the barbarian turned and motioned the remaining orc to come on. It did, rushing out of the tunnel on four spider legs. It held three clubs that it swung in a deadly dance, and its lower jaw stuck out and dripped a sizzling venom. It stared down Angre with six unblinking eyes. — Entry in the discovered journal of the wizard Prant Tro in the spider tunnels below the Blackrock Mountains

Sporcs have the furry lower half of a spider and the muscular torso of a rampaging orc. They have four legs capable of climbing over any surface and four arms capable of wielding a variety of hand weapons. Their facial features are a mixture of spider and orc, with a hog-like snout accentuated by three pairs of eyes that run up its brow. Their powerful lower jaw has a pair of spider mandibles that drip toxic venom.

Sporc

Large monstrosity, chaotic evil

Armor Class 19 (natural armor)
Hit Points 209 (22d10 + 88)
Speed 30 ft., climb 30 ft.

STR	DEX	CON	INT	WIS	CHA
18 (+4)	16 (+3)	18 (+4)	10 (+0)	12 (+1)	2 (+1)

Skills Perception +5, Stealth +7
Damage Immunities poison
Condition Immunities poisoned
Senses darkvision 120 ft., passive Perception 15
Languages Abyssal, Orc
Challenge 9 (5,000 XP)

Fey Ancestry. The sporc has advantage on saving throws against being charmed, and magic can't put the sporc to sleep.
Spider Climb. The sporc can climb difficult surfaces, including hanging upside down on ceilings, without needing to make an ability check.
Sunlight Sensitivity. While in sunlight, the sporc has disadvantage on attack rolls, as well as on Wisdom (Perception) checks that rely on sight.
Web Walker. The sporc ignores movement restrictions caused by webbing.
Wild Swing. When reduced to half their hit points, sporcs begin swinging wildly, fighting with no concern for their own safety. While doing so, they have advantage on their attack rolls and all attacks against them have advantage.
Void Sight. Magical darkness doesn't impede the sporc's darkvision.
Innate Spellcasting. The sporc's innate spellcasting ability is Wisdom (spell save DC 13, +5 to hit with spell attacks). It can cast the following spells, requiring no material components:
At will: *dancing lights, web*
1/day each: *darkness, faerie fire*

Actions

Multiattack. The sporc makes one Bite attack, and two other attacks.
Bite. *Melee Weapon Attack:* +8 to hit, reach 5 ft., one target. *Hit:* 7 (1d6 + 4) piercing damage plus 14 (4d6) poison damage.
Great Axe. *Melee Weapon Attack:* +8 to hit, reach 5 ft., one target. *Hit:* 10 (1d12 + 4) slashing damage.
Longbow. *Ranged Weapon Attack:* +7 to hit, range 150/600 ft., one target. *Hit:* 7 (1d8 + 3) piercing damage.
Web. *Ranged Weapon Attack:* +7 to hit, range 100/400 ft. one target. *Hit:* target is restrained (escaped DC 16).

Spriggan

The tavern was busy, but we'd gotten our usual table near the fireplace. The hearth was warm and inviting, and it was drawing many in out of the cold rain. Sandra was sipping delicately at her wine, while that big oaf OTATO! was already into his third pitcher of cheap ale. A quartet of musicians launched into a jaunty melody, and that was all the encouragement the barbarian needed. He danced around the room with a pitcher in each hand, sloshing the brew over everyone and everything. A band of ugly gnomes picked that unfortunate moment to wander in out of the storm. The barbarian shouted "Dwarves!" and picked up one of the newcomers. The angry, sputtering gnome wasn't having it, and all four of them instantly became giants whose heads touched the ceiling. — Benisi Harpstring, elven bard recounting the barfight at the Broken Goblet

Spriggans are ugly, stocky gnomes with a bulbous nose and reddish eyes. They have shaggy dark mustaches and ratty beards, both unkempt and caked with dirt and filth. Spriggans are among the ugliest and certainly the most foul tempered of all gnomes. At one moment a normal-sized gnome, a spriggan can grow to giant-sized in an instant, gaining immense strength and taking unsuspecting opponents by surprise.

Spriggan

Small fey, chaotic evil

Armor Class 15 (chain shirt)
Hit Points 36 (8d6 + 8)
Speed 20 ft.

STR	DEX	CON	INT	WIS	CHA
8 (−1)	16 (+3)	13 (+1)	11 (+0)	11 (+0)	8 (−1)

Skills Nature +2, Perception +2, Stealth +5, Survival +2
Senses darkvision 60 ft., passive Perception 12
Languages Sylvan
Challenge 3 (700 XP)

Innate Spellcasting. The spriggan's innate spellcasting ability is Constitution (spell save DC 11). The spriggan can innately cast the following spells, requiring no material components:
At will: *druidcraft*
1/day: *shatter*
Magic Resistance. The spriggan has advantage on saving throws against spells and other magical effects.

Actions

Multiattack. The spriggan makes two Shortsword attacks.
Shortsword. *Melee Weapon Attack:* +5 to hit, reach 5 ft., one target. *Hit:* 6 (1d6 + 3) piercing damage.
Enlarge (1/day). The spriggan's size triples in all dimensions, and its weight is multiplied by 10. This growth increases its size from Small to Large. The spriggan remains changed for one hour, or until it takes a bonus action to end the effect. The spriggan has advantage on Strength checks and Strength saving throws, and the spriggan's weapons grow to match its new size. While these weapons are enlarged, the spriggan's attacks deal an additional die of damage on a hit.

Stank Hog

I've slept in a longhouse with Northmen who didn't bathe for weeks … and that smell was like a field of flowers compared to that damned hog. We stumbled into a field in the Gundlock Hills and found a dozen wild hogs and their piglets grazing on the grasses. They were ugly things, stout and hairless, with big tusks. One charged, and Skalton pulled out his blade, ready to provide us with dinner. The hog was faster, though, and caught him in the thigh with its tusks. But the blast from its flanks as it charged away finished off the warrior. He vomited and collapsed to the ground, rubbing furiously at his eyes. The hog took his head off when it charged again. — Aldir Strugg, who was rescued from a tree by farmers who drove off the angry herd of stank hogs

The stank hog is somewhat larger than its cousin, the common wild swine, reaching a shoulder height of 40 inches, a length of six feet, and weighing up to 500 pounds. Protruding from an elongated muzzle, a single set of curved and pointed tusks reaches a length of 10 to 12 inches upon maturity. Stank hogs are nearly devoid of fur, with only sparse, bristly hairs poking upward from their thick, dark-gray hides. Each of its feet has four toes that end in two larger frontal hooves and two smaller rear hooves. Its short tail ends with a tuft of bristly hair and twitches when the animal is agitated.

Stank Hog

Large beast, unaligned

Armor Class 13 (natural armor)
Hit Points 45 (6d10 + 12)
Speed 40 ft.

STR	DEX	CON	INT	WIS	CHA
16 (+3)	11 (+0)	14 (+2)	4 (–3)	8 (–1)	3 (–4)

Skills Perception +1
Senses passive Perception 11
Languages —
Challenge 2 (450 XP)

Stank's Revenge. Any piercing attack from the flank or rear has a 10% chance of popping the inflated anal gland of the stank hog, releasing the noxious flatulence and causing the full effect as described under the mephitic gas action. Additionally, any piercing or slashing critical hit from the flank or rear has a 50% chance of popping the inflated anal gland and triggering the mephitic gas action, the mighty blow cutting deep into the stank hog's thick hide and puncturing the gas-filled gland. If stank's revenge is activated, the hog can no longer use the mephitic gas attack until it is able to heal for one week.

Actions

Bite. *Melee weapon attack:* +5 to hit. *Hit:* 10 (2d6 + 3) piercing damage.

Cut and Run. *Melee weapon attack:* +5 to hit. *Hit:* 12 (2d8 + 3) slashing damage. The stank hog charges its opponent, often emerging from the cover of thick underbrush, and attempts to gore with its tusks and keep running to the safety of more underbrush, if present, or simply to put space between itself and the opponent. Any opponent gored in such a manner must make a DC 12 Dexterity saving throw or be knocked prone. The hog may or may not release its mephitic gas attack during this charge.

Mephitic Gas (recharge 3–6). While making an attack, the stank hog lets forth a vile gust of air accumulated in its specialized anal gland. Roll 1d20. On a result of less than 10, the anal gland deflates and adheres to itself, rendering the mephitic gas for that stank hog unusable until it completes a long or short rest. A result of 10 or higher creates a 10-foot-diameter gas cloud; 15 or higher creates a 20-foot-diameter gas cloud; and a roll of 20 creates a 30-foot-diameter gas cloud. The effect is immediate and profound, affecting all creatures within the cloud. Any creature that starts its turn within the gaseous cloud or enters the cloud on its turn must make a successful Constitution saving throw, the save DC equaling the stank hog's roll, or become incapacitated. While incapacitated from the mephitic gas, the creature lies upon the ground with eyes stinging and vomit flowing. An incapacitated creature may make another saving throw at the start of its turn, ending the effect upon itself on a success. The mephitic gas lasts for 1d4 + 1 rounds, lingering in the same area unless a strong wind disperses it. The stank hog is immune to its own and other stank hogs' mephitic gas.

Stank Piglet

Small beast, unaligned

Armor Class 12
Hit Points 7 (2d6)
Speed 30 ft.

STR	DEX	CON	INT	WIS	CHA
10 (+0)	14 (+2)	10 (+0)	4 (–3)	8 (–1)	8 (–1)

Skills Perception +1
Senses passive Perception 11
Languages —
Challenge 1/2 (100 XP)

Stank's Revenge. Any piercing attack from the flank or rear has a 10% chance of popping the inflated anal gland of the piglet, releasing the noxious flatulence and causing the full effect as described under the mephitic gas action. Additionally, any piercing or slashing critical hit from the flank or rear has a 50% chance of popping the inflated anal gland and triggering the mephitic gas action, the mighty blow cutting deep into the piglet's tender hide and puncturing the gas-filled gland. If stank's revenge is activated, the piglet can no longer use the mephitic gas attack until able to heal for one week.

Actions

Bite. *Melee weapon attack:* +2 to hit. *Hit:* 3 (1d4) piercing damage.

Mephitic Gas (recharge 6). While making an attack, the stank hog lets forth a vile gust of air accumulated in its specialized anal gland. Roll 1d20. On a result of less than 10, the anal gland deflates and adheres to itself, rendering the mephitic gas for that stank hog unusable until it completes a long or short rest. A result of 10 or higher creates a five-foot-diameter gas cloud; 15 or higher creates a 10-foot-diameter gas cloud. The effect is immediate and profound, affecting all creatures within the cloud. Any creature that starts its turn within the gaseous cloud or enters the cloud on its turn must make a successful Constitution saving throw, the save DC equaling the stank hog's roll, or become incapacitated. While incapacitated from the mephitic gas, the creature lies upon the ground with eyes stinging and vomit flowing. An incapacitated creature may make another saving throw at the start of its turn, ending the effect upon itself on a success. The mephitic gas lasts 1d4 + 1 rounds, lingering in the same area unless a strong wind disperses it. The stank hog is immune to its own and other stank hogs' mephitic gas.

TOME OF HORRORS

STEGOCENTIPEDE

The sound coming down the darkened hallway was like hundreds of creatures running at once. A tap-tap-tap-tap! that went on forever. But I couldn't place the shush-shush-shush! sound accompanying those incessant taps. When I saw it, it all made sense. It was about 20 feet long and sidewinding back and forth on hundreds of legs. It raised nasty-looking spikes along its armored back when it saw us. A dangerous stinger waved behind it, raised and ready to strike. I've seen insects — and some big ones at that — but nothing quite as mean and built for inflicting pain as this thing. — Kilmori Ract, displaying the severed head of the stegocentipede to awed villagers in Doan

Stegocentipedes are arthropods grown to stunning size. They are rumored among sages to have come to the Material Plane from another plane or dimension, though no proof has been found to support this theory. It is based chiefly on the fact that nothing else like them exists. A typical stegocentipede is 18 feet long, but there is much variety among the species. A stegocentipede raises its spines instinctively when it enters combat, and it moves constantly in a back-and-forth, sawing motion as it fights.

STEGOCENTIPEDE

Huge beast, unaligned

Armor Class 14 (natural armor)
Hit Points 76 (9d12 + 18)
Speed 40 ft.

STR	DEX	CON	INT	WIS	CHA
19 (+4)	15 (+2)	14 (+2)	1 (−5)	10 (+0)	6 (−2)

Condition Immunities charmed, prone, restrained
Senses darkvision 60 ft., passive Perception 10
Languages —
Challenge 4 (1,100 XP)

Spines. A creature that makes a melee attack against a stegocentipede while within five feet of the stegocentipede must make a successful DC 12 Dexterity saving throw or take 6 (1d8 + 2) slashing damage from spines on the stegocentipede's carapace.

ACTIONS

Multiattack. The stegocentipede makes one Bite attack and one Sting attack.
Bite. *Melee Weapon Attack:* +6 to hit, reach 5 ft., one target. *Hit:* 8 (1d8 + 4) piercing damage.
Sting. *Melee Weapon Attack:* +6 to hit, reach 10 ft., one target. *Hit:* 13 (2d8 + 4) piercing damage and the target must make a successful DC 12 Constitution saving throw or be poisoned. While poisoned, the creature takes 7 (2d6) poison damage at the start of its turn. A poisoned creature repeats the saving throw at the start of its turn, ending the effect on itself with a success.

Stone Maiden

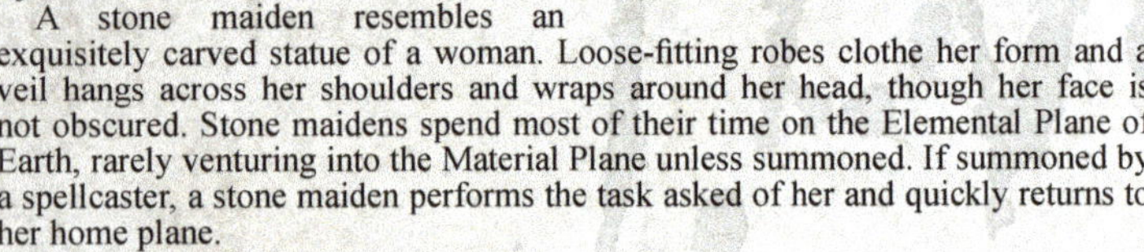

The riddle on the scrolls led us high into the Stonehearts near Mount Daergyd. They spoke of ancient guardians, but all we found were statues of woman covered in vines and dust. The round altar was surrounded by 20-foot-tall pillars with carved bull heads atop them. Chains draped from pillar to pillar. The Chisel of Zemlya sat in the center of the altar. All we had to do was find its companion mystical hammer then destroy both together. If we succeeded, no one would ever combine those tools to carve the names of their enemies in stone and end their life. "Rockbreaker" Voons stepped between the statues, but one reached out and grabbed his leg, sending him sprawling forward. Each of the stone women rose as one, and we knew we had finally found the guardians.
— Lucelyn Abbestot, speaking to the temple priests while being healed of her injuries

A stone maiden resembles an exquisitely carved statue of a woman. Loose-fitting robes clothe her form and a veil hangs across her shoulders and wraps around her head, though her face is not obscured. Stone maidens spend most of their time on the Elemental Plane of Earth, rarely venturing into the Material Plane unless summoned. If summoned by a spellcaster, a stone maiden performs the task asked of her and quickly returns to her home plane.

Stone Maiden

Medium elemental, neutral

Armor Class 17 (natural armor)
Hit Points 102 (12d8 + 48)
Speed 30 ft.

STR	DEX	CON	INT	WIS	CHA
18 (+4)	11 (+0)	18 (+4)	15 (+2)	16 (+3)	20 (+5)

Saving Throws Str +7, Con +7, Cha +8
Skills Perception +6, Persuasion +8
Damage Resistances cold, fire; bludgeoning, piercing, and slashing from nonmagical attacks
Damage Immunities necrotic, poison
Damage Vulnerabilities thunder
Condition Immunities exhaustion, paralyzed, petrified, poisoned, unconscious
Senses darkvision 60 ft., passive Perception 16
Languages Common, Terran
Challenge 8 (3,900 XP)

Earth Magic Immunity. The stone maiden is immune to any spell or magical effect that employs or manipulates earth or stone, including her own *spike growth* spell.
Earth Mastery. If the stone maiden and a creature are standing on the ground, the creature suffers a –1 to its attack and damage rolls against the stone maiden and has disadvantage on grappling checks made against the stone maiden.
Innate Spellcasting. The stone maiden's innate spellcasting ability is Charisma (spell save DC 16, +8 to hit with spell attacks). She can innately cast the following spells, with no need for material components or concentration:
At will: *meld into stone, spike growth, stone shape*
2/day: *move earth, wall of stone*

Actions

Multiattack. The stone maiden makes two Longsword attacks or two Slam attacks.
Longsword. *Melee Weapon Attack:* +7 to hit, reach 5 ft., one creature. *Hit:* 13 (2d8 + 4) slashing damage.
Slam. *Melee Weapon Attack:* +7 to hit, reach 5 ft., one creature. *Hit:* 11 (2d6 + 4) bludgeoning damage.
Animate Rocks **(recharge 4–6).** The stone maiden causes a pile of rocks she can see within 100 feet of her to animate into a humanoid shape. The rock form has statistics identical to the stone maiden, except it may use only Slam attacks. The rocks act under the control of the stone maiden, but do not require her concentration, and return to their lifeless state when reduced to 0 hit points or when they are more than 100 feet from the stone maiden.

Stroke Lad

The plan was to approach the new "lord" of the manor and convince him to give up his false claim to Lord Galifrin's inheritance, on behalf of his lordship, of course. The usurper's servants, all willowy young women and handsome lads, met us at the door and ushered us into the hall. What a hall! What once no doubt was a refined hall of taste and decorum had been replaced by perverse artwork, scandalous sculptures, and a profusion of gold leaf that hinted at ill breeding, if not madness. The new "lord" of Whitsomber was no man but instead a fey creature with the twisting horns of a goat and a wicked smile. We presented our case, and he calmly stepped down from a gaudy throne, removed one long silk glove, and slapped Sir Ector, withering the brave knight's body to that of a crooked old man. — Sir Cedric of Reme, knight errant

Fey of the darkest kind, stroke lads are tall, slender, delicately featured beings with the mien of a jaded aristocrat. Their heads feature a pair of goat's horns that are kept at a glossy sheen. They dress in fine silks, drape themselves with jewelry, and wield scepters or other symbols of nobility and authority. While stroke lads prefer to avoid combat, letting their servants take care of ruffians, their ability to wither limbs and bodies with a touch make them fearsome foes.

Stroke Lad

Medium fey, neutral evil

Armor Class 14
Hit Points 97 (13d8 + 39)
Speed 30 ft.

STR	DEX	CON	INT	WIS	CHA
14 (+2)	18 (+4)	16 (+3)	15 (+2)	12 (+1)	16 (+3)

Skills Deception + 6, Intimidation +6, Persuasion +6
Damage Resistances bludgeoning, piercing, slashing
Condition Immunities charmed, frightened
Senses darkvision 60 ft., passive Perception 11
Languages Common, Sylvan
Challenge 6 (2,300 XP)

Innate Spellcasting. The stroke lad's innate spellcasting ability is Charisma (spell save DC 14, +6 to hit with spell attacks). It can cast the following spells, requiring no material components:
At will: *charm, dancing lights, detect evil and good*
1/day each: *confusion, detect thoughts, dispel magic*
Magic Resistance. The stroke lad has advantage on saving throws against spells and other magical effects.
Magic Weapons. The stroke lad's weapon attacks are magical.

Actions

Multiattack. The stroke lad makes two Withering Touch attacks.
Withering Touch. *Melee Weapon Attack:* +7 to hit, reach 5 ft., one target. *Hit:* 22 (4d8 + 4) necrotic damage.

Surf Lurker

Carvac decided he wasn't going to wait for us. He pushed the old, vine-covered boat off the beach and rowed out onto the blue depths of the Cærulean, headed for the rock column to look for the next series of glyphs. He was shouting the symbols to us, describing them as best he could in his thick Northlander accent. Suddenly, two sinuous, scaled serpents with fish-like heads and wide, webbed wings launched themselves out of the clear water. They slammed into Carvac and wrapped him in their long tentacles. It was only a miracle that he stayed standing. The ever-jumpy wizard Bolam fired off a ball of flame — I can't recall how many times that has happened — and hit the boat square. I've never seen something go up in a blaze so quickly. I spotted Carvac's body floating in the bay before a tentacle rose up and sucked him under. — Bethelema LaCroix, describing the creatures that killed the Northlander to his family

Surf lurkers resemble medium-sized serpents with mottled blue-green scales that aid in camouflage. Their thin, membranous wings are normally kept closely folded against their bodies, but they unfurl them when they leap from hiding to surprise their prey. Their heads resemble predatory fish more than snakes, and sport stabbing fangs that secrete a toxic venom used to subdue smaller prey. While they normally hunt smaller fish or surface creatures that venture near the ocean, lurkers have no qualms about attacking larger victims such as sailors or unfortunate beachcombers.

Surf Lurker

Medium monstrosity, unaligned

Armor Class 16 (natural armor)
Hit Points 99 (18d8 + 18)
Speed 30 ft., fly 30 ft., swim 30 ft.

STR	DEX	CON	INT	WIS	CHA
12 (+1)	15 (+2)	12 (+1)	3 (−4)	16 (+3)	3 (−4)

Skills Stealth +6
Senses passive Perception 13
Languages —
Challenge 4 (1,100 XP)

Camouflage. Surf lurkers gain advantage on all Dexterity (Stealth) checks while in water.

Actions

Multiattack. The surf lurker makes six Tentacle attacks, uses Reel, and makes one Bite attack.

Bite. *Melee Weapon Attack:* +3 to hit, reach 5 ft., one target. *Hit:* 19 (4d8 + 1) damage plus 11 (2d10) poison damage. The lurker has advantage on targets grappled by one or more of its tentacles.

Tentacles. *Melee Weapon Attack:* +7 to hit, reach 50 ft., one creature. *Hit:* The target is grappled (escape DC 14). Until the grapple ends, the target is restrained and has disadvantage on Strength checks and Strength saving throws, and the creature can't use the same tendril on another target. The lurker can automatically grapple a target with its remaining tentacles; each tentacle adds 1 to the target's escape DC. The surf lurker has advantage on all bite attacks against targets grappled by its tentacles.

Drown. A lurker with a grappled target attempts to submerge and drown its target (see Suffocation rules).

Reel. The lurker pulls one grappled creature up to 25 feet closer to it.

Swarm of Adamantine Wasps

When the iron bells rang, a swarm of metallic insects buzzed out of the tower, swarming down the steep spiraling stairs and catching us halfway up the flight. Synder leaped over the rail and fell, trusting to his ring to let him float to the ground so far below. That was his mistake, as the wasps simply chased him down and swarmed his floating body. His frozen corpse broke into hundreds of icy chunks when he finally hit the ground. — Edgren of Sunderland, on his first failed attempt to conquer the Labyrinth Hive of the Apocrita Queen

Adamantine wasps are flying constructs with a deadly sting. They are one-foot-long silver wasps that often fly in swarms to bring down larger prey. The wasps are constructs created to guard or patrol areas. Their bodies are segmented like a normal wasp with a head, thorax, and abdomen, with its metallic pieces seamlessly fitted together. An adamantine stinger protrudes from the wasp's abdomen. Its wings are formed of paper-thin adamantine. Their poison freezes the blood of those they sting. Adamantine wasps are non-intelligent and are programmed to carry out simple tasks that might include phrases such as "guard this room" or "attack any who enter." The wasps fight until destroyed when performing their tasks.

Swarm of Adamantine Wasps

Large swarm of Tiny constructs, unaligned

Armor Class 18 (natural armor)
Hit Points 133 (14d10 + 56)
Speed 5 ft., fly 40 ft.

STR	DEX	CON	INT	WIS	CHA
14 (+2)	16 (+3)	19 (+4)	3 (–4)	8 (–1)	1 (–5)

Saving Throws Dex +7, Con +8
Skills Perception +3, Stealth +7
Damage Resistances bludgeoning, fire, piercing, slashing
Damage Immunities acid, cold, poison, psychic; bludgeoning, piercing, and slashing from nonmagical attacks
Condition Immunities blinded, charmed, deafened, frightened, grappled, paralyzed, petrified, poisoned, prone, restrained, stunned
Senses blindsight 60 ft., passive Perception 13
Languages —
Challenge 11 (7,200 XP)

Swarm. The swarm can occupy another creature's space and vice versa, and the swarm can move through any opening large enough for a Tiny adamantine wasp. The swarm can't regain hit points or gain temporary hit points.

Actions

Multiattack. The swarm makes two Icy Stingers attacks.
Icy Stingers. *Melee Weapon Attack:* +7 to hit, reach 0 ft., one creature in the swarm's space. *Hit:* 14 (4d6) piercing damage, or 7 (2d6) piercing damage if the swarm has half of its hit points or fewer. The target must make a DC 17 Constitution saving throw, taking 18 (4d8) cold damage on a failed save, or half as much damage on a successful one. In addition, on a failed save the target gains a level of cold-based exhaustion.

Swarm of Bladecoins

The greedy halfling Pirtson shouted in delight when he saw the gold and silver coins gleaming in the stone fountain. I never really liked him that much, and I'm sure he's the reason some of my belongings — the compass, that gem I won from that drunken gambler, a few of my coins — went missing. He dove headfirst into that pile of coins. When he surfaced, it took him a moment to feel the pain of the thousands of cuts slicing across his face and arms. When he did, he shrieked as his wounds began to bleed. The coins themselves rose up in a tornado around the thief then, slicing him to ribbons before we could do anything else. No one seemed to be moving too fast to help the halfling. We'd all had items go missing since he joined our circle. — Ellyn Trailfinder, after retreating from Rappan Athuk

A bladecoin swarm appears to be nothing more than a pile of brass or copper coins. However, when the swarm senses intruders entering the area it is tasked with guarding, it swirls upward into a cyclonic tornado composed of hundreds of coins with razor-sharp edges. The swarms are often placed to deter would-be thieves.

Swarm of Bladecoins

Large swarm of Tiny constructs, unaligned

Armor Class 14 (natural armor)
Hit Points 75 (10d10 + 20)
Speed 5 ft., fly 30 ft.

STR	DEX	CON	INT	WIS	CHA
10 (+0)	15 (+2)	14 (+2)	3 (–4)	8 (–1)	1 (–5)

Skills Stealth +8
Damage Resistances acid, bludgeoning, piercing, slashing
Damage Immunities cold, poison, psychic
Condition Immunities blinded, charmed, deafened, frightened, grappled, paralyzed, petrified, poisoned, prone, restrained, stunned
Senses blindsight 60 ft., passive Perception 9
Languages —
Challenge 5 (1,800 XP)

Swarm. The swarm can occupy another creature's space and vice versa, and the swarm can move through any opening large enough for a Tiny bladecoin. The swarm can't regain hit points or gain temporary hit points.
Distraction. A creature that starts its turn in the swarm's space must succeed on a DC 14 Dexterity saving throw or be blinded and deafened until the start of its next turn.

Actions

Multiattack. The swarm makes two Slash attacks.
Slashes. *Melee Weapon Attack:* +5 to hit, reach 0 ft., one creature in the swarm's space. *Hit:* 18 (4d8) slashing damage, or 9 (2d8) slashing damage if the swarm has half its hit points or fewer, and 4 (1d8) slashing damage at the end of its next turn.

Swarm of Carnivorous Fish

We thought the hole in the raft when we struck the river rock was going to be the worst of it. Sure, we'd all get a little wet, but once we pulled the boat ashore and repaired the damage, we'd be off again. We were treading water when something tugged at my legs. And again. And again. Sahaen the silk merchant screamed and tried to scramble back onto the raft. His legs were gone below the knees, and his blood pooled in the water. We scattered then, thrashing our way to shore as the bites and nips continued. Of the seven merchants sharing the raft, three of us made it to shore. — Jewelry merchant Ingo Dievoet, on a trip up the Quell River through the Seething Jungle

A carnivorous fish swarm attacks prey as it crosses through the rivers they call home. The swarm's initial bites draw blood, which send the school into a frenzy that can strip the meat from the bone in a matter of moments. Swarms of piranhas are most commonly encountered.

Swarm of Carnivorous Fish

Medium swarm of tiny beasts, unaligned

Armor Class 12
Hit Points 36 (8d8)
Speed 0 ft., swim 40 ft.

STR	DEX	CON	INT	WIS	CHA
12 (+1)	14 (+2)	10 (+0)	1 (–5)	7 (–2)	2 (–4)

Damage Resistance bludgeoning, piercing, slashing
Condition Immunities charmed, frightened, grappled, paralyzed, petrified, prone, restrained, stunned
Senses darkvision 60 ft., passive Perception 8
Challenge 1 (200 XP)

Blood Frenzy. The swarm has advantage on melee attack rolls against any creature that doesn't have all its hit points.
Swarm. The swarm can occupy another creature's space and vice versa, and the swarm can move through any opening large enough for a Tiny creature. The swarm can't regain hit points or gain temporary hit points.
Water Breathing. The swarm can breathe only underwater.

Actions

Bites. *Melee Weapon Attack:* +4 to hit, reach 0 ft., one creature in the swarm's space. *Hit:* 14 (4d6) piercing damage or 7 (2d6) if the swarm has fewer than half its starting hit points.

Swarm of Eye Spiders

"See? The eyes are moving." Two-Fang Saracen stopped in front of one of the portraits in the great hall. He peered close at the image of an ancient king wearing a silver and ruby crown. He lifted his hammer above his shoulder, paused for a second, and then slammed the heavy weapon into the painting. The blow easily punched a hole through the canvas — and the wall behind it. The eyes were indeed moving. They came boiling out of the wall in a swarm. — Freen "One-Eye" D'Edgeros, on how he lost his eye

Eye spiders are tiny constructs formed from eyeballs discarded by the scholars of the Great Repository in the City of Brass. They resemble spiders composed completely of eyeballs with a larger eye (presumably taken from a larger creature) serving as the monster's central body. Small eyes that have been sewn, chained, or stitched together function as the creatures' legs.

Swarm of Eye Spiders

Medium swarm of Tiny constructs, unaligned

Armor Class 13 (natural armor)
Hit Points 45 (10d8)
Speed 20 ft., climb 20 ft.

STR	DEX	CON	INT	WIS	CHA
13 (+1)	13 (+1)	10 (+0)	1 (–5)	9 (–1)	3 (–4)

Damage Resistances bludgeoning, piercing, and slashing
Damage Immunities lightning, poison; bludgeoning, piercing, and slashing from nonmagical attacks that aren't adamantine
Condition Immunities charmed, exhaustion, frightened, paralyzed, petrified, poisoned, prone, restrained, stunned
Senses darkvision 60 ft., passive Perception 9
Languages understands the language of its creator but can't speak
Challenge 3 (700 XP)

Distraction. Any living creature that begins its turn with the swarm in its space must succeed on a DC 14 Constitution save or be frightened for one round.
Swarm. The swarm can occupy one or more other creatures' spaces and vice versa, and the swarm can move through an opening large enough for a Tiny eye spider. The swarm can't regain hit points or gain temporary hit points.

Actions

Slam. *Melee Weapon Attack:* +3 to hit, reach 0 ft., one creature in the swarm's space. *Hit:* 4 (1d8) bludgeoning damage or 2 (1d4) bludgeoning damage if the swarm has half its starting hit points or fewer.

Bonus Actions

Mind Ruin. The swarm flashes and pulsates. Any creature caught within its space when it does so has its mind suddenly filled with thousands of tangled visual images composed of text, passages, and secrets that the eyes of the swarm have seen over the centuries. The creature must succeed on a DC 14 Wisdom saving throw or be confused, as if by a *confusion* spell. If the target fails three consecutive saving throws, the condition is permanent until cured by *greater restoration* or other magic.

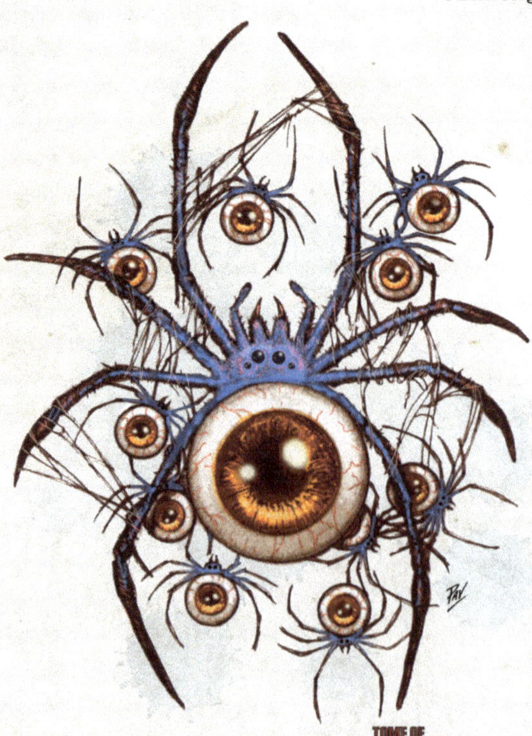

Swarm of Flying Scorpions

From a distance we thought the cloud was just a swarm of locusts, but as it neared the image resolved, and to our horror they were flying scorpions. Each had a scorpion's body, complete with deadly stinger, but also a pair of wings like a beetle. Seeing the danger, we quickly set to finding shelter. Most of the members of the expedition were able to throw up some tents or rig bedding into makeshift barriers. The rest we buried beneath the shifting sands. — Algrid Henswaithe, University of the Vast

Flying scorpions swarms are clouds of hundreds, sometimes thousands, of the small, predatory arachnids, each with beetle-like wings. The scorpions swarm enemies, stinging them repeatedly with their poisonous tails.

Swarm of Flying Scorpions

Medium swarm of tiny beast, unaligned

Armor Class 12 (natural armor)
Hit Points 22 (5d8)
Speed fly 30 ft.

STR	DEX	CON	INT	WIS	CHA
3 (–4)	13 (+1)	10 (+0)	1 (–5)	7 (–2)	1 (–5)

Damage Resistances bludgeoning, piercing, slashing
Condition Immunities charmed, frightened, grappled, paralyzed, petrified, prone, restrained, stunned
Senses blindsight 10 ft., passive Perception 8
Languages —
Challenge 1 (200 XP)

Swarm. The swarm can occupy another creature's space and vice versa, and the flying scorpion swarm can move through any opening large enough for a Tiny creature. The flying scorpion swarm can't regain hit points or gain temporary hit points.

Actions

Stings. *Melee Weapon Attack:* +3 to hit, reach 0 ft., one target in the swarm's space. *Hit:* 16 (6d4 + 1) poison damage, or 8 (3d4 + 1) poison damage if the swarm has half or fewer hit points.

TOME OF HORRORS

Swarm of Hostile Birds

A green and purple portal opened in the sky above Cailin Lee, a deep bruise floating in the air and swirling at an impossible speed. Flocks of starlings took flight from the trees and wheeled toward the circling bands, flying in great rings around the widening gyre. With a flash, the portal's glowing interior collapsed, leaving an image burned on our vision. We realized trouble had come to the fortress when the massive flocks of cawing birds began dropping fast into our courtyard, pecking and slashing at everyone who had gathered to stare at the strange phenomenon. — Report from Commander Megyn Friar on strange behavior of the birds in the area

A swarm of hostile birds is a collection of feathered avians that fly in a twisting mass. The birds swoop and dive to attack creatures, pecking with their beaks and slashing with their talons. The flights are often composed of the same type of bird, such as starlings or magpies, but some larger birds might be found mixed into their number.

Swarm of Hostile Birds
Medium swarm of tiny beasts, unaligned

Armor Class 12
Hit Points 31 (7d8)
Speed 10 ft., fly 50 ft.

STR	DEX	CON	INT	WIS	CHA
6 (–2)	14 (+2)	10 (+0)	3 (–4)	12 (+1)	6 (–2)

Damage Resistances bludgeoning, piercing, slashing
Condition Immunities charmed, frightened, grappled, paralyzed, petrified, prone, restrained, stunned
Senses passive Perception 11
Challenge 1/4 (50 XP)

Swarm. The swarm can occupy another creature's space and vice versa, and the swarm can move through any opening large enough for a Tiny creature. The swarm can't regain hit points or gain temporary hit points.

Actions

Beaks. *Melee Weapon Attack:* +4 to hit, reach 5 ft., one target in the hostile bird swarm's space. *Hit:* 7 (2d6) piercing damage or 3 (1d6) piercing if the swarm has half its initial hit points or fewer.

Swarm of Miniature Mermaids

We found it! Gombrie pushed open the massive brass doors and led us into the Aquarium Vault of Verthrimon. The first thing we found was a wall of glass that held back an ocean of water. Colorful fish swam in lazy circles. There was even a shark! I remember seeing something small swim toward the glass, then another, and another. I was amazed. Mermaids! Tiny mermaids! I remember them singing such a beautiful melody. — Holy warrior Jurgen DeFetterlind, found wandering the Haunted Steppes while dragging the bodies of his four friends in a net

Miniature mermaid swarms consist of tiny mermaids that swim together like a school of fish. They raise their voices together in a song that can charm anyone they encounter. They swarm prey that enters their watery depths, drowning them.

Swarm of Miniature Mermaids
Large swarm of Small humanoids (merfolk), neutral

Armor Class 13
Hit Points 60 (11d10)
Speed 10 ft., swim 40 ft.

STR	DEX	CON	INT	WIS	CHA
12 (+1)	16 (+3)	10 (+0)	8 (–1)	14 (+2)	17 (+3)

Skills Perception +4
Damage Resistances bludgeoning, piercing, slashing
Condition Immunities charmed, frightened, grappled, paralyzed, petrified, prone, restrained, stunned
Senses passive Perception 14
Languages Aquan, Common
Challenge 3 (700 XP)

Amphibious. The swarm can breathe air and water.
Smothering Embrace. While in water, a creature in the swarm's space is at risk of suffocating. It must succeed on a DC 13 Constitution saving throw to hold its breath or begin choking. A choking creature can survive a number of rounds equal to its Constitution modifier (minimum of one round) before dropping to 0 hit points and dying.
Swarm. The swarm can occupy another creature's space and vice versa, and the swarm can move through any opening large enough for a Small mermaid. The swarm can't regain hit points or gain temporary hit points.

Actions

Bites. *Melee Weapon Attack:* +5 to hit, reach 0 ft., one creature in the swarm's space. *Hit:* 21 (6d6) piercing damage, or 10 (3d6) piercing damage if the swarm has half its initial hit points or fewer.
Haunting Melody (recharge 6). The voices of the dozens of miniature mermaids harmonize into a haunting melody. Each creature within 30 feet of the swarm that can hear it must succeed on a DC 13 Charisma saving throw or be charmed by the swarm for one minute. A creature can repeat the saving throw at the end of each of its turns, ending the effect on itself on a success. If a creature's saving throw is successful or the effect ends for it, the creature is immune to the swarm's Haunting Melody for the next 24 hours.

Swarm of Stirges

I heard the scuttling and squeaking a moment before Ash pulled open the trapdoor in the ceiling. I expected a horde of rats to drop down on the thief, but it was much worse. Dozens of bat-like creatures poured out of the room above us. They hooked onto Ash's leather armor and stuck their long needle-like snouts into his flesh, rooting out every opening they could find. I'd seen a stirge feed before, and it was easy to knock the thing off and kill it. But a swarm? — Gwinneth the Stout, Priestess of Muir

Stirge swarms are flocks of the bloodsucking creatures. The individual stirges look like a cross between a bat and a mosquito. It has sharp pincers on its legs that allow it to grab hold of prey. They use their long proboscises to stab and suck their victims dry.

Swarm of Stirges

Medium swarm of Tiny beasts, unaligned

Armor Class 15 (natural armor)
Hit Points 58 (13d8)
Speed 10 ft., fly 40 ft.

STR	DEX	CON	INT	WIS	CHA
3 (–4)	19 (+4)	10 (+0)	1 (–5)	12 (+1)	6 (–2)

Skills Perception +5
Damage Resistances bludgeoning, piercing, slashing
Condition Immunities charmed, frightened, grappled, paralyzed, petrified, prone, restrained, stunned
Senses darkvision 60 ft., passive Perception 15
Languages —
Challenge 5 (1,800 XP)

Swarm. The swarm can occupy another creature's space and vice versa, and the swarm can move through any opening large enough for a Tiny creature. The swarm can't regain hit points or gain temporary hit points.

Actions

Blood Drain. *Melee Weapon Attack:* +6 to hit, reach 5 ft., one creature. *Hit:* 15 (6d4) piercing damage, and the stirges attach to the target. While attached, the stirges don't attack. Instead, at the start of each of the swarm's turns, the target loses 15 (6d4) hit points due to blood loss.

The swarm can detach itself by spending 5 feet of its movement. It does so after it drains 30 hit points of blood from the target or the target dies. A creature, including the target, can use its action to detach the stirges.

Swarm of Undead Bats

Broll and I found the goats dead outside the caves. He muttered something about vampire bats, but neither of us worried. It was just past midday, and we had no plans on hanging around after the sun went down. The fluttering of leathery wings from the cave mouth surprised us. Bat don't fly during the day, do they? These did. Although how they flew at all with their broken, twisted bodies was horrifying to behold. I ran. Broll did too, but he just wasn't fast enough. I hate to think of him lying amid all those dead goats, but I can't go back there. Never. — Brack Parks, telling the village elders where to find Goatherder Broll's body

Undead bat swarms are collections of dead bats that still fly as if they were living, breathing creatures. The bats attack with hundreds of tiny bites as they swarm their prey.

Swarm of Undead Bats

Medium swarm of Tiny undead, chaotic evil

Armor Class 12
Hit Points 22 (5d8)
Speed 0 ft., fly 30 ft.

STR	DEX	CON	INT	WIS	CHA
5 (–3)	15 (+2)	10 (+0)	2 (–4)	12 (+1)	4 (–3)

Damage Resistances bludgeoning, piercing, slashing
Damage Immunities poison
Condition Immunities charmed, frightened, grappled, paralyzed, petrified, poisoned, prone, restrained, stunned
Senses blindsight 60 ft., darkvision 60 ft., passive Perception 11
Languages —
Challenge 1/4 (50 XP)

Echolocation. The swarm can't use its blindsight while deafened.
Keen Hearing. The swarm has advantage on Wisdom (Perception) checks that rely on hearing.
Swarm. The swarm can occupy another creature's space and vice versa, and the swarm can move through any opening large enough for a Tiny bat. The swarm can't regain hit points or gain temporary hit points.

Actions

Bites. *Melee Weapon Attack:* +4 to hit, reach 0 ft., one creature in the swarm's space. *Hit:* 5 (2d4) piercing damage, or 2 (1d4) piercing damage if the swarm has half its hit points or fewer.

Swarm of Undead Hummingbirds

We heard a thwip-thwip-thwip through the sunflowers and saw hundreds of tiny flitting bodies moving quickly among the stalks. Paisley darted into the flowers, singing a tune to draw the hummingbirds to her. She was always talking to the animals. She came screaming out of the flowers a moment later, a swarming mass of tiny birds darting close behind her. She was bleeding from hundreds of tiny pinpricks on her skin. The birds were horrible to behold, with broken bodies, twisted necks, and scabrous holes in their feathered skin. — Teely Ravenstot, former druid-in-training

Undead hummingbird swarms are composed of hundreds to thousands of dead hummingbirds. The tiny birds flit and dart about as they move, but seem to follow a single, focused mind when pursuing prey. Their pecks deal little damage, but in large numbers they can kill larger creatures by swarming over their bodies.

Swarm of Undead Hummingbirds

Medium swarm of Tiny undead, chaotic evil

Armor Class 16
Hit Points 27 (6d8)
Speed 10 ft., fly 60 ft.

STR	DEX	CON	INT	WIS	CHA
1 (−5)	21 (+5)	10 (+0)	1 (−5)	10 (+0)	6 (−2)

Skills Perception +4, Stealth +9
Damage Vulnerabilities bludgeoning
Damage Resistances piercing, slashing
Damage Immunities poison
Condition Immunities charmed, frightened, grappled, paralyzed, petrified, poisoned, prone, restrained, stunned
Senses darkvision 60 ft., passive Perception 15
Languages —
Challenge 2 (450 XP)

Swarm. *The swarm can occupy another creature's space and vice versa, and the swarm can move through any opening large enough for a Tiny creature. The swarm can't regain hit points or gain temporary hit points.*

Actions

Pierce. *Melee Weapon Attack:* +5 to hit, reach 5 ft., one creature. *Hit:* 1 piercing damage. If the target is a creature, the wound bleeds for 1 necrotic damage on each subsequent turn. The wound continues to bleed until it is cured by magical healing.

Swarm of Undead Rats

O'tez jumped over the pit and grabbed hold of the wall on the other side. The elf was the most-nimble person I'd ever seen. Except … the wall beyond the pit wasn't solid. As soon as he put his weight against it, it tilted outward in a 12-foot section that sent him backward into the pit. He rolled when he landed and came up without a scratch. "It's all right," he shouted up from the hole. "The floor is soft." Why was it soft? He found out a moment later when the rats — hundreds of them — began to squirm and writhe around him, biting and slashing. We looked on in horror, for the rats themselves were dead things with broken bodies oozing disease. — Wulfe the Brave, the first to run from the Whisper Vault

An swarm of undead rats consists of hundreds of undead rodents that squirm and writhe as if alive, until you stop to look at their broken bodies and lifeless eyes. Their insides ooze through their fur, making them a disgusting mass to deal with.

Swarm of Undead Rats

Medium swarm of Tiny undead, chaotic evil

Armor Class 10
Hit Points 24 (7d8 − 7)
Speed 30 ft.

STR	DEX	CON	INT	WIS	CHA
9 (−1)	11 (+0)	9 (−1)	2 (−4)	10 (+0)	3 (−4)

Damage Resistances bludgeoning, piercing, slashing
Damage Immunities poison
Condition Immunities charmed, frightened, grappled, paralyzed, petrified, poisoned, prone, restrained, stunned
Senses darkvision 30 ft., passive Perception 10
Languages —
Challenge 1/4 (50 XP)

Keen Smell. The swarm has advantage on Wisdom (Perception) checks that rely on smell.
Swarm. The undead rat swarm can occupy another creature's space and vice versa, and the swarm can move through any opening large enough for a Tiny rat. The swarm can't regain hit points or gain temporary hit points.

Actions

Bites. *Melee Weapon Attack:* +2 to hit, reach 0 ft., one creature in the swarm's space. *Hit:* 7 (2d6) piercing damage, or 3 (1d6) piercing damage if the swarm has half of its hit points or fewer.

Tangagumak

The snow blinded us, even as the cold crept through the thick layers of seal skin we had traded for in Nieuburg. We were pushing northward through the Hyperborean Way when the squalls turned into a deadly blizzard, halting our progress. Gunnter dropped into the snow, his lips blue as he stammered incoherently. Sallo tried casting a spell to conjure a blaze, but her brittle fingers barely moved as she murmured her incantation. Finally, we all huddled together over Gunnter, hoping our combined body heat would save us. I thought I was hallucinating when polar bears wearing golden armor rose up out of the snow. The warmth of their fur as they carried us back to their cave was like a pleasant dream. — Eaddard Dimouk, thought lost in the Northlands until he reappeared four months later speaking of spellcasting polar bears

The tangagumak are ursine humanoids native to cold northern climates that resemble upright polar bears, save with grasping hands and the glint of intelligence in their dark eyes. Though they are fierce hunters, the tangagumak are a peaceful race and slow to anger unless their families are threatened, in which case they are brave and merciless. Tangagumak society is tribal, usually led by elder female chiefs, with senior hunters, priests, and warriors making up an advisory council. Most communities make their living by hunting, fishing, and whaling. Skilled swimmers, tangagumak do not use boats, preferring to face the fish, seals, and whales of the frozen seas on their own, armed only with their teeth and claws. Tangagumak are also superb artisans and crafters, creating fine weapons and armor, as well as splendid carvings and other works of art.

Tangagumak

Large humanoid, lawful neutral

Armor Class 13 (natural armor)
Hit Points 28 (3d10 + 12)
Speed 30 ft., swim 30 ft.

STR	DEX	CON	INT	WIS	CHA
20 (+5)	10 (+0)	16 (+3)	10 (+0)	13 (+1)	10 (+0)

Skills Perception +3, Survival +3
Senses passive Perception 13
Languages Common, Tangagumak
Challenge 2 (450 XP)

Keen Smell. Tangagumak have advantage on Wisdom (Perception) checks that rely on smell.
Natural Swimmer. Tangagumak have advantage on Strength (Athletics) checks related to swimming.

Actions

Multiattack. The tangagumak makes one Bite and one Claw attack, or one Bite and one Spear attack.
Bite. *Melee Weapon Attack:* +7 to hit, reach 5 ft., one target. *Hit:* 9 (1d8 + 5) piercing damage.
Claw. *Melee Weapon Attack:* +7 to hit, reach 5 ft., one target. *Hit:* 8 (1d6 + 5) slashing damage.
Spear. *Melee or Ranged Weapon Attack:* +7 to hit, reach 5 ft. or range 20/60 ft., one target. *Hit:* 8 (1d6 + 5) piercing damage.

Tangagumak Warrior

Tangagumak warriors are ferocious, equally at home with sword and bow as with their own natural weaponry. They engage in a number of spiritual practices intended to enhance their martial prowess, including fasting, meditation, vision quests, and living apart from other tangagumak, emerging only if called upon by their chief in defense of the tribe.

Warriors wear elaborate breastplates inscribed with tribal icons and protective runes and bear finely crafted greatswords as symbols of rank. These greatswords are works of art, often handed down for generations. Foreigners and non-tangagumak are not allowed to wield these sacred weapons; a tangagumak warrior who sees one in the possession of an outsider immediately attacks to retrieve it.

Tangagumak Warrior

Large humanoid, lawful neutral

Armor Class 16 (breastplate)
Hit Points 127 (15d10 + 45)
Speed 30 ft., swim 30 ft.

STR	DEX	CON	INT	WIS	CHA
20 (+5)	12 (+1)	16 (+3)	10 (+0)	13 (+1)	10 (+0)

Saving Throws Dex +4, Con +6
Skills Athletics +8, Perception +4, Survival +4
Senses passive Perception 14
Languages Common, Tangagumak
Challenge 5 (1,800 XP)

Keen Smell. Tangagumak have advantage on Wisdom (Perception) checks that rely on smell.
Natural Swimmer. Tangagumak have advantage on Strength (Athletics) checks related to swimming.

Actions

Multiattack. The tangagumak warrior makes one Bite and two Claw attacks, or one Bite and two Greatsword attacks.
Bite. *Melee Weapon Attack:* +8 to hit, reach 5 ft., one target. *Hit:* 9 (1d8 + 5) piercing damage.
Claw. *Melee Weapon Attack:* +8 to hit, reach 5 ft., one target. *Hit:* 8 (1d6 + 5) slashing damage.
Greatsword. *Melee Weapon Attack:* +8 to hit, reach 5 ft., one target. *Hit:* 12 (2d6 + 5) slashing damage.
Greatbow. *Ranged Weapon Attack:* +4 to hit, range 150/600 ft., one target. *Hit:* 6 (1d10 + 1) thunder damage.

Tangagumak Shaman

The tangagumak worship a pantheon of nature gods, including those who provide good hunting, control the weather, and send bounty from the sea. Different communities worship the gods under different names, but their roles are almost always similar. Tangagumak shamans act as intercessors between mortals and the gods, performing ceremonies and leading others in worship. They also act as tribal healers and storytellers, keeping the community's historical lore and passing it to their successors.

Tangagumak Shaman

Large humanoid, lawful neutral

Armor Class 13
Hit Points 90 (12d10 + 24)
Speed 30 ft., swim 30 ft.

STR	DEX	CON	INT	WIS	CHA
20 (+5)	10 (+0)	14 (+2)	17 (+3)	16 (+3)	10 (+0)

Saving Throws Str +2, Con +2
Skills Athletics +9, History +6, Intimidation +4, Perception +5, Survival +5, Athletics +9
Senses passive Perception 15
Languages Common, Tangagumak
Challenge 4 (1,100 XP)

Keen Smell. Tangagumak have advantage on Wisdom (Perception) checks that rely on smell.
Natural Swimmer. Tangagumak have advantage on Strength (Athletics) checks related to swimming.
Spellcasting. The tangagumak shaman is a 5th-level spellcaster. Its spellcasting ability is Wisdom (spell save DC 14, +6 to hit with spell attacks). The shaman has the following cleric spells prepared:
Cantrips (at will): *guidance, light, mending, sacred flame*
1st level (4 slots): *bless, cure wounds, protection from evil and good, shield of faith*
2nd level (3 slots): *aid, hold person, spiritual weapon*
3rd level (2 slots): *mass healing word, spirit guardian*

Actions

Multiattack. The tangagumak shaman makes one Bite and two Claw attacks.
Bite. *Melee Weapon Attack:* +7 to hit, reach 5 ft., one target. *Hit:* 9 (1d8 + 5) piercing damage.
Claw. *Melee Weapon Attack:* +7 to hit, reach 5 ft., one target. *Hit:* 8 (1d6 + 5) slashing damage.

Thunder Terrier

Thunder rolled through the clear blue sky, but there was not the hint of a storm or lightning. Dods saw the pup first, but it was unlike any dog I've seen before or since. It was as big as a horse, running at us with its tongue lolling from the side of its mouth, its spittle flying. Danila cast a quick spell and a grove of trees rose in its path. The pup tore one of the saplings out of the ground and gave it a mighty shake before casting it aside and running headlong at us once more. When it stopped, it dropped into a crouch, its head between its paws, as if it was ready to play. "See? It's friendly," Dods said, just before the dog barked and a peal of thunder knocked us off our feet. — Explorer Whinney T. Perringson, writing in The Dog Titans of the Blackrock Mountains

Thunder terriers are extraordinarily rare, found most often in the company of storm giants and cloud giants who raise them as pets. Though similar to Yorkshire, Scottish, or West Highland terriers, the coloring of their fur ranges from sky blue to an almost sparkling teal. Like the smaller breed for which they are named, thunder terriers are natural ratters with a disposition to be excitable and gregarious. Thunder terrier pups can be reared and trained like any other dog, though the cost for feeding them is enormous and the likelihood of collateral damage is quite high.

Thunder Terrier
Large monstrosity, unaligned

Armor Class 13 (natural armor)
Hit Points 75 (10d10 + 20)
Speed 50 ft.

STR	DEX	CON	INT	WIS	CHA
18 (+4)	13 (+1)	14 (+2)	7 (−2)	12 (+1)	8 (−1)

Skills Perception +5, Stealth +3
Damage Immunities thunder
Senses passive Perception 15
Languages —
Challenge 3 (700 XP)

Keen Hearing and Smell. The thunder terrier has advantage on Wisdom (Perception) checks that rely on hearing or smell.

Actions

Bite. *Melee Weapon Attack:* +6 to hit, reach 5 ft., one target. *Hit:* 11 (2d6 + 4) piercing damage. If the target is a creature, it must succeed on a DC 14 Strength saving throw or be knocked prone.

Thundering Bark (recharge 5–6). The thunder terrier emits a thundering bark in a 60-foot cone. Each creature in this area must make a DC 12 Constitution saving throw. On a failed save, a creature takes 9 (2d8) thunder damage, is pushed 10 feet away from the terrier, and is deafened for one minute. On a successful save, the creature takes half as much damage and isn't pushed or deafened.

In addition, unsecured objects completely within the area of effect are automatically pushed 10 feet away from the terrier by the bark's effect, and the bark emits a thunderous boom audible out to 300 feet.

Toad, Fey Giant

Anke stepped onto the lily pad, testing its weight, as she followed the light dancing over the water. She was the smallest of us all and the most agile; no way was she going into the lake, which would surely have happened if that brute Windle had taken the step. Anke bounced once, and the lily pad miraculously held her. She made the leap to the second, then the third, as if the lily pads were steppingstones placed just for her across the water. She jumped onto the fourth just as it rose up beneath her, throwing her off balance. She pinwheeled her arms for balance, but was too late. She fell forward, but she never hit the water. This giant purple and pink frog beneath the lily pad snatched her into its mouth with its long tongue. The thing sank beneath the waters and we never saw her cheery smile again. — Morgan Adewale, found mourning beside a marshy offshoot of the Star Sea

Little about this enormous toad is ordinary, from its graceful wings to its colorful purple and pink skin to its bright, shining eyes. The amphibian has poisonous skin that can kill anyone touching the creature. It attacks by biting its enemies, but far worse is the chance that it swallows its prey whole, trapping them until they are digested or drowned as it swims back into the waters where it often hides. But don't think you're safe away from the water, for the frog can take to the air on its wings to give chase.

Fey Giant Toad
Large fey, chaotic neutral

Armor Class 14 (natural armor)
Hit Points 42 (5d10 + 15)
Speed 30 ft., fly 50 ft., swim 30 ft.

STR	DEX	CON	INT	WIS	CHA
17 (+3)	17 (+3)	16 (+3)	3 (−4)	10 (+0)	12 (+1)

Skills Perception +3
Senses passive Perception 13
Languages Sylvan
Challenge 2 (450 XP)

Innate Spellcasting. A demonic mist's spellcasting ability is Charisma (spell save DC 13), and requires no material components for the following spells:
3/day each: *dancing lights*
1/day each: *entangle, faerie fire*

Keen Smell. The fey giant toad has advantage on Wisdom (Perception) checks that rely on smell.

Poison Hide. A creature that touches the fey giant toad or hits it with an unarmed or natural weapon attack takes 3 (1d6) poison damage from the toad's poisonous hide.

Actions

Bite. *Melee Weapon Attack:* +5 to hit, reach 10 ft., one target. *Hit:* 10 (2d6 + 3) piercing damage, and the target is grappled (escape DC 13).

Swallow. The fey giant toad makes one bite attack against a Medium or smaller target it is grappling. If the attack hits, the target is swallowed, and the grapple ends. The swallowed target is blinded and restrained, it has total cover against attacks and other effects outside the fey giant toad, and it takes 3 (1d6) acid damage at the start of each of the fey giant toad's turns. The fey giant toad can swallow only one target at a time.

If the fey giant toad dies, a swallowed creature is no longer restrained by it and can escape from the corpse using 5 feet of movement, exiting prone.

TOME OF HORRORS

TROLL, BLACK

The troll hunt had been going well; three singed heads were in the sack already, and we hoped to add two more before the day was done. Tall Grass spotted troll spoor, three of them with one being much larger. Such great sport! We followed, and the largest turned out to be a rare black troll! The horn was sounded, and the hounds set upon the smaller ones. — Sir Cedric of Reme, knight errant

Black trolls are larger and more fearsome cousins of the common troll. Some sages postulate that black trolls were created through magical augmentation, but who would be foolish enough to augment a troll? These trolls are if anything more rapacious in their appetites than their more common kin, though it should be noted that they will not eat other trolls. Black trolls mate with each other to produce more black trolls, but they also mate with other types of trolls, although these unions do not produce black trolls.

BLACK TROLL
Large giant, chaotic evil

Armor Class 16 (natural armor)
Hit Points 94 (9d10 + 45)
Speed 30 ft.

STR	DEX	CON	INT	WIS	CHA
21 (+5)	12 (+1)	20 (+5)	11 (+0)	13 (+1)	7 (–2)

Skills Perception +4, Stealth +4
Damage Resistances bludgeoning, piercing, and slashing from nonmagical attacks
Damage Immunities fire
Senses darkvision 60 ft., passive Perception 14
Languages Common, Giant
Challenge 8 (3,900 XP)

Keen Smell. The troll has advantage on Wisdom (Perception) checks that rely on smell.
Fire Absorption. When the black troll is subjected to fire damage, it takes no damage and instead regains a number of hit points equal to the fire damage dealt. In addition, until the end of its next turn, the black troll deals an additional 3 (1d6) fire damage with each of its attacks.
Regeneration. The black troll regains 10 hit points at the start of its turn. If the troll takes cold damage, this trait doesn't function at the start of the troll's next turn. The troll dies only if it starts its turn with 0 hit points and doesn't regenerate.

ACTIONS

Multiattack. The black troll makes one Bite attack and two Claw attacks.
Bite. *Melee Weapon Attack:* +8 to hit, reach 5 ft., one creature. *Hit:* 8 (1d6 + 5) piercing damage.
Claw. *Melee Weapon Attack:* +8 to hit, reach 5 ft., one target. *Hit:* 12 (2d6 + 5) slashing damage.

Sea Troll

Large giant, chaotic evil

Armor Class 16 (natural armor)
Hit Points 94 (9d10 + 45)
Speed 30 ft., swim 30 ft.

STR	DEX	CON	INT	WIS	CHA
18 (+4)	14 (+2)	20 (+5)	7 (–2)	9 (–1)	5 (–3)

Skills Perception +2
Senses darkvision 60 ft., passive Perception 12
Languages Giant
Challenge 7 (2,900 XP)

Keen Hearing. The sea troll has advantage on Wisdom (Perception) checks that rely on hearing.
Regeneration. The sea troll regains 10 hit points at the start of its turn. If the troll takes acid or thunder damage, this trait doesn't function at the start of the troll's next turn. The troll dies only if it starts its turn with 0 hit points and doesn't regenerate.
Limited Amphibiousness. The sea troll can breathe air and water but begins to suffocate if not submerged in the sea at least once a day for one minute.

Actions

Multiattack. The troll makes one Piscine Mutation attack and two Claw attacks.
Claw. *Melee Weapon Attack:* +7 to hit, reach 5 ft., one target. *Hit:* 11 (2d6 + 4) slashing damage.
Piscine Mutations. The sea troll has one or more of the following attack options, provided it has the appropriate anatomy:
Bite. *Melee Weapon Attack:* +7 to hit, reach 5 ft., one target. *Hit:* 11 (2d6 + 4) piercing damage.
Poison Quills. *Melee Weapon Attack:* +7 to hit, reach 5 ft., one creature. *Hit:* 8 (1d8 + 4) poison damage, and the target must succeed on a DC 12 Constitution saving throw or be poisoned for one minute. The target can repeat the saving throw at the end of each of its turns, ending the effect on itself on a success.
Tentacle. *Melee Weapon Attack:* +7 to hit, reach 10 ft., one target. *Hit:* 8 (1d8 + 4) bludgeoning damage, and the target is grappled (escape DC 16) if it is a Medium or smaller creature.

Troll, Sea

The docks were aflame from a careless lantern thrown at the beasts that had climbed up the pier's pilings. Their forms stood out against the flames, and no two were the same. I saw quills rising like an urchin on some, tentacles waving on a few, and large pincers on others. They were taller than the sailors fleeing the burning ships, whom they snatched up and tossed into the water where other monsters swam. The dockworkers ran forward to stop them, but it was obvious that the docks were a lost cause. At least Muir answered my prayer that the creatures not find their way into town. — Pier Master Bastille Manten Granger, on the sea troll attack on Jah Sezar

Sea trolls live near the large bodies of water of the world. Due to mutations, sea trolls have become viable hunters on land and in the water. Those that have mostly piscine diets have even taken on some of the physical traits of their prey (see **Piscine Mutations** under **Actions**). Due to their extended time spent in the water, sea trolls have a heightened sense of hearing similar to echo location instead of smell. Their bodies are more resistant to fire as well. However, they are vulnerable to thunder damage, so much so that it arrests the regenerative properties of their flesh.

Troll Pony

It was an odd thing that answered the sea druid's underwater summons. The four creatures — ponies, she called them — had scales and powerful tails. But they were the ugliest things I'd ever seen. Like a boar and a moose mashed into one face. Three of us drank potions for the underwater ride, and Goleenda cast a spell she used frequently to dive beneath the ship to search for damage. But I have to admit the creatures were fast in the water, getting us to the underwater shipwreck in record time. — Delphira Enesi, on the successful search for The Steel Lady's Tears.

Troll ponies are not equines of any kind, but they do make tough and steady beasts of burden, or even mounts, much like ponies. While trolls would be more likely to eat a troll pony than domesticate it, the people of the coastal regions where troll ponies are native see them as troll-like on three counts. First, they are semi-aquatic, much like the local sea trolls. Second, their hides are so tough it is joked that a troll pony is as hard to hurt as a troll. Third, and perhaps most decisively, troll ponies, like trolls, have faces that make camels look elegant and personable.

Troll Pony

Large beast, unaligned

Armor Class 13 (natural)
Hit Points 45 (6d10 + 12)
Speed 60 ft., swim 60 ft.

STR	DEX	CON	INT	WIS	CHA
18 (+4)	13 (+1)	15 (+2)	2 (–4)	12 (+1)	5 (–3)

Skills Perception +3
Resistances slashing damage from nonmagical attacks
Senses passive Perception 13
Languages —
Challenge 1 (200 XP)

Semi-aquatic. A troll pony suffers no penalties in underwater movement or combat and can remain underwater for up to an hour without needing to surface for breath.

Actions

Multiattack. The troll pony makes one Ram attack, one Tusks attack, and two Claw attacks. Instead of the two Claw attacks, it can choose to make a single Tail Slap.
Ram. *Melee Weapon Attack:* +4 to hit, reach 5 ft., one target. *Hit:* 6 (1d4 + 4) bludgeoning damage.
Tusks. *Melee Weapon Attack:* +4 to hit, reach 5 ft., one target. *Hit:* 7 (1d6 + 4) slashing damage.
Claw. *Melee Weapon Attack:* +4 to hit, reach 5 ft., one target. *Hit:* 7 (1d6 + 4) slashing damage.
Tail Slap. *Melee Weapon Attack:* +4 to hit, reach 10 ft., one target. *Hit:* 13 (2d8 + 4) bludgeoning damage.

Training a Troll Pony

A troll pony raised from birth by humanoids can serve as a pack animal or, with proper training, bear a rider, even in combat, on land or sea. Wild-born troll ponies are not typically trainable, especially not for riding. Training a captive-bred troll pony as a combat mount takes six weeks of work followed by a successful DC 20 Wisdom (Animal Handling) check.

Troll ponies bond heavily to one rider at a time and behave poorly when ridden by unfamiliar people. During the first month with a new rider, all ride checks are made at disadvantage, and the new rider must be sure to ride the troll pony every day to establish a good relationship. Troll ponies also respond poorly to rough handling or abuse, requiring a balance of firm boundaries and gentle patience. Once a troll pony bonds to a new rider, however, it becomes a courageous and loyal companion, often compared to a large, ugly dog.

Well-bred troll pony "pups" are worth 700 gp apiece on the animal market, while a well-trained adult costs three times that at a minimum. Professional trainers charge 1,000 gp to rear or train a troll pony. Cheaper troll ponies may be available in small, coastal towns where they are native, but these are likely to be better suited for hauling than riding.

We made our way to the intersection of the Charcoal and Obsidian bridges, joining the throngs waiting to enter the City of Brass. A low chanting rumbled around us, and we turned to find a massive elephant stomping slowly toward us. It carried a host of visitors whose wealth allowed them to ride in style above the rabble crowding the bridge. The elephant's massive bronze tusks swung over our heads as it passed. I swear the elephant looked wiser and more intelligent than those it carried. — Menlo Top, describing the sights witnessed on his visit to the legendary City of Brass

Tusk lords are towering, intelligent elephants with charcoal skin and ruby red eyes. They have oversized and upward-curving bronze-colored tusks. The tusk lords are believed to hail from a world destroyed ages ago. Scholars say only a dozen of these creatures are left in all the realms of existence, and it is believed that all work on the Charcoal Bridge on the Plane of Molten Skies. Some claim they are the last hierophants of a now-destroyed god.

Tusk Lord
Gargantuan monstrosity, neutral

Armor Class 20
Hit Points 444 (24d20 + 192)
Speed 30 ft.

STR	DEX	CON	INT	WIS	CHA
30 (+10)	13 (+1)	27 (+8)	17 (+3)	22 (+6)	16 (+3)

Saving Throws Str +16, Con +14, Wis +12, Cha +9
Skills Arcana +9, History +9, Nature +9, Perception +12, Religion +9
Damage Resistances bludgeoning, piercing, and slashing from nonmagical attacks
Damage Immunities acid, cold, fire, lightning, poison, thunder
Condition Immunities charmed, frightened, poisoned
Senses darkvision 120 ft., passive Perception 22
Languages understands all but speaks only Tusk Lord
Challenge 19 (22,000 XP)

Immortal. The tusk lord does not need to breathe, eat, or sleep. It will not die of old age but may still be killed.

Improved Sense of Smell. The tusk lord has advantage on Perception checks that rely on scent.

Innate Spellcasting. The tusk lord's innate spellcasting ability is Wisdom (spell save DC 20, +12 to hit with spell attacks). It can innately cast the following spells, with no need for material components or concentration:

2/day each: *antimagic field, etherealness, globe of invulnerability*

Sealed Mind. The tusk lord is immune to mind-altering magic such as charm, compulsion, fear, illusion, or sleep.

Wish Granting. At its discretion, the tusk lord may grant the wish of a creature (as the *wish* spell). The tusk lord does so only if presented with a pleasing whale song. Magical reproductions of such a noise automatically qualify; otherwise, a creature must succeed on a DC 20 Charisma (Performance) check to create a reasonable facsimile by mundane means. The tusk lord may grant only one wish per creature.

Actions

Multiattack. The tusk lord makes one Gore attack and two Stomp attacks.

Gore. *Melee Weapon Attack:* +16 to hit, reach 15 ft., one creature. *Hit:* 37 (6d8 + 10) piercing damage.

Stomp. *Melee Weapon Attack:* +16 to hit, reach 15 ft., one creature. *Hit:* 32 (4d10 + 10) bludgeoning damage, and the target must succeed on a DC 20 Strength saving throw or be knocked prone.

Unmasked Priest of Tsathoggus

The masked priests dragged us into the greenstone chamber, lifting the ropes binding our hands over hooks attached to a long silver pole. They swung the pole with us attached out over the 20-foot-wide pit, and we looked down into the frog-filled swamp so out of place in this temple. Only when we saw the unmasked priest with his vaguely frog-like features did we understand the dreadful worshippers we had stumbled upon. — "Thistle" Grafter, after escaping the Cult of the Frog God near Tegel Manor

The unmasked priests of Tsathoggus openly revel in the deformities their worship of the loathsome Frog God cause on their mortal flesh. Their skin is often misshapen and deformed, vaguely frog-like, glazed over with an oozing film that drips down their scarred cheeks. Some have bulging eyes like a toad.

Unmasked Priest of Tsathoggus

Medium humanoid (human), chaotic evil

Armor Class 17 (*+1 scale mail*)
Hit Points 127 (17d8 + 51)
Speed 30 ft., swim 30 ft.

STR	DEX	CON	INT	WIS	CHA
16 (+3)	12 (+1)	16 (+3)	14 (+2)	18 (+4)	8 (–2)

Saving Throws Wis +8, Cha +2
Skills Medicine +8, Religion +6
Damage Resistances necrotic, psychic
Senses darkvision 60 ft., passive Perception 14
Languages Common, Tsathar
Challenge 10 (5,900 XP)

Special Equipment. The unmasked priest of Tsathoggus wears a set of green *+1 scale mail* and wields a black enameled *unholy mace* (see sidebar).
Amphibious. The unmasked priest can breathe air and water.
Fetid Blessing. Whenever the unmasked priest deals acid or poison damage, it ignores resistance to those damage types and deals an additional 7 (2d6) damage of the same type.
Spellcasting. The unmasked priest is a 12th-level spellcaster. Its spellcasting ability is Wisdom (spell save DC 15, +7 to hit with spell attacks). It has the following cleric spells prepared:

Cantrips (at will): *acid splash, guidance, mending, poison spray, thaumaturgy*
1st level (4 slots): *bane, inflict wounds, protection from evil and good, shield of faith*
2nd level (3 slots): *acid arrow, hold person, lesser restoration, spiritual weapon*
3rd level (3 slots): *caustic burst*, create food and water, dispel magic, tongue of the frog god**
4th level (3 slots): *blight, control water*
5th level (2 slots): *insect plague*
6th level (1 slot): *harm*
*see sidebar

Actions

Unholy Mace. Melee Weapon Attack: +8 to hit, reach 5 ft., one target. *Hit:* 7 (1d6 + 4) bludgeoning damage. If the target is good-aligned, it takes an additional 3 (1d6) poison damage.

Caustic Burst

3rd-level evocation
Casting Time: 1 action
Range: 60 feet
Components: V, S, M (an acid pitted ruby worth 5 gp)
Duration: Instantaneous
You launch a ball of viscous acid from your open hand which lands at a point you choose within range and then splashes in a 10-foot radius. Each creature in the area centered on that point must make a Dexterity saving throw. A target takes 6d4 acid damage on a failed saving throw, or half as much damage on a successful saving throw. If a target took acid damage, it takes an additional 3d4 acid damage at the start of its next turn.
At Higher Levels. When you cast this spell using a spell slot of 4th level or higher, the damage increases by 1d4 for each slot level above 3rd.

Tongue of the Frog God

3rd-level transmutation
Casting time: 1 action
Range: 15 feet
Duration: Concentration, up to 1 minute
This spell conjures a long, swollen tongue that grows from your mouth. This tongue can be used as a whip like appendage to grab objects and has a strength score equivalent to your own. The tongue may also be used to attack opponents. On a successful hit, the tongue inflicts 4d8 bludgeoning damage and the target is grappled. You may use a bonus action to increase the grapple to restrained. You are tied, by the tongue, to the target as long as it is grappled or restrained. If you have a target grappled or retrained by your tongue you may not speak or cast any spells that require a verbal component.

While you have a target grappled or restrained by your tongue, you may use a bonus action to squeeze it for 4d8 bludgeoning damage.

The tongue has your AC and can be severed if it suffers damage equal to 1/10th your maximum hit points. Damage to the tongue does not count against your own hit points. If the tongue is destroyed, it dissolves into nothing and your tongue returns to normal.

Unholy Mace

Weapon (mace), uncommon (requires attunement)
This black-iron mace seems to glow with a very dim, sickly green light, and its head is adorned with curved, almost thorn-like spikes. You have a +1 bonus to attack and damage rolls made with the *unholy mace*. In addition, if you strike a good-aligned creature, you deal an additional 1d6 poison damage.

VARGOUILLE

The vault was filled with unnamable horrors. Eman fell against the wall, trying to keep down the greasy mutton from that roadside inn. He didn't succeed. Jurise was made of sterner stuff and pushed past the vomiting thief, but even she made a face at the heads sitting on the stone ledges around us. "What madness is this?" she whispered, drawing her blade just to have it ready. It's a good thing she did. From among the rotting heads of hundreds of beings rose a flock of creatures with the faces of demons. They flew on bat wings as they swept over us. — Excerpt from the long-winded description Symmes the Loquacious gave of evil-winged fiends released on the countryside

A vargouille is a hideous, disgusting, and vile creature that is little more than a severed head with bat wings. The creature is slightly larger than a human head with a foot-long wingspan. These creatures from the Abyss flap through the air in search of prey to infect with potent diseases that perpetuate their abominable kind. They delight in causing pain and live to bestow a demonic curse on their victims. Those so cursed develop demonic features, and soon die as their head rips itself away from their body and unfurls its own bat wings.

VARGOUILLE

Tiny fiend, chaotic evil

Armor Class 12 (natural armor)
Hit Points 13 (3d4 + 6)
Speed 5 ft., 30 ft.

STR	DEX	CON	INT	WIS	CHA
6 (+0)	14 (+2)	14 (+2)	4 (–3)	7 (–2)	2 (–4)

Damage Resistances cold, fire, lightning
Damage Immunities poison
Condition Immunities poisoned
Senses darkvision 60 ft., passive Perception 8
Languages understands Abyssal and Infernal, and any languages it new before becoming a fiend, but is unable to speak
Challenge 1 (200 XP)

ACTIONS

Bite. *Melee Weapon Attack:* +4 to hit, reach 5 ft., one target. *Hit:* 5 (1d6 + 2) piercing damage plus 10 (3d6) poison damage.
Demon's Kiss. If an incapacitated target is within five feet of the vargouille, the vargouille can kiss that creature, which must succeed on a DC 12 Charisma saving throw or become cursed. The cursed target loses 1 point of Charisma at the end of each hour, as its facial features take on a fiendish aspect. The curse is held at bay by direct sunlight or the *daylight* spell. Once the cursed target's Charisma drops to 2, it suffers an excruciating, violent death as its head tears away from its body to become a new vargouille. The curse can be ended only by a *remove curse* or *greater restoration* spell. The physical changes are undone when the curse ends through these means.
Stunning Shriek. The vargouille unleashes a piercing shriek. Creatures within 30 feet of the vargouille that hear the shriek must succeed on a DC 12 Wisdom saving throw or be frightened and stunned until the end of the vargouille's next turn. While frightened in this way, a target is stunned. If the creature's saving throw is successful, then it is immune to the vargouille's shrieks for the next hour.

WAKANDAGI

If ye plan on rowin' across Lake Aur and pannin' for gold, be wary when the water parts and breaks. It inn't the lake, but the things in the lake. They'll smash yer boat with their horns, then feast on yer bones when they drag you under. You might see their heads, like stags they are, but that's just to fool ye. They are serpents, and mean ones at that. I don't think they care 'bout the gold in the lake, but they know it brings fools like ye lookin' fer it. — Jorgan "Old Gab" Crostover, overseer of the locks on the River of Gold

The fierce wakandagi resembles an eel or serpent but with the head and antlers of a stag. Known for their fierce territoriality, they are held sacred by many wilderness-dwelling folk and are considered guardians of sacred spots. Travelers who defend themselves against attacks by the wakandagi may find themselves in trouble with local priests and their communities.

Wakandagi dwell in streams and lakes and are known to aggressively defend their territory, often tearing holes in the bottom of boats with their antlers, then attacking as their victims splash helplessly in the water. The males become particularly violent during rutting season in the spring.

WAKANDAGI

Large beast, unaligned

Armor Class 16
Hit Points 102 (12d10 + 36)
Speed 20 ft., swim 40 ft.

STR	DEX	CON	INT	WIS	CHA
16 (+3)	16 (+3)	16 (+3)	1 (–5)	13 (+1)	4 (–3)

Skills Perception +5
Senses passive Perception 15
Challenge 3 (700 XP)

Amphibious. Wakandagi can breathe both air and water.
Keen Smell. The wakandagi has advantage on Wisdom (Perception) checks that rely on smell.
Magic Resistance. The wakandagi has advantage on saving throws against spells and other magical effects.

ACTIONS

Bite. *Melee Weapon Attack:* +6 to hit, reach 10 ft., one target. *Hit:* 14 (3d6 + 4) piercing damage.
Gore. *Melee Weapon Attack:* +6 to hit, reach 5 ft., one target. *Hit:* 13 (2d8 + 4) piercing damage.

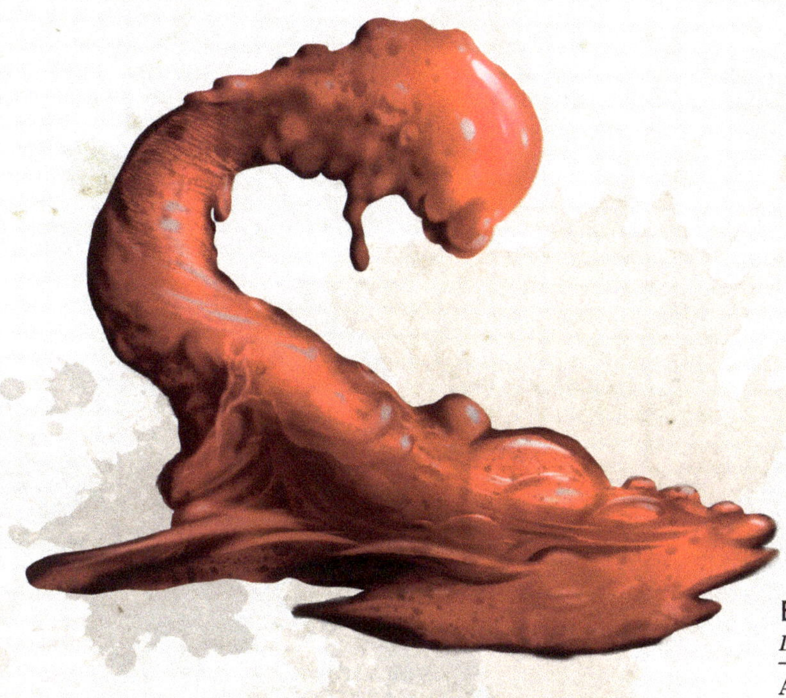

Weird, Blood

The fountain looked entirely innocent, with angel-faced cherubs holding lotuses as they stood among playful dolphins. How deceiving! Kirtsu flipped the stone switch on the edge of the fountain, and the pipes hidden within gurgled and groaned … and torrents of dark blood began to spurt from the idyllic imagery to rapidly fill the bowl. Kirtsu stepped back, but it was too late. A serpent of blood rose from the basin and grabbed the halfling around the waist. He was lifted up and vanished into the pool with a splash. — Zuhari Glass, on the discovery of the Blood Cult of Tsathar in Harwood Forest

Blood weirds are virtually unknown and rarely encountered unless summoned to the Material Plane. Before summoning the weird, casters often fill a large basin or font with the blood of slain foes or captives. Blood weirds wait patiently in their pool for potential prey. When a foe wanders too close, the weird lashes out and wraps itself around the opponent.

Blood Weird

Large elemental, chaotic evil

Armor Class 16 (natural armor)
Hit Points 105 (14d10 + 28)
Speed 0 ft., swim 60 ft.

STR	DEX	CON	INT	WIS	CHA
18 (+4)	16 (+3)	15 (+2)	11 (+0)	10 (+0)	10 (+0)

Saving Throws Con +5
Skills Perception +6, Stealth +9
Damage Resistances bludgeoning; bludgeoning, piercing, and slashing from nonmagical attacks
Damage Immunities poison
Condition Immunities exhaustion, grappled, paralyzed, poisoned, prone, restrained, unconscious
Senses blindsight 30 ft., passive Perception 16
Languages Abyssal, Common
Challenge 8 (3,900 XP)

Invisible in Blood. The blood weird is invisible while fully immersed in blood.

Blood Bound. The blood weird dies if it spends more than two consecutive rounds outside a large body of blood.

Extinguish. When the blood weird successfully hits a Medium or smaller target holding a torch, exposed lantern, or other nonmagical source of fire with its Constrict attack, that fire source is extinguished.

Regeneration. The blood weird regains 10 hit points at the start of its turn if it has at least 1 hit point and is at least partially immersed in blood. If the blood weird takes fire damage, this trait doesn't function at the start of the blood weird's next turn. The blood weird dies only if it starts its turn with 0 hit points and doesn't regenerate.

Actions

Multiattack. The blood weird makes one Constrict attack and uses Siphon Blood.

Constrict. *Melee Weapon Attack:* +7 to hit, reach 10 ft., one target. *Hit:* 18 (4d6 + 4) bludgeoning damage. If the target is Medium or smaller, it is grappled (escape DC 16) and pulled five feet toward the blood weird. Until this grapple ends, the target is restrained, the blood weird tries to drown it, and the blood weird can't grapple another target.

Siphon Blood. A grappled creature must make a DC 16 Constitution saving throw. On a failure, it takes 14 (4d6) necrotic damage, and the blood weird regains hit points equal to half the amount of necrotic damage dealt.

WEIRD, FUNGUS

Mama Alfose had let us stay at her cottage while we were traveling to the Crescent City. Londru thought it would be a nice thing if we did a few chores around the place before we headed out, and as usual he went overboard. While the rest of us were chopping wood and cleaning out the hog pens, he went to clear out some brush. Turned out that brush was alive, for a long snake thing made of fungi and plants sprang out and attacked. We came running and jumped into the fight. It was tough — you don't wear your armor while mucking hogs, after all — but in the end we put it down. Damn thing wasn't dead dead, though, for it rose back up before we left. Our wizard Rangi burned it out. I hope that did the trick. — Ultär son of Ultär, adventurer

Fungus weirds are masses of fungi, mosses, and plants from other planes. They have a degree of sentience and can be communicated with, though their thought process, wants, and needs are truly alien. At rest, the fungus weird looks like a pile of brambles, downed limbs, fungi, and mosses. When roused, it can extend a 10-foot-long serpentine body or stalk and attack with surprising speed. Their spores can induce sleep, leaving a victim to lie in slumber while the weird decides if it is going to eat it or not.

FUNGUS WEIRD

Large plant, unaligned

Armor Class 15 (natural armor)
Hit Points 60 (8d10 + 16)
Speed 30 ft.

STR	DEX	CON	INT	WIS	CHA
17 (+3)	17 (+3)	14 (+2)	10 (+0)	12 (+1)	13 (+1)

Skills Perception +5, Stealth +5
Damage Resistances acid; bludgeoning, piercing, and slashing from nonmagical attacks
Damage Immunities poison
Condition Immunities exhaustion, grappled, paralyzed, poisoned, restrained, prone, unconscious
Senses darkvision 60 ft., passive Perception 15
Languages —
Challenge 3 (700 XP)

Ambusher. In the first round of combat, the fungus weird has advantage on attack rolls against any creature it has surprised.
Camouflage. The fungus weird has advantage on Dexterity (Stealth) checks it makes while in its pool.
Fungus Bound. A fungus weird's "pool" is not a pool at all, but an entanglement of leaves, branches, mosses, fungi, and plants. The fungus weird dies if it leaves this area or if the area is destroyed.
A creature that enters the fungus weird's pool must succeed on a DC 13 Strength saving throw or be restrained by the entangling plants. A creature restrained by the plants can use its action to make a DC 13 Strength check, freeing itself on a success.
Rejuvenation. A destroyed fungus weird reforms in 24 hours if its pool is still intact, regaining all its hit points and becoming active again.
Surprise Attack. If the fungus weird surprises a creature and hits it with an attack during the first round of combat, the target takes an extra 14 (4d6) damage from the attack.

ACTIONS

Bite. *Melee Weapon Attack:* +5 to hit, reach 5 ft., one target. *Hit:* 16 (3d8 + 3) piercing damage, and the target is grappled (escape DC 13). Until this grapple ends, the target is restrained, and the fungus weird can't grapple another target.
Sleep Spores. The fungus weird ejects spores at one creature it can see within five feet of it. The target must succeed on a DC 13 Constitution saving throw or be poisoned for one minute. The poisoned creature is incapacitated as it slumbers. The target can repeat the saving throw at the end of each of its turns, ending the effect on itself on a success.

WEREDACTYL

Lunscray led our horses into the narrow canyon, following the rocky path he promised would get us through a gap in the Kulgera Ridge. We were making good time when one of the scouts noticed the six obese men and women sitting on a high ledge watching us. How they had climbed to that height was inconceivable. They laughed among themselves and pointed down at our caravan. Someone screamed when one of them leaped from the cliff, falling right at us. That fat blob of a man sprouted wings as he fell and gave a shriek as he became an angry, birdlike creature. The others matched the shriek as they too launched off the cliff. — Vizzin Shaw, exploring the Seething Jungle for a route across the Kulgera Ridge

Weredactyls in their human form are fat, slouching humanoids with protruding faces, low foreheads, and sagittal crests. Their were-form is a pterodactyl with long human fingers at the wing-joint and human eyes. In hybrid form, their arms and legs are more developed, and their wings and beaks are small, too small to enable flight in the case of the wings. They are naturally stupid even in human form, which many skelzis exploit to gain loyal (albeit dimwitted) servants.

WEREDACTYL

Medium humanoid (shapechanger), chaotic evil

Armor Class 12
Hit Points 44 (8d8 + 8)
Speed 30 ft. (human or hybrid form); 10 ft., 50 ft. flying (pterodactyl form)

STR	DEX	CON	INT	WIS	CHA
16 (+3)	15 (+2)	12 (+1)	7 (−2)	10 (+0)	8 (−1)

Damage Immunity bludgeoning, piercing, and slashing damage from nonmagical attacks that aren't silver
Senses darkvision 60 ft., passive Perception 10
Languages Common, Skelzi
Challenge 2 (450 XP)

Shapechanger. The weredactyl can use its action to polymorph into a pterodactyl-humanoid hybrid or into a pterodactyl, or back into its true form, which is humanoid. Its statistics are the same in each form. Any equipment it is wearing or carrying isn't transformed. It reverts to its true form if it dies.

ACTIONS

Multiattack. The weredactyl makes two melee attacks or two ranged attacks.
Peck (pterodactyl or hybrid form only). *Melee Weapon Attack:* +5 to hit, reach 5 ft., one target. *Hit:* 6 (1d6 + 3) piercing damage.
Claw (hybrid form only). *Melee Weapon Attack:* +5 to hit, reach 5 ft., one target. *Hit:* 6 (1d6 + 3) slashing damage. If two Claw attacks hit the same target on the weredactyl's turn, the target must make a successful DC 12 Dexterity saving throw or be grappled (escape DC 11).
Handaxe (human or hybrid form only). *Melee or Ranged Weapon Attack:* +5 to hit, reach 5 ft. or range 20/60 ft., one target. *Hit:* 6 (1d6 + 3) slashing damage.

Witch Tree

We were still miles from town when the rain caught up to us, a real gully washer that soaked us to our skin. We found a grove of willow trees and happily ducked under their drooping branches. The impromptu shelter was still wet, but it kept the worst of the rain off us. Little did we know we'd walked willingly into the lion's den. We had just spread our blankets to rest when the tree reached down grabbed Hanslon. I looked up from the ground to find a bark-skinned woman formed from the tree trunk looking back at me. — Phineous G. Babblebrook, halfling explorer

From a distance, a witch tree is almost indistinguishable from a normal willow. Up close, however, a witch tree appears to be a tall, beautiful woman formed from a willow tree. The trees fronds form the woman's hair and fingers, while the branches and trunk create her arms and torso. The willow's roots form the woman's legs and feet. The witch tree's skin is thick and dark, resembling the bark of a tree. Witch trees gain nutrients from the soil where they take root, but they have a particular fondness for living flesh, particularly that of gnomes and orcs. As such, groves of these creatures can be found near such settlements.

Witch Tree

Huge plant, chaotic evil

Armor Class 16 (natural armor)
Hit Points 94 (9d12 + 36)
Speed 20 ft.

STR	DEX	CON	INT	WIS	CHA
21 (+5)	10 (+0)	19 (+4)	7 (−2)	12 (+1)	16 (+3)

Skills Perception +4
Damage Vulnerabilities fire
Damage Resistances cold; bludgeoning, piercing, and slashing from nonmagical attacks
Damage Immunities acid
Condition Immunities charmed, exhaustion, frightened
Senses darkvision 60 ft., tremorsense 60 ft., passive Perception 14
Languages Abyssal, Common, Goblin, Sylvan
Challenge 8 (3,900 XP)

False Appearance. As long as the witch tree remains motionless, it is indistinguishable from a normal willow tree.
Innate Spellcasting. The witch tree's innate spellcasting ability is Constitution (spell save DC 14). It can cast the following spells, requiring no material components:
5/day: *enthrall*
1/day: *dominate monster*
Tendrils. The witch tree's tendrils can be cut, have an Armor Class of 15, 10 hit points, immunity to poison and psychic damage, and the witch tree's damage vulnerabilities, resistances, and other immunities. Cutting a creature free of the tendrils deals no damage to the witch tree. The tendrils can also be broken if a creature takes an action and succeeds on a DC 17 Strength check.

Actions

Multiattack. The witch tree uses its Constrict ability and makes four Tendril attacks.
Tendril. Melee Weapon Attack: +8 to hit, reach 15 ft., one target. *Hit:* 15 (3d6 + 5) bludgeoning damage and the target is grappled (escape DC 16). A grappled creature is restrained.
Constrict. All grappled creatures must make a DC 16 Constitution saving throw, taking 15 (3d6 + 5) bludgeoning damage, or half as much damage on a successful saving throw.

Wolf, Shadow

Longtooth led us into the box canyon, that old hound's nose to the ground as he tracked the scent of the deer. It was our dinner, but we should have just let it go. But that old dog found that deer all right ... or at least what was left of it. The animal was torn to shreds on the ground, its blood still warm where it had fallen. Porthos drew his blade, but at what? Nothing was in that canyon with us. That's when a wolf howled — the signal to attack — and shadowy shapes squeezed out of the narrowest of gaps in the rocks around us. I still blame that dog for getting us into that mess.
— Crymm "One Arm" Gloomreaver, remembering the day he lost his sword arm

Shadow wolves are nocturnal hunters that hate all living creatures. Their eyes flash with a crimson fire when prey is sighted. Shadow wolves prefer to attack from ambush, using the shadows and darkness to their advantage. When prey wanders nearby, a shadow wolf leaps to the attack. A shadow wolf pack leads its prey into an ambush and then strikes when opponents are completely unaware.

Shadow Wolf

Medium undead, chaotic evil

Armor Class 14
Hit Points 32 (5d8 + 10)
Speed 50 ft.

STR	DEX	CON	INT	WIS	CHA
8 (−1)	18 (+4)	14 (+2)	6 (−2)	10 (+0)	8 (−1)

Skills Stealth +6
Damage Vulnerabilities radiant
Damage Resistances acid, cold, fire, lightning, thunder; bludgeoning, piercing, and slashing from nonmagical attacks
Damage Immunities necrotic, poison
Condition Immunities exhaustion, frightened, grappled, paralyzed, petrified, poisoned, prone, restrained
Senses darkvision 60 ft., passive Perception 10
Languages —
Challenge 1 (200 XP)

Amorphous. The shadow wolf can move through a space as narrow as one inch wide without squeezing.
Shadow Stealth. While in dim light or darkness, the shadow wolf can take the Hide action as a bonus action. Its stealth bonus is also improved to +8.
Sunlight Weakness. While in sunlight, the shadow wolf has disadvantage on attack rolls, ability checks, and saving throws.

Actions

Strength Drain. *Melee Weapon Attack:* +6 to hit, reach 5 ft., one creature. *Hit:* 13 (2d8 + 4) necrotic damage, and the target's Strength score is reduced by 1d4. The target dies if this reduces its Strength to 0. Otherwise, the reduction lasts until the target finishes a short or long rest. If the target is a creature, it must also succeed on a DC 12 Strength saving throw or be knocked prone.
If a non-evil humanoid dies from this attack, a new shadow rises from the corpse 1d4 hours later.
Bay (recharge 5–6). The shadow wolf lets out a fearful howl. All creatures within 40 feet who hear it must succeed on a DC 12 Wisdom saving throw or become frightened for one minute. A frightened creature may repeat the saving throw at the end of each of its turns, ending the effect on itself on a success.

Woodwose

We ignored the dryad's warnings and proceeded deeper into the forest, laughing the whole time at the thought that we, the Five from Kyrgos, would fear some story of a mighty tree man who haunts the shadowed depths. We learned our lesson soon enough, for we came upon a crooked old man with skin like moss-covered bark, a beard of leaves, and a wicked glint in the gnarled knots he called eyes. At first we sought to parley; many creatures of the forest dark will talk if approached with honor and respect. Not this one, for he let out a sound like wind whistling through dead limbs and leapt to attack. Many Fists' warclub just bounced off the man, and our attacks were as useless as slicing at a tree bole. The wood man grew spines along his arms and slashed at us, all the while calling upon the powers of the forest to bring down thorny vines and call forth hungry bears. — Sir Cedric of Reme, knight errant

The woodwose, or green men, are wicked male counterparts of the dryad. Guardians and protectors of forests and woodlands, woodwose have a cruel streak, feeling it better to bury an intruder among the trees than to ever let them leave their forested sanctuaries. Due to their malign nature, woodwoses do not associate with dryads, most sprites, or other benign woodland creatures. They do however sometimes form bonds and alliances with other evil fey creatures (such as quicklings). The woodwose stands five feet tall and weighs about 150 pounds. Its skin is dark brown and rough, and course to the touch. Its hair is dark greenish-brown. A woodwose's eyes are deep chestnut brown.

Woodwose

Medium fey, neutral evil

Armor Class 16 (natural armor)
Hit Points 150 (20d8 + 60)
Speed 30 ft.

STR	DEX	CON	INT	WIS	CHA
17 (+3)	16 (+3)	18 (+4)	13 (+1)	16 (+3)	18 (+4)

Saving Throws Con +8, Wis +7
Skills Nature +7, Stealth +7
Damage Vulnerabilities fire
Damage Resistances bludgeoning, piercing, and slashing damage from nonmagical attacks
Senses darkvision 60 ft., passive Perception 13
Languages Common, Sylvan
Challenge 10 (5,900 XP)

Innate Spellcasting. The woodwose's innate spellcasting ability is Wisdom (spell save DC 15, +7 to hit with spell attacks). It can cast the following spells, requiring no material components:
At will: *entangle, pass without trace, shillelagh, speak with plants*

Plant Passivism. Plant creatures will not willingly attack the woodwose. They can be forced to do so through magical or other means. If the woodwose or its allies attack a plant creature, the effect is broken until the woodwose completes a long rest.

Plant Sense. The woodwose can sense any creature within 60 feet that is in contact with vegetation.

Spellcasting. The woodwose is a 9th-level spellcaster. Its spellcasting ability is Wisdom (spell save DC 15, +7 to hit with spell attacks). It has the following spells prepared:
Cantrips (at will): *detect magic, guidance, resistance*
1st level (4 slots): *cure wounds, faerie fire, longstrider, thunder wave*
2nd level (3 slots): *gust of wind, locate animals and plants, moonbeam*
3rd Level (3 slots): *call lightning, dispel magic, plant growth*
4th Level (3 slots): *dominate beast, giant insect, ice storm*
4th Level (1 slot): *insect plague*

Wood Immunity. A woodwose is unaffected by weapons made of wood or spells that have primarily a wooden component. Weapons that have damaging parts that are primarily metal (such as arrows or spears) affect the woodwose normally.

Actions

Multiattack. The creature makes one Club attack and one Punch attack.

Club. *Melee Weapon Attack:* +7 to hit, reach 5 ft., one target. *Hit:* 21 (4d8 + 3) bludgeoning damage.

Punch. *Melee Weapon Attack:* +7 to hit, reach 5 ft., one target. *Hit:* 12 (2d8 + 3) bludgeoning damage.

ZOMBIE, AQUEOUS

Caulfield cast the net over the first dead thing as it clambered onto the ship, pinning it to the deck. Tree melted the next one with a well-placed bolt of flame to the face. That left the last one to me, and it was a gruesome ordeal. My blade cut through its guts with ease, releasing a gusher of saltwater and blood. I slipped in the gore, and that was a good thing, as the zombie spewed a spray of salt from its mouth that tore the wood off the main mast. — Pollax, traveling aboard the Ocean's Countess

Aqueous zombies are the remains of victims sacrificed to the sea and the gods of the deep. The ritual to create them is quite gruesome and involves stuffing the still-living sacrifice with dried sea salt and blood until their stomach bursts, at which point they are drowned.

AQUEOUS ZOMBIE

Medium undead, neutral evil

Armor Class 9
Hit Points 30 (4d8 + 12)
Speed 20 ft., swim 20 ft.

STR	DEX	CON	INT	WIS	CHA
13 (+1)	8 (−1)	16 (+3)	3 (−4)	6 (−2)	5 (−3)

Saving Throws Wis +0
Damage Immunities poison
Condition Immunities Exhaustion, Poisoned
Senses darkvision 60 ft., passive Perception 8
Languages understands the languages it knew in life but can't speak
Challenge 1/2 (100 XP)

Undead Fortitude. If damage reduces the aqueous zombie to 0 hit points, it must make a Constitution saving throw with a DC of 5 + the damage taken, unless the damage is radiant or from a critical hit. On a success, the aqueous zombie drops to 1 hit point instead.

ACTIONS

Multiattack. The aqueous zombie makes two Slam attacks.
Slam. *Melee Weapon Attack:* +3 to hit, reach 5 ft., one creature. *Hit:* 4 (1d6 + 1) slashing damage.
Salt Spray (recharge 5–6). The aqueous zombie ejects a salt spray in a 10-foot line that is five feet wide. Each creature in that line must make a DC 13 Dexterity saving throw, taking 7 (2d6) bludgeoning damage, or half as much damage on a successful one.

ZOMBIE, BRAMBLE

We found all the servants dead in the brambles out front of the manor house, a wall of bodies tangled in the vines. Most were shriveled corpses wasting to nothing in the blazing sun. The vines themselves whipped and thrashed as we tried to retrieve the corpses. In the end, we set the mass on fire to end the horror. The blaze drew the royal family from their home. Or what was left of them. Vines wrapped tightly around their bodies, the thorns digging into their dead flesh. They raised their red claws as they advanced. — Report delivered to Sir Rhonic Ort by the knights of Albor Broce sent to investigate Harlow Manor outside the capital city

A bramble zombie is what happens when a medium creature addicted to bramble berries dies. Bramble zombies retain no personality, memory, or abilities from their previous existence. They mindlessly defend the **bramble** (see monster entry) that created them and have no other purposes or goals. Other than the possible red thorn-claws, bramble zombies look like dead bodies, usually 10–15 times as decomposed as they should be compared to when they died. Bramble zombies never smell bad, however, and their decomposition process is dry and dusty, as if they're turning directly into soil while skipping the stages in between. Since they spend so much time sitting still near the quick-growing bramble, older bramble zombies often have bramble vines growing all over or through themselves.

BRAMBLE ZOMBIE

Medium undead, neutral

Armor Class 17 (natural armor)
Hit Points 207 (18d8 + 126)
Speed 15 ft.

STR	DEX	CON	INT	WIS	CHA
22 (+6)	6 (−2)	24 (+7)	5 (−3)	10 (+0)	2 (−4)

Saving Throws Str +10, Con +11
Damage Vulnerabilities bludgeoning
Damage Immunities poison, psychic
Condition Immunities charmed, frightened, poisoned, stunned, unconscious
Senses tremorsense 120 ft., passive Perception 10
Languages —
Challenge 12 (8,400)

Loyal to the Bramble. A bramble zombie is incapable of actions contrary to the well-being of the bramble that created it. It will die before causing harm or allowing harm to befall its bramble.
Temporary. Bramble zombies decay much more quickly than ordinary corpses. After a year of service, they crumble to a soil-like dust. If at all possible, bramble zombies make sure to crumble near the roots of their bramble, to nourish it with their remains. Bramble zombies also die if their bramble dies.

ACTIONS

Multiattack. The bramble zombie makes one Bite attack and two Claw attacks.
Bite. *Melee Weapon Attack:* +10 to hit, reach 5 ft., one target. *Hit:* 10 (1d8 + 6) piercing damage + 3d6 poison damage.
Claw. *Melee Weapon Attack:* +10 to hit, reach 5 ft., one target. *Hit:* 8 (1d4 + 6) slashing damage plus 5 (2d4) poison damage.

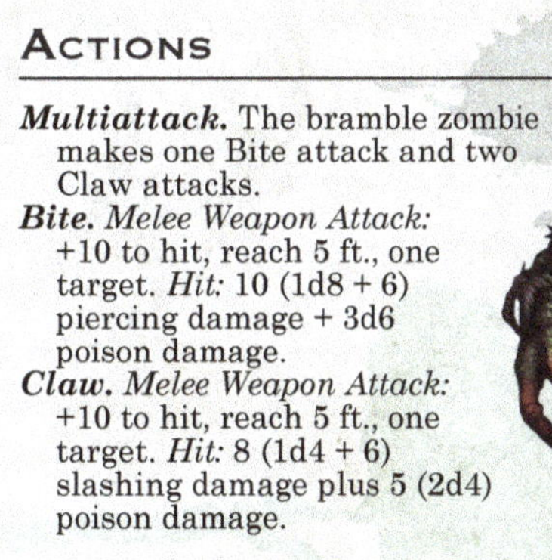

Zombie, Carcharodon

As we crossed the Sea of the Dead, we fought off the many horrors spawned by that cursed place. Bloated zombies clambered aboard, undead gulls stripped the flesh from the unwary, and even the weevils in our biscuits animated and attacked. By far the worst were the undead sharks, a massive Carcharodon foremost among them. It came from below, savaging our hull and shaking the ship like an ape going after fruit. — Captain Elisa Bounapert of the Wastrel's Daughter

Zombie carcharodons are giant undead sharks that roam the seas, looking to sate their never-ending hunger on the ships and sailors of the world. Schools of normal sharks may be found swimming alongside their larger zombie brethren. They often fall victim to the frenzied thrashing of the undead carcharodon when it tastes blood in the water.

Carcharodon Zombie
Gargantuan undead, neutral evil

Armor Class 13 (natural armor)
Hit Points 332 (19d20 + 133)
Speed 0 ft., swim 60 ft.

STR	DEX	CON	INT	WIS	CHA
30 (+10)	6 (−2)	24 (+7)	1 (−5)	3 (−4)	5 (−3)

Damage Immunities poison
Condition Immunities exhaustion, poisoned
Senses blindsight 60 ft., passive Perception 6
Languages —
Challenge 18 (20,000 XP)

Blood Frenzy. The carcharodon zombie has advantage on melee attack rolls against any creature that doesn't have all its hit points.

Turn Resistance. The carcharodon zombie has advantage on saving throws against any effect that turns undead.

Undead Fortitude. If damage reduces the carcharodon zombie to 0 hit points, it must make a Constitution saving throw with a DC of 5 + the damage taken, unless the damage is radiant or from a critical hit. On a success, the carcharodon zombie drops to 1 hit points instead.

Actions

Multiattack. The carcharodon zombie makes two Bite attacks.

Bite. *Melee Weapon Attack:* +10 to hit, reach 5ft., one target. *Hit:* 22 (3d10 + 6) piercing damage.

Zombie, Goblin

I've seen cheap armies before. For instance, the Star Kings cut corners by handing out pikes to peasants, while the overlord of Kaff used cut-rate mercs who cut and run. But zombie goblins? This Everik "the Dark Lord" was scraping the bottom of the barrel here. Even so, the little buggers kept coming and coming; our arms grew tired from slaying and the reaper started to call its horn long before we were through the last of them. — Big Joanne, mercenary

Pound for pound, zombie goblins might be the least effective zombies, but necromancers looking to cut costs or those who lack access to large numbers of human zombies often choose this route. Goblin shamans who work with the materials they have often have large numbers of zombie goblin servants. Either way, they are weak individually but dangerous in greater numbers. Even a mediocre wannabe dread lord can bring dozens of the things to battle.

Goblin Zombie

Small undead, neutral evil

Armor Class 11 (leather armor)
Hit Points 13 (3d6 + 3)
Speed 15 ft.

STR	DEX	CON	INT	WIS	CHA
13 (+1)	10 (+0)	12 (+1)	3 (–4)	6 (–2)	5 (–3)

Saves Wis +0
Damage Immunities poison
Condition Immunities poisoned
Senses darkvision 60 ft., passive Perception 8
Languages can't speak but understands the languages it knew in life
Challenge 1/4 (50 XP)

Undead Fortitude. If damage reduces the zombie goblin to 0 hit points, it must make a Constitution saving throw with a DC of 5 + the damage taken, unless the damage is radiant or from a critical hit. On a success, the zombie goblin drops to 1 hit point instead.

Actions

Bite. *Melee Weapon Attack:* +3 to hit, reach 5 ft., one target. *Hit:* 4 (1d6 + 1) piercing damage.

Zombie, Gug

Can a gug even be zombified? That was the question we were throwing around that evening as we sipped ales down at the Sudden Happenstance. Well, as it turned out, Hille's master had a fresh gug corpse and we were just drunk enough to think of it as possible, but not so drunk as to not be able to do it. We did and regretted it. True, it lacked most of the fearsome defenses that a gug has, but it still had four arms and a gaping maw that could swallow a deer, or in this case, a Hille. — Päuk, apprentice mage.

While its flesh is not of this word, a gug is certainly flesh and blood enough to die, and if it can die, it can be animated as undead. The zombie gug is even more horrific than it was in life, with its flesh rotting in long strips that seem to decay into nothingness as they break off from the body, its eyes slack and staring, its four limbs moving with terrible slowness yet incredible strength. Zombie gugs are sometimes created when gugs are summoned to this realm and then left to guard an area for so long that even their alien bodies wither and die, yet they remain on guard for eons to come.

Gug Zombie

Large undead, neutral evil

Armor Class 17 (natural armor)
Hit Points 190 (20d10 + 80)
Speed 40 ft.

STR	DEX	CON	INT	WIS	CHA
17 (+3)	18 (+4)	19 (+4)	11 (+0)	16 (+3)	11 (+0)

Saving Throws Wis +7
Skills Athletics +11, Acrobatics +12, Perception +7, Stealth +8, Survival +7
Damage Immunities poison
Condition Immunities poisoned
Senses darkvision 60 ft., passive Perception 17
Languages understands Undercommon but can't speak
Challenge 10 (5,900 XP)

Compression. A gug can contort and distend its bodies in unnatural ways, allowing them to fit through any space large enough for a Small creature to fit without squeezing, and can move through any space large enough for a Tiny creature, but moves at a speed of five feet while doing so.

Undead Fortitude. If damage reduces the zombie gug to 0 hit points, it must make a Constitution saving throw with a DC of 5 + the damage taken, unless the damage is radiant or from a critical hit. On a success, the zombie drops to 1 hit point instead.

Actions

Multiattack. The gug makes one Bite attack and two Claw attacks.
Bite. *Melee Weapon Attack:* +7 to hit, reach 5 ft., one target. *Hit:* 14 (2d10 + 3) piercing damage.
Claw. *Melee Weapon Attack:* +7 to hit, reach 15 ft., one target. *Hit:* 24 (6d6 + 3) slashing damage.

Zombie, Juju

Helmgat had a bodyguard, a cloaked figure who stood menacingly behind him at all times and glared from the depths of a hood so deep we couldn't make out anything save for two red eyes. Nasty work, but when you're desperate you take the jobs you can find. In the end, Helmgat tried to stiff us. When we protested, his bodyguard threw off its cloak to reveal a rotting corpse. No zombie moved like that, smooth with the motions of a skilled warrior, or fought with such intelligence and cunning. As we closed in, it knocked over a flagon of oil onto the charcoal fireplace in the center of the table and hustled itself and its charge out the back. — Tara the Wise, adventurer

Juju zombies retain memories and talents they had in life, and some even retain their names and personalities. They are most often created by dark rituals but can also be accidently animated when a corpse is slain by powerful necromantic magic. Self-willed, they make difficult undead servants, for their loyalty must be earned, not simply commanded. However, their intelligence and unique skill sets make them terrible foes, and thus excellent bodyguards and lieutenants.

Juju Zombie

Medium undead, neutral evil

Armor Class 16 (chain mail)
Hit Points 39 (6d8 + 12)
Speed 30 ft.

STR	DEX	CON	INT	WIS	CHA
20 (+5)	16 (+3)	15 (+2)	4 (−3)	10 (+0)	14 (+2)

Skills Acrobatics +7, Athletics +9
Damage Resistances fire
Damage Immunities cold, lightning, poison
Condition Immunities exhaustion, poisoned
Senses darkvision 60 ft., passive Perception 10
Languages understands the languages it knew in life but can't speak
Challenge 3 (700 XP)

Undead Fortitude. If damage reduces the zombie to 0 hit points, it must make a Constitution saving throw with a DC of 5 + the damage taken, unless the damage is radiant or from a critical hit. On a success, the zombie drops to 1 hit point instead.
Magic Resistance. The zombie has advantage on saving throws against spells and other magical effects.

Actions

Multiattack. The juju zombie makes two Longsword attacks, or one Longsword attack and one Slam attack.
Longsword. *Melee Weapon Attack:* +7 to hit, reach 5 ft., one target. *Hit:* 9 (1d8 + 5) slashing damage, or 10 (1d10 + 5) slashing damage if used with two hands.
Slam. *Melee Weapon Attack:* +7 to hit, reach 5 ft., one target. *Hit:* 12 (2d6 +5) bludgeoning damage.

Zombie, Mummy

We barely had time to mourn Shafa. Our brave fighter had blundered into one too many traps and taken a swinging scythe to the head. As Sister Catherine pronounced him too far gone, he stirred and sat up. His body had already begun to desiccate and smell like the mummies we had fought, frankincense and myrrh wafting from his moaning mouth. As he rose, he blamed us, especially Miroini our trapfinder, for his death. We had to put him down before he used that greatsword of his to finish off Miroini. Even with her healing powers, Sister Catherine says he may never walk straight again. — Algrid Henswaithe, University of the Vast

Certain cursed temples or those built to glorify dark gods in the lands of Khemit animate all living creatures that die within them. These corpses rise as mummy zombies, not nearly as powerful as true mummies and lacking the funeral wrappings. Their flesh is desiccated and often infused with the substances used to mummify the dead, which sometimes hides their walking corpse status under wafts of perfumed air. These undead retain some semblance of the minds they had in life, though twisted with hatred toward their companions who "let them die," and can use many of the skills they had in life, though not anything as complex as spellcasting.

Mummy Zombie

Medium undead, chaotic evil

Armor Class 11
Hit Points 17 (2d8 + 8)
Speed 20 ft.

STR	DEX	CON	INT	WIS	CHA
20 (+5)	13 (+1)	13 (+1)	2 (–4)	2 (–4)	2 (–4)

Damage Vulnerabilities fire
Damage Resistances cold
Damage Immunities necrotic, poison; bludgeoning, piercing, and slashing damage from nonmagical attacks
Condition Immunities charmed, exhaustion, frightened, paralyzed, poisoned
Senses darkvision 60 ft., passive Perception 6
Languages —
Challenge 2 (450 XP)

Actions

Multiattack. The mummy zombie makes two Claw attacks.
Claw. *Melee Weapon Attack:* +7 to hit, reach 5 ft., one target. *Hit:* 9 (1d6 + 5) slashing damage plus 7 (2d6) necrotic damage.

Zombie, Otyugh

What's fouler than an otyugh? A zombie otyugh. No, this is not some kind of joke; we fought one during the Darkhold campaign. Seems the Wight Kings had been using live otyughs as disposals, just tossing bits and scraps down to them when the unused corpse parts started to pile up. Tidy, for necromancers at least. When the war turned against them, they zombified their waste eaters and sent them against our lines. Line breakers they were, and it took an iron stomach to stand that smell as hundreds of pounds of rotting flesh and worse came barreling at you. I saw many a brave warrior felled as they retched their guts out. — Big Joanne, mercenary

While they can be created through the normal means of creating zombies, must zombie otyughs come into being through accident. While immune to mundane diseases, these offal eaters from time to time consume too much necrotic flesh. The result is a magical disease that eats the otyugh from the inside, turning it into a perverse and even fouler version of its living self.

Otyugh Zombie
Large undead, neutral evil

Armor Class 14 (natural armor)
Hit Points 114 (12d10 + 48)
Speed 30 ft.

STR	DEX	CON	INT	WIS	CHA
16 (+3)	11 (+0)	19 (+4)	6 (–2)	13 (+1)	6 (–2)

Saving Throws Con +7, Wis +4
Damage Immunities poison
Condition Immunities poisoned
Senses darkvision 120 ft., passive Perception 11
Languages —
Challenge 5 (1,800 XP)

Limited Telepathy. The otyugh zombie can magically transmit simple messages and images to any creature within 120 feet of it that can understand a language. This form of telepathy doesn't allow for the receiving creature to telepathically respond.

Undead Fortitude. If damage reduces the otyugh zombie to 0 hit points, it must make a Constitution saving throw with a DC of 5 + the damage taken, unless the damage is radiant or from a critical hit. On a success, the zombie drops to 1 hit point instead.

Actions

Multiattack. The otyugh zombie makes one Bite attack and two Tentacle or Tentacle Slam attacks.

Bite. *Melee Weapon Attack:* +6 to hit, reach 5 ft., one target. *Hit:* 12 (2d8 + 3) piercing damage. If the target is a creature, it must succeed on a DC 15 Constitution saving throw against disease or become poisoned until the disease is cured. For every 24 hours that elapse, the target must repeat the saving throw, reducing its hit point maximum by 5 (1d10) on a failure. The disease is cured on a success. The target dies if the disease reduces its hit point maximum to 0. This reduction to the target's hit point maximum lasts until the disease is cured.

Tentacle. *Melee Weapon Attack:* +6 to hit, reach 10 ft., one target. *Hit:* 7 (1d8 + 3) bludgeoning damage plus 4 (1d8) piercing damage. If the target is Medium or smaller, it is grappled (escape DC 13) and restrained until the grapple ends. The otyugh has two tentacles, each of which can grapple one target.

Tentacle Slam. The otyugh zombie slams creatures grappled by it into each other or a solid surface. Each creature must succeed on a DC 14 Constitution saving throw or take 10 (2d6 + 3) bludgeoning damage and be stunned until the end of the otyugh's next turn. On a successful save, the target takes half the bludgeoning damage and isn't stunned

Zombie, Poisonous Snake

Latina was digging her hands through the damp soil, trying to find the gems supposedly buried beneath the sunflowers. She saw it as the perfect opportunity to grab a little gold to make all of the deaths worth it. She ended up falling facedown into the soil as the undead snakes wrapped around her arms and began biting repeatedly with their deadly poison. — Calystto Myrt, describing the Fungus Druid's underground greenhouse known as the Mushroom Grotto

Poisonous zombie snakes are undead serpents that deliver a deadly bite. The tiny asps are created using vipers. Their bodies often show the wounds that caused their deaths. Necromancers and other evil sorcerers occasionally animate entire barrels of the serpents to provide added defenses for their homes.

Poisonous Snake Zombie

Tiny undead, neutral evil

Armor Class 10 (natural armor)
Hit Points 5 (1d4 + 3)
Speed 20 ft., swim 20 ft.

STR	DEX	CON	INT	WIS	CHA
2 (–4)	10 (+0)	16 (+3)	1 (–5)	6 (–2)	3 (–4)

Damage Immunities poison
Condition Immunities exhaustion, poisoned
Senses blindsight 10 ft., darkvision 60 ft., passive Perception 8
Languages —
Challenge 1/8 (25 XP)

Undead Fortitude. If damage reduces the zombie snake to 0 hit points, it must make a Constitution saving throw with a DC of 5 + the damage taken, unless the damage is radiant or from a critical hit. On a success, the zombie poisonous snake drops to 1 hit point instead.

Actions

Bite. *Melee Weapon Attack:* +2 to hit, reach 5 ft., one target. *Hit:* 1 piercing damage, and the victim must make a DC 13 Constitution saving throw, taking 9 (2d8) points of poison damage on a failed save, or half as much on a successful save. If the poison damage reduces the target to 0 hit points, the target is stable but poisoned for one hour, even after regaining hit points, and is paralyzed while poisoned in this way.

TOME OF HORRORS

Zombie, Sphinx

Karmeiko's Treasury of Desert Legend *spoke of a sphinx guarding the pass through the Broken Mountains. I came prepared, having memorized a dozen carefully selected riddles that were sure to allow us passage. It was all for naught, for as we crested the pass and came within sight of the sphinx, it turned its milky white eyes on us with a vacant stare. I was saddened to see a once noble and learned beast turned into this foul perversion of life. As it charged, I responded with flame and lightning. — Algrid Henswaithe, University of the Vast*

Sphinx are often bound by magic to guard a place or secret lore. The magic that keeps them in service sometimes survives the magic-user who bound them, leaving the sphinx trapped. If lucky, enough food and water is provided to keep the sphinx alive for centuries; if not, they eventually succumb, trapped by the bounds of magic. These sphinxes, maddened by their callous treatment and needless deaths, animate as zombies, but zombies far more intelligent than others of their ilk.

Sphinx Zombie

Large undead, neutral evil

Armor Class 11 (natural armor)
Hit Points 168 (16d10 + 80)
Speed 30 ft., fly 40 ft.

STR	DEX	CON	INT	WIS	CHA
22 (+6)	6 (−2)	20 (+5)	3 (−4)	10 (+0)	5 (−3)

Saving Throws Wis +3
Damage Immunities poison, psychic; bludgeoning, piercing, and slashing from nonmagical attacks
Condition Immunities charmed, frightened, poisoned
Senses darkvision 60 ft., passive Perception 8
Languages understands the languages it knew in life but can't speak
Challenge 5 (1,800 XP)

Magic Weapons. The zombie's weapon attacks are magical.
Undead Fortitude. If damage reduces the zombie to 0 hit points, it must make a Constitution saving throw with a DC of 5 + the damage taken, unless the damage is radiant or from a critical hit. On a success, the zombie drops to 1 hit point instead.

Actions

Multiattack. The zombie makes two Claw attacks.
Claw. Melee Weapon Attack: +9 to hit, reach 5 ft., one target. *Hit:* 17 (2d10 + 6) slashing damage.

APPENDIX 1

ANIMATED OBJECTS

Various mundane and magical items take on a life of their own after long exposure to latent magical energies or through purposeful experimentation by powerful sorcerers. Rules for creating animated objects are listed below. Though not a comprehensive list of every possible object that could become animate, it should provide enough information to create unique objects to throw at your unsuspecting players.

CREATING AN ANIMATED OBJECT

When creating an animated object, you must first decide the size of the object. The five creature statistics listed below provide the foundation for an animated object of Tiny, Small, Medium, Large, or Huge size. Gargantuan objects, though possible to animate, are not included.

TINY ANIMATED OBJECT

Tiny construct, unaligned

Armor Class 12
Hit Points 28 (8d4 + 8)
Speed 20 ft.

STR	DEX	CON	INT	WIS	CHA
10 (+0)	14 (+2)	13 (+1)	1 (−5)	5 (−3)	1 (−5)

Skills Perception −1
Damage Immunities poison, psychic
Condition Immunities blinded, charmed, deafened, exhaustion, frightened, paralyzed, petrified, poisoned
Senses blindsight 60 ft. (blind beyond this radius), passive Perception 9
Languages —
Challenge 1/2 (100 XP)

Antimagic Susceptibility. The animated object is incapacitated while in the area of an *antimagic field*. If targeted by *dispel magic*, the animated object must succeed on a Constitution saving throw against the caster's spell save DC or fall unconscious for one minute.
Constructed Nature. An animated object doesn't require air, food, drink, or sleep.
False Appearance. While the animated object remains motionless, it is indistinguishable from a normal object of its type.

ACTIONS

Multiattack. The animated object makes two Slam attacks.
Slam. *Melee Weapon Attack:* +4 to hit, reach 5 ft., one target. *Hit:* 4 (1d4 + 2) bludgeoning damage.

SMALL ANIMATED OBJECT

Small construct, unaligned

Armor Class 12
Hit Points 44 (8d6 + 16)
Speed 25 ft.

STR	DEX	CON	INT	WIS	CHA
14 (+2)	14 (+2)	15 (+2)	1 (−5)	5 (−3)	1 (−5)

Skills Perception −1
Damage Immunities poison, psychic
Condition Immunities blinded, charmed, deafened, exhaustion, frightened, paralyzed, petrified, poisoned
Senses blindsight 60 ft. (blind beyond this radius), passive Perception 9
Languages —
Challenge 1 (200 XP)

Antimagic Susceptibility. The animated object is incapacitated while in the area of an *antimagic field*. If targeted by *dispel magic*, the animated object must succeed on a Constitution saving throw against the caster's spell save DC or fall unconscious for one minute.
Constructed Nature. An animated object doesn't require air, food, drink, or sleep.
False Appearance. While the animated object remains motionless, it is indistinguishable from a normal object of its type.

ACTIONS

Multiattack. The animated object makes two Slam attacks.
Slam. *Melee Weapon Attack:* +4 to hit, reach 5 ft., one target. *Hit:* 5 (1d6 + 2) bludgeoning damage.

MEDIUM ANIMATED OBJECT

Medium construct, unaligned

Armor Class 12
Hit Points 60 (8d8 + 24)
Speed 30 ft.

STR	DEX	CON	INT	WIS	CHA
16 (+3)	14 (+2)	17 (+3)	1 (−5)	5 (−3)	1 (−5)

Skills Perception −1
Damage Immunities poison, psychic
Condition Immunities blinded, charmed, deafened, exhaustion, frightened, paralyzed, petrified, poisoned
Senses blindsight 60 ft. (blind beyond this radius), passive Perception 9
Languages —
Challenge 2 (450 XP)

Antimagic Susceptibility. The animated object is incapacitated while in the area of an *antimagic field*. If targeted by *dispel magic*, the animated object must succeed on a Constitution saving throw against the caster's spell save DC or fall unconscious for one minute.
Constructed Nature. An animated object doesn't require air, food, drink, or sleep.
False Appearance. While the animated object remains motionless, it is indistinguishable from a normal object of its type.

ACTIONS

Multiattack. The animated object makes two Slam attacks.
Slam. *Melee Weapon Attack:* +5 to hit, reach 5 ft., one target. *Hit:* 7 (1d8 + 3) bludgeoning damage.

LARGE ANIMATED OBJECT

Large construct, unaligned

Armor Class 13
Hit Points 76 (8d10 + 32)
Speed 30 ft.

STR	DEX	CON	INT	WIS	CHA
18 (+4)	16 (+3)	19 (+4)	1 (−5)	5 (−3)	1 (−5)

Skills Perception −1
Damage Immunities poison, psychic
Condition Immunities blinded, charmed, deafened, exhaustion, frightened, paralyzed, petrified, poisoned
Senses blindsight 60 ft. (blind beyond this radius), passive Perception 9
Languages —
Challenge 3 (700 XP)

Antimagic Susceptibility. The animated object is incapacitated while in the area of an *antimagic field*. If targeted by *dispel magic*, the animated object must succeed on a Constitution saving throw against the caster's spell save DC or fall unconscious for one minute.
Constructed Nature. An animated object doesn't require air, food, drink, or sleep.
False Appearance. While the animated object remains motionless, it is indistinguishable from a normal object of its type.

ACTIONS

Multiattack. The animated object makes two Slam attacks.
Slam. *Melee Weapon Attack:* +6 to hit, reach 5 ft., one target. *Hit:* 9 (1d10 + 4) bludgeoning damage.

HUGE ANIMATED OBJECT

Huge construct, unaligned

Armor Class 13
Hit Points 92 (8d12 + 40)
Speed 40 ft.

STR	DEX	CON	INT	WIS	CHA
20 (+5)	16 (+3)	21 (+5)	1 (−5)	5 (−3)	1 (−5)

Skills Perception −1
Damage Immunities poison, psychic
Condition Immunities blinded, charmed, deafened, exhaustion, frightened, paralyzed, petrified, poisoned
Senses blindsight 60 ft. (blind beyond this radius), passive Perception 9
Languages —
Challenge 4 (1,100 XP)

Antimagic Susceptibility. The animated object is incapacitated while in the area of an *antimagic field*. If targeted by *dispel magic*, the animated object must succeed on a Constitution saving throw against the caster's spell save DC or fall unconscious for one minute.
Constructed Nature. An animated object doesn't require air, food, drink, or sleep.
False Appearance. While the animated object remains motionless, it is indistinguishable from a normal object of its type.

ACTIONS

Multiattack. The animated object makes two Slam attacks.
Slam. *Melee Weapon Attack:* +7 to hit, reach 5 ft., one target. *Hit:* 11 (1d12 + 5) bludgeoning damage.

THEMES

After you choose the animated object's size, next choose a theme. Each theme adds a variety of features to the base animated object, such as the ensnaring theme that gives the animated object the Hard to Grasp trait, or adjusts features of the object, such as the animalistic theme that modifies the creature's method of locomotion.

Each animated object must have at least one theme, but it can have more. Increase the animated object's Challenge rating by 1 for each theme you add to it beyond the first theme, rounding down for Tiny animated objects. For example, a Small animalistic ensnaring animated object would have a Challenge rating of 2 while a Tiny animalistic ensnaring animated object would have a Challenge rating of 1. If you use two themes that replace or modify the same feature (such as animalistic and paraphernalia, which both modify the Slam attack), pick one theme's modification and ignore the other theme's modification; do not apply both modifications to the same creature.

An animated object uses its Constitution modifier when setting the saving throw DC for its traits and actions (DC equal to 8 + the object's proficiency bonus + its Constitution modifier).

ANIMALISTIC THEME

This theme applies to animated objects that look like animals, such as figurines of griffons or children's toy animals. An animalistic animated object retains its statistics except as noted below.

Speed. The animated object's method of locomotion changes. Choose one of the following:

Increased Movement. The animated object's walking speed increases by 20 feet.

Unique Movement. The animated object has a climbing, flying, or swimming speed of 30 feet.

New Action: Multiattack. The animated object's Multiattack action changes to: The animated object makes one Bite attack and two Claw attacks.

New Action: Bite. The animated object's Slam attack is replaced with a Bite attack. This attack deals the same damage as the Slam, except it deals piercing damage instead of bludgeoning damage.

New Action: Claw. The animated object has a Claw attack. This attack deals slashing damage, and its damage dice are half of the animated object's Slam damage dice (rounded down to the nearest damage die). Otherwise, this attack works like the animated object's Slam attack. For example, a Tiny object's claw attack would use a d2 (half of a d4) as its base damage die while Medium and Large objects would use a d4 (half of a d8 and d10).

ENSNARING THEME

This theme applies to animated objects that are used to tie or wrap objects, such as chains, rope, drapes, and blankets. An ensnaring animated object retains its statistics except as noted below.

Hard to Grasp. The animated object has advantage on ability checks and saving throws made to escape a grapple.

Skill Proficiency: Athletics. The animated object is proficient in Strength (Athletics) checks.

New Action: Smother. The animated object has the Smother action, which allows it to wrap itself around its target's throat, chest, or face. This action works like the animated object's Slam attack, except it deals double the Slam attack's damage dice to the target and the target is grappled (escape DC equal to 8 + the animated object's Athletics). Until this grapple ends, the target is restrained, blinded, and at risk of suffocating, and the animated object can't smother another target. The animated object can still use its Slam action while grappling a target. For example, a Tiny object's smother attack would have a base damage of 4d4 + 2 while a Large object would do 4d10 + 4.

FORTIFIED THEME

This theme applies to animated objects made of a sturdy material, such as stone statues or metal cauldrons. A fortified animated object retains its statistics except as noted below.

Armor Class. The animated object has Armor Class equal to 12 + its Dexterity modifier.

Damage Resistances. The animated object has resistance to bludgeoning, piercing, and slashing damage from nonmagical attacks.

Blunting Form. Any nonmagical piercing or slashing weapon made of metal that hits the animated object begins to dull. After dealing damage, the weapon takes a permanent and cumulative −1 penalty to damage rolls. If its penalty drops to −5, the weapon is too dull to deal damage and can't be used to deal damage again until a creature spends 10 minutes sharpening the weapon.

HUMANOID THEME

This theme applies to animated objects that are humanoid in shape, such as toy soldiers or dress mannequins. A humanoid animated object retains its statistics except as noted below.

Ability Score. The animated object's Intelligence increases to 6.

Skill Proficiency: Perception. The animated object's proficiency bonus is doubled for its Wisdom (Perception) checks.

Languages. The animated object understands Common but speaks only through the use of its Mimicry trait.

Mimicry. The animated object can mimic humanoid voices. A creature that hears the sounds can tell they are imitations with a successful Wisdom (Insight) check.

New Action: Multiattack. The animated object's Multiattack action changes to: The animated object makes two Slam attacks or two attacks with its chosen weapon. Alternatively, the animated object can make one Slam attack and one attack with its chosen weapon.

New Action: Weapon Attack. The animated object has one weapon suitable for a creature of its size and shape. It is proficient with that weapon.

MONSTROUS THEME

This theme applies to animated objects that are often monstrous in appearance, and they contain some substance that they unleash on their enemies, including objects such as a horrifying amalgam of cobbled-together parts that emits bursts of springs and gears, a barrel that spews ale on those nearby, or a wardrobe infested with thousands of spiders. A monstrous animated object retains its statistics except as noted below.

Contents. The animated object is filled with a substance that it can eject on its enemies. Choose one of the following damage types: acid, bludgeoning, cold, fire, lightning, piercing, poison, slashing, or thunder. The animated object deals this type of damage when a creature comes into contact with its contents.

Pervasive Contents. A creature that touches the animated object or hits it with a melee attack while within five feet of it takes half the animated object's Slam damage dice (rounded down to the nearest damage die) of the type related to its contents. If the animated object uses its Spew Contents, this trait doesn't function until the end of the animated object's next turn.

New Action: Spew Contents (recharge 6). The animated object spews its contents in a cone. Each creature in that area must make a Dexterity saving throw, taking quadruple the animated object's Slam damage dice of the type related to its contents on a failed save, or half as much damage on a successful one. The cone is 15 feet for Tiny, Small, and Medium animated objects, and it is 30 feet for Large and Huge animated objects.

PARAPHERNALIA THEME

This theme applies to animated objects that are objects in the most mundane sense, such as standard traveling equipment, kitchen cookware, or bedroom furniture. These objects often defy specificity, and this theme serves as a catch-all theme for animated objects that don't fit into any of the other themes. Animated objects with this theme usually don't have other themes. A paraphernalia animated object retains its statistics except as noted below.

Speed. The animated object has a flying speed, and it can hover. Its flying speed is 20 feet at Tiny and increases by 10 feet for each size above Tiny.

Ability Score. The animated object's Dexterity increases by 4.

Saving Throw. The animated object has proficiency in Dexterity saving throws.

Weaponized Form. The animated object's Slam attack deals bludgeoning, piercing, or slashing damage, your choice, each time it attacks as the object uses all aspects of its form to damage its enemies.

POSSESSED THEME

This theme applies to an animated object that has been possessed by some otherworldly force, such as an angel, demon, or devil. A possessed animated object can't be possessed by more than one entity, and the entity possessing it must be good or evil. A possessed animated object retains its statistics except as noted below.

Alignment. The animated object's alignment is the same as the entity possessing it.

Type. The animated object is a construct but it counts as a celestial (if good) or a fiend (if evil) for spells and features, such as *protection from evil and good* and a paladin's Divine Sense.

Damage Immunities. The animated object is immune to necrotic damage (if evil) or radiant damage (if good).

Senses. The animated object has truesight with a radius of 30 feet.

Languages. The animated object knows the Abyssal, Celestial, and Infernal languages, and it has telepathy with a radius of 60 feet.

Magic Resistance. The animated object has advantage on saving throws against spells and other magical effects.

New Reaction: Otherworldly Presence. When a creature the animated object can see targets it with an attack, the animated object shows a glimpse of the entity possessing it. The attacker must succeed on a Wisdom saving throw or the attack misses, and the attacker is frightened until the end of its next turn.

Examples of Animated Objects

Below are examples of some animated objects:

Cart

Medium construct, unaligned

Armor Class 13 (natural armor)
Hit Points 38 (7d8 + 7)
Speed 30 ft.

STR	DEX	CON	INT	WIS	CHA
14 (+2)	11 (+0)	13 (+1)	1 (–5)	3 (–4)	1 (–5)

Damage Immunities poison, psychic
Condition Immunities blinded, charmed, deafened, exhaustion, frightened, paralyzed, petrified, poisoned
Senses blindsight 60 ft. (blind beyond this radius), passive Perception 6
Languages —
Challenge 2 (450 XP)

Antimagic Susceptibility. The animated car is incapacitated while in the area of an *antimagic field*. If targeted by *dispel magic*, the cart must succeed on a Constitution saving throw against the caster's spell save DC or fall unconscious for one minute.
Charge. If the animated cart moves at least 20 feet straight toward a target and then hits it with a slam attack on the same turn, the target takes an extra 9 (2d8) bludgeoning damage. If the target is a creature, it must succeed on a DC 15 Strength saving throw or be knocked prone.

Actions

Slam. *Melee Weapon Attack:* +4 to hit, reach 5 ft., one target. *Hit:* 13 (2d10 + 2) bludgeoning damage.

Chain

Medium construct, unaligned

Armor Class 12
Hit Points 60 (8d8 + 24)
Speed 30 ft.

STR	DEX	CON	INT	WIS	CHA
16 (+3)	14 (+2)	17 (+3)	1 (–5)	5 (–3)	1 (–5)

Skills Athletics +5, Perception –1
Damage Immunities poison, psychic
Condition Immunities blinded, charmed, deafened, exhaustion, frightened, paralyzed, petrified, poisoned
Senses blindsight 60 ft. (blind beyond this radius), passive Perception 9
Languages —
Challenge 2 (450 XP)

Animated Object Theme. The chain's theme is ensnaring.
Antimagic Susceptibility. The chain is incapacitated while in the area of an *antimagic field*. If targeted by *dispel magic*, the chain must succeed on a Constitution saving throw against the caster's spell save DC or fall unconscious for one minute.
Constructed Nature. An animated object doesn't require air, food, drink, or sleep.
False Appearance. While the chain remains motionless, it is indistinguishable from a normal chain.
Hard to Grasp. The chain has advantage on ability checks and saving throws made to escape a grapple.

Actions

Multiattack. The chain makes two Slam attacks.
Slam. *Melee Weapon Attack:* +5 to hit, reach 5 ft., one target. *Hit:* 7 (1d8 + 3) bludgeoning damage.
Smother. *Melee Weapon Attack:* +5 to hit, reach 5 ft., one target. *Hit:* 12 (2d8 + 3) bludgeoning damage, and the target is grappled (escape DC 13). Until this grapple ends, the target is restrained, blinded, and at risk of suffocating, and the chain can't smother another target. The chain can still use its Slam while grappling the target.

APPENDIX 2

HAZARDS

The following hazards can prove deadly to unprepared adventurers:

GREEN SLIME

Green slime is corrosive, slick, and adhesive, sticking to anything it comes into contact with. Metal, flesh, and organic material is especially vulnerable to the corrosive properties of the slime. It is often found in warm, humid caverns and ruins, and is noticeable as it clings to ceilings and walls, and covers floors, usually in five-foot squares.

Green slime can detect movement within 30 feet and drops on unsuspecting victims when they are below it; it is unable to move so it must depend on unwitting prey. If a creature is aware of the presence of the slime, it can attempt to avoid the hazard by succeeding on a DC 10 Dexterity saving throw.

The green slime secretes acid and does 5 (1d10) acid damage to any creature it contacts. This damage continues on each of the creature's turns until it uses an action to remove or destroy the slime. Much like its more evolved ooze relatives, the green slime is doubly caustic to nonmagical wood and metal, doing 11 (2d10) acid damage against objects of these types.

Green slime is vulnerable to and can be destroyed by fire, cold, radiant damage, sunlight or any disease curing magic.

BROWN MOLD

Brown mold is an ectotherm that feeds on the warmth of the environment surrounding it. When within 30 feet of brown mold, the temperature is noticeably colder, often to the point of freezing depending on the size of the brown mold patch. It is common for brown mold to cover a 10-foot square, but it isn't unusual for patches to be much larger.

Creatures that come within 10 feet of brown mold or start their turn within 10 feet of the mold must succeed on a DC 12 Constitution saving throw. A failed save results in 22 (4d10) cold damage, or half as much on a successful saving throw.

Exposure to fire causes the brown mold to rapidly expand and grow in the direction of the fire. Exposure to cold instantly destroys brown mold.

APPENDIX 3

MONSTERS BY CHALLENGE RATING

CR 0

Pterodactyl
Nupperibo Devil

CR 1/8

Mus
Mandragora
Cat, Undead Feral
Poisonous Snake Zombie

CR 1/4

Lesser Bone needle
Spiny Horror
Swarm of Hostile Birds
Fyr
Spore Rat
Goblin Zombie
Rat, Shadow
Swarm of Undead Bats
Swarm of Undead Rats

CR 1/2

Fungus Bat
Musk Ox
Stank Piglet
Tiny Animated Object
Ara
Steel Elf
Dire Corby
Giant Sea Leech
Gillmonkey
Gribbon
Leechfolk
Pyrolisk
Crystal Ooze
Fungal Creeper
Aqueous Zombie
Crawling Hand

CR 1

Crawling Offspring
Dinosaur, Pteranodon
Greater Bone needle
Platybelodon
Sea Cow
Swarm of Carnivorous Fish
Swarm of Flying Scorpions
Troll Pony
Pewter Knight
Small Animated Object
Drake, Fire
Bog Nixie
Nixie
Quickling
Vargouille
Dark Creeper
Skelzi
Skelzi, Vampiric
Cave Fisher
Flowershroud
Jupiter Bloodsucker
Bog Corpse
Corpsespun
Draug
Lacedon
Shadow Wolf

CR 2

Bone Cobbler
Denizen of Ong
Cave Scorpion
Dinosaur, Allosaurus
Dinosaur, Hadrosaur
Fei Shei
Monstrous Crayfish
Stank Hog
Tyrannosaurus Rattus
Cart
Chain
Medium Animated Object
Fey Giant Toad
Demon, Abrikandilu
Olithagorian Thrall
Stygian Mane
Styx Mane
Ara Cleric
Craniform
Tangagumak
Weredactyl
Fen Witch
Jelly, Whip
Blood Kaktos
Cobra Flower
Green Brain
Hoar Spirit
Mummy Zombie
Swarm of Undead Hummingbirds

CR 3

Dinosaur, Raptor
Dire Ape
Wakandagi
Large Animated Object
Lesser Flesh Golem
Sepulchral Guardian
Swarm of Eye Spiders
Drake, Ice
Dokkaebi
Filth Fairy
Spriggan
Wind Fey
Burning Dervish
Ice Mane
Skitterdark
Craniform Priestess
Dark Stalker
Inphidian
Mus Sorcerer
Mus Swashbuckler
Swarm of Miniature Mermaids
Death Worm
Thunder Terrier
Stunjelly
Algoid
Fungus Weird
Ghoul of Khemit
Hyaenodon, Undead
Juju Zombie

CR 4

Bonesucker
Death Weaver
Ant Lion
Baboonwere
Dinosaur, Ankylosaurus
Stegocentipede
Huge Animated Object
Blood Mane
Demon, Cacodemon
Aberrant Giant
Berberoka
Shell Folk
Tangagumak Shaman
Dinosaur, Raptors, Mutant
Arcanoplasm
Caterwaul
Churr
Drider-Goblin
Surf Lurker
Shroom
Bloody Bones
Draug Captain
Fear Guard
Groaning Spirit

CR 5

Blood Orchid
Cerebral Stalker
Forest Stalker
Swarm of Stirges
Niutomi
Swarm of Bladecoins
Basalt Warhound
Smoke Elemental
Grimstalker
Alu Demon
Chaos Knight
Demon, Daraka
Hellstoker Devil
Hydrodemon
Mezzalorn Demon
Nerizo Demon
Tangagumak Warrior
Drider-Goblin Spellcaster
Gronk
Corpsespinner
Livestone
Egui
Ekimmu
Ghul
Ice Wraith
Murder Born
Murder Crow
Otyugh Zombie
Red Jester
Sphinx Zombie

CR 6

Dinosaur, Iguanodon
Rhacos
Buxiu Immortal Guard
Gray Nisp
Stroke Lad
Demon, Amaimon
Demon, Gallu
Olithagorian
Silent Assassin
Tormentor Devil
Half-Ogre Enforcer
Jokao
Nazalor
Duppy
Masked Spirit

CR 7

Blood Orchid Savant
Cave Bear
Fluttercat
Charonademon
Sea Troll

CR 8

Blood Weird
Stone Maiden
Black Troll
Soul Vampire
Gnarlwood
Witch Tree
Binguai
Bone Reaper
Gholle
Greater Shadow

CR 9

Singa
Devil, Flayer
Fox Demon
N'gathau Warrior
Soul Hammer
Sea Giant
Sporc
Mi-Go

CR 10

Silaaal
Dinosaur, Diplodocus
Woodwose
Faceless
Nabasu
Nysrock
Piscodemon
Stirge Demon
Unmasked Priest of Tsathoggus
Greater Abyssal Basilisk
Guardian Shade
Gug Zombie

CR 11

Swarm of Adamantine Wasps
Sequana Genie
Carapace Symbiont

CR 12

Horror from Below
Shining Child
Dinosaur King, Triceratops
Dinosaur King, Tyrannosaurus
Celestial Paragon
Golem, Shedu
Hundred-eyed demon
Shrroth
Bramble Zombie

CR 13

Volcano Giant

CR 14

Forest Child

CR 15

Huangshe'yao
Teratashia, Demon Princess of Dimensions

CR 16

Devil, Ghaddar
Deepmind
Monster of Set
Mummy, Lightning-Quick

CR 17

Demon Lord, Beluiri The Temptress
Bramble

CR 18

Grexias the Destroyer
Modar the Huntress
N'Gathau, Aagash the Broken
N'Gathau, Asagin the Assassin
Rauuka The Ravager
Veenes the Blademistress
Veruard the Creator, the Razor of Abaddon
Carcharodon Zombie

CR 19

Tusk Lord
Demi-Lich

CR 20

Immortal Master
Bake Kujira

21

Vepar

CR 22

Ha-Naga
Golem, Mithral
Ammon, Duke of Malbolge,
  Keeper of the Kennels,
Lord of the Ditches, Arch Devil
Devil, Alastor the Executioner, Arch Devil
Devil, Arch Devil, Titivilus, Duke of Dis
Devil, Baalzebal, Prince of Stygia,
  Lord of Flies, Arch Devil
Devil, Baaphel, Grand Duke of Covetous
Regent of Belial, Arch Devil
Devil, Belial, Prince of Covetous,
  Lord of Lusts, Arch Devil
Gorson, Blood Duke of Aplistia, Arch Devil
Mammon, The Miser, Prince of Aplistia,
  Arch Devil
Moloch, Arch Devil
Xaphan, The Burning Duke, Duke of Infernus,
  Arch Devil
Living Lake

CR 23

Azure Dragon
Afanc

CR 24

Devil, Caasimolar, Former President of Hell,
  Arch Devil
Lilith, Former Queen of Hell, Arch Devil
Kaiju, Galazon

CR 25

Greater Demi-Lich

CR 26

Kaiju, Daguros

CR 28

The Lightbringer, Prince of Darkness,
Prince of Infernus, Arch Devil
Kaiju, Xarakhan

APPENDIX 4

MONSTERS BY TYPE

ABERRATION
Blood Orchid
Blood Orchid Savant
Bone Cobbler
Bonesucker
Cerebral Stalker
Crawling Offspring
Death Weaver
Denizen of Ong
Ha-Naga
Horror from Below
Huangshe'yao
Shining Child
Silaaal

BEAST
Ant Lion
Cave Bear
Cave Scorpion
Dinosaur King, Triceratops
Dinosaur King, Tyrannosaurus
Dinosaur, Allosaurus
Dinosaur, Ankylosaurus
Dinosaur, Diplodocus
Dinosaur, Hadrosaur
Dinosaur, Iguanodon
Dinosaur, Pteranodon
Dinosaur, Raptor
Dire Ape
Fei Shei
Fluttercat
Forest Stalker
Fungus Bat
Greater Bone needle
Lesser Bone needle
Monstrous Crayfish
Musk Ox
Platybelodon
Pterodactyl
Rhacos
Sea Cow
Spiny Horror
Stank Hog
Stank Piglet
Stegocentipede
Swarm of Carnivorous Fish
Swarm of Flying Scorpions
Swarm of Hostile Birds
Swarm of Stirges
Troll Pony
Tyrannosaurus Rattus
Wakandagi

BEAST (SHAPECHANGER)
Baboonwere

CELESTIAL
Celestial Paragon
Niutomi
Singa

CONSTRUCT
Buxiu Immortal Guard
Cart
Chain
Golem, Mithral
Golem, Shedu
Huge Animated Object
Large Animated Object
Lesser Flesh Golem
Medium Animated Object
Pewter Knight
Sepulchral Guardian
Small Animated Object
Swarm of Adamantine Wasps
Swarm of Bladecoins
Swarm of Eye Spiders
Tiny Animated Object

DRAGON
Azure Dragon
Drake, Fire
Drake, Ice

ELEMENTAL
Basalt Warhound
Blood Weird
Sequana Genie
Smoke Elemental
Stone Maiden

FEY
Bog Nixie
Dokkaebi
Fey Giant Toad
Filth Fairy
Fyr
Gray Nisp
Grimstalker
Nixie
Quickling
Spriggan
Stroke Lad
Wind Fey
Woodwose

FIEND
Burning Dervish
Chaos Knight
Faceless

FIEND (DEMON)
Alu Demon
Blood Mane
Charonademon
Demon Lord, Beluiri The Temptress
Demon, Abrikandilu
Demon, Cacodemon
Demon, Daraka
Demon, Gallu
Fox Demon
Hundred-eyed demon
Hydrodemon
Ice Mane
Mezzalorn Demon
Nabasu
Nerizo Demon
Nysrock
Piscodemon
Shrroth
Silent Assassin
Skitterdark
Stirge Demon
Stygian Mane
Styx Mane
Teratashia, Demon Princess of Dimensions
Vargouille
Vepar

FIEND (DEVIL)
Ammon, Duke of Malbolge, Keeper of the Kennels, -Lord of the Ditches, Arch Devil
Demon, Amaimon
Devil, Alastor the Executioner, Arch Devil
Devil, Arch Devil, Titivilus, Duke of Dis
Devil, Baalzebal, Prince of Stygia, Lord of Flies, Arch Devil
Devil, Baaphel, Grand Duke of Covetous Regent of Belial, Arch Devil
Devil, Belial, Prince of Covetous, Lord of Lusts, Arch Devil
Devil, Caasimolar, Former President of Hell, Arch Devil
Devil, Flayer
Devil, Ghaddar
Gorson, Blood Duke of Aplistia, Arch Devil
Hellstoker Devil
Lilith, Former Queen of Hell, Arch Devil
Mammon, The Miser, Prince of Aplistia, Arch Devil
Moloch, Arch Devil
Nupperibo Devil
The Lightbringer, Prince of Darkness, Prince of Infernus, Arch Devil
Tormentor Devil
Xaphan, The Burning Duke, Duke of Infernus, Arch Devil

FIEND (N'GATHAU)
Grexias the Destroyer
Modar the Huntress
N'gathau Warrior
N'Gathau, Aagash the Broken
N'Gathau, Asagin the Assassin
Rauuka The Ravager
Soul Hammer
Veenes the Blademistress
Veruard the Creator, the Razor of Abaddon

FIEND (PRIMORDIAL)
Olithagorian
Olithagorian Thrall

GIANT
Aberrant Giant
Berberoka
Black Troll
Jokao
Nazalor
Sea Giant
Sea Troll
Volcano Giant

GIANT (HALF-OGRE)

Half-Ogre Enforcer

HAZARD

Brown Mold
Green Slime

HUMANOID

Ara
Ara Cleric
Dark Creeper
Dark Stalker
Immortal Master
Mus
Mus Sorcerer
Mus Swashbuckler
Shell Folk
Skelzi
Skelzi, Vampiric
Tangagumak
Tangagumak Shaman
Tangagumak Warrior

HUMANOID (CRANIFORM)

Craniform
Craniform Priestess

HUMANOID (ELF)

Steel Elf

HUMANOID (HUMAN)

Unmasked Priest of Tsathoggus

HUMANOID (INPHIDIAN)

Inphidian

HUMANOID (MERFOLK)

Swarm of Miniature Mermaids

HUMANOID (SHAPECHANGER)

Weredactyl

MONSTROSITY

Dinosaur, Raptors, Mutant
Afanc
Arcanoplasm
Bake Kujira
Caterwaul
Cave Fisher
Churr
Death Worm
Deepmind
Dire Corby
Drider-Goblin
Drider-Goblin Spellcaster
Fen Witch
Giant Sea Leech
Gillmonkey
Greater Abyssal Basilisk
Gribbon
Gronk
Kaiju, Daguros

Kaiju, Galazon
Kaiju, Xarakhan
Leechfolk
Monster of Set
Pyrolisk
Sporc
Surf Lurker
Thunder Terrier
Tusk Lord

MONSTROSITY (EXTRAPLANAR)

Corpsespinner

MONSTROSITY (SHAPECHANGER)

Soul Vampire

OOZE

Carapace Symbiont
Crystal Ooze
Jelly, Whip
Living Lake
Stunjelly

OOZE (FUNGUS)

Livestone

PLANT

Algoid
Blood Kaktos
Bramble
Cobra Flower
Flowershroud
Fungal Creeper
Fungus Weird
Gnarlwood
Jupiter Bloodsucker
Mi-Go
Spore Rat
Witch Tree

PLANT (FUNGUS)

Green Brain
Mandragora
Shroom

UNDEAD

Aqueous Zombie
Bloody Bones
Bog Corpse
Bone Reaper
Bramble Zombie
Corpsespun
Crawling Hand
Greater Shadow
Ice Wraith
Rat, Shadow
Red Jester

UNDEAD (BEAST)

Cat, Undead Feral
Hyaenodon, Undead
Murder Crow

Otyugh Zombie
Poisonous Snake Zombie
Shadow Wolf
Swarm of Undead Bats
Swarm of Undead Hummingbirds
Swarm of Undead Rats

UNDEAD (EXTRAPLANAR)

Gug Zombie

UNDEAD (GENIE)

Ghul

UNDEAD (GHOUL)

Lacedon

UNDEAD (GIANT)

Binguai

UNDEAD (HUMANIOD)

Groaning Spirit
Hoar Spirit
Draug
Draug Captain
Duppy
Egui
Fear Guard
Gholle
Ghoul of Khemit
Goblin Zombie
Juju Zombie
Mummy Zombie
Mummy, Lightning-Quick
Murder Born
Sphinx Zombie

UNDEAD (LICH)

Demi-Lich
Greater Demi-Lich

UNDEAD (SPIRIT)

Ekimmu
Forest Child
Guardian Shade
Masked Spirit

UNDEAD (ZOMBIE, BEAST)

Carcharodon Zombie